of love & life

ISBN 978-0-276-44278-0

www.readersdigest.co.uk

The Reader's Digest Association Limited, 11 Westferry Circus, Canary Wharf, London E14 4HE

For information as to ownership of copyright in the material of this book, and acknowledgments, see last page.

# of love & life

Three novels selected and condensed
by Reader's Digest

The Reader's Digest Association Limited, London

CONTENTS

Cecelia Ahern

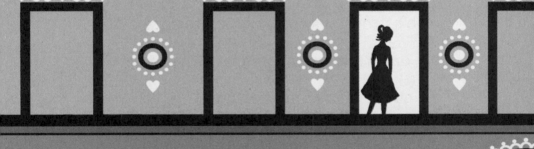

Thanks for the Memories

When Justin Hitchcock overcomes his needle phobia and donates a pint of blood, he's proud that he's helped to save a life. If only there was some way the recipient could thank him, he muses: a basket of muffins would be nice, or his dry-cleaning collected, even a newspaper and coffee delivered to his door every morning. But what's the likelihood of that?

Prologue

CLOSE YOUR EYES and stare into the dark.

My father's advice when I couldn't sleep as a little girl. He wouldn't want me to do that now but I've set my mind to the task regardless. I'm staring into that immeasurable blackness that stretches far beyond my closed eyelids. Though I lie still on the ground, I feel perched at the highest point I could possibly be; clutching at a star in the night sky with my legs dangling above cold black nothingness. I take one last look at my fingers wrapped round the light and let go. Down I go, falling, then floating, and, falling again, I wait for the land of my life.

I know now, as I knew as that little girl fighting sleep, that behind the gauzed screen of shut-eye, lies colour. It taunts me, dares me to open my eyes and lose sleep. Flashes of red and amber, yellow and white speckle my darkness. I refuse to open them. I rebel and I squeeze my eyelids together tighter to block out the grains of light, mere distractions that keep us awake but a sign that there's life beyond.

But there's no life in me. None that I can feel, from where I lie at the bottom of the staircase. My heart beats quicker now, the fighter in the ring, a red boxing glove pumping victoriously into the air, refusing to give up. It's the only part of me that cares. It fights to pump the blood round to heal, to replace what I'm losing. But it's all leaving my body as quickly as it's sent; forming a deep black ocean of its own around me where I've fallen.

Rushing, rushing, rushing. We are always rushing. Never have enough time here, always trying to make our way there. The phone rings again and I acknowledge the irony. I could have taken my time and answered it now.

Now, not then.

I could have taken all the time in the world on each of those steps. But we're always rushing. All, but my heart. That slows now. I don't mind so much.

I place my hand on my belly. If my child is gone, and I suspect this is so, I'll join it there. There . . . where? Wherever. It; a heartless word. He or she so young; who it was to become, still a question. But there, I will mother it.

There, not here.

I'll tell it: *I'm sorry, sweetheart, I'm sorry I ruined your chances, my chance—our chance of a life together. But close your eyes and stare into the darkness now, as Mummy is doing, and we'll find our way together.*

There's a noise in the room and I feel a presence.

'Oh God, Joyce, oh God! Can you hear me, love? Oh God. Good Lord, not my Joyce, don't take my Joyce! Hold on, love, I'm here. Dad is here.'

I don't want to hold on and I feel like telling him so. I hear myself groan, an animal-like whimper and it shocks me, scares me. I have a plan, I want to tell him. I want to go, only then can I be with my baby.

Then, not now.

He's stopped me from falling but I haven't landed yet. Instead he helps me balance on nothing, to hover while I'm forced to make the decision. I want to keep falling but he's calling the ambulance and he's gripping my hand with such ferocity it's as though it is *he* who is hanging onto dear life. As though I'm all he has. He's brushing the hair from my forehead and weeping loudly. I've never heard him weep. Not even when Mum died. I remember that I am all he has. The blood continues to rush through me. Rushing, rushing, rushing. Maybe I'm rushing again. Maybe it's not my time to go.

I feel the rough skin of old hands squeezing mine, and their intensity and their familiarity force me to open my eyes. Light fills them and I glimpse his face, a look I never want to see again. He clings to his baby. I know I've lost mine; I can't let him lose his. In making my decision I already begin to grieve. I've landed now, the land of my life.

And, still, my heart pumps on.

Even when broken it still works.

One Month Earlier

One

'BLOOD TRANSFUSION,' Dr Fields announces from the podium of a lecture hall in Trinity College's arts building, 'is the process of transferring blood or blood-based products from one person into the circulatory system of another. Blood transfusions may treat medical conditions, such as massive blood loss due to trauma, surgery, shock and where the red-cell-producing mechanism fails.

'Here are the facts. Three thousand donations are needed in Ireland every week. Only three per cent of the Irish population are donors, providing blood for a population of almost four million. One in four people will need a transfusion at some point. At least one hundred and fifty people in this room will need a blood transfusion at some stage in their lives.'

Five hundred heads turn left, right and around. A hand is raised.

'Yes?'

'How much blood does a patient need?'

'How long is a piece of string, dumb-ass,' a voice from the back mocks.

'It's a very good question.' She frowns into the darkness. 'This is what Blood For Life Week is all about. It's about asking all the questions you want, learning all you need to know about blood transfusions before you possibly donate today, tomorrow, the remaining days of this week on campus, or maybe regularly in your future.'

The main door opens and light streams into the dark lecture hall. Justin Hitchcock enters, the concentration on his face illuminated by the white light of the projector. Under one arm are multiple piles of folders, each one slipping by the second. A knee shoots up to hoist them back in place. His right hand carries both an overstuffed briefcase and a dangerously balanced Styrofoam cup of coffee. He slowly lowers his hovering foot down to the floor, as though performing a Tai chi move, and somebody sniggers. *Hold it, Justin. Woman on podium, five hundred kids. All staring at you. Say something. Something intelligent.*

'I'm confused,' he announces to the darkness. There are twitters in the room and he feels all eyes on him as he moves back towards the door to check the number. *Don't spill the coffee. Don't spill the damn coffee.*

He opens the door, allowing shafts of light to sneak in again and the students in its line shade their eyes.

Laden down with items, he manages to hold the door open with his leg. He looks back to the number on the outside of the door and then back to his sheet, the sheet that, if he doesn't grab it that very second, will float to the ground. He makes a move to grab it. Wrong hand. Styrofoam cup of coffee falls to the ground. Closely followed by sheet of paper. *Dammit! There they go again, twitter, twitter. Nothing funnier than a lost man who's spilled his coffee and dropped his schedule.*

'Can I help you?' The lecturer steps down from the podium.

Justin brings his entire body back into the lecture hall and darkness resumes. 'Well, it says here . . . well, it said there,' he nods his head towards the sodden sheet on the ground, 'that I have a class here now.'

'Enrolment for international students is in the exam hall.'

He frowns. 'No, I—'

'I'm sorry.' She comes closer. 'I thought I heard an American accent. Mature students are next door.' She adds in a whisper, 'Trust me, you don't want to join this class.'

Justin clears his throat. 'Actually I'm lecturing the History of Art and Architecture class.'

'You're lecturing?'

'Guest lecturing. Believe it or not.' He blows his hair up from his sticky forehead. *A haircut, remember to get a haircut. There they go again, twitter, twitter. A lost lecturer, who's spilled his coffee, dropped his schedule, is about to lose his folders and needs a haircut. Definitely nothing funnier.*

'Professor Hitchcock?'

'That's me.' He feels the folders slipping from under his arm.

'Oh, I'm so sorry,' she whispers. 'I didn't know . . .' She catches a folder for him. 'I'm Dr Sarah Fields from the IBTS. The Faculty told me that I could have a half-hour with the students before your lecture.'

'Oh, well, nobody informed me of that, but that's no problemo.' *Problemo?* He shakes his head at himself and makes for the door.

'Professor Hitchcock?'

He stops at the door. 'Yes?'

'Would you like to join us?'

I most certainly would not. No. Just say no.

'Um . . . nn–es.' *Nes?* 'I mean yes.'

Twitter, twitter, twitter. Lecturer caught out. Forced into doing something he clearly didn't want to do by attractive young woman in white coat claiming to be a doctor of an unfamiliar initialised organisation.

'Great. Welcome.' She places the folder back under his arm and returns to the podium to address the students.

'OK, attention, everybody. Back to the initial question of blood quantities. A car accident victim may require up to thirty units of blood. A bleeding ulcer could require anything between three and thirty units of blood. A coronary artery bypass may use between one and five units of blood. Now you see why we *always* want donors.'

Justin takes a seat in the front row and listens with horror.

'Does anybody have any questions?'

Can you change the subject?

'Do you get paid for giving blood?'

'Not in this country, I'm afraid.'

'Does the person who is given blood know who their donor is?'

'Donations are usually anonymous to the recipient but products in a blood bank are always individually traceable.'

'Can anyone give blood?'

'Good question. I have a list here of contraindications to being a blood donor. Please all study it carefully and take notes if you wish.' Dr Fields places her sheet under the projector and her white coat lights up with a rather graphic picture of someone in dire need of a donation.

People groan and the word 'gross' travels round the tiered seating like a Mexican wave. Twice by Justin. Dizziness overtakes him and he averts his eyes from the image.

'Oops, wrong sheet,' Dr Fields says cheekily, slowly replacing it with the promised list.

Justin searches with great hope for needle or blood phobia in an effort to eliminate himself as a possible blood donor. No such luck— not that it mattered, as the chances of him donating a drop of blood to anyone are as unlikely as ideas in the morning.

Dr Fields moves on. 'Remember, your body will replace the liquid part of the donation within twenty-four hours. With a unit of blood at almost a pint and everyone having eight to twelve pints of blood in their body, the average person can easily spare one.'

Pockets of juvenile laughter at the innuendo.

'Everybody, please.' Dr Fields claps her hands. 'It's all well and good that we can have a laugh but at this time I think it's important to note the fact that someone's *life* could be depending on you right now.'

How quickly silence falls upon the class. Even Justin stops talking to himself.

'**P**rofessor Hitchcock.' Dr Fields approaches Justin, who is arranging his notes at the podium while the students take a five-minute break.

'Please call me Justin, Doctor.'

'Please call me Sarah.' She holds out her hand. 'I just want to make sure we'll see each other later?'

'Later?'

'Yes, later. As in . . . after your lecture,' she smiles.

Is she flirting? It's been so long, how am I supposed to tell? Speak, Justin, speak. 'Great. A date would be great.'

She purses her lips to hide a smile. 'OK, I'll meet you at the main entrance at six and I'll bring you across myself.'

'Bring me across where?'

'To where we've got the blood drive set up. It's beside the rugby pitch.'

'The blood drive . . .' He's immediately flooded with dread. 'Ah, I don't think that—'

'And then we'll go for a drink after?'

'You know what? I'm just getting over the flu so I don't think I'm eligible for donating.' He parts his hands and shrugs.

'Are you on antibiotics?'

'No, but that's a good idea, Sarah. Maybe I *should* be . . .'

'Oh, I think you'll be OK,' she grins.

'No, you see, I've been around some pretty infectious diseases lately. Malaria, smallpox, the whole lot. I was in a very tropical area.' He remembers the list of contraindications. 'And my brother, Al? Yeah, he's a leper.' *Lame, lame, lame.*

'Really?' She lifts an eyebrow and though he fights it with all his will, he cracks a smile. 'How long ago did you leave the States?'

Think hard, this could be a trick question. 'I moved to London three months ago,' he finally answers truthfully.

'Oh, lucky for you. If it was two months you wouldn't be eligible.'

'Now hold on, let me think . . .' He scratches his chin. 'Maybe it *was* two months ago. If I work backwards from when I arrived . . .' He trails off, while counting his fingers.

'Are you afraid, Professor Hitchcock?' she smiles.

'Afraid? No!' He guffaws. 'But did I mention I have malaria?' He sighs at her failure to take him seriously. 'Well, I'm all out of ideas.'

'I'll see you at six. Oh, and don't forget to eat beforehand.'

'Of course, because I'll be *ravenous* before my date with a giant homicidal needle,' he mumbles as he watches her leave.

The students begin filing back into the room and he tries to hide the smile of pleasure on his face, mixed as it is. Finally the class is his.

OK, my little twittering friends. It's pay-back time.

They're not yet all seated when he begins.

'Art,' he announces to the lecture hall, and he hears the sounds of pencils and notepads being extracted from bags. 'The products of human creativity.' He doesn't stall to allow them time to catch up. In fact, it is time to have a little fun. His speech speeds up.

'The creation of beautiful or significant things.'

'Sir, could you say that again, plea—'

'No,' he interrupts. 'Engineering,' he moves on, 'the practical application of science to commerce or industry.' Total silence now. 'Creativity and practicality. The fruit of their merger is architecture.' *Faster, Justin!*

'Architecture-is-the-transformation-of-ideas-into-a-physical-reality. The-complex-and-carefully-designed-structure-of-something-especially-with-regard-to-a-specific-period. To-understand-architecture-we-must-examine-the-relationship-between-technology-science-and-society.'

'Sir, can you—'

'No.' But he slows slightly. 'We examine how architecture through the centuries has been shaped by society, how it continues to be shaped, but also how it, in turn, shapes society.'

He pauses, looking around at the youthful faces staring up at him, their minds empty vessels waiting to be filled.

He will transport them from the stuffy lecture theatre of the prestigious Dublin college to the rooms of the Louvre Museum, hear the echoes of their footsteps as he walks them through the Cathedral of Saint-Denis, to Saint-Germain-des-Prés and Saint-Pierre de Montmartre. They'll know not only dates and statistics but the smell of Picasso's paints, the feel of baroque marble, the sound of the bells of Notre-Dame.

They'll experience it all, right here in this classroom.

They're staring at you, Justin. Say something.

He clears his throat. 'This course will teach you how to analyse works of art and how to understand their historical significance. It will enable you to develop an awareness of the environment while also providing you with a deeper sensitivity to the culture and ideals of other nations.' He allows a silence to fall. Do their hearts beat wildly with excitement as his does, just thinking about all that is to come? Even after all these years, he still feels the same enthusiasm for the buildings, paintings and sculptures of the world. He looks again at their faces and has an epiphany. *You have them! They're hanging on your every word, just waiting to hear more. You've done it, they're in your grasp!*

Someone farts and the room explodes with laughter.

He sighs, his bubble burst, and continues his talk in a bored tone. 'My name is Justin Hitchcock and in my guest lectures scattered throughout the course, you will be introduced to European painting through, for example, the Italian Renaissance and French Impressionism. There'll also be an introduction to European architecture. Greek temples to the present day. Volunteers to help me hand these out?'

And so it was another year. He wasn't at home in Chicago now; he had chased his ex-wife and daughter to live in London and was flying back and forth between there and Dublin for his guest lectures. A different country perhaps but another class of the same. Another group displaying an immature lack of understanding of his passions.

It doesn't matter what you say now, pal, from here on in the only thing they'll go home remembering is the fart.

'**W**hat is it about fart jokes, Bea?'

'Oh, hi, Dad.'

'What kind of a greeting is that?'

'Oh, gee whiz, wow, Dad, so great to hear from you. It's been, what, ah shucks, three hours since you last phoned?'

'Fine, you don't have to go all porky pig on me. Is your darling mother home yet from a day out at her new life?'

'Yes, she's home.'

'And has she brought the delightful Laurence back with her?' He can't hold back his sarcasm. 'Laurence,' he drawls, 'Laurence of A— inguinal hernia.'

'Oh, you're such a geek. Would you ever give up talking about his trouser leg,' she sighs with boredom.

Justin kicks off the scratchy blanket of the cheap Dublin hotel he's staying in. 'Really, Bea, check it next time he's around. Those trousers are far too tight for what he's got going on down there. There should be a name for that. Something-itis.' *Balls-a-titis.*

'There are only four TV channels in this dump, one in a language I don't even understand. You know, in my wonderful home back in Chicago, I had two hundred channels.' *Dick-a-titis. Dickhead-a-titis. Ha!*

'None of which you watched.'

'But one had a choice not to watch those deplorable house-fixer-upper channels and music channels of naked women dancing around.'

'I appreciate *one* going through such an upheaval, Dad. It must be very traumatic for you, a sort-of grown man, while I, at sixteen years old, had to take this huge life adjustment of parents getting divorced and a move from Chicago to London all in my stride.'

'You got two houses and extra presents, what do you care?' he grumbles. 'And it was your idea.'

'It was my idea to go to *ballet school* in London, not for your marriage to end!'

'Oh, *ballet school*. I thought you said, "Break up, you *fool*." My mistake. Hey, you think I was going to stay in Chicago while you're all the way over this side of the world?'

'You're not even in the same country right now,' she laughs.

'Ireland is just a work trip. I'll be back in London in a few days. Honestly, Bea, there's nowhere else I'd rather be,' he assures her.

'I'm thinking of moving in with Peter,' she says far too casually.

'So what is it about fart jokes?' he asks again, ignoring her.

'I take it you don't want to talk about me moving in with Peter?'

'You're a child. You and Peter can move into the Wendy house, which I still have in storage. I'll set it up in the living room.'

'I'm eighteen. Not a child any more. I've lived alone away from home for two years now.'

'One year alone. Your mother left *me* alone the second year to join you, remember.'

'You and Mum met at my age.'

'And we did not live happily ever after.'

Bea sighs and steers the conversation back to safer territory. 'Why are your students laughing at fart jokes, anyway? I thought your seminar was for postgrads who'd elected to choose your boring subject.'

'Along with my postgraduate classes, I was asked to speak to first-year students throughout the year too, an agreement I may live to regret, but no matter. On to my day job and far more pressing matters, I'm planning an exhibition at the gallery on Dutch painting in the seventeenth century. You should come see it.'

'No, thanks.'

'Well, maybe my postgrads over the next few months will be more appreciative of my expertise.'

'You know, your students may have laughed at the fart joke but I bet at least a quarter of them donated blood.'

'They only did it because they heard they'd get a free KitKat afterwards,' Justin huffs. 'You're angry at me for not giving blood?'

'I think you're an asshole for standing up that woman.'

'Don't use the word "asshole", Bea. Anyway, who told you that I stood her up?'

'Uncle Al.'

'Uncle Al is an asshole. And you know what else, honey? You know what the good doctor said today about donating blood? That the donation is anonymous to the recipient. Hear that? *Anonymous.* So what's the point in saving someone's life if they don't even know you're the one who saved them?'

'Dad!'

'What? Come on, Bea. Lie to me and tell me you wouldn't want a bouquet of flowers for saving someone's life?'

Bea protests but he continues.

'Or a little basket of those, whaddaya call 'em muffins that you like, coconut—'

'Cinnamon,' she laughs, finally giving in.

'A little basket of cinnamon muffins outside your front door with a little note tucked into the basket saying, "Thanks, Bea, for saving my life. Anytime you want anything done, like your dry-cleaning picked up, or your newspaper and a coffee delivered to your front door every morning, a chauffeur-driven car for your own personal use, front-row tickets to the opera . . ." Oh, the list could go on and on. It could be like one of those Chinese things; you know the way someone saves your life and then you're for ever indebted to them. It could be nice having someone tailing you; catching pianos flying out of windows and stopping them from landing on your head, that kind of thing.'

Bea calms herself. 'I hope you're joking.'

'Yeah, of course I'm joking. The piano would surely kill them and that would be unfair. You think I'm selfish, don't you?'

'Dad, you uprooted your life, left a great job, nice apartment and flew thousands of miles to another country just to be near me—of course I don't think you're selfish.'

Justin smiles to himself.

'But if you're not joking about the muffin basket, then you're definitely selfish. And if it was Blood For Life Week in my college, I would have taken part. But you have the opportunity to make it up to that woman.'

'I just feel like I'm being bullied into this entire thing. I was going to get my hair cut tomorrow, not have people stab at my veins.'

'Remember, if you do give blood, a tiny little needle isn't gonna kill you. In fact, the opposite may happen, it might save someone's life and you never know, that person could follow you around for the rest of your life leaving muffin baskets outside your door and catching pianos before they fall on your head. Now wouldn't that be nice?'

In a blood drive beside Trinity College's rugby pitch, Justin tries to hide his shaking hands from Sarah, who smiles encouragingly and talks him through everything as though giving blood is the most normal thing in the world.

'Now I just need to ask you a few questions. Have you read, understood and completed the health and lifestyle questionnaire?'

Justin nods, words failing him in his clogged throat.

'OK, we're all set. I'm just going to do a haemoglobin test.'

'Does that check for diseases?' He looks nervously at the equipment in the van. *Please don't let me have any diseases. That would be too embarrassing. Not likely anyway. Can you even remember the last time you had sex?*

'No, this just measures the iron in your blood.' She takes a pinprick of blood from the pad of his finger. 'Blood is tested later for diseases and STDs.'

'Must be handy for checking up on boyfriends,' he jokes.

She quietens as she carries out the quick test.

Justin lies supine on a cushioned bench and extends his left arm.

Sarah wraps a pressure cuff round his upper arm, making the veins more prominent, and she disinfects his inner elbow.

Don't look at the needle, don't look at the needle.

He looks at the needle and the ground swirls beneath him. His throat tightens. 'Is this going to hurt?' Justin swallows hard.

'Just a little sting,' she smiles, approaching him with a cannula in her hand. He smells her sweet perfume and it distracts him momentarily. As she leans over, he sees down her V-neck sweater. A black lace bra. 'I want you to take this in your hand and squeeze it repeatedly.'

'What?' he laughs nervously.

'The ball.' She smiles at him again. 'It's to help speed up the process.'

'Oh.' He pumps at top speed.

Sarah laughs. 'Not yet. And not that fast, Justin.'

Sweat rolls down his back. His hair sticks to his clammy forehead. *You should have gone for the haircut, Justin.* 'Ouch.'

'That wasn't so bad, was it?' she says softly.

Justin's heart beats loudly in his ears. He pumps the ball in his hand to the rhythm of his heartbeat. He imagines his heart pumping the blood, the blood flowing through his veins. Fifteen minutes later, he looks at his pint of blood with pride. He doesn't want it to go to some stranger, he wants to bring it to the hospital himself and present it to someone he really cares about, someone special, for it's the first thing to come straight from his heart in a very long time.

Two

I OPEN MY EYES SLOWLY. Slowly, objects come into focus. I move my eyes around. I'm in a hospital. A television high up on the wall. Green fills its screen. I focus more. Horses. Jumping and racing. Dad must be in the room. I lower my eyes and there he is with his back to me in an armchair. I see his tweed cap appearing and disappearing behind the back of the chair as he bounces up and down.

The horse racing is silent. So is he. I wonder if it's my ears that aren't allowing me to hear him. He springs out of his chair now and he raises his fist at the television, quietly urging his horse on.

The television goes black. He raises his hands up in the air and beseeches God. He puts his hands in his pockets, feels around and pulls the material out. They're empty. He pats down his chest, feeling for money. Grumbles. So it's not my ears.

He turns to feel around in his overcoat beside me and I shut my eyes quickly. I'm not ready yet. Nothing has happened to me until they tell me. Last night will remain a nightmare in my mind until they tell me it was true.

I hear him rooting around in his overcoat, I hear change rattling and I hear the clunk as the coins fall into the television. I risk opening my eyes again and there he is back in his armchair, cap bouncing.

My curtain is closed to my right but I can tell I share a room with others. I don't know how many. It's quiet. There's no air in the room; it's stuffy with stale sweat. The giant windows that take up the entire wall to my left are closed. I see a bus-stop across the road. A woman waits by the stop, shopping bags by her feet and on her hip sits a baby, bare chubby legs bouncing in the Indian summer sun. I look away immediately. Dad is watching me. He is leaning out over the side of the armchair, twisting his head round. 'Hi, love.'

'Hi.' I feel I haven't spoken for such a long time, and I expect to croak. But I don't. My voice is pure, pours out like honey. As if nothing's happened. But nothing has happened. Not yet. Not until they tell me.

With both hands on the arms of the chair he slowly pulls himself up. Like a seesaw, he makes his way over to the side of the bed. Up and down, down and up. He was born with a leg-length discrepancy, his left leg longer than his right. Despite the special shoes he was given in later years, he still sways, the motion instilled in him since he learned to walk. He hates wearing those shoes and, despite our warnings and his back pains, he goes back to what he knows. I'm so used to the sight of his body going up and down, down and up. I recall as a child holding his hand and going for walks. How my arm would move in perfect rhythm with him. Being pulled up as he stepped down on his right leg, being pushed down as he stepped on his left.

He was always so strong. Always so capable. Always fixing things. Lifting things, mending things. A handyman for the entire street. His legs were uneven, but his hands, always and for ever, steady as a rock.

He takes his cap off as he nears me, clutches it with both hands. 'Are you . . . em . . . they told me that . . .' He swallows hard and his thick messy eyebrows furrow and hide his glassy eyes. 'You lost . . .'

My lower lip trembles.

His voice breaks when he speaks again. 'You lost a lot of blood, Joyce. They . . . they did a transfusion of the blood thingy on you so you're em . . . you're OK with your bloods now.'

My hands automatically go to my belly. I look to him hopefully, only realising now how much I have convinced myself the awful incident in the labour room was all a terrible nightmare. Perhaps I imagined my baby's silence that filled the room in that final moment. Perhaps there were cries that I just didn't hear. Maybe I just didn't hear the first little miraculous breath of life that everybody else witnessed.

Dad shakes his head sadly. No, it had been me that had made those screams instead.

My body shakes terribly and I can't stop it. The tears; they well, but I stop them from falling. If I start now I know I will never stop. I'm making a noise. Groaning. Grunting. A combination of both. Dad grabs my hand and holds it hard. He doesn't say anything. But what can a person say? I don't even know.

I doze in and out. I wake and remember a conversation with a doctor and wonder if it was a dream. *Lost your baby, Joyce, we did all we could . . . blood transfusion . . .* Who needs to remember something like that? No one. Not me.

When I wake again the curtain beside me has been pulled open. There are three small children running around, chasing one another round the bed while their father, I assume, calls to them to stop in a language I don't recognise. Their mother, I assume, lies in bed.

Dad calls over to them. 'Where are you lot from, then?'

'Excuse me?' her husband asks.

'I said where are you lot from, then?' Dad repeats. 'Not from around here, I see.' Dad's voice is cheery and pleasant. No insults intended. No insults ever intended.

'We are from Nigeria,' the man responds.

'Nigeria,' Dad replies. 'Where would that be then?'

'In Africa.' The man's tone is pleasant too. Just an old man starved of conversation, trying to be friendly, he realises.

'Ah, Africa. Never been there myself. Is it hot there? I'd say it is. Hotter than here. Get a good tan, I'd say, not that you need it,' he laughs. 'Do you get cold here?' Dad wraps his arms round his body and pretends to shiver. 'Cold?'

'Yes,' the man laughs. 'Sometimes I do.'

'Thought so. I do too and I'm from here,' Dad explains. 'The chill gets right into my bones. But I'm not a great one for heat either. Skin goes red, just burns. My daughter, Joyce, goes brown. That's her over there.' He points at me and I close my eyes quickly. 'She was on one of those Spanish islands a few months back and came back black, she did. Well, not as black as you, you know, but she got a fair ol' tan on her. Peeled, though. You probably don't peel.'

The man laughs politely. That's Dad. Never means any harm but has never left the country in his entire life. A fear of flying holds him back. Or so he says.

'Anyway, I hope your lovely lady feels better soon. It's an awful thing to be sick on your holliers.'

With that I open my eyes.

'Ah, welcome back, love. I was just talking to these nice neighbours of ours.' He seesaws up to me again, his cap in his hands. 'You know I think we're the only Irish people in this hospital. The nurse that was here a minute ago, she's from Sing-a-song or someplace like that.'

'Singapore, Dad,' I smile.

'That's it. They all speak English, though, the foreigners do. Sure, isn't that better than being on your holidays and having to do all that signed-languagey stuff.'

'Dad,' I smile, 'you've never been out of the country in your life.'

'Haven't I heard the lads at the Monday Club talking about it? Frank was away in that place last week—oh, what's that place?' He shuts his eyes and thinks hard. 'The place where they make the chocolates?'

'Switzerland.'

'No.'

'Belgium.'

'No,' he says, frustrated now. 'The little round ball-y things all crunchy inside. You can get the white ones now but I prefer the original dark ones.'

'Maltesers?' I laugh, but feel pain and stop.

'That's it. He was in Maltesers.'

'Dad, it's Malta.'

'That's it. He was in Malta.' He is silent. 'Do they make Maltesers?'

'I don't know. Maybe. So what happened to Frank in Malta?'

He squeezes his eyes shut again and thinks. 'I can't remember what I was about to say now.' Silence. He hates not being able to remember. He used to remember everything.

'Did you make any money on the horses?' I ask.

'A few bob. Enough for a few rounds at the Monday Club tonight.'

'But today is Tuesday.'

'It's on a Tuesday on account of the bank holiday,' he explains, see-sawing round to the other side of the bed to sit down.

I can't laugh. I'm too sore and it seems some of my sense of humour was taken away with my child.

'You don't mind if I go, do you, Joyce? I'll stay if you want, I really don't mind, it's not important.'

'Of course it's important. You haven't missed a Monday night for twenty years.'

'Well,' he takes my hand, 'you're more important than a few pints and a singsong.'

'What would I do without you?' My eyes fill again.

'You'd be just fine. Besides,' he looks at me warily, 'you have Conor.'

I look away. What if I don't want Conor any more?

'I tried to call him last night on the hand phone but there was no answer. But maybe I tried the numbers wrong,' he adds quickly. 'There are so many more numbers on the hand phones.'

'Mobiles, Dad,' I say distractedly.

'Ah, yes. The mobiles. He keeps calling when you're asleep. He's going to come home as soon as he can get a flight. He's very worried.'

'That's nice of him. Then we can get down to the business of spending the next ten years of our married life trying to have babies.' Back to business. A nice little distraction to give our relationship some sort of meaning.

'Ah now, love . . .'

The first day of the rest of my life and I'm not sure I want to be here. I know I should be thanking somebody for this but I really don't feel like it. Instead I wish they hadn't bothered.

I watch the three children playing together on the floor of the hospital, little fingers and toes, chubby cheeks and plump lips—the faces of their parents clearly etched on theirs. My heart drops into my stomach and it twists. My eyes fill again and I have to look away.

'Mind if I have a grape?' Dad chirps like a little canary.

'Of course you can. Dad, you should go home now, go get something to eat. How did you get here?' It suddenly occurs to me that he hasn't been into the city for years. It all became too fast for him, buildings suddenly sprouting up where there weren't any, roads with traffic going in different directions from before. With great sadness he sold his car too, his failing eyesight too much of a danger for him and others on the roads. Seventy-five years old, his wife dead ten years. Now he has a routine of his own, content to stay around the local area, chatting to his neighbours, church every Sunday and Wednesday, Monday Club every Monday (apart from the bank holidays when it's on a Tuesday), his crosswords, puzzles and TV shows, his garden.

'Fran from next door drove me in.' He pops another grape into his mouth. 'Almost had me killed two or three times. Enough to let me know there is a God if ever there was a time I doubted.'

'Do you still believe in your God now, Dad?' It comes out crueller than I mean to but the anger is almost unbearable.

'I do believe, Joyce.' As always, no offence taken. 'The Lord acts in mysterious ways, in ways we often can neither explain nor understand, tolerate nor bear. I understand how you can question Him now—we all do at times. When your mother died I . . .' He trails off and abandons the sentence as always, the furthest he will go to being disloyal about his God, the furthest he will go to discussing the loss of his wife. 'But this time God answered all my prayers. He saved you. He kept my girl alive and for that I'll be for ever grateful to Him, sad as we may be about the passing of another.'

I have no response to that, but I soften.

He pulls his chair closer to my bedside. 'And I believe in an afterlife,' he says, a little more quietly now. 'That I do. I believe in the paradise of heaven, up there in the clouds, and everyone that was once here is up there. Including the sinners, for God's a forgiver, that I believe.'

'Everyone?' I fight the tears. I fight them from falling. If I start I know I will never stop. 'What about my baby, Dad? Is my baby there?'

He looks pained. We hadn't spoken much about my pregnancy. Early days and we were all worried, nobody more than he. Only days ago we'd had a minor falling-out over my asking him to store our spare bed in his garage. I had started to prepare the nursery, you see . . .

Five months to go. Some people, my father included, would think preparing the nursery at four months is premature but we'd been waiting six years for a baby, for this baby. Nothing premature about that.

'Ah, love, you know I don't know . . .'

'I was going to call him Sean if it was a boy,' I hear myself finally say aloud. 'Grace, if it was a girl. After Mum. She would have liked that.'

His jaw sets at this and he looks away. Anyone who doesn't know him would think this has angered him. I know this is not the case. I know it's the emotion gathering in his jaw, like a giant reservoir, waiting for those rare moments when the drought within him calls for those walls to break and for the emotions to gush.

'I used to talk to him. Sing to him. I wonder if he heard.'

Silence while I imagine a future that will never be with little imaginary Sean. Of singing to him every night, of marshmallow skin and splashes at bathtime. Of kicking legs and bicycle rides. Anger at a missed life—no, worse—a lost life, overrides my thoughts.

'I wonder if he even knew.'

'Knew what, love?'

'What was happening. Did he think I was sending him away? I hope he doesn't blame me. I was all he had and—' I stop. Torture over for now. I feel seconds away from screaming with such terror, I must stop. 'Where is he now, Dad? How can you die when you haven't even been born yet?'

'Ah, love.' This time he thinks about it. Long and hard. He pats my hair, with steady fingers takes the strands from my face and tucks them behind my ears. He hasn't done that since I was a little girl. 'I think he's in heaven, love. Oh, there's no thinking involved—I know so. He's up there with your mother, yes he is. Sitting on her lap while she plays rummy with Pauline, robbing her blind and cackling away. She'll be tellin' him all about you, she will, about when you were a baby, about your first day of school and your last day of school and every day in between, and he'll know all about you so that when you walk through those gates up there, as an old woman far older than me now, he'll look up from rummy and say, "Ah, there she is now. The woman herself. My mammy." Straight away he'll know.'

The lump in my throat, so huge I can barely swallow, prevents me from saying the thank you I want to express, but perhaps he sees it in my eyes because he nods in acknowledgment.

'There's a nice chapel here, love. Maybe you should go visit, when you're good and ready. Just sit there and think. I find it helpful.'

I think it's the last place in the world I want to be.

'It's a nice place to be,' Dad says, reading my mind.

'It's a rococo building, you know,' I say suddenly, and have no idea what I'm talking about. 'It's famous for the stucco work which adorns the ceiling. It's the work of French stuccadore, Barthélemy Cramillion.'

'Is that so, love? When did he do that, then?'

'In 1762.' So precise. So inexplicable that I know it.

'That long? I didn't know the hospital was here since then.'

'It's been here since 1757,' I reply. I can't stop myself, almost like my mouth is on autopilot. 'It was designed by the same man who did Leinster House. Richard Cassells was his name. One of the most famous architects of the time.'

I don't know where the words are coming from, don't know where the knowledge is coming from. Like a feeling of *déjà vu*—these words, this feeling are familiar but I haven't heard them or spoken them in this hospital. I think maybe I'm making it up but I know somewhere deep inside that I'm correct.

Dad is confused. 'I didn't know you had an interest in that kind of thing, Joyce. How do you know all that?'

I frown. Suddenly frustration overwhelms me and I shake my head aggressively. 'I want a haircut,' I say angrily, blowing my fringe off my forehead. 'I want to get out of here.'

'OK, love.' Dad's voice is quiet. 'A little longer, is all.'

Get a haircut! Justin blows his fringe out of his eyes and glares with dissatisfaction at his reflection in the mirror.

Until his image caught his eye, he was packing his bag to go back to London while whistling the happy tune of a recently divorced man who'd just been laid by the first woman since his wife. Well, the second time that year, but the first that he could recall with some small degree of pride. Now, standing before the full-length mirror, his whistling stalls. He corrects his posture, vowing that he will get his body back in order. Forty-three years old, he is handsome and he knows it, but it's not a view that is held with arrogance. He possesses the common sense enabling him to recognise he was born with good genes and features that were in proportion. He should be neither praised nor blamed for this. It's just how it is.

At almost six feet, he is tall, his shoulders broad, his hair still thick and chestnut brown, though greying at the sides. This he does not mind. For Justin, moving on and change are what he expects, though he didn't expect his particular philosophy of ageing and greying to apply to his marriage. Jennifer left him two years ago to ponder this, though not just this, but for a great many other reasons too. So many, in fact, he wishes he had taken out a pen and notepad and listed them as she bellowed at him in her tirade of hate.

Through strands of his long fringe hanging over his eyes, he has a vision of the man he expects to see. Leaner, younger. Any faults, such as the expanding waistline, are partly due to age and partly of his own doing, because he took to beer and takeaways for comfort during his divorce process rather than walking or the occasional jog.

Repeated flashbacks of the previous night draw his eyes back to the bed, where he and Sarah finally got to know one another intimately.

Blood For Life Week is over, much to Justin's relief, and Sarah has moved on from the college, back to her base. On his return to Dublin this month he coincidentally bumped into her in a bar, that he just happened to know she frequented, and they went from there. He wasn't sure if he would see her again though his inside jacket pocket was safely padded with her number.

He has to admit that while the previous night was indeed delightful—a few too many bottles of Château Olivier, which until last night he's always found disappointing despite its ideal location in Bordeaux, in a lively bar on the Green, followed by a trip to his hotel room—he feels much was missing from his conquest. He acquired some Dutch courage from his hotel minibar before calling round to see her, and by the time he arrived, he was already incapable of serious conversation or, more seriously, incapable of conversation. Despite ending up in his bed, he feels that Sarah did care about the conversation. He feels that perhaps there were things she wanted to say to him, and perhaps did say while he saw those sad blue eyes boring into his and her rosebud lips opening and closing, but which his whiskey wouldn't allow him to hear.

With his second seminar in two months complete, Justin throws his clothes into his bag. Friday afternoon, time to fly back to London. Back to his daughter, and his younger brother, Al, and sister-in-law, Doris, visiting from Chicago. He departs the hotel, steps out onto the cobbled side streets of Temple Bar and into his waiting taxi.

'The airport, please.'

'Here on holiday?' the driver asks immediately.

'No.' Justin looks out of the window.

'Working?' The driver starts the engine.

'Yes.'

'Where do you work?'

'A college.'

'Which one?'

Justin sighs. 'Trinity.'

'So where are ye off to? Off on holiday?'

'Nope.'

'What is it then?

'I live in London.' *And my US social security number is . . .*

'And you work here?'

'Yep.'

'Ah. So what do you do in London?'

I'm a serial killer who preys on inquisitive cab drivers.

'Lots of different things.' Justin sighs and caves in as the driver waits for more. 'I'm the editor of the *Art and Architectural Review*, the only truly international art and architectural publication,' he says proudly. 'I started it ten years ago and still we're unrivalled. Highest selling magazine of its kind.' *Twenty thousand subscribers, you liar.*

There's no reaction.

'I'm also a curator.'

The driver winces. 'You've to touch dead bodies?'

Justin scrunches his face in confusion. 'What? No.' He rolls his eyes, throws off his suit jacket, opens another of his shirt buttons and lowers the window. His hair sticks to his forehead. Still. A few weeks have gone by and he still hasn't been to the barber's. He blows his fringe out of his eyes.

They stop at a red light and Justin looks to his left. A hair salon.

'Hey, would you mind pulling over on the left just for a few minutes?'

'Look, Conor, don't worry about it. Stop apologising,' I say into the phone tiredly. He exhausts me. 'Dad is here with me now and we're going to get a taxi to the house together.'

Outside the hospital, Dad holds the door open for me and I climb into the taxi. Finally I'm going home but I don't feel the relief I was hoping for. There's nothing but dread. I dread meeting people I know and having to explain what has happened, over and over again. I dread walking into my house and having to face the half-decorated nursery. I dread having to go to work instead of taking the leave I had planned. I dread seeing Conor. I dread going back to a loveless marriage with no baby to distract us. I dread living every day of the rest of my life while Conor drones on and on down the phone about wanting to be here for me, when it seems my telling him *not* to come home has been my mantra for the past few days. I want to be on my own to grieve. I want to feel sorry for myself without sympathetic words and clinical explanations. I want to be illogical, self-pitying, self-examining, bitter and lost for just a few more days, please, world, and I want to do it alone.

Though that is not unusual in our marriage.

Conor's an engineer. He travels abroad to work for months before coming home for one month and going off again. I used to get so used to my own company and routine that for the first week of him being home I'd be irritable and wish he'd go back. That changed over time, of course. Now that irritability stretches to the entire month of him being home. And it's become glaringly obvious I'm not alone in that feeling.

When Conor took the job all those years ago, it was difficult being away from one another for so long. I used to visit him as much as I could but it was difficult to keep taking time off work. The visits got shorter, rarer, then stopped.

I always thought our marriage could survive anything as long as we both tried. But then I found myself having to try to try. I dug to get to the beginning of the relationship. What was it, I wondered, that we had then that we could revive? Ah. Love. A small simple word. If only it didn't mean so much, our marriage would be flawless. Sitting in the taxi beside Dad, while listening to Conor over the phone, I realise I've stopped pretending.

'Where is Conor?' Dad asks as soon as I've hung up. He looks for the handle on the car door, to roll the window down.

'It's electronic, Dad. There's the button. He's still in Japan. He'll be home in a few days.'

'I thought he was coming back yesterday.' He puts the window all the way down and is almost blown away. He has a mini-battle with the button before finally figuring out how to leave a small gap at the top for air to enter the stuffy taxi.

'Ha! Gotcha,' he smiles victoriously, thumping his fist at the window.

I wait until he's finished fighting with the window to answer. 'I told him not to.'

'You told who what, love?'

'Conor. You were asking about Conor, Dad.'

'Ah, that's right, I was. Home soon, is he?'

I nod.

The day is hot and I blow my fringe up from my sticky forehead. I feel my hair sticking to the back of my clammy neck. Brown and scraggy, it weighs me down and once again I have the overwhelming urge to shave it all off. I become agitated in my seat and Dad, sensing it again, knows not to say anything. I've been doing that all week: experiencing anger beyond comprehension. Then I become weepy and feel such loss inside me it's as if I'll never be filled again. I prefer the anger. Anger is hot and filling and gives me something to cling onto.

We stop at a set of traffic lights and I look to my left. A hair salon.

'Pull over here, please. Wait in the car, Dad. I'll be ten minutes. I'm just going to get a quick haircut. I can't take it any more.'

The taxi directly in front of us indicates and moves over to the side of the road too. We pull up behind it.

A man ahead of us gets out of the car and I freeze with one foot out of the car, to watch him. He's familiar and I think I know him. He pauses and looks at me. We stare at one another for a while. He scratches at his left arm; something that holds my attention for far too long. The moment is unusual and goose bumps rise on my skin. The last thing I want is to see somebody I know, and I look away quickly.

He looks away from me too and begins to walk.

I start walking towards the hair salon and it becomes clear that our destination is the same. My walk becomes mechanical, awkward, self-conscious. Something about him makes me disjointed. Unsettled.

He holds open the door to the salon and smiles. Handsome. Fresh-faced. Tall. Broad. Athletic. Perfect. Is he glowing? I must know him.

'Thank you,' I say.

'You're welcome.'

We both pause, look at one another. I think he's about to say something else but I quickly look away and step inside.

The salon is empty and two staff members are sitting down chatting. They are two men; one has a mullet, the other is bleached blond. They see us and spring to attention.

'Which one do you want?' the American says out of the side of his mouth.

'The blond,' I smile.

'The mullet it is, then,' he says.

My mouth falls open but I laugh.

'Hello there, loves.' The mullet man approaches us. 'How can I help you?' He looks back and forth from the American to me. 'Who is getting their hair done today?'

'Well, both of us, I assume, right?' American man looks at me and I nod.

'Oh, pardon me, I thought you were together.'

I realise we are so close our hips are almost touching. We both take one step away in the opposite direction.

'You two should try synchronised swimming,' the hairdresser laughs, but the joke dies when we fail to react. 'Ashley, you take the lovely lady. Now come with me.'

He leads his client to a chair. The American makes a face at me while being led away and I laugh again.

'Right, I just want two inches off, please,' the American says. 'The last time I got it done they took, like, twenty off. Please, just two inches,' he stresses. 'I've got a taxi waiting outside to take me to the airport, so as quick as possible too, please.'

His hairdresser laughs. 'Sure, no problem. Are you going back to America?'

The man rolls his eyes. 'No, I'm not going to America, I'm not going on holiday and I'm not going to meet anyone at arrivals. I'm just going to take a flight. Away. Out of here. You Irish ask a lot of questions.'

'Do we?'

'Y—' he stalls and narrows his eyes at the hairdresser.

'Gotcha,' the hairdresser smiles, pointing the scissors at him.

'Yes, you did.' Gritted teeth. 'You got me good.'

I chuckle aloud and he immediately looks at me. He seems slightly confused. Maybe we do know each other. Maybe he works with Conor. Maybe I showed him a property. Maybe he's famous and I shouldn't be staring. I become embarrassed and I turn away again quickly.

My hairdresser wraps a black cape round me. 'So what will it be for you, madam?'

'All off,' I say, trying to avoid my reflection but I feel cold hands on the sides of my hot cheeks, raising my head, and I am forced to stare at myself face to face. My cheeks are sunken, small black rings below my eyes, red lines like eyeliner still sting from my night tears. But apart from that, I still look like me. Despite this huge change in my life, I look exactly the same. Tired, but me. I don't know what I'd expected. A totally changed woman, someone that people would look at and just know had been through a traumatic experience. Yet the mirror told me this: you can't know everything by looking at me. You can *never* know by looking at someone.

I'm five foot five, with medium-length hair that lands on my shoulders. My hair colour is midway between blonde and brown. I'm a medium kind of person. Not fat, not skinny; I'm neither outgoing nor shy, but a little of both, depending on the occasion. I never overdo anything and enjoy most things I do. When I drink I get tipsy but never fall over or get ill. I like my job, don't love it. I'm pretty, not stunning, not ugly; don't expect too much, am never too disappointed. I'm never overwhelmed or under it either; just nicely whelmed. I look in the mirror and see this medium average person. A little tired, a little sad, but not falling apart. I look to the man beside me and I see the same.

'Excuse me?' The hairdresser breaks into my thoughts. 'You want it *all* off? Are you sure? You've such healthy hair.' He runs his fingers through it. 'Is this your natural colour?'

'Yes, I used to put a little colour in it but I stopped because of the—' I'm about to say 'baby'. My eyes fill and I look down.

'Stopped because of what?' he asks.

'Oh, em . . .' *Don't cry. Don't cry. If you start now you will never stop.* 'Chemicals,' I mumble. 'I stopped because of chemicals.'

'Right, this is what it'll look like,' he says, taking my hair and tying it back. 'How about we do a Meg Ryan in *French Kiss*?' He pulls hairs out in all directions and I look like I've stuck my fingers in an electric socket. 'Or else we can do this.' He messes about with my hair some more.

'Can we hurry this along? I've got a taxi waiting outside too.' I look out of the window. Dad is chatting to the taxi driver. They're both laughing and I relax a little.

'O . . . K. Something like this really shouldn't be rushed.'

'It's fine. I'm giving you permission to hurry. Just cut it all off.'

'Well, we must leave a few inches on it, darling. We don't want Sigourney Weaver in *Aliens*, do we? We'll give you a side-swept fringe, very sophisticated, show off those high cheekbones. What do you think?'

I don't care about my cheekbones. I want it all off. 'Actually, how about we just do this?' I take the scissors from his hand, cut my pony-tail, and then hand them both back to him.

He gasps. But it sounds more like a squeak. 'Or we could do that. A . . . bob.'

American man's mouth hangs open at the sight of my hairdresser with a large pair of scissors and ten inches of hair dangling from his hand. He turns to his hairdresser and grabs the scissors before he makes another cut. 'Do not,' he points, 'do *that* to me!'

Mullet man sighs and rolls his eyes. 'No, of course not, sir.'

The American starts scratching his left arm again. 'I must have got a bite.' He tries to roll up his shirtsleeve and I squirm in my seat, trying to get a look at his arm.

'Could you please sit still?'

'Could you please sit still?'

The hairdressers speak in perfect unison. They look to one another and laugh. 'Something funny in the air today,' one of them comments and American man and I look at each other. Funny, indeed.

My hairdresser places a finger under my chin and tips my face back to the centre. He begins to shape my hair into style now and as each strand falls my head feels lighter. The hair that grew the day we bought the cot, too soon, but we were so excited . . . Snip. The hair that grew the day we decided the names. Snip. The hair that grew the day we announced it to friends and family. Snip. The day of the first scan. The day I found out I was pregnant. The day my baby was conceived. Snip. Snip. Snip.

The more painful recent memories will remain at the root for another little while. I will have to wait for them to grow until I can be rid of them too and then all traces will be gone and I will move on.

I reach the till as the American pays for his cut.

'That suits you,' he comments, studying me.

I go to tuck some hair behind my ear self-consciously but there's nothing there. I feel lighter, light-headed, delighted with giddiness, giddy with delight. 'So does yours.'

'Thank you.'

He opens the door for me.

'Thank you.' I step outside.

'You're far too polite,' he tells me.

'Thank you,' I smile. 'So are you.'

'Thank you,' he nods.

We laugh and look at each other curiously. He gives me a smile, then walks to his taxi, glancing back twice.

I float to my taxi and we both pull our doors closed at the same time. The taxi driver and Dad look at me like they've seen a ghost.

'What?' My heart beats wildly. 'What happened? Tell me.'

'Your hair,' Dad simply says, his face aghast. 'You're like a boy.'

As the taxi gets closer to my home in Phisboro, my stomach knots tighter.

'That was funny how the man in front kept his taxi waiting too, Gracie, wasn't it?'

'Joyce. And yes,' I reply, my leg bouncing with nerves.

'Is that what people do now when they get their hairs cut?'

'Do what, Dad?'

'Leave taxis waiting outside for them.'

'I don't know.'

He pulls himself closer to the taxi driver. 'I say, Jack, is that what people do when they go to the barber's now?'

'What's that?'

'Do they leave their taxis outside waiting for them?'

'I've never been asked to do it before,' the driver answers politely.

Dad sits back satisfied. 'That's what I thought. There's Patrick.' He waves. 'I hope he doesn't wave back.' He watches his friend from the Monday Club with two hands on his walking frame. 'And David out with the dog.' He waves again. 'Home sweet home,' he announces.

Conor and I have lived in the redbrick terraced house in Phisboro since our marriage ten years ago. The houses have been here since the forties, and over the years we've pumped our money into modernising ours. Finally it's how we want it. A black railing encloses a small patch of a front garden where the rosebushes my mother planted preside.

Dad lives in an identical house two streets away, the house I grew up in.

The front door to my house opens just as the taxi drives off. Dad's neighbour Fran smiles at me from my own front door. 'Oh, your hair!' she says first, then gathers herself. 'I'm sorry, love, I meant to be out of here by the time you got home.' She opens the door fully. She is wearing a single Marigold glove on her right hand.

Dad looks nervous and avoids my eye.

'What were you doing, Fran? How on earth did you get into my house?' I try to be as polite as I can but the sight of someone in my house without my permission both surprises and infuriates me.

She laughs nervously and pulls off her single Marigold. 'Oh, your dad gave me a key. I thought that . . . well, I put down a nice rug in the hallway for you. I hope you like it.'

I stare at her in utter confusion.

'Never mind, I'll be off now.' She walks by me, grabs my arm and squeezes hard. 'Take care of yourself, love.'

'Dad.' I look at him angrily. 'What the hell is this?' I push into the house, looking at the disgusting dusty rug on my beige carpet. 'Why did you give a near stranger my house keys so she could come in and leave a rug? I am not a charity!'

He takes off his cap and scrunches it in his hands. 'She's not a stranger, love. She's known you since the day you were brought home from the hospital—'

Wrong story to tell at this moment, and he knows it.

'I don't care!' I splutter. 'I hate this ugly piece of shit rug!' I drag it outside and then slam the door shut. I'm fuming and I look at Dad to shout at him again. He is looking at the floor sadly. My eyes follow his.

Various shades of faded brown stains, like red wine, splatter the beige carpet. My blood.

Dad's voice is quiet, injured. 'I thought it would be best for you to come home with that gone.'

'Oh, Dad.'

'Fran has been here for a little while every day now and has tried different things on it. It was me that suggested the rug.'

I despise myself. 'I'm sorry, Dad. I don't know what came over me. I'll . . . I'll call around to Fran at some stage and thank her properly.'

'Right,' he nods, 'I'll leave you at it, so. I'll bring the rug back to Fran. I don't want any neighbours seeing it outside and telling her so.'

'No, I'll put it back where it was. It's too heavy for you to bring all the way around. I'll return it to her soon.' I retrieve it from the outside path. I drag it back into the house with more respect, laying it down so that it hides the scene where I lost my baby.

Dad pats my shoulder. 'You're having a hard time, that I know. I'm only round the corner if you need me for anything.'

With a flick of his wrist, his tweed cap is on his head and I watch him seesaw down the road. He disappears round the corner and I close the door. Alone. Silence. Just me and the house.

It seems as though the nursery upstairs vibrates through the walls and floor. Thump-thump. Thump-thump. As though like a heart, it's trying to push out the walls and send blood flowing down the stairs, through the hallways to reach every little nook and cranny. I walk away from the stairs, the scene of the crime, and wander around the rooms. I see that Fran has tidied around. The cup of tea I was drinking is gone from the coffee table in the living room. The galley kitchen hums with the sound of the dishwasher Fran has set. The taps and draining boards glisten, the surfaces are gleaming. Straight through the kitchen the door leads to the back garden. My mum's rosebushes line the back wall. Dad's geraniums peep up from the soil.

Upstairs the nursery still throbs.

I notice the red light on the answering machine in the hall flashing. Four messages. I flick through the list of registered phone numbers and recognise friends' numbers. I leave the answering machine, not able to listen to their condolences quite yet. Then I freeze. I go back. I flick through the list again. There it is. Monday evening. 7.10 p.m. Again at 7.12 p.m. My second chance to take the call. The call I had foolishly rushed down the stairs for and sacrificed my child's life.

They have left a message. With shaking fingers, I press play.

'Hello, this is Xtra-vision, Phisboro calling about the DVD *The Muppet's Christmas Carol*. It says on our system that it's one week late. We'd appreciate it if you could return it as soon as possible, please.'

I inhale sharply. Tears spring in my eyes. What did I expect? A phone call worthy of losing my baby? Something so urgent that I was right to rush for it? Would that somehow warrant my loss?

My entire body trembles with rage and shock. Breathing in shakily, I make my way into the living room. I look straight ahead to the DVD player. On top is the DVD I rented while minding my goddaughter. I reach for the DVD, throw it hard across the room. It knocks our collection of photographs off the top of the piano.

I open my mouth. And I scream. I scream the loudest I can possibly go. It's deep and low and filled with anguish. I scream again. One scream after another from the pit of my stomach, from the depths of my heart, until I am out of breath and my throat burns.

Upstairs, the nursery continues to vibrate. Thump-thump, thump-thump. It beckons me, the heart of my home beating wildly. I go to the staircase, grab the banister, feeling too weak even to lift my legs. I pull myself upstairs. I reach for the handle and open the door.

A half-painted wall of Buttercup Dream greets me. A cot with a mobile of little yellow ducks dangling above. A bunny rabbit sits up enthusiastically inside the cot. He smiles stupidly at me. I take my shoes off and step barefoot onto the soft shagpile carpet. I pick up the rabbit and carry it around the room with me while I run my hands over the shiny new furniture, clothes and toys. I open a music box and watch as the little mouse inside begins to circle round and round after a piece of cheese to a mesmerising tinkling sound.

'I'm sorry, Sean,' I whisper, and my words catch in my throat. 'I'm so, so sorry.'

'**I** can't find any food in the apartment; we're going to have to get takeout,' Justin's sister-in-law, Doris, calls into the living room as she roots through the kitchen cabinets.

'So maybe you know the woman.' Justin's younger brother, Al, sits on the plastic garden furniture chair in Justin's half-furnished living room.

'No, you see, that's what I'm trying to explain. It's *like* I know her but at the same time, I didn't know her at all.'

'You recognised her.'

'Yes. Well, no.' *Kind of*.

'And you don't know her name.'

'No. I definitely don't know her name.'

'Hey, am I talking to myself?' Doris interrupts again. 'I said there's no food here so we're going to have to get takeout.'

'Yeah, sure, honey,' Al calls automatically. 'Maybe she's a student of yours or she went to one of your talks.'

'There's hundreds of people at a time,' Justin shrugs. 'And mostly they sit in darkness.'

'Actually, forget the takeout,' Doris calls. 'You don't have any plates or cutlery—we're going to have to eat out.'

'And just let me get this clear, Al. When I say "recognise", I mean I didn't actually know her face. I just got a feeling. Like she was familiar.'

'Maybe she just looked like someone you know.'

'Hey, is anybody listening to me?' Doris interrupts them, standing at the living-room door with her inch-long leopard-print nails on her skintight leather trouser-clad hips. Thirty-five-year-old Italian-American fast-talking Doris had been married to Al for the past ten years and is regarded by Justin as a lovable but annoying younger sister.

'Yeah, sure, honey,' Al says again, not taking his eyes off Justin. 'Maybe it was that *déjà vu* thingy.'

'Yes!' Justin clicks his fingers. 'Or perhaps *vécu*, or *senti*,' he rubs his chin, lost in thought. 'Or *visité*.'

'What the heck is that?' Al asks as Doris pulls over a cardboard box filled with books, to sit on, and joins them.

'*Déjà vu* is French for "already seen" and it describes the experience of feeling that one has witnessed or experienced a new situation previously, but I don't think this thing today with me and the woman was *déjà vu*.' Justin frowns and sighs.

'Why not?'

'Because *déjà vu* relates to just *sight* and I felt . . . oh, I don't know.' I *felt*. '*Déjà vécu* is translated as "already lived", which explains the experience that involves more than sight, but of having a weird knowledge of what is going to happen next. *Déjà senti* specifically means "already felt", which is exclusively a mental happening and *déjà visité* involves an uncanny knowledge of a new place, but that's less common. No,' he shakes his head, 'I definitely didn't feel I had been at the salon before.'

They all go quiet.

Al breaks the silence. 'Well, it's definitely *déjà* something. Are you sure you didn't just sleep with her before?'

'Al!' Doris hits her husband across the arm. 'Why didn't you let me cut your hair, Justin, and who are we talking about anyway?'

'You own a doggy parlour.' Justin frowns.

'Dogs have hair,' she shrugs.

'Let me try to explain this,' Al interrupts. 'Justin saw a woman yesterday at a hair salon in Dublin and he says he recognised her but didn't know her face, and he felt that he knew her but didn't actually know her.' He rolls his eyes melodramatically, out of Justin's view.

'Oh my God,' Doris sings, 'I know what this is.'

'What?' Justin asks, taking a drink from a toothbrush holder.

'It's obvious.' She holds her hands up. 'It's past-life stuff.' Her face lights up. 'You knew the woman in a *paaast liiife*,' she pronounces the words slowly. 'I saw it on *Oprah*.' She nods her head, eyes wide.

'Not more of this crap, Doris. It's all she talks about now. She sees somethin' about it on TV and that's all I get, all the way from Chicago.'

'I don't think it's past-life stuff, Doris, but thanks. The woman was familiar, that's all. Maybe she just looked like someone I knew at home. No big deal.' *Forget about it and move on.*

'Well, you started it with your *déjà* stuff,' Doris huffs. 'How do you explain it?'

Justin shrugs. 'The optical pathway delay theory.'

They both stare at him, dumb-faced.

'One theory is that one eye may record what is seen fractionally faster than the other, creating that strong recollection sensation upon the same scene being viewed milliseconds later by the other eye. Basically it's the product of a delayed optical input from one eye, closely followed by the input from the other eye, which should be simultaneous. This misleads conscious awareness and suggests a sensation of familiarity when there shouldn't be one.'

Silence.

'Believe it or not, honey, I prefer your past-life thing,' Al snorts.

'Thanks, sweetie.' Doris places her hands on her heart, over-whelmed. 'Anyway, as I was saying when I was *talking to myself* in the kitchen, there's no food, cutlery or crockery here so we'll have to eat out. Look at how you're living, Justin. I'm worried about you.' Doris looks around the room with disgust and her backcombed, hairsprayed, dyed red hair follows the movement. 'You've moved all the way over to this country on your own, you've got nothing but garden furniture and unpacked boxes in a basement that looks like it was built for students.'

'This is a Victorian masterpiece, Doris. It was a real find, and it's the only place I *could* find with a bit of history as well as having affordable rent. All the place needs is a bit of TLC and it'll be fine,' Justin says.

'Which is why I'm here.' Doris claps her hands with glee.

'Great.' Justin's smile is tight. 'Let's go get some dinner now. I'm in the mood for a steak.'

'But you're vegetarian, Joyce.' Conor looks at me as if I've lost my mind. I probably have. I can't remember the last time I ate red meat but I have a sudden craving for it now that we've sat down at the restaurant.

'I'm not vegetarian, Conor. I just don't like red meat.'

'But you've just ordered a medium-rare steak!'

'I know,' I shrug. 'I'm just one crazy cat.'

'Have you chosen the wine yet?' the waiter asks Conor.

I quickly grab the menu. 'Actually I would like to order this one, please.' I point to the menu.

'Sancerre 1998. That's a very good choice, madam.'

'Thank you.' I have no idea whatsoever why I've chosen it. It's too expensive and I usually drink white, but I act naturally because I don't want Conor to think I've lost my mind. He already thought I was crazy when he saw I'd chopped all my hair off. He needs to think I'm back to my normal self in order for me to be able to say what I'm going to say tonight.

The waiter returns with the bottle of wine.

'You can do the tasting,' Al says to Justin, 'seeing as it was your choice.'

Justin picks up the glass of wine, dips his nose into the glass and inhales deeply.

I inhale deeply and then swivel the wine in the glass. I take a sip and hold it on my tongue, suck it in and allow the alcohol to burn the inside of my mouth. Perfect.

'Lovely, thank you.' I place the glass on the table again.

Conor's glass is filled and mine is topped up.

'It's beautiful wine.' I begin to tell him the story.

'I found it when Jennifer and I went to France years ago,' Justin explains. 'She was there performing in the Festival des Cathédrales de Picardie with the orchestra. On one of her nights off in Paris we found this beautiful little fish restaurant tucked away down one of the cobbled alleys of Montmartre. We ordered the special, sea bass, but you know how much of a red wine fanatic I am—even with fish I prefer to drink red—so the waiter suggested we go for the Sancerre. You can drink red Sancerre cooled exactly like white, at twelve degrees. But when not chilled, it's also good with meat. Enjoy.' He toasts his brother and sister-in-law.

Conor is looking at me with a frozen face. 'Montmartre? Joyce, you've never been to Paris before. How do you know so much about wine? And who the hell is Jennifer?'

I pause, snap out of my trance and suddenly hear the words of the story I had just told. I do the only thing I can do under the circumstances. I start laughing. 'Gotcha.'

'Gotcha?' he frowns.

'They're the lines of a movie I watched the other night.'

'Oh.' Relief floods his face and he relaxes. 'Joyce, you scared me there for a minute. I thought somebody had possessed your body.' He smiles. 'What film is it from?'

'Oh, I can't remember.' I wave my hand dismissively.

'You don't like anchovies now?' He looks down at the little collection of anchovies I've gathered in a pile at the side of my plate.

'Give them to me, bro,' Al says, lifting his plate closer to Justin's. 'I love 'em. How you can have a Caesar salad without anchovies is beyond me. Is it OK that I have anchovies, Doris?' he asks sarcastically. 'The doc didn't say anchovies are going to kill me, did he?'

'Not unless somebody stuffs them down your throat, which is quite possible,' Doris says through gritted teeth.

'Thirty-nine years old and I'm being treated like a kid.'

'Thirty-five years old and the only kid I have is my husband,' Doris snaps, picking an anchovy from the pile and tasting it. 'So, Justin, tell me about this lady you're seeing.'

Justin frowns. 'Doris, it's really no big deal, I told you I just thought I knew her.' *And she looked like she thought she knew you too.*

'No, not her,' Al says loudly with a mouthful of anchovies. 'She's talking about the woman you were banging the other night.'

'Al!' Food wedges in Justin's throat.

'Joyce,' Conor says with concern, 'are you OK?'

My eyes fill as I try to catch my breath from coughing.

'Here, have some water.' He pushes a glass in my face.

People around us are staring, concerned.

I'm coughing so much I can't even take a breath to drink. Conor gets up from his chair and comes around to me. I stand up in panic, overturning my chair behind me in the process.

'**A**l, Al, do something!' Doris panics. 'He's going purple.'

Al coolly stands up and positions himself behind his brother. He wraps his arms round his waist, and pumps hard on his stomach.

On the second push, the food is dislodged from Justin's throat.

As a third person races to my aid, or rather to join the growing panicked discussion of how to perform the Heimlich manoeuvre, I suddenly stop coughing. Three faces stare at me in surprise.

'Are you OK?' Conor asks, patting my back.

'Yes,' I whisper, embarrassed by the attention we are receiving. 'I'm fine, thank you. Everyone, thank you so much for your help.' I sit down quickly, trying to ignore the stares. 'God, that was embarrassing.'

'That was odd; you hadn't even eaten anything.'

I shrug. 'I don't know, something caught when I inhaled.'

I feel a nudge from behind me as our neighbour leans over to our table. 'Hey, for a minute there I thought you were going into labour, ha-ha! Didn't we, Margaret?' He looks at his wife and laughs.

'No,' Margaret says, her face turning puce. 'No, Pat.'

'Huh?' He's confused. 'Well, *I* did anyway. Congrats, Conor.' He turns back to face his table, and we hear murmured squabbling.

Conor's face falls and he reaches for my hand. 'Are you OK?'

'That's happened a few times now,' I explain, and instinctively place my hand over my flat stomach.

'Oh, Joyce.' His grip on my hand tightens as I speak; he squeezes my wedding ring into my skin and it hurts.

A wedding ring but no marriage.

'Conor,' is all I say. I give him a look and I know he knows what I'm about to say. He's seen this look before.

'No, no, no, no, Joyce, not this conversation now.' He holds his hands up in defence. 'You—*we*—have been through enough this week.'

'Conor, no more distractions.' I lean forward with urgency.

We've had this conversation in some form or another on an annual basis over the last five years and I wait for the usual retort from Conor. That no one says marriage is easy, we promised one another, he's determined to work at it. I wait for his usual comments. I realise minutes later they still haven't come. I look up and see he is battling tears and is nodding in what looks like agreement.

I take a breath. This is it.

Justin eyes the dessert menu.

'You can't have any, Al.' Doris plucks the menu out of her husband's hands and snaps it shut.

'Why not? Am I not allowed to even read it?'

'Your cholesterol goes up just reading it.'

Justin zones out as they squabble. He shouldn't be having any either. He really shouldn't, but his eyes hover above one item on the menu like a vulture watching its prey.

'Any dessert for you, sir?' the waiter asks.

Go on. 'Yes. I'll have the . . .'

Banoffee pie, please,' I blurt out to the waiter, to my own surprise.

Conor's mouth drops. Oh dear. My marriage has just ended and I'm ordering dessert. I bite my lip and stop a nervous smile from breaking out.

To new beginnings. To the pursuit of . . . somethingness.

Three

A CHIME WELCOMES ME to my father's humble home. Apologetic, short and clipped. It says, *sorry, Dad, sorry to disturb you. Sorry the thirty-three-year-old daughter you thought you were long ago rid of is back home after her marriage has fallen apart.*

Dad opens the door, looks at me blankly and then down at the suitcases round my feet. 'What's this?'

'You . . . you told me I could stay for a while.'

'I thought you meant till the end of *Countdown*.'

'Oh . . . well, I was hoping to stay for a bit longer than that.'

'Long after I'm gone, by the looks of it.' He surveys his doorstep. 'Come in, come in. Where's Conor? Something happen to the house? You haven't mice again, have you? It's the time of the year for them.'

'Dad, I've never called round to stay here because of mice.'

'There's a first time for everything. Your mother used to do that.

Hated the things. Used to stay at your grandmother's for the few days while I ran around here like that cartoon cat trying to catch them. Tom or Jerry, was it?' He squeezes his eyes closed tight to think, then opens them again, none the wiser, and carries my suitcases into the hall.

'Dad?' I say, frustrated. 'I thought you understood me on the phone. Conor and I have separated.'

'Separated what?'

'Ourselves.'

'What on earth are you talking about, Gracie?'

'Joyce. We're not together any more. We've split up.'

He puts the bags down by the hall's wall of photographs, there to provide any visitor who crosses the threshold with a crash course on the Conway family history, and works his way into the kitchen. 'Cuppa?'

I stay in the hall looking around at the photos and breathe in that smell. The smell that's carried around every day on every stitch of Dad's back, like a snail carries its home. I always thought it was the smell of Mum's cooking that drifted around the rooms and seeped into every fibre, including the wallpaper, but it's ten years since Mum has passed away. Perhaps the scent was her; perhaps it's still her.

'What are you doin' sniffin' the walls?'

I jump, startled and embarrassed at being caught, and make my way into the kitchen. It hasn't changed since I lived here and it's as spotless as the day Mum left it, nothing moved, not even for convenience's sake. I watch Dad move slowly about, resting on his right foot to access the cupboards below, and then using the extra inches of his left leg as his own personal footstool to reach above.

It's rare I'm around the area so early on in the day. Usually I'd be at work showing property around the city. It's so quiet now with everyone at work, I wonder what on earth Dad does in this silence.

'What were you doing before I came?'

'Thirty-three years ago or today?'

'Today.' I try not to smile because I know he's serious.

'Quiz.' He nods at the kitchen table where he has a page full of puzzles and quizzes. Half of them are completed. 'I'm stuck on number six. Have a look at that.' He brings the cups of tea to the table, managing not to spill a drop despite his swaying. Always steady.

'"Which especially influential critic summed up one of Mozart's operas as having 'too many notes'?"' I read the clue aloud.

'Mozart,' Dad shrugs. 'Haven't a clue about that lad at all.'

'Emperor Joseph the Second,' I say.

Dad's eyebrows go up in surprise. 'How did you know that, then?'

I frown. 'I must have just heard it some wh—do I smell smoke?'

He sits up straight and sniffs the air like a bloodhound. 'Toast. I made it earlier. Had the setting on too high and burned it. They were the last two slices, as well.'

'Hate that.' I shake my head. 'Where's Mum's photograph from the hall?'

'Which one? There are thirty of her.'

'You've counted?' I laugh.

'Nailed them up there, didn't I? Forty-four photos in total.'

'So where is it?'

'Right where it always is,' he says unconvincingly.

We both look at the closed kitchen door, in the direction of the hall table. I stand up to go out and check. These are the kinds of things you do when you have time on your hands.

'Ah ah,' he jerks a floppy hand at me. 'Sit yourself down.' He rises. 'I'll go out and check.' He closes the kitchen door behind him, blocking me from seeing out. 'She's there all right,' he calls to me. 'Hello, Gracie, haven't you been there all along watchin' your daughter sniffin' the walls, thinkin' the paper's on fire. But sure isn't it only madder she's gettin', leaving her husband and packing in her job.'

I haven't mentioned anything to him about taking leave from my job, which means Conor has spoken to him, which means Dad knew my reasons for being here from the first moment he heard the doorbell. I have to give it to him, he plays stupid very well. He returns to the kitchen and I catch a glimpse of the photo on the hall table.

'Ah!' He looks at his watch in alarm. 'Ten twenty-five! Let's go inside quick!' He grabs his weekly television guide and his cup of tea and rushes into the television room.

'What are we watching?' I follow him into the living room.

'*Murder, She Wrote.* That Jessica Fletcher is a great one for catching the murderers. Then over on the next channel we'll watch *Diagnosis Murder*, where the dancer solves the cases.' He takes a pen and circles it on the TV page.

I'm captivated by Dad's excitement. He sings along with the theme tune, making trumpet noises with his mouth.

'Come in here and lie on the couch and I'll put this over you.' He picks up a tartan blanket draped over the back of the green velvet couch and places it gently over me, tucking it in around my body so tightly I can't move my arms. It's the same blanket I rolled on as a baby, the same blanket they covered me with when I was home sick from school and was allowed to watch television on the couch. I watch Dad with fondness, remembering the tenderness he always showed me as a child, feeling right back there again.

Until he sits at the end of the couch and squashes my feet.

'What do you think, Gracie—will Betty be a millionaire by the end of the show?'

I have sat through an endless number of half-hour morning shows over the last few days and now we are watching the *Antiques Roadshow*. Betty is seventy years old, from Warwickshire, and is currently waiting with anticipation as the dealer tries to price the old teapot she has brought with her. I watch the dealer handling the teapot delicately and a comfortable, familiar feeling overwhelms me.

'Sorry, Betty,' I say to the television, 'it's a replica made in the early twentieth century. You can see from the way the handle is shaped. Clumsy craftsmanship.'

'Is that so?' Dad looks at me with interest.

We listen as the dealer repeats my remarks. Poor Betty is devastated.

'How do you know all that about the pots, Gracie? Read it in one of your books maybe?'

'Maybe.' I have no idea. I get a headache thinking about this new-found knowledge.

Dad catches the look on my face. 'Why don't you call a friend or something? Have a chat.'

I know I should. 'I should probably give Kate a call.'

'The big-boned girl? The one who ploughed you with poteen when you were sixteen?'

'That's Kate,' I laugh. He has never forgiven her for that.

'She was a messer, that girl. Has she come to anything?'

'She just sold her shop in the city for two million to become a stay-at-home mother.' I try not to laugh at the shock on his face.

His ears prick up. 'Ah, sure, give her a call. Have a chat. You women like to do that. Good for the soul, your mother always said. Your mother loved talking, was always blatherin' on to someone or other about somethin' or other.'

'Wonder where she got that from?' I say under my breath as I escape to my bedroom to phone Kate. I enter the room, practically unchanged since the day I left it. My box bedroom can only fit a bed and a wardrobe but it was my whole world. My only personal space then and, at thirty-three years old, my only space now. Who knew I'd find myself back again? The wallpaper is floral and wild; completely inappropriate for a space of rest. The carpet is brown, stained from spilt perfume and make-up. New additions to the room are old and faded brown leather suitcases lying on top of the wardrobe, gathering dust since Mum died. Dad never goes anywhere, a life without Mum, he decided long ago, enough of a journey for him.

The duvet cover is the newest introduction. New, as in, over ten years old; Mum purchased it when my room became the guest room. I moved out a year before she died, to live with Kate, and I wish every day since that I hadn't, all those precious days of not waking up to hear her long yawns that turned into songs, talking to herself as she made her verbal diary with Gay Byrne's radio show on in the background. She loved Gay Byrne; I think she had a thing for him. Dad hated him. I think he knew about her thing.

He likes to listen to him now, though, whenever he's on. I think he reminds him of a precious time spent with Mum. When she died, Dad surrounded himself with all the things she adored. He put Gay on the radio every morning, watched Mum's television shows, bought her favourite biscuits on his weekly shopping trip even though he never ate them. He liked to see them on the shelf when he opened the cupboard. He liked to remind himself that his entire world hadn't fallen apart. Sometimes we need all the glue we can get, just to hold ourselves together.

At sixty-five years old, he was too young to lose his wife. At twenty-three I was too young to lose my mother. At fifty-five she shouldn't have lost her life, but cancer stole it from her and us all.

Mum never met Conor but I don't know whether she would have liked him. Mum loved people with high spirits, people that lived and exuded that life. Conor is never overexcited. Never, in fact, excited at all. Just pleasant, which is just another word for nice. Marrying a nice man gives you a nice marriage but never anything more. And nice is

OK when it's among other things but never when it stands alone.

The only negative thing Dad ever said about Conor was, 'Sure, what kind of man likes *tennis*?' A GAA and soccer man, Dad had spat the word out as though just saying it had dirtied his mouth.

Dad blamed our failure to produce a child on the little white tennis shorts Conor sometimes wore. I know he said it to put a smile on my face; sometimes it worked, other times it didn't, but it was a safe joke because we all knew it wasn't the tennis shorts or the man wearing them that was the problem.

I sit down on the duvet cover and I turn on my mobile, which has been switched off for days, and it begins to beep as a dozen messages filter through. I have already made my calls to those near, dear and nosy. Quick snappy phone calls made by a strangely upbeat woman who'd momentarily inhabited my body. She even attempted a bit of humour, which some members of the near, dear and nosy coped well with while others seemed almost insulted—not that she cared, for it was her party and she was crying if she wanted to.

It will be a long time before I can speak in my own voice to people other than the woman I am calling now.

Kate picks up on the fourth ring.

'Hello,' she shouts and I jump. There are manic noises in the background, as though a mini-war has broken out.

'Joyce!' she yells and I realise I'm on speakerphone. 'I've been *calling* you and *calling* you. Derek, SIT DOWN. Sorry, I'm just doing the school run. I've to bring six kids home, then a quick snack before I bring Eric to basketball and Jayda to swimming. Want to meet me there at seven? Jayda is getting her ten-metre badge today.'

Jayda howls in the background about hating ten-metre badges.

'How can you hate it when you've never had one?' Kate snaps. Jayda howls even louder and I have to move the phone from my ear. 'JAYDA! GIVE MUMMY A BREAK! DEREK, PUT YOUR SEAT BELT ON! If I have to brake suddenly, you will go FLYING through the windscreen and SMASH YOUR FACE IN. Hold on, Joyce.'

There is silence while I wait. Suddenly Kate's voice is back and it sounds as though calm has been restored.

'OK, you're off speakerphone. I'll probably be arrested for holding the phone, not to mention cast off the car-pool list, like I give a flying fuck about that.'

'Fuck, Fuck, Fuck,' I hear a crowd of kids chanting.

'Jesus, Joyce, I better go. See you at the leisure centre at seven? It's my only break. Or else I have tomorrow. Tennis at three or gymnastics at six? I can see if Frankie is free to meet up too.'

Frankie. Christened Francesca but refuses to answer to it. Dad was wrong about Kate. She may have sourced the poteen but technically it was Frankie that held my mouth open and poured it down my throat. As a result of this version of the story never being told, he thinks Frankie's a saint, very much to Kate's annoyance.

'I'll take gymnastics tomorrow,' I smile as the children's chanting gets louder. Kate's gone and there's silence.

'Gracie!' Dad yells.

'It's *Joyce*, Dad.'

'I got the conundrum in *Countdown*!' Dad arrives at the door. 'I was the only one that got the conundrum. The contestants hadn't a clue. Simon won anyway, goes through to tomorrow's show. He's been the winner for three days now and I'm half bored lookin' at him. He has a funny-looking face; you'd have a right laugh if you saw it. Do you want a HobNob? I'm going to make another cuppa.'

'No, thanks.' I lie back on my bed and cover my head with a pillow. He uses so many *words*.

'Well, I'm having one. I have to eat with my pills. Supposed to take it at lunch but I forgot.'

'You took a pill at lunch, remember?'

'That was for my heart. This is for my memory. Short-term memory pills.'

I take the pillow off my face to see if he's being serious. 'And you forgot to take it?'

He nods.

'Oh, Dad.' I start to laugh. 'You are medicine enough for me. Well, you need stronger pills. They're not working, are they?'

'They'd bloody well work if I remembered to take them.'

'Dad, thanks for not asking any questions about Conor.'

'Sure, I don't need to. I know you'll be back together in no time.'

'No, we won't,' I say softly.

'Is he stepping out with someone else?'

'No, he's not. And I'm not. We don't love each other.'

'But you married him, Joyce. You both promised each other in the house of Our Lord, I heard you myself with my own ears. What is it with you young people these days, breaking up and remarrying all the time? What happened to keeping promises?'

I sigh. How can I answer that? 'Would you rather I kept my promise to spend the rest of my life with Conor, but not love him and be unhappy?'

'No one's happy all the time, love.'

'I understand that, but what if you're *never* happy. Ever.'

He thinks about that for what looks like the first time and I hold my breath until he finally speaks. 'I'm going to have a HobNob.' Halfway down the stairs he shouts back rebelliously, 'A *chocolate* one.'

'I'm on a vacation, bro, why are you dragging me to a gym?' Al half walks, half skips alongside Justin in an effort to keep up with his lean brother's long strides.

'I have a date with Sarah next week,' Justin power-walks from the tube station, 'and I need to get back into shape.'

'I didn't realise you were *out* of shape,' Al pants, and wipes trickles of sweat from his beetroot face.

'Never mind *my* having to work out, look at yourself. Your doctor's already told you to drop a few hundred pounds.'

'Fifty pounds . . .' gasp, 'aren't exactly . . .' gasp, 'a few *hundred*, and don't start on me too.' Gasp. 'Doris is bad enough.' Wheeze. Cough. 'What she knows about dieting is beyond me. The woman doesn't eat. She's afraid to bite a nail in case they've too many calories.'

'Doris's nails are real?'

'Them and her hair is about all.'

'I can't believe Doris's *hair* is real too,' Justin says.

'All but the colour. She's a brunette. Italian, of course. Dizzy.'

'Yeah, she is a bit dizzy. All that past-life talk about the woman at the hair salon.' Justin laughs. *So how do you explain it?*

'I meant *I'm* dizzy.' Al glares at him and reaches out to hold onto the nearby railing.

'Oh . . . Think you can make it another hundred yards or so?'

'Depends on the "or so",' Al snaps.

'It's about the same as the week *or so* vacation that you and Doris were planning on taking. Looks like that's turning into a month.'

'Well, we wanted to surprise you, and Doug is well able to take care of the shop while I'm gone. The doc advised me to take it easy. With heart conditions being in the family history, I really need to rest up.'

'You told the doctor there's a history of heart conditions in the family?' Justin asks.

'Yeah, Dad died of a heart attack. Who else would I be talkin' about?'

Justin is silent.

'Besides, you won't be sorry, Doris will have your apartment done up so nice that you'll be glad we stayed. You know she did the doggy parlour all by herself?'

Justin's eyes widen.

'I know,' Al beams proudly. 'So, how many of these seminars will you be doing in Dublin? Me and Doris might accompany you on one of your trips over there, you know, see the place Dad was from.'

'Dad was from Cork.'

'Oh. Does he still have family there? We could go and trace our roots, what do you think?'

'That's not such a bad idea.' Justin thinks of his schedule. 'I have a few more seminars ahead. You probably won't be here that long, though.' He eyes Al sideways. 'And you can't come next week because I'm mixing that trip with a date with Sarah.' He changes the subject. 'Let's do an hour at the gym.'

'*One hour?*' Al almost explodes. 'What are you planning on doing on the date, rock-climbing?'

'It's just lunch.'

Al rolls his eyes. 'What, you have to chase and kill your food? Anyway, you wake up tomorrow morning after your first workout for a whole year, you won't be able to *walk*, never mind screw.'

I wake up to the sound of banging pots and pans coming from downstairs. I didn't sleep well last night between the thoughts in my head and the sound of the cistern flushing every hour after Dad's toilet breaks. When he was asleep, his snores rattled through the walls of the house.

Despite the interruptions, my dreams during my rare moments of sleep are still vivid in my mind. They almost feel real, like memories, though who's to know how real even they are, with all the altering our minds do? I remember being in a park, though I don't think I was me. I twirled a young girl with white-blonde hair around in my arms while a woman with red hair looked on smiling. We had a picnic . . .

I swing my legs out of the bed and groan with pain, suddenly feeling an ache in both legs from my hips, right down my thighs, all the way down to my calf muscles. I try to move the rest of my body and feel paralysed with the pain; my shoulders, biceps, triceps, back muscles and torso. I massage my muscles in complete confusion and make a note in my head to go to the doctor. I'm sure it's my heart, so full of pain it has needed to ooze its ache around the rest of my body just to relieve itself.

I throw a dressing gown round me and slowly, as stiff as a board, make my way downstairs, trying my best not to bend my legs.

The smell of smoke is in the air again and I notice as I'm passing the hall table that Mum's photograph once again isn't there. Something urges me to slide open the drawer beneath the table and there she is, lying face down in the drawer. Tears spring in my eyes, angry that something so precious has been hidden away. I decide to say nothing for now, assuming Dad has his reasons. I slide the drawer closed, feeling as if I'm burying her all over again.

When I limp into the kitchen, chaos greets me. There are pots and pans everywhere, tea towels, egg shells and what looks like the contents of the cupboards covering the counters.

'Morning, love.' Dad sees me and steps up onto his left leg to give me a kiss on the forehead.

I realise it's the first time in years somebody has made my breakfast for me, but it's also the first time for many years that Dad has had somebody to cook breakfast for. He's excited.

I watch him poking the sausages around, trying to get all sides evenly cooked.

'I'll have sausages too.'

'But you're one of those vegetarianists.'

'Vegetarian. And I'm not any more.'

'Sure, of course you're not. You've only been one since you were fifteen years old after seeing that show about the seals. Tomorrow I'll wake up and you'll be tellin' me you're a man. Saw it on the telly once. This woman brought her husband live on the telly in front of an audience to tell him that she decided that she wanted to turn her—'

Feeling frustrated with him, I blurt out, 'Mum's photo isn't on the hall table.'

Dad freezes, a reaction of guilt, and this makes me somewhat angry, as though I had convinced myself before that the mysterious midnight photograph-mover had broken in and done the dirty deed himself. I'd almost prefer that. 'Why?' is all I say.

He keeps himself busy, clattering with plates and cutlery now. 'Why what? Why are you walking like that is what I want to know?'

'I don't know,' I snap, and limp across the room to take a seat at the table. 'Maybe it runs in the family.'

'Hoo hoo hoo,' Dad hoots and looks up at the ceiling, 'we've got a live one here, boss! Set the table like a good girl.'

He brings me right back and I can't help but smile. And so I set the table and Dad makes the breakfast and we both limp around the kitchen pretending everything is as it was and for ever shall be. World without end.

'So, Dad, what are your plans for the day? Are you busy?'

A forkful of sausage, egg, bacon, black pudding, mushroom and tomato stops on its way into my dad's open mouth. Amused eyes peer out at me from under his wildly wiry eyebrows. 'Plans, you say? Well, let's see, Gracie. I was thinking of after I finish my fry in approximately fifteen minutes, I'd have another cuppa tea. Then while I'm drinking me tea I might sit down in this chair at this table, or maybe that chair where you are, the exact venue is TBD. Then I'll go through yesterday's answers of the crossword to see what we got correct and what was incorrect. Then I'll do the Sudoku, then the word game. I see we've to try and find *nautical* words today. Then I'm going to cut out my coupons and all that will fill my early morning right up, Gracie. Then I'd say I'll have another cuppa after all of that and then my programmes start.' He finally shovels the food into his mouth and egg drips down his chin. He doesn't notice and leaves it there.

'So basically, according to your schedule, you're doing exactly the same thing as yesterday.'

'Oh, no, it's not the same at all.' He thumbs through his TV guide and stabs a greasy finger on today's page. '*Animal Hospital* is on instead of the *Antiques Roadshow*. It'll be doggies and bunnies today instead of Betty's fake teapots.' He picks up his highlighter and marks another show, his tongue licking the corners of his mouth in concentration as though he was decorating a manuscript.

'The Book of Kells,' I blurt out of nowhere, though that is nothing odd these days. My random ramblings are becoming something of the norm. 'Let's go into town today. Do a tour of the city, go to Trinity College and look at the Book of Kells.'

Dad stares at me and munches. 'You want to go to Trinity College. The girl who never wanted to set foot near the place for either studies or excursions with me and your mother, suddenly out of the blue wants to go. If you don't want to watch the *Animal Hospital* show just say so. You don't have to go darting into the city. There's such a thing as changing channels.'

'You're right, Dad, and I've been doing some of that recently.'

'Is that so? I hadn't noticed, what with your marriage breaking up, your not being a vegetarianist any more, your not mentioning a word about your job and your moving in with me, and all.'

'I need to do something new,' I explain. 'I've got the big remote control of life in my hands and I'm ready to start pushing some buttons.'

He stares at me for a moment then puts a sausage in his mouth.

'We'll get a taxi into town,' I continue, 'and catch one of those tour buses. What do you think? I'll have a shower and we'll leave in an hour. Ha! That rhymes.' I limp out of the kitchen, leaving my bewildered father behind with egg on his chin.

'I doubt I can walk at this speed, Gracie,' Dad says, trying to keep up with me as we dodge pedestrians on Grafton Street.

'Sorry, Dad.' I slow down and link his arm. Despite his corrective footwear he still sways and I sway with him. 'Dad, are you ever going to call me Joyce?'

'What are you talkin' about? Sure, isn't that your name?'

I look at him with surprise. 'Do you not notice you always call me Gracie?'

He seems taken aback but makes no comment and keeps walking.

'I'll give you a fiver, every time you call me Joyce today,' I smile.

'That's a deal, Joyce, Joyce, Joyce. Oh, how I love you, Joyce,' he chuckles. 'That's twenty quid already!' He nudges me and says seriously, 'I didn't notice I called you that, love. I'll do my best. You remind me so much of her, you know.'

'Ah, Dad, really?' I'm touched; I feel my eyes prick with tears. He never says that. 'In what way?'

'You both have little piggy noses.'

I roll my eyes.

'I don't know why we're walking further away from Trinity College. Wasn't it there that you wanted to go to?'

'Yes, but the tour buses leave from Stephen's Green. We'll see it as we're passing. I don't really want to go in there now anyway.' I don't know why. Not going just feels right. Internal compass says so.

Justin darts through the front arch of Trinity College and bounds up the road to Grafton Street. Lunchtime with Sarah. He beats away the nagging voice within him telling him to cancel her. *Give her a chance. Give yourself a chance.* He needs to try, he needs to remember that not every meeting with a woman is going to be the same as the first time he laid eyes on Jennifer. The thump-thump, thump-thump feeling that made his entire body vibrate. He thought about how he'd felt on his date with Sarah. Nothing but flattery that she was attracted to him and excitement that he was back out in the dating world again. Plenty of feelings about her and the situation but nothing *for* her. He had more of a reaction to the woman in the hair salon a few weeks ago.

Conscious that he'll be late for Sarah, he attempts to break into a run, but the aches and pains in his over-exercised body almost cripple him. Instead he limps along, trailing behind what seem to be the two slowest people on Grafton Street, one of whom is singing happily to himself and swaying. *Drunk at this hour, honestly.*

Dad takes his time, meandering up Grafton Street as though he has all the time in the world. I suppose he does, compared to everybody else, though a younger person would think differently. Sometimes he stops and points at things, joins circles of spectators to watch a street act and, like a rock in a stream, sends people flowing around him; he's completely oblivious. He sings as we move up and down, down and up. 'Grafton Street's a wonderland. There's magic in the air . . .' He looks at me and smiles and sings.

So this is what you do when you take your time. You breathe slowly. You open your eyes wider and look at everything. Take it all in. Talk about it. Find out the answers you didn't know to yesterday's crosswords. *Slow down.* Hold up the people behind you for all you care, feel them kicking at your heels but maintain your pace. Don't let anybody dictate your speed.

Though if the person behind me kicks my heels one more time . . .

Dad suddenly stops walking near the top of Grafton Street, enthralled by the sight of a mime artist nearby. As I'm linking his arm, I'm forced to a sudden stop too, causing the person behind to run straight into me. That is it.

'Hey!' I spin round. 'Watch it!'

He grunts at me in frustration and power-walks off. 'Hey yourself,' an American voice calls back.

I'm about to shout again but his voice silences me.

'Look at that,' Dad marvels, watching the mime trapped in an invisible box. He laughs. 'Now where do we go from here?' He spins round beside me, looking about. He walks off in another direction, straight through a group of parading Hare Krishnas.

The American in a sandy duffle coat turns round again, throws me one last dirty look before he hurries on in a huff.

Still, I stare. If I was to reverse the frown. That smile. Familiar.

'Gracie, this is where you get the tickets. I've found it,' he shouts.

'OK, Dad.' I continue to watch the duffle coat moving further away. I don't—correction, can't—move my eyes away from him. I mentally throw a cowboy's rope round his body and begin to pull him back towards me.

He suddenly stops dead in his tracks. Yee-ha.

Please turn. I pull on the rope.

He spins round, searches the crowd. For me?

'Who are you?' I whisper.

'It's me!' Dad is beside me again. 'You're just standing in the middle of the street.'

'I know what I'm doing,' I snap. 'Here, go get the tickets.' I hold out some money.

I step away from the Hare Krishnas, keeping my eye on the duffle coat, hoping he'll see me.

His eyes continue to search the street and then they ever so slowly fall upon mine. I remember him in the second it takes them to register me. 'Him' from the hair salon.

What now? Perhaps he won't recognise me at all.

He holds up a hand. Waves. Suddenly Grafton Street is empty. And silent. Just me and him. Funny how that happened. How thoughtful of everyone. I wave back. He mouths something to me.

Sorry. He's sorry. I try to figure out what to mouth back but I'm smiling. Nothing can be mouthed when smiling, it's impossible.

'I got the tickets!' Dad shouts. 'Twenty euro each—it's a crime, that is. Seeing is for free, I don't know how they can charge us to use our eyes.'

Suddenly I hear the traffic again, feel the sun and breeze on my face, feel my heart beating wildly in my chest as my blood rushes around in frenzied excitement. I feel Dad tugging on my arm.

'It's leaving now. Come on, Gracie, it's leaving. It's a bit of a walk up the road, we have to go. Near the Shelbourne Hotel.'

A steady flow of pedestrians gather at the top of Grafton Street to cross the road, blocking my view of him. I feel Dad pulling me back and so I begin to move with him down Merrion Row, walking backwards, trying to keep him in sight.

'Dammit! I can't see him.'

'Who, love?'

'A guy I think I know.' I stop walking backwards and stand in line with Dad, continuing to look down the street and scouring the crowds.

'Well, unless you know that you know him for sure, I wouldn't be stopping to chat in the city,' Dad says protectively. 'What kind of a bus is this at all, Gracie? It looks a bit odd, I'm not sure about this.'

I ignore him and let him lead the way onto the bus, while I'm busy searching furiously through the, curiously, plastic windows. The crowd finally moves on from in front of where he stood.

'He's gone.'

'Is that so? Can't have known him too well then, if he just ran off.'

I turn my attention to my father. 'Dad, that was the weirdest thing.'

'I don't care what you say, there's nothing weirder than this.' Dad looks around us in bewilderment.

Finally I too look around the bus and take in my surroundings. Everyone else is wearing a Viking helmet, with life jackets on their laps.

'OK, everybody,' the tour guide speaks into the microphone, 'we finally have everyone on board. Let's show our new arrivals what to do. When I say the word I want you all to rooooooar just like the Vikings did! Let me hear it!' Dad and I jump in our seats, and I feel him cling to me, as the entire bus roars.

'I'm Olaf the White, and welcome aboard the Viking Splash bus! Historically known as DUKWs, or more affectionately Ducks. We are sitting in the amphibious version of the General Motors vehicle built during World War Two. Designed to withstand being driven onto beaches in fifteen-foot seas to deliver cargo or troops from ship to shore, they are now more commonly used as rescue and underwater recovery vehicles in the US, UK and other parts of the world.'

'Can we get off?' I whisper in Dad's ear.

He swats me away, enthralled.

'This particular vehicle weighs seven tonnes and has six wheels. As you can see, it has been outfitted with comfortable seats, a roof, roll-down sides to protect you from the elements, because as you all know, after we see the sights around the city, we have a "splashdown" into the water with a fantastic trip around the Grand Canal Docks!'

Everyone cheers and Dad looks at me, eyes wide like a little boy.

'Sure, no wonder it was twenty euro. A bus that goes into the water! Wait till I tell the lads at the Monday Club about this. Big mouth Donal won't be able to beat this story for once.' He turns his attention back to the tour operator, who, like everyone else on the bus, is wearing a Viking helmet with horns. Dad collects two, props one on his head and hands the other, which has blonde side plaits attached, to me.

'Olaf, meet Heidi.' I pop it on my head and turn to Dad.

He roars quietly in my face.

'Sights along the way include our famous city cathedrals, St Patrick's and Christ Church, Trinity College, Government buildings, Georgian Dublin . . .'

'Ooh, you'll like this one,' Dad elbows me.

'. . . and of course *Viking Dublin*!'

Everyone roars again, including Dad, and I can't help but laugh.

Justin frantically searches over the shaven heads of a group of Hare Krishnas who have begun to parade by him and obstruct his view of his woman in the red coat. Before him, a mime artist, dressed in a black leotard, with a painted white face, red lips and a striped hat, appears suddenly. They stand opposite one another, each waiting for the other to do something, Justin praying for the mime to grow bored and leave. He doesn't. Instead, the mime squares his shoulders, looks mean, parts his legs and lets his fingers quiver around his holster area.

Keeping his voice down, Justin speaks politely. 'Hey, I'm really not in the mood for this. Would you mind playing with someone else, please?'

Looking forlorn, the mime begins to play an invisible violin.

Justin hears laughter and realises he has an audience. *Great.*

'Here I am!' a voice calls beyond the crowd.

There she is! She recognised me!

Justin shuffles from foot to foot, trying to catch sight of her red coat.

The crowd turns and parts, to reveal Sarah, looking excited by the scene.

The mime mimics Justin's obvious disappointment, plastering a look of despair on his face and hunching his back so that his arms hang low and his hands almost scrape the ground.

'Oooooooo,' goes the crowd, and Sarah's face falls.

Justin nervously replaces his look of disappointment with a smile. He makes his way through the crowd, greets Sarah quickly and leads her speedily away from the scene while people clap and some drop coins into a container nearby.

Justin continues to look around for the red coat as they make their way to the restaurant for lunch, which he now definitely wants to cancel. *Tell her you have unfortunately made a mistake and that you have a lecture, right now. Tell her, tell her!*

But instead he finds himself continuing to walk with her, his eyes jumping around like an addict needing a fix. In the basement restaurant, they are led to a quiet table in the corner. *Yell 'FIRE' and run!*

Such a coincidence he bumped, quite literally, into the woman from the salon again. Though Dublin's a small town. Since being here he's learned that everyone pretty much knows everyone, or somebody related to somebody. But the woman, he would definitely have to stop calling her that. He should give her a name. *Angelina.*

'What are you thinking about?' Sarah leans across the table.

Or Lucille. 'Coffee. I'm thinking about coffee. I'll have a black coffee, please,' he says to the waitress clearing their table.

'You're not eating?' Sarah asks, disappointed and confused.

'No, I can't stay as long as I'd hoped. I have to get back to the college earlier than planned.' His leg bounces beneath the table.

'Oh, OK, well,' Sarah studies the menu, 'I'll have a chef's salad and a glass of the house white, please,' she says to the waitress and then to Justin, 'I have to eat or I'll collapse, I hope you don't mind.'

'No problem,' he smiles. *Even though you ordered the biggest salad on the menu. How about the name, Susan? Does my woman look like a Susan? My woman? What the hell is wrong with me?*

'We are now turning into Dawson Street, so named after Joshua Dawson, who also designed Grafton, Anne and Henry Streets. On your right you will see the Mansion House, which houses the Lord Mayor of Dublin.' All horned Viking helmets turn to the right. Cameras are suspended from the open windows.

'To your right you will see St Anne's Church, which was designed by Isaac Wells in 1707. The interior dates back to the seventeenth century.'

'Actually the Romanesque façade wasn't added until 1868, and that was designed by Thomas Newenham Deane,' I whisper to Dad.

'Oh,' Dad says slowly at this, eyes widening. 'I didn't know that.'

My eyes widen at my own piece of information. 'Me neither.'

'We are now on Nassau Street, we will pass Grafton Street on the left in just a moment.'

Dad starts singing, 'Grafton Street's a wonderland.' Loudly.

The American woman in front of us turns round, her face beaming. 'Oh, do you know that song? My father used to sing that song. He was from Ireland. Oh, I would love to hear it again; can you sing it for us?'

A chorus of, 'Oh, yes, please do . . .' from around us.

No stranger to singing in public, Dad begins singing and the entire bus joins in, moving from side to side.

Justin watches with growing impatience as Sarah slowly picks at her salad. Her fork playfully pokes at a piece of chicken; the chicken hangs on, falls off, grabs on again and manages to hang on while she waves it around, using it as a sledgehammer to knock pieces of lettuce over to see what's beneath. Finally she stabs a piece of tomato.

'Are you sure you're not hungry, Justin? You seem to be really studying this plate,' she smiles, waving another forkful of food around, sending red onion and Cheddar cheese tumbling back to the plate.

'Yeah, sure, I wouldn't mind having some.' He'd ordered and finished a bowl of soup in the time it had taken her to have five mouthfuls.

'You want me to feed it to you?' she flirts.

'Well, I want more on it than that, for a start.' The more food he can squeeze in his mouth, the quicker this frustrating experience will be over. He knows that his woman, *Veronica*, is probably long gone by now, but sitting here, watching Sarah burn more calories playing with her food than ingesting them, isn't going to confirm that for him.

'OK, here comes the aeroplane,' she sings.

'More.' At least half of it has fallen again during its 'takeoff'. Justin takes the fork from her and begins stabbing at as much as he can. Chicken, corn, lettuce, beetroot, tomato, cheese; he manages it all. 'Now, if the lady pilot would like to bring her plane in to land . . .'

She giggles, shovels it in, laughing all the while, barely fitting it all into Justin's mouth. When he's finally swallowed it all, he looks at his watch and then again at her plate.

'OK, now you do it.' *You're such a shit, Justin.* 'Come on.' He gathers as much food as possible and 'flies' it into her open mouth.

She laughs while trying to fit it all in. For almost a full minute she's unable to speak in her attempts to chew in as ladylike a manner as possible. Juices, dressing and food dribble down her chin and when she finally swallows, her lipstick-smudged mouth smiles at him to reveal a great big piece of lettuce stuck between her teeth.

'That was fun,' she smiles.

'Are you finished? Can I take the plate?' the waitress asks.

Sarah begins to answer, 'N—' but Justin jumps in.

'Yes, we are, thank you.' He avoids Sarah's stare.

'Actually I'm not quite finished, thank you,' Sarah says sternly.

Justin's leg bounces beneath the table, his impatience growing. *Salma. Sexy Salma.* An awkward silence falls between them.

'I'm sorry, Salma, I don't mean to be rude—'

'Sarah.'

'What?'

'My name is Sarah. You called me Salma.'

'Oh. What? Who's Salma? God. Sorry. I don't even know a Salma.'

She speeds up her eating, obviously dying to get away from him now.

He says more softly, 'It's just that I have to get back to the college—'

'Earlier than planned. You said.' She smiles quickly and her face falls immediately as she looks back down at her plate.

Justin cringes inside, knowing his behaviour is uncharacteristically rude. He stares at her: beautiful face, great body, intelligent. There is absolutely nothing wrong with this woman at all. It is Justin's own distraction that is the problem, the feeling that a part of him is somewhere else. A part of him, in fact, that feels so nearby, he is almost compelled to run out and catch it.

The problem is he doesn't know what he is trying to catch, or who. In a city of one million people, he can't expect to walk outside this door and find the same woman standing on the pavement. And is it worth leaving the beautiful woman sitting with him in this restaurant, in order just to chase a good idea?

He stops bouncing his leg up and down and settles back into his chair. 'Sarah,' he sighs, and means it this time when he says, 'I'm very sorry.'

She looks up at him, chews quickly and swallows. Her face softens. 'OK.' She wipes away the crumbs around her plate, shrugging. 'I'm not looking for a marriage here, Justin. Lunch is all this is.'

'I know that.'

'Or shall we say just coffee, in case mentioning the former sends you running out yelling "Fire"?' She acknowledges his empty cup.

He reaches out to grab her hand. 'I'm sorry.'

'OK,' she repeats. The air clears. Her plate is cleared away. 'I suppose we should get the bill—'

'Have you always wanted to be a doctor?'

'Whoa.' She pauses midway opening her wallet. 'It's just intense either way with you, isn't it?' But she's smiling.

'I'm sorry.' Justin shakes his head. 'Let's have a coffee before we leave. Hopefully I'll have time to stop this from being the worst date you've ever been on.'

She shakes her head, smiling. 'It was almost the worst but you pulled it right back there with the doctor question.'

Justin smiles. 'So. Have you?'

She nods. 'Ever since James Goldin operated on me when I was five years old. He saved my life.'

'Wow. That's young for a serious operation.'

'I was in the yard at lunch break, I fell during a game of hopscotch and hurt my knee. The rest of my friends were discussing amputation but James Goldin came running over and gave me mouth-to-mouth. Just like that, the pain went away. And that's when I knew.'

'That you wanted to be a doctor?'

'That I wanted to marry James Goldin.'

Justin smiles. 'And did you?'

'Nah. Became a doctor instead.'

'You're good at it.'

'Yes, because you can tell that from a needle insertion at a blood donation,' she smiles. 'Everything OK in that department?'

'My arm's a little itchy but it's fine.'

'Itchy? It shouldn't be itchy, let me see.'

He goes to roll up his sleeve and stops. 'Could I ask you something? Is there any way that I can find out who my blood went to?'

She shakes her head. 'The beauty of this is that it's completely anonymous.'

'But someone, somewhere would know, wouldn't they?'

'Of course. Products in a blood bank are always individually traceable. It's documented throughout the entire process of donation, testing, separation into components, storage and administration to the recipient, but you can't know who received your donation.'

'But you just said that it's documented.'

'That information can't be released. Justin, the blood you donated was not transfused directly into somebody's body exactly as it came from your vein. It was broken up and separated into red blood cells, white blood cells, platelets—'

'I know, I know, I know all of that.'

'There's nothing I can do. Why are you so keen to know?'

He thinks about it for a while. 'I'm just interested to know who I helped, if I helped them at all and if I did, how they are. I feel like . . . no, it sounds stupid, you'll think I'm insane. It doesn't matter.'

'Tell me.' Her piercing blue eyes watch him over her cup.

'This is the first time I've said this aloud, so forgive me for speaking while I think. At first, it was a ridiculous macho ego trip. I wanted to know whose life I saved. But then over the last few days I haven't been able to stop thinking about it. I feel differently. Genuinely different. Like I've given something away. Something precious.'

'It is precious, Justin. We need more donors all the time.'

'I know, but not—not like that. I just feel like there's someone out there walking around with something inside them that I gave them and now I'm missing something—'

'The body replaces the liquid part of your donation within twenty-four hours.'

'No, I mean, I feel like I've given away a part of me, and that somebody else has been completed because of that part of me and . . . this sounds crazy. I just want to know who that person is. I just feel like there's a part of me missing and I need to get out there and grab it.'

'You can't get your blood back, you know,' Sarah jokes weakly.

'I should never try to discuss something so illogical with a doctor, I suppose,' he says.

'You sound like a lot of people I know, Justin. You're just the first person I've heard blame it on a blood donation.'

Silence.

'Well,' Sarah says as she reaches behind her chair to get her coat, 'you're in a rush so we should really move now.'

They make their way down Grafton Street in a comfortable silence that's occasionally dotted with small talk. They stop walking at the Molly Malone statue, across the road from Trinity College.

'You're late for your class.'

'No, I've got a little while before I—' He looks at his watch and then remembers his earlier excuse. He feels his face redden. 'Sorry. I really had a lovely time,' he says awkwardly. 'Should we . . . you know, I'm feeling really uncomfortable right now with her watching us.'

Molly stares down at them with her bronze eyes.

Sarah laughs. 'You know maybe we could make arrangements to—'

'Roooooaaaaaaaarrrrrrrrr!!'

Justin almost leaps out of his skin with fright, startled by the intense screaming coming from the bus stopped at the traffic lights beside him. Sarah yelps with fright. Beside them more than a dozen men, women and children, all wearing Viking helmets, are waving their fists in the air and laughing and roaring at passers-by. Sarah and the dozens of others crowded around them on the pavement start laughing.

Justin, whose breath has caught in his throat, is silent, for he can't take his eyes off the woman laughing uproariously with an old man; a helmet on her head, long blonde plaits flowing each side.

'We certainly got them, Joyce,' the old man laughs.

Look at me, Justin wills her. Her eyes stay on the old man's. *Turn round! Look at me just once!* The traffic lights flash to amber. Her head remains turned, completely lost in conversation.

The lights turn green and the bus slowly moves off up Nassau Street. He starts to walk alongside it, quickening his pace and breaking into a jog. He can hear Sarah calling after him but he can't stop.

'Hey!' he calls.

Not loud enough; she doesn't hear him. The bus picks up speed and Justin's jog breaks into a run.

'Joyce!' he blurts out. The surprising sound of his own yell is enough to stop him in his tracks. What on earth is he doing? He tries to catch his breath, tries to centre himself in the whirlwind he feels caught up in. A Viking helmet appears from the window. He can't make out the face but he knows it has to be her.

The whirlwind stops momentarily while he holds up a hand in salute. A hand appears out of the window and the bus rounds the corner onto Kildare Street, leaving Justin, heart beating wildly, to look down the empty street.

Who are you, Joyce?

'**W**hy are you hanging your head out of the window?' Dad pulls me in, wild with worry. 'You might not have much to live for but, for Christ's sake, you owe it to yourself to live it.'

'Did you hear somebody calling my name?' I whisper to Dad, my mind a whirl.

'Oh, she's hearing voices now,' he grumbles. He turns his attention back to Olaf.

'On your left is Leinster House, the building that now houses the National Parliament of Ireland. Parts of the building, which was formerly the Royal College of Surgeons—'

'Science,' I say loudly, still largely lost in thought.

'Pardon me?' He stops talking and heads turn once again.

My face flushes. 'I was just saying that it was the Royal College of Science.'

'Oh,' he gets flustered. 'Excuse me, I'm mistaken. Parts of the building, which was formerly the . . . the Royal College of,' he looks pointedly at me, '*Science*, have served as the seat of the Irish government since 1922 . . .'

I tune out. 'Remember I told you about the guy who designed the Rotunda Hospital?' I whisper to Dad. 'Richard Cassells. He designed this too. It's been claimed that it formed a model for the design of the White House.'

'Is that so?' Dad says.

'Really?' The American woman twists round in her seat to face me. She speaks loudly. Very loudly. Too loudly. 'Honey, did you hear that? This lady says the guy who designed this, designed the White House.'

'No, I didn't actually—' Suddenly I notice the tour operator is glaring at me. All eyes, ears and horns are on us. 'Well, I said it's been *claimed* that it formed a *model* for the design of the White House,' I say quietly. 'It's just that James Hoban, who won the competition for the design of the White House in 1792, was an Irishman. He studied architecture in Dublin and would have more than likely studied the design of Leinster House,' I finish off quickly.

The people around me ooh and aah about that titbit of information.

'We can't hear you!' someone at the top of the bus shouts out.

'Stand up, Gracie.' Dad pushes me up.

'Dad . . .' I slap him away.

'Hey, Olaf, give her the microphone!' the woman shouts to the tour operator. He grudgingly hands it over and folds his arms.

'Eh, hello.' I repeat my comments, and the people up front nod with interest.

'And this is all part of your government's buildings too?' The American woman points to the buildings either side.

I look uncertainly at Dad and he nods at me with encouragement. 'The building to the left is the National Library and the National Museum is on the right. The National Library and the National Museum were originally home of the Dublin Museum of Science and Art, which opened in 1890. Both were designed by Thomas Newenham Deane and his son Thomas Manly Deane after a competition held in 1885 and were constructed by the Dublin contractors J. and W. Beckett, who demonstrated the best of Irish craftsmanship in their construction. The museum is one of the best surviving examples of Irish decorative stonework, woodcarving and ceramic tiling. The National Library's most impressive feature is the entrance rotunda. The exterior of the building is characterised by its array of columns and pilasters in the Corinthian order—'

Loud clapping interrupts my talk—coming from only one person: Dad. The rest of the bus is silent. An imaginary piece of tumbleweed blows down the aisle, landing at a grinning Olaf the White. I quickly sit down. Olaf grabs the microphone from me. 'Now, everybody, let's rooooooooaaaaaar!'

The silence is broken as everybody comes to life again.

Dad leans into me to whisper in my ear. 'How did you know all that, love?'

My mouth opens and closes but nothing comes out. How on earth did I know all of that?

Four

MY EARS IMMEDIATELY SIZZLE as I enter the school gymnasium that same evening, and spy Kate and Frankie huddled together on the bleachers, looking deep in conversation. Kate is talking and Frankie looks as though her dog's been hit by a car, a face I'm familiar with, as I was the one to deliver the news, and the blow, that broke three of the sausage dog's legs. Now Kate looks as though she's been caught in the act as she glances in my direction. Frankie freezes too. Looks of surprise, then guilt and then a smile to make me think they've just been discussing the weather, rather than the events in my life.

My friends hug me tight, which I find surprisingly comforting. The pity in their faces hammers home my great loss and I realise that swaddling myself in a nest with Dad does not hold the super healing powers I'd hoped for, for every time I leave the house I have to feel it all, all over again. Wrapped in Kate and Frankie's arms I could easily morph into the baby that they in their minds are coddling, but I don't, because if I start now, I know I'll never stop.

We sit on the bleachers away from the other parents. I spot Kate's children, six-year-old Eric and my five-year-old goddaughter, Jayda, the *Muppet's Christmas Carol* fanatic I have sworn not to hold anything against. They are enthusiastically hopping about and chirping like crickets. Eleven-month-old Sam sleeps beside us in a stroller, blowing bubbles from his chubby lips. I watch him fondly, then remember again and look away. Ah, remembering. That old chestnut.

'How's work, Frankie?' I ask, wanting everything to be as it was.

'Busy as usual,' she responds, and I detect guilt, perhaps even embarrassment. When something tragic has happened, you'll find that you, the tragic*ee*, become the person that has to make everything comfortable for everyone else.

'How's Crapper?' I fill the uncomfortable silence and ask after Frankie's dog.

'He's doing well; his legs are healing nicely. Still howls when he sees your photograph, though. Sorry I had to move it from the fireplace.'

'Doesn't matter. In fact I was going to ask you to move it. Kate, you can get rid of my wedding photo too.' Divorce talk. Finally.

'Ah, Joyce,' she shakes her head and looks at me sadly, 'that's my favourite photo of me. I looked so good at your wedding. Can I not just cut Conor out?'

'Or draw a little moustache on him,' Frankie adds. 'Or better yet, give him a personality. What colour should that be?'

I bite my lip guiltily to hide a smile. I'm not used to this kind of talk of my ex-. It's disrespectful and I'm not sure I'm completely comfortable with it. But it is funny.

Frankie softens her voice. 'So, Joyce, how are you?'

I have debated whether to tell them. Short of carting me off to the madhouse I have no idea how anybody will react to what's been happening to me, or even how they should react. But after today's experience, I side with the part of my brain that is anxious to reveal.

'This is going to sound really odd so bear with me on this.'

Kate grabs my hand. 'Say whatever you want. Just release.'

Frankie rolls her eyes.

'Thanks.' I slowly slip my hand out of hers. 'I keep seeing this guy. I think I know him but at the same time, I know I don't. I've seen him precisely three times now, the most recent being today, when he chased after my Viking bus. And I think he called out my name. Though I may have imagined that because how on earth could he know my name? Unless he knows me, but that brings me back to my being sure that he really doesn't. What do you think?'

'Hold on, I'm way back at the Viking bus part,' Frankie slows me down. 'You say you have a Viking bus?'

'I don't *have* one. I was on one. With Dad. It goes into the water too. You wear helmets with horns and go "aaaagh" at everyone.' I go close to their faces and wave my fists at them. They stare back blankly. I sigh and slide back on the bench. 'So anyway, I keep seeing him.'

'OK,' Kate says slowly, looking at Frankie.

There's an awkward silence as they worry about my sanity. I join with them on that.

Frankie clears her throat. 'So this man, Joyce, is he young, old, or indeed a Viking upon your magic bus that travels the high waters?'

'Late thirties, early forties. He's American. We got our hair cut together. That's where I saw him first.'

'Which is lovely, by the way.' Kate gently fingers a few front strands.

'Dad thinks I look like Peter Pan,' I smile.

'So maybe he remembers you from the hair salon,' Frankie reasons.

'It even felt weird at the salon. There was a . . . recognition or a *something*.'

Frankie smiles. 'Welcome to the world of singledom.'

I rub my eyes wearily. 'I know I sound insane, I'm tired and probably imagining things where there is nothing to be imagined. The man I'm supposed to have on the brain is Conor and he's not. He's really not. Right now, I feel nothing but relieved,' I continue. 'Isn't that terrible?'

'Is it OK for me to feel relieved too?' Kate asks.

'You hated him?' I ask sadly.

'No. He was fine. He was nice. I just hated you not being happy.'

'I hated him,' Frankie chirps up.

'We spoke briefly yesterday. It was odd. He wanted to know if he could take the espresso machine.'

'The bastard,' Frankie spits. 'It's mind games, Joyce. Be careful. First it's the espresso machine and then it's the house and then it's your soul. And then it's that emerald ring that belonged to his grandmother that he claims you stole but that you recall more than clearly when you first went to his house for lunch and he said, "help yourself" and there it was.' She scowls.

I look to Kate for help.

'Her breakup with Lee.'

'Ah. Well, it's not going to get like your breakup with Lee.'

Frankie grumbles.

'Christian went for a pint with Conor last night,' Kate says. 'Hope you don't mind.'

'Of course I don't. They're friends. Is he OK?'

'Yeah, he seemed fine. He's upset about the, you know . . .'

'Baby. You can say the word. I'm not going to fall apart.'

'He's upset about the baby and disappointed the marriage didn't work but I think he thinks it's the right thing to do. He's going back to Japan in a few days. He said you're putting the house on the market.'

'I don't like being there any more and we bought it together, so it's the right thing to do.'

'But are you sure? Where will you live? Is your dad not driving you insane?'

As a tragicee and future divorcee, you'll also find that people will question you on the biggest decision you've ever made in your life as though you hadn't thought about it at all before.

'Funnily enough, no,' I smile as I think about him. 'He's actually having the opposite effect. I'm going to stay with him until the house is sold and I find somewhere else to live.'

'That story about the man . . . apart from him, how are you *really*? We haven't seen you since the hospital and we were so worried.'

'I know. I'm sorry about that.' I'd refused to see them when they came to visit, and I'd sent Dad out to the corridor to send them home, which of course he didn't, and so they'd sat by my side for a few minutes while I stared at the wall, thinking about the fact I was staring at a wall, and then they left. 'I really appreciated you coming, though.'

'No, you didn't.'

'OK, I didn't then, but I do now.'

I think about that, about how I am now, *really*. Well, they asked.

'I eat meat now. And I drink red wine. I hate anchovies and I listen to classical music. Last night I listened to Handel's "*Mi restano le lagrime*" from Act Three of *Alcina* on Lyric FM before going to sleep, and I actually knew the words but have no idea how. I know a lot about Irish architecture but not as much as I know about French and Italian. I've read *Ulysses*. Today I'm particularly vexed about talk of bulldozing a hundred-year-old building in Old Town, Chicago, and so I plan to write a letter. I bet you're wondering how I knew about that. Well, I read it in the recent edition of the *Art and Architectural Review*, the only truly international art and architectural publication. I'm a subscriber now.' I take a breath. 'Ask me anything, because I'll probably know the answer and I've no idea how.'

Stunned, Kate and Frankie look at each other.

'Maybe with the stress of constantly worrying about you and Conor over with, you're able to concentrate on things more,' Frankie suggests.

I consider that but not for long. 'I dream almost every night about a little girl with white-blonde hair who every night gets bigger. And I hear music—a song I don't know. When I'm not dreaming about her I have vivid dreams of places I've never been, eating foods I've never tasted and am surrounded by strange people that I seem to know so well. A picnic in a park with a woman with red hair. A man with green feet. And sprinklers.' I think hard. 'Something about sprinklers. When I wake up I have to remember all over again that my dreams are not real and that my reality is not a dream. I find that next to impossible, but not completely, because Dad is there with a smile on his face and sausages in the frying pan, and for some unknown reason hiding Mum's photograph in the hall table drawer. And after the first few moments of my waking day when everything is crap, I keep thinking about an American man that I don't even know.'

The girls' faces are a mixture of sympathy, worry and confusion.

I don't expect them to say anything—they probably think I'm crazy—and so I look out to the kids on the gymnasium floor and watch as Eric takes to the balance beam. His face is a picture of nervous concentration. He raises his eyes briefly to see if his mother is watching and in that one moment, loses balance and falls straight down, the beam unfortunately positioned between his legs. His face is one of horror.

Frankie snorts again. Eric howls. Kate runs to her child. Sam continues to blow bubbles.

I leave.

Driving back to Dad's, I try not to glance at my house as I pass. My eyes lose the battle with my mind and I see Conor's car parked outside. Since our final meal together at the restaurant we have talked a few times, each conversation varying in degrees of affection for one another, the last, at the lower end of the scale. But each time I hung up the phone, I felt that my weak goodbye wasn't a goodbye. It was more of a 'see you around'.

I pull the car over and stare up at the house we've lived in for almost ten years. Didn't it deserve more than a few weak goodbyes?

I ring the doorbell and there's no answer. Through the front window I can see everything in boxes, the walls naked, the surfaces bare. I turn my key in the door and step inside. I'm about to call his name when I hear the soft tinkle of music drifting from upstairs. I make my way up to the nursery and find Conor sitting on the soft carpet, tears streaming down his face as he watches the mouse chase the cheese. I cross the room and reach for him. On the floor, I hold him close and rock him gently. I close my eyes and drift away.

He stops crying and looks up at me slowly. 'What?'

'Hmm?' I snap out of my trance.

'You said something. In Latin.'

'No, I didn't.'

'Yes, you did. Just there. Since when do you speak Latin?'

'I don't.'

'You must, you just said it.'

'Conor, I don't recall saying anything.' He glares at me, something pretty close to hate in his eyes, and I swallow hard.

A stranger stares back at me in a tense silence. 'OK.' He gets to his feet and moves towards the door. No more questions, no more trying to understand me. He no longer cares. 'Patrick will be acting as my solicitor now.'

Fantastic, his shit-head brother. 'OK,' I whisper.

He stops at the door and turns round, grinds his jaw as his eyes take in the room. A last look at everything, including me, and he's gone.

The final goodbye.

I have a restless night in bed at Dad's as more images flash through my mind like lightning. A church. Bells ringing. Sprinklers. A tidal wave of red wine. Old buildings with shopfronts. Stained glass.

A view through banisters of a man with green feet, closing a door behind him. A baby in my arms. A girl with white-blonde hair.

A casket. Tears. Family dressed in black.

Park swings. My hands pushing a child. Me swinging as a child. A seesaw. A chubby young boy raising me higher in the air, as he lowers himself to the ground. Laughter. Me and the same boy in swimming togs. Suburbs. A woman in a white dress. Cobbled streets. Cathedrals. Confetti. Hands, fingers, rings. Shouting. Slamming.

The man with green feet closing the door.

Sprinklers again. A chubby young boy chasing me and laughing. A drink in my hand. Lecture halls. Music.

View from the banisters of the man with green feet closing a door. A bottle in his hand. Pills in his hand too. The man's eyes seeing mine before the door closes. My hand on a doorknob. The door opening. Empty bottle on the ground. Bare feet with green soles. A casket.

Sprinklers. Rocking back and forth. Humming that song. Long blonde hair covering my face and in my small hand. I open my eyes with a gasp, heart drumming in my chest. I fumble in the darkness for the bedside lamp, reach for my mobile and dial with trembling fingers.

'Conor?' My voice is shaking.

'Joyce, it's three a.m.,' he croaks.

'I know, I'm sorry.'

'What's wrong? Are you OK?'

'Yes, yes, I'm fine, it's just that, well, I—I had a dream. Or a night-mare . . .' I stop myself and try to focus. '*Perfer et obdura; dolor hic tibi proderit olim?*'

'What?' he says groggily.

'The Latin that I said earlier, is that what I said?'

'Yeah, it sounds like it. Jesus, Joyce—'

'Be patient and tough; someday this pain will be useful to you,' I blurt out. 'That's what it means.'

He is quiet and then he sighs. 'OK, thanks.'

'Somebody told me that, if not when I was a child, but then tonight, they told me.'

'You don't have to explain.'

Silence.

'I'm going back to sleep now. Are you OK, Joyce? Do you want me to call someone for you or . . .?'

'No, I'm fine. Perfect.' My voice catches in my throat. 'Good night.'

He's gone. A single tear rolls down my cheek and I wipe it away before it reaches my chin. Don't start, Joyce. Don't you dare start now.

As I make my way downstairs the following morning, I spy Dad placing Mum's photograph back on the hall table. He hears me approaching, whips out his handkerchief and pretends he's dusting it.

'Ah, there she is. Muggins has risen from the dead.'

'Yes, well, the toilet flushing every fifteen minutes kept me awake for most of the night.' I kiss the top of his almost hairless head and go into the kitchen. I sniff the smoky atmosphere. 'Did you burn toast again?'

He doesn't hear me and takes his usual seat in the path of the sun's beam, props his glasses on the base of his nose and continues his Sudoku. I check the toaster. 'It's on the right setting, I don't understand how it's still burning.' I look inside. No crumbs. I check the bin, no toast thrown out. I sniff the air again. Dad fidgets. Nervously. Aha. I narrow my eyes and race around the kitchen, opening cupboards, searching inside each of them.

He looks worried. 'Have you lost your mind? What are you doing?'

'Did you take your pills?' I ask, coming across the medicine cabinet.
'What pills?'

With a response like that, there's definitely something up.

'Your heart pills, memory pills, vitamin pills.'

'No, no and . . .' He thinks for a while. 'No.'

I bring them over to him, line them up on the table. He relaxes a little. Then I continue searching the cupboards and I feel him tense. I pull on the cereal cupboard knob—

'Water!' he shouts, and I jump and bang the door closed.

'Are you OK?'

'Yes,' he says calmly. 'I just need a glass of water for my pills.'

Suspiciously, I fill a glass with water and deliver it to him. I return to the cereal cupboard.

'Tea!' he shouts. 'Sure, we'll have a cup of tea. Sit down there and I'll make it for you. You've been through such a tough time and you've been great about it all. So brave. Trophy brave, as a man says.'

'Dad,' I warn. He stops dithering and sighs in surrender.

I open the cupboard door and look inside. Nothing odd, just the porridge I eat every morning and Sugar Puffs that I never touch. Dad lets out a hearty harrumph. Hold on a minute. I reach for the Sugar Puffs that I never eat and never see Dad eat. As soon as I lift it I know that it's empty of cereal. I look inside.

'Dad, you promised me!' I hold the packet of cigarettes in front of his face.

'I only had one, love.'

'You have not had *only* one. That smell of smoke every morning is not burnt toast. You lied to me!'

'One a day is hardly going to kill me.'

'That's exactly what it's going to do. You've had bypass surgery, you're not supposed to smoke at all!' I tell him. 'I'm calling your doctor.'

He jumps out of his chair. 'No, love, don't do that.'

I march out to the hall and he chases after me. Up, down, down, up.

'Ah, you wouldn't do that to me. If the cigarettes don't kill me, she will. She's a battleaxe, that woman.'

I pick up the phone that's beside Mum's photograph and dial the emergency number I've memorised. The first number that comes to my mind when I need to help the most important person in my life.

'If Mum knew what you were doing she would go berserk—oh.'

I stall, then ask him, 'That's why you hide the photograph?'

Dad looks down at his hands and nods sadly. 'She made me promise I'd stop. If not for me, for her. I didn't want her to see.'

'Hello?' There's a response on the other end of the phone. 'Hello? Is that you, Dad?' a young girl with an American accent says.

'Oh,' I snap out of it and Dad looks pleadingly at me. 'Pardon me,' I speak into the phone. 'Hello?'

'Oh, I'm sorry, I saw an Irish number and thought you were my dad,' the voice on the other end explains.

'That's OK,' I say, confused. 'I was looking for . . .' Dad shakes his head wildly and I stall.

'Tickets to the show?' the girl asks.

I frown. 'To what show?'

'The Royal Opera House.'

'Sorry, who is this? I'm confused.'

'I'm Bea.'

'Bea.' I look at Dad questioningly and he shrugs. 'Bea who?'

'Well, who is this?' Her tone is harder.

'My name is Joyce. I'm sorry, Bea, I think I've dialled the wrong number. You said you saw an Irish number? Have I called America?'

'No, don't worry.' Happy there isn't a stalker at the other end, her tone is friendly again. 'You've called London,' she explains. 'I saw the Irish number and thought you were my dad. He's flying back tonight to make it to my show tomorrow and I was worried because I'm still a student and it's such a huge deal and I thought he was . . . sorry, I have absolutely no idea why I'm explaining this to you but I'm so nervous.' She laughs. 'Technically, this is his emergency number.'

'Funny, I dialled my emergency number too,' I say faintly. 'Your voice is familiar, Bea. Do I know you?'

'I don't think so. Don't know anyone in Ireland apart from my dad, who is a man and American, so unless you're my dad trying to be funny . . .'

'No, no, I'm not trying to be . . .' I feel weak at the knees. 'This may sound like a stupid question but, are you blonde?'

Dad holds his head in his hands and I hear him groan.

'Yeah! Why, do I sound blonde?'

I have a lump in my throat and must stop speaking. 'Just a silly guess,' I force out.

'Good guess,' she says curiously. 'Well, I hope everything's OK. You said you dialled your emergency number?'

'Yes, thanks, everything's fine.'

Dad looks relieved.

She laughs. 'Well, this is weird. I better go. Nice talking to you.'

'Nice talking to you too, Bea. Best of luck with your ballet show.'

We say our goodbyes and with a shaking hand I replace the handset.

'You silly dope, did you just dial the Americas?' Dad says, putting his glasses on and pressing a button on the phone. 'Joseph down the road showed me how to do this when I was getting the cranky calls. You can see who's called you and who you've called too. There it is. First few numbers are 0044. Where's that?'

'That's the UK.'

'Why on earth did you do that? Were you trying to trick me? Christ, that alone was enough to give me a heart attack.'

'Sorry, Dad.' I lower myself to the bottom stair, feeling shaky. 'I don't know where I got that number from.'

'Well, that sure taught me a lesson,' he says insincerely. 'I'll never smoke again. Give me those cigarettes and I'll throw them out.'

I hold my hand out, feeling dazed.

He snaps the packet up and shoves it deep into his trouser pocket. He narrows his eyes. 'What's up with you?'

'I'm going to London,' I blurt out.

'What?' His eyes almost pop out of his head.

'I have to find some answers to . . . something. I have to go to London. Come with me,' I urge, standing up.

He begins to walk backwards with his hand held protectively over his pocket containing the cigarettes. 'I can't go,' he says nervously.

'Why not?'

'Sure, I've never been away from here in my life!'

'All the more reason to go away now,' I urge him intensely. 'If you're going to smoke, you might as well see outside of Ireland before you kill yourself. Come to London with me, Dad. Please.'

'But, but,' he keeps moving backwards, his eyes wide, 'I can't miss the Monday Club.'

'We'll go tomorrow morning, be back before Monday, I promise.'

'But, I don't have a passport.'

'You just need photo ID.'

We're approaching the kitchen now.

'But we've nowhere to stay.' He passes through the door.

'We'll book a hotel.'

'It's too expensive.'

'We'll share a room.'

'But . . . but,' he bumps into the kitchen table and can move back no further. His face is a picture of terror. 'I've never been on a plane before.'

'There's nothing to it. You'll probably have a great time up there. And I'll be right beside you, talking to you the whole time.'

He looks unsure. 'What will I pack? What will I need for over there? Your mother usually packed all my going-away bags.'

'I'll help you pack,' I smile, getting excited. 'This is going to be so much fun—you and me on our first overseas holiday!'

Dad looks excited for a moment, then the excitement fades. 'No, I'm not going. I can't swim. If the plane goes down, I can't swim. I don't want to go over the seas. I'll fly with you but not over the seas.'

'Dad, we live on an island; *everywhere* we go outside of this country has to be over the sea. And there are life jackets on the plane. They show you what to do in case of emergencies, but believe me there won't be one. I've flown dozens of times without so much as a hiccup. You'll have a great time. And imagine all the things you'll have to tell the gang at the Monday Club? They'll hardly believe their ears, they'll want to hear your stories all day.'

A smile slowly creeps onto Dad's lips.

'**F**ran's outside, Dad. We have to go!'

'Hold on, love, I'm just making sure everything's OK.'

'Everything's fine,' I assure him. 'You've checked five times already.'

'You can never be too sure. You hear these stories of televisions malfunctioning and toasters exploding and people coming back from their holidays to a pile of smouldering ashes instead of their house.' He checks the socket switches in the kitchen for the umpteenth time.

Beep, beeeeeeep. Fran presses down on the horn.

'OK, so.' He takes a last look around and makes his way to the door. I watch his figure swaying. Dressed in his Sunday finest: a three-piece suit, shirt and tie, extra-shined shoes and his tweed cap, of course, which he'd never be seen without outside the house. He stalls at the hall table and reaches for the photograph of Mum.

'You know your mother was always at me to go to London with her.' He pretends to wipe a smudge on the glass but really he runs his finger over Mum's face.

'Bring her with you, Dad.'

'Ah, no, that'd be silly,' he says unsurely. 'Wouldn't it?'

'I think it'd be a great idea. The three of us will go and have a great time.'

His eyes tear up and with a simple nod of the head, he slides the photo frame into his overcoat pocket and exits the house to more of Fran's beeping. 'Ah, there you are, Fran,' he calls to her as he sways down the garden path. 'You're late, we've been waiting for you for ages.'

As I slide the key into the lock the phone sitting just inside the hall begins ringing. I look at my watch. Seven a.m. Who on earth would be calling at seven a.m?

Fran's car beeps again and I turn round angrily and see Dad leaning over Fran's shoulder, pushing his hand down on the steering wheel. 'Come on, love, we've a plane to catch!' he laughs uproariously.

I ignore the ringing phone and hurry to the car with the bags.

'There's no answer.' Justin paces the living room in a panic. He tries the number again. 'Why didn't you tell me about this yesterday, Bea?'

Bea rolls her eyes. 'Because I didn't think it'd be such a big deal. People get wrong numbers all the time.'

Answering machine. Dammit! Do I leave a message?

He hangs up and frantically dials again.

Bored with his antics, Bea sits on the garden furniture in the living room and looks around the dustsheet-covered room. 'When is Doris going to have this place finished?'

'After she starts,' Justin snaps, dialling again.

'My ears are burning,' Doris sings, appearing at the door in a pair of leopard-print overalls. 'Buzzy-Bea, sweetie, so lovely to see you!' She rushes to her niece and they embrace. 'We are so excited about your performance tonight, you have no idea. Little Buzzy-Bea all grown up and performing in the *Royal Opera House*.' Her voice rises to a screech. 'Oh, we are so proud, aren't we, Al?'

Al enters the room with a chicken leg in his hand. 'Mmm-hhm.'

Doris looks him up and down with disgust, and then turns back to her niece. 'A bed for the spare room arrived yesterday morning so you'll actually have something to sleep on when you stay. Also, I got some paint and fabric samples so we can start planning your room design but I'm only designing according to feng shui rules.'

Bea freezes. 'Oh gee, great.'

'I know we'll have such fun!'

Justin glares at his daughter. 'That's what you get for withholding information.'

'What information? What's going on?'

'Dad is having a conniption fit,' Bea explains.

'I told him to go to the dentist already. He has an abscess, I'm sure of it,' Doris says matter-of-factly.

'I told him too,' Bea agrees.

'No, not that. The woman,' Justin says intensely. 'Remember the woman I was telling you about?'

'Sarah?' Al asks.

'No!'

'Who can keep up with you?' Al shrugs. 'Certainly not Sarah, especially when you're running at top speed after buses, leaving her behind.'

Justin cringes. 'I apologised.'

'To her voicemail,' Al chuckles. 'She is never going to answer your calls again.'

'The *déjà vu* woman?' Doris gasps, realising.

'Yes.' Justin gets excited. 'Her name is Joyce and she called Bea yesterday.'

'A woman named Joyce rang yesterday,' Bea agrees. 'But I do believe there's more than one Joyce in the world.'

Ignoring her, Doris gasps again. 'How can this be? How do you know her name?'

'I heard somebody call her that on a Viking bus. And *yesterday* Bea got a *phone call*, on her *emergency* number, that no one but me has, from a *woman in Ireland*.' Justin pauses for dramatic effect. 'Called Joyce.'

There's a silence. Justin nods. 'Yep, I know, Doris. Spooky, huh?'

Frozen in place, Doris widens her eyes. 'Spooky, all right. Besides from the Viking bus.' She turns to Bea. 'You're eighteen years old and you've given your father an *emergency* number?'

Justin groans with frustration and starts dialling again.

Bea's cheeks pink. 'Before he moved over, Mum wouldn't let him call at certain hours because of the time difference. So I got another number. He's the only one that has it and every time he calls he seems to have done something wrong.'

'Not true,' Justin objects.

'Sure,' Bea responds breezily, flicking through a magazine. 'And I'm not moving in with Peter.'

'You're right, you're *not*. Peter,' he spits out the name, 'picks strawberries for a living.'

'Peter is an *IT consultant*.' Bea holds her hands out in confusion.

Choosing this moment to butt in, Doris turns to Justin. 'Sweetie, you know I'm all for this stuff with the *déjà vu* lady, but you got nothing but a coincidence. And I'm all for coincidences but this is . . . well, a pretty dumb one.'

'I have not got nothing, Doris, and that sentence is atrocious. I have got a *name* and now I have a *number*. And that, Doris Hitchcock, means that I got something!'

'It also makes you a stalker,' Bea says under her breath.

You are now leaving Dublin. We hope you enjoyed your stay.

Fran pulls over at the drop-off section, busy with people quickly unloading bags. Dad stands still, like the rock thrown into the stream again, and takes it all in, as I lift the bags from the boot. Eventually he snaps out of it and surprises us all by offering Fran a hug.

Once inside, in the hustle and bustle of one of Europe's busiest airports, Dad holds onto my arm tightly. We go to the computers to check in.

'What are you doing? Getting the sterling pounds out?'

'It's not an ATM, this is check-in, Dad.'

'I wouldn't trust this yoke.' He looks over the shoulder of the man beside us. 'Excuse me, is your yokey-mabob working for you?'

'*Scusi?*'

Dad laughs. 'Scoozy-woozy to you too.'

'*Mi dispiace tanto, signore, la prego di ignorarlo, è un vecchio sciocco e non sa cosa dice,*' I apologise to the Italian man. I have no idea what I've said but he returns my smile and continues checking in.

'You speak Italian?' Dad looks surprised but I haven't time to respond as he hushes me as an announcement is made. 'Whisht, Gracie, it might be for us. We better hurry.'

'We have two hours until our flight.'

'Where do we go now?' he asks once I retrieve our boarding passes from the machine.

'To check our bags in.'

'Hello,' the lady behind the counter smiles.

'Hello,' Dad says chirpily.

'How many bags are you checking in?'

'Two.'

'Did you pack your own bags?'

'Yes.'

'No.' Dad nudges me and frowns. 'You packed my bag for me, Gracie.'

I sigh. 'Yes, but you were with me, Dad. We packed it together.'

'Not what she asked.' He turns back to the lady. 'Is that OK?'

'Yes.' She continues, 'Did anybody ask you to carry anything for them on the plane?'

'N—'

'Yes,' Dad interrupts me again. 'Gracie put a pair of her shoes in my bag because they wouldn't fit in hers. She brought three pairs. *Three.*'

'Do you have anything sharp or dangerous in your hand luggage—scissors, tweezers, lighters or anything like that?'

'No,' I say.

Dad squirms and doesn't respond.

'Dad.' I elbow him. 'Tell her no.'

'No,' he finally says.

'Have a pleasant trip.' She hands us back our IDs.

'Thank you. You have very nice lipstick,' Dad adds.

I take deep breaths as we approach the security gates and I try to remind myself that this is Dad's first time in an airport. I collect a clear plastic bag and fill it with my make-up and his pills, and we make our way through the maze that is the security queue.

'I feel like a little mouse,' Dad comments. 'Will there be cheese at the end of this?' He gives a wheezy laugh. Then we are through to the metal detectors.

'Just do what they say,' I tell him while taking off my belt and jacket. 'You won't cause any trouble, will you?'

'Trouble? Why would I cause trouble? What are you doing? Why are you taking your clothes off, Gracie?'

I groan quietly.

'Sir, could you please remove your shoes, belt, overcoat and cap?'

'What?' Dad laughs at him.

'Remove your shoes, belt, overcoat and cap.'

'I will do no such thing. You want me walking around in my socks?'

'Dad, just do it,' I tell him.

'If I take my belt off, my trousers will fall down,' he says angrily.

'You can hold them up with your hands,' I snap. 'Just do it.' An extremely long queue of irritated travellers is forming behind us.

'Empty your pockets, please.' An older and angrier-looking security man steps in.

Dad looks uncertain.

'Oh my God, Dad, this is not a joke. Just do it.'

'Can I empty them away from her?'

'No, you'll do it right here.'

'I'm not looking.' I turn away, baffled.

I hear clinking noises as Dad empties his pockets.

'Sir, you were told you could not bring these things through with you.'

I spin round to see the security man holding a lighter and toenail clippers in his hands, the packet of cigarettes is in the tray with the photograph of Mum. And a banana.

'Dad!' I say.

'Stay out of this, please.'

'Don't speak to my daughter like that. I didn't know I couldn't bring them. She said scissors and tweezers and water and—'

'OK, we understand, sir, but we're going to have to take these from you.'

'But that's my good lighter, you can't take it from me! And what'll I do without my clippers?'

'We'll buy new ones,' I say through gritted teeth.

'OK,' he waves his hands rudely at them, 'keep the damn things.'

'Sir, please remove your cap, overcoat, shoes and belt.'

'He's an old man,' I say to the security guard in a low voice so that the gathering crowd behind us don't hear. 'He needs a chair to sit on to take off his shoes. And he shouldn't have to take them off as they're corrective footwear. Can you not just let him through?'

'The nature of his right shoe means that we must check it,' the man begins to explain but Dad overhears and explodes.

'Do you think I have a BOMB IN MY SHOE? Sure, what kind of eejit would do that? Is my banana really a GUN, do you think?' He waves the banana around at the staff, making shooting sounds. Dad reaches for his cap. 'Or maybe I've a GRENADE under my—'

He doesn't have the opportunity to finish as everything goes crazy. He is whisked away before my eyes and I am taken to a small cell-like room and ordered to wait.

After fifteen minutes of sitting alone in the bare interrogation room, I hear the door in the next room open, then close, then Dad's voice, as always, louder than everyone else's.

'Who are you travelling with?'

'Gracie.'

'Are you sure about that, Mr Conway?'

'Of course! She's my daughter, ask her yourself!'

'Her passport tells us her name is Joyce. Is she lying to us, Mr Conway? Or are you lying?'

'I'm not lying. Oh, I meant Joyce, I meant to say Joyce.'

'Are you changing your story now?'

'What story? I got the name wrong, is all. My wife is Gracie, I get confused.'

'Where is your wife?'

'She's not with us any more. She's in my pocket. I mean the photograph of her is in my pocket. At least, it *was* in my pocket until the lads out there took her and put her in the tray. Will I get my toenail clippers back, do you think? They cost me a bit.'

'Mr Conway, you were told sharp items and lighter fluid are not permitted on the flights.'

'I know that, but my daughter, Gracie, I mean, Joyce, went mad at me yesterday when she found my pack of smokes hidden in the Sugar Puffs and I didn't want to take the lighter out of my pocket or she'd lose her head again. I apologise for that.'

'Mr Conway, why did you refuse to take off your shoes?'

'I have holes in me socks!'

There is a silence. 'What was the reason for your refusal to remove your belt?'

'My trousers would have fallen down and you'd be arrestin' me for a whole lot more than this, believe you me.'

'You haven't been arrested, Mr Conway. We just need to ask you some questions. We need to ascertain if you are a threat to the safety of our passengers.'

'What do you mean, a threat?'

The security officer clears his throat. 'Well, it means finding out if you are a member of any gangs or terrorist organisations.'

I hear Dad roar with laughter. 'Terrorist organisations? I am, all right. The Monday Club is all I'm a member of. Meet every Monday, a bunch of lads and lasses gettin' together for a few pints and a singsong. Though if you're lookin' for juice, Donal's family were pretty heavily involved in the IRA all right.'

I hear the man questioning him clear his throat again. 'Donal?'

'Donal McCarthy. Ah, leave him alone, he's ninety-seven, and I'm talkin' about way back when his dad fought. The only rebellious thing he's able to do now is whack the chessboard with his cane and that's only because he's frustrated he can't play.' Dad laughs and sighs in the long pause that follows. 'Do you think I could get a cuppa?'

'We won't be much longer, Mr Conway. What is the nature of your visit to London?'

'I'm going because my daughter dragged me here, last minute. She gets off the phone yesterday morning and looks at me with a face as white as a sheet. I'm off to London, she says, like it's somethin' you just do last minute. Ah, maybe it is what you young people do, but not for me. Not what I'm used to at all, at all. Never been on a plane before, you see. But because of recent, well, troubles, shall we say, I decided to come with her. And that's no crime, is it?'

'What recent troubles, Mr Conway?'

'Lost her little baby a few weeks back, you see. Lost a little of herself too, if I'm to be honest with you. Lost the husband too just last week. Mind you, she got a little somethin' she never had before. Can't put my finger on exactly what, but whatever it is, I don't think it's such a bad thing. Generally things aren't goin' right for her and sure, what kind of a father would I be to let her go off on her own in this state? Here, take my bloody cap. My Joyce wants to go to London and you fellows should let her. If I have to go without my cap and my shoes and my belt and my overcoat, well then, that's fine by me, but my Joyce isn't going to London without me.'

Well, if that isn't enough to break a girl.

'Mr Conway, you do know that you get your clothing back once you go through the metal detector?'

'What?' he shouts. 'Why the hell didn't she tell me that? Honestly, you'd think she almost *wants* the trouble sometimes.'

Any tears that had welled very quickly dried.

Finally the door to my cell opens and I'm a free woman.

'**D**oris, you cannot move the stove in the kitchen. Al, tell her.'

'Why not?'

'Honey, first of all it's heavy and second of all, it's gas. You are not qualified to move around kitchen appliances,' Al explains, and prepares to bite into a doughnut.

Doris whisks it away from him. 'You two don't seem to understand that it's bad feng shui to have a stove facing a door. The person at the stove may instinctively want to glance back at the door, which creates a feeling of unease, which can lead to accidents.'

'Perhaps removing the stove altogether will be a safer option for Dad.'

'You have to give me a break,' Justin sighs, sitting down at the new kitchen table and chairs. 'Come on, sweetheart, let's get out of here.'

'Where are you two going? Can I come?' Al asks.

'I'm going to the dentist and Bea has rehearsals for tonight.'

'Good luck, Blondie.' Al ruffles her hair. 'We'll be cheering for you.'

'Thanks.' She grinds her teeth and fixes her hair. 'Oh, that reminds me. One more thing about the woman on the phone, Joyce?'

What, what, what? 'What about her?'

'She knows that I'm blonde.'

'How did she know?' Doris asks, with surprise.

'She said she just guessed. But that's not it. Before she hung up she said, "Best of luck with your ballet show." I don't remember telling her anything about my show being specifically ballet.'

Justin immediately looks to Al, a little more concerned now that it involves his daughter, but adrenaline still surges. 'What do you think?'

'I think, watch your back, bro. She could be a fruit-cake.'

Justin looks at his daughter. 'Did she sound like a fruit-cake?'

'I dunno,' Bea shrugs. 'What does a fruit-cake sound like?'

Justin, Al and Bea all turn to stare at Doris. 'What?' she squeals.

'No.' Bea shakes her head at her father. 'Nothing like that, at all.'

'What's this for, Gracie?'

'It's a sick bag.'

'What does this do?'

'It's a table.'

'How do you get it down?'

'By unlatching it, at the top.'

'Sir, please leave your tabletop up until after takeoff.'

Silence.

'What's that yoke?'

'An ejector seat for people who ask three million questions.'

'What's it, really?'

'For reclining your chair.'

'Sir, could you stay upright until after takeoff, please?'

Silence.

'What does that do?'

'A light.'

'And that one?'

'Yes, sir, can I help you?'

'Eh, no, thanks.'

'You pressed the button for assistance.'

'Oh, I didn't know. Can I have a drink of water?'

'We can't serve drinks until after takeoff, sir.'

I take deep breaths and pretend that I don't know him. I continue reading my book, *The Golden Age of Dutch Painting: Vermeer, Metsu and Terborch*, and convince myself this was not a bad idea.

'Where are the toilets?'

'To the top and on the left but you can't go until after takeoff.'

Dad's eyes widen. 'And when will that be?'

'In just a few minutes.'

'In just a few minutes, that,' he takes the sick bag out from the seat pocket, 'won't be used for what it's supposed to be used for.'

'We will be in the air in just a few minutes more, I assure you.' The stewardess quickly leaves before he asks another question.

I sigh.

'Don't you be sighing until after takeoff,' Dad says, and the man next to me laughs and tries to turn it into a cough.

Dad looks out of the window and I revel in the moment of silence.

'Oh oh oh,' he sings, 'we're moving now, Gracie.'

As soon as we're off the ground, Dad is quiet, agog at the blue and calm above the fluffy world of clouds. Dad blesses himself.

The fasten seat belt sign goes off with a bing. Dad takes down the tabletop and takes out his photograph of Mum. He places her on the table, facing out of the window, and they both watch the endless sea of white clouds disappear further below us and don't say a word for the remainder of the flight.

Five

'WELL, I MUST SAY, that was absolutely marvellous. Marvellous indeed.' Dad pumps the pilot's hand up and down enthusiastically. We are standing by the just-opened door of the plane, with a queue of hundreds of irritated passengers huffing and puffing down our necks.

'OK, Dad, we should move on now. We're holding everybody up.'

'Oh, is that so? Thanks again, folks. 'Bye now. Might see you on the way back,' he shouts over his shoulder as I pull him away.

We make our way through the tunnel adjoining the plane to the terminal and Dad says hello and tips his hat to everyone we pass.

'You really don't have to say hello to everybody, you know.'

'It's nice to be important, Gracie, but it's more important to be nice. Particularly when in another country,' says the man who hasn't left the province of Leinster for ten years.

'Will you stop shouting?'

'I can't help it. My ears feel funny.'

'Either yawn or hold your nose and blow. Your ears will pop.'

He stands by the conveyor belt, purple-faced, with his cheeks puffed out and his fingers over his nose. He takes a deep breath and pushes. He lets out a fart.

The conveyor belt jerks into motion and like flies around a carcass, people suddenly swoop in front of us to block our view, as though their life depends on grabbing their bags this very second.

'There's your bag.' I step forward. 'I'll get it, you'll hurt your back.'

'Step back, love, I can do it.' He passes over the yellow line and grabs his bag, only to realise that the strength he once had is gone and he finds himself walking alongside it, while tugging away. Ordinarily I would rush to help him but I'm doubled over laughing. All I can hear is Dad saying, 'Excuse me, excuse me,' to people as he tries to keep up with his moving luggage. He does a full lap of the conveyor belt and by the time he gets back to where I stand (though I'm still doubled over) somebody has the common sense to help the out-of-breath grumbling old man.

He pulls his bag over to me, his face scarlet.

'I'll let you get your own bag,' he says, pulling his cap further down over his eyes with embarrassment.

As I collect my bag from the belt, I am aware that there is not a clear purpose for this trip at all. A wild-goose chase is all it is. Completely irrational behaviour.

What does it mean to dream about somebody you've never met, almost every night, and then have a chance encounter with them over the phone? I had called my dad's emergency number; she had answered her dad's emergency phone number. Is it a mere coincidence that an ordinary right-thinking person would ignore or am I right to feel that something more lies beneath this? My hope is that this trip will have some answers for me. Panic begins to build as I watch Dad reading a poster on the far side of the room. I have no idea what to do with him.

Suddenly Dad's hand flies to his head and then his chest and he darts towards me with a manic look in his eyes. He grabs my arm and starts to pull me along.

'What's wrong? Where are we going?'

'We're going to Westminster.'

'What? Why? No! Dad, we have to go to the hotel to leave our bags.'

He stops walking and whips round. His voice shakes with the adrenaline. 'The *Antiques Roadshow* are having a valuation day today from nine thirty to four thirty in the afternoon in a place called Banqueting House. Sure we might even get to see Michael Aspel. *Michael Aspel*, Gracie. Christ Almighty, let's get out of here.' He shoots off through the sliding doors, with nothing to declare but temporary insanity, and takes a confident left.

I stand in the arrivals hall. I sigh and wait. Dad appears from the direction he went off in, seesawing and pulling his bag behind him at top speed.

'You could have told me that was the wrong way,' he says, passing me and heading in the opposite direction.

Dad rushes through Trafalgar Square, pulling his suitcase behind him. Finally, after we've taken a few wrong turns since surfacing from the tube station, Banqueting House is eventually in view, a seventeenth-century former royal palace, and though I am sure I have never visited it before, it stands before me, a familiar sight.

We wait outside to enter the reception area of Banqueting House. There are TV vans, camera and sound people going in and out of the building, and cameras filming the queue. Many people have brought picnic baskets, and as Dad looks around with a grumbling stomach I feel like a guilty mother who hasn't properly equipped her child. I'm also concerned for Dad that we won't make it past the front door.

'Dad, I don't want to worry you but I really think that we're supposed to have something with us. Everybody else has things with them to be valued.'

Dad looks around and notices for the first time. His face falls.

'Maybe they'll make an exception for us,' I add quickly but I doubt it.

We shuffle along slowly in the queue and Dad has a great time chatting to everybody. After queuing for an hour and a half, we have been invited to two houses for afternoon tea. Up ahead, just beyond the doors, I see an elderly couple being turned away due to having no items with them. Dad sees this too and looks at me, his eyes worried.

'Eh . . .' I look around quickly for something.

Both entrance doors have been held open for the flowing crowd. Just inside the main entrance, behind the opened door is a wooden waste basket posing as an umbrella stand. While no one is looking I turn it upside down, emptying the few scrunched balls of paper and broken umbrellas out. I kick them behind the door just in time to hear, 'Next.'

I carry it up to the reception desk and Dad's eyes almost pop out of his head at the sight of me.

'Welcome to Banqueting House,' the young woman greets us.

'Thank you,' I smile innocently.

'How many objects have you brought today?' she asks.

'Oh, just the one.' I raise the bin onto the table.

'Oh, wow, fantastic.' She runs her fingers along it. 'Once you enter the hall you'll see there are many queues. Please join the queue for the appropriate discipline.'

'What queue should we join for this thing?' Dad looks at the item as though there's a bad smell.

'Well, what is it?' she smiles.

'We were hoping you'd tell us that,' I say politely.

'I'd suggest miscellaneous. Once you reach the expert's table, simply show your item and he or she will tell you all about it.'

'Which table do we go to for Michael Aspel?'

'Unfortunately Michael Aspel isn't actually an expert, he is the host, so he doesn't have a table of his own.'

Dad looks devastated.

'There is the chance that your item may be chosen for television,' she adds quickly, sensing Dad's disappointment. 'The expert shows the object to the television team and a decision is made whether to record it, depending on rarity, quality, what the expert can say about the object and, of course, value. If your object is chosen, you'll be taken to our waiting room and made up before talking to the expert about your object in front of the camera for about five minutes. You would meet Michael Aspel under those circumstances. And the exciting news is that for the first time, we are broadcasting the show live, in, ooh let's see,' she examines her watch, 'in one hour.'

Dad's eyes widen. 'But five *minutes*? To talk about that thing?' Dad explodes and the woman laughs.

'Do enjoy your day,' she says finally, calling the next person in line forward.

As soon as we enter the busy hall, I immediately look up at the ceiling of the double-cubed room, already knowing what to expect: nine huge canvases commissioned by Charles I, to fill the panelled ceiling.

'Here you go, Dad.' I hand him the waste basket. 'I'm going to take a look around this beautiful building while you look at the junk people are putting inside it.'

As I wander the rooms, the feeling that I've been here before comes over me in a wave. I find a quiet corner and secretly produce my mobile.

'Manager, deputy head corporate treasury and investor solutions desk, Frankie speaking.'

'My God, that's a ridiculous quantity of words.'

'Joyce! Hi!' Her voice is hushed and behind her, the stock-trading in the Irish Financial Services Centre offices, sounds manic. 'How are you?'

'I'm fine. I'm in London. With Dad.'

'What? With your dad? What are you doing there?'

'I just decided to come over last minute.' For what, I have no idea. 'We're currently at the *Antiques Roadshow*. Don't ask.'

I leave the quiet rooms behind me and enter the gallery of the main hall. Below me I can see Dad wandering around the crowded hall.

'Have we ever been to Banqueting House together?'

'Refresh my memory, where is it and what does it look like?'

'It's at the Trafalgar Square end of Whitehall. It's a seventeenth-century former royal palace designed by Inigo Jones in 1619.' What does it look like? I close my eyes. 'From memory, the roofline is balustrade. The street façade has two orders of engaged columns, Corinthian over Ionic, above a rusticated basement, which lock together in a harmonious whole.'

'Joyce? Are you reading from a tourist guide?'

I snap out of it. 'No.'

'Our last trip to London consisted of Madame Tussauds, a night in G-A-Y and a party back in a man named Gloria's flat. It's happening again, isn't it? That thing you were talking about?'

'Yes.' I slump into a chair in the corner, feel a rope beneath me and jump back up. I quickly move away from the antique chair, looking around for security cameras.

'Has your being in London got anything to do with the American man?'

'Yes,' I whisper.

'Oh, Joyce—'

'Listen, Frankie. Yesterday I panicked about something and called Dad's doctor, a number that is practically engraved in my head, as it should be. I couldn't possibly get it wrong, right?'

'Right.'

'Wrong. I ended up dialling a UK number and a girl named Bea answered the phone. She'd seen an Irish number and thought it was her dad calling. So from our short conversation I figure out that her dad is American but was in Dublin and was travelling to London last night to see her in a show today. And she has blonde hair. I think Bea is the little girl I keep dreaming about seeing on the swings and playing in the sand, all at different ages.'

Frankie is quiet.

'I know I sound insane, Frankie, but this is what's happening.'

'I know this is *not* something you'd be inclined to make up,' she says quickly. 'But even as I take you seriously please do keep in consideration the fact that you've had a traumatic time and what you're currently experiencing could be due to high levels of stress.'

'I've already considered that.' I groan. 'I need help.'

'We'll only consider insanity as a last resort. Let me think for a second.' She sounds as though she's writing it down. 'So basically, you have seen this girl, Bea—'

'Maybe Bea.'

'OK, OK, let's just say it is Bea. You've seen her grow up?'

'Yes. From birth to I don't know . . . Teenager.'

'OK, so who else is in the scenes with Bea?'

'Another woman. With a camera.'

'But never your American man?' ·

'No. So he probably has nothing to do with this at all.'

'Let's not rule anything out. So when you view Bea and the lady with the camera, are you part of the scene or viewing them as an outsider?'

I close my eyes and think hard, see my hands pushing the swing, feeling the water from the sprinklers spray and tickle my skin . . . 'No, I'm part of it. They can see me.'

'OK.' She is silent.

'What, Frankie, what?'

'OK. So you see a child, a mother and they both see you?'

'Yes.'

'Would you say that in your dreams you're viewing this girl grow up through the eyes of a father?'

'Oh my God,' I whisper. The American man?

'OK, we're onto something here. I don't know what, but it's something very weird. What else do you dream about?'

'It's all very fast, images just flashing by.'

'Try and remember.'

'Sprinklers in a garden. A chubby young boy. A woman with long red hair. I hear bells. I'm at a funeral. Then at college. Then with the woman and young girl. Sometimes she's smiling and holding my hand, sometimes she's shouting and slamming doors.'

'Hmm . . . she must be your wife.'

I bury my head in my hands. 'Frankie, this sounds so ridiculous.'

'What you should do is, every time you get a flash of something, or suddenly know something you never knew, then write it down and tell me. I'll help you figure this out.'

'Thank you.'

'So apart from the place you're in now, what kinds of things do you suddenly just know about?'

'Em . . . mostly buildings. And art. I spoke Italian to a man at the airport. And Latin, I spoke Latin to Conor the other day.'

'Wow, Joyce, it's like you've got a crash course in an entire college education you never had.'

The door to the gallery opens and a flustered-looking young girl with a headset rushes in. 'Joyce Conway?' she asks me, out of breath.

'Yes.' My heart beats a mile a minute. Please let Dad be OK.

'Your father wants you to join him in the green room. He's going live with Michael Aspel in just a few minutes with his item and he wants you to join him because he says you know more about it. There's very little time and we need to get you made up.'

'Live with Michael Aspel . . .' I trail off. I realise I'm still holding the phone. 'Frankie,' I say, dazed, 'put on BBC, quick. You're about to witness me getting into very big trouble.'

I half walk, half run behind the girl with the headset, to get to the green room, and arrive panting and nervous to see Dad sitting on a make-up chair facing a mirror, a cup and saucer in his hand, his bulbous nose being powdered for his close-up.

'Ah, there you are, love,' Dad says grandly. 'Everybody, this is my daughter and she'll be the one to tell us all about my lovely piece here that caught the eye of Michael Aspel.' This is followed by a chuckle and he sips at his tea. 'There's Jaffa Cakes over there if you want them.'

Evil little man.

Justin is sitting in the dentist's waiting room, sandwiched between two old dears carrying on a conversation about someone called Rebecca, who should leave a man called Timothy. *Shut up, shut up, shut up!*

The 1970s television in the corner announces that the *Antiques Roadshow* is about to begin.

Justin groans. 'Does anybody mind if I change the channel?'

'I'm watching it,' says a young boy no older than seven years old.

Justin grunts in frustration.

'Excuse me.' Justin finally interrupts the women to his right and left. 'Would one of you ladies like to swap places with me, so that you can continue this conversation more privately?'

'No, don't worry, love, there's nothing private about this conversation, believe you me. Eavesdrop all you like.'

'I wasn't eavesdropping. Your *lips* were quite literally in my *ear*, and I'm not sure if Charlie or Graham or Rebecca would appreciate that.'

'Oh, Ethel,' one of the women laughs, 'he thinks we're talking about *real* people.'

Justin turns his attention back to the television in the corner.

'. . . And welcome to our first *live Antiques Roadshow* special coming to you from Banqueting House, London.'

Oh, I've been there. A nice example of Corinthian and Ionic locked together in a harmonious whole.

Ethel leans across Justin and rests her elbow on his thigh. 'So anyway, Margaret—'

He zones in on the television so as not to grab both their heads and smash them together.

'So what do we have here?' Michael Aspel asks. 'Looks like a designer waste basket to me,' he says as the camera takes a close-up on the piece propped on the table.

Justin's heart begins to palpitate.

'Do you want me to change it now, mister?' The boy flicks through the channels at top speed.

'No!' he shouts. Margaret and Ethel jump and go silent. 'Go back, go back, go back!' He grabs the remote control from the boy and flicks back through the channels. He stops when he comes upon the close-up of Joyce, whose eyes are looking uncertainly to the left and right, as though she has just landed in the cage of a Bengal tiger at feeding time.

In the Irish Financial Services Centre, Frankie is racing through the offices searching for a television. She finds one and starts fiddling with the buttons. She finds Joyce and Henry live on BBC. She gasps and holds her hands up to her mouth. And then she laughs and throws her fist at the screen. 'You go, Joyce!'

'*Em* . . .' Joyce is saying, 'well, we found it . . . I mean we *put* it, put this beautiful . . . extraordinarily . . . eh, wooden . . . bucket inside our front porch. For umbrellas.'

'Yes, and it may have been used for that too,' the appraiser says. 'Where did you get it from?'

Joyce's mouth opens and closes for a few seconds and Henry jumps in. There is a glint in his eye and he ignores the expert and takes on a posh accent to direct his answer at Michael Aspel, whom he addresses as though he's the Pope.

'Well, Michael, I was given this by my great-great-grandfather Joseph Conway, who was a farmer in Tipperary. He gave it to my grandfather Shay. My grandfather gave it to my father, Paddy-Joe, and then when he died, I took it.'

'I see, and do you have any idea where your great-great-grandfather may have got this?'

'He probably stole it from the Brits,' Henry jokes. Joyce elbows her father, Frankie snorts, and in a dentist's waiting room in London, Justin throws his head back and laughs loudly.

'Well, the reason I ask is because this is a fabulous item you have. It's a rare nineteenth-century English Victorian era upright jardinière planter—'

'I love gardening, Michael,' Henry interrupts the expert, 'do you?'

Michael smiles at him politely and the expert continues, 'It has wonderful hand-carved Black Forest-style plaques set in the Victorian ebonised wood framing on all four sides. Inside it has what looks like an original tole-painted tin liner. Superb condition, ornate patterns carved into the solid wood panels. An absolutely wonderful piece to have by your front door too.'

'Worth a few quid, is it?' Henry asks, dropping the posh accent.

'We'll get to that part,' the expert says.

In the dental surgery's waiting room, Justin is glued to the television, glued to Joyce's face.

'Is she a friend, love?' Ethel asks.

Justin studies Joyce's face and smiles. 'Yes, she is. Her name is Joyce.'

Margaret and Ethel ooh and aah.

Onscreen, the expert asks, 'How does between one thousand five hundred and one thousand seven hundred pounds sound to you?'

'Sterling pounds?' the old man asks, flabbergasted.

The camera zooms in on Joyce's and her father's face. They are both gobsmacked.

'Now there's an impressive reaction,' Michael laughs. 'Good news from this table, let's go over to our porcelain table . . .'

'Justin Hitchcock,' the receptionist calls.

The room is quiet. They all look around at one another.

'Justin,' she repeats, raising her voice.

'That must be him,' Ethel says. 'Yoohoo!' she sings.

'Somebody's in love, ooohey-ooohey,' Margaret sings.

'Louise,' Ethel says to the receptionist, 'why don't I go in now while this young man runs down to Banqueting House to see his lady?'

Justin stands and follows the receptionist down the hallway to the surgery. Adrenaline once again surges through his body. 'Actually, hold on. My tooth is fine now.' He holds out his hands and shrugs as if it's all no big deal. 'No pain at all. In fact, chomp, chomp, chomp,' he says as he snaps his teeth together. 'Look, completely gone. What am I even doing here? Can't feel a thing. I need to go to Banqueting House.'

She glares at him, killing his excitement. 'You're not escaping again. Come now. Dr Montgomery won't be happy if you don't show for your appointment again.' She urges him along.

Dr Montgomery greets him. 'Hello, trying to run off on me again, Justin?'

'No. Well, yes. Well, no, not run off exactly but I realised that there's somewhere else I should be and . . .'

By the time he's finished his excuse he realises he's wearing a protective gown and reclining in the chair.

'Blah blah blah, was all I heard, I'm afraid, Justin,' Dr Montgomery says cheerily.

Justin sighs.

The red light on the camera goes off and I grab Dad's arm.

'Dad, we have to go now,' I say with urgency.

'Not now,' Dad responds in a David Attenborough-style loud whisper. 'Michael Aspel is right over there.' He prepares to approach Michael Aspel, who is standing alone by the porcelain table with his finger in his ear. 'Must get waxy build-up, like me,' Dad whispers. 'He should use that stuff you got for me. Pop! Comes right out.'

'It's an earpiece, Dad. He's listening to the people in the control room. He's very busy.'

'No, I think it's a hearing aid. Let's go over to him and remember to speak up and mouth your words clearly. I have experience with this.'

I block his path. 'Dad, if we do not leave this place right now, we will find ourselves locked in a cell. Again.'

Dad laughs. 'Ah, don't exaggerate, Gracie.'

'I'm *bloody* Joyce,' I hiss. 'I don't think you understand the serious-ness of our situation. We have just stolen a seventeen-hundred-pound Victorian waste basket from a once-upon-a-time royal palace and talked about it live on air.'

Dad looks at me quickly, his bushy eyebrows raised. For the first time in a long time I can see his eyes. They look alarmed. And rather watery and yellow at the corners, and I make a note to ask him about that later, when we are not running from the law. Or the BBC.

The production girl gives me wide eyes from across the room. Heads are turning to stare at us. They know.

'OK, we have to go now. I think they know.'

'It's no big deal. We'll put it back.' He speaks as though it *is* a big deal. 'We haven't even taken it off the premises—that's no crime.'

'OK, it's now or never. Grab it quick, so we can put it back.'

Dad grabs the waste basket from the table and we make our way through the crowd. I see the young girl with the headset pushing her way through the crowd too.

'Quick, Dad, quick.'

We make it to the door of the hall and start towards the main entrance. I look back and catch the girl with the headset talking into her mike, urgently. She starts to run but gets caught behind two men in brown overalls carrying a wardrobe. We speed up. Down the stairs, we grab our bags from the cloakroom and then up and down, down and up, all the way along the marble-floored hallway.

Dad reaches for the oversized gold handle on the main door and we hear, 'Stop! Wait!'

We slowly turn round, and I prepare to defend our honour.

'Where are you two going in such a hurry?' the man asks, making his way towards us.

'It was her,' Dad says straight away, thumb pointed at me.

My mouth falls open.

'It was both of you, I'm afraid,' he smiles. 'You left your microphones and packs on. Worth a bit, these are.' He fiddles round the back of Dad's trousers and unclips his battery pack. 'Could have got into a bit of trouble if you'd escaped with this,' he laughs.

Dad looks relieved until I ask nervously, 'Were these turned on, the entire time?'

'Eh,' he studies the pack and flicks the switch to the off position. 'They were.'

'Who would have heard us?'

'Don't worry, they wouldn't have broadcast your sound while they went to the next item.'

I breathe a sigh of relief.

'But internally, whoever was wearing headphones on the floor would have heard,' he explains, removing Dad's mike. 'Oh, and the control room too,' he adds.

After he shuffles back to the fair, we place the umbrella stand back by the entrance door while no one is looking, fill it with the broken umbrellas and exit the scene of the crime.

'So, Justin, any news?' Dr Montgomery asks.

Justin, who is reclined in the chair, with two surgically gloved hands *and* apparatus shoved in his mouth, is unsure of how to answer.

Dr Montgomery chuckles. 'I might start getting offended one of these days, if people continue to ignore me when I ask questions.' He leans in over Justin. 'Hate to say I told you so,' he continues, 'but the cavity that you wouldn't let me look at during your last visit has become infected and now the tissue is inflamed.'

He taps around some more. Justin concentrates on the television suspended from the wall in the corner of the room. Sky News's red banner at the bottom of the screen screams it's breaking news again and though it's muted and too far away for him to read what exactly it is that they are breaking, it provides a welcome distraction.

The broadcaster is currently standing outside Westminster, but as Justin can't hear a thing he has no idea what he's talking about. He tries to lip-read while Dr Montgomery comes at him with a needle. His eyes widen as he catches sight of something on the television and he tries to sit up. For once, Justin doesn't care about the needle. He must try to communicate this as best as possible. Unable to move or close his mouth, he begins to make deep noises from the back of his throat.

'OK, don't panic. Just one more minute. I'm nearly there.'

He leans over Justin again, blocking his view of the television, and Justin squirms in his seat, trying to see the screen.

'My goodness, Justin, please stop it. The needle won't kill you, but I might if you don't stop wriggling.' Chuckle, chuckle.

'Ted, I think maybe we should stop,' his assistant says.

'Is he having a fit of some sort?' Dr Montgomery asks her.

Justin rolls his eyes and makes noises from the back of his throat.

'TV?' Dr Montgomery finally removes his fingers from Justin's mouth.

All three focus on the screen, the other two concentrating on the news while Justin watches the background where Joyce and her father have wandered into the path of the camera's angle, them at the front, Big Ben in the background. Seemingly unaware, they carry out what looks like a seriously heated conversation, their hands gesturing wildly.

'Look at those two idiots at the back,' Dr Montgomery laughs.

Suddenly Joyce's father pushes his suitcase over to Joyce and then storms off in the other direction.

Yeah, thanks, that's very mature,' I shout after Dad who has just stormed off, leaving his suitcase behind with me. He is going in the wrong direction. Again. I sit on my case and wait for him to realise the error of his ways and come back. It's evening now and I just want to get to the hotel and have a bath. My phone rings.

'Hi, Kate.'

She is laughing hysterically.

'Well, it's nice to hear *somebody* is in a good mood.'

'Oh, Joyce, you are the best dose of medicine, you really are.'

'What do you mean?' I can hear children's laughter in the background.

'Do me a favour and raise your right hand.'

'Why?'

'Just do it. It's a game the kids taught me,' she giggles.

'OK,' I sigh, and raise my right hand.

I hear the kids howl with laughter in the background.

'Tell her to wiggle her right foot,' Jayda shouts down the phone.

'OK,' I laugh. This is putting me in a much better mood. I wiggle my right foot and they laugh again. I can even hear Kate's husband howling in the background, which suddenly makes me uncomfortable again. 'Kate, what exactly is this?'

Kate can't answer, she's laughing so much.

'Tell her to hop up and down!' Eric shouts.

'No.' I'm irritated now.

'She did it for Jayda,' he begins to whinge, and I sense tears.

I quickly hop up and down. They howl again.

'By any chance,' Kate wheezes through her laughter, 'is there anyone around you who has the time?'

'What are you talking about?' I frown, looking around. I see Big Ben behind me, I'm still not sure of the joke, and as I turn back round only then see the camera crew in the distance. I stop hopping.

'**W**hat on earth is that woman doing?' Dr Montgomery steps closer to the television. 'Is she dancing?'

'Oo han ee ha?' Justin says, feeling the effects of his numbed mouth.

'Of course I can see her,' he responds. 'I think she's doing the hokey-cokey. See? You put your left leg in,' he begins to sing.

Justin, relieved that his sightings of Joyce aren't all in his mind, begins to bounce up and down in his seat, impatiently. *Hurry! I need to get to her.*

Dr Montgomery glances at him curiously, pushes Justin back in the chair and places the instruments in his mouth again. 'You're not going anywhere until I have filled this cavity. You'll have to take antibiotics for the abscess. Whoever this Joyce lady is, you can thank her for curing your fear of needles. You didn't even notice I'd injected you.'

I succeed in hailing a black cab and I send the driver in the direction of the dapper old man who is easily spotted on the pavement, swaying like a drunken sailor amid the crowd's vertical stream. Like a salmon, he swims upstream, pushing against the throng of people going in the opposite direction. Not doing it just for the sake of it, not to be deliberately different, or even noticing he's the odd one out.

'Dad,' I call out of the open window, 'come on, get in the car.'

He ignores me and holds a cigarette to his mouth, inhaling long and hard, so much so that his cheeks look concave.

'Dad, don't be like this. Just get in the car and we'll go to the hotel.'

He continues walking, looks straight ahead, as stubborn as anything. I've seen this face so many times before. The 'I'm right, you're wrong' look that has set his chin in that defiant stance, jutting outwards like Cork and Kerry's rugged coastline to the rest of the land.

'Look, we don't even have to talk. You can ignore me in the car too. And in the hotel. Don't talk to me all night, if it'll make you feel better.'

'You'd like that, wouldn't you?' he huffs.

'Honestly?'

He looks at me.

'Yes.'

He tries not to smile. Scratches the corner of his mouth with his yellow-stained cigarette fingers to hide how he softens. The smoke rises into his eyes and I think of his yellow eyes, think of how piercingly blue they used to be when, as a little girl, I'd watch him sitting at the kitchen table, while he dismantled a radio or a clock or a plug. I'd watch him, transfixed, afraid to speak, afraid to breathe, afraid to break the spell he'd cast on the contraption he was fixing, the muscles in his arms tanned from the gardening, flexing and unflexing as his fingers tackled the problem. His fingernails, always with a trace of dirt under the surface. His right forefinger and middle finger, yellow from the nicotine. Yellow, but steady. Uneven, but steady.

Finally he stops walking. He throws his cigarette on the ground and stomps it out with his chunky shoe. The cab stops. I throw the life-saving ring round his body and we pull him out of his stream of defiance and into the boat.

He is silent for a record amount of time. Ten, maybe fifteen, minutes. Finally words start spilling out of his mouth, as though they'd been queuing up impatiently behind his closed lips during the rare silence. Now the lips open and the words fly out in all directions like projectile vomit. 'You may have got a sherbet but I hope you know that I haven't a sausage.'

'What?'

'You heard me.'

'Yes, but . . .'

'Sherbet dab, *cab*. Sausage and mash, *cash*,' he explains. 'It's the ol' Chitty Chitty.'

I try to work that out in my head.

'Bang Bang, *rhyming slang*,' he finishes. 'He knows exactly what I'm talking about,' he nods at the driver.

'He can't hear you.'

'Why? Is he mutt and jeff?'

'What?'

'Deaf.'

'No,' I nod my head, feeling dazed and tired. 'When the red light is off, they can't hear you.'

'Like Joe's hearing aid,' Dad responds. He leans forward and flicks the switch in the back of the cab. 'Can you hear me?' he shouts.

'Yeah, mate.' The driver looks at him in the mirror. 'Loud and clear.'

Dad smiles and flicks the switch again. 'Can you hear me now?'

There is no response, the driver quickly glances at him in the rearview mirror, concern wrinkling his forehead, while trying also to keep an eye on the road.

Dad chuckles. I bury my face in my hands.

'This is what we do to Joe,' he says mischievously. 'Sometimes he can go a whole day without realising we turned his hearing aid off. Every half-hour he shouts, "JAYSUS, IT'S VERY QUIET IN HERE!"' Dad laughs and flicks the switch again, "'Allo, guv,' he says pleasantly.

'All right, Paddy,' the driver responds.

I wait for Dad's gnarled fist to go through the slit in the window. It doesn't. Instead his laughter filters through.

'I feel like being on my tod tonight. Could you tell me where there's a good jack near my hotel, so I can go for a pig without my teapot.'

The young driver studies Dad's innocent face in the mirror; he always means well, never intending insults. But he doesn't respond and continues driving.

I look away so Dad isn't embarrassed, but I feel rather superior and hate myself for it. Moments later, at a set of traffic lights, the hatch opens and the driver passes a piece of paper through.

'There's a list of a few there, mate. I'd suggest the first one, that's my favourite. Does good loop and tucker right about now, if you know what I mean,' he smiles and winks.

'Thank you.' Dad's face lights up. He studies the paper closely, then folds it carefully and slides it into his top pocket, proudly. 'It's just that this one here, is being a merry ol' soul, if you know what *I* mean. Make sure she gives you a good bit of rifle.'

The driver laughs and pulls over at our hotel: three-star and only ten minutes' walk from main theatres, Oxford Street, Piccadilly and Soho.

Dad gets out of the car and pulls his case along to the revolving doors at the hotel entrance. I watch him while waiting for my change. The doors are going round so fast, I can see him trying to time his entrance. Finally he makes a run for it and his suitcase gets stuck outside, jamming the revolving doors and trapping him inside.

'Help! Someone!' I hear Dad call.

I take my time getting out of the cab. 'By the way, what did he call me?' I ask the driver, calmly ignoring the calls behind me.

'A merry old soul?' he asks. 'It means arsehole,' he laughs, and then he pulls away, leaving me at the side of the street with my mouth gaping.

I notice the knocking has quietened and turn to see that Dad has been freed at last. I hurry inside.

'I can't give you a credit card, but I can give you my word,' Dad is saying slowly and loudly to the woman behind the reception desk.

'It's OK, here you go.' I slide my credit card across the counter.

The receptionist smiles politely and taps away on the computer. 'You're sharing a room?' she asks.

'Yes,' I respond with dread.

'Two Uncle Teds, I hope?'

She frowns.

'Beds,' I say quietly. 'He means beds.'

'Yes, they're twin beds, Mr Conway.'

The room is standard and it's clean, and that's good enough for me. Our beds are far enough apart for my liking, there's a television and a minibar, which hold Dad's attention while I run a bath.

'I wouldn't mind a drop of fine,' he says, his head disappearing into the minibar.

'You mean wine.'

'Fine and dandy, *brandy*.'

I finally slide down into the soothing bathwater, the suds rise like the foam atop an ice-cream float. I lie back, feel tiny bubbles all over my body pop as they touch my skin . . . There's a knock on the door.

I ignore it.

BANG! BANG!

'What?' I shout.

'Oh, sorry, thought you'd fallen asleep or something, love. You have to be careful in those things. Could nod off and slip under the water and drown. Happened to one of Amelia's cousins. You know Amelia. Visits Joseph sometimes, down the road.'

'Dad, I appreciate your concern but I'm fine.'

'OK.'

Silence.

'Actually, it's not that, Gracie. I'm just wonderin' how long you'll be in there for?'

I grab the yellow rubber duck sitting at the side of the bath and I strangle it.

'Love?' he asks in a little voice.

I take a deep breath, breathe out slowly. 'About twenty minutes, Dad, is that OK?'

Silence. I close my eyes again.

'Eh, love. It's just that you've been in there twenty minutes already and you know how my prostate is—'

I don't hear any more, because I'm climbing out of the bath. I throw a towel round me and open the door, bow and hold my arm out to the toilet. 'Your chariot awaits you, sir.'

Embarrassed, he shuffles inside and closes the door behind him. It locks.

Wet and shivering, I browse through the half-bottles of red wine in the minibar. I pick one up and study the label. Immediately an image flashes through my mind. A picnic basket with this bottle inside, an identical label, red and white chequered cloth laid out on the grass, a little girl with blonde hair twirling in a pink tutu. I am lying on the chequered cloth, barefoot, trousers rolled above my ankles. *Hairy* ankles. I feel a hot sun beating down on my skin, the little girl twirls before the sun. A hand appears before me, a glass of red wine in it. I look to her face. Red hair, lightly freckled, smiling adoringly. At me.

Justin, she's singing. *Earth to Justin!*

Then it's gone. I'm back in the hotel room, my hair dripping bathwater onto the carpet. Dad is watching me curiously. 'Earth to Joyce,' he's singing.

I clear my throat. 'You're done?'

Dad nods and his eyes follow me to the bathroom. On the way there, I stop and turn. 'By the way, I've booked a ballet show for tonight if you'd like to come. We need to leave in an hour.'

'OK, love,' he nods softly, and watches after me with a familiar look of worry in his eyes. I've seen that look as a child, I've seen it as an adult and a million times in between. It's as though I've taken the stabilisers off my bicycle for the very first time and he's running along beside me, holding on tight, afraid to let me go.

Six

DAD LINKS MY ARM TIGHTLY as we slowly make our way to Covent Garden. Having booked our tickets so late we are seated in the lower slips almost at the top of the tremendous theatre. The view of the stage is restricted, yet the view of the boxes opposite is perfect. Squinting through the binoculars situated near the seat, I spy on the people filling the boxes. No sign of my American man. *Earth to Justin?* I hear the woman's voice in my head and wonder if Frankie's theory about seeing the world from his eyes was correct.

Dad is enthralled by our view. He takes the photograph of Mum from his pocket and places her on the velvet balcony ledge. 'Best seat in the house, indeed,' he says, his eyes filling.

The conductor taps and the orchestra plays the opening bars of Tchaikovsky's ballet music. Apart from Dad snorting when the male principal dancer appears onstage wearing tights, it runs smoothly and we are both entranced by the story of *Swan Lake*. I look away from the prince's coming-of-age party and study those sitting in the boxes through my opera glasses, moving from left to right, a row of unfamiliar faces until . . . My eyes widen as I reach the familiar face, the man from the hair salon I now know from Bea's biography in the programme, to be Mr Hitchcock. *Justin Hitchcock?* He watches the stage, entranced, leaning so far over the balcony it looks as though he'll topple over the ledge.

Dad elbows me. 'Would you stop looking around you, and keep your eye on the stage. He's about to kill her.'

I try to hold my eyes on the prince but I can't. A magnetic pull turns my face back down to the box, anxious to see who Mr Hitchcock is sitting with. Beside him is the woman with long red hair who holds the camera in my dreams. Beside her is a sweet-looking gentleman and behind them, squashed together, are a young man pulling uncomfortably at his tie, a woman with big curly red hair and a large round man. I flick through my memory files. The chubby boy from the sprinkler scene and seesaw? Perhaps. But the other two, I don't know. I move my eyes back to Justin Hitchcock.

Suddenly the music changes, and his expression changes. I know instantly that Bea is onstage, and I turn to watch. There she is among the flock of swans. Her long blonde hair is tied up in a bun, covered by a neat headdress. I recall the image of her in the park as a little girl, twirling and twirling in her tutu, and I'm filled with pride. How far she has come. How grown up she is now. My eyes fill.

'**O**h, look, Justin,' Jennifer says breathily beside him.

He is looking. He can't take his eyes off his daughter. She looks so grown-up. It seems like only yesterday she was twirling for him and Jennifer in the park across from their house, a little girl with a tutu and dreams and now . . . His eyes fill and he looks beside him to Jennifer, to share a look, share the moment but at the same time, she reaches for Laurence's hand. He looks away quickly, back to his daughter. A tear falls and he reaches into his front pocket for his handkerchief.

A handkerchief is raised to my face, catches my tear before it drips from my chin.

'What are you crying for?' Dad says loudly, dabbing at my chin roughly, as the curtain lowers for the interval.

'Oh, nothing . . . I just think it's beautiful. What do you think?'

'I think those lads have definitely got socks down their tights.'

I laugh and wipe my eyes. 'Do you think Mum's enjoying it?'

He smiles and stares at the photo. 'She must be, she hasn't turned round once since it started. Unlike you, who's got ants in her pants.'

'Do you miss her?'

'It's been ten years, love.'

It stings that he can be so dismissive. I fold my arms and look away, silently fuming.

Dad leans closer and nudges me. 'And every day, I miss her more than I did the day before.'

Oh. I immediately feel guilty.

'It's like my garden, love. Everything grows. Including love. And with that growing every day how can you expect missing her to ever fade away? Everything builds, including our ability to cope with it. That's how we keep going.'

I shake my head, in awe of some of the things he comes out with. Philosophical and otherwise. And this from a man who's been calling me his teapot (lid, *kid*) since we landed.

'And I just thought you liked pottering,' I smile.

'Ah, there's a lot to be said for pottering. You know Thomas Berry said that gardening is an active participation in the deepest mysteries of the universe? There are lessons in pottering.'

'Like what?' I try not to smile.

'Well, even a garden grows stranglers, love. It grows them naturally, all by itself. They creep up and choke the plants that are growing from the very same soil as they are. We each have our demons, our self-destruct button. Even in gardens. Pretty as they may be. If you don't potter, you don't notice them.'

He eyes me and I look away, choosing to clear my already-clear throat. Sometimes I wish he'd just stick to laughing at men in tights.

'Justin, we're going to the bar, are you coming?' Doris asks.

'No,' he says, in a huff like a child, folding his arms.

'Why not?' Al squeezes further into the box to sit beside him. 'You'll be here on your own.'

'So?'

'Mr Hitchcock, would you like me to get you a drink?' Bea's boyfriend, Peter, asks.

'Mr Hitchcock was my father, you can call me Al. Like the song.' He punches him playfully on the shoulder.

'OK, Al, but I actually meant Justin.'

'You can call *me* Mr Hitchcock.' Justin looks at him like there's a bad smell in the room.

'We don't have to sit with Laurence and Jennifer, you know.'

Laurence. Laurence of Ahernia who has elephantitis of the—

'Yes, we do, Al, don't be ridiculous,' Doris interrupts.

Al sighs. 'Well, give Petey an answer, do you want us to bring you back a drink?'

Yes. But Justin can't bring himself to say it and instead shakes his head sulkily.

'OK, we'll be back in fifteen.'

Al gives him a comforting brotherly pat on his shoulder before they all leave him alone in the box to stew over Laurence and Jennifer and Bea and Chicago and London and Dublin and now Peter, and how exactly his life has ended up.

Two minutes later and already tired of feeling sorry for himself, he looks through his opera glasses and begins spying on the trickles of people seated below him who'd stayed in their seats for the interval. Nothing exciting. He moves to the boxes opposite. They are empty, everyone choosing to have their pre-ordered drinks in the nearby bar. He cranes his neck up higher. *How on earth can anyone see anything from there?*

Up there, there are a small number of people chatting. He moves along from right to left. Then stops. Rubs his eyes. He squints through the opera glasses again and sure enough, there she is. With the old man. Every scene in his life was beginning to be like a page from *Where's Wally?*

She is looking through her opera glasses too, scanning the crowd below them both. Then she raises her opera glasses, moves slowly to the right and . . . they both freeze, staring. He waves. She slowly does the same. The old man beside her puts his glasses on and squints in his direction, mouth opening and closing the entire time.

Justin holds his hand up, a 'wait' sign. *Hold on, I'm coming up to you.* He holds his forefinger up. *One minute. Hold on, I'll be one minute*, he tries to signal.

She gives him the thumbs up and he breaks into a smile.

He drops the opera glasses and stands up immediately. The door to the box opens and in walks Laurence.

'Justin, I thought maybe we could have a word,' he says politely.

'No, Laurence, not now, sorry.' He tries to move past him.

'I promise not to take up too much of your time. Just a few minutes while we're alone. To clear the air, you know?'

'Yeah, I appreciate that, buddy, I really do, but I'm in a really big hurry right now.' He tries to inch by him.

'A hurry?' Laurence says, raising his eyebrows. 'But . . . ah.' He stops, realising. 'I see. Well, I just thought I'd give it a try. If you're not ready to have the discussion yet, that's understandable.'

'No, it's not that.' Justin looks through his opera glasses and up at Joyce, feeling panicked. She's still there. 'It's just that I really am in a hurry to get to somebody. I have to go, Laurence.'

Jennifer walks in just as he says that. Her face is stony.

'Honestly, Justin. Laurence just wanted to be a gentleman and talk to you like an *adult*. Something, it seems, you have forgotten how to be.'

'No, no, look, Jennifer.' *I used to call you Jen. So formal now, a lifetime away from that memorable day in the park.* 'I *really* don't have time for this right now. You don't understand, I have to go.'

'You can't go. The ballet is about to begin. Don't tell me you're walking out on your daughter too.'

Doris and Al enter the box. Al holds a pint of cola in his hand and an oversized bag of crisps.

'Tell him, Justin.' Doris folds her arms and taps her long pink fake nails against her thin arms. '*Remind* him of the heart disease in your family so that he may think twice before eating and drinking that crap.'

'What heart disease?' Justin holds his hands to his head while on the other side of him, Jennifer drones on and on.

'Your *father*, dying of a *heart attack*,' she says impatiently.

Justin freezes. 'No, no, you don't have to worry about that, Al.'

'See?' He looks at Doris.

'That's not what the doctor said, sweetheart. We have to be more careful if it runs in the family.'

'No, it doesn't run in the—' Justin stalls. 'I really have to go now.'

'No, you will not,' Jennifer blocks him. 'You are not going anywhere until you *apologise* to Laurence.'

'It's really all right, Jen,' Laurence says awkwardly.

I call her Jen, not you!

Voices come at him from all sides, wah wah wah, he is unable to make out the words. He feels hot and sweaty, dizziness grips him.

Suddenly the lights dim and the music begins and he has no choice but to take his seat again, beside a fuming Jennifer, an insulted Laurence, a silent Peter, a worried Doris and a hungry Al, who decides to munch loudly in his left ear, on the packet of potato crisps.

He sighs and looks up at Joyce. *Help.*

It seems the squabble in Mr Hitchcock's box has ended. Deep inside, my heart drums like a *djembe*. He saw me, he wanted to come to me. I feel relieved that following my instincts, however flighty, paid off. When I calm my nerves slightly I turn my attention back to the stage where Bea takes my breath away and causes me to sniffle through her performance like a proud aunt.

'Dad, can I ask you something?' I lean close to him and whisper.

'He's just after telling that girl that he loves her but she's the wrong girl.' He rolls his eyes. 'Eejit. The swan girl was in white and that one is in black. They don't look alike at all.'

'She could have changed for the ball. No one wears the same thing every day.'

He looks me up and down. 'You only took your bathrobe off *one day* last week. Anyway, what's up with you?'

'Well, it's that, I, em, something has happened and, well . . .'

'Spit it out for Christ's sake, before I miss anything else.'

I give up whispering in his ear and turn to face him. 'I've been given something, or more, something very special has been *shared* with me. It's completely inexplicable and it doesn't make any sense at all, in an Our Lady of Knock kind of way, you know?' I laugh nervously.

No, he doesn't know. Dad looks angry I've used Mary's apparition in County Mayo during the 1870s as an example of nonsense.

'OK, perhaps that was a bad example. What I mean is, it breaks every rule I've ever known. I just don't understand *why*.'

'Gracie.' Dad lifts his chin. 'Knock, like the rest of Ireland, suffered great distress over the centuries from evictions and famines, and Our Lord sent His Mother to visit with His oppressed children.'

'No, I don't mean why did Mary appear, I mean why has this . . . this *thing* happened to me? This thing I've been given.'

'Oh. Well, is it hurting anyone? Because if it's not and if you've been given it, I'd stop callin' it a "thing" and start referring to it as a "gift".'

A gift. I'd never thought of it like that.

'But I don't understand *why* and *how* and—'

'What is it with people these days?' he hisses. 'In my day, something *just was*. None of this analysis a hundred times over. Sometimes, love, you just need to forget all of those Whys and Hows and Becauses and enrol in a little lesson called "Thank You". Look at this story here.' He points at the stage. 'Do you hear anybody here giving out about the fact *she*, a *woman*, has been turned into a *swan*? Have you met anyone lately who happens to have been turned into a swan?'

I laugh and whisper, 'No.'

'Yet look at it. This bloody thing has been famous the world over for centuries. We have non-believers, intellectuals, cynicists, all kinds of what-have-yous in here tonight, but all of them want to see that fella in the tights end up with that swan girl, so she'll be able to get out of that lake. Only with the love of one who has never loved before, can the spell be broken. Why? Who the hell cares why? Do you think your woman with the feathers is going to ask *why*? No. She's going to say *thank you* because then she can move on and wear nice dresses and go for walks, instead of having to peck at soggy bread in a stinky lake every day for the rest of her life.'

I have been stunned to silence.

During the standing ovation, Justin spies Joyce's father helping her into a red coat, the same one from their Grafton Street collision. She begins to move to her nearby exit with her father in tow.

'Justin.' Jennifer scowls at her ex-husband, who is more busy spying through his opera glasses up at the ceiling than at his daughter bowing.

He puts the glasses down and claps loudly, cheering.

'Hey, guys, I'm going to go to the bar and keep some good seats for us.' He starts moving towards the door.

'It's already reserved,' Jennifer shouts after him, over the applause.

He holds his hand up to his ear and shakes his head. 'Can't hear you.'

He escapes and runs down the corridors, trying to find his way upstairs to the lower slips. People begin to exit their boxes, crowding the corridors and making it impossible for Justin to push past.

He has a change of plan: he'll rush to the exit and wait for her there. That way he can't miss her.

'**L**et's get a drink, love,' Dad says as we slowly amble behind the crowd exiting the theatre. 'I saw a bar on this floor.'

We stop to read some directions.

'There's the Amphitheatre bar, this way,' I say, looking out constantly for Justin Hitchcock.

A woman usher announces that the bar is open only for cast, crew and family members.

'That's great, we'll have some peace and quiet so,' Dad says to her, tipping his cap as he walks by. 'Oh, you should have seen my grand-daughter up there. Proudest day of my life,' he says, putting his hand on his heart.

The woman smiles and allows us entry.

'Come on, Dad.' After we've bought our drinks, I drag him deep into the room to sit at a table in the far corner, away from the growing crowd. I wring my hands nervously and look around for him. *Justin.*

Bea's mother enters with the two unknown people from the box, and the chubby man I recognise. But no Mr Hitchcock.

'There she is,' I whisper.

'Who?'

'One of the dancers. She was one of the swans.'

'How do you know? They all looked the same. Even the nancy boy thought they were the same. Sure, didn't he profess his love to the wrong woman? The bloody eejit.'

There's no sign of Justin and I begin to worry that this is another wasted opportunity. Perhaps he has left early.

'Dad,' I say urgently, 'I'm just going to take a look around for some-body. Please do *not* move from this chair. I'll be back soon.'

Justin gives up. He must have missed her and he was stupid to think there was only one exit. He sighs with frustration. He wishes he could transport himself back in time to the day in the salon and relive the moment properly this time. His pocket vibrates, snapping him out of his daydream.

'Bro, where the heck are you?'

'Hi, Al. I saw the woman again.'

'The Sky News woman? The Viking woman?'

'Yeah, yeah, her.'

'The *Antiques Roadshow* wo—'

'YES! For Christ's sake, do we have to go through this again?'

'Whatever, hurry back up here before Jennifer has a conniption fit.'

Justin sighs. 'I'm coming.' He snaps his phone shut and takes one last look down the street. Among the crowd something catches his eye, a red coat. He races outside.

'Joyce!' he calls. 'Joyce, wait!'

She keeps walking, unable to hear him.

He bumps and pushes past the crowd, until finally she's just inches from him.

'Joyce,' he says breathlessly, reaching out and grabbing her arm.

She spins round, a face twisted in surprise and fright. A stranger.

She hits him over the head with her leather bag.

'Ow! Hey! Jesus!'

Apologising, he slowly makes his way back to the theatre, rubbing his sore head. He reaches for the main door. It doesn't open. He rattles it slightly a few times. Within seconds, he pulls and pushes the door with full force, kicking at it with frustration.

'Hey, hey, hey! We're closed! Theatre's closed!' a member of staff informs him from behind the glass.

When I return to the bar, I thankfully find Dad sitting in the corner where I'd left him. Only he's not alone. Perched on the chair beside him is Bea.

'Hi.' I approach them, terrified by what verbal diarrhoea may have slipped out of his mouth already.

'Ah, there you are, love. Thought you'd abandoned me. This nice girl came to see if I was OK, seeing as someone tried to throw me out again.'

'I'm Bea,' she smiles, and I can't help but notice how self-assured and confident she is.

'Hello, Bea.'

'Do I know you?' Frown lines appear on her porcelain forehead.

'Em . . .'

'This is my daughter, Gracie,' Dad butts in, and for once I don't correct him.

'Oh, Gracie,' Bea shakes her head. 'No. I was thinking of someone else. Nice to meet you.'

We shake hands. 'You were wonderful tonight. I was so proud,' I say.

'Proud? Oh, yes, your father told me you designed the costumes,' she smiles. 'They were beautiful. I'm surprised I hadn't met you until now, we had been dealing with Linda for all the fittings.'

My mouth drops, Dad shrugs nervously and sips on what looks to be a new pint. A fresh lie for a fresh pint. The price of his soul.

'Oh, I didn't design them . . . I just . . .' You just what, Joyce? 'I just supervised,' I say dumbly. 'What else has he been telling you?' I nervously sit down and look around for her father, hoping this isn't the moment he chooses to enter and greet me, in the midst of this ridiculous lie.

'Well, just as you arrived he was telling me about how he'd saved a swan's life,' she smiles.

'Single-handedly,' they add in unison and laugh.

'Ha-ha,' I force out and it sounds fake. 'Is that true?' I ask him.

'Oh, ye of little faith. It's great to save a life, it really, really is,' Dad says. 'Unless you've done it, you have no idea.'

'My father, the hero,' I smile.

Bea laughs at Dad. 'You sound exactly like my father.'

My ears perk up. 'Is he here?'

She looks around. 'No, not yet. I don't know *where* he is. Probably hiding from my mom and her new boyfriend, not to mention my boyfriend,' she laughs. 'But that's another story. Anyway, he considers himself Superman—'

'Why?' I interrupt and try to rein myself in.

'About a month ago, he donated blood,' she smiles and holds her hands up. 'Ta-da! That's it!' She laughs. 'But he thinks he's some kind of hero that's saved somebody's life. I mean, I don't know, maybe he has. It's *all* he talks about. He donated it at a mobile unit at the college where he was giving a seminar—you guys probably know it, it's in Dublin. Trinity College? Anyway, I wouldn't mind, but he only did it because the doctor was cute and for that Chinese thing, what do you call it? The thing where you save someone's life and they're for ever indebted to you or something?'

Dad shrugs. 'I don't speak Chinese. Or know any.'

Bea laughs. 'Anyway, he figured if he was going to save someone's life he deserved to be thanked every day for the rest of his life by the person he *saved*.'

'How would they do that, then?' Dad leans in.

'Deliver a muffin basket, collect his dry-cleaning, a newspaper and coffee delivered to his door every morning, a chauffeur-driven car, front-row tickets to the opera . . .' She rolls her eyes and then frowns. 'I can't remember what else but they were ridiculous things. Anyway, I told him he may as well have a slave if he wants that kind of treatment, not save someone's life.' She laughs and Dad does too.

I make an *oh* shape with my mouth but nothing comes out.

'Don't get me wrong, he's a really thoughtful guy,' she adds quickly, misunderstanding my silence. 'And I was proud of him for donating blood as he's absolutely terrified of needles. He has a *huge* phobia,' she explains to Dad, who nods along in agreement. 'That's him there.' She opens her locket round her neck and if I have regained my power of speech, it is quickly lost again.

On one side of the locket is a photograph of Bea and her mother, and on the other side is the photograph of her and her father when she was a little girl, in the park on that summer day that is clearly embedded in my memory.

Dad takes the gold locket in his old fingers. 'Where was this?'

'The park near where we used to live. In Chicago. I'm five years old there, with my dad, but I love this photograph. It was such a special day.' She looks at it fondly. 'One of the best.'

I smile too, remembering it.

'Photograph!' somebody in the bar calls out.

'Dad, let's get out of here,' I whisper.

'OK, love, just after this pint—'

'No! Now!' I hiss.

'Group photo! Come on!' Bea says, grabbing Dad's arm.

'Oh!' Dad looks pleased.

'No, no no no no no.' I try to smile to hide my panic.

'Just one photo, Gracie,' she smiles. 'We have to get the lady who's responsible for all these beautiful costumes.'

A woman on the other side of the group throws me a look of horror, on hearing this. Dad laughs. I'm stiff beside Bea, who throws one arm round me and the other arm round her mother.

'Everyone say Tchaikovsky!' Dad shouts.

The camera flashes.

Justin enters the room.

The crowd breaks up.

I grab Dad, and run.

Back in our hotel room it's lights out for Dad and me. Lying flat and still on my back, I attempt to process the day's events. My body once again becomes the subject of Zulu drumming as my heartbeat intensifies. I feel its pounding against the springs in the mattress beneath me.

The reason for these internal war drums? The revelation that Bea's dad, Justin, donated blood a month ago in Dublin, the same month

I fell down the stairs and changed my life for ever, plays over and over in my mind. Coincidence? A resounding yes. Something more? A shaky possibility. A *hopeful* possibility.

When is a coincidence just a coincidence, though? And when, if at all, should it be seen as something more? At a time like this? When I am lost and desperate, grieving for a child that was never born, and tending to my wounds after a failed marriage? It is during troubled times like these that people see straight, though others watch with concern and try to convince them that they don't. When you're in trouble you look harder for answers than those who aren't, and it's those answers that help you through.

This blood transfusion—is it the explanation for the sudden arrival of alien memories, the reason for such a deep connection to Justin? Is this the answer that my heart is currently raging within me in order to realise? I breathe in slowly through my nose and exhale, I close my eyes gently and place my hands over my chest, feeling the thump-thump, thump-thump that is raging within me. Time to slow everything down now, time to get answers.

Taking the bizarre as a given for just one moment: if I did indeed receive Justin's blood during my transfusion, then my heart is now sending his blood round my body. Some of the blood that once flowed through his veins, keeping him alive, now rushes through mine, helping to keep me alive. Something that came from his heart, that beat within him, that made him who he is, is now a part of me.

At first I shiver at the thought, but on further reflection, I suddenly don't feel so lonely, feel glad of the company within me.

I sigh wearily, knowing nothing in my life makes sense any more, and not just since the day I fell down the stairs. I had been falling for quite some time before that. That day was the day I'd landed. The first day of the rest of my life, quite possibly thanks to Justin Hitchcock.

From the darkness I hear a wheezing, short rasps drifting into the atmosphere.

'Dad?' I whisper. 'Are you OK?'

The wheezing gets louder and my body freezes.

'Dad?'

Then it's followed by a snort. And a loud guffaw. 'Michael Aspel,' he splutters through his laughter. 'Christ Almighty, Gracie.'

I smile with relief as his laughter intensifies. I giggle. He laughs harder on hearing me, and I on hearing him. Thoughts of the umbrella stand, going live with Michael Aspel, the group cheering 'Tchaikovsky!' at the camera, cause us to roar even more.

'Oh, my stomach,' he howls.

I can't stop and Dad's high-pitched wheezing sets me off even more. I don't think I've ever heard him laugh so much and so heartily. From the pale light seeping through the window beside Dad, I see his legs rise in the air and kick around with glee.

We wheeze and roar and laugh, sit up, lie down, roll around and try to catch our breaths. We stop momentarily and there is silence. Dad farts and we are off again.

Hot tears roll from the sides of my eyes and it occurs to me how close happiness and sadness are. Such a thin line, a thread-like divide that in the midst of emotions, it trembles, blurring the territory of exact opposites. The movement is minute, like the thin thread of a spider's web that quivers under a raindrop. Here in my moment of unstoppable laughter, my body is racked by emotion and therefore steps ever so slightly over the mark, and into sadness. Tears of sadness gush down my cheeks as my stomach continues to shake and ache with happiness.

I think of Conor and me; how quickly a moment of love was snapped away to a moment of hate. One comment to steal it all away. Of how love and war stand upon the very same foundations. How despair can be altered by one simple smile offered by a stranger; confidence can become fear through the arrival of one uneasy presence. Just as Kate's son had wavered on the balance beam and in an instant his excitement had turned to pain. Everything is on the verge; a tremble sends things toppling. How similar emotions are.

Dad stops his laughter so abruptly it concerns me and I reach for the light. He throws the covers off his body and shuffles into the bathroom, grabbing his travel bag and refusing to meet my eyes. I look away. How quickly such comfort with someone can shift to awkwardness.

Dad makes his way back to bed wearing a different pair of pyjama bottoms and with a towel tucked under his arm. I turn off the light, both of us quiet now. I feel lost again when only moments ago I'd been found. My answers of only minutes ago are again transformed into questions.

'I can't sleep, Dad.' My voice sounds childlike.

'Close your eyes and stare into the dark, love,' Dad responds sleepily.

Seven

'SO ARE YOU ALL red-bused out of it?' Frankie asks.

I'm seated at the desk in my hotel room, on the phone to the girls who are huddled round the phone in Kate's house with me on loud-speaker. I'd spent the morning looking around London with Dad, taking photographs of him standing awkwardly in front of anything typically English: red buses, postboxes, police horses, pubs, Buckingham Palace, and a completely unaware transvestite, as he was so excited to see 'a real one', who was nothing like the local priest who'd lost his mind and wandered the streets wearing a dress, in his home town of Cavan when he was young.

While I sit at the desk, he is lying on his bed watching a rerun of *Strictly Come Dancing*, drinking a brandy and licking the sour cream and onion off Pringles before depositing the soggy crisps in the bin.

I've made a conference call, partly to share the latest news, but more for help and a plea for sanity strengthening.

'Your *kid* just puked on me,' Frankie says.

'Oh, that is not puke, that's just a little dribble.'

'No, *this* is dribble . . .'

There's silence.

'Frankie, you are disgusting.'

'OK, girls, girls, please can you two stop, just this once?'

'Sorry, Joyce, but I can't continue this conversation until it is out of here. It's crawling around biting things, climbing on things, drooling on things. It's very distracting. Can't Christian mind it?'

I try not to laugh.

'Do not call my child "it". And no, Christian is busy.'

'He's watching football.'

'He doesn't like to be disturbed, particularly by you. Ever.'

'Well, you're busy too. How do I get it to come with me?'

There's a silence.

'Come here, little boy,' Frankie says uneasily.

'His name is Sam. You're his godmother, in case you've forgotten.'

'No, I haven't forgotten *that*. Just his name.' Her voice strains, as though she's lifting weights. 'Wow, what do you feed it?'

Sam squeals like a pig. Frankie snorts back.

'Frankie, give him to me. I'll bring him in to Christian.'

'OK, Joyce,' Frankie begins in Kate's absence, 'I've done some research on the information you gave me yesterday and I've brought some paperwork with me, hold on.' I hear papers being ruffled.

'What's this about?' Kate asks, returning.

'This is about Joyce jumping into the mind of the American man, thereby possessing his memories, skills and intelligence,' Frankie responds.

'What?' Kate shrieks.

'I found out that his name is Justin Hitchcock,' I say excitedly.

'How?' Kate asks.

'His surname was in his daughter's biography in last night's ballet programme, and his first name, well, I heard that in a dream.'

There's silence. I imagine them giving each other *that* look.

'What the hell is going on here?' Kate asks, confused.

'Google him, Kate,' Frankie orders. 'Let's see if he exists.'

'He exists, believe me,' I confirm.

'No, sweetie, you see, the way these stories work is, we're supposed to think you're crazy for a while before eventually believing you. So let us check up on him and then we'll go from there. While Kate's doing that, I looked into the idea of sharing memories—'

'What?' Kate shrieks again. 'Sharing memories? Are you both out of your mind?'

'No, just me,' I say tiredly, resting my head on the desk.

'Surprisingly enough, it turns out that you're not clinically insane. I went online and did some research. It turns out you're not alone in feeling that.'

I sit up, suddenly alert.

'I came across websites with interviews with others who have admitted to experiencing somebody else's memories and who have also acquired their skills or tastes.'

'Oh, you two are having me on. I knew this was a set-up. I knew it was out of character for you to drop by, Frankie,' said Kate.

'This isn't a set-up,' I assure Kate.

'So you're trying to tell me honestly that you've magically acquired somebody *else's* skills?'

'She speaks Latin, French and Italian,' Frankie explains.

'And what about tastes?' Kate is not convinced.

'She eats meat now,' Frankie says matter-of-factly.

'But why do you think these are somebody else's skills? Why can't she just have learned Latin, French and Italian by herself and decided that she likes meat all by herself, like a normal person?'

'Look, Kate, I agree with you about the change of diet being a natural thing, but in all fairness, Joyce did learn three languages overnight without *actually* learning them.'

'Oh.'

'And I have dreams of Justin Hitchcock's private childhood moments.'

'Where the hell was I when all of this was happening?'

'Making me do the hokey-cokey live on Sky News,' I huff.

I watch the time on the bottom of the television as both Frankie and Kate laugh heartily at the other end. After three minutes, the laughter stops.

'So as I was saying,' Frankie says, catching her breath, 'there are other, eh . . .'

'Freaks?' Kate suggests.

'. . . *cases* where people have spoken of similar things. The only thing is, these are all people who have had heart transplants, which is nothing to do with what you've been through, so that blows that theory.'

Thump-thump, thump-thump. In my throat again. 'Listen. He donated blood. The same month that I went into hospital.'

'So?' Kate says.

'She received a blood transfusion,' Frankie explains. 'Not all that different to the heart transplant theory I just mentioned.'

We all go quiet.

Kate breaks the silence. 'OK, so, I still don't get it.'

'Well, it's practically the same thing, isn't it?' I say. 'Blood comes from the heart.'

Kate gasps. 'It came straight from his heart,' she says dreamily.

'Oh, so now blood transfusions are romantic to you,' Frankie comments. 'Let me tell you about what I got from the net. Because of reports from several heart transplant recipients of unexpected side effects, Channel Four made a documentary about whether it's possible that in receiving a transplanted organ, a patient could inherit some of their donor's memories, tastes, desires and habits as well. It questions science's understanding of how the memory works, featuring scientists who are pioneering research into the intelligence of the heart and the biochemical basis for memory in our cells.'

'So if they think that the heart holds more intelligence than we think, then the blood which is pumped from someone's heart could carry that intelligence?' Kate asks. 'So in transfusing his blood, he transfused his memories too? And his love of meat and languages,' she adds a little tartly.

Nobody wants to say yes to that question. Everybody wants to say no. Apart from me. I've had a night to warm to the idea already.

'This can easily be solved,' Kate says excitedly. 'You can just find out who your blood donor was.'

'She can't.' Frankie, as usual, dampens her spirits. 'That kind of information is confidential. Besides, it's not as though she received all of his blood. He could only have donated less than a pint in one go. Then it's separated into white blood cells, red blood cells, plasma and platelets. What Joyce would have got, if Joyce received it at all, is only a part of his blood. It could even have been mixed with somebody else's.'

'His blood is still running through my body,' I add. 'It doesn't matter how much of it there is. And I remember feeling distinctly odd as soon as I opened my eyes in the hospital.'

A silence answers my ridiculous statement, as we all consider the fact that my feeling 'distinctly odd' had nothing to do with my transfusion and all to do with the unspeakable tragedy of losing my baby.

'We've got a Google hit for Mr Justin Hitchcock.' Kate fills the silence.

My heart beats rapidly. Please tell me I'm not making it all up, that he exists, that he's not a figment of my delusional mind. That the plans I've put in place already are not going to scare away some random person.

'OK, Justin Hitchcock was a hatmaker in Massachusetts. Hmm. Well, at least he's American. You have any knowledge of hats, Joyce?'

I think hard. 'Berets, bucket hats, fedoras, tweed caps.'

Dad stops licking his Pringle and looks at me. 'Panama hat.'

'Panama hat,' I repeat to the girls.

'Cowboy hat,' Frankie says, sounding deep in thought. She snaps out of it. 'Wait a minute, what are we doing? Anybody can name hats.'

'You're right, it doesn't feel right. Keep reading,' I urge.

'Justin Hitchcock moved to Deerfield in 1774,' Kate continues, 'where he served as a soldier and fifer in the Revolution . . .'

'Hold on,' Frankie takes over. 'There's another Justin Hitchcock below that. New York sanitation department—'

'No,' I say with frustration. 'I already know he exists. This is ridiculous. Add Trinity College to the search; he did a seminar there.'

Tap-tap-tap. 'No. Nothing for Trinity College. I'm adding the words, art, architecture, French, Latin, Italian to the search,' Frankie says over the tap-tap-tap sound.

'Aha! Gotcha, Justin Hitchcock! *Guest* lecturer at Trinity College, Dublin. The Faculty of Arts and Humanities. Department of Art and Architecture. Bachelor's degree, Chicago, Master's degree, Chicago, PhD Sorbonne University. Special interests are History of Italian Renaissance and baroque sculpture, Painting in Europe 1600–1900. External responsibilities include founder and editor of the *Art and Architectural Review*. He is the co-author of *The Golden Age of Dutch Painting: Vermeer, Metsu and Terborch* . . .'

'So he exists,' Kate says, as though she's just found the Holy Grail.

Feeling more confident now I say, 'Try his name with the London National Gallery.'

Kate continues reading, 'He is a curator of European Art at the National Gallery, London. Oh my God, Joyce, he works in London. You should go see him.'

'Hold your horses, Kate,' Frankie objects. 'She might freak him out and end up in a padded cell. He might not even be the donor. And even if he is, it doesn't explain anything.'

'We'll have to figure out a way to find out,' Kate offers.

'It's him,' I say confidently.

'So what are you going to do about it?' Kate asks.

'What makes you think I haven't done something already?'

Justin holds the phone to his ear and paces the small office in the National Gallery. 'No, no, Simon, I said *Dutch* Portraits. The Age of Rembrandt and Frans Hals. I've written a book about that subject so it's something I'm more than familiar with.' *A half-written book you stopped working on two years ago, liar.*

There is a knock on the door. 'Just a minute,' he calls out.

The door opens anyway and his colleague, Roberta, enters. She tries to manoeuvre her way through the obstacle course that is his cluttered office to reach his desk.

'Sorry, Justin,' she whispers, carrying a small basket in her hand. 'I didn't know you were on the phone. This was at reception for you. I'll just put it here.' She tiptoes out of the room.

He nods at her and then tries to concentrate on the conversation, picking up where he left off. 'The exhibition will include sixty works, all painted between 1600 and 1680.' He eyes the hamper suspiciously, feeling as though something is about to jump out at him.

'Yes, Simon, in the Sainsbury Wing. If there's anything else you need to know please do contact me here at the office.'

He hurries his colleague off the phone and hangs up. Underneath the wicker handle, the contents of the small hamper are covered by a chequered cloth. He stands back and lifts it slowly, preparing to jump away at any moment.

A dozen or so muffins stare back at him.

His heart thumps. He searches the basket for a card. Taped to the other side is a small white envelope. With shaking hands, he rips it rather clumsily from the basket and slides the card out. In the centre of the card in neat handwritten script it simply says: *Thank you . . .*

Justin power-walks through the halls of the National Gallery. He spots Roberta in the hallway. 'Roberta! Where did you get this hamper?' He holds it out to her.

'At reception. I was returning from my break when Charlie asked me to give it to you. Is there something wrong?'

'Charlie.' He thinks hard. 'He's at the Sir Paul Getty entrance?'

She nods.

'OK, thank you, Roberta.' He dashes off to the East Wing, the basket swinging from his hand.

'Finished for the day, Little Red Riding Hood?'

Justin, noticing he was skipping along with the basket, stops abruptly and spins round to face Charlie, a security guard, over six foot tall. 'I was wondering who gave you this basket?'

'A delivery guy from . . .' Charlie moves over to behind his small desk and riffles through some papers. He retrieves a clipboard.

'Harrods. Zhang Wei,' he reads. 'Why? Something wrong with the muffins?' He runs his tongue over his teeth and clears his throat.

Justin's eyes narrow. 'How did you know they were muffins?'

Charlie refuses to meet his stare. 'Had to check, didn't I? This is the National Gallery. You can't expect me to accept a package without knowing what's in it.'

Justin studies Charlie, whose face has pinked. He spies crumbs stuck to the corners of his mouth. He removes the chequered cloth from his hamper and counts. Eleven muffins.

'Don't you think it's odd to send a person eleven muffins?'

'Odd?' Eyes wander, shoulders fidget. 'Dunno, mate.'

'Wouldn't it seem more obvious to send a *dozen* muffins?'

Shoulders shrug. Fingers fidget. His body language tells Justin that he's finished with the conversation.

Justin whips out his cellphone as he exits to Trafalgar Square. 'Bea, it's Dad.'

'I'm not talking to you.'

'Why not?'

'Peter told me what you said to him at the ballet last night,' she snaps. 'You interrogated him on his *intentions* all night.'

'I'm your father, that's my job.'

'No, what you did is the job of the Gestapo,' she fumes. 'I swear, I'm not speaking to you until you *apologise* to him.'

'So I asked him a few questions, so what? Bea, he's not good enough for you.'

'No, he's not good enough for *you*. Well, I don't care what you think of him, it's me that's supposed to be happy.'

'He picks *strawberries* for a living.'

'He is an *IT consultant*! You will apologise to Peter and if you do not, I will not answer your phone calls and you can deal with your little dramas all by yourself.'

'Wait, wait, wait. Just one question.'

'Dad, I—'

'Did-you-send-me-a-hamper-of-a-dozen-cinnamon-muffins?' he rushes out with.

'What? No!'

'No?'

'No muffins! No conversations, no *nothing* until you apologise.'

'OK,' he sighs. 'Sorry.'

'Not to *me*. To *Peter*.'

'OK, but does that mean you won't be collecting my dry-cleaning on your way over tomorrow? You know where it is, it's the one beside the tube station—' The phone clicks. He stares at it in confusion. *My own daughter hung up on me? I knew this Peter was trouble.*

He thinks again about the muffins and dials again. He clears his throat. 'Jennifer, it's Justin.'

'Hello, Justin.' Her voice is cold. Used to be so warm. Like honey. No, like hot caramel. But now? He listens to the silence on the other end. Ice.

'I'm just calling to see whether you'd sent me a hamper of muffins.' As soon as he's said it, he realises how ridiculous this call is. Of course she didn't send him anything. Why would she?

'I beg your pardon?'

'I received a basket of muffins at my office today along with a thank-you note, but the note failed to reveal the sender's identity. I was wondering if it was you.'

Her voice is amused now. No, not amused, mocking. 'What would I have to thank you for, Justin?'

It's a simple question, but knowing her as he knows her, it has implications far beyond the words, and so Justin jumps and snaps at the bait. Bitter Justin is back. 'Oh, I don't know, twenty years of marriage, perhaps. A daughter. A good living. A roof over your head.' He knows it's a stupid statement. 'Travel all over the world. Clothes and more clothes. A new kitchen . . .'. And he goes on, like a man from the nineteenth century who'd been keeping his wife accustomed to a good life she would otherwise have been without, ignoring the fact that she had made a good living herself, playing in an orchestra that travelled the world.

At the beginning of their married life they had no choice but to live with Justin's mother. They were young and had a baby to rear, the reason for their hasty marriage, and as Justin was still attending college by day, bartending at night and working at an art museum at the weekend, Jennifer had made money playing the piano at an up-market restaurant in Chicago. At the weekends, she would return home in the early hours of the morning, her back sore and tendinitis in her middle finger, but that all went out of his mind when she'd dangled the line with that seemingly innocent question.

She had known that this tirade would come and he gobbles, gobbles, gobbles on the bait that fills his mouth. Finally running out of steam, he stops.

Jennifer is silent.

'Jennifer?'

'Yes, Justin.' Icy.

Justin sighs with exhaustion. 'So, was it you?'

'It most certainly wasn't me.' Click and she's gone.

Fuming, Justin charges down the North Terrace steps, sits down by one of the fountains, places the basket by his feet and bites into a muffin. Crumbs fall at his feet, attracting a flock of pigeons with intent in their beady black eyes. Afraid of falling missiles from those that circle his head, he picks up his basket and shoos them away with all the butchness of an eleven-year-old.

Justin breezes in the front door of his home, leaving it open behind him, and is immediately greeted by Doris, with a paint palette in her hand. 'OK, so I've narrowed it down,' she begins, thrusting dozens of colours in his face. Her long leopard-print nails are each decorated with a diamanté jewel. She wears an all-in-one snakeskin jumpsuit, and her feet wobble dangerously in patent lace-up ankle stilettos. Her painted lips match her shock of red hair. He watches them with severe irritation as they open and close.

The random words he hears are, 'Gooseberry Fool, Celtic Forest, English Mist and Woodland Pearl, all *calm* tones, would look so good in this room *or* Wild Mushroom, Nomadic Glow and Sultana Spice. The Cappuccino Candy is one of my faves but I don't think it'll work next to that curtain, what do you think?' She waves a fabric in front of his face. He doesn't respond but takes deep breaths and counts to ten in his mind.

'Hello? Justin?' She snaps her fingers in his face. 'Hel-lo?'

'Maybe you should give Justin a break, Doris. He looks tired.' Al looks nervously at his brother.

'OK, but just one more thing. Bea will love her room done in Ivory Lace. And Petey too. Imagine how romantic this will be for—'

'ENOUGH!' Justin screams at the top of his lungs, not wanting his daughter's name and the word romantic to share the same sentence.

Doris jumps and stops talking immediately. Her hand flies to her chest. Al stops drinking, his bottle freezes just below his lips.

'Doris.' Justin takes a deep breath and tries to speak as calmly as possible. 'Enough of this, please. Enough of this Cappuccino Nights—'

'Candy,' she interrupts, and quickly silences again.

'Whatever. This is a Victorian house, from the nineteenth century, not some painted lady from an episode of *Changing Rooms*. It needs *sophistication*, it needs to be *researched*, it needs furniture *of* the period, colours *of* the period, not a room that sounds like Al's dinner menu.'

'Hey!' Al speaks up.

Justin takes a deep breath and says gently, 'I think it needs somebody else for the job. Maybe it's just bigger than you thought it was going to be. Please tell me you understand.'

She nods slowly and he breathes a sigh of relief.

Suddenly the paint palettes go flying across the room as Doris lets rip, 'You pretentious little bastaaaaard!'

'Doris!' Al leaps up out of his armchair, or at least, makes a great attempt to.

She walks aggressively towards Justin, pointing her sparkly animal-print nail at him, like a weapon.

'Listen here, you silly little man. I have spent the last two weeks researching this dump of a basement in the kinds of libraries and places you wouldn't even think *exist*. I've been to dark, dingy dungeons where people smell of old . . . things.' Her nostrils flare and her voice deepens, threateningly. 'I purchased every historic period paint brochure that I could get my hands on and applied the colours in accordance with the colour rules at the end of the nineteenth century. I have matched the Dulux colours as closely as I possibly could to your historic period paint and I've been to secondhand, thirdhand, even *antique* stores and seen furniture in such disgusting derelict conditions, I almost set up the ISPCF. I've seen things crawling around dining-room tables and sat in chairs so rickety I could smell the black death that killed the last person who died sitting right in it. I have sanded down so much pine, I have splinters in places you don't wanna see. So.' She prods him in the chest with her dagger nail. 'Don't. Tell. Me. That *this* is too big for me.'

She clears her throat. 'But despite what you said, I will finish this project. I will do it in spite of you and I will do it for your brother, who might be dead next month and you don't even care.'

'Dead?' Justin's eyes widen.

With that, she turns on her heel and storms off into her bedroom. She sticks her head out of the doorway. 'By the way, just so you know, I would have banged the door behind me VERY LOUDLY to show just how angry I am but it's currently out in the back yard ready for sanding and priming, before I paint it . . .' and this she spits out rebelliously, 'Ivory Lace.'

I shift from foot to foot nervously outside the open door of Justin's home. Should I press the bell now? Simply call his name into the room? Would he call the police and have me arrested for trespassing? Oh, this was such a bad decision. Frankie and Kate had persuaded me to present myself to him. I had hopped in a taxi to Trafalgar Square, to catch him at the National Gallery before he left. I'd been so close to him as he'd been on the phone, heard his calls to people as he asked them about the basket. I'd felt oddly comfortable just watching him, without his knowing, revelling in the secret thrill of being able to see him for who he is instead of viewing his life from his own memories.

His anger at whoever was on the phone—most likely his ex-wife—convinced me it was the wrong time to approach him and so I'd followed him. *Followed*, not stalked. I'd taken my time while trying to build up the courage to talk to him. Would I mention the transfusion or not? Would he think I was crazy or be open to listening, or even believing?

But once on the tube, the timing again wasn't right. It was overcrowded, people were pushing and shoving, avoiding eye contact, never mind first-time introductions or conversations about studies into the possible intelligence of blood. And so after pacing up and down his road, feeling like both a schoolgirl with a crush and a stalker at the same time, I now find myself standing outside the door, with a plan. But my plan is once again being compromised as Justin and his brother Al begin to talk about something I know I shouldn't be hearing, about a family secret I am more than familiar with already.

I move my finger away from the doorbell, keep hidden from all the windows and I bide my time.

Justin looks to his brother in panic. 'Al, what was she talking about? About you being dead next month.'

'No, no, no,' Al laughs. 'She said, *might* be dead. That's distinctly different. Hey, you got away lightly there, bro. Good for you. I think that

Valium is really helping her. Cheers.' He holds up his bottle.

'Hold on, hold on. Al, what are you talking about? There's something you haven't told me? What did the doctor say?'

'The doctor told me exactly what I've been telling you for the last two weeks. If any members of a person's immediate family developed coronary heart disease at a young age, i.e., a male under fifty-five years old, well then, we have an increased risk of coronary heart disease.'

'Have you high blood pressure?'

'A little.'

'Have you high cholesterol?'

'A lot.'

'So, all you do is make lifestyle changes, Al. It doesn't mean you're going to be struck down like . . . like . . .'

'Dad?'

'No.' He frowns and shakes his head. 'Al, you're not going to have a heart attack.'

'It's my fortieth birthday next week. That's what age Dad was when he died.' He lowers his eyes and peels the label from his beer.

'That's what this is about?' Justin's voice softens. 'Dammit, Al, that's what this is all about? Why didn't you say something earlier?'

'I just thought that I'd spend some time with you before, you know, just in case . . .' His eyes tear up and he looks away.

Tell him the truth.

'Al, listen, there's something you should know.' His voice trembles and he clears his throat. *You've never told anyone.* 'Dad was under a huge amount of pressure at work. He had a lot of difficulties, financial and otherwise, that he didn't tell anyone. Not even Mom.'

'I know, Justin. I know.'

'You know?'

'Yeah, I get it. He didn't just drop dead for no reason. He was stressed out of his mind. And I'm not, I know that. But ever since I was a kid, I've had this feeling hanging over me that it's gonna happen to me too. It's been playing on my mind for as long as I can remember and now that my birthday's next week and I'm not in the greatest of shape . . . Things have been real busy at the business and I haven't been looking after myself. Never could do it like you could, you know?'

'Hey, you don't have to explain it to me.'

'Remember that day we spent with him on the front lawn? With the sprinklers? Just hours before Mom found him . . . Well, remember the whole family playing around?'

'They were good times,' Justin smiles, fighting back the tears.

'Dad was holding the hose and spraying us both. He seemed in such good humour. And it was real hot. Do you remember it being real hot?'

'Yeah.'

'And Dad had his pants rolled up to his knees and his shoes and socks off. And the grass was getting all wet and his feet were all covered in grass and he just kept chasing us around and around . . .' He smiles into the distance. 'That was the last time I saw him.'

It wasn't for me.

Justin's memory flashes through the image of his father closing the living-room door. Justin had run into the house from the front yard to go to the bathroom; as far as he knew, all the members of his family were still outside playing. But when he was coming downstairs, he spotted his dad coming out of the kitchen, walking down the hall. Justin, wanting to jump out and surprise him, crouched down and watched him from behind the banister.

But then he saw in his hand the bottle of liquid that was always locked away in the cabinet in the kitchen and only taken out on special occasions when his dad's family came over from Ireland to visit. When they all drank from that bottle they would change, they would sing and laugh and tell stories and sometimes cry. He wasn't sure why that bottle was in his dad's hands now. Did he want to sing and laugh and tell stories today? Did he want to cry?

Then Justin saw the bottle of pills in his hand too. He hoped his dad wasn't sick and he hoped he didn't want to cry. He watched as he closed the door behind him with the pills and bottle of alcohol in his hands. He should have known then what his dad was about to do but he didn't. Thinks of that moment over and over and tries to force himself to call out and stop him. But the nine-year-old Justin stays crouched on the stair, waiting for his dad to come out so he can jump out and surprise him. As time went by he began to feel that something wasn't right, but he didn't quite know why.

After minutes that felt like hours, Justin stood up. He could hear Al screaming with laughter outside. He could still hear Al laughing when he went inside and saw the green feet on the floor. He remembers the sight of those feet so vividly, Dad lying on the floor like a big green giant. He remembers following those feet and finding his dad on the floor, staring lifeless at the ceiling.

He didn't say anything. Didn't try to help him because though he didn't understand much at that time, he knew that it was too late for help. He just slowly backed out of the room, closed the door behind him and ran out to the front lawn to his mom and younger brother.

Five minutes they had. Five more minutes of everything being exactly the same. He was nine years old on a sunny day with a mom and a dad and a brother, and he was happy and Mom was happy and the neighbours smiled at him normally like they did all the other kids. Five more minutes of everything being the same, until his mom went into the house and then everything changed. Five minutes later, he wasn't happy, neither was Mom, and the neighbours smiled at him with such a sadness he wished they didn't bother smiling at all. The five extra minutes wasn't long enough.

Mom told them Dad had suffered a heart attack.

Justin could never bring himself to tell anyone he knew the truth, half because he wanted to believe the lie and half because he thought his mother had started to believe it too. He hadn't even told Jennifer, because saying it out loud made it true and he did not want to validate his father dying that way. And now, their mother gone, he was the only person who knew the truth about his dad. The story of their father's death that had been fabricated to help them had ended up hanging like a black cloud over Al and was a burden for Justin.

He wanted to tell Al the truth right now, he really did. But how could it help him? Surely knowing the truth would be far worse, and he'd have to explain how and why he'd kept it from him all these years . . . But then he would no longer have to shoulder all the burden. Perhaps there would be finally some release for him. It could help Al's fear of heart failure and they could deal with it together.

'Al, there's something I have to tell you,' Justin begins.

The doorbell rings suddenly. A sharp sting of a ring.

'Is someone gonna get that?' Doris yells, breaking the silence.

Justin walks to the door. The door is ajar and he pulls it open. Before him, on the railings, hangs his dry-cleaning. Nobody is there. He steps outside and runs up the basement steps to see who has left it there, but apart from the skip, the front lawn is empty.

'Who is it?' Doris calls.

'Nobody,' Justin responds, confused. He unhooks his dry-cleaning from the railing and carries it inside.

'You're telling me that cheap suit just pressed the doorbell itself?' she asks, still angry at him from before.

'I don't know. It's peculiar. Bea was going to collect this tomorrow. I hadn't arranged a delivery with the dry-cleaners.'

'Maybe it's a special delivery, for being such a good customer because by the looks of it, they dry-cleaned your entire wardrobe.'

'Yeah, and I'll bet the special delivery comes with a big bill,' he grumbles. 'I had a little falling-out with Bea earlier; maybe she organised this as an apology.'

'Oh, you are a stubborn man.' Doris rolls her eyes. 'Do you ever think for a second that it's *you* who should be making the apologies?'

Justin narrows his eyes at her. 'Did you talk to Bea?'

'Hey, look, there's an envelope on this side,' Al points out, interrupting the beginnings of another fight.

Justin's heart immediately leaps to his mouth as he catches sight of the familiar envelope. He opens it and gulps hard, reading the note. He takes out the card he received on the muffin basket earlier, and he holds the two cards together so that they make a complete sentence. Reading the words causes a chill to run through his body.

Thank you . . . For Saving My Life.

I lie in the skip, breathless, heart beating at the speed of a humming-bird's wings. I'm like a child playing hide-and-seek. Please, Justin, don't find me like this, at the bottom of the skip in your garden, covered in plaster and dust. I hear his footsteps move further away, back down the steps to his basement flat, and the door closes.

What on earth have I become? A coward. I chickened out and rang the doorbell to stop Justin telling the story about his father to Al and then, afraid of playing God to two strangers, I ran, leapt and landed in the bottom of a skip. How metaphorical. I'm not sure I'll ever be able to speak to him. I don't know how I'll ever find the words to explain how I'm feeling. Justin would never believe me if I told him—but actions speak louder than words.

As I brush dust, paint and wood from my clothes and clamber out of the skip, I try to remember what other things Bea mentioned her father wanted to have done, by the person he saved.

'Justin, calm down, for creep's sake. You're making me nervous.' Doris sits on a stepladder and watches Justin pace up and down the room.

'I can't calm down. Do you not understand what this means?' He hands her the two cards.

Her eyes widen. 'You saved someone's life?'

'Yeah.' He shrugs and stops pacing. 'It's really no big deal. Sometimes you just gotta do what you gotta do.'

'He donated blood,' Al interrupts his brother's failed attempt at modesty.

'*You* donated blood?'

'It's how he met Vampira, remember?'

'Her name is *Sarah* not Vampira.'

'So you donated blood to get a date.' Doris folds her arms. 'Is there nothing you do for the greater good of humanity or is it *all* just for yourself?'

'Hey, I have donated plenty of my time to helping organisations which are in need of my expertise. Something I don't *have* to do, but which I have agreed to do *for them*.'

'Yeah and I bet you charge them per word. That's why he says "oops-a-daisy" instead of "shit" when he stubs his toe.'

Al and Doris dissolve into laughter, hitting each other in their fit.

Justin takes a deep breath. 'Let's get back to the matter at hand. *Who* is sending me these notes and running these errands?' He begins pacing again. 'Maybe this is Bea's idea of a joke. She's the only person I had the conversation with about deserving thanks in return for saving a life.'

Please, don't be Bea.

'Man, you are selfish,' Al laughs.

'No.' Doris shakes her head, her long earrings whip against her cheeks with each movement, her back-combed hairsprayed hair as still as a microphone head. 'Bea wants nothing to do with you until you apologise. No words can describe how much she hates you right now.'

'But she must have told somebody or this wouldn't be happening. Doris, find out from Bea who she spoke to about this.'

'Huh.' Doris lifts her chin and looks away. 'You said some pretty nasty things to me before. I don't know if I can help you.'

Justin falls to his knees and shuffles over to her. 'Please, Doris. I am so, so sorry for what I said. I underestimated you.'

'So I'm a good interior designer?' Doris lifts her chin.

'A *great* designer.'

'How great?'

'Greater than . . .' he stalls. 'Andrea Palladio.'

'Is he better than Ty Pennington?'

'He was an Italian architect in the sixteenth century, widely considered the most influential person in the history of Western architecture.'

'Oh. OK. You're forgiven.' She holds out her hand. 'Give me your phone and I'll call Bea.'

Moments later they are all seated round the new kitchen table listening to Doris's half of the phone conversation.

'OK, Bea told Petey, and the costume supervisor for *Swan Lake*. And her father.'

'The costume supervisor? Do you guys still have the programme?'

Doris disappears to her bedroom and returns with the ballet programme. She flicks through the pages.

'No,' Justin shakes his head on reading her biography, 'I met this woman that night and it's not her. But her father was there? I didn't see her father. The person must be Irish or have received medical attention in an Irish hospital.'

Al shrugs. 'Maybe her dad's Irish, or was in Ireland.'

'Give me that programme, I'm calling the theatre.'

'Justin, you can't just call her up.' Doris dives for the programme in his hand, but he dodges her. 'What are you going to say?'

'All I need to know is if her father is Irish or was in Ireland during the past month. I'll make the rest up as I go along.'

Al and Doris look at each other worriedly while he leaves the kitchen to make the call. 'Did you do this?' Doris asks Al quietly.

'No way.' Al shakes his head, his chins wobbling.

Five minutes later Justin returns. 'She remembered me from last night and, no, it's not her or her father. So either Bea told somebody else or . . . it must be Peter fooling around. I'm gonna get that—'

'Grow up, Justin. It's not him,' Doris says sternly. 'Start looking elsewhere. Call the dry-cleaners, call the guy who delivered the muffins.'

'I have already. They were charged to a credit card and they can't release the owner's details.'

'Your life is just one big mystery. Between the Joyce woman and these mysterious deliveries, you should hire a private investigator,' Doris responds. 'Oh! I just remembered.' She reaches into her pocket and hands him a piece of paper. 'Speaking of private investigators. I got this for you. I've had it for a few days but didn't say anything because I didn't want you going on a wild-goose chase and making a fool of yourself. But seeing as you're choosing to do that anyway, here.'

She hands him the piece of paper with Joyce's details.

'I called International Directory Enquiries and gave them the number of the Joyce person that showed up on Bea's phone last week. They gave me the address that goes with it. I think it'd be a better idea to find this woman, Justin. Forget this other person. It seems very odd behaviour to me. Who knows who's sending you these notes? Concentrate on the woman; a nice healthy relationship is what you need.'

He barely reads the page before putting it in his jacket pocket, totally uninterested, his mind elsewhere.

'Hey, it could be the Joyce woman that's sending the messages,' Al pipes up.

'Don't be ridiculous, Al,' Justin dismisses him. 'I met her in a hair salon. Anyway, who says it's a woman that's doing this?'

'Well, it's obvious,' Al replies. 'Because you were given a *muffin basket*.' He scrunches up his nose. 'Only a woman would think of sending a muffin basket. Or a gay guy.'

'*I* was the one who thought of the muffin basket!' Justin puffs.

'Yeah, like I said. Woman or gay guy,' he grins.

Justin falls back in his chair. 'You two are no help.'

'Hey, I know who could help you.' Al sits up. 'Vampira,' he says spookily.

'I've already asked her for help. She won't tell me where my blood went and she won't ever speak to me again either.'

'On account of you running away from her after a Viking bus?'

'That had something to do with it.'

'Gee, Justin, you really have a beautiful way with women.'

'Well, at least *somebody* thinks I'm doing something right.' He stares at the two cards he's placed in the centre of the table.

Who are you?

'You don't have to ask Sarah straight out.' Al gets excited. 'Maybe you could snoop around a bit in her office.'

'No, that would be wrong,' Justin says unconvincingly. 'I could get into trouble. I could get *her* into trouble. Besides, I've treated her so badly.'

'So a really lovely thing to do,' Doris says slyly, 'would be to drop by her office, and tell her you're sorry. As a friend.'

A smile slowly creeps onto each of their faces.

'But can you take a day off work next week, to go to Dublin?' Doris asks, breaking their evil moment.

'I've already accepted an invitation from the National Gallery in Dublin,' Justin says excitedly. 'To give a talk on Terborch's *Woman Writing a Letter*.'

Eight

AT SEVEN FIFTEEN the next morning, just before Justin leaves his flat for work, he stands poised at the front door, hand on the door handle.

'Justin, where's Al?' Doris shuffles out of her bedroom in her slippers and robe. 'He wasn't in bed when I woke up.'

Justin holds a finger to his lips, hushing her, and jerks his head in the direction of the door.

'Is the blood person out there?' she whispers excitedly. He nods. They press their ears up against the door and Doris's eyes widen. '*I can hear!*' she mouths.

'OK, on three,' he whispers and they mouth together, *One, two*—He pulls the door open with full force. 'HA! Gotcha!' he shouts.

'Aaaah!' the postman screams with fright, dropping envelopes by Justin's feet. He fires a package at Justin and holds another parcel by his head in defence.

'Aaaah!' Doris shouts.

Justin doubles over as the package hits between his legs. He falls to his knees, his face turning red as he gasps for air. The postman remains cowered, his knees bent, his head covered by a package.

'Justin,' Doris exclaims as she picks up an envelope and hits Justin across the arm, 'you idiot! It's the postman.'

'Yes,' he rasps, and makes choking sounds. 'I can see that now.' He takes a moment to compose himself. 'It's OK, sir, you can lower your package now. I'm sorry to have frightened you.'

The postman slowly lowers the parcel. 'What was that about?'

'I thought you were someone else. I'm sorry.' He looks to the envelopes on the floor. Bills. 'Is there nothing else for me?'

His left arm starts to niggle at him again. Tingling as though a mosquito has bitten him. He starts to scratch. The tingling becomes more intense and he digs his nail into his skin, scratching over and over. Beads of sweat break out on his forehead.

The postman shakes his head and starts to back away.

'Did nobody give you anything to deliver to me?' Justin climbs back to his feet and moves closer, unintentionally appearing threatening.

'No, I said no.' The postman rushes up the steps.

'Leave the man alone. You almost gave him a heart attack.' Doris continues picking up the envelopes. 'If you ever do meet this person, I advise you rethink the "Ha! Gotcha!" routine.'

Justin pulls up the sleeve of his shirt and examines his arm, expecting to find red lumps or a rash, but there are no marks on his skin apart from the scratch marks he has made himself.

Doris shuffles back into the kitchen. 'Al?' her voice echoes around the kitchen. 'Where are you?'

'Help! Help me! Someone!' In the distance they hear Al's voice, muffled as though his mouth is stuffed with socks.

Doris gasps, 'Baby?' Justin hears the fridge door opening. 'Al?' She sticks her head in the fridge. She returns to the living room, shaking her head, alerting Justin to the fact that her husband was not in the fridge after all.

Justin rolls his eyes. 'He's outside, Doris.'

'Then for goodness' sake help him!'

He opens the door and Al sits slumped on the ground at the base of the steps, T-shirt soaked with sweat, legs spandex-clad and crumpled underneath him, still in the same position as when he'd fallen.

Doris pushes by Justin aggressively, and charges towards Al. She falls to her knees. 'Baby? Are you OK? Did you fall down the stairs?'

'No,' he says weakly, his chins resting on his chest.

'No, you're not OK or no, you didn't fall down the stairs?' she asks.

'The first one,' he says with exhaustion. 'No, the second. Hold on, what was the first?'

She shouts at him now as though he is deaf. 'The first was, are you OK? And the second was, did you fall down the stairs?'

'No,' he responds, rolling his head back to rest it against the wall.

'No what, baby? Come on, don't go to sleep on me, don't you dare go anywhere.' She slaps his face. 'You have to stay conscious.'

Justin knows his brother is fine, lack of fitness being his only problem. He goes to the kitchen for some water for Al.

'My heart . . .' Al is panicking when Justin returns. His hands are scraping at his chest and he's gasping for air.

'Are you having a heart attack?' Doris shrieks. 'Don't you dare have a heart attack, do you hear me?' She picks up a newspaper from the ground, starts hitting Al across the arm with each word. 'Don't. You. Dare. Even. *Think*. Of. Dying. Before. Me. Al. Hitchcock.'

'Ow,' he rubs his arm, 'that hurts.'

'Hey, hey, hey!' Justin breaks it up. 'Give me that paper, Doris. Where did you get it?' He tries to grab it out of her hands but she dodges him each time.

'It was just there, beside Al,' she shrugs. 'Paperboy delivered it.'

'They don't have paperboys around here,' he says.

'Then I guess it's Al's.'

'There's a coffee-to-go too,' Al, finally getting his breath back, manages to say.

'A coffee-to-WHAT?' Doris screeches. 'You bought a coffee?' She begins spanking him again with the newspaper. 'No wonder you're dying!'

'Hey,' he crosses his arms over his body protectively, 'it's not mine. It was outside the door with the newspaper when I got here.'

'It's mine.' Justin snatches the paper from Doris's hands and the coffee-to-go that is on the ground beside Al.

'There's no note attached.' She narrows her eyes and looks from one brother to the other and back. 'Trying to defend your brother is only going to kill him in the long run, you know.'

'I might do it more often, then,' he grumbles, shaking the newspaper and hoping for a note to fall out. He checks the coffee cup for a message. Nothing. Yet he's sure it's for him. He focuses then on the front page. Above the headline, he notices the instruction, 'P. 42.'

He battles with the oversized pages to get to the correct point. Finally he opens it up on the classified pages. He scans the advertisements.

'Eternally grateful recipient wishes to thank Justin Hitchcock, donor and hero, for saving life. Thank you.'

He holds his head back and howls with laughter. Doris and Al look at him with surprise.

'Al.' Justin lowers himself to his knees before his brother. 'I need you to help me now.' His voice is urgent. 'Did you see anybody when you were jogging back to the house?'

'No.' Al's head rolls tiredly from one side to the other. 'I can't think.'

'Think.' Doris slaps his face lightly.

'That's not entirely necessary, Doris.'

'They do it in the movies. Go on, tell him, baby.'

'I don't know,' Al whinges. 'By the time I got to the house, I couldn't breathe, let alone see. I don't remember anyone. Sorry, bro. Man, I was so scared. All of these black dots were in front of my eyes and I was getting so dizzy and—'

'OK,' Justin leaps to his feet and runs up the stairs to the front yard. He runs to the drive entrance and looks up and down the street. It's busier now; at seven thirty there is more life as people leave their homes to head for work and the traffic noise level has picked up.

'THANK YOU!' Justin shouts at the top of his lungs. A few people turn round to look at him but most keep their heads down as another man loses his mind on a Monday morning in the city.

'I CAN'T WAIT TO READ THIS!' He waves the newspaper around in the air, shouting up the road and down. *What do you say to someone whose life you saved? Say something deep. Say something funny. Say something philosophical.*

'I'M GLAD YOU'RE ALIVE!' he shouts.

'Eh, thanks.' A woman scurries past him with her head down.

'EM, I WON'T BE HERE TOMORROW!' Pause. 'IN CASE YOU'RE PLANNING ON DOING THIS AGAIN.' He lifts the coffee into the air and waves it around, sending droplets to jump from the small drinking hole and burn his hand. Still hot. Whoever it was, they weren't here that long ago. 'EM. GETTING THE FIRST FLIGHT TO DUBLIN TOMORROW MORNING. ARE YOU FROM THERE?' he shouts to the wind. 'ANYWAY, THANKS AGAIN.' He waves the paper in the air and turns to face the house.

Doris and Al are standing at the top of the stairs, their arms folded, their faces a picture of concern. Al has caught his breath. Justin puts his hand in his pocket and strolls back towards the house. Feeling a piece of paper in his hand, he retrieves it and reads it quickly before tossing it into the skip. He has saved a person's life just as he thought; he must focus on the most important matter at hand. He makes his way to the flat, trying to appear as dignified as possible.

From the bottom of the skip, I lie in the discarded bathtub and listen as the voices recede and the door to the flat finally closes. A crumpled ball of paper has landed nearby and I reach for it and open it up, smoothing out the edges. My heart starts its rumba beat again as I see my first name, Dad's address and his phone number scrawled upon it.

'Where on earth have you been? What happened to you, Gracie?'

'Joyce,' is my response as I burst into the hotel room, breathless and covered in dust. 'Don't have time to explain.' I rush around the room, throwing my clothes into my bag, taking a change of clothes and hurrying by Dad, who's sitting on the bed, to get to the bathroom.

'I tried calling you on your hand phone,' Dad calls to me.

'Yeah? I didn't hear it ring.' I struggle to squeeze into my jeans and brush my teeth at the same time.

I hear his voice saying something. Mumbles but no words.

'Can't hear you, brushing my teeth!'

Silence while I finish and then back to the room.

'That's because when I called it, I heard it ringing here in the bedroom. It was on top of your pillow. I was worried about you,' he says.

'You needn't have been.' I hop around with one shoe on, while searching everywhere for the other.

'So I called downstairs to reception to see if they knew where you were.'

'Yeah?' I give up looking for my shoe and concentrate on inserting my earrings. My fingers are trembling with the adrenaline of the Justin situation.

'So then I walked up and down the road, checking all of the shops that I know you like, asking all the people in them if they'd seen you.'

'You did?' I say, distracted. 'Where the hell is my shoe?'

'And along the way,' Dad continues, and I hold back my aggravation, 'I met a policeman and I told him I was very worried, and he walked me back to the hotel and told me to wait here for you but to call this number if you didn't come back after twenty-four hours.'

'Oh, that was nice of him.' I open the wardrobe, still searching for my shoe, and find it still full of Dad's clothes. 'Dad!' I exclaim. 'You forgot your other suit. And your good jumper!'

I look at him, I realise, for the first time since I entered the room, and only now notice how pale he looks, how old, perched at the edge of his single bed, his case half-packed beside him. In one hand is the photograph of Mum, in the other is the card the policeman gave him. The fingers that hold them tremble; his eyes are red and sore-looking.

'Dad,' I say as panic builds inside me, 'are you OK?'

'I was worried,' he repeats again in the tiny voice I'd as good as ignored since I'd entered the room. He swallows hard. 'I didn't know where you were.'

'I was visiting a friend,' I say softly, joining him on the bed.

'Oh. Well, this friend here was worried.' He gives a weak smile. I'm jolted by how fragile he appears. He looks like an old man.

I look at his bag. 'Did you pack that yourself?'

'Tried to. Thought I got everything.' He looks away from the open wardrobe, embarrassed.

'OK, well, let's take a look in it and see what we have.' It startles me to hear myself speaking to him as though addressing a child.

'Aren't we running out of time?' he asks.

'No,' my eyes fill with tears and I speak more forcefully than I intend, 'we have all the time in the world, Dad.' I distract those tears from falling by lifting his case onto the bed, but when I open the case I feel my composure slip again. It is a mess, though I shouldn't be surprised as Dad has never had to pack a suitcase in his life. I think what upsets me is the possibility that at seventy-five years old, after ten years without his wife, he simply doesn't know how to, or else my being missing for a few hours has prevented him from accomplishing it. A simple thing like that, my steady-as-a-rock father cannot do. Instead he sits on the edge of the bed twisting his cap round in his gnarled trembling fingers.

Things are crumpled in small balls with no order at all as though they have been packed by a child. I find my shoe inside some bathroom towels. I take my shoe out and put it on my foot without saying anything, as though it's the most normal thing in the world. The towels go back to where they belong. I start folding and packing all over again.

'We have all the time in the world, Dad,' I repeat. Though this time, it's for my own benefit.

On the tube, on the way to the airport, Dad keeps checking his watch and fidgeting in his seat.

'Have you to be somewhere?' I smile.

'The Monday Club.' He looks at me with worried eyes. He's never missed a week, not even when I was in hospital.

'But today is Monday.'

'I just don't want to miss this flight. We might get stuck over here.'

'There's more than one flight a day, you know.'

'Good.' He looks relieved. 'I might even make evening Mass. Oh, they won't believe everything I tell them tonight,' he says with excitement. 'Donal will drop dead when everybody listens to me and not to him for a change.' He settles back into his seat and watches out of the window as the blackness of the underground speeds by. I take out my mobile and start planning my next move.

'Frankie, it's me. Justin Hitchcock is getting the first plane to Dublin tomorrow morning and I need to know what he's doing fast.'

'Give me an hour, I'll get back to you.'

Two hours later, just as Dad and I are about to board, I receive a phone call from Frankie. 'He's going to be in the National Gallery tomorrow morning at ten thirty. He's giving a talk on a painting called *Woman Writing a Letter*. It sounds fascinating.'

'Oh, it is, it's one of Terborch's finest. In my opinion.'

Silence.

'You were being sarcastic, weren't you?' I realise. 'OK, well, does your uncle Tom still run that company?' I smile mischievously and Dad looks at me curiously.

'What are you planning?' Dad asks suspiciously once I've hung up.

'I'm having a little bit of fun.'

'Shouldn't you get back to work? It's been weeks now. Conor called your hand phone while you were gone this morning, it slipped my mind to tell you. He's in Japan. He wanted to know why the house hadn't got a For Sale sign in the garden yet.'

'Oh, I haven't forgotten.' I'm agitated by Conor's call. 'I'm selling it myself. I have my first viewing tomorrow.'

He looks unsure and he's right to because I'm lying through my teeth, but all I have to do is call around my list of clients who I know to be looking for a similar property.

While we shuffle along the queue to board the plane, I text a few clients to see if they're interested in a viewing. Then I ask my trusty photographer to take the shots. As we take our seats on the plane, I have already arranged the photographs and For Sale sign for later today and a viewing appointment for tomorrow. Both teachers at the local school, the woman and her husband will view the house during their lunch break. At the bottom of the text is the mandatory 'Was so sorry to hear about what happened. Have been thinking of you. See you tomorrow, Linda xx.' I delete it straight away.

Dad looks at my thumb working over the buttons on my phone with speed. 'You'll get arthritis in your thumb and it's not much fun, I can tell you that.'

I press send and switch the phone off.

'You weren't lying about the house?' he asks.

'No,' I say, confidently now.

'Well, I didn't know that, did I? I didn't know what to tell him.'

Score one to me.

'That's OK, Dad, you don't have to feel in the middle of all this.'

'Well, I am.'

Score one to him.

'Well, you wouldn't have been if you hadn't answered *my* phone.'

Two one.

'You were missing all morning—what was I supposed to do, ignore it?'

Two all.

'He was concerned about you, you know. He thought you should see someone. A professional person.'

Off the charts.

'Did he now?' I fold my arms, wanting to call him straight away and rant about all the things I hate about him and that have always annoyed me. The cutting of his toenails in bed, his nose-blowing every morning that almost rattled the house, his inability to let people finish their sentences, his stupid party coin trick that I fake laughed to every time he did it, including the first, his inability to sit down and have an adult conversation about our problems, his constant walking away during our fights . . . Dad interrupts my silent torture of Conor.

'He said you called him in the middle of the night, spurting Latin.'

'Really?' I feel anger surge. 'What did you say?'

He looks out of the window as we pick up speed down the runway.

'I told him you made a fine fluent Italian-speaking Viking too.' I see his cheeks lift and I throw my head back and laugh.

All even.

He suddenly grabs my hand. 'Thanks for all this, love. I had a great time.' He gives my hand a squeeze.

Justin walks through arrivals at Dublin airport on Tuesday morning to see, behind the barricade, a man in a dark suit holding a large white placard with Justin's surname written in large capitals. Underneath are those two magical words: THANK YOU.

Those words had captured his attention on billboards, newspapers, radio and television adverts all day and every day, since the first note arrived. They were constantly in his head, *thank you, thank you, thank you*. The more he heard them and reread the short notes, the more alien they became, as though he was seeing the sequence of those particular letters for the first time in his life—like music notes, so familiar, so simple, but which, when arranged in a different way, become masterpieces.

Now he takes a step back from those two words. Just as with paintings in a gallery, the words themselves dictate the angle from which they should be approached and the position from which they should best be contemplated. He has found the correct angle now. He can now see the weight they hold. They have a sense of purpose, the strength of beauty and ammunition. Rather than a polite utterance heard a thousand times a day, 'Thank you' now has meaning.

He approaches the man holding the sign. 'Hello.'

'Mr Hitchcock?' The six-foot man's eyebrows are so dark and thick Justin can barely see his eyes.

'Yes,' he says suspiciously. 'Is this car for a *Justin* Hitchcock?'

The man consults a piece of paper in his pocket. 'Yes, it is, sir. Is that still you or does it change things?'

'Ye-es,' he says slowly, contemplatively. 'That's me.'

'You don't seem so sure,' the driver says, lowering the sign. 'Where are you going this morning?'

'Shouldn't you know that?'

'I do. But the last time I let somebody in my car as unsure as you, I delivered an animal rights activist directly into an IMFHA meeting.'

Unfamiliar with the initials, Justin asks, 'Is that bad?'

'The President of the Irish Masters of Fox Hounds Association thought so. He was stuck at the airport with no car, while the lunatic I collected was splashing red paint around the conference room.'

'Well, I'm going to the National Gallery.' Pause. 'I'm *pro* the National Gallery. I'm going to talk about painting, not turn people into canvases as a method of venting my frustration. Though if my ex-wife was in the audience I'd run at her with a paintbrush,' he laughs, and the driver responds with a blank glare.

'I wasn't expecting anybody to greet me,' Justin yaps at the chauffeur's heels, out of the airport into the grey October day. 'Nobody at the gallery informed me you'd be here,' he tests him as they hurry across the pedestrian walkway through the parachuting raindrops.

'I didn't know about the job until late last night when I got a call. I was supposed to be going to my wife's aunt's funeral today.' He roots around his pockets for the car parking ticket and slides it into the machine to validate it.

'Oh, I'm sorry to hear that.'

'So was I. I hate funerals.' He stops walking and turns to face Justin with a look of intense seriousness on his face. 'They always give me the giggles,' he says. 'Does that ever happen to you?'

Justin is unsure whether to take him seriously or not but the driver doesn't crack even the slightest smile. Justin pictures his father's funeral when he was nine years old. The two families huddled together at the graveyard round the dirty open hole in the ground where the casket was placed. His dad's family had flown over from Ireland, bringing with them the rain, which was unusual for Chicago's hot summer. They stood beneath umbrellas, he close to his Aunt Emelda, who held the umbrella in one hand, the other hand tightly on his shoulder, Al and his mother beside him under another umbrella. Justin hated Aunt Emelda's hand being there on his shoulder, though he knew she was trying to be helpful. It felt heavy and tight, as though she was holding him back, afraid he'd scuttle into the big hole in the ground where his father was going. Maybe Aunt Emelda could read his mind, for Justin *had* thought about jumping into that damp dark hole.

If he could leap into the hole before anybody could catch him, maybe when the ground was closed over on top of them, they would both be together. He could have him all to himself, without having to share him with Mom or Al, and there they could play and laugh together, where it was darker. Maybe Dad just didn't like the light;

maybe all he wanted was for the light to go away so that it wouldn't make his eyes squint and his fair skin burn and freckle and itch, as it always did when the sun came out. When that hot sun was in the sky it annoyed his dad, and he would have to sit in the shade while he and his mom and Al would play outside.

As his dad's casket was lowered into the hole, his mother let out howls that made Al cry too. Even Dad's brother, Seamus, who always looked like he wanted to laugh, had a trembling lip and a vein that jutted out of his neck like a body builder, which made Justin think there was another person inside Uncle Seamus, just bursting to get out if Uncle Seamus would let him. Justin didn't cry like everyone else because he felt assured that Dad had finally escaped the light. His dad would no longer have to sit alone in the shade.

Justin realises the driver is staring at him intently. 'No,' he says quietly, clearing his throat and adjusting his eyes to the world of thirty-five years later. Time travel of the mind; a powerful thing.

'That's us over there.' The driver presses the button on his keys and the lights of an S-class Mercedes light up.

Justin's mouth drops. 'Do you know who organised this?'

'No idea.' The driver holds the door open for him. 'I just take the orders from my boss.'

'Could you find out from your boss who's paying for this?'

'I could try.'

'That would be great.' *I'll have gotcha then!* Justin relaxes into the leather seat, stretches his legs out fully and closes his eyes, barely able to hold back his smile.

'I'm Thomas, by the way,' the driver introduces himself. 'I'm here for you all day so wherever you want to go after this, just let me know.'

'For the entire day?' He saved a rich person's life. Yes! He should have mentioned more to Bea than muffins and daily newspapers. A villa in the South of France. What an idiot he was not to have thought more quickly. 'After the gallery, do you mind bringing me to D'Olier Street? I need to visit somebody in the blood donor clinic.'

'No problem, boss.'

The October gust huffs and puffs and attempts to blow the last of the leaves off the nearby trees. I watch as one leaf lets go, dances around in the air before falling to the ground. I'm not fond of autumn. Not fond of watching things so sturdy wither as they lose against nature, the higher power they can't control.

'Here comes the car,' I comment to Kate.

We're standing across the main road from the National Gallery, behind the parked cars, shaded by the trees rising above and over the gates of Merrion Square.

'You paid for *that*?' Kate says. 'You really are nuts.'

'Tell me something I don't know. Actually, I paid half. That's Frankie's uncle driving—he runs the company. Pretend you don't know him if he looks over.'

'I don't know him.'

'Good, that's convincing.'

'Joyce, I have never seen that man in my life.'

'Wow, that's really good.'

'How long are you going to keep this up, Joyce? The London thing sounded fun but really, all we know is that he donated blood.'

'To me.'

She looks doubtful. 'You can't know that.'

'I can. That's the funny thing.'

The Mercedes pulls up by the gates of the gallery. Justin emerges, a beam from ear to ear, and I'm happy to see that next month's mortgage payment has gone to good use. I shall worry about that, and everything else in my life, when the time comes.

He still has the aura I felt from the day I first laid my eyes on him in the hair salon—a presence that makes my stomach bounce.

The leaves around me rustle as another soft breeze blows and I'm not sure if I imagine that it carries to me the smell of his aftershave, the same scent as from the hair salon. I have a brief flash of him picking up a parcel wrapped in emerald-green paper, which sparkles under Christmas tree lights. It's tied with a large red bow and my hands are momentarily his as he carefully peels back the tape from the paper, taking care not to rip it. I am struck by his tenderness for the package, until his thoughts are momentarily mine and I am in on his plans to pocket the paper and use it on the unwrapped presents he has sitting out in the car. Inside is a bottle of aftershave and a shaving set. A Christmas gift from Bea.

'He's handsome,' Kate whispers. 'I support your stalking campaign one hundred per cent, Joyce.'

'It's not a stalking campaign,' I hiss, 'and I'd have done this if he was ugly.'

'Can I go in and listen to his talk?' Kate asks.

'No!'

'Why not? He's never seen me; he won't recognise me. At least I can go and listen to him to see what he's like.'

'What about Sam?'

'Do you want to mind him for a little while?'

I freeze.

'Oh, forget that,' she says quickly. 'I'll bring him in with me.'

'No, no, it's OK. I can mind him.' I swallow and push her away gently. 'Go in and enjoy yourself. We'll be fine here, won't we?'

Sam puts his socked toe in his mouth in response.

'I promise I won't be long.' Kate leans into the stroller, gives her son a kiss and dashes across the road and into the gallery.

'So . . .' I look around nervously. 'It's just you and me, Sean.'

He looks at me with his big blue eyes and mine instantly fill.

I look around to make sure nobody has heard me. I mean Sam.

Justin takes his place at the podium in the lecture hall. A packed room of faces stares back at him. A late arrival, a young woman, enters the room and quickly takes a place among the crowd.

'Good morning, ladies and gentlemen. I am here to talk about this painting: *Woman Writing a Letter*, by Terborch, a Dutch baroque artist from the seventeenth century who was largely responsible for the popularisation of the letter theme. This painting—well, not this painting alone—this genre of letter-writing is a personal favourite of mine, particularly when in this current age it seems a personal letter has almost become extinct.' He stops. *Almost but not quite, for there's somebody sending me notes.* His eyes narrow as he studies his audience. Somebody here could be the mystery note-writer. He studies the woman who arrived a little late as he says half of this and another young woman behind her for the second half, wondering if they are reading deeper into his words. He almost laughs aloud at himself at his assumption that, first, the person whose life he saved would be in this room; secondly, that it would be a young woman; and thirdly, attractive. Which makes him ask himself what exactly was he hoping to come out of this current drama?

I push Sam's stroller into Merrion Square. Burnt oranges, reds and yellows of the autumn foliage litter the ground and, with each gentle breeze, hop alongside us like inquisitive robin redbreasts. I choose a bench along the quiet walk and turn Sam's stroller round so that he faces me.

Sam points a tiny finger up at the sky and makes sounds.

'Tree,' I tell him, which makes him smile, and his mother is instantly recognisable. The vision has the same effect as a boot hitting my stomach. I take a moment to catch my breath. 'Sam, while we're here we should really discuss something,' I say.

His smile widens.

'I have to apologise for something.' I clear my throat. 'I haven't been paying much attention to you lately, have I? The thing is . . . The thing is, I couldn't bear to look at you . . .' I trail off as his grin widens.

'Oh, here.' I lift him out of the buggy and sit him on my lap. I breathe in the top of his head, his wispy hairs so silky like velvet, his body so chubby and soft in my arms, I want to squeeze him tighter. 'The thing is,' I say quietly to the top of his head, 'it broke my heart to look at you, to cuddle you like I used to, because each time I saw you, I remembered what I'd lost.' He looks up at me and babbles in response. I kiss his nose. 'I shouldn't have taken it out on you but you're not mine, and that's so hard.' My eyes fill and I let the tears fall. 'I wanted to have a little boy or girl so that just like when you smile, people could say, oh look, you're the picture of your mummy. People say I look like my mum. And I love hearing that, Sam, I really do, because I miss her and I want to be reminded of her every single day. But looking at you was different. I didn't want to be reminded I'd lost my baby every single day.'

'Ba-ba,' he says.

I sniffle. 'Ba-ba gone, Sam. Sean for a boy, Grace for a girl.' I wipe my nose. Sam, uninterested in my tears, looks away and studies a bird. He points a chubby finger again. 'Bird,' I say through my tears.

'Ba-ba,' he responds.

I smile and wipe my eyes as yet more tears stream down. 'But there's no Sean or Grace now.' I hug him tighter and let my tears fall. The bird hops a few inches and then takes off, disappearing into the sky.

'Ba-ba gone,' Sam says, holding his hands out, palms up.

I watch it fly into the distance, still visible like a speck of dust against the pale blue sky. My tears stop. 'Ba-ba gone,' I repeat.

'**W**hat do we see in this painting?' Justin asks.

Silence as everyone views the projected image.

'Well, let us state the obvious first. A young woman sits at a table writing a letter. We do not know what she is writing but her soft smile suggests she is writing to a loved one or perhaps a lover . . .'

'**S**o how did that go?' Thomas the driver asks as Justin gets back into the car after his talk.

'I saw you standing at the back of the room. You tell me.'

'Well, I don't know much about art but you certainly knew how to talk a lot about one girl writing a letter.'

Justin smiles.

'Were you looking for somebody?' Thomas asks. 'In the crowd. I noticed you looking around a few times. A woman, is it?' he grins.

Justin smiles, and shakes his head. 'I have no idea. You'd think I was crazy if I told you.'

'**S**o, what do you think?' I ask Kate as we walk around Merrion Square and she fills me in on Justin's lecture.

'What do I think?' she repeats. 'I think he seems like a lovely man. I think that no matter what your reasons are for feeling connected to him or attracted to him, they're not important. You should stop all this running around and just introduce yourself.'

I shake my head. 'No can do.'

'Why not? He seemed to be interested when he was chasing your bus down the road, and when he saw you at the ballet.'

'He doesn't want anything to do with me.'

'How do you know that?'

'I know.'

'*How?* And don't tell me it's because of some mumbo-jumbo thing you saw in your tea leaves.'

'He's too busy looking for the woman whose life he saved; he's no longer interested in me. He had my contact details, Kate, and he never called. Not once. In fact, he went so far as to throw them in a skip, and don't ask me how I know that.'

'Knowing you, you were probably lying in the bottom of it.'

I keep tightlipped.

Kate sighs. 'How long are you going to keep this up?'

I shrug. 'Not much longer.'

'What about work? What about Conor?'

'Conor and I are done. There's nothing more to say. Four years of separation and then we'll be divorced. As for work, I've already told them I'm going back next week—my diary is already full with appointments—and as for the house—shit!' I pull up my sleeve to find my watch. 'I have to get back. I'm showing the house in an hour.'

'O<small>K</small>, this is it.' Justin stares out of the car window and up to the second floor, which houses the blood donor clinic.

He nervously asks for Sarah at reception and is told to wait in the waiting room. Around him men and women on their lunch breaks from work sit in their suits and read the newspapers, waiting to be called for their blood donations. When the last person leaves him alone in the room, Sarah appears at the door.

'Justin.' She isn't icy, she isn't tough or angry. Quiet. Hurt. That's worse. He'd rather she was angry.

'Sarah.' He stands to greet her. 'I can't stay long, I have to get to the airport for a flight, but I wanted to call by and see you. Can we talk?'

'Yes, sure.' She enters the reception and sits down, arms still folded.

'Oh.' He looks around. 'Don't you have an office, or something?'

'This is nice and quiet.'

'Where is your office?'

Her eyes narrow with suspicion and he gives up that particular line of questioning and quickly takes a seat beside her.

'I'm here, really, to apologise for my behaviour the last time we met. Well, every time we met and every moment after that. I really am sorry.'

She nods, waiting for more.

Dammit, that's all I had! Think, think. You're sorry and . . .

'I didn't mean to hurt you. I got very distracted that day with those crazy Vikings and, uh . . .' *Think!* 'Could I go to the men's room? If you wouldn't mind. Please.'

She looks a little taken aback but directs him. 'Sure, it's straight down the hall at the end.'

S<small>tanding</small> outside, where a newly hammered 'For Sale' sign is attached to the front wall, Linda and her husband, Joe, are pressing their faces up against the window and gawking into the living room. A protective feeling comes over me. Then as soon as it comes, it vanishes. Home is not a place—not this place, anyway.

'Joyce? Is that you?' Linda slowly lowers her sunglasses. 'Your hair, you look so different.'

'Hi, Linda. Hi, Joe.' I hold out my hand to greet them.

Linda has other plans and reaches out to offer me a huge, tight hug. 'Oh, I'm so sorry for you.' She squeezes me. 'Poor you.'

A nice gesture, if perhaps I'd known her a bit longer than just to show her three houses over a month ago.

She lowers her voice to a whisper. 'Did they do that at the hospital?' She eyes my hair.

'Eh, no,' I chirp. 'They did that at the hair salon.' I turn the key in the door and allow them to enter first.

'Oh,' she breathes excitedly, and her husband smiles and takes her hand. I have a flashback of Conor and me ten years ago, coming to view the house. It had reeked inside, had old carpets and rotting windows. It was disgusting and a money pit, and we loved it as soon as we stood where Linda and her husband stand right now.

We had it all ahead of us back then, when Conor was the Conor I loved and I was the old me; a perfect match. Then Conor became who he is now and I became the Joyce he no longer loved. As the house became more beautiful, our relationship became uglier. Every minute detail of what was wrong in our marriage we attempted to fix by getting a new couch, replacing the draughty windows. If only we'd put that much time and concentration into self-improvement rather than home improvement. Neither of us thought to fix the draught in our marriage. It whistled through the growing cracks while neither of us was paying attention until we both woke up one morning with cold feet.

'I'll show you around downstairs, but, em,' I look up at the nursery door, no longer vibrating as it had when I first returned home. It is just a door, quiet and still. Doing what a door does. Nothing. 'I'll let you wander around upstairs by yourselves.'

'Are the owners still living here?' Linda asks.

I look around. 'No. No, they're long gone.'

As Justin makes his way down the hall to the toilet, he examines each of the names on the doors, looking for Sarah's office. He has no idea where to start but maybe if he can find the folder that deals with blood taken from donors at Trinity College in early autumn, then he'll be closer to finding out.

He sees her name on the door, enters and closes it quietly behind him. He runs to the filing cabinets and starts riffling through them. Moments later the doorknob turns. He drops the file back into the cabinet, turns towards the door and freezes. Sarah looks at him, shocked.

'Justin? What are you doing in my office?'

You're an educated man, think of something smart.

'I took a wrong turn.'

She folds her arms. 'Why don't you tell me the truth now?'

'I was on my way back and I saw your name on the door and I thought I'd come in and have a look around, see what your office is like. I have this thing where I believe that an office really represents what a person is like and I thought that if we're to have a future tog—'

'We're not going to have a future.'

'Oh. I see. But if we *were* to—'

'No.'

He scans her desk and his eyes fall upon a photograph of Sarah with her arms round a young blonde girl and a man.

Sarah follows his gaze. 'That's my daughter, Molly.' She tightens her lips then, angry at herself for saying anything.

'You have a daughter? How old is she?'

'Six.'

'I didn't know you had a daughter.'

'You don't know a lot of things about me. You never stuck around long enough on our dates to talk about anything that wasn't about you.'

Justin cringes, his heart falls. 'Sarah, I'm so sorry.'

'So you said, so sincerely, right before you came into my office and started rooting around.'

'I wasn't rooting—'

Her look is enough to stop himself from telling another lie. Nothing about her is rough or aggressive. She is filled with disappointment; not for the first time, an idiot like Justin has let her down.

'The man in the photo?'

'I would have been happy to tell you about him before,' she says softly. 'In fact, I remember trying to on at least two occasions.'

'I'm sorry,' he repeats, feeling so small he almost can't see over her desk. 'I am hugely embarrassed and disappointed in myself.' And he realises he actually means it from the bottom of his heart. 'I am going through some strange things at the moment.'

'Find me someone who isn't. We all have crap to deal with, Justin. Just please do not drag me into yours.'

'Right.' He nods and offers another apologetic, embarrassed smile before exiting her office, rushing down the stairs and into the car, feeling two foot tall.

'What's that?'

'I don't know.'

'Do you think it will come off?'

'I've no idea. Let's ask Joyce.'

I hear Linda and Joe mumbling together in the hallway. I've left them to their own devices and have been standing in the galley kitchen, drinking a black coffee and staring out at my mother's rosebushes.

'Joyce, could we show you something for a moment?'

'Sure.'

I put the coffee cup down and make my way to the hall. They are on their hands and knees examining the stain by the stairs. My stain.

'I think it might be wine,' Joe says, looking up at me. 'Did the owners say anything about the stain?'

'Eh . . .' My legs wobble slightly and for a moment I think my knees are going to go. 'It's been cleaned a few times already, as far as I know. Would you be interested in keeping the carpet?'

Linda makes a face while she thinks. 'I think wooden floors would be lovely. Don't you?' she asks Joe.

'Yeah,' he nods. 'A nice pale oak.'

'Yeah,' she agrees. 'No, I don't think we'd keep this carpet.'

I hadn't intended to keep the owners' details from them deliberately—there's no point as they'll see it on the contract anyway. I had assumed they knew that the property was mine, but it was their misunderstanding, and as they poked holes in the decorations and the choice of room layout, I didn't think it would be necessary to make them uncomfortable by pointing it out now.

'You seem keen,' I smile, watching their faces aglow with warmth.

'We are,' she grins. 'We have been so fussy but now the situation has changed and we need to find somewhere bigger as soon as we can, seeing as we're expanding, or I'm expanding,' she jokes nervously, and it's only then that I notice her small bump beneath her shirt.

'Oh, wow . . .' Wobble of knees again, eyes fill, please let this moment be over quickly, please make them look away from me. They have tact and so they do. 'That's fantastic, congratulations,' my voice says.

'So that room upstairs would be perfect.' Joe nods to the nursery.

'Oh, of course, that's just wonderful.'

'I can't believe they don't want any of the furniture,' Linda says, looking around. 'They're not taking *anything*?'

'No,' I smile, looking around. 'Nothing but the rosebushes in the back garden.' And a suitcase of memories.

Justin falls into the car with a giant sigh.

'What happened to you?'

'Nothing. Could you just drive directly to the airport now, please? I'm a little behind time.' Justin places his elbow on the window ledge and covers his face with his hand, hating himself, hating the selfish miserable man he has become. He and Sarah weren't right for one another but what right had he to use her like that?

'I've got something that will cheer you up,' Thomas says, reaching for the glove compartment.

'No, I'm really not in the—' Justin stops, seeing Thomas retrieve a familiar envelope from the compartment. He hands it over to him.

'Where did you get this?'

'My boss told me to give it to you before you got to the airport.'

'Your boss.' Justin narrows his eyes. 'What's his name?'

Thomas is silent for a while. 'John,' he finally replies.

'John Smith?' Justin says, his voice thick with sarcasm.

'The very man.'

Knowing he'll squeeze no information from Thomas, he turns his attention back to the envelope. He circles it slowly in his hand, trying to decide whether to open it or not. He could leave it unopened and end all of this now, get his life back in order.

'Well? Aren't you going to open it?' Thomas asks.

Justin continues to circle it in his hand. 'Maybe.'

Dad opens the door to me, his iPod in his ears, the control pad in his hand. He looks my outfit up and down.

'OOH, YOU LOOK VERY NICE TODAY, GRACIE,' he shouts at the

top of his voice, and a man walking his dog across the road turns to stare. 'WERE YOU OUT SOMEWHERE SPECIAL?'

I smile. Light relief at last. I put my finger on my lips and take the earphones out of his ears.

'I was showing the house to some clients of mine.'

'Did they like it?'

'They're going to come back in a few days to measure. So that's a good sign. But I don't think they want a lot of the furniture. Would it be OK if I stored it in your garage?'

'My woodwork studio?'

'That you haven't been in for ten years.'

'I've been in there,' he says defensively. 'Oh, all right then, you can put your things in there. Will I ever get rid of you at all, at all?' he says with a slight smile on his face.

I sit at the kitchen table and Dad immediately busies himself, filling the kettle as he does for everyone who enters the kitchen.

'So how did the Monday Club go last night? I bet Donal McCarthy couldn't believe your story. What was his face like?'

'He wasn't there,' Dad says, turning his back to me as he takes a cup and saucer out for himself and a mug for me. 'He died at the weekend. His funeral's tomorrow. We spent the night talking about him and all his old stories that he told a hundred times.'

'Oh, Dad, I'm so sorry.'

'Ah, well. If he hadn't have gone over the weekend, he would have dropped dead when he'd heard I met Michael Aspel. Maybe it was just as well,' he smiles sadly.

I feel for Dad. It is such a trivial thing compared with the loss of a friend, but he had been so excited to share his stories with his great rival. We both sit in silence.

'You'll keep the rosebushes, won't you?' Dad asks finally.

I know immediately what he's talking about. 'Of course I will. I thought that it'd look good in your garden.'

He looks out of the window and studies his garden, probably deciding where he'll plant it.

'You have to be careful with moving, Gracie. Too much shock causes a serious, possibly a grave decline.'

I smile sadly. 'I'll be fine, Dad. Thanks for caring.'

He keeps his back turned. 'I was talking about the roses.'

My phone rings, vibrates along the table and almost hops off the edge. 'Hello?'

'Joyce, it's Thomas. I just left your young man off at the airport.'

'Oh, thank you so much. Did he get the envelope?'

'Eh, yeah. About that: I gave it to him all right but I've just looked in the back seat of the car and it's still there.'

'What?' I jump up from the kitchen chair. 'Go back, go back! Turn the car round! You have to give it to him. He's forgotten it!'

'You see, the thing is, he wasn't too sure on whether he wanted to open it or not.'

'What? Why?'

'I don't know, love! I gave it to him when he got back into the car before we got to the airport, just like you asked. He seemed very down and so I gave him the envelope and he sat there looking at it and I asked him if he was going to open it and he said maybe.'

'Maybe,' I repeat. Had I done something to upset him? Had Kate said something to him? 'He was upset when he came out of the gallery?'

'No, not the gallery. We stopped off at the blood donor clinic on D'Olier Street before the airport.'

Oh my God, maybe he'd discovered it was me who'd received his blood and he wasn't interested. 'Thomas, do you know if he opened it?'

'Did you seal it?'

'No.'

'Then there's no way of my knowing. I didn't see him open it. I'm sorry. Do you want me to drop it at your house on the way back from the airport?'

'Please.'

An hour later Thomas gives me the envelope. I can feel the tickets still inside and my heart falls. 'Here, Dad.' I slide the envelope across the kitchen table. 'A present for you.'

'What's in it?'

'Front-row seats to the opera for next weekend,' I say sadly. 'It was a gift for somebody else, but he clearly doesn't want to go.'

'The opera.' Dad makes a funny face though he opens the envelope anyway as I get up to make some more coffee.

'Oh, I think I'll pass on this opera thing, love, but thanks anyway.'

I spin round. 'Oh, Dad, why? You liked the ballet and you didn't think that you would.'

'Yes, but I went to that with you. I wouldn't go to this on my own.'

'You don't have to. There are two tickets.'

'No, there aren't.' He turns the envelope upside-down and shakes it. A loose piece of paper falls out and flutters to the table.

My heart skips a beat.

Dad peers down at the note. '"Accompany me",' he says slowly. 'Ah, love, that's awful nice of you—'

'Show me that.' I grab it from his hands, disbelievingly, and read it for myself. Then I read it again. And again and again.

'*Accompany me? Justin.*'

Nine

'HE WANTS TO MEET ME,' I tell Kate nervously. We are seated on a split-level viewing balcony at Kate's local swimming pool. Below us Eric and Jayda splash noisily in their swimming class. Beside us Sam is sitting in his stroller, looking around.

'Did you not think that this would eventually happen? Really, Joyce, you've been taunting the man for weeks. And if he did save your life, as you're insisting he did, wouldn't he want to meet the person whose life he saved? Boost his male ego? Come on, it's the equivalent of a white horse and a shiny suit of armour.'

'No, it's not.'

'It is in his male eyes. His male *wandering* eyes,' she spits out aggressively.

My eyes narrow as I study her closely. 'Is everything OK? You're beginning to sound like Frankie.'

'Stop biting your lip, it's starting to bleed. Yes, everything's great.'

'OK, here I am,' Frankie makes her announcement as she breezes through the door and joins us on the bleachers. 'Issue number one for discussion today is why do we have to constantly meet in these places with all these *things* crawling around?' Frankie looks at all the toddlers.

'What happened to cool bars, new restaurants, shop openings? Remember we used to go out and have *fun*?'

'I have plenty of fun,' Kate says a little too defensively.

Frankie doesn't hear the unusual tone in Kate's voice, or does hear it and decides to push anyway. 'Yes, at dinner parties for other couples who haven't been out for a month either. For me, that's not so fun.'

'You'll understand when you have kids.'

'I don't plan to have any. Is everything OK?'

'Yes, she's "great",' I say to Frankie, using my fingers as inverted commas.

'Oh, I see,' Frankie says slowly and mouths 'Christian' at me.

I shrug.

'Is there anything you want to get off your chest?' Frankie asks.

'Actually, yes.' Kate turns to her with fire in her eyes. 'I'm tired of your little comments about my life. If you're not happy here or in my company, then piss off somewhere else.'

Frankie is silent for a moment as she observes her friend. 'OK,' she says perkily and turns to me. 'My car is parked outside; we can go to the new bar down the road.'

'We're not going anywhere,' I protest.

'Ever since you left your husband and your life has fallen apart, you've been no fun,' she says to me sulkily. 'And as for you, Kate, ever since you got that new Swedish nanny and your husband's been eyeing her up, *you've* been absolutely miserable. As for me, I'm tired of hopping from one night of meaningless sex to another, and having to eat microwave dinners alone every evening. There, I've said it.'

My mouth falls open. So does Kate's. I can tell we are both trying our best to be angry with her but her comments are so spot-on, it's actually quite humorous. She nudges me with her elbow and chuckles mischievously in my ear. The corners of Kate's lips begin to twitch too.

'I should have got a manny,' Kate finally says.

'Nah, I still wouldn't trust Christian,' Frankie responds. 'You're being paranoid, Kate,' she assures her seriously. 'I've been around there, I've seen him. He adores you and she is not attractive at all.'

'You think?'

'Uh-huh,' she nods, but when Kate looks away, mouths 'gorgeous' to me. 'OK,' she claps her hands, causing Sam to jump with fright, 'what's this session's meeting been called for?'

'Justin wants to meet Joyce,' Kate explains, and snaps at me, 'Stop biting your lip.'

I stop.

'Ooh, great,' Frankie says excitedly. 'So what's the problem?' She sees my look of terror.

'He's going to realise that I'm me.' I bite my lip again.

'This is really reminding me of the old days. You are thirty-three years old, Joyce, why are you acting like a teenager?'

'Because she's in love,' Kate says, bored, turning to face the swimming pool and clapping her coughing daughter, Jayda, whose face is half under the water.

'She can't be in love.' Frankie rolls her nose up in disgust.

'Is that normal, do you think?' Kate, beginning to get worried about Jayda, tries to get our attention.

'Of course it's not normal,' Frankie responds. 'She hardly knows the guy.'

'Girls, eh, stop for a minute,' Kate tries to butt in. 'Is she OK, do you think?'

'Are you in love?' Frankie looks at me as though I've just said I want to have a sex change.

I smile just as the lifeguard crashes into the water to save Jayda.

'You'll have to take us over to Ireland with you,' Doris says with excitement, placing a vase on the kitchen windowsill. The flat is almost finished. 'We need to be nearby just in case something happens. They could be a murderer, a serial stalker who dates people and then kills them. I saw something like that on *Oprah*.'

'I am not taking you both to the opera with me,' Justin says.

'What if she's a celebrity?' Doris says excitedly. 'Oh my God, she could be! I think she is! Jennifer Aniston could be sitting in the front row of the opera and there could be a place free beside her. Oh my God, what if it is?' She turns to Al with wide eyes. 'Justin, you *have* to tell her I'm her biggest fan.'

'Whoa, whoa, whoa, *how on earth* have you come to that conclusion? We don't even know if it's a woman,' Justin sighs.

'Yeah, Doris,' Al joins in. 'It's probably just a normal person.'

Justin rolls his eyes. 'Yeah,' he imitates his tone, 'because celebrities aren't normal people, they're really underworld beasts.'

'We're going to Dublin tomorrow,' Doris says with an air of finality. 'It's your brother's birthday and a weekend in Dublin, in a very nice hotel like the Shelbourne Hotel—I've, I mean *Al* has always wanted to stay there—would be a perfect birthday present for him, from you.'

'I can't afford the Shelbourne Hotel, Doris.'

'Well, we'll need somewhere close to a hospital in case he has a heart attack. In any case, we're all going!' She claps her hands excitedly.

'**D**oris, is this really necessary?' Justin moans from the bathroom.

'Yes!' she calls. 'This is what we're here for. We have to make sure you're going to look right tonight. Hurry up.'

Doris and Al are sitting on the end of their bed in a Dublin hotel, not the Shelbourne, much to Doris's dismay. It is more of a Holiday Inn, but it's central to the city and shopping streets. As soon as they'd landed earlier that morning, Justin had been all set to show them around the sights, the museums, churches and castles, but Doris and Al had other things on their minds. Shopping. The Viking tour was as cultured as they got and Doris had howled when water had sprayed her in the face on entry into the River Liffey.

There were only hours to go until the opera, until he would finally discover the identity of this mystery person. He was filled with anxiety, excitement and nerves at the thought of it.

He fixes his tie and exits the bathroom. He is greeted by silence.

'What?' he says nervously. 'Something wrong? Is there a stain?'

Doris rolls her eyes and shakes her head. 'Ha-ha very funny. Now seriously, stop wasting time and show us the real suit.'

'Doris!' Justin exclaims. 'This is the real suit!'

'That's your best suit?' she drawls, looking him up and down.

'I think I recognise that from our wedding.' Al's eyes narrow.

Doris stands up and picks up her handbag. 'Take it off,' she says.

'**T**hese are too formal, Kate.' I turn my nose up at the dresses she has chosen. 'It's not a ball, I just need something . . .'

'Sexy,' Frankie says, waving a little dress in front of me. I've met them in the city for help on what to wear to tonight's opera.

'It's an opera, not a nightclub.' Kate whips it away from her. They both turn away and continue to root through the rails.

'Aha! I got it,' Frankie announces.

'No, I've found the perfect one.'

They both spin round with the same dresses in their hand, Kate holding one in red, Frankie holding the black. I chew on my lip.

'Stop it!' they say in unison.

'**O**h my God,' Justin whispers.

'What? You've never seen a pink pinstripe before? It's divine. Justin? Earth to Justin? What on earth are you looking at? Oh, she's pretty.'

'That's Joyce,' he whispers. He had once read that a blue-throated hummingbird had a heart rate of one thousand two hundred and sixty beats per minute, and he'd wondered how on earth anything could survive that. He understood now. With each beat, his heart pushed out blood and sent it flowing round his body. He felt his entire body throb.

'That's Joyce?' Doris asks, shocked. 'The phone woman? Well, she looks . . . *normal*, Justin. What do you think, Al?'

Al looks Joyce up and down and nudges his brother. 'Yeah, she looks real *normal*. You should ask her out once and for all.'

'Why are you both so surprised she looks normal?' Thump-thump.

'Well, sweetie, the very fact that she exists is a surprise,' Doris snorts. 'The fact that she's *pretty* is damn near a miracle. Go on, ask her out for dinner tonight.'

'I can't tonight, I've got the opera!'

'Opera shopera. Who cares about that?'

'You have been talking about it nonstop for over a week. And now it's opera shopera?' Thump-thump. Thump-thump.

'Well, I didn't want to alarm you before but I was thinking about it on the plane on the way over and . . .' she takes a deep breath, 'it can't be Jennifer Aniston. Sorry, Al.' She touches his arm apologetically.

'What? But I brought my autograph book!'

Justin can barely think, everything is happening too fast. Joyce, far more beautiful up close than he remembers, is beginning to move away now. He has to do something quick. *Think, think, think!*

'Ask her out tomorrow night,' Al suggests.

'I can't! My exhibition is tomorrow.'

'Skip it. Call in sick.'

'I can't, Al! I've been working on this for months, I'm the damn curator, I *have* to be there.' Thump-thump, thump-thump.

'If you don't ask her out, I will.' Doris pushes him.

Joyce starts to move away.

Do something!

'Joyce!' Doris calls out.

'Jesus Christ.' Justin tries to turn round and scarper in the other direction but both Al and Doris block him.

'Justin Hitchcock,' a voice says loudly and he stops trying to break through their barrier and slowly turns round. The lady standing beside Joyce is familiar. She has a baby in a stroller beside her.

'Justin Hitchcock.' The girl reaches her hand out. 'Kate McDonald. I was at your talk last week in the National Gallery. It was incredibly interesting.' She smiles brightly. 'I didn't know you knew Joyce.' She elbows Joyce. 'Joyce, you never said! I was at Justin Hitchcock's talk just last week! Remember I told you?'

Joyce's eyes are wide and startled. She looks from her friend to Justin and back again.

'She doesn't know me, exactly,' Justin finally speaks up and feels a slight tremble in his voice. 'We've passed one another on many occasions but never had the opportunity to meet properly.' He holds out his hand. 'Joyce, I'm Justin.'

She reaches out to take his hand and static electricity rushes through as they get a quick shock from each other.

They both let go quickly. 'Whoa!' She pulls back.

'Oooh,' Doris sings.

'It's static electricity, Doris. Caused when the air and materials are dry. They should use a humidifier in here,' Justin says like a robot.

Frankie cocks her head and tries not to laugh. 'Charming.'

'I tell him that all the time,' Doris says angrily.

After a moment, Joyce extends her hand again to finish the handshake properly. 'Sorry, I just got a—'

'That's OK, I got it too,' he smiles.

They remain holding hands, just staring at one another. A line of Doris, Justin and Al standing opposite Joyce's party of three. Doris clears her throat noisily. 'I'm Doris, his sister-in-law.' She reaches diagonally over Justin and Joyce's handshake to greet Frankie.

'I'm Frankie.' They shake hands. While they are doing so, Al reaches over diagonally to shake hands with Kate.

'Would you like to go for dinner tonight with Justin?' Doris blurts out.

'Tonight?' Joyce's mouth drops.

'She would *love* to,' Frankie answers for her.

'*Tonight*, though?' Justin turns to face Doris with wide eyes.

'Oh, it's no problem, Al and I want to eat alone anyway,' she smiles.

'Are you sure you wouldn't rather stick to your *other* plans tonight?' Joyce says, slightly confused.

'Oh, no,' Justin shakes his head, 'I'd love to have dinner with you. Unless of course *you* have plans?'

Joyce turns to Frankie. 'Tonight? I have that *thing*, Frankie . . .'

'Oh, no, don't be silly. It doesn't really make a difference now, does it?' She widens her eyes. 'Where are you taking her?' She smiles sweetly at Justin.

'The Shelbourne Hotel?' Doris says. 'At eight?'

'Oh, I've always wanted to eat there,' Kate sighs. 'Eight suits her fine,' she responds.

Justin smiles and looks at Joyce. 'Does it?'

Joyce seems to consider this, her mind ticking at the same rate as his heart.

'You're *absolutely* sure you're happy to cancel your other plans for tonight?' Frown lines appear on her forehead.

Guilt overcomes him as he thinks of whoever he is currently making arrangements to stand up. He gives a single nod and is unsure of how convincing it seems.

Sensing this, Doris begins to pull him away. 'Well, it was wonderful to meet you all but we really better get back to shopping. Nice to meet you, Kate, Frankie, Joyce sweetie.' She gives her a quick hug. 'Enjoy dinner. At eight. Shelbourne Hotel. Don't forget now.'

'Red or black?' Joyce holds up the two dresses to Justin, before he's pulled away.

He considers this carefully. 'Red.'

'Black it is, then,' she smiles, mirroring their first and only conversation from the hair salon, the first day they met.

He laughs and allows Doris to drag him away.

'What the hell did you do that for, Doris?' Justin asks as they walk back towards their hotel.

'You've gone on and on about this woman for weeks and now you've finally got a date with her. What's so wrong with that?'

'I have *plans* tonight! I can't just stand the person up.'

'You don't even know who they are!'

'It doesn't matter, it's still rude.'

'Justin, seriously, listen to me. This whole thank you message thing could honestly be somebody playing a cruel joke.'

Justin sighs.

'Would you rather risk going to something where you have no idea what or who to expect? Or go to dinner with a pretty lady, who you are absolutely crazy about and have been thinking about for weeks?'

'Come on,' Al joins in, 'when's the last time you felt like this about anyone? I don't even think you were like this with Jennifer.'

Justin smiles.

'Ok, I'm coming!' I call down the stairs to Kate, Frankie and Dad.

'I've got the camera ready!' Kate hollers.

Dad starts making trumpet noises as I walk down the stairs and I laugh. I keep an eye on Mum's photo on the hall table as I walk down the steps. I wink at her as I pass.

As soon as I step into the hall and turn to them in the kitchen, they all go quiet. My smile fades. 'What's wrong?'

'Oh, Joyce,' Frankie whispers, 'you look beautiful.'

I sigh with relief and join them in the kitchen.

'Do a twirl.' Kate films with the video camera.

I spin in my new red dress while Sam claps his podgy hands.

'Mr Conway, you haven't said anything!' Frankie nudges him. 'Isn't she beautiful?'

We all turn to face Dad, who has gone silent, eyes filled with tears. He nods up and down quickly, but no words come.

'Oh, Dad.' I wrap my arms round him. 'It's only a dress.'

'You look beautiful, love,' he manages to say. 'Go get him, kiddo.' He gives me a kiss on the cheek and hurries into the living room, embarrassed by his emotion.

'So,' Frankie says, smiling, 'have you decided whether it's going to be dinner or the opera tonight?'

'I still don't know.'

'He asked you out to dinner,' Kate says. 'Why do you think he'd rather go to the opera?'

'Because firstly, *he* didn't ask me out for dinner. His sister-in-law did. And I didn't say yes. *You* did.' I glare at Kate. 'I think it's killing him not knowing whose life he saved. He didn't seem so convinced at the end, before he left the shop, did he?'

'Stop reading so much into it,' Frankie says. 'He asked you out so go out.'

'But he looked guilty to be standing the opera date up.'

'I don't know,' Kate disagrees. 'He seemed to really want you at that dinner.'

'It's a tough decision,' Frankie summarises. 'I would *not* like to be in your shoes.'

'Hey, they're my shoes,' Kate says, insulted. 'Why can't you just come clean and tell him that it's you?'

'My way of coming clean was supposed to be him seeing me at the opera. This was going to be it, the night he found out.'

'So go to dinner and tell him that it was you all along.'

'But what if he goes to the opera?'

We talk in circles for a while longer until my head is spinning. When the taxi arrives, Dad walks me to the door.

'I don't know what you girls were in such deep conversation about but I know you've to make a decision about something. Have you made it?' Dad asks softly.

I swallow hard. 'I don't know what the right decision is.'

'Of course you do. You always take your own route, love.'

'What do you mean?'

He looks out to the garden. 'See that trail there?'

'The garden path?'

He shakes his head and points to a track in the lawn where the grass has been trampled on and the soil is slightly visible beneath. 'You made that path.'

'What?' I'm confused now.

'As a little girl,' he smiles. 'We call them "desire lines" in the gardening world. They're the tracks and trails that people make for themselves. You've always avoided the paths laid down by other people, love. You've always gone your own way. You've never taken the official route,' he chuckles to himself. 'You're certainly your mother's daughter, cutting the corners, creating spontaneous paths, while I'd stick to the routes and make my way the long way round.' He smiles as he reminisces.

We both study the small well-worn ribbon of trampled grass across the garden leading to the path.

'Desire lines,' I repeat. 'I suppose desire isn't linear. There is no straightforward way of going where you want.'

'Do you know what you're going to do now?' he asks.

I smile and kiss him on his forehead. 'I do.'

I step out of the taxi at Stephen's Green and immediately see the crowds flowing towards the Gaiety Theatre, all dressed in their finest for the National Irish Opera's production. I'm filled with nerves, with anticipation, and with the greatest hope I have ever felt in my life, that the final part of my plan will come together.

I stand halfway between the Shelbourne Hotel and the Gaiety Theatre. I look from one to the other, close my eyes and wait to feel the pull. Which way to go. Right to the Shelbourne. Left to the Gaiety. My heart drums in my chest.

I turn to the left and stride confidently towards the theatre. Inside the bustling entrance foyer, I purchase a programme and make my way to my seat. No time for pre-performance drinks; if he shows up early and sees I'm not here I would never forgive myself. Front-row tickets— I could not believe my luck but I had called the very moment the tickets had gone on sale to secure these precious seats.

I take my seat. The atmosphere is magical. Thousands of people buzzing with excitement, orchestra tuning, the air rich with perfumes and aftershaves, pure honey.

I look to my right at the empty chair and shiver with excitement.

An announcement explains that the performance will begin in five minutes, that those who are late will be forbidden entry until a break. Hurry, Justin, hurry, I plead, my legs bouncing beneath me with nerves.

Justin speed-walks from his hotel and up Kildare Street. He stops walking at the top of the road. The Shelbourne Hotel is directly beside him, the Gaiety Theatre two hundred yards to his right.

He closes his eyes and takes deep breaths. Breathes in the fresh October air of Dublin city.

Which way to go. Which way to go.

The performance has begun and I cannot take my eyes off the door to my right-hand side. Beside me is an empty seat. Despite the announcement, a few people have been permitted entry. If Justin does not come now, he may not be able to be seated until after the interval.

I turn round once more and my heart skips a beat as the door beside me opens.

Justin pulls on the door and as soon as he enters the room, all heads turn to stare at him. He looks around quickly for Joyce.

The maître d' approaches. 'Welcome, sir. How can I help you?'

'Good evening. I've booked a table for two, under Hitchcock.' He looks around nervously. 'Is she here yet?'

'No, sir, you are the first to arrive. Would you like me to show you to your table or would you rather have a drink before?'

'The table, please.' If she arrives and sees he isn't at the table, he will never forgive himself.

He is led to a table for two in the centre of the dining room. 'Sir, would you like to see the menu or wait for the other party?'

'I'll wait, thank you.' He watches the door.

It has been over an hour. The chair beside me remains empty and cold. The woman next to it glances occasionally at it and at me. I am twisted round, eye on the door, and she smiles politely, sympathetically. It brings tears to my eyes. I feel utterly alone. The interval begins; everybody stands up and exits to the bar. I sit and I wait.

The more lonely I feel, the more hope that springs in my heart. He may still come. He may still feel this is as important to him as it is to me. Dinner with a woman he's met once or an evening with a person whose life he helped save, a person who has done exactly what he wished and thanked him in all the ways he asked.

Perhaps it wasn't enough.

'**W**ould you like to see the menu now, sir?'

'Em,' he looks at the clock. She's a half-hour late but he remains hopeful. 'She's just running a little late, you see,' he explains.

'Of course, sir.'

'I'll have a look at the wine menu, please.'

'**G**o get him,' Dad said. Well, I didn't. I've been stood up by a man who'd rather have dinner with me. As nonsensical as it should be, it is crystal clear to me. I wanted him to be here. I wanted the connection

I felt, that he caused, to be the thing that brought us together, not a chance meeting in a department store, a few hours before. It seems so fickle for him to choose me over something far more important.

Perhaps I should be happy he chose dinner with me. I look at my watch. Perhaps he is there right now, waiting for me. But what if I leave here and he arrives, missing me? No. I am best to stay put.

But if he is at the restaurant now, and I am here, then he has been alone for over an hour. Why then wouldn't he run a few hundred yards to seek out the mystery date? Unless he took one look through the door, saw that it was me and refused to come in. I am overwhelmed by the thoughts in my head.

Before I know it, the opera is over. I walk out to the cold night air. My tears feel cold against my skin as the breeze hits them.

Justin empties the last of his second bottle of wine into his glass and slams it back onto the table unintentionally. He has lost all coordination by now, he can barely read the time on his watch but he knows it's gone past a reasonable hour for Joyce to show.

He has been stood up. By the one woman he's had any sort of interest in since his divorce. Not counting poor Sarah. He had never counted poor Sarah.

I am a horrible person.

'I'm sorry to disturb you, sir,' the maître d' says politely, 'but we have received a phone call from your brother, Al? He wanted to pass on the message that he is still alive and that he hopes you are, em, well, that you're enjoying your night.'

'Alive?'

'Yes, sir, he said you would understand, as it's twelve o'clock. His birthday? I'm also sorry to tell you that we are closing for the evening. Would you like to settle your bill?'

Justin looks up at him, bleary-eyed. 'I've been stood up.'

'I'm sorry, sir.'

'Oh, don't be. I deserve it. I stood up a person I don't even know.'

'Oh. I see.'

'But they have been so kind to me. So, so kind. They gave me muffins and coffee, a car and a driver, and I've been so horrible to him or her.' He stops suddenly. *It might be still open!*

'Here.' He thrusts his credit card at him. 'I might still have time.'

I stroll around the quiet streets of the neighbourhood. I told the taxi driver to let me out round the corner so that I could clear my head and be rid of my tears by the time Dad sees me, who I'm sure is currently sitting up in his armchair as he used to do when I was younger, alert and eager to find out what had happened.

I walk by my old house, which I successfully managed to sell only days ago, not to the eager Linda and Joe, who found out it was my home and were afraid that the stairs that caused my fall would be too dangerous for Linda during her pregnancy. Nobody takes responsibility for their actions, I notice. It wasn't the stairs, it was me. I was rushing. It was my fault. Simple as that. Something I'm going to have to dig deep to forgive.

The money for the house is to be halved and shared between Conor and me. I will have to start hunting for something smaller, something cheaper. I have no idea what he will do—an odd realisation.

I stop outside our old home and stare up at the red bricks. The building that housed my once-upon-a-time dreams stands for someone else now, as it did for the people before us, and I feel happy to let it go. Happy that was another time and that I can begin again, anew, though bearing the scars of before. They represent wounds that have healed.

It's midnight when I return to Dad's house and behind the windows is blackness. There isn't a single light on, which is unusual.

I open my bag to get my keys and bump against my mobile phone. It lights up to show I have missed ten calls, eight of which are from the house. I had it on silent at the opera and, knowing that Justin didn't have my number, I didn't think to look at it. I scramble for my keys and I'm through the door like a rocket, turning on all the lights.

'Dad?' I call in the hallway. No answer.

I walk to the kitchen and flick the switch. A full cup of tea sits on the kitchen table. 'Dad?' I say more loudly now, walking into the living room and turning on the light.

His pills have all been spilled on the floor, all the containers opened and emptied, all the colours mixed.

I panic now, running upstairs, turning on all the lights as I yell at the top of my lungs, 'DAD! DAD! WHERE ARE YOU?' Tears are flowing now. He is not in his bedroom, or the bathroom, not in my room. All I can hear is the drumbeat of my heart in my ears, in my throat.

'DAD!' I yell. I start pulling open wardrobes, searching under his bed. I look out of the back window and into the garden: no sign of him.

My knees too weak to stand, I sink onto the top stair on the landing and try to figure out where he could be.

Then I think of the spilled pills on the floor and I yell the loudest I have *ever* shouted in my life. 'DAAAAAAD!'

Silence greets me and I have never felt so alone. Then. 'Joyce?' A voice calls from the front door, which I've left open. 'Joyce, it's me, Fran.' She stands there in her dressing gown.

'Dad is gone.' My voice trembles.

'He's in the hospital, I was trying to call y—'

'What? Why?' I stand up and race down the stairs. 'I have to go to him.' I rush around searching for my car keys. 'Which one is he in?'

'Joyce, relax, love, relax.' Fran's arms are round me. 'I'll drive you.'

I run down the corridors, trying to find the correct room. A nurse stops me and helps. I shouldn't be allowed in at this time but she can tell I'm distraught, wants to calm me by showing me he's all right. She allows me a few minutes.

I follow her down a series of corridors and finally she leads me into his room. I see Dad lying in bed, tubes attached to his wrists and nose, his skin deathly pale, his body so small under the blankets in the bed.

'Dad.' I try to remain calm but my voice comes out muffled.

'It's OK, love. I just got a shock, is all. Thought my heart was acting up again, went to take my pills but then I got dizzy and they all fell. Something to do with sugar, they tell me.'

'Diabetes, Henry,' the nurse smiles. 'The doctor will be around to explain it all to you in the morning.'

I sniffle, trying to remain calm.

'Ah, come here, you silly sod.' He lifts his arms towards me.

I rush to him and hug him tight, his body feeling frail but protective.

'I'm not going anywhere on you now. Hush, now.' He runs his hands through my hair and pats my back comfortingly. 'I hope I didn't ruin your night, now. I told Fran not to bother you.'

'Of course you should have called me,' I say into his shoulder. 'I got such a fright when you weren't home.'

'Well, I'm fine. You'll have to help me, though, with all this stuff,' he whispers. 'I told the doctor I understand but I don't really,' he says, a little worried. 'He's a real snooty type.' He ruffles up his nose.

'Of course I will.' I wipe my eyes and try to compose myself.

'So, how did it go?' he asks, perking up. 'Tell me all the good news.'

'He, em,' I purse my lips, 'he didn't show up.' My tears start again.

Dad is quiet; sad then angry, then sad again. He hugs me again, tighter this time. 'Ah, love,' he says gently. 'He's a bloody fool.'

Justin finishes explaining the story of his disastrous weekend to Bea, who is sitting on the couch, her mouth open in shock.

'I can't believe I missed all this. I'm so bummed!'

'Well, you wouldn't have missed it if you'd been talking to me,' Justin teases.

'Thank you for apologising to Peter. I appreciate it. He appreciates it.'

'I was acting like an idiot; just didn't want to admit my little girl was all grown-up.'

'You better believe it,' she smiles. 'God,' she thinks back to his story, 'I still can't imagine somebody sending you all that stuff. Who could it be? The poor person must have waited and waited for you at the opera.'

Justin covers his face and winces. 'Please stop, it's killing me.'

'But you chose Joyce. You must have really liked her.'

'She must have really not liked me because she didn't show up. No, Bea, I'm over it now. It's time to move on. If you can't remember anyone else you told, then we'll never know.'

Bea thinks hard. 'I only told Peter, the costume supervisor and her father. But what makes you think it wasn't either of them?'

'I met the costume supervisor that night. She didn't act like she knew me, and she's English—why would she have gone to Ireland for a blood transfusion? I called her and asked her about her father. He's Polish.'

'Hold on, where are you getting that from? She wasn't English, she was Irish,' Bea frowns. 'They both were.'

Thump-thump. Thump-thump.

'Justin,' Laurence enters the room with cups of coffee, 'I was wondering when you have a minute, if we could have a word.'

'Not now, Laurence,' Justin says, moving to the edge of his seat. 'Bea, where's your ballet programme? Her photograph's in it.'

'Honestly, Justin.' Jennifer arrives at the door with her arms folded. 'Could you please just be respectful for one moment.'

Bea runs to her room, and returns waving the programme in her hand, ignoring them. As does Justin. He flicks through it quickly.

'There!' he stabs his finger on the page.

'Guys,' Jennifer steps in between them, 'we have to settle this now.'

'Not now, Mum. Please!' Bea yells. 'This is important! That's not her.' She shakes her head furiously. 'That's not the woman I spoke to.'

'Well, what did she look like?' Justin is up on his feet now.

'Let me think, let me think.' Bea panics. 'I know! Mum! Where are the photographs we took of the first night I stood in for Charlotte in the ballet?'

'Oh, em—' Jennifer looks from Justin to Bea with confusion.

'Quick.'

'They're in the corner kitchen cupboard,' Laurence says, frowning.

'Yes, Laurence!' Justin punches the air. 'Go get them, quick!'

Alarmed, Laurence runs into the kitchen, while Justin paces.

'Here they are.' Bea snaps them out of his hand. Jennifer tries to interject but Bea and Justin's speech and movements are on fast forward.

Bea shuffles through the photos at top speed. 'You weren't in the room at the time, Dad. You had disappeared somewhere but we all got a group photo and, here it is!' She rushes to her dad. 'That's them. The woman and her father, at the end.' She points.

Silence.

'Dad?'

Silence.

'Dad, are you OK?'

'Justin?' Jennifer moves in closer. 'He's gone very pale, get him a glass of water, Laurence, quick.'

'Dad.' Bea clicks her fingers in front of his eyes. 'Are you with us?'

'It's her,' he whispers.

'Her who?' Jennifer asks.

'The woman whose life he saved.' Bea jumps up and down excitedly.

'*You* saved a woman's life?' Jennifer asks, shocked. '*You?*'

'It's Joyce,' he whispers.

Bea gasps. 'The woman who phoned me?'

He nods.

Bea gasps again. 'The woman you stood up?'

Justin closes his eyes, and silently curses himself.

'You saved a woman's life and then *stood her up?*' Jennifer laughs.

'Bea, where's your phone? She called you, remember? Her number was in your phone.'

'Oh, Dad, that was ages ago. My phone log only holds ten recent numbers. That was weeks ago!'

'Dammit!'

'I gave it to Doris, remember? She wrote it down. You called the number from your flat!'

You threw it in the skip, you jerk! The skip! It's still there!

'Here.' Laurence runs in with the glass of water, panting.

'Laurence.' Justin reaches out, takes him by the cheeks and kisses his forehead. 'I give you my blessing. Jennifer,' he does the same and kisses her directly on the lips, 'good luck.'

He runs out of the apartment as Bea cheers him on, Jennifer stares as she wipes her lips with disgust and Laurence wipes the spilt water from his clothes.

As Justin sprints from the tube station to his house, rain pours from the clouds like a cloth being squeezed. He doesn't care, he just laughs, unable to believe that Joyce was the woman all along. He should have known. It all makes sense now, her asking him if he was sure he wanted to make new dinner plans, her friend being at his talk, all of it!

He turns the corner into his drive and sees the skip now filled to the brim with items. He jumps in and begins sorting through it.

From the window, Doris and Al stop packing their suitcases and watch him with concern. 'Dammit, I really thought he was getting back to normal,' Al says. 'Should we stay?'

I lie in bed, staring at the ceiling, trying to process my life. Dad is still in hospital undergoing tests and will be home tomorrow. With nobody around, it has forced me to think about my life and I have worked my way through despair, guilt, sadness, anger, loneliness, depression and cynicism, and have finally found my way to hope.

It's eleven p.m. when the phone rings. Thinking it's Dad I hurry downstairs, grab the phone and sit on the bottom stair. 'Hello?'

'It was you all along.'

I freeze. My heart thuds. 'Justin?'

'I saw the photograph of you and your father with Bea. That's the night she told you about my donation. About wanting thank yous. Why didn't you say anything to me? All those times I saw you? Did you follow me or . . . or, what's going on, Joyce?'

'Are you angry with me?'

'No! I mean, I don't know. I don't understand. I'm so confused.'

'Let me explain.' I take a deep breath and try to steady my voice. 'I didn't follow you to any of the places we met so please don't be concerned. I'm not a stalker. Something happened when I received my transfusion and *whatever* that was, when your blood was transfused into mine, I suddenly felt connected to you. I kept turning up at places you were at, like the hair salon. It was all a coincidence.' I'm speaking too fast now but I can't slow down. 'And then Bea told me you'd donated blood around the same time that I'd received it and . . .'

'You mean, you don't know for sure if it is my blood that you received? Because I couldn't find out, nobody would tell me. Did somebody tell you?'

'No. Nobody told me. They didn't need to. I—'

'Joyce.' He stops me and I'm immediately worried by his tone.

'I'm not some *weird* person, Justin. Trust me. I have never experienced what I have over the past few weeks.' I tell him the story. Of experiencing his skills, his knowledge, of sharing his tastes. He is quiet. 'Say something, Justin.'

'I don't know what to say. It sounds . . . odd.'

'It is odd, but it's the truth. This will sound even worse but I feel like I've gained some of your memories too.'

'Really?' His voice is cold, far away. I'm losing him.

'Memories of the park in Chicago, Bea dancing in her tutu on the red and white chequered cloth, the seesaw with Al, the sprinklers, the—'

'Whoa, whoa, whoa. Stop now. Who's told you these things?'

'Nobody, I just know them!' I rub my eyes tiredly. 'I know it sounds bizarre, Justin, I really do, but this is my life and these are the things that are happening to me. If you don't believe me then I'm sorry, but please know that this is not a joke or a hoax or any kind of set-up.'

He is quiet for a while. And then, 'I want to believe you.'

'You feel something between us?'

'I feel that.' He speaks very slowly as though pondering every letter of every word. 'The memories, tastes and hobbies and whatever else of mine that you mentioned, are things that you could have seen me do or heard me say. You saw the photo in Bea's locket, you've been to my talks, you've read my articles. I may have revealed things about myself in them, in fact I know I have. How can I know that you knowing these things is through a transfusion? How do I know that—no offence—that you're not some lunatic young woman who's convinced herself of some crazy story she read in a book or saw in a movie?'

I sigh. I have no way of convincing him.

'I'm sorry, Joyce,' he begins to end the conversation.

'No, wait,' I stop him. 'Aren't you going to even try to believe me?'

He sighs deeply. 'I thought you were somebody else, Joyce. I don't know why because I'd never even met you, but I thought you were a different kind of person. This . . . this I don't understand. This, I find . . . it's not right, Joyce.'

Each sentence is a stab through my heart.

'You've been through a lot, by the sound of it, perhaps you should . . . talk to someone.'

'Why don't you believe me? Please, Justin. There must be something I can say to convince you. Something I know that you haven't written in an article or a book or told anyone in a lecture . . .' I trail off, thinking of something. No, I can't use that.

'Goodbye, Joyce. I hope everything works out for you, really I do.'

'Wait! There is one thing. One thing that only you could know.'

He pauses. 'What?'

I squeeze my eyes shut and take a deep breath. Do it or don't do it. Do it or don't. I open my eyes and blurt it out. 'Your father.'

'What about him?' His voice is ice cold.

'I know what you saw,' I say softly. 'How you could never tell anyone.'

'What the hell are you talking about?'

'I know about you being on the stairs, seeing him through the banisters. I see him too. I see him with the bottle and the pills closing the door. Then I see the green feet on the floor—'

'STOP IT!' he yells, and I'm shocked to silence.

But I must keep trying.

'I know how hard it must have been for you as a child—'

'You know nothing,' he says coldly. 'Absolutely nothing. Please stay away from me. I don't ever wish to hear from you again.'

'OK.' My voice is a whisper but he has already hung up.

I sit on the steps of the dark empty house and listen as the cold October wind rattles the building.

So that's that.

One Month Later

Ten

'NEXT TIME WE SHOULD take the car, Gracie,' Dad says as we make our way down the road back from our walk in the Botanic Gardens. I link his arm and I'm lifted up and down with him as he sways. Up and down, down and up. The motion is soothing.

'No, you need the exercise, Dad.'

'Speak for yourself,' he mutters. 'Howya, Sean? Miserable day, isn't it?' he calls across the street to the old man on his Zimmer frame.

'Terrible,' Sean shouts back.

'So what did you think of the apartment, Dad?'

'I'm not sure. It seemed awful small and there was a funny man that went into the flat next door. Don't think I liked the look of him . . . Good afternoon, Graham. Miserable day, isn't it?' he says to the neighbour passing.

'Awful day, Henry,' Graham responds.

'Anyway, I don't think you should take that apartment, Gracie. Hang on here a little longer until something more appropriate pops up.'

'Dad, we've seen ten apartments and you don't like any of them. You can't keep me at home for ever, you know.'

'For ever's been and gone, my love. There's no budging you. You're the Stonehenge of grown-up children living at home.'

'Can I go to the Monday Club again tonight? I've to finish off the game of chess I started with Larry.'

'Larry just keeps positioning his pawns so that you'll lean over and he can see down your top. That game will never end.' Dad rolls his eyes. 'You need to get more of a social life than hanging around with the likes of Larry and me.'

'I like hanging around with you.'

He smiles to himself, pleased. We turn into Dad's house and sway up the small garden path to the front door.

The sight of what's on the doorstep stops me in my tracks.

A small hamper of muffins, covered in plastic wrapper and tied with a pink bow. I look at Dad, who steps right over them and unlocks the front door. His movement makes me question my eyesight. Have I imagined them? 'Dad! What are you doing?' Shocked, I look around behind me but nobody's there.

Dad winks at me before closing the door in my face.

I reach for the envelope that is taped to the plastic and with trembling fingers slide the card out. *Thank you . . .*

'I'm sorry, Joyce.' I hear a voice behind me. I twirl round.

There he is, standing at the garden gate, a bouquet of flowers in his hands, the sorriest look on his face. He is a vision; he takes my breath away with one look, his proximity to me almost too much to bear.

'Justin . . .' Then I'm utterly speechless.

'Do you think,' he takes a step forward, 'you could find it in your heart to forgive a fool like me?' He stands at the end of the garden.

I'm unsure what to say. It's been a month. Why now?

'On the phone, you hit a sore point,' he says, clearing his throat. 'Nobody knows that about my dad. I don't know how you did.'

'I told you how.'

'I don't understand it.'

'Neither do I.'

'But then I don't understand most ordinary things that happen every day. I don't understand what my daughter sees in her boyfriend. I don't understand how my brother has defied the laws of science by not turning into an actual potato chip. I don't know how Doris can open the milk carton with such long nails. I don't understand why I didn't beat down your door a month ago and tell you how I felt . . .'

I take in the sight of his face, his curly hair covered by a woolly hat, his small nervous smile. He studies me back and I shiver, but not from the cold. I don't feel it now. The world has been heated up for me.

Frown lines appear on his forehead as he looks at me.

'What?'

'Nothing. You just remind me so much of somebody right now. It's not important.' He clears his throat, smiles.

'Eloise Parker,' I guess, and his grin fades.

'How the hell do you know that?'

'She was your next-door neighbour who you had a crush on for years. When you were five years old you picked flowers from your front yard and brought them to her house. She opened the door before you got up the path and stepped outside wearing a blue coat and a black scarf,' I say, pulling my blue coat round me tighter.

'Then what?' he asks, shocked.

I shrug. 'You dropped them on the ground and chickened out.'

He shakes his head softly and smiles. 'How on earth . . .?' He narrows his eyes. 'What else do you know about Eloise Parker?'

I smile and look away. 'You lost your virginity to her when you were sixteen, in her bedroom when her mom and dad were away.'

He rolls his eyes and lowers the bouquet so that it faces the ground. 'Now you see, *that* is not fair. You are not allowed to know stuff like that about me.'

I laugh.

'You were christened Joyce Bridget Conway but you tell everyone your middle name is Angeline,' he retaliates.

My mouth falls open.

'You had a dog called Bunny when you were a kid.' He lifts an eyebrow, cockily.

I narrow my eyes.

'You got drunk on poteen when you were,' he closes his eyes and thinks hard, 'fifteen. With your friends Kate and Frankie.'

He takes a step closer to me with each piece of knowledge and that smell, the smell of him I've dreamed of being near gets closer and closer.

'Your first French kiss was with Jason Hardy when you were ten. You're not the only one who's allowed to know stuff.' He takes a step closer and can't move any nearer now.

My heart takes out a trampoline and enrols in a marathon session of leaping. I hope Justin doesn't hear it whooping with joy.

'Who told you all of that?'

'Getting me here was a big operation,' he smiles. 'Big. Your friends had me run through a series of tests to prove I was sorry enough to be deemed worthy of coming here.'

I laugh, shocked that Frankie and Kate could finally agree on something. Silence. We are so close, if I look up at him my nose will touch his chin. I keep looking down.

'You're still afraid to sleep in the dark,' he whispers, taking my chin in his hand and lifting it so that I can look nowhere else but at him.

'Unless somebody's with you,' he adds with a small smile.

'You cheated on your first college paper,' I whisper.

'You used to hate art.' He kisses my forehead.

'You lie when you say you're a fan of the *Mona Lisa*.' I close my eyes.

'You had an invisible friend named Horatio until you were five.' He kisses my nose and I'm about to retaliate but his lips touch mine so softly, the words give up, fainting before they reach my voice box.

I am faintly aware of Fran exiting her house and saying something to me, but everything is blurred in the distance as I get lost in the moment with Justin, as I create a new memory for him, for me.

'Forgive me?' he says as he pulls away.

'I have no choice but to. It's in my blood,' I smile. I look down at the flowers in his hands, which have been crushed between us. 'Are you going to drop these on the ground too and chicken out?'

'Actually, they're not for you.' His cheeks redden even more. 'They're for somebody at the blood clinic whom I really need to apologise to. I was hoping you would come with me, help explain the reason for my crazy behaviour, and maybe she could explain a few things to us in turn.'

I look back to the house and see Dad spying at us from behind the curtain. He gives me the thumbs up and my eyes fill.

'He was in on this too?'

'He called me a worthless silly sod.' He makes a face and I laugh.

I blow Dad a kiss as I begin slowly to walk away. I feel him watching me, and feel Mum's eyes on me too, as I walk down the garden path, cut across the grass and follow the desire line I had created as a little girl, out onto the pavement leading away from the house I grew up in.

Though this time, I'm not alone.

Cecelia Ahern

Profile

Born: September 30, 1981, Dublin
Likes: her gorgeous new twin nephews
Dislikes: the yellow line at airport baggage carousels that no one stands behind
Best advice: anything her mum tells her

As I walked through a gloriously sunny Covent Garden on my way to meet Cecelia Ahern, I was amazed to see the paparazzi camped outside the elegant hotel where she was staying. Were they there to photograph Cecelia? I wondered. 'Wouldn't that be grand,' she laughed moments later, as we chatted. 'I'm hoping it means that George Clooney is staying in the hotel as his latest film premiered in London last night. He'd be a sight for sore eyes over breakfast now, wouldn't he?' Cecelia Ahern has such a warm, delightful personality that within a few minutes you feel as though you've known her for ages.

Since the publication of her first novel, *PS, I Love You*, Cecelia has gone from one success to another. *Thanks for the Memories* is her fifth best seller and *PS, I Love You* has been made into a film. She has also co-written an award-winning American TV series called *Samantha Who?*, about a woman with amnesia. 'I can hardly believe it all,' Cecelia admits. 'From the moment they started filming *PS, I Love You*, I began searching for a dress for the premiere. In the end I had one made, but then the day before I saw *the* perfect dress and that's what I wore in the end. It was a fantastic night—do you know there are *three* red carpets that snake up and down, which you have to walk along, smiling for the cameras!'

Cecelia is at her happiest when she is writing, usually in

the kitchen of her Dublin home, but she also loves to encourage young readers. Her novels are all very different but centre on a woman whose life has hit rock bottom, and who must begin a new journey. 'I don't like them described as "fairy tales",' Cecelia told me. 'In fairy tales women are saved by men, but the women in my stories save themselves.'

So has Cecelia ever donated blood, like Justin Hitchcock in *Thanks for the Memories*? 'Not yet. But it's something I really want to do. So I will. I promise.'

Jane Eastgate

THE CHOICE
Nicholas Sparks

Travis Parker has all that a man could want: a good job, loyal friends, even a waterfront home in small-town North Carolina. In short, he's living the good life—boating, swimming and regular barbecues with his good-natured buddies and their families— and is convinced that a serious relationship would only cramp his style. Until a gorgeous young woman moves in next door . . .

PROLOGUE

February 2007

STORIES ARE AS UNIQUE as the people who tell them, and the best stories are those in which the ending is a surprise. At least, that's what Travis Parker recalled his dad telling him when he was a child. Travis remembered the way his dad would sit on the bed, his mouth curling into a smile as Travis begged for a story. 'What kind of story do you want?' his dad would ask.

'The best one ever,' Travis would answer.

Usually, his dad would sit quietly for a few moments, and then he'd put his arm around Travis and launch into a story that often kept Travis awake long after his dad had turned out the lights. There was always adventure and danger and excitement and journeys that took place in and around the small coastal town of Beaufort, North Carolina, the place Travis Parker grew up in and still called home. Strangely, most of them included bears. Grizzly bears, brown bears, Kodiak bears . . . his dad wasn't a stickler for detail when it came to a bear's natural habitat. He focused on hair-raising chase scenes through the sandy lowlands, giving Travis nightmares about crazed polar bears on Shackleford Banks until he was well into middle school. Yet no matter how frightened the stories had made him, he would inevitably ask, 'What happened next?'

To Travis, those days seemed like the innocent vestiges of another era. He was forty-three now and, as he parked his car in the parking lot of Carteret General Hospital, where his wife had worked for the past ten years, he thought again about the words he'd always said to his father.

After stepping out of the car, he reached for the flowers he'd brought. The last time he and his wife had spoken, they'd had an argument and, more than anything, he wanted to take back his words and make amends. He was under no illusions that the flowers would make things better between them, but he wasn't sure what else to do. It went without saying that he felt guilty about what had happened, but married friends had assured him that guilt was the cornerstone of any good marriage. 'Everyone makes mistakes,' they'd said, and though he'd nodded as if he believed them, he knew they would never understand what he was going through. They couldn't. After all, their wives were still sleeping beside them every night; none of them had ever been separated for three months, none of them wondered whether their marriage would ever return to what it once had been.

As he crossed the parking lot, he thought about both of his daughters, his job, his wife. At the moment, none of them gave him much comfort. He felt as though he was failing in practically every area of his life. Lately, happiness seemed as distant and unattainable to him as space travel. He hadn't always felt this way. There had been a long period during which he remembered being very happy. But things change. People change. Mistakes are made, regrets form, and all that's left are repercussions.

Shaking his head, he approached the hospital, picturing himself as a child listening to his father's stories. His own life had been the best story ever, he mused, the kind of story that should have ended on a happy note. As he reached for the door, he felt the familiar rush of memory and regret.

Only later, after he let the memories overtake him once again, would he allow himself to wonder what would happen next.

PART ONE
One

May 1996

'THIS IS RIDICULOUS. Tell me again why I agreed to help you with this.' Matt, red-faced and grunting, continued to push the spa towards the recently cut square at the far edge of the deck. His feet slipped, and he could feel sweat pouring from his forehead into his eyes, making them sting. It was hot, way too hot for early May. Even Travis's dog,

Moby, was hiding in the shade and panting, his tongue hanging out.

Travis Parker, who was pushing the massive box alongside him, managed to shrug. 'Because you thought it would be fun,' he said. He lowered his shoulder and shoved; the spa, which must have weighed 400 pounds, moved another couple of inches. At this rate, it should be in place, oh . . . sometime next week.

'This is ridiculous,' Matt said, heaving his weight into the box, thinking that what they really needed was a team of mules. His back was killing him.

'You've already said that.'

'And it isn't fun,' Matt grunted.

'You said that, too.'

'And it isn't going to be easy to install.'

'Sure it is,' Travis said. He stood and pointed to the lettering on the box. 'See? It says right here, EASY TO INSTALL.'

From his spot beneath the tree, Moby, a purebred boxer, barked in agreement, and Travis smiled, looking way too pleased with himself.

Matt scowled, trying to catch his breath.

'As I recall, you said Joe and Laird would be here to help us with your "little project" and that Megan and Allison would cook some burgers, and we'd have beer.'

'They're coming,' Travis said.

'You said that four hours ago.'

'They must be running a little late.'

'*Uh-huh,*' Matt answered.

He was scowling again. It was Saturday—Saturday! His day of recreation and relaxation, his chance to escape from the grindstone, the break he earned after five days at the bank, the kind of day he *needed*. He was a loan officer, for God's sake! He was supposed to push paper, not hot tubs! He could have been golfing! He could have gone to the beach!

He paused. Who was he kidding? Had he not been here, he would have spent the day with Liz's parents, which was the main reason he'd agreed to Travis's request in the first place. But that wasn't the point. He lowered his shoulder, feeling bitter.

'This isn't fun, you know?'

Travis winked. 'You said that already, remember?'

'**W**ow!' Joe commented, lifting an eyebrow as he walked the perimeter of the hot tub. By then, the sun was beginning its descent, streams of gold reflecting off the bay. In the distance, a heron broke from the trees and gracefully skimmed the surface. Joe and Megan, along with Laird and Allison, had arrived with kids in tow, and Travis was showing them around. 'This looks great! You two did all of this today?'

Travis nodded, holding his beer. 'It wasn't so bad,' he said. 'I think Matt even enjoyed it.'

Joe glanced at Matt, who lay flattened in a lawn chair off to the side of the deck, a cold rag over his head. Even his belly—Matt had always been on the podgy side—seemed to sag.

'I can see that.'

'Was it heavy?'

'Like an Egyptian sarcophagus!' Matt croaked. 'One of those gold ones that only cranes can move.'

Joe laughed. 'Can the kids get in?'

'Not yet. I just filled it, and the water will take a little while to heat up. The sun will help, though.'

'The sun will heat it within minutes,' Matt moaned. 'Within seconds!'

Joe grinned. He, Laird, Travis and Matt had been at school together since kindergarten. 'Tough day, Matt?'

Matt removed the rag and scowled at Joe. 'You have no idea. And thanks for showing up on time.'

'Travis said to be here at five. If I had known you needed help, I would have come earlier.'

Matt slowly shifted his gaze to Travis.

'How's Tina doing?' Travis said, changing the subject. 'Is Megan getting any sleep?'

Megan was chatting with Allison at the table on the far end of the deck, and Joe glanced briefly in her direction. 'Some. Tina's cough is gone, and she's been able to sleep through the night again. But I think Megan's no longer wired to sleep since she became a mom.' He turned to Matt. 'Where's Liz?' he asked.

'She should be here any minute,' Matt answered. 'She spent the day with her parents.'

'Lovely,' Joe commented.

'Be nice. They're good people.'

'I seem to recall you saying that if you had to sit through one more of your father-in-law's stories about his prostate cancer or listen to your mother-in-law fret about Henry getting fired again, you were going to stick your head in the oven.'

Matt struggled to sit up. 'I never said that!'

'Yes, you did.' Joe winked as Matt's wife, Liz, rounded the corner of the house with Ben toddling just in front of her. 'But don't worry. I won't say a word.'

Matt's eyes darted nervously from Liz to Joe and back again, checking to see if she'd heard.

'Hey, y'all!' Liz called out with a friendly wave, leading little Ben by the hand. She made a beeline for Megan and Allison. Ben broke away and toddled towards the other kids in the yard.

Joe saw Matt sigh in relief. He grinned and lowered his voice. 'So . . . Matt's in-laws. Is that how you conned him into coming here?'

'I might have mentioned it,' Travis smirked.

Joe laughed.

'What are you guys saying?' Matt called out suspiciously.

'Nothing,' they said in unison.

Later, with the sun down and the food eaten, Travis listened to the sound of the kids splashing away in the spa and felt a wave of satisfaction wash over him. This was his favourite kind of evening, whiled away to the sound of shared laughter and familiar banter. One minute Allison was talking to Joe; the next minute she was chatting with Liz and then Laird or Matt, and so on for everyone seated around the outdoor table. No pretences, no attempts to impress, no one trying to show anyone up. His life, he sometimes thought, resembled a beer commercial, and, for the most part, he was content simply to ride the current of good feeling.

Travis looked around the table, pleased that his childhood friends were still a part of his life. It didn't always turn out that way. At thirty-two, he knew that life was sometimes unpredictable. What were the odds that the four of them would find themselves in their early thirties still spending weekends together? Pretty small, he thought. But somehow, after heading off to four different colleges with differing career goals, they had each moved back here to Beaufort. They were more like family than friends.

And, miraculously, the wives got along, too. Laird had been the first to marry—he and Allison had tied the knot the summer after they graduated from Wake Forest. Joe and Megan walked down the aisle a year later after falling in love during their senior year at North Carolina. Matt, who'd gone to Duke, met Liz here in Beaufort, and they were married a year after that. Travis had been the best man at all three weddings.

Some things had changed, of course, largely because of the new additions to the families. Laird wasn't always available to go mountain biking. Joe couldn't join Travis on the spur of the moment to go skiing in Colorado as he used to, and Matt had all but given up trying to keep up with him on most things. But that was OK. They were all still available enough, and among the three of them—and with enough planning—he was still able to make the most of his weekends.

Lost in thought, Travis hadn't realised that the conversation had lapsed. 'Did I miss something?' he asked.

'I asked if you'd talked to Monica lately,' Megan said, her tone letting Travis know he was in trouble. All six of them, he thought, took a bit too much interest in his love life. The trouble with married people was that they seemed to believe that everyone they knew should get married, too.

'Not recently,' he said.

'Why not? She's nice.'

'She broke up with me, remember?'

'So? It doesn't mean she doesn't want you to call.'

'I thought that's exactly what it meant.'

Megan, along with Allison and Liz, stared at him as if he were just plain dense. The guys, as usual, seemed to be enjoying this.

Megan leant back in her chair. 'I think you have commitment issues. What's the longest you've ever dated someone? Two months? Four months?'

Travis pondered the question. 'I guess I'd have to say . . . I can't remember.'

'In other words, not long enough to remember?'

'What can I say? I've yet to meet any woman who could measure up to any of you.'

He could tell she was pleased by his words. He'd learned long ago that flattery was his best defence at moments like these, especially since it was sincere. Megan, Liz and Allison were terrific. All heart and loyalty and generous common sense.

'Well, I'm just saying that I think you should give her a call,' she persisted.

'I'll think about it,' he said, knowing he wouldn't. He rose from the table, angling for an escape. 'Anyone need another beer?'

When little Josie had her second temper tantrum at a little before nine, Allison scooped her into her arms and gave Laird *the look*, the one that said it was time to go so that they could get the kids in bed. Laird didn't bother arguing, and when he stood up from the table, Megan glanced at Joe, Liz nodded at Matt, and Travis knew the evening was at an end. Parents might believe themselves to be the bosses, but in the end it was the kids who made the rules.

Megan, Joe and Liz rose and started to clean up the table, but Travis waved them off.

'I'll get it in a while. No big deal.'

When they were gone, he wandered over to the stereo, sorted through the CDs, and chose *Tattoo You* by the Rolling Stones, then cranked up the volume. He pulled out another beer on his way back to his chair. He then sat down, threw his feet up on the table, and leant back. Moby sat beside him.

'Just you and me for a while,' he said. He had a sneaking suspicion that Stephanie, his younger sister, might swing by later. She was coming in from Chapel Hill, where she was working towards a master's degree in biochemistry. Though she would stay at their parents' place, she was usually wired after the drive and in the mood to talk, and their parents would already be in bed.

Travis stared out over the water. Beside him, Moby whined. 'You want to go get your ball?' Travis finally said.

Moby stood up so quickly, he almost knocked over the chair.

It was the music, she thought, that proved to be the clincher in what had already been one of the most miserable weeks of her life. Loud music. OK, nine o'clock on a Saturday night wasn't so bad, especially since he obviously had company. But eleven o'clock? When he was alone and playing fetch with his dog?

From her back deck, she could see him just sitting there, in the same shorts he'd worn all day, feet on the table, tossing the ball and staring at the creek. What on earth could he be thinking?

Maybe she shouldn't be so hard on him. It was his house, right? King of the castle and all that. He could do what he wanted. But that wasn't the problem. The problem was that he had neighbours, including her, and she had a castle, too, and neighbours were supposed to be considerate. And truth be told, he'd crossed the line. Not just because of the music. In all honesty, she liked the music he was listening to and usually didn't really care how loud or how long he played it. The problem was with his dog, Nobby, or whatever he called him. More specifically, what his dog had done to her dog.

Molly, she was certain, was pregnant.

Molly, her beautiful, sweet, purebred collie—the first thing she'd bought herself after finishing her physician assistant rotations at the Eastern Virginia School of Medicine—had noticeably gained weight during the past couple of weeks. And her nipples seemed to be growing. Add it up, and Molly was definitely on her way to birthing a litter of puppies that no one on earth was ever going to want. A boxer and a collie? She scrunched up her face as she tried to imagine how the puppies would look.

It had to be that man's dog. When Molly was in heat, that dog had staked out her house like a private detective, and he was the only dog she'd seen wandering around the neighbourhood in weeks. But would her neighbour even consider fencing his yard? No. His motto seemed to be 'My dog shall be free!' It didn't surprise her. He seemed to live his own life by the same irresponsible motto. On her way to work, she saw him running, and when she got back, he was out biking or kayaking or in-line skating or shooting baskets in his front drive with a group of neighbourhood kids. God forbid the man should work a minute of overtime, and she knew that he didn't work at all on Fridays. And what kind of job let you head off every day wearing jeans and a T-shirt? She suspected it more than likely required an apron and name tag.

OK, maybe she wasn't being entirely fair. He was probably a nice guy. His friends—who appeared normal enough and had kids to boot— seemed to enjoy his company and were over there all the time. But what about those puppies? Gabby felt anxious at the thought of the future. What if no one wanted them? She couldn't imagine taking them to the pound. She wasn't going to have them murdered.

This wasn't what she'd dreamt about when she'd first seen the house earlier this year. Even though it wasn't in Morehead City, where her boyfriend, Kevin, lived, it was just minutes across the bridge. It was small and almost half a century old and a definite fixer-upper by Beaufort standards, but the view along the creek was spectacular. The yard was big enough for Molly to run in, and, best of all, she could afford it. Just barely, what with all the loans she'd taken out for PA school. But loan officers were pretty understanding when it came to making loans to people like her. Professional, educated people.

Not like Mr My-Dog-Shall-Be-Free and I-Don't-Work-Fridays.

She drew a deep breath, reminding herself that the man might be a nice guy. He always waved to her whenever he saw her pulling in from work, and she vaguely remembered that he'd dropped off a basket of cheese and wine to welcome her to the neighbourhood when she'd moved in a couple of months back. She hadn't been home, but he'd left it on the porch, and she'd promised herself that she'd send a thankyou note, one that she never quite got around to writing.

Her face scrunched up again. OK, she wasn't perfect, either, but this wasn't about a forgotten thankyou note. This was about Molly and that man's wandering dog, and now was as good a time as any for them to discuss the situation.

She stepped off the back deck and started towards the tall row of hedges that separated his house from hers. Part of her wished Kevin were with her, but that wasn't going to happen. Not after their spat this morning, which started after she'd casually mentioned that her cousin was getting married. Kevin, buried in the sports section of the news-paper, hadn't said a word in response, preferring to act as if he hadn't heard her. Anything about marriage made the man go as silent as a stone, especially lately. She supposed that she shouldn't have been surprised—they'd been dating almost four years (a year less than her cousin, she was tempted to point out), and if she'd learned one thing about him, it was that if Kevin found a topic uncomfortable, then more than likely he wouldn't say anything at all.

But Kevin wasn't the problem. Nor was the fact that lately she felt as though her life weren't quite what she'd imagined it would be. And it wasn't the terrible week at the office, either, one in which she'd been puked on three—*three!*—times on Friday alone, which was an all-time record, at least according to the nurses, who didn't bother to hide their smirks. Nor was she angry about Adrian Melton, the married doctor at her office who liked to touch her whenever they spoke, his hand lingering just a bit too long for comfort. And she surely wasn't angry at the fact that through it all, she hadn't once stood up for herself.

No siree, this had to do with Mr Party being a responsible neighbour, one who was going to own up to the fact that he had as much of a duty to find a solution to their problem as she did.

As Gabby marched through the grass, the dew moistened the tips of her toes through her sandals. Trying to figure out exactly where to begin, she barely noticed. Courtesy dictated that she head first to the front door and knock, but, with the music blaring, she doubted he'd even be able to hear it. Besides, she wanted to get this over with while she was still worked up and willing to confront him head-on.

Up ahead, she spotted an opening in the hedges and headed towards it. It was probably the same one that Nobby snuck through to take advantage of poor, sweet Molly. Her heart squeezed again, and this time she tried to hold on to the feeling. This was important. Very important.

Focused as she was on her mission, she didn't notice the tennis ball flying towards her as she emerged from the opening. She did, however, distantly register the sound of the dog galloping towards her a second before she was bowled over and hit the ground.

As she lay on her back, Gabby noted dully that there were way too many stars in a too-bright, out-of-focus sky. For a moment, she wondered why she couldn't draw breath, then quickly became more concerned with the pain that was coursing through her. All she could do was lie on the grass and blink with every throb.

From somewhere far away, she heard a jumble of sounds, and the world slowly started coming back into focus. She tried to concentrate and realised she was hearing voices. Or, rather, a single voice. It seemed to be asking if she was OK.

At the same time, she gradually became conscious of a succession of warm, smelly breezes on her cheek. She blinked once more, turned her head slightly and was confronted with an enormous, furry, square head. Nobby, she concluded fuzzily.

'Ahhhh . . .' she whimpered, trying to sit up. As she moved, the dog licked her face.

'Moby! Down!' the voice said, sounding closer. 'Are you OK? Maybe you shouldn't try to get up yet.'

'I'm OK,' she said, finally raising herself into a seated position. She took a couple of deep breaths, still feeling dizzy. Wow, she thought, that hurt. In the darkness, she sensed someone squatting beside her.

'I'm really sorry,' the voice said.

'What happened?'

'Moby accidentally knocked you down. He was going after a ball.'

'Who's Moby?'

'My dog.'

'Then who's Nobby?'

'What?'

She brought a hand to her temple. 'Never mind.'

'Are you sure you're OK?'

'Yeah,' she said, still dizzy but feeling the pain subside to a low throb. As she began to rise, she felt her neighbour place his hand on her arm, helping her up.

'Some welcome, huh?' he asked.

His voice still sounded far away, but she knew it wasn't, and when she faced him, she found herself focusing up at someone at least six inches taller than her own five foot seven. She wasn't used to that, and as she tilted her head upwards, she noticed his angled cheekbones, wavy brown hair and gleaming white teeth. Up close, he was good-looking—really good-looking—but she suspected that he knew it as well. Lost in thought, she opened her mouth to say something, then closed it again, realising she'd forgotten the question.

'I mean, here you are, coming over to visit, and you get slammed by my dog,' he went on. 'Like I said, I'm really sorry. Usually he pays a bit more attention. Say hey, Moby.'

The dog was sitting on his haunches, acting pleased as punch, and with that, she suddenly remembered the purpose of her visit. Beside her, Moby raised a paw in greeting. It was cute, but she wasn't about to fall for it. This was the mutt who'd not only tackled her, but ruined Molly as well. He probably should have been named Mugger. Or better yet, Pervert.

'You sure you're OK?'

The way he asked made her realise that this wasn't the sort of confrontation she'd wanted, and she tried to summon the feeling she'd had on her way over.

'I'm fine,' she said, her tone sharp.

For an awkward moment, they eyed each other without speaking.

Finally he motioned over his shoulder with his thumb. 'Would you like to sit on the deck? I'm just listening to some music.'

'Why do you think I want to sit on the deck?' she snapped.

He hesitated. 'Because you were coming over?'

Oh, yeah, she thought. That.

She held up her hands, impatient to get this over with. 'I came over here because I wanted to talk to you . . .'

She broke off when he slapped at his arm. 'Me, too,' he said before she could get started again. 'I've been meaning to drop by to welcome you to the neighbourhood. Did you get my basket?'

She heard a buzzing near her ear and waved at it. 'Yes. Thank you for that,' she said, slightly distracted. 'But what I wanted to talk about . . .'

She trailed off when she realised he wasn't paying attention. Instead, he was fanning the air between them. 'You sure you don't want to head to the deck?' he pressed. 'The mosquitoes are vicious around the bushes here.'

'Fine,' she relented. 'We can talk on the deck.'

A moment later, they were in the clear, moving quickly. 'I hate mosquitoes, which is why I've got some citronella candles going on the table. That's usually enough to keep them away. They get much worse later in the summer.' He left just enough space between them so they wouldn't accidentally bump. 'I don't think we've formally met, by the way. I'm Travis Parker.'

She felt a flicker of uncertainty. She wasn't here to be his buddy, but expectation and manners prevailed. 'I'm Gabby Holland.'

'Nice to meet you.'

'Yeah,' she said. She made a point of crossing her arms as she said it, then subconsciously brought a hand to the dull ache at her ribs.

Staring at her profile, Travis could tell that she was angry. Somehow he knew the anger was directed at him, though he had no idea why. Aside from being tackled by the dog, that is. But that wasn't quite it, he decided. He remembered the expressions that his kid sister, Stephanie, was famous for, ones that signalled a slow build-up of resentment over time, and that's how Gabby seemed to be acting now. As if she'd worked herself up to this. But there the similarities with his sister ended. While Stephanie had grown up to become a certifiable beauty, Gabby was attractive in a similar but not quite perfect kind of way. Her blue eyes were a little too wide set, her nose was just a bit too big, and red hair was always hard to pull off, but somehow these imperfections lent an air of vulnerability to her natural good looks.

In the silence, Gabby tried to collect her thoughts. 'I was coming over because I wanted to talk to you.'

'Hold on,' he said as they reached the deck. 'Before you begin, why don't you sit down?' Dropping into his chair, Travis leant back and put his feet on the table.

'I'd rather remain standing, thank you.'

Travis squinted and shaded his eyes with his hands.

'But I can barely see you,' he said. 'The porch lights are shining behind you.'

She threw up her hands in exasperation. 'Fine!' she said. She pulled out a chair and took a seat. 'I came over because I wanted to talk to you . . .' she began.

He raised his eyebrows. 'You've already said that.'

'I know!' she said. 'I've been trying to tell you, but you haven't let me finish!'

He saw her glare at him, but he still had no idea what she was so wound up about. After a second, she began to speak, a bit hesitantly at first, and then the words came more quickly. She talked about how she'd found the house and how excited she'd been, and how owning a home had been her dream for a long time, before the topic wandered to Molly and how Molly's nipples were getting bigger. At first, Travis had no idea who Molly was—which lent that part of the monologue a surreal quality. But he gradually realised that she was Gabby's collie. After that, she began talking about ugly puppies and murder, but it made little sense until she started gesturing at Moby. Then it dawned on him that she believed Moby was responsible for Molly getting pregnant.

He wanted to tell her that it wasn't Moby, but she was on such a roll, he thought it best to let her finish. By that point, her story had veered back on itself. Bits and pieces of her life continued to come tumbling out, little snippets that sounded unrehearsed and unconnected, along with bursts of anger randomly directed his way.

A few times, she paused, and in those moments, he tried to respond. But that didn't work, either, because she immediately overrode him. Instead, he listened and—at least in those moments when she wasn't insulting him or his dog—sensed a trace of desperation, even a little confusion, as to what was happening in her life. He felt a surge of compassion for her, and when her tirade finally wound down, he thought he saw tears. He rose quickly, grabbed a few napkins from near the grill, and brought them to her. He offered her one, and she wiped the corner of her eyes. Now that she'd calmed down, he noted she was even prettier than he'd first realised.

She drew a shaky breath. 'The question is, what are you going to do?' she finally asked.

He hesitated. 'Let's start at the beginning. Are you really sure Molly's pregnant?'

'Of course I'm sure! Didn't you hear a word I said?'

'Have you had her checked by a vet?'

'I'm a physician assistant. I know when someone's pregnant.'

'With people, I'm sure you do. But with dogs, it's different.'

'How would you know?'

'I've had a lot of experience with dogs. Actually, I—'

Yeah, I'll bet, she thought, cutting him off with a wave. 'She's moving slower and her nipples are swollen. What else could it be?'

'What if she has an infection? That would cause swelling.'

Gabby opened her mouth to speak, then closed it when she realised that she hadn't thought of that. An infection *could* cause swelling in the nipples—mastitis or something like that. However, it wasn't one or two nipples, it was all of them. 'She's going to have puppies. And you're going to have to help me find homes for them, since I'm not taking them to the pound.'

'I'm sure it wasn't Moby.'

'I knew you were going to say that.'

'But you should know—'

She shook her head furiously and stood. 'You're going to have to take some responsibility here. And I hope you realise it's not going to be easy to find homes for them.'

'But—'

'What on earth was that about?' Stephanie asked.

Gabby had disappeared into the hedge; a few seconds later, he'd seen her enter her home through the sliding-glass door. He was still sitting at the table, feeling slightly shell-shocked, when he spotted his sister approaching.

'How long have you been here?'

'Long enough,' she said. She saw the cooler near the door and pulled out a beer. 'Still charming the girlfriends, I see.'

'She's not my girlfriend. She's my neighbour. Actually, that's the first time I've ever met her.'

'Impressive,' Stephanie observed, taking a seat.

'What?'

'You know—making someone hate you so quickly. That's a rare gift. Usually you have to know a person better first.'

'Very funny.'

'I thought so. And Moby . . .' She turned towards the dog and lifted a scolding finger. 'You should know better.'

'It's not Moby's fault.'

'So you said. Not that she wanted to hear it, of course.' Stephanie leant back, evaluating her brother. 'She was kind of cute, don't you think?'

'I didn't notice.'

'Yeah, sure you didn't. I saw the way you were ogling her.'

'My, my. You're in quite a mood this evening.'

'I should be. The exam I just finished was a killer.'

'Poor baby. Life as a perpetual student is so much harder than actually earning a living.'

'Look who's talking? You were in school longer than me. Which reminds me . . . how do you think Mom and Dad would feel if I told them I wanted to stay in for another couple of years to get my PhD?'

At Gabby's house, the kitchen light flashed on. Distracted, Travis took a moment to answer.

'They'd probably be OK with it. You know Mom and Dad.'

'I know. But lately I get the feeling that they want me to meet someone and settle down.'

'Join the club. I've had that feeling for years.'

'Yeah, but it's different for me. I'm a woman. My biological clock is ticking.'

The kitchen light next door flashed off and another flashed on in the bedroom. He wondered if Gabby was turning in for the night.

'You've got to remember, Mom was married at twenty-one,' Stephanie went on. 'By twenty-three, she already had you.' She waited for a response but got nothing. 'But then again, look how well you turned out. Maybe I should use that as my argument.'

Her words filtered in slowly. 'Is that an insult?'

She smirked. 'Just checking to see if you're paying attention to me or whether you're thinking about your new friend over there.'

'She's not a friend,' he said.

'Not now,' his sister said. 'But I get the feeling she will be.'

Gabby wasn't sure how she felt after leaving her neighbour's. She closed her door and leant against it while she tried to regain her equilibrium.

Maybe she shouldn't have gone over there, she thought. It certainly hadn't done any good. Not only had he not apologised, he'd gone so far as to deny that his dog was responsible. Still, as she finally moved away from the door, she found herself smiling. At least she'd done it. She'd stood up for herself. She normally wasn't very good at speaking her mind. Not to Kevin about the fact that his plans for their future seemed to go only as far as the next weekend. Or to Dr Melton about the way she felt when he touched her. Not even to her mom, who always seemed to have opinions on how Gabby could improve herself.

She stopped smiling when she caught sight of Molly sleeping in the corner. A quick peek was enough to remind her that the end result hadn't changed. As she replayed the evening, she felt a wave of embarrassment. She knew she'd been rambling, but after being knocked down, she had lost her focus, and then her frustration had rendered her completely unable to stop talking. Her mother would have had a field day with that one. She loved her mother, but her mother was one of those ladies who never lost control. It drove Gabby crazy. More than once during her teenage years, she'd wanted to take her mother by the arms and shake her, just to elicit a spontaneous response. Of course, it wouldn't have worked. Her mother would simply have allowed the shaking to continue until Gabby was finished, then smoothed her hair and made some comment like: 'Well, Gabrielle, now that you've gotten that out of your system, can we discuss this like ladies?'

Ladies. Gabby couldn't stand that word. When her mother said it, she was often plagued by a sweeping sense of failure, one that made her think she had a long way to go and no map to get there.

Of course, her mother couldn't help the way she was any more than Gabby could. Her mother was a walking cliché of southern womanhood, having grown up wearing frilly dresses and being presented to the community's elite at the Savannah Christmas Cotillion, one of the most exclusive debutante balls in the country. She had also served as treasurer for the Tri Delts at the University of Georgia, another family tradition, though, while in college, academia was far less important to her than working towards a 'Mrs' degree, which she believed to be the only career choice for a proper southern lady. It went without saying that she wanted the 'Mr' part of the equation to be worthy of the family name. Which essentially meant rich.

Enter her father, a successful real estate developer and general contractor, who, if not as rich as some, was certainly well-off. Gabby used to wonder how two such different people could ever have fallen in love. While her mom loved the pheasant at the country club, Dad preferred biscuits and gravy at the local diner. But love each other they did—of this, Gabby had no doubt. Even now, when she visited, she would find her parents snuggled up on the couch together. She had to admit that, for whatever reason, they suited each other.

Much to her mother's endless disappointment, Gabby, unlike her three honey-blonde sisters, had always been more like her father. Even as a child, she preferred overalls to dresses, adored climbing trees, and spent hours playing in the dirt. After work, she and her dad would play catch or shoot baskets while her mom watched from the kitchen window disapprovingly. More often than not, her sisters could be seen standing beside her, their mouths agape.

While Gabby liked to tell people about the free spirit she'd been as a child, in reality, she'd ended up straddling both her parents' visions of the world, mainly because her mom was an expert when it came to the manipulative power of motherhood. Because of a raised eyebrow here and a little comment there, Gabby ended up in dance lessons and was formally presented at the Savannah Christmas Cotillion. If her mother was proud that night—and she was, by the look on her face—Gabby by that time felt as if she was finally ready to make her own decisions, some of which she knew her mother wouldn't approve of. Sure, she wanted to get married and have children someday, but, by then, she'd realised that she also wanted a career. More specifically, she wanted to be a doctor.

Oh, Mom said all the right things when she found out, but then the subtle guilt offensive began. Her mom would sometimes frown and wonder aloud whether it was possible to work full-time as a doctor and be a wife and mother. 'But if work is more important to you than family,' her mom would say, 'then by all means, become a doctor.'

Gabby tried to resist her mother's campaign, but, in the end, she settled on PA school instead of medical school. The reasons made sense. She'd still see patients, but her hours would be stable—definitely a more family-friendly option. She couldn't deny that family was important to her. That's the thing about being the product of happily married parents. You grow up thinking the fairy tale is real, and that you're entitled to live it. So far, though, it wasn't working out as planned. She and Kevin had dated long enough to fall in love, survive the ordinary ups and downs that break most couples apart, and even talk about the future. She had decided he was the one she wanted to spend her life with, and she frowned, thinking about their most recent argument.

As if sensing Gabby's distress, Molly struggled to her feet and waddled over. Gabby stroked her fur. 'I wonder if it's stress,' Gabby said. 'Do I seem stressed to you?'

Molly didn't answer, but she didn't have to. Gabby knew she was stressed. It didn't help that, aside from Kevin, she didn't have any friends here. She'd barely got to know anyone outside the office, and, truth be told, her neighbour was the first person she'd spoken to since she'd moved in. Thinking back, she supposed she could have been nicer about the whole thing, especially since he did seem like a friendly guy. And, once she'd started babbling, he hadn't interrupted her once, which was sort of refreshing, too.

It was remarkable now that she thought about it. Considering how crazy she must have sounded, he hadn't got upset or snapped at her. And then there had been a moment after he'd handed her the napkin that she'd caught him staring at her in a way that suggested he'd found her attractive as well. It had been a long time since something like that had happened, and it made her feel good about herself.

She went into the bedroom and slipped into a pair of sweat pants. Molly trailed behind her and Gabby motioned towards the door.

'You ready to go outside?' she asked.

Molly's tail started to wag as she moved towards the door. Gabby inspected her closely. She still looked pregnant, but maybe her neighbour had a point. She should take her to the vet, if only to be sure. She stepped onto the back deck and watched as Molly padded down the steps. The stars spread across the sky in random, intricate patterns that, aside from the Big Dipper, she'd never been able to discern, and she resolved that she'd buy a book on astronomy tomorrow, right after lunch. She'd spend a couple of days learning the basics, then invite Kevin to spend a romantic evening at the beach, where she'd point to the sky and ever so casually mention something astronomically impressive. And, tomorrow, she'd figure out what to do about Molly, too. She'd find homes for every one of those puppies.

But first, she'd take her to the vet.

Two

IT WAS SHAPING UP to be one of those days when Gabby wondered why she'd decided to work in a paediatric office. She'd had the chance, after all, of working in a cardiology unit at the hospital in her home town, which had been her plan all the way through PA school. She had loved assisting in challenging surgeries, and it had seemed like a perfect fit until her final rotation, when she had happened to work with a paediatrician who'd filled her head with ideas about the nobility and joy of caring for infants.

Despite the job offer in cardiology, she'd accepted a position with Drs Furman and Melton in Beaufort, North Carolina. Dr Furman struck her as oblivious, and Dr Melton struck her as a flirt, but it was an opportunity to be nearer to Kevin. For the most part, she loved working with the kids. It was the parents who drove her crazy, the neurotic, know-it-all parents who thought that since she wasn't technically a physician and was relatively young, she was little more than an overpaid nurse.

It was half past noon when she finished with her last patient of the morning. Clutching her bag, she made her way to her car, knowing she didn't have much time. Her next appointment was in forty-five minutes, but assuming she wasn't held up at the vet's, she would be OK. It was one of the nice things about living in a small town of fewer than four thousand people. Everything was only minutes away. While Morehead City—five times the size of Beaufort—was just across the bridge that spanned the Intracoastal Waterway, the short distance was enough to make this town feel distinct and isolated, like most of the towns 'down east', which was what the locals called this part of the state. ·

Beaufort was a pretty place, especially the historic district.

Wide streets, shady trees and a little more than a hundred restored homes occupied several blocks, eventually giving way to Front Street and a short boardwalk that overlooked the marina. Slips were occupied by leisure and working boats of every shape and size; a magnificent yacht worth millions might be docked next to a small crab boat on one side, with a lovingly maintained sailboat on the other. There were a couple of restaurants with gorgeous views, covered patios and picnic tables. On the opposite side of the street, there were real estate offices mingled with art shops and tourist traps.

A few minutes later, Gabby pulled into her driveway. Molly met her on the porch, took her time smelling the flowerbed until she took care of business, then hopped into the passenger seat.

The Down East Veterinary Clinic was only a couple of minutes away. The building in which it was housed—a rustic, weathered Victorian—looked less like an office than a home. The screen door opened with a loud squeak, and Gabby felt Molly tug at her leash as she approached the front desk. Before she could speak, the receptionist stood.

'Is this Molly?' she asked.

Gabby didn't bother to hide her surprise. Living in a small town still took some getting used to. 'Yeah. I'm Gabby Holland.'

'Nice to meet you. I'm Terri. We were wondering when you'd get here. You have to get back to work, right?' She grabbed a clipboard. 'Let me get you set up in a room. You can do the paperwork there. That way, the vet can see you right away.'

'Great,' Gabby said. 'I really appreciate it.'

The receptionist proceeded down the hallway to a small room furnished with a metal table and plastic chair and handed the clipboard to Gabby. 'Just fill that out and I'll let the doctor know you're here.'

Terri left them alone and Gabby took a seat, then filled out the paperwork while Molly wandered the room.

A few minutes later, the door opened, and the first thing Gabby noticed was the white smock; an instant later, she saw the name embroidered in blue. She was just about to speak, but sudden recognition made it impossible.

'Hi, Gabby,' Travis said. 'I take it this is Molly.' He squatted and rubbed Molly's neck. 'Hey, girl. How you feeling?'

'You're . . . you're the vet?' Gabby stammered.

Travis nodded as he continued to scratch Molly's neck. 'Along with my dad. He started the clinic and I joined him after I finished school.'

This couldn't be happening.

'Why didn't you say anything the other night?'

He looked up. 'You mean about me being the vet? I tried to tell you, but you wouldn't let me.'

'You should have said something anyway.'

'I don't think you were in any mood to hear it. But that's water under the bridge. No hard feelings.' He smiled. 'Let me check this girl out, OK? I know you have to get back to work, so I'll make this quick.'

She could feel her anger rising at his nonchalant 'No hard feelings'. Part of her wanted to leave right then. Unfortunately, he was already beginning to prod Molly's belly. Chagrined, she crossed her arms while he readied the stethoscope. He listened, moved the stethoscope, listened again, then examined her nipples. Finally, he slipped on a rubber glove with a snap and did a quick internal.

'Well, she's definitely pregnant,' he said, removing the glove and tossing it into the bin. 'From the look of things, she's about seven weeks along.'

'I told you.' She glared at him. And Moby is responsible, she refrained from adding.

Travis reached for the clipboard and flipped the page.

'Just so you know, Moby's not responsible.'

'Oh, no? What makes you so sure?'

He started making notes. 'Well, for one thing, he's been neutered.'

There are moments when mental overload can render words impossible. All at once, Gabby saw a mortifying montage of herself babbling and crying and finally storming off. She did have a vague memory of him trying to tell her something.

'Neutered?' she said.

'Uh-huh.' He looked up from the clipboard. 'Two years ago. My dad did it here in the office.'

'Oh . . .'

'I tried to tell you that, too. But you left before I had a chance. I felt bad about it, so I stopped by on Sunday to tell you, but you were out.'

It took some effort, but she uncrossed her arms. 'I guess I owe you an apology.'

'No hard feelings,' he said again. 'I know you're in a rush, so let me tell you a bit about Molly, OK? The gestation period lasts nine weeks, so you've got another two weeks. There's nothing you need to do, but keep in mind that she'll want a cool, dark place to have her puppies, so you might want to put some old blankets down in the garage. You have a door from the kitchen, right?'

She nodded, feeling as if she were shrinking.

'Just leave it open and she'll probably start wandering in there. We call it nesting and it's perfectly normal. Odds are she'll have the puppies when it's quiet, at night, or while you're at work. They know how to nurse right away, so you don't need to be concerned about that.'

She nodded again, feeling ever smaller.

'Other than that, there's not much more you need me to tell you. If there are any problems, you know where I live.'

She cleared her throat. 'OK.'

When she said nothing else, he smiled and began to move to the door. 'That's it. You can take her back home if you'd like.'

'Thanks,' Gabby mumbled. 'And again, I'm really sorry . . .'

He held up his hands. 'It's no problem. Really. You were upset, and Moby does wander the neighbourhood. It was an honest mistake. I'll see you around, OK?'

Once Travis—Dr Parker—left the examination room, Gabby waited for a long moment to be certain he was gone. Then she went to the receptionist's desk, where she quietly paid her bill. By the time she got back to work, the only thing Gabby knew for certain was that she'd never live down what she'd done, and it was in her best interests to avoid him for a while. Not for ever, of course. Something reasonable. Like the next fifty years.

Travis stood by the window, watching as Gabby led Molly back to the car. He was smiling to himself. Though he barely knew her, he'd seen enough to conclude that she was one of those people whose expressions were a window to their every feeling. It was a rare quality. He often felt that too many people lived their lives pretending. Gabby, he felt certain, would never be that way.

Pocketing his keys, he headed for his truck, with the promise that he'd be back from lunch in half an hour. He retrieved his cooler—he packed his lunch every morning—and drove to his usual spot. A year ago he'd purchased a plot of land overlooking Shackleford Banks Island at the end of Front Street, with the thought that one day he'd build his dream home there. The only problem was that he wasn't quite sure what that entailed. Part of him dreamt of throwing up a rustic little shack like the kind he'd seen in the Florida Keys, something with lots of character that appeared a hundred years old on the outside but was surprisingly bright and roomy on the inside. But then he'd reason that the lot was better suited to something more family-friendly. That rendered the image of his dream home fuzzier, since it no doubt included a future wife and kids, neither of which he was even close to imagining.

Sometimes, the way he and his sister had turned out struck him as strange, since she, too, was in no hurry to marry. Their parents had been married for almost thirty-five years, and Travis could no more picture either of them single than he could picture himself flapping his arms and zooming into the clouds. Sure, he'd heard the stories of how they'd met on a church group camping trip while they were in high school. One touch and 'Bing, bang, boom, just like that,' Dad would say, 'I knew she was the one for me.'

So far, there'd never been a 'bing, bang, boom' for Travis. Nothing even close. There had been girlfriends, of course. But the breakups were almost always mutual. He wasn't right for them, and they weren't right for him. He seldom thought about finding permanence or his soul mate, but in the rare times he did, he always imagined finding someone who shared the same active, outdoor passions he did. He wanted to experience life. No, change that. He *needed* to experience life.

He'd been that way for as long as he could remember. Growing up, Travis had been organised and capable when it came to school, but, more often than not, just as happy with a B instead of an A. School just didn't excite him the way riding his bike at breakneck speed or surfing in the Outer Banks did. He was an X Games kind of kid, even before there was such a thing, and by thirty-two, he'd pretty much done it all.

In the distance, he could see wild horses congregating near the dunes of Shackleford Banks and, as he watched them, he reached for his sandwich. Turkey on wheat with mustard, an apple and a bottle of water; he had the same thing every day, after the exact same breakfast of oatmeal, scrambled egg whites and a banana. As much as he craved the occasional adrenaline rush, his diet couldn't be more boring. He preferred plain and predictable to anything exotic, and over the years he had cut out the junk.

As he enjoyed his sandwich, he wondered at the direction of his thoughts. It wasn't like him. He wasn't usually prone to deep reflection. It had to be Gabby, he thought, though for the life of him, he couldn't understand why. He barely knew her, and he doubted whether he'd even had a chance to meet the real Gabby Holland yet. Still, he was glad she'd come by, if only to give them a chance to start over as neighbours. The last thing he wanted was for Gabby to feel any reason to avoid him. Maybe he'd invite her over the next time his friends visited.

Yeah, he thought, I'll do that. The decision made, he gathered his cooler and started back towards his truck. When he got in, he found himself wondering whether Gabby had ever gone surfing or snow-boarding, or if she would be up for either of them. As he started the engine, he tried to convince himself it didn't matter. Except for the fact that, somehow, it did.

Over the next two weeks, Gabby became an expert in making a covert entry and exit, at least when it came to her house.

She had no other choice. She'd made a fool of herself, and Travis had compounded the matter by being so forgiving, which obviously meant that coming and going required a new set of rules, one in which avoidance was Rule Number 1.

She'd had to learn Travis's schedule, of course. It wasn't hard—a quick peek at the clock when he was about to pull out in the morning while she watched from her kitchen. Returning home from work was even easier; he was usually out on the boat or the Jet Ski by the time she arrived, but, on the downside, that made evenings the worst. Because he was *out there,* she had to stay *in here,* no matter how glorious the sunset, and unless she went over to Kevin's, she'd find herself studying the astronomy book, the one she'd purchased in the hope of impressing Kevin while they did some stargazing. Which, unfortunately, hadn't happened yet.

She supposed she could have been more grown-up about it all, but the last thing she wanted was to make an even worse impression than she already had. Besides, she had other things on her mind.

Kevin, for one. Most evenings, he swung by for a little while, and he'd even stayed over last weekend after his customary round of golf. Kevin adored golf. And a couple of days ago, while sitting on the couch, he'd told her how much he loved her. By the way he was talking, she kind of got the impression that she should consider moving in with him. Which was good. It was the closest he'd come to talking about their future, but . . .

But what? Was living together a step towards the future or just a way to continue the present? Did she really need him to propose? She thought about it. Well . . . *yes*. But not until he was ready. Which led, of course, to the question that had begun to creep in whenever they were together: would he ever be ready?

Thinking about this gave her a headache. What she really wanted to do was to sit outside on the deck with a glass of wine and forget everything for a while. But Travis Parker was on his back deck, flicking through a magazine. So she was stuck inside on a Thursday night again.

She wished Kevin wasn't working late so they could do something together. She knew he was dedicated to building his business—but he was heading off to Myrtle Beach for a convention first thing in the morning, and she wouldn't have a chance to see him until next Wednesday. Kevin's dad had started one of the largest insurance brokerages in eastern North Carolina, and Kevin was taking on more responsibility at their office in Morehead City. His dad spent fewer than twenty hours a week in the office these days, which usually left Kevin working closer to sixty. And left her stuck inside on nights like this.

Maybe she should just head over to Atlantic Beach and watch the sun go down. She could take Molly. She got up from the couch and turned off the television. Molly wasn't around, and, guessing she was in the garage, she headed that way. The door was open, and when she walked in and turned on the light, the first thing she noticed was the collection of wiggling fur balls surrounding Molly. Gabby called out to her. A moment later, however, she began to scream.

Travis had just gone into the kitchen to pull a chicken breast from the refrigerator when he heard the sudden, frantic pounding on his door.

'Dr Parker? . . . Travis? . . . Are you in there?'

When he opened the door, Gabby's face was pale and terrified.

'You've got to come,' she gasped. 'Molly's in trouble.'

Travis reacted on instinct. As Gabby began racing back to her house, he retrieved a medical bag from behind the passenger seat in the truck. By then, Gabby had disappeared into the house. Travis followed a moment later and spotted her in the kitchen, near the open door that led to the garage.

'She's panting and vomiting,' she said as he hurried to her side. 'And . . . something's hanging out of her.' Travis took in the scene, instantly recognising the prolapsed uterus and hoping he wasn't too late.

'Let me wash my hands,' he said quickly. He scrubbed his hands briskly at the kitchen sink.

'Is she going to be OK?'

'I'll know in a couple of minutes how serious it is.' Holding up his hands like a surgeon, he nodded towards the bag on the floor. 'Could you bring that in for me? Just put it over there, as close to Molly as you can get, OK?'

'OK,' she said, trying not to panic.

Travis approached the dog carefully, noting with some relief that Molly was conscious. He focused on the tubular mass that protruded from her.

'What now?' Gabby asked.

'Just hold her and whisper to her. I need you to help keep her calm.'

When Gabby was in place, Travis squatted next to the dog. He gently checked the uterus and Molly twitched slightly.

'What's wrong with her?'

'It's a uterine prolapse. It means that part of the uterus has turned inside out, and it's protruding.' He felt the uterus, turning it gently to see if there were any ruptures. 'Reach into the bag,' he said. 'There should be some saline. And I'll need the lubricating jelly, too.'

'What are you going to do?'

'I need to clean the uterus, and then I'm just going to manipulate it a bit. I want to try to reduce it manually. If we're lucky, it'll contract back in on its own. If not, I'll have to bring her in for surgery.'

Gabby found the saline and the jelly and handed them over. She couldn't bear to watch, so she concentrated on Molly, while Travis worked quietly. She didn't know how long they were in the garage—it could have been ten minutes or it could have been an hour—but finally, she saw him lean back.

'Is it over?' she ventured. 'Is she all right?'

'Yes and no,' he said. 'Her uterus is back in place, and it seemed to contract without any problems, but she needs to go to the clinic for a couple of days while she gets her strength back. She'll need some antibiotics and fluids and an X-ray.'

'What about the puppies?'

'We'll take them. They need to be with their mamma.'

Gabby felt her shoulders relax. For the first time, she smiled. 'I don't know how to thank you,' she said.

'You just did.'

After cleaning up, Travis carefully loaded Molly into his truck while Gabby gathered up the puppies. Once all six were settled, Travis opened the driver's-side door and tossed his bag onto the front seat. 'I'll let you know how it goes,' he said.

'I'm coming.'

'It would be better if she got some rest, and if you're in the room that might not happen. Don't worry—I'll take good care of her. I'll be with her all night. You have my word on that.'

She hesitated. 'Are you sure?'

'She'll be fine. I promise.'

'I still think I should come with you.'

'Don't you have to work tomorrow?'

'Yes. But so do you.'

'True, but this is my job. It's what I do. And besides, I have a cot. If you came, you'd have to sleep on the floor.'

'You mean you wouldn't give me the cot?'

He climbed into the truck. 'I suppose I could if I had to,' he said, grinning. 'But I'm concerned about what your boyfriend would think if you and I spent the night together.'

'How did you know I have a boyfriend?'

He reached for the door. 'I didn't,' he said, sounding faintly disappointed. Then he smiled, recovering. 'Call me tomorrow, OK?'

'Yeah,' she relented. 'OK.'

Travis closed the door and she heard the engine rattle to a start. He leant out the window. 'Don't worry,' he said again. 'She's going to be fine.'

After he left, Gabby wandered to the bedroom and stood in front of the dressing table. Despite her exhaustion and unruly hair, she didn't look as bad as she feared. The thought pleased her, though she wasn't sure why. Unaccountably, she recalled the disappointment on Travis's face when she'd told him about her boyfriend, and she flushed. She'd certainly been wrong about Travis Parker, wrong about everything from the beginning. He'd been so steady during the emergency. It amazed her, but it was his job, after all, she reminded herself.

With that, she called Kevin, who was immediately sympathetic.

After finding his son crashed on the cot, and a dog in the recovery room, Max Parker listened as Travis explained what had happened. The old man filled two cups with coffee and brought them both to the table. 'Not bad for your first time,' Max said. With his white hair and bushy white eyebrows, he was the picture of a well-liked, small-town veterinarian.

'Have you ever treated a dog for it?'

'Never,' Max admitted. 'Treated a horse once, though. You know how rare it is. Molly seems to be doing fine now. She sat up and wagged her tail when I came in this morning. How late were you up with her?'

Travis sipped the coffee with gratitude. 'Most of the night. I wanted to make sure it didn't recur.'

'It usually doesn't,' he said. 'It's a good thing you were there. Have you called the owner yet?'

'No. But I will.' He wiped his face. 'Man, I'm exhausted.'

'Why don't you go get some sleep? I can handle things here, and I'll keep an eye on Molly.'

'I don't want to put you out.'

'You're not,' Max said with a grin. 'Don't you remember? You're not supposed to be here. It's Friday.'

A short time later, after checking in on Molly, Travis pulled into his driveway and got out of the car. He stretched his arms overhead, then headed over to Gabby's. He stepped onto her porch and was about to knock when he heard the sound of approaching footsteps and the door swung open. Gabby straightened, surprised to see him.

'Oh, hey,' she said. 'I was just thinking that I should call you.'

Though barefoot, she was dressed in slacks and an off-white blouse, her hair fastened loosely by an ivory clip. He noted again how attractive she was.

'Since I was on my way home, I thought I'd let you know in person. Molly's doing fine.'

'You're sure?'

He nodded. 'I did an X-ray, and I didn't see any indication of internal bleeding. Once she got some fluids in, she seemed to get her strength back. She could probably come home later today, but I'd like to keep her one more night, just to be safe. Actually, my dad will watch her for a while. I was up most of the night, so I'm going to bed, but I'll check on her myself later.'

'Can I see her?'

'Sure,' he said. 'The puppies are doing well, too, by the way. They're cute as bugs.'

She smiled. 'I just want to thank you again,' she said.

For an awkward beat, they faced each other silently.

'Would you like a cup of coffee?' she offered. 'I just brewed a pot.' She felt a mixture of relief and disappointment when he shook his head.

'No, thanks. I'd rather not be awake when I'm trying to sleep.'

She laughed. 'Funny.'

'I try,' he said. He turned to step off the porch.

Despite herself, Gabby called to him as he reached the yard. 'Before you go, could you tell me what time you think you'll be at the clinic? To check on Molly, I mean?'

'I'm not sure. How about you tell me what time you take lunch, and I'll meet you there.'

'A quarter to one?'

'I'll be there,' he promised. He took a couple of steps backwards. 'And, by the way, you look fantastic in that outfit,' he added.

What *on earth just happened?*

That pretty much summed up Gabby's mental state for the rest of the morning. It didn't matter whether she was doing a well-baby check (twice), diagnosing ear infections (four times), giving a vaccination (once) or recommending an X-ray (once); she felt herself operating on autopilot, only half-present, while another part was still back on the porch, wondering if Travis had actually been flirting with her and whether maybe, just maybe, she'd sort of liked it.

After finishing with her last patient, Gabby stuffed her stethoscope into the pocket of her lab coat and checked her watch. She had a few minutes until she had to leave. She ran a hand through her undisciplined curls, thinking she was definitely making too big a deal about it. It probably didn't mean anything. After all they'd gone through the night before, he'd become something like a friend—her first friend in a new town at the start of her new life. She liked the sound of that. She smiled at the thought before it gave way to a frown.

Then again, maybe it wasn't such a good idea. Being friendly with a neighbour was one thing, making friends with a flirty guy was something completely different. As innocent as the visit to the vet might be, it had a vaguely *unfaithful* feeling about it.

She hesitated. I'm going crazy, she thought.

She'd done nothing wrong. He hadn't, either. And nothing was going to come of their little flirtation, even if they were neighbours. She and Kevin had been a couple since their senior year at the University of North Carolina. After college, he commuted to her PA school in Norfolk to see her; she drove down to Morehead City to see him. They fought and made up, broke up and reunited. Through it all, he'd remained the laid-back, easy-going guy he always had been. Where she would worry, he would shrug; in her pessimistic moments, he remained unconcerned. That was why, she thought, they got along so well. They balanced each other. There would be no contest if the choice came down to Kevin or Travis, not even close.

Having reached clarity on the issue, she decided it didn't matter whether Travis was flirting. He could flirt all he wanted. She knew exactly what she wanted in her life.

She was sure of it.

Just as Travis had promised, Molly was much better. Her tail thumped with enthusiasm and, despite the presence of her puppies—most of which were sleeping and resembled furry little balls—she got up without a struggle when Gabby entered and trotted towards her before applying a few sloppy licks.

'I'm so glad you're better,' Gabby whispered, stroking her fur.

'I am, too,' Travis's voice echoed behind her from the doorway. 'She's a real trouper, and she's got a wonderful disposition.'

Gabby turned and saw him leaning against the door.

'I think I was wrong,' he said, walking towards her, holding an apple. 'She could probably go home tonight, if you want to pick her up after work. She's doing even better than I predicted.' He squatted and lightly snapped his fingers. 'Aren't you a good girl,' he said. Surprising her, Molly left Gabby's side to go to him.

'And these little guys are doing great, too,' he went on. 'If you do take them home, make sure you put together some sort of pen to keep them contained. Otherwise, it can get kind of messy. And be sure to line it with newspaper.'

She barely heard him as, despite herself, she noted again how good-looking he was. It annoyed her that she couldn't get past that every time she saw him. It was as if his appearance constantly set off alarm bells in her, and, for the life of her, she didn't know why. He was tall and lean, but she'd seen lots of guys like that. What was it about him?

'You OK?' he said. 'You seem distracted.'

'Just tired,' she lied. She motioned to Molly. 'I guess she's taken a liking to you.'

'Oh, yeah,' he said. 'We've been getting along great. I think it was the jerky treats I gave her. Jerky treats are the way to a dog's heart.'

'I'll remember that,' she said, quickly regaining composure.

When one of the puppies began to whine, Molly returned to the open cage, and Travis stood and polished the apple on his jeans. 'So what do you think?' he asked.

'About what?'

'About Molly. Do you want to take her home tonight or not?'

'Oh, that,' she said, flustered. She cleared her throat. 'I think I'll take her home. If you're sure it won't hurt her.'

'She'll be fine,' he assured her. He took a bite of his apple, then motioned towards her with it. 'You know, I thought you'd be more excited about the fact she's OK.'

'I am excited.'

'You don't seem excited.'

'What's that supposed to mean?'

'I don't know,' he said. He took another bite of his apple. 'Based on the way you showed up at my door, I guess I figured that you'd show a bit more emotion. Not only about Molly, but the fact that I happened to be there to help.'

'And I've already told you I appreciate it,' she said. 'How many times do I have to thank you?'

'I don't know. How many do you think?'

'I wasn't the one who asked.'

He lifted an eyebrow. 'Actually, you were.'

Oh, yeah, she thought. 'Well, fine,' she said, throwing up her hands.

Thank you again. For all you did.' She enunciated the words as if he were hard of hearing.

He laughed. 'Are you like this with your patients, or just around me?'

'Like what?'

'So serious.'

She could feel the flame rising in her cheeks. 'I don't know what you're talking about.'

He smirked. 'OK.'

She opened her mouth, wanting to say something witty to put him in his place, but before anything sprang to mind, he tossed the remains of the apple in the garbage and turned to rinse his hands.

'Listen. I'm glad you're here for another reason, too,' he said over his shoulder. 'I'm having a little get-together tomorrow with friends and I was hoping you'd be able to swing by.'

She blinked, unsure if she'd heard him right. 'Like a date?'

'No, like a get-together. With friends.' He turned off the tap and began to dry his hands. 'I'm hooking up the parasail for the first time this year. It should be a blast.'

'Are they mainly couples? The people going?'

'Except for my sister and me, all of them are married.'

She shook her head. 'I don't think so. I have a boyfriend.'

'Great. Bring him along.'

'We've been together almost four years.'

'Like I said, he's more than welcome to come.'

She wondered if she'd heard him right and stared at him. 'He can't come. He'll be out of town for a few days.'

'Then if you've got nothing else to do, come on over.'

'I'm not so sure that's a good idea.'

'Why not?'

'I'm in love with him.'

'You can be in love with him at my place. Like I said, it's going to be fun. Have you ever been parasailing?'

'No. But that's not the point.'

'You don't think he'd be happy if you came over?'

'Exactly.'

'So, he's the kind of guy who doesn't like you to have fun?'

'No!'

'He doesn't want you to meet new people?'

'Of course he does!'

'It's settled then,' he said. He headed towards the door before pausing. 'People will start showing up around ten thirty. All you need to bring is a bathing suit. We'll have beer and wine and soda, but if you're particular about what you drink, you might want to bring your own.'

'I just don't think . . . .'

He held up his hands. 'I'll tell you what. You're welcome to come if you'd like. But no pressure, OK?' He shrugged. 'I just figured it would give us a chance to get to know each other.'

She knew she should have said no. But instead, she swallowed through the sudden dryness in her throat. 'Maybe I will,' she said.

Three

As the sun came slanting through the blinds, Gabby found her fuzzy pink slippers and shuffled to the kitchen to pour herself a cup of coffee, looking forward to a leisurely Saturday morning. But before she'd taken her first sip, she remembered that she needed to check on Molly. She was happy to find that Molly was nearly back to normal. The puppies seemed healthy, too, latched onto Molly like fuzzy barnacles. But, oh, the stench!

It didn't just smell—the odour assailed her like the Force in a *Star Wars* movie. As she began to gag, she vaguely remembered that Travis had suggested she build a pen to keep the puppies contained. Who knew puppies could poop so much? She spent the next half-hour holding her breath as she cleaned up the garage.

What a way to start the weekend. To top it off, her coffee was now lukewarm, and the water had gone cold before her shower was finished. Great. Just great.

Where was the fun? she grumbled to herself as she threw on her clothes. Here it was, the weekend, and Kevin was nowhere to be found. Even when he was around, their weekends weren't anything like the ones when she'd visited him during her school breaks. Back then, every visit was filled with new experiences and people. Now he spent part of every weekend at the golf course.

She shook her head, thinking she was making too much of it. Their relationship was just going through some growing pains. Moving out onto her back deck, she saw that outside it was one of those impossibly beautiful mornings, and Travis was heading down to the dock wearing nothing but low-slung plaid Bermudas. She could see the muscle striations in his arms and back as he walked, and she took a step backwards, hoping he wouldn't spot her. In the next instant, however, she heard him calling out to her.

'Hey, Gabby!' He waved. 'Can you believe how beautiful the day is already?'

He started to jog towards her and she took a deep breath.

'Hey, Travis.'

'How's Molly doing?'

Gabby cleared her throat. 'She's fine. Thanks.'

'And the puppies?'

'They seem OK, too. But they made quite a mess.'

'They'll do that. That's why it's a good idea to keep them in a smaller area.'

He flashed those white teeth in a familiar grin, way too familiar, even if he was the Hunk-Who-Saved-Her-Dog.

She crossed her arms. 'Yeah, well, I didn't quite get to it.'

'Why not?'

Because you distracted me, she thought. 'I guess I just forgot.'

'Your garage must smell to high heaven.'

She shrugged.

'Listen, it doesn't have to be complicated. But pooping is all puppies do for the first couple of days. It's like the milk runs right through them. But you've got the pen up now, right?'

She tried her best to keep a poker face but obviously failed.

'You don't?' he asked.

Gabby shifted from one foot to the other. 'Not exactly.'

'Why not?'

Gabby shrugged. 'I'm not sure I need one.'

He stared at her in obvious bafflement. 'As your vet, I'm going to come right out and say that I don't think you've made the right decision.'

'Thanks for your opinion,' she snapped.

He continued to stare at her. 'All right, then. Suit yourself. You're going to come to my house around ten thirty, right?'

'I don't think so.'

'Why not?'

'Because I don't think it's a good idea.'

'Why not?'

'Because.'

'I see,' he said, sounding exactly like her mother.

'Good.'

'Is something bothering you?'

'No.'

'Have I done something to upset you?'

Yes, a little voice answered. *You and your damn muscles.* 'No.'

'Then what's the problem?'

'There's no problem.'

'Then what's up with the way you're acting?'

'I'm not acting any way.'

The smile was gone, as was all the friendliness he'd shown earlier. 'Yeah, you are. I drop a basket off to welcome you to the neighbourhood, I save your dog, I invite you over to have some fun on my boat today—all this after you screamed at me for no reason, mind you—and now you're treating me like I have the plague. Since you moved next door, I've tried to be nice, but every time I see you, you seem angry at me. I just want to know why?'

'Because,' she said, knowing she sounded like a sulky fifth-grader. She just couldn't think of anything else to say.

He studied her face closely. 'Because why?'

'It's none of your business.'

He let her answer settle into the silence.

'Whatever,' he finally said. He turned on his heels, shaking his head as he walked towards the steps. He was already on the grass when Gabby took a step forward.

'Wait!' she called out.

Travis slowed to a halt. He turned to face her. 'Yeah?'

'I'm sorry,' she offered. 'I'm sorry for the way I've been treating you. For the way I've made you think I'm not grateful for the things you've done.'

'And?'

She felt herself shrink, something that seemed to happen only in his presence.

'And,' she hesitated, then said, 'You're right. I haven't been treating you the way I should, but, to be honest, I'd rather not go into the reasons why.' She forced a smile. 'Would it be possible for us to start over?'

He seemed to mull this over. 'I don't know.'

'Huh?'

'You heard me,' he said. 'The last thing I need in my life is a crazy neighbour. I don't mean to hurt your feelings, but I learned a long time ago to call 'em like I see 'em.'

'That's not fair.'

'No?' He didn't bother to hide his scepticism. 'I think I'm being more than fair. But I'll tell you what—if you're willing to start over, I'm willing to start over. But only if you're certain you want that.'

'I am.'

'OK, then,' he said. He retraced his steps to the deck. 'Hi,' he offered, holding out his hand. 'My name is Travis Parker and I want to welcome you to the neighbourhood.'

She stared at his hand. After a moment, she took it and said, 'I'm Gabby Holland. It's a pleasure to meet you.'

'What do you do?'

'I'm a physician assistant,' she said, feeling slightly ridiculous. 'How about you?'

'I'm a veterinarian,' he said. 'Where are you from?'

'Savannah, Georgia,' she answered. 'And you?'

'From here,' he said. 'Born and raised.'

'Do you like it here?'

'What's not to like? Beautiful weather, zero traffic.' He paused. 'And, for the most part, nice neighbours, too.' He motioned over his shoulder. 'Hey, my friends and I are heading out on the boat today. Would you like to join us?'

She squinted up at him. 'I would, but I have to build a pen for the puppies my dog, Molly, had two nights ago. I don't want you to have to wait for me.'

'Need some help? I've got some extra planks of wood and some crates in the garage. It won't take long.'

She hesitated, then smiled. 'In that case, I'd love to come.'

'You invited the new neighbour over, huh?' Stephanie asked. 'What's her name again?'

'Gabby,' Travis answered, pulling the boat closer to the dock. 'She should be here any minute.' The rope tightened and then slackened as the boat was manoeuvred into place. They'd just lowered it into the water and were tying it up to the dock to load the coolers.

'She's single, right?'

'Technically, she has a boyfriend.'

'So?' Stephanie grinned. 'When have you ever let that stop you?'

'Don't read anything into this. He's out of town, and she had nothing to do, so I invited her along.'

'Uh-huh.' Stephanie nodded. 'You think she's attractive, don't you?'

Travis looked at his sister. 'Why do I get the feeling that this is going to be a long day?'

'I have no idea.'

'Do me a favour, OK? Go easy on her.'

'What do you mean?'

'You know what I mean. Just . . . let her get used to everyone before you start on her.'

Stephanie cackled. 'You do realise who you're talking to, right?'

'I'm just saying that she might not understand your humour.'

'I promise to be on my best behaviour.'

'So . . . you ready to go skinny-dipping?' Stephanie asked.

Gabby blinked, unsure she'd heard her right. 'Excuse me?'

A minute earlier, Stephanie had walked over wearing a long T-shirt and holding a couple of beers. Handing one to Gabby, she'd introduced herself as Travis's sister and led her to some chairs along the back deck while Travis finished up.

'Oh, not right now,' Stephanie drawled. 'It usually takes a couple of beers before everyone is loose enough to drop their drawers.'

'Skinny-dipping?'

'You did know that Travis is a nudist, right?' She nodded towards the Slip 'n' Slide Travis had set up earlier. 'After that, we generally go Slip 'n' Sliding.'

Though her head felt as though it were spinning, Gabby nodded almost imperceptibly. Then she heard Stephanie's laughter.

'I was only kidding!' she hooted. 'Do you honestly think I'd go skinny-dipping with my brother around? *Ewww*! That's gross! But I'm sorry. My brother warned me to take it easy on you. For whatever reason, he thinks my humour takes some getting used to.'

Gee, I wonder why. 'Really?' Gabby said.

'Yeah, but if you ask me, we're two peas in a pod. Where do you think I learned it?' Stephanie leant back in her seat as she adjusted her sunglasses. 'Travis tells me you're a physician assistant?'

'Yeah. I work at the children's clinic. How about you?'

'I'm a student,' she said. She took a sip of beer. 'I'm thinking of making it my career.'

For the first time, Gabby laughed and felt herself begin to relax. 'Do you know who else is coming?'

'Oh, probably the same old crew. My brother has these three friends he's known for ever, and I'm sure they'll be here along with their wives and kids. Travis doesn't bring the parasail boat out too much anymore, which is why he keeps it docked at the marina. Usually he takes the ski boat, because wakeboarding or water-skiing is a lot easier. But parasailing is great. Have you ever been?'

'No.'

'You'll love it. And Travis knows what he's doing. That's how he earned extra spending money while he was in college. Or, at least, that's what he claims. Actually, I'm fairly certain that everything he earned was used to buy the boat; they're very expensive.'

'So he's quite the shrewd businessman, huh?'

Stephanie laughed. 'Oh, yeah. My brother. A budding Donald Trump. Actually, he doesn't much care about money. I mean, sure, he earns a living and pays his own way, but anything left over goes to new boats or Jet Skis or trips here and there. He's been everywhere. Europe, Central and South America, Australia, Africa, Bali, China, Nepal . . .'

'Really?'

In the distance, a car door slammed.

'Here come the Clampetts,' Stephanie remarked. 'Or, if you prefer, the Brady Bunch. Brace yourself. Our relaxing morning is about to end.'

Gabby turned and spotted a rowdy group rounding the side of the house. Chatter and shouts rang out as the three children ran in front of the adults, wobbling as if they were constantly on the verge of falling. Stephanie leant closer. 'It's easy to distinguish them, believe it or not. Megan and Joe are the ones with blonde hair. Laird and Allison are the tall ones. And Matt and Liz are . . . less thin than the others.'

The corners of Gabby's mouth curled up slightly. 'Less thin?'

'I didn't want to call them plump. But I was just trying to make it easy for you.'

Stephanie rose from her seat. Introductions were made to Megan, Allison and Liz while they watched the kids chasing one another. Joe, Laird and Matt, meanwhile, strolled down to the dock, loaded up with towels and coolers, to greet Travis.

'Hey! Y'all ready?' Travis called out. 'We're good to go, here.'

Gabby trailed a step behind the group, adjusting the T-shirt she'd worn over her bikini and shorts.

The men were already in the boat when they got to the dock. The kids were dressed in life jackets and were handed to Joe. Laird held out his hand to help the women into the boat. Gabby stepped in, concentrating on keeping her balance amid the rocking, surprised at the size of the boat. It was longer than Travis's ski boat by a good five feet, with bench seats that ran along both sides, which was where most of the kids and adults seemed to congregate. Stephanie and Allison made themselves comfortable at the front. At the back of the boat was a large platform and crank, along with Travis, who stood behind the wheel. Joe was untying the line that held the boat in place, while Laird rolled it up.

'Sit by me,' Stephanie commanded Gabby.

Gabby sat, and from the corner of her eye, she saw Travis grab a baseball hat he had tucked into a corner compartment. The cap, which she'd always believed looked goofy on grown men, somehow suited his carefree demeanour.

'Everyone ready?' he called.

He didn't wait for an answer, and the boat rumbled forward. They reached the mouth of the creek and turned south, into the waters of Back Sound. Shackleford Banks loomed ahead, grass threaded along the dunes.

Gabby leant towards Stephanie. 'Where are we going?'

'Most likely Cape Lookout. We'll probably make for the inlet, then out into Onslow Bay. Afterwards, we'll either picnic on Shackleford Banks or at Cape Lookout. Hold on for a second . . .' She turned towards Travis. 'Hey, Trav! Can I drive?'

He raised his head. 'Since when do you want to drive?'

'Now. It's been a while.'

'Later.'

'I think I should drive.'

'Why?'

Stephanie shook her head, as if marvelling at the stupidity of men. She rose from her spot. 'I'll be back, OK? I have to talk to my idiot brother.'

As Stephanie made her way towards the rear of the boat, Allison nodded towards her. 'Don't let her scare you. She and Travis always talk to each other that way.'

'I take it they're close.'

'They're best friends, even if both would deny it.'

Allison watched Stephanie lecturing Travis, one hand on the boat to steady herself, the other hand gesturing.

'How did you and Travis meet?' she asked Gabby.

'We live next door to each other, actually.'

'And?'

'And . . . well, it's kind of a long story. But to make it short, my dog, Molly, had some trouble when she had her puppies, and Travis was kind enough to come over and treat her. After that, he invited me to come.'

'He's got a way with animals. Kids, too. Speak of the devil . . . Hey, Travis.'

'Hey,' he said. 'Should be fun today, huh?' Behind him, Stephanie was perched behind the wheel. 'Hopefully it won't get too windy.'

Allison looked around. 'I don't think it will.'

'Why?' Gabby pressed. 'What happens if it's windy?'

'Nothing good when you're parasailing,' Travis answered. 'Basically, the chute could collapse, the lines could get tangled, and that's the last thing you want in a parachute.'

Gabby had an image of herself spinning out of control as she rushed towards the water.

'Don't worry,' Travis reassured her. 'If I even suspect a problem, no one goes up.'

'Hold on!' Stephanie shouted, rotating the wheel.

Travis instinctively grabbed the side of the boat as it hit a large wake and the bow rose and fell with a thud. Allison rushed towards her daughter, Josie, who'd fallen and was already beginning to cry.

Travis took a seat beside Gabby and leant back, planting his feet wide. 'So, how'd you like my sister?'

With the sun behind him, his features were difficult to discern. 'I like her. She's . . . unique.'

'She seems taken with you, too. If she didn't like you, believe me, she would have let me know.'

Gabby studied Travis, suddenly grasping what had happened. 'She sent you back here to talk to me, didn't she?'

'Yeah,' he admitted. 'She reminded me that you were my guest and that I'd be rude if I didn't make sure you were comfortable.'

'I'm fine.' She waved a hand. 'I'm perfectly happy enjoying the view.'

'Have you ever been over to Cape Lookout?' Travis asked.

'No.'

'It's a national park and there's a cove that's great for little kids because the waves don't break there. On the Atlantic side, there's an unspoilt white-sand beach, which is almost impossible to find any more.'

They turned towards the inlet. Behind them, Beaufort grew smaller; up ahead, the waters of Onslow Bay embraced the Atlantic. The three couples at the front of the boat were as transfixed by the view as Gabby was, and even the kids sat contentedly on laps, their bodies relaxed. Gabby could feel the wind whipping through her hair and the balm of the summer sun.

'Hey, Trav,' Stephanie called out, 'is this OK?'

'Let's go a bit farther. I want to make sure we have enough room. We've got a rookie on board.'

Stephanie nodded, and the boat accelerated.

Gabby leant towards him. 'How does this work, by the way?'

'It's easy,' he said. 'First, I fill the parachute and get it ready to accept the harnesses by using that bar over there.' He pointed towards the corner of the boat. 'Then you and your partner put the harnesses on, I clip those to the long bar and you take a seat on the platform. I start the crank, and you lift off. It takes a couple of minutes to reach the right height and then . . . well, you float around. You get a great view of Beaufort and the lighthouse, and, because the weather's been so clear, you might get to see some dolphins, porpoises, rays, sharks and even turtles. We might slow the boat, let you dunk your feet, and then go up again. It's a blast.'

'Sharks?'

'Of course. It's the ocean. But there's nothing to be afraid of. They won't bother you.'

'I don't know . . .'

'How about if I'm with you? Then would you try it?'

She hesitated, then gave a quick nod. 'I'll think about it,' she offered. 'I'm not promising anything.'

'Fair enough.' He winked as he flashed a smile.

Gabby tried to ignore the leaping sensation in her stomach. Instead, she reached in her bag for some lotion and began nervously to apply it to her face, trying to regain some distance.

'Stephanie tells me you're a world traveller.'

'I've travelled a bit.'

'She made it sound like more than that. Like you've pretty much been everywhere.'

He shook his head. 'I wish. Believe me, there are lots of places I haven't seen.'

Stephanie began to slow the boat and Travis sat up straighter. When his sister glanced at him, he nodded and stood up. Stephanie lowered the throttle, allowing the boat to slow even further.

'We're ready,' he said, and moved to a storage box. Pulling out the parachute, he asked, 'Are you up for a new experience?'

Gabby swallowed. 'I can't wait.'

Once the parachute was filled and the harnesses strapped on, Joe and Megan lifted off first, followed by Allison and Laird, then Matt and Liz. One by one, the couples sat on the platform and were lifted into the air, the towrope unwinding until they were a hundred feet up. From Gabby's spot on the boat, they looked small and inconsequential as they drifted over the water. Travis, who'd taken the wheel from Stephanie, kept the boat at a steady speed, then finally brought it to a gradual halt, allowing the riders to drift towards the sea. Just as their feet grazed the water, he'd gun the throttle and the parachute would rush skywards like a kite being pulled by a boy running in the park.

Gabby felt herself growing nervous as her turn approached. Travis tossed aside his baseball cap. 'C'mon,' he said to her, 'I'll help you with your harness.'

Liz handed over the life preserver. 'It's so much fun,' she said. 'You're going to love it.'

Travis led Gabby to the platform. After hopping up, he bent over, offering a hand. She could feel the warmth in it as he helped her up. The harness lay crumpled, and he pointed towards two open loops. 'Step in those and pull it up. I'll tighten it for you.'

She held her body steady against the tugs of the canvas straps. 'That's it?'

'Almost. When you sit on the platform, keep the wide strap underneath your thighs. You don't want it under your backside, because that doesn't support your weight as well. And you might want to take off your T-shirt, unless you don't mind getting it wet.'

She slipped off her T-shirt, trying not to feel nervous.

Travis hooked up the straps of her harness to the bar, then his own. He smiled. 'Just relax and enjoy, OK?'

A second later, Joe pushed the throttle, the chute filled, and Gabby and Travis were lifted from the deck. They rose diagonally towards the sky. Gabby gripped the canvas straps so hard that her knuckles turned white while the boat grew smaller. She felt Travis touch her shoulder.

'Look over there,' he said, pointing. 'There's a pod of dolphins. Near the banks.'

As she marvelled at the sight, her nervousness started to subside. Instead, she began to soak up the view—the town, the boats, the water. It was extraordinary to drift along at this elevation, coasting on a wind current as if she were a bird.

'Are you willing to be dipped? I promise it'll be fun.'

'Let's do it,' she agreed.

Travis engaged Joe in a quick series of hand signals, and, beneath her, the whine of the boat suddenly diminished. The parachute began to descend. Staring at the rapidly approaching water, she scanned the surface to make sure nothing was lurking below. The parachute dipped lower and lower and she felt cold water splash on her lower body. Then the boat accelerated and they shot skywards again. Gabby felt adrenaline surge through her body and didn't bother trying to hide her grin.

Travis nudged her. 'See? It wasn't bad at all.'

'Can we do that again?' she asked.

Travis and Gabby rode for another quarter hour. Then each couple rode once more. By then, the kids were getting bored. Travis steered the boat towards the cove at Cape Lookout and stopped. Joe tossed the anchor overboard, removed his shirt, and followed the anchor into the water. The water was waist-deep and, with practised ease, Matt handed him a cooler. Matt took off his shirt and jumped in; Laird handed him a cooler and then followed him into the water, while Travis jumped in, carrying a small, portable grill and bag of charcoal briquettes. Simultaneously, the mothers hopped in the water and took hold of the kids. Gabby stood in the back of the boat, thinking she should have helped, while Stephanie, seemingly oblivious to the commotion, lay sprawled on the seats at the front of the boat, soaking up the sun.

'I'm on vacation, so I feel no need to volunteer my services,' Stephanie announced. 'And they're so good at it, I feel no guilt about being a slacker. As Confucius once said, "He who does nothing is the one who does nothing."'

Gabby furrowed her brow. 'Did Confucius really say that?'

Sunglasses in place, Stephanie shrugged. 'No, but who cares? Did you really want to carry coolers and tents all the way to the beach?' She sat up. 'OK, the coast is clear. We're good to go.' She slung her beach bag over her shoulder. 'You gotta know when to be lazy. Done correctly, it's an art form that benefits everyone.'

Gabby hesitated. 'I don't know why, but I like the way you think.'

Stephanie laughed. 'Of course you do,' she said. 'It's good to know I'm not the only one who understands that essential truth.'

She jumped overboard. 'C'mon. And by the way, don't think twice about anything you did or didn't do. Doing these things makes these people feel manly and motherly, which is *just* the way the world *should* work. As single women, all we have to do is enjoy it.'

Setting up the camp—like getting off and unloading the boat—was informally ritualised, with everyone apparently knowing exactly what to do. A pop-up tent was set in place, blankets were spread, and the charcoal was lit. In keeping with her inactivity on the boat, Stephanie simply grabbed a beer and a towel, picked a spot, and resumed sunbathing. Gabby, unsure of what else to do, spread her towel and did exactly the same thing. She lay there trying to ignore the fact that everyone else—aside from Stephanie—seemed to be doing something.

'How was it with Travis?' Stephanie asked.

'Fine,' Gabby said.

'I think he likes you.'

'And I think you believe we're still in seventh grade.'

'What? You don't care?'

'No.'

'Because you have a boyfriend?'

'Among other reasons.'

Stephanie laughed. 'Oh, that's good. If I didn't know you, I might even have believed you.'

'You don't know me!'

'Oh . . . I know you. Believe it or not, I know exactly who you are.'

'Oh yeah? Where am I from?'

'I don't know.'

'Tell me about my family?'

'I can't.'

'Then you don't really know me, do you?'

After a moment, Stephanie rolled over to face her. 'Yes,' she said. 'I do.' She couldn't hide the challenge in her tone. 'OK, how about this? You're a good girl and always have been, but, deep down, you think there's more to life than always following the rules and there's a part of you that craves the unknown. If you're honest with yourself, Travis is part of that. You're selective when it comes to sex, but once you commit to someone, the standards you would normally hold yourself to go out of the window. You think you'll marry your boyfriend, but can't help but wonder why you don't have a ring on your finger yet. You love your family, but you wanted to make your own decisions about who you become, which is why you live here. Even so, you worry your choices will earn your family's disapproval. How am I doing so far?'

As she'd spoken, Gabby had grown pale. Interpreting a direct hit, Stephanie propped herself on an elbow. 'You want me to go on?'

'No,' Gabby said.

'I was right, wasn't I?'

Gabby exhaled sharply. 'Not about everything.'

'Where was I wrong?'

Instead of answering, Gabby shook her head and rolled back onto her towel. 'I don't want to talk about it.'

Gabby expected Stephanie to persist, but instead, Stephanie simply shrugged and lay back on her towel, as if she'd never said anything.

Gabby could hear the sounds of children frolicking in the surf, and distant, indistinguishable strains of conversation. Her head spun at

Stephanie's assessment; it was as if the woman had known her all her life and were privy to her darkest secrets.

'By the way, in case you're freaking out, I should tell you that I'm psychic.'

Gabby sat up as a wave of relief washed over her, even though she knew the concept was preposterous. 'Really?'

Stephanie laughed. 'No, of course not! I just inserted your "amazingly personal experiences" into pretty much every woman who ever lived. Well, except for the part about Travis. I guessed about that. But it's pretty amazing, huh? I study that, by the way. I've been part of half a dozen studies and it always amazes me that, once you cut through the clutter, people are pretty much the same. Oh, and in case you were curious, Travis isn't seeing anyone. He's not only single, but he's eligible.'

'I wasn't curious.'

'Since you have a boyfriend, right?'

'Right. But even if I didn't have a boyfriend, I wouldn't have been curious.'

Stephanie laughed. 'Yes, of course. How could I have been so wrong? I guess I must have been fooled by the way you keep staring at him.'

'I haven't been staring.'

'Oh, don't be so touchy. After all, he's been staring at you, too.'

From her spot on her towel, Gabby inhaled the scent of charcoal, hot dogs, burgers and chicken wafting on a gentle breeze. Stephanie had been uncharacteristically quiet since her last comment. In some people, that would have struck Gabby as discomfort or shyness; in Stephanie, it came across as the kind of confidence Gabby had always secretly coveted. Because Stephanie was so comfortable with herself, she made Gabby feel comfortable around her, which, she had to admit, was a feeling she had been missing lately. For a long time, she hadn't been comfortable at home; she still wasn't comfortable at work; and she was less than confident about where things were going with Kevin.

As for Travis—he definitely made her uncomfortable. Well, when he wasn't wearing his shirt, anyway. Sneaking a look, she spotted him sitting in the sand near the water's edge, building sandcastles with the three toddlers. He seemed to be having as much fun as they were, and the sight of him made her want to smile. She forced herself not to, on the off chance he might see it and get the wrong idea.

The aroma finally forced Gabby to sit up. Off to the side, she saw Laird standing over the portable grill, wielding a pair of tongs. Megan was lining up bags of potato crisps and buns and Tupperware containers on a small fold-up table, while Liz was setting out condiments along with paper plates and plastic utensils. Joe and Matt were behind them, tossing a football back and forth. She couldn't remember a weekend from her childhood where a group of families got together to enjoy one another's company in a gorgeous spot simply because it was . . . Saturday.

'Food's ready!' Laird shouted.

Gabby slipped her shirt over her bathing suit and wandered over, surprised by how hungry she was. Over her shoulder, she saw Travis doing his best to herd the kids forward, scurrying around them like a sheepdog. The three of them rushed to the grill where Megan stood guard.

'Line up on the blanket,' she ordered, and the toddlers—obviously out of well-trained habit—did exactly as they were told.

'Megan has magic powers with kids,' Travis observed over Gabby's shoulder. He was breathing heavily, his hands on his hips. 'I wish they listened to me like that. I have to resort to chasing them until I'm about to pass out.'

'But you seem like such a natural.'

'I love playing with them, not herding.' He leant towards her conspiratorially. 'Anyway, in a little while, they'll start getting cranky. That's when I let their parents take over.'

'In other words, when the going gets tough, the tough get going.'

'I think when the time comes, I might just volunteer your services.'

'Gee, thanks.'

'No problem. Hey—you hungry?'

'Starved.'

By the time they reached the food, the kids were seated on the blanket with hot dogs and diced fruit. Liz, Megan and Allison sat near enough to monitor, but far enough away to converse. Joe, Matt and Laird sat on the coolers with their plates on their knees, bottles of beer propped up in the sand.

'Burgers or chicken?' Gabby enquired.

'I like chicken. But the burgers are supposed to be terrific. I just never really acquired the taste for red meat.'

'I thought all men ate burgers.'

'Then I guess I'm not a man.' He straightened up. 'Which, I must say, is really going to surprise and disappoint my parents.'

She laughed. 'Well . . .' She nodded towards the grill. 'They clearly saved the last piece of chicken for you.'

They reached for some plates as they eyed the side dishes spread out on the table—beans, potato, cucumber and fruit salads. Travis dropped the chicken onto his plate, then lifted a burger from the side of the grill and added it to Gabby's.

He scooped some fruit salad onto his plate; Gabby added a taste of pretty much everything. When she was finished, she looked at both their plates with an almost guilty expression, which Travis thankfully didn't seem to notice.

'Would you like a beer?' he asked.

'Sounds great.'

He reached into the cooler and fished out a Coors Light, then grabbed a bottle of water for himself.

'Gotta drive the boat,' he explained. He lifted his plate in the direction of the dunes. 'How about we sit over there?'

'Lead the way.'

They trudged towards a low dune, a spot shaded by a sickly salt-poisoned tree bent by years of ocean breezes. Travis lowered himself to the sand and Gabby sat down next to him.

'Coming out here reminds me of high school,' Travis remarked. 'I can't tell you how many weekends we spent here back then.'

'I'll bet that was fun.'

'It was,' he said. 'One night, Joe, Matt, Laird and I were out here sitting around a bonfire, drinking beer, telling jokes and laughing, and I remember thinking life couldn't get any better.'

'Sounds like a Budweiser commercial. Aside from the fact that you were underage and the whole thing was illegal.'

'And you never did anything like that, right?'

'Actually, no,' she said. 'I didn't.'

'Really? Never?'

'Why do you look so surprised?'

'I don't know. I just don't see you as someone who grew up following all the rules.' When he saw her expression, he backtracked. 'Don't get me wrong. I just meant that you strike me as someone who's independent and always up for new adventures.'

'You don't know anything about me.'

As soon as she said it, she remembered saying pretty much the same thing to Stephanie.

He absently moved his fruit with his fork. 'I know that you moved away from your home, that you bought your own house, that you're making it on your own. To me, that means independence. And as for adventurous—you're here with a bunch of strangers, aren't you? You went parasailing and overcame the thought of sharks to get dipped in the water. I think that's admirable.'

She blushed, liking Travis's response much better than his sister's. 'Maybe,' she conceded. 'But it's not like travelling around the world.'

'Don't let that fool you. You think I wasn't nervous when I left? I was terrified. I mean, it's one thing to tell your friends what you're going to do, and it's another thing entirely actually to get on the plane and land in a country where barely anyone speaks English. Have you travelled?'

'Not much. Aside from a spring break I spent in the Bahamas, I've never been out of the country.' She paused, then asked, 'Where are you going next? Your next big adventure?'

'Nothing too far-flung. I'm going to the Grand Tetons to do some camping.'

'Are you going alone?'

'No,' he said. 'I'm going with my dad. I can't wait.'

Gabby made a face. 'I can't imagine going off on a trip with either one of my parents.'

'Why not?'

'Well, first off, my mom is the kind of lady who believes that staying in anything less than a five-star hotel is roughing it. And my dad has never shown interest in anything other than fishing. Besides, he wouldn't go anywhere without Mom.'

'They must be very proud of you,' Travis said.

'What makes you say that?'

'Why wouldn't they be?'

Why indeed? she wondered. Let me count the ways. 'Let's just say that I'm pretty sure my mom prefers my sisters. And, trust me, they're just like her.'

'And that means she can't be proud of you?'

She took a bite of her burger, taking her time before responding. 'It's complicated,' she demurred.

'How so?' he persisted.

'For one thing, I have red hair. My sisters are all blonde. I'm twenty-six and still single, and I want a career, none of which fits the image of the daughter my mother wants. She has definite ideas about the role of women, especially southern women of proper social standing.'

'I'm getting the sense that you and your mother don't get along.'

'Ya think?'

'Maybe she's jealous,' he said. 'Here you are, making your own life with your own goals and dreams, dreams independent of the world you grew up in. It takes courage to do something different, and maybe what you think is disappointment in you is actually, at some deeper level, her own disappointment in herself.' He took a bite of chicken and added, 'I have a feeling that both of them are extremely proud of you, even if they don't know how to show it.'

His comments were unexpected and strangely affecting. She leant towards him slightly. 'I don't know if you're right, but thanks anyway. And I don't want you to get the wrong impression. I mean, we talk on the phone every week and we're civil. It's just that I sometimes wish things were different.'

Travis said nothing in response, and Gabby found herself relieved that he didn't try to offer a solution or advice. When she'd related similar feelings to Kevin, his first instinct had been to come up with a game plan to change things. She set her plate aside, pulled up her legs, and wrapped her arms around her knees. 'Tell me—what's the best thing about being a vet?'

'The animals,' he said. 'And the people. But that's probably what you expected me to say, right?'

For the next half-hour, they sat together talking in a way that felt remarkably familiar. She talked more about her mother and father and their polar personalities; she told him a bit about her sisters and what it was like to grow up with so much pressure to conform. She filled him in on college and PA school, mentioning Kevin only in passing. Somehow, talking to Travis reminded her that she'd become the woman she was going to be long before meeting Kevin. By the time the conversation wound down, Megan and Liz had packed most of the food back inside the coolers. Laird and Allison had gone for a walk. Matt had half his body buried in sand by the toddlers, who were raining sand into his face.

Just then, a Frisbee landed near Gabby's feet and she saw Joe approaching. 'I think it's time we rescued Matt,' he called out. He pointed towards the Frisbee. 'You up for it?'

Travis looked at her. 'Do you mind?'

'No, go ahead.'

'I have to warn you—it's not going to be pretty.' He stood up and shouted. 'Hey, kids? Are you guys ready to see the World Champion Frisbee expert in action?'

'Yay!' came the chorus. They dropped their shovels and dashed towards the water.

As Travis jogged down to the waterline and sloshed in, Gabby found herself following his movements with something like affection. Spending time with Travis wasn't at all the way she'd imagined it would be. There was no pretension and he seemed to have an intuitive feel for when to stay silent or when to respond. Gabby reflected on this as she watched him dive for the Frisbee. He bungled the catch, allowing the Frisbee to hit him in the chest, and landed in the surf with a dramatic cascade of water. The toddlers squealed with delight.

Gabby was still trying to make sense of her reaction to Travis when he finally emerged from the ocean and started towards her, shaking the water from his hair. A moment later, he plopped down on the sand beside her, and, when they accidentally touched, Gabby had the briefest flash of them sitting together just like this on a hundred different weekends in the future.

Four

THEY SPENT ANOTHER HOUR at the beach before reloading the boat, and, by late afternoon, they were cruising through the inlet. Travis stopped to buy some shrimp from a local fisherman; by the time they finally docked, all three toddlers were sound asleep. The adults were windblown and content, their faces darkened by the hours in the sun.

Once the boat was unloaded, the couples departed one by one, until only Gabby, Stephanie and Travis remained. Travis was on the dock with Moby; he'd already spread the parachute on the dock so it could dry and was rinsing off the boat with a garden hose.

Stephanie stretched her arms overhead. 'I guess I should be on my way, too. Dinner with the folks tonight. Let me say goodbye to Travis.'

Gabby nodded as Stephanie leant over the deck railing.

'Hey, Trav!' she shouted. 'I'm outta here. Thanks!'

'Glad you could come!' he shouted with a wave.

'You might want to toss something on the grill! Gabby just said she's starving!'

Before Gabby could say anything, she saw Travis give a thumbs up. 'I'll be up in a minute!' he shouted.

Stephanie sauntered by Gabby, obviously pleased with her social engineering.

'Why'd you say that?' Gabby hissed.

'Because I'm going to be with my parents. I don't want my poor brother to have to spend the rest of the evening alone. He likes to have people around.' She slung her bag over her shoulder. 'Hey, it was great getting to know you. I'm glad we had the chance to meet.' She removed her sunglasses and wiped them with her shirt. 'See you again?'

'Sure,' Gabby said, still thrown by what had just happened.

Stephanie went to the patio door, slid it open and vanished inside, cutting through the house to the front door. Travis was already strolling up, Moby trotting happily by his side. For the first time today, he'd put on a short-sleeved shirt, though he'd left it unbuttoned.

'Let me get the coals going. Shrimp kebabs OK?'

She debated only an instant. 'Just give me a few minutes to change?'

While Travis got the coals going, Gabby checked on Molly, finding her sleeping soundly along with the puppies.

She took a quick shower before changing into a light cotton skirt and blouse. After drying her hair, she put on just a bit of mascara. When she stepped back from the mirror, it occurred to her that it had been years since she'd had dinner with a man other than Kevin. Was her decision something she should feel guilty about? The day had been harmless—technically, she'd spent more time with Stephanie than she had with Travis. So what was the big deal?

You're dining alone tonight, of course, a little voice whispered.

But was that really a problem? Stephanie had been right. She *was* hungry again, and her neighbour had food. It wasn't as though she were going to sleep with him. She had no intention of even kissing him. They were friends, that's all. And if Kevin were here, she was sure that Travis would have invited him along, too.

But he's not here, the little voice insisted. *Will you tell Kevin about your cosy dinner for two?*

'Definitely. I'll definitely tell him,' she muttered, trying to silence the voice. There were times when she absolutely hated that little voice. It sounded just like her mother.

Thus decided, she looked at herself one last time in the mirror and, pleased with what she saw, slipped out through the patio door and started across the lawn.

As Gabby weaved her way between the hedges and then appeared at the edge of his lawn, Travis caught the movement from the corner of his eye and found himself staring unabashedly as she approached. When she stepped onto the deck, he felt a strange shift in the atmosphere.

'Hey,' she said simply. 'How long until dinner?'

'A couple of minutes,' he answered. 'Your timing is perfect.'

She looked at the skewered shrimps and brightly coloured peppers and onions.

'Wow,' she murmured. 'They look great.'

'Do you want anything to drink?' He gestured towards the opposite end of the deck. 'I think there's some beer and soda left over in the cooler.'

She crossed the deck and Travis watched as she flipped open the lid and pulled out two beers. When she returned to hand him one, he felt her fingers graze his. He twisted open the cap and took a long pull, looking down the line of the bottle at her. In the silence, she stared at the water. The sun, hovering over the trees, was still bright, but its heat had diminshed and shadows were gradually stretching across the lawn.

'How's Molly?' he asked.

'She seems fine. She was sleeping when I checked on her.' She looked around. 'Where's Moby?'

'I think he wandered round to the front. He got bored with my cooking once he realised I wasn't about to offer him any scraps.'

'Is there anything I can do to help?'

'Not really. Unless you want to grab some plates from the kitchen?'

'Be happy to.' She nodded. 'Where are they, exactly?'

'In the cupboard to the left of the sink. And would you mind bringing some silverware, too? It's in the drawer near the dishwasher.'

As soon as she turned to enter the house, Travis found himself studying her. There was definitely something about Gabby that interested him. It wasn't simply that she was attractive. Her straightforward intelligence and unforced humour suggested a grounded sense of right and wrong. Beauty and earthy common sense were a rare combination.

By the time she emerged, the kebabs were ready. He loaded a couple on each plate before they took their seats at the table. Beyond them, the slow-moving creek reflected the sky like a mirror.

'This looks delicious,' she said.

'Thank you.'

She took a sip of her beer and motioned to the boat. 'Are you going out again tomorrow?'

'I don't think so. Tomorrow I'll probably go riding.'

'Horseback riding?'

He shook his head. 'Motorcycle. In college, I bought a beat-up 1983 Honda Shadow with the goal of restoring it and making a quick profit. Let's just say it wasn't quick and I doubt I'll ever make a profit. But I can say I did all the work myself.'

'That must be rewarding.'

'*Pointless* is probably a better word. It has a tendency to break down, and genuine parts are impossible to find. Have you ever gone riding?'

'No. Too dangerous.'

'Danger depends more on the rider and the conditions than the bike.'

'But yours breaks down.'

'True. But I like to live life on the edge.'

'I've noticed that about your personality.'

'Is that good or bad?'

'Neither. But it's definitely unpredictable. Especially when I try to reconcile it with the fact that you're a veterinarian. It's such a stable-sounding profession. When I think of veterinarians, I automatically think family man.'

'In other words, boring. Like the most exciting thing I should do is golf.'

She thought of Kevin. 'There are worse things.'

'Just to let you know, I am a family man.' Travis shrugged. 'Except for the family part.'

'That's kind of a prerequisite, don't you think?'

'I think that being a family man is more about having the proper world view than the actual condition of having a family.'

'Nice try.'

She squinted at him, feeling the effects of the beer.

'So tell me about your boyfriend. Is he a family man?'

'None of your business,' she said.

'OK, don't tell me—at least not yet. Is he tall?'

'What does that matter?'

'It doesn't. I'm just making conversation.'

'Then let's talk about something else. I have a question about vet school,' she added, apropos of nothing, but no longer caring about the direction of their conversation. It felt good just to relax, to bask in the pleasure of Travis's company. 'I know it's dumb, but I've always wondered how much anatomy you have to study. As in, how many different kinds of animals?'

'Just the major ones,' he said. 'Cow, horse, pig, dog, cat and chicken.'

'Wow. I thought it was hard just doing people.'

'Yeah, but remember: most people won't sue me if their chicken dies. Your responsibility is much greater.' He paused, then motioned to her bottle as he stood. 'Want another?'

She hadn't even realised she'd finished. 'I'd better not.'

'I won't tell anyone.'

'That's not the point. I don't think my boyfriend would appreciate it.'

'Then it's a good thing he's not here, isn't it? Besides, we're just getting to know each other. What harm is there in that?'

'Fine.' She sighed. 'Last one, though.'

He brought two more over and opened hers. As soon as she took a drink, she heard a voice inside her whisper, *You shouldn't be doing this*.

'You'd like him,' she said, trying to re-establish some boundaries between them. 'He's a great guy.'

'I'm sure he is.'

'And yes, to answer your earlier question, he's tall.'

'I thought you didn't want to talk about him.'

'I don't. I just want you to know I love him.'

'Love is a wonderful thing. I love being in love.'

'Spoken like a man with plenty of experience. But keep in mind that true love lasts for ever.'

'Poets would say that true love always ends in tragedy. I'm not saying I agree. Like you, I'm more of a happy-ending romantic. My parents have been married for ever, and that's what I want to have one day, too.'

Gabby couldn't help thinking that he was very good at this sort of flirty banter—and then reminded herself that he'd had a lot of practice.

'Did you know that I almost bought your house?' he asked. 'It was for sale at the same time this one was. I liked the floor plan better on yours, but this one already had the deck and the boathouse and a lift. It was a tough choice.'

'And now you've even got a hot tub.'

'You like that?' He cocked an eyebrow. 'We could get in later.'

'I don't have my suit.'

'Bathing suits are optional, of course.'

She rolled her eyes. 'I don't think so.'

He stretched. 'How about just our feet, then.'

'I could probably handle that.'

On the other side of the creek, the setting sun was changing the sky to a golden palette of colours. Gabby stared across the water, feeling a sense of well-being she hadn't experienced for a long time.

'Tell me about Africa,' she said. 'Is it as otherworldly as it seems?'

'It was for me,' he said. 'I kept wanting to go back. Like something in my genes recognised it as home.'

She was quiet for a moment.

'How long were you there?'

'Which time?'

'How many times have you been there?'

'Three.'

She tried to imagine living a life so free but somehow failed. 'Tell me about all of them.'

They talked quietly for a long time, dusk giving way to darkness. Halfway through his stories, he rose from the table and brought back two bottles of water, respecting her earlier comment, and the appreciation she felt added to her growing sense of affection. Though she knew it was wrong, she was unable to stop it.

By the time they got up to take the dishes into the house, stars were twinkling overhead. Travis rinsed the dishes, then they wandered back outside to the hot tub. He flipped open the cover while Gabby removed her sandals. A moment later, they were sitting beside each other, their feet swishing back and forth. Gabby stared upwards at the sky.

'What are you thinking about?' Travis asked.

'The stars,' she said. 'I just bought an astronomy book and I'm trying to see if I remember anything.'

'Do you?'

'Just the big ones. The obvious ones.' She pointed towards the house. 'Go straight up from the chimney and you'll see Orion's Belt. Betelgeuse is on Orion's left shoulder, and Rigel is the name of his foot. The bright star over there is Sirius.'

Travis spotted Orion's Belt, but he couldn't make out the others.

He pointed over her shoulder. 'I can see the Big Dipper. Right over there. That's the only one I can always find.'

'It's also known as the Big Bear, or Ursa Major. I just love the names, even if I can't make out all the constellations yet. The Pleiades, Cassiopeia . . . their names sound like music.'

'I take it this is a new hobby of yours?'

'It's more like good intentions buried in the detritus of daily life. But for a couple of days there, I was really into it.'

He laughed. 'At least you're honest.'

'I know my limitations. I wish I knew more, but I do know that some stars are so far away that their light takes millions of years just to reach us.' She was quiet for a long moment. 'Sorry. I'm probably boring you.'

'Not at all. In fact, I'll never think of stars in the same way again.'

'You're teasing me.'

'Absolutely not,' he said seriously.

His gaze held hers. She had the sudden sense that he was about to kiss her, and she quickly turned away, moving her feet nervously in the water.

'I think my feet are getting wrinkled,' she said.

'Do you want me to get a towel?'

'No, that's OK. But I should probably be going. It's getting late.'

He stood up and offered a hand. 'I'll walk you back.'

'I'm sure I can find my way.'

'Just to the bushes, then.'

At the table, she picked up her sandals and spotted Moby heading their way. He trotted up to them just as they stepped onto the grass, his tongue flapping happily. Moby circled them before charging towards the water, as if making sure nothing was hiding. He came to a stop with front paws slapping, then charged off in another direction.

'Moby is a dog with boundless curiosity and enthusiasm,' Travis observed.

'Kind of like you.'

'Kind of. Except I don't roll in fish guts.'

She smiled. The grass was soft underfoot and they reached the hedge a moment later. 'I had a wonderful time today,' she said. 'And tonight, too.'

'So did I. And thanks for the astronomy lesson.' Travis shuffled his feet, then looked at Gabby. 'What are you doing tomorrow?'

'Nothing really. I have to go to the grocery store. Why?'

'Do you want to come with me?'

'On your motorcycle?'

'I want to show you something. And it'll be fun, I promise. I'll even bring lunch.'

She hesitated. It was a simple question, and she knew what the answer should be, especially if she wanted to keep her life from getting complicated. Instead, she found herself beginning to smile.

'Sure,' she said. 'What time?'

If he was surprised by her answer, he didn't show it. 'How about eleven? I'll give you a chance to sleep in.'

She raised a hand to her hair. 'Well, listen, thanks again.'

'Yeah, you too. See you tomorrow.'

For an instant, she thought she'd simply turn and leave. But again their eyes met, and before she realised what was happening, Travis pulled her towards him and kissed her. It took an instant for her brain to register what was happening and then she pushed him back.

'What are you doing?' she gasped.

'I couldn't help it.' He shrugged, seeming not the least bit apologetic. 'It just seemed like the right thing to do.'

'You know I have a boyfriend,' she repeated, knowing that deep down she hadn't minded the kiss at all and hating herself for it.

'I'm sorry if I made you uncomfortable,' he said.

'It's fine,' she said, holding up her hands. 'Just forget about it. But it's not going to happen again, OK?'

'Right.'

She turned and started through the hedge, breathing fast. He'd kissed her! She still couldn't believe it. Though she intended to march straight to her door, she snuck a look over her shoulder and was mortified to realise he'd seen her. He raised a hand in a wave.

'See you tomorrow,' he called out.

She didn't bother to respond, since there was really no reason to. She pulled the sliding patio door closed behind her and marched to her bedroom, doing her best to work up the anger she felt the situation merited. It would have worked, but for the shaky legs and hammering heart, and the lingering realisation that Travis Parker found her desirable enough to want to kiss her.

After Gabby had left, Travis's thoughts kept returning to her. As Moby bounded through the yard, Travis couldn't shake the memory of the way her eyes crinkled when she smiled or the awe in her voice as she'd named the stars.

No question, he was definitely interested in her. It was odd, though. If history were any guide, she really wasn't his type. She didn't strike him as particularly delicate or touchy—he seemed to attract those types of women in droves. When he teased her, she teased him right back; when he pushed the boundaries, she had no qualms about putting him in his place. The whole day struck him as a tantalising dance, in which each of them had taken turns leading, one pushing, the other pulling, and vice versa. He wondered if a dance like that could go on for ever.

Gabby's first thought on waking the next morning was that she liked to think of herself as a good person. It wasn't last night's kiss that had her doubting her integrity. She hadn't had anything to do with that—that was all Travis. No, her guilt had more to do with the fact that she'd willingly returned for dinner. What had she been thinking?

She'd called Kevin last night after she'd got back to her house. As his cellphone rang, she'd prayed he wouldn't detect the guilt in her tone. No problem there, she'd quickly realised; they could barely hear each other at all.

'Hey, sweetie,' she said, 'I just wanted to call—'

'Hey, Gabby!' he interrupted. 'It's really loud in here, so speak up.'

He shouted so loudly that she had to hold the phone away from her ear. 'I can tell.'

'What?'

'I said it sounds noisy!' she shouted back. 'I take it you're having a good time?'

'I can barely hear you! What did you say?'

In the background, she heard a woman's voice asking if he wanted another vodka and tonic. Kevin's answer was lost in the cacophony.

'Where are you?' she asked.

'I'm not sure of the name. Just some club.'

'What kind of club?'

'Just someplace these other guys wanted to go. No big deal.'

'I'm glad you're having a good time.'

'Speak up!'

She brought her fingers to the bridge of her nose and squeezed. 'I just wanted to talk. I miss you.'

'Yeah, miss you, too, but I'll be home in a few days. Let me call you back tomorrow, OK?'

'Sure.'

'Love you!'

'Love you, too.'

Gabby hung up, annoyed. She'd just wanted to talk to him, but she supposed she should have known better. Conventions had a way of turning grown men back into adolescents. No harm in it. She didn't believe for a moment that he had got himself into trouble or done anything he'd regret.

Like kiss someone else?

She threw back the covers, really wishing she could stop thinking about that. She didn't want to remember the way Travis's lips had felt against hers or the electric spark she'd felt because of it. Still, as she headed for the shower, something else was bugging her, something she couldn't quite put her finger on. Turning on the water, she found herself wondering if—in the brief instant it had happened—she'd also kissed him back.

'**G**ood morning,' Kevin said into the phone, just as Gabby was getting ready to leave. She moved the receiver to her other shoulder.

'Oh, hey,' she answered. 'How are you?'

'Good. Listen, I'm sorry about the call last night.'

'It's OK. You sounded like you were having fun.'

'It was less thrilling than you probably think. I should have known I was in trouble when those guys started doing shots right after dinner, but someone had to keep an eye on them. Anyhow, I'll probably crush them in the golf tournament today. They'll be too hung over even to hit the ball.'

'Who were they?'

'Just some other brokers from Charlotte and Columbia. How about you? What did you end up doing?'

She hesitated. 'Not too much.'

'Hey, I was thinking. Maybe you and I could head down to Miami for a long weekend. One of the guys I was talking to just got back from South Beach, and he said there were a couple of great golf courses nearby.'

She paused. 'Have you ever thought about going to Africa?'

'Africa?'

'Yeah. Or someplace in Europe? Like Greece?'

'Not really. What made you think of that?'

'No reason,' she said.

Travis stepped up onto Gabby's porch and knocked. A moment later, she appeared in the doorway, the phone to her ear. Motioning to the phone, she waved him inside. He stepped into the living room. She pointed to the couch and vanished into the kitchen, the swinging doors swaying behind her.

He took a seat and waited. And waited. Finally, she stepped back into the living room.

'I'm sorry. I know I'm a little late, but the phone's been ringing off the hook all morning.'

Travis stood, thinking that Gabby had grown even prettier overnight, which made no sense at all. 'No big deal,' he answered.

Kevin's call left her wondering again what she was doing, and she willed herself to stop thinking about it. 'Let me just get my things,' she said. 'Where are we going, by the way?'

'Just for a ride,' he said. 'Over the bridge, all the way down Bogue Banks to Emerald Isle, back over the bridge, then we'll wind our way back to this place I want to show you.'

'Where?'

'It's a surprise.'

'It sounds exciting.'

'Don't build it up too much. It's just this place I like to go—nothing spectacular.'

She raised a sardonic eyebrow. 'Have you taken a lot of women there?'

'No,' he said. 'Actually, you'll be the first.'

She waited to see if he would add anything else, but for once he seemed serious.

By that time, they'd reached the drive and Travis motioned towards the bike. 'This is it.'

The chrome on the bike made Gabby squint and she put on a pair of sunglasses.

'Your pride and joy?'

'Frustration and angst.'

'You're not going to start whining about how hard it is to get parts again, are you?'

He made a face, then chuckled. 'I'll try to keep it to myself.'

She walked to the motorcycle. He gave her a helmet, and she fastened it beneath her chin and threw her leg over the seat. 'Where do I put my feet?'

Travis unfolded the rear pegs. 'There's one on each side. And try not to touch the exhaust with your leg. It gets very hot.'

'Good to know. What about my hands?'

'They'll be around me, of course.'

'Such a ladies' man,' she said. 'Why, if you were any smoother, I wouldn't even be able to hold on, would I?'

Travis put on his helmet and in a single, smooth motion climbed on and started the bike. She could feel the slight vibration through her seat and felt a distinct anticipatory thrill. Travis eased the machine forward and onto the street. Gabby reached for his hips. As soon as she touched him, her stomach flipped over. As the motorbike began to accelerate, she told herself to keep her hands steady.

They had soon left the quiet confines of their neighbourhood behind them. Gabby slowly got the hang of leaning when Travis leant, and, a few turns later, they were making their way through Beaufort and over the small bridge to Morehead City. Now the road widened to two lanes and was clogged with weekend beach traffic. They veered towards the bridge that crossed the Intracoastal Waterway and the traffic slowed to a crawl. When they reached the highway that bisected Bogue Banks Island, the traffic heading for Atlantic Beach evaporate and Travis began to pick up speed.

She held him to keep herself steady, intensely conscious of the outline of his back muscles through the thin fabric of his shirt. Despite her best intentions, she was beginning to accept the reality of the attraction she felt for him.

They drifted in an almost dream-like silence past one town, then another—Atlantic Beach, Pine Knoll Shores and Salter Path. At Emerald Isle, the most westerly town on Bogue Banks, Travis slowed for a turning car, and Gabby felt herself lean into him. She wondered if he had noticed the way their bodies were pressed together. Though she willed herself to pull away, she didn't.

There was something happening here, something she didn't quite understand. She loved Kevin and wanted to marry him; that feeling hadn't changed. And yet she couldn't deny that spending time with Travis seemed . . . right, somehow. It seemed an impossible contradiction, and, as they crossed the bridge at the far end of the island, heading towards home, she gave up trying to resolve it.

They made their way up the highway, then turned and cut through Morehead City, passing by the Atlantic Beach bridge and completing the loop on their way back to Beaufort. Minutes later, they were cruising past restaurants and the marina on their way down Front Street. Travis finally pulled onto a large grassy lot near the end of the block, bordered by a Georgian house on one side and a Victorian one on the other. He turned off the engine and removed his helmet.

'Here we are,' he said, ushering her off the bike. 'This is what I wanted to show you.'

There was something in his voice that kept her from making light of what seemed to be nothing more than a vacant lot, and, for a moment, Gabby simply watched as he stared across the road to Shackleford Banks. Removing her helmet, she walked towards him. Reaching his side, she sensed he would tell her what this was all about when he was ready.

'In my opinion, this place has one of the most beautiful views anywhere along the coast,' he finally said. 'It's not like an ocean view, where all you see is waves and water. Here, there's always something new to see. There are always sailboats and yachts streaming towards the marina; if you come out here at night, you can see the crowds along the waterfront and listen to the music. I've seen porpoises and rays passing through the channel and wild horses over on the island.'

'You come out here a lot?'

'Twice a week, maybe. This is where I come to think.'

'I'm sure the neighbours are thrilled about that.'

'It's not like they can do anything about it. I own it.'

'Really?'

'Why do you sound so surprised when you say that?'

'I'm not sure. Buying a lot just sounds so . . . domestic. Like you're the kind of guy who has long-term plans.'

'And you don't see me like that?'

'Well, how about this: you continually surprise me.'

'Like when you brought Molly to the clinic and realised I was a veterinarian?'

'I'd rather not talk about that.'

He laughed. 'Then let's eat.'

She followed him back to the motorcycle, where he unpacked a basket and a blanket he'd attached to the back of the bike. After leading her up a small incline, he spread the blanket and motioned for her to sit. Once they were both comfortable, he started removing Tupperware containers.

'What's on the menu?' she asked.

'Three different kinds of cheese, crackers, kalamata olives and grapes—it's more of a snack than a lunch.'

'Sounds perfect.' She reached for the crackers and then sliced some cheese. 'There used to be a house here, right? I can't imagine that this particular spot has been vacant for a hundred and fifty years.'

'You're right,' he said. 'It burnt down when I was a kid. Most of these historic homes had fallen into disrepair, and the one here had been abandoned for years. One winter night, I guess a couple of vagrants lit a fire inside to stay warm. The place went up in minutes, and the next day it was just this smouldering pile. The town bulldozed it away and the lot kind of got forgotten until I tracked down the owner in New Mexico and made a low offer on it. He accepted it immediately.'

'And you're going to build a house here?'

'That's part of my long-term plan, anyway, being that I'm so domestic and all.'

Travis grabbed an olive and popped it into his mouth, then put cheese on a cracker. 'You ready to tell me about your boyfriend yet?'

Gabby's thoughts returned to her conversation wiht Kevin. 'Are we back to this again?'

'I'm just thinking of you. When does he arrive in town? I don't want to get you in any trouble.'

'I appreciate your concern, but I'm a big girl. And, not that it matters, but he'll be coming home on Wednesday. Why?'

'Because I've enjoyed getting to know you these last couple of days.'

'And I've enjoyed getting to know you.' Gabby smiled.

'But are you sorry it's coming to an end?'

'It doesn't have to come to an end. We'll still be neighbours.'

'And I'm sure your boyfriend wouldn't mind if I took you out for another motorcycle ride, or went for a picnic with you, right?'

The answer was obvious and her expression became more serious. 'He probably wouldn't be too happy about it.'

'So it'll be ending.'

'We can still be friends.'

He shook his head. 'There's no such thing as *being friends*. Not with single men and women our age. It just doesn't work like that, unless you're talking about someone you've known for a very long time. And besides, I'm not sure I want to be friends.'

'Why not?'

'Because most likely I'd find myself wanting more than that.'

She said nothing. Travis watched her, unable to read her expression. Finally he shrugged. 'I don't think you'd want to be friends with me, either. You'd probably end up falling for me, too, and doing something you'd regret.'

'It sounds like you've got the whole thing figured out.'

'I do.'

'Except for the part about me falling for you.'

'You can't see that happening?'

'I have a boyfriend.'

'And you're going to marry him?'

'As soon as he asks. That's why I moved here.'

'Why hasn't he asked you yet?'

'Why are you so curious?'

'Because,' he said, his eyes steady on hers, 'if I was him, and you moved up here to be with me, I would've asked you already.'

She looked away, and, when she spoke, her voice was soft. 'Don't ruin this for me, OK?'

'Ruin what?'

'This. Today. Yesterday. Last night.' She took a deep breath. 'This weekend has meant a lot to me, if only because I finally felt I'd made a friend. A couple of them, actually. I didn't realise how much I'd missed having friends in my life. Spending time with you and your sister reminded me of how much I left behind when I moved here. I mean, I'm not sorry I made the decision I did, but it's hard sometimes. When you say things like you just said, and I know you don't mean them, it just trivialises everything.'

'What makes you think I didn't mean what I said?' Travis countered. 'I meant every word. But I understand that you don't want to hear it. Let me just say that I hope your boyfriend realises how lucky he is. I'm sorry if that makes you uncomfortable, and I won't say it again.' He grinned. 'But I had to say it once.'

She looked away, liking what he had said despite herself. Travis turned towards the water, allowing her the silence she needed; unlike Kevin, he always seemed to know how to respond.

'We should probably be heading back, don't you think?' He motioned towards the bike. 'You should check on Molly.'

'Yeah,' she agreed. 'That's probably a good idea.'

They packed up the remains of the food, then folded up the blanket and retraced their steps to the motorcycle. Travis refastened the blanket and basket, then put on his helmet. Gabby did the same, and they pulled out of the lot a moment later. Gabby clung to Travis's hips, trying and failing to convince herself that he'd said similar things to dozens of different women in the past.

A short time later, they pulled into her drive, and Travis brought the motorcycle to a halt. Gabby dismounted. Standing before him, she felt an awkwardness she hadn't experienced since high school.

'Thanks for today,' she said. She handed Travis the helmet, watching as he placed it on the seat.

'My pleasure,' he said. 'I guess I'll see you around?'

'Hard not to, us being neighbours and all.'

He nodded. 'Do me a favour? If this whole boyfriend thing doesn't work out, give me a call.'

'I might just do that.'

He turned the handlebars and started walking the motorcycle backwards, getting into position to leave her drive. He was about to start the engine when he looked at her again. 'Would you have dinner with me tomorrow night?'

She crossed her arms. 'I can't believe you just asked me that.'

'A man's got to seize the moment. It's kind of my motto.'

She took a step backwards, but, in spite of her reservations, she found herself smiling at his persistence. 'How about if I make you dinner tonight instead? At my place. Seven o'clock.'

'Sounds great,' he said, and a moment later she was standing in the drive, wondering if she had taken temporary leave of her senses.

Five

WITH THE SUN beating down and the water from the hose icy cold, Travis was having a hard time keeping Moby in one place. The short leash didn't seem to help much. Moby hated baths. He'd given Travis his best 'how could you do this to me?' expression as he was being walked round to the back of the house, but Travis had shaken his head.

'Don't blame me. I didn't tell you to roll in dead fish, did I?'

Moby loved to roll in dead fish, the more foul-smelling the better. Now, out at the back, with the leash secured to the deck railing, he danced from side to side trying to avoid getting even more wet than he already was.

'It's only water, you big baby,' Travis scolded. He set aside the hose and poured a third of a bottle of shampoo on Moby's back. He scrubbed for a few minutes and rinsed again.

Once he was satisfied that Moby was clean, Travis took the dog to another part of the deck and secured him again. He'd learned that if allowed to roam immediately after a bath, Moby would return to the scene of the crime as quickly as possible. Now, the boxer shook away the excess water and lay down on the deck with a grunt.

Afterwards, Travis mowed the lawn. As he pushed the mower, he kept glancing reflexively towards Gabby's house. A few minutes earlier, he'd seen her leave the garage and hop in her car. If she'd seen him, she hadn't shown it. She'd simply backed out, then headed towards town. He'd never met anyone quite like her. And now she'd invited him to dinner. He didn't know what to make of that.

Wondering about all of this was new to him. But, then again, he couldn't remember the last time he'd enjoyed himself so thoroughly with a woman. After finishing the lawn, he dragged the mower back to the garage, noting that Gabby still hadn't returned. She'd left the garage door cracked open and Molly wandered out into the yard, then turned round and headed back inside.

Back in his kitchen, Travis downed a glass of iced tea in one long gulp. He thought again about their upcoming dinner and wondered what would happen. He was, he realised for the first time in his dating life, nervous that he might do something wrong.

Gabby made the short drive to the grocery store and pulled into the crowded lot. Slinging her bag over her shoulder, she got out of the car, located a trolley and entered the store.

She'd spotted Travis mowing the lawn earlier, but she'd ignored him, needing somehow to feel more in control than she actually was. Her nice, orderly little world had been thrown out of whack, and she needed time to regain her composure.

Insidethe store, Gabby made her way to the produce section, where she collected some fresh green beans, the ingredients for a salad and a box of pasta. Knowing that Travis liked chicken, she put a packet of breasts in the trolley, thinking that a bottle of Chardonnay would go well with them. She scanned the limited selection of wines for a winery that she recognised. There were two from Napa Valley, but she chose something from Australia, thinking it sounded a little more exotic.

The checkout lines were long, but at last she made it back to her car. Glancing in the rearview mirror, she paused for a moment, staring at herself as if through someone else's eyes.

She was drawn to Travis; she couldn't deny that. It wasn't just that he was handsome and that he made her feel desirable. It had something to do with his natural exuberance and with the fact that he had lived a life so different from hers, and yet they still spoke the same language. She'd never met anyone like him. Most people she'd known seemed to live their lives as if marking off goals on a score sheet. Get a job, get married, buy a house, have kids; and, until this weekend, she realised, she'd been no different. Somehow, compared with the choices he'd made and the places he'd visited, her life seemed so banal.

But would she do it differently if she could? She doubted it. Her experiences had formed her into the woman that she'd become. And yet, as she started the engine, she knew that wasn't the question that mattered. The choice before her was this: Where do I go from here?

It is never too late to change things. The thought frightened her even as it excited her. A few minutes later, she was heading towards Beaufort, feeling as if somehow she'd been given the chance to start over.

The sun had drifted across the sky by the time Gabby got home. She reached for the bags and brought them inside. She put the wine into the refrigerator along with the chicken, then set a pot of water on the stove for the pasta. While it was heating, she mixed the ingredients for salad together with a bit of cheese and the kalamata olives Travis had introduced her to that day.

She added the pasta to the water, and sautéed the chicken in olive oil, wishing she could have done something a bit fancier. She set the oven to warm, added some broth to the bowl with the chicken, and put it in, hoping that would keep it from drying out. She drained the pasta and put it in a bowl.

In her bedroom, she laid out some clothes and took a shower. On the bed were a new pair of jeans and a beaded, low-cut shirt. She dressed and then slipped on sandals and a dangly pair of earrings. She stepped in front of the floor mirror and was pleased with the way she looked.

With time running out, she set out some candles throughout the house and was adding the last of them to the table when she heard Travis knocking. She stood up straight, trying to compose herself, then made her way to the door.

When the door opened, Travis found himself unable to turn away. Nor could he find his voice. Instead, he stared wordlessly at Gabby, trying to sort through the jumble of emotions that began to crowd his heart.

Gabby smiled at his obvious discomfiture. 'Come in,' she said. 'I've just about got everything ready.'

Travis followed her inside, trying not to stare.

'I was about to open a bottle of wine. Would you like a glass?'

'Please.'

In the kitchen, she picked up the opener, then reached into the fridge for the bottle.

Travis stepped forward. 'I can get that for you.'

As he opened the bottle, Travis watched her retrieve two glasses from the cupboard. She set them on the counter, and Travis noted the label. 'I've never had this kind before. Is it any good?'

'I have no idea.'

'Then I guess it'll be new for both of us.' He poured, handing one glass to her, trying to read her expression.

'Would you like to go sit outside?' she asked.

'Love to.'

They took a seat in the rockers she'd placed near the door. Gabby took a sip of her wine, glad for something to take the edge off her nerves.

'I like your view,' Travis said gamely. 'It reminds me of mine.'

Gabby laughed. 'Unfortunately, I haven't learned to enjoy it the way you do.'

'Very few people do. It's kind of a lost art these days. Watching the creek flow by is a little like smelling the roses.'

'Maybe it's a small-town thing,' she speculated.

Travis eyed her with interest. 'Tell me honestly, are you enjoying life in Beaufort?' he asked.

'It has its good points.'

'I hear the neighbours are terrific.'

'I've only met one.'

'And?'

'He has a tendency to ask loaded questions.'

Travis grinned. He loved her sense of play.

'But to answer your question,' she went on, 'yes, I do like it here. I think I'm learning to love the slower pace of life.'

'You make it sound like Savannah is as cosmopolitan as New York or Paris.'

'It isn't.' She looked over her glass at him. 'But I will say that Savannah is definitely closer to New York than Beaufort.'

He leant back in his rocker, the picture of ease. 'Do you think you'll ever move back?'

'I don't think so,' she said. 'Don't get me wrong. I think it's a great place, and it's one of the most beautiful cities in the South. I love the way the city is laid out. It has the most beautiful squares—and some of the houses that front them are stunning. When I was a little girl, I used to imagine myself living in one of them. For a long time, it was a dream of mine. But as I grew older, I began to realise that it was more my mom's dream than my own.'

'Can you imagine yourself staying here, in Beaufort?'

She thought about her answer, sensing there was more to the question than there appeared. 'I suppose that depends. It's not exactly exciting, but, on the other hand, it's not a bad place to raise a family.'

'And that's important?'

She turned towards him with a faint air of challenge. 'Is there anything more important?'

'No,' he agreed evenly, 'there isn't. I'm evidence of that belief because I lived it. Beaufort is the kind of place where Little League baseball generates more conversation than the Super Bowl, and I like thinking that I can raise my kids where the little world they live in is all they know. That they'll never grow jaded, the way city kids do.'

'It's nice to hear you say something like that,' Gabby said. 'A lot of people don't think that way.'

'I love this town.'

'Not that,' she said, smiling. 'I was talking about the way you said you wanted to raise your kids. It seems like you've given it a lot of thought.'

'I have,' he conceded.

'You know, the more I've got to know you, the more you've come to strike me as impossibly well-adjusted.'

'I could say the same about you,' he responded. 'Maybe that's why we get along so well.'

She stared at him, feeling the crackle of tension between them. 'You ready for dinner?'

'That sounds great.'

Taking their wineglasses, they returned to the kitchen. Gabby motioned for Travis to sit at the table while she got things ready, and, as he watched her, Travis felt a sense of contentment settle upon him. At dinner, he ate two pieces of chicken, and complimented Gabby extravagantly on her cooking, until she giggled, begging him to stop. He asked her repeatedly about her childhood in Savannah, and she finally relented, regaling him with girlhood stories that made them both chuckle. In time, the sky turned grey and then blue and finally black. The candles burnt lower, and they poured the last of the wine into their glasses, both aware that they were sitting across from a person who just might change the course of their lives for ever if they weren't careful.

After dinner was over and Travis had helped Gabby to clean up, they retreated to the couch, nursing the last of their wine and sharing stories from their pasts. As the evening wore on, Travis inched closer, casually slipping his arm round Gabby. She leant into him, content to watch the play of silver moonlight outside as it filtered through the clouds.

'What are you thinking about?' Travis asked at one point, breaking a particularly long yet comfortable silence.

'I was thinking how natural this whole weekend has seemed.' Gabby looked at him. 'Like we've known each other for ever.'

He pulled her tighter. 'The more I get to know you, the more you surprise me. I like that.'

'What are neighbours for?'

'Is that still all I am to you? Just a neighbour?'

Gabby glanced away without responding.

Travis went on, 'I know it makes you uncomfortable, but I can't leave without telling you that just being neighbours isn't enough for me.'

'Travis—'

'Let me finish, OK?' he said. 'Earlier today, you told me how much you'd missed having friends around, and I've been thinking about that. It made me realise that even though I have friends, I've been missing something that all my friends have. Laird and Allison, Joe and Megan, Matt and Liz, all have each other. I don't have that in my life, and, until you came along, I wasn't sure I even wanted it. But now . . .'

She picked at the beadwork on her shirt, resisting his words and yet welcoming them, too.

'I don't want to lose you, Gabby. I can't imagine seeing you walk to your car in the morning and pretending that none of this ever happened. I can't imagine not sitting here with you on the couch, like we're doing now.' He swallowed. 'And right now, I can't imagine being in love with any other woman.'

Gabby wasn't sure she'd heard him right, but when she saw the way he was staring at her, she knew he meant it. And with that, she felt the last of her defences falling away and knew she had fallen in love with him as well.

The phone rang, shattering her thoughts, and Travis turned away. Gabby leant forward to answer it, her voice betraying nothing: 'Oh, hey, how are you? . . . Not much . . . Uh-huh . . . I was running some errands . . . What's been going on there?'

As she listened to Kevin's voice, a rush of guilt washed over her.

'Oh, that's great. Congratulations. I'm glad you won . . .'

Gabby leant back against the couch, trying to keep her voice steady, wishing she hadn't answered, wishing he hadn't called. 'No, nothing's wrong. I'm just tired, I guess . . . No, nothing to worry about. It's been a long weekend.' It wasn't a lie, but it wasn't the truth, either, which made her feel even worse. Travis was staring downwards, listening.

'I will,' she went on. 'Yeah, you, too . . . Uh-huh . . . OK . . . I do, too. And have fun tomorrow. Bye.'

Hanging up the phone, she seemed preoccupied for a moment. Travis knew enough not to say anything.

'That was Kevin,' she said.

'I figured.'

'He won a tournament today.'

'Good for him.'

A silence descended between them.

'I think I need some fresh air,' she finally said, rising from the couch. She made her way to the sliding door and stepped outside. Travis watched her go, wondering if he should join her or whether she needed to be alone. But he felt he needed to be with her, now more than ever.

He made his way out of the door and joined her against the rail. In the moonlight, her skin was pearly, her eyes darkly luminous.

'I'm sorry,' he said.

'Don't be. There's nothing for you to be sorry for.' She forced a smile. 'It's my fault, not yours. I knew what I was getting into.'

Gabby could sense that he wanted to touch her, but she knew she shouldn't let the evening progress any further. Yet she couldn't break the spell that Travis's declaration had cast over her. It didn't make sense. It took time to fall in love, more than a single weekend, yet somehow it had happened. She sensed Travis's nervousness as he stood beside her and took a step closer to him. When he turned to face her, she slipped her arms round his neck. She could hear the little voice inside warning her to stop. But another urge had taken hold of her, and she knew it was pointless to deny it.

Travis pulled her tight against him, noticing how her body seemed to fit against his. As they stood holding each other, he felt as if he'd reached the end of a long journey. When he whispered, 'I love you, Gabby Holland' against her ear, he'd never felt more sure of anything.

Gabby sank into him.

'I love you, too, Travis Parker,' she whispered, and as they stood in each other's arms, Gabby couldn't imagine wanting anything more than what was happening now, all regrets and reservations swept aside.

He kissed her again and again. She ran her hands over his chest and shoulders, feeling the strength in the arms that held her, knowing that this was what the weekend had been building towards all along. They kissed on the deck for a long time. Finally she pulled back and took his hand to lead him inside, past the living room and towards the bedroom.

Though they both returned to work on Monday, over the next two days, Travis and Gabby spent every free moment together. They made love on Monday morning before work, had lunch together at a café in Morehead City, and, that evening, they took Moby for a walk on the beach near Fort Macon.

Afterwards, they stopped at the grocery store and Travis picked up the ingredients for a chicken Caesar salad. In the kitchen, he grilled the chicken and Gabby rinsed the lettuce leaves at the sink. They curled up on the couch after dinner and, that night, they lay in each other's arms until long after midnight.

On Tuesday evening, they sat on Travis's deck.

'What's going to happen next?' Travis asked.

Gabby rotated a water glass in her hands. 'I'm not sure,' she said in a low voice.

'You're going to tell him about us, aren't you?'

'I don't know,' she said. 'I really don't.' She turned to Travis, her eyes filled with tears. 'Don't get mad at me. Please don't. Believe me when I say that I know how this makes you feel, because it makes me feel the same way. But as much as I care about you, we're not the same people. For you, it's easy—we love each other, so we should be together. But Kevin is important to me, too.'

'What about all those things you said?' Travis asked, trying not to sound as scared as he felt.

Her smile was pained. 'I love you, Travis, I really do. If I thought of this as a weekend fling, I'd put it behind me now and then go back to imagining a future with Kevin. But it's not going to be that easy. I have to make a choice between the two of you. Kevin's not perfect, but I know what to expect. Or at least until you came along, I thought I did. But now . . .'

She paused, and Travis could see her hair moving slightly in the breeze. She hugged her arms tightly to her body.

'We've only known each other for a few days, and I've started wondering whether you would feel the same way about me in the future as you do right now, or whether this will just end up like all your previous relationships. As much as we think we know each other, we don't. All I know is that I fell in love with you, and I've never been more frightened about anything in my entire life.'

She stopped. Travis rubbed his brow.

'You're right,' he admitted. 'Your choice is different from mine. But you're wrong if you think this was just a fling for me. I might have started out thinking along those lines, but . . .' He reached for her hand. 'That's not how it ended up. The more time we spent together, the more I could imagine it lasting in the future. That's never happened to me before, and I'm not sure it'll ever happen again. I've never been in love with anyone before you came along—not real love, anyway. Not like this, and I'd be a fool if I let you slip away without a fight.'

He ran a hand through his hair, drained.

'I don't know what else I can tell you, Gabby, other than that I can imagine spending the rest of my life with you. I know that sounds crazy. But I've never been more sure of anything. And if you give me a chance, I'm going to live the rest of my life proving to you that you made the right decision.'

For a long moment, neither of them said anything. Gabby wanted to run away, and she wanted to stay here for ever—a reflection of the impossible bind she'd got herself into. She patted his knee. 'Will you do something for me?'

'Of course,' he said.

'Will you make love to me? And not think to yourself that it might be the last time it ever happens?'

'That's two things.'

She didn't dignify his answer with a response. Instead, she held out her hand to him. As they moved towards the bedroom, she broke into the tiniest of smiles, finally knowing what she had to do.

PART TWO
Six

February 2007

TRAVIS TRIED to shake free of those memories from nearly eleven years ago, wondering why they'd resurfaced with such clarity. Was it because he was now old enough to realise how unusual itwas to fall in love so quickly? Or simply because he missed the intimacy of those days? He didn't know.

Lately, it seemed he didn't know a lot of things. There were people who claimed to have all the answers, though Travis had never believed them. But if there were one person who could answer any question, his question would be this: how far should a person go in the name of true love?

He could pose the question to a hundred people and get a hundred different answers. Most were obvious: a person should sacrifice, or accept, or forgive, or even fight if need be. But none of these would help him now. Thinking back, he recalled events he wished he could change, tears he wished had never been shed, time that could have been better spent, and frustrations he should have shrugged off. Life, it seemed, was full of regret, and he yearned to turn back the clock so he could live parts of his life over again. One thing was certain: he should have been a better husband. And as he considered the question of how far a person should go in the name of love, he knew what his answer would be. Sometimes it meant a person should lie.

And soon, he had to make his choice as to whether he would.

The fluorescent lights and white tiles underscored the sterility of the hospital. Travis moved slowly down the corridor, steeling himself to head over and talk to Gabby. But the vivid parade of memories earlier had drained him, and he stopped, knowing a few more minutes to collect his thoughts wouldn't make any difference.

He ducked into a small reception room and took a seat. Watching the steady, rhythmic movement in the corridor, he realised that despite the never-ending emergencies, the staff had a routine here, much as he had his own routines at home. It was inevitable for people to try to create a sense of normality in a place where nothing was normal. His mornings were a case in point, for every one was the same. Six fifteen alarm; a minute to get out of bed and nine minutes in the shower, another four minutes to shave and brush his teeth, and seven minutes to get dressed. After that, he'd hurry downstairs to pour cereal; he'd check backpacks for homework and make peanut-butter-and-jelly sandwiches for lunches while his sleepy daughters ate their breakfast. At exactly seven fifteen they'd troop out of the door, and he'd wait with them at the end of the driveway for the school bus.

Lisa and Christine were six and eight, and as he watched them venture out to start another day, he often felt his heart clench with worry. Perhaps that was common, but recently he dwelled on things he never had before. Sometimes he would find himself replaying the morning over and over, searching for clues to their well-being.

It shouldn't have been like this. Gabby should have been with him. Gabby should have been the one tying shoes and adjusting the blankets. She was good at things like that, as he'd known she would be from the very beginning. In the days that followed their first weekend together, he'd known, at some deep level, that he'd never find a better mother or more perfect complement to him.

Their courtship hadn't been quite as uncomplicated for her. She was the one torn between two men vying for her love. Travis could remember her pained expression on the morning she knew Kevin would be arriving back in town. She had barely touched her breakfast; when he had kissed her goodbye, she'd responded with only the flicker of a smile. The hours had crawled by without a word. Travis had busied himself at work and made calls to find homes for Molly's puppies, knowing it was important to Gabby. Eventually, after work Travis went to check on Molly. She didn't return to the garage after he let her out. Instead, she lay in the tall marsh grass that fronted Gabby's property, staring towards the street as the sun sank lower in the sky.

It was well after dark when Gabby had turned ino the drive. He remembered the steady way she had looked at him as she stepped out of the car. Without a word, she had sat down beside him on the steps. Molly wandered up and began to nuzzle her.

'Hey,' Travis said, breaking the silence.

'Hey.' Her voice sounded drained of emotion.

'I think I found homes for all of the puppies,' he offered.

'Yeah?'

He nodded, and the two of them sat together without speaking.

'I'm always going to love you,' he said, searching and failing to find adequate words to comfort her.

'I believe you,' she whispered. She looped her arm through his and leant her head against his shoulder. 'That's why I'm here.'

Travis had never liked hospitals, but Gabby had thrived working here at Carteret General, energised by the steady buzz of activity. Soon after they met, Gabby had left the paediatrician's office and had taken a job in the emergency room. There'd recently been a letter in the mailbox, something from the administrator's office announcing plans to honour her tenth year working at the hospital.

A small plaque would be hung in her honour in one of the corridors, though as yet it hadn't happened.

He doubted that she cared. Gabby hadn't taken the job at the hospital because she might one day receive a plaque.

Travis shifted in his seat, conscious of the papers in his pocket. Where once he'd kept them in his desk, he now found it impossible to go about his daily life without them, even though they portended the end of everything he held dear.

It seemed strange that they could signal the official end of his marriage. They were codified words, nothing more, but the power afforded them now seemed almost malevolent. Where, he wondered, was the humanity in those phrases? Where was the emotion governed by these laws? Where was the acknowledgment of the life Travis and Gabby had led together? And why in God's name had Gabby wanted them drawn up in the first place?

It shouldn't have ended like this, and it was certainly not an outcome he had foreseen when he'd proposed to Gabby. He remembered their autumn trip to New York. While Gabby had been at the hotel spa, he'd sneaked over to West 47th Street for the engagement ring. They'd taken a carriage ride through Central Park, and, beneath a full-moon sky, he'd asked for her hand in marriage and was overcome by the passionate way she'd wrapped her arms round him while whispering her consent.

And then? Life, he supposed. In between her shifts at the hospital, she planned the wedding. Eighty people in a small, weathered chapel on Cumberland Island in spring 1997. They honeymooned in Cancún, which ended up being an idyllic choice for both of them. Gabby wanted someplace relaxing, and they spent hours lying in the sun and eating well. He wanted a bit more adventure, so she learned to scuba-dive, and she joined him on a day trip to see the nearby Aztec ruins.

The give-and-take of the honeymoon set the tone for the marriage. Their dream house was constructed by their first anniversary; Gabby was pregnant a couple of months later. After Christine was born, Gabby cut back on her hours, and they worked out a schedule that ensured one of them was always home with the baby. When Lisa followed two years later, neither of them noticed much of a change, other than added joy and excitement in the house.

Christmases and birthdays came and went. Max eventually retired, leaving Travis to take over the clinic. Gabby limited her hours even more and had enough time to volunteer at school. On their fourth anniversary, they went to Italy and Greece; for their sixth, they spent a week on safari in Africa. Travis taught his daughters to wakeboard and ski; he coached their soccer teams in the fall. On the rare occasions when he stopped to reflect on his life, he wondered if anyone in the world felt as blessed as he did.

Not that things were always perfect. Years ago, he and Gabby had gone through a rough patch. But even then, he had never truly believed their marriage to be in jeopardy. Nor, he suspected, had she. Marriage, each of them realised intuitively, was about compromise and forgiveness. It was about balance. He and Gabby had had that for years, but right now they didn't, and the realisation left him wishing there was something, anything, he could do to restore that delicate balance between them.

Travis knew he couldn't postpone seeing her any longer, and he rose from his seat. Holding the flowers he'd brought, he started down the corridor. His legs were shaky, and he could feel the beginning of a headache, a dull throb at the back of his head. He was falling apart. He'd lost eighteen pounds in the past twelve weeks, and in the mirror he could see that his cheeks had hollowed out. He reached the door and pushed it open, forcing himself to smile as he saw her. 'Hi, sweetheart.'

He waited for her to stir, but nothing happened, and in the long, empty silence that followed, Travis felt an ache like a physical pain in his heart. It was always like this. Stepping into the room, he set the flowers on the windowsill, then took a seat in the chair by the bed and reached for her hand. Her skin was pale, almost waxy, and her body seemed smaller. Still, she was as remarkable to him as she had been the first time he'd seen her. It amazed him that he'd known her almost eleven years. Not because the length of time was extraordinary, but because those years seemed to contain more . . . *life* than the first thirty-two years without her. It was the reason he'd come to the hospital today; it was the reason he came every day. He couldn't imagine being anywhere else.

Eighty-four days had passed since the accident, and now he had to make a choice. He had no idea what to do. He'd been searching for answers in the Bible and in the writings of Aquinas and St Augustine. Occasionally he would find a striking passage, but nothing more than that. He would close the book and find himself staring out of the window as if hoping to find the solution somewhere in the sky.

He seldom drove straight home from the hospital. Instead, he would drive across the bridge and walk the sands of Atlantic Beach. He knew his daughters were as upset as he was, and he needed time to compose himself. It would be unfair to subject them to his angst.

Always they asked about her, but usually he didn't know what to tell them. They were mature enough to understand that Mommy wasn't well and had to stay in the hospital. They understood that when they visited, it would seem as if Mommy were asleep. But he couldn't bring himself to tell them the truth about her condition. Instead, he would cuddle with them on the couch and thumb through the photo albums Gabby had assembled with care. Travis would tell stories associated with each photograph and, as he stared at Gabby's radiant face in the photos, his throat would tighten at the knowledge that he'd never seen anyone more beautiful.

Later, after the girls had gone to bed, he would put away the albums and sit alone on the couch, weighed down by the sadness he felt inside. Sometimes Stephanie would call. Their conversations were filled with their usual banter, but it was somehow stilted at the same time, for he

knew she wanted him to forgive himself. Despite her sometimes flip-
pant remarks, he knew what she was really saying—that it wasn't his
fault. That she and others were worried about him. To head her off,
he'd always say that he was doing fine, for the truth was something he
knew she didn't want to hear—that not only did he doubt he'd ever be
fine again, but he wasn't even sure he ever wanted to be.

Warm bands of sunlight stretched towards them. Travis squeezed
Gabby's hand and winced at the pain in his wrist. It had been in a cast
until a month ago; the bones in his arm had fractured and his ligaments
had torn in half.

'The girls are good,' he began. 'Christine finished her Lucky Charms
at breakfast, and Lisa was close. I know you worry about how much
they eat, but they've been pretty good about nibbling on the snacks
I put out after school.'

Outside the window, a pigeon landed on the sill. It walked a few
steps one way, then back again, before finally settling in place as it did
on most days. It seemed, somehow, to know when it was time for Travis
to visit. There were times he believed it was an omen of sorts, though of
what, he had no idea.

'We do homework after dinner. You'd be excited at how well
Christine is doing in math. We've been using those flashcards you
bought and she didn't miss a single question on her latest test.'

The sound of the cooing pigeon was audible through the glass.

'And Lisa's doing well. For her birthday, she wants a princess theme.'

He cleared his throat, trying to act as naturally as he could. He had
no idea whether she heard him; the medical community seemed
divided on that. Some swore that coma patients could hear—and possibly remember—conversations; others said just the opposite. Travis
didn't know whom to believe, but he chose to live his days on the side
of the optimists.

'Other than that, not much new is going on,' he said. 'My dad's still
covering for me at the clinic. It's like he never left. People still adore him.'

He heard a knock at the door and saw Gretchen walk in. In the past
month, he'd come to depend on her. Unlike the other nurses, she
maintained faith that Gabby would emerge from all of this just fine.
'Hey, Travis,' she chirped. 'Sorry for interrupting, but I've got to hook
up a new IV.'

When Travis nodded, she approached Gabby. 'I'll bet you're starving, honey,' she said. 'Just give me a second, OK?'

She worked quickly, removing one IV bag and replacing it with another, all the while keeping up a steady stream of conversation. 'I know you're sore from your workout this morning. We really went at it, didn't we? I was proud of you.'

Every morning and evening, a nurse came in to flex and stretch Gabby's limbs. Bend the knee, straighten it out; flex the foot up, then push it down. They did this for every joint and muscle in Gabby's body.

After she finished hanging the bag, Gretchen checked the flow and adjusted the sheets, then turned to Travis.

'Are you doing OK today?'

'I don't know,' he said.

Twelve weeks ago, Gabby was rolled into the emergency room on a gurney, unconscious and bleeding heavily from a gash on her shoulder. The physicians concentrated first on the gash because of the heavy blood loss, though, in retrospect, Travis wondered whether a different approach would have changed things.

He didn't know, nor would he ever. Like Gabby, he'd been rolled into the emergency room; like Gabby, he'd spent the night unconscious. But the following day, he woke up in pain with a mangled arm, while Gabby never woke up at all.

The doctors didn't try to conceal their concern. Brain injuries were always serious, they said, but they were hopeful that all would be well in time.

In time.

He sometimes wondered if doctors realised that time was something finite. He doubted it. No one really understood the choice that lay before him. On the surface, it was simple. He would do exactly what Gabby wanted, exactly as she'd made him promise.

But what if . . .

And that was the thing. He stayed awake at night considering the question. In the darkness, he would toss and turn, wishing for someone else to make the choice for him. More often than not, he'd wake in the morning with a tear-drenched pillow in the place where Gabby should have been. And the first words out of his mouth were always the same.

'I'm so sorry, sweetheart.'

The choice Travis now had to make had its roots in two distinct events. The first event related to a couple named Kenneth and Eleanor Baker. The second event, the accident itself, had occurred on a rainy, windy night twelve weeks ago.

The accident was simple to explain, similar to many in that a series of isolated and seemingly inconsequential mistakes somehow came together and exploded in the most horrific of ways. In mid-November, they'd driven to the RBC Center in Raleigh to see David Copperfield perform onstage. Travis was running late at the clinic, and they got a late start out of Beaufort. In his haste, Travis forgot his umbrella, despite the ominous clouds and building wind. That was mistake number one.

By the time they'd left the theatre, rain was pouring down hard, and Travis remembered standing with Gabby, wondering how best to get to their car. They bumped into friends who'd also seen the show and who offered to walk Travis to his car so he wouldn't get wet. But Travis declined the offer and bolted into the rain, splashing through ankle-deep puddles on the way to his car. He was soaked to the bone by the time he crawled in, especially his feet. That was mistake number two.

Because it was late, and because they both had to work the following morning, on the way home Travis drove fast despite the wind and rain, trying to save a few minutes in a drive that normally took two and a half hours. Though it was difficult to see through the windshield, he drove in the passing lane, racing past cars with more cautious drivers. That was mistake number three. Gabby asked him repeatedly to slow down. More than once, he did as she asked, only to speed up again as soon as he could. By the time they reached Goldsboro, she'd become so angry that she'd stopped speaking to him. She leant her head back and closed her eyes, refusing to talk. That was mistake number four.

The accident could have been avoided had none of the other things happened. Had he taken his umbrella, he might not have run to his car. Had he not run to the car in the rain, his feet might have stayed dry. Had he slowed the car, he might have been able to control it. Had he respected Gabby's wishes, they wouldn't have argued, and she would have been watching and stopped him before it was too late.

Near Newport, there's a wide, easy bend in the highway intersected by a set of traffic lights. By that point in the drive—less than twenty minutes from home—the itch in his feet was driving him crazy. His shoelaces had tightened with the moisture, and no matter how hard he tried to push his shoes off, the toe of one foot would slip from the heel of the other. He leant forward, his eyes barely above the dashboard, and reached for one shoe with his hand. Glancing downwards, he struggled with the knot and didn't see the light turn yellow.

When the knot finally did come free, he lifted his eyes, but it was already too late. The light had turned red, and a truck was entering the intersection. Instinctively, he hit the brakes and the car's tail began to swerve on the rain-slicked road. The car careered out of control. At the last instant, it avoided the truck only to hurtle off the highway and towards the pines. The mud was even more slippery, and there was nothing he could do. He turned the wheel and nothing happened. For an instant, the world seemed to be moving in slow motion. The last thing he remembered was the sickening sound of shattering glass and twisting metal.

Gabby didn't even have time to scream.

Travis brushed a loose strand of hair from Gabby's face and tucked it behind her ear, listening to his stomach as it gurgled. As hungry as he was, he couldn't bear the idea of eating.

In the first weeks after the accident, he'd been almost frantic about making sure the evening nurse had his cell number handy. After a month, because Gabby was breathing on her own, she was moved from the intensive care unit to a private room, and he was certain the change would wake her. But as the days passed with no change at all, his manic energy was replaced by a quiet, gnawing dread. At three months, he knew, most patients who remained in a coma were moved to a nursing home for long-term care. That day was today, and he was supposed to let the administrator know what he wanted to do. But that wasn't the only choice he was facing. His major choice had to do with Kenneth and Eleanor Baker, but he wasn't ready to think about them just yet.

The house they built was the kind of place in which Travis could imagine spending the rest of his life. Despite its newness, it had a lived-in quality that Gabby had worked hard to create. She wanted a home that made people feel comfortable as soon as the door was opened.

She was the one who oversaw the details that had made the house come alive. While Travis conceived the structure in terms of square footage and building materials, Gabby introduced eclectic elements he'd never have considered. She wanted big oak beams and a vaulted, soft pine ceiling in the living room. She spent long weekends shopping for antique furniture and knick-knacks. Guessing that they'd spend a lot of time on the wraparound porch, she insisted on an outdoor grill and a seating area located so that they could sit outside without getting wet during storms.

On their first night in their new home, as they lay on the canopy bed, Gabby rolled towards Travis with an expression of pure contentment, her voice almost a purr: 'This place, with you by my side, is where I'll always want to be.'

The kids had been having problems, even if he didn't mention them to Gabby. Not surprising, of course, but, most of the time, Travis was at a loss as to what to do. At eight years old, Christine was throwing temper tantrums, and Lisa, who'd always had a generally sunny disposition, was crying herself to sleep. From downstairs, Travis could hear her weeping on the monitor and he'd have to pinch the bridge of his nose to keep from joining in. On those nights, he would climb the stairs to the girls' bedroom and lie beside Lisa, stroking her hair as she whimpered, 'I miss Mommy' over and over.

Almost too choked up to speak, he would simply say, 'I know. I do, too.'

He couldn't begin to take Gabby's place, and he didn't try. What that left, however, was a hole where Gabby used to be, an emptiness he didn't know how to fill. Gabby, he knew now, had taken a far greater share of the child-care responsibility than he had, and he regretted it. There were so many things he didn't know how to do, things that Gabby had made seem easy.

In the past couple of weeks, things had improved. Kind of. Christine still threw her tantrums and Lisa still cried at night, but they'd adapted to life without their mom. They didn't ask about her as much, and they rarely visited. It was hard for them to go, for they didn't know what to say or even how to act. 'Just talk to her,' he would tell them, and they would try, but their words would trail off into nothing when no response was forthcoming.

Seven

BY MIDAFTERNOON, the sky was turning cloudy, and it was time for Gabby's routine. One day, Travis had asked Gretchen if it would be OK if he did an afternoon workout with Gabby.

'I think she'd like that,' Gretchen had said.

She had walked him through the process, making sure he understood that every muscle and every joint needed attention. While Gretchen and the other nurses always started with Gabby's fingers, Travis started with her toes. He lowered the sheet and reached for her foot, then began flexing her toes up and down.

Travis had come to love doing this for her. The feel of her skin against his was enough to rekindle a dozen memories: the way he'd rubbed her feet while she'd been pregnant, the slow, intoxicating back rubs by candlelight.

He finished with her toes and moved to her ankles; when that was done, he flexed her knees, bending them both to her chest and then straightening them.

'Does that feel good, sweetheart?'

That feels wonderful. Thanks. I was feeling a little stiff.

He knew he'd imagined her answer, but her voice seemed to rise from nowhere when he worked with her like this. Sometimes he wondered whether he was going crazy. 'How are you doing?'

Bored out of my head, if you want to know the truth. Thanks for the flowers. They're lovely. Did you get them from Frick's?

'Where else?'

How are the girls? Tell me the truth this time.

'They're OK. They miss you though; it's hard on them. Sometimes I don't know what to do.'

They'll be OK. They're tougher than they look.

'I know. They take after you.'

Travis imagined her looking him over, her expression wary.

I'm worried about you. You look skinny. You've got to take care of yourself. For the girls. For me.

'I'll always be here for you.'

I know. I'm afraid of that, too. Do you remember Kenneth and Eleanor Baker?

Travis stopped flexing. 'Yes.'

Then you know what I'm talking about.

He sighed. 'Yes.'

He began working on her fingers and arms. He bent over and kissed her on the forehead. 'I miss you so much.'

I miss you, too.

His throat clenched as he finished the exercise routine, knowing Gabby's voice would begin to fade away again. 'You know you've got to wake up, right? The girls need you. I need you.'

I know. I'm trying. Will you sit with me a while longer?

'Of course.'

And hold my hand?

He nodded, covering her with the sheet once more. He sat in the chair by the bed and took her hand. Outside, the pigeon had come back, and, beyond it, heavy clouds shifted in the sky, transforming into images from other worlds. He kissed her fingertips and brought her hand to his cheek, feeling her warmth and wishing for even the tiniest of movements, but nothing happened.

Eleanor Baker was a thirty-eight-year-old housewife with two boys she adored. Eight years ago, she'd come into the emergency room vomiting and complaining about a blinding pain in the back of her head. Gabby happened to be working that day, though she didn't treat Eleanor. She knew nothing about her until the following Monday, when she learned that Eleanor had been placed in the ICU when she didn't wake up on Sunday morning. Her coma was caused by a severe case of bacterial meningitis.

Her husband, Kenneth, a gregarious, friendly history teacher at East Carteret High School, spent his days at the hospital. Over time, Gabby got to know him. He adored his wife and children, drank Mountain Dew by the litre, and was a devout Catholic.

Travis knew all this because Gabby spoke about him after work.

Weeks turned into months and Eleanor Baker was eventually moved to a nursing home. Months then passed into years, and Gabby would occasionally bump into Kenneth Baker at the grocery store. Always the conversation would turn to how Eleanor was doing. There was never any change.

But over the years, as they continued to run into each other, Gabby noticed that Kenneth had changed. 'She's still going,' was the way he casually began to describe her condition. Where there had once been a light in his eyes when he spoke about Eleanor, there was now only blankness. In the cereal aisle or frozen food section, he mentioned one horrible event after another: he'd lost his job, lost his house, his oldest kid had dropped out of high school, and the younger one had been arrested again for dealing drugs. *Again.* That was the word Gabby emphasised when she told Travis about it later. She also said she was pretty sure he'd been drunk when she'd run into him. 'I just feel so bad for him,' Gabby said. 'Sometimes I think it might have been easier if his wife had died instead.'

Staring out of the window, Travis thought about Kenneth and Eleanor Baker. He had no idea whether Eleanor was still alive. Since the accident, he'd replayed those conversations in his head nearly every day. He wondered whether Eleanor and Kenneth Baker had been brought into their lives for a reason. How many people, after all, knew anyone who'd been in a coma? And if there was some sort of reason, what was it? To warn him that he was doomed? That his daughters would lose their way? Those questions terrified him, and he awoke every morning with the thought that even if they were struggling, which was normal, he would still insist that the girls behave at home and in school. Because this is what Gabby would have done.

His in-laws sometimes thought he was too hard on the girls. That wasn't surprising. His mother-in-law, in particular, had always been judgmental. In the beginning, Travis and Gabby spent the mandatory holidays in Savannah, and Gabby always came home stressed. Once their daughters were born, Gabby told her parents she wanted to start her own holiday traditions and that while she would love to see them, her parents would have to come to Beaufort. They never did.

After the accident, however, they checked into a hotel in Morehead City and the three of them were often in Gabby's room together. While they never said they blamed him for the accident, Travis could feel it in the way they kept their distance.

In time, they had to go back, and now they sometimes came up at weekends. When they did, Travis tried to stay away from the hospital. He told himself that it was because they needed time alone with their daughter. What he didn't like to admit was that he also stayed away because they reminded him that he was responsible for Gabby being in the hospital in the first place.

His friends had reacted as he'd expected. Allison, Megan and Liz prepared dinners in shifts for the first six weeks. Between them and his mother—who was there every afternoon and most weekends—Travis was seldom alone with his daughters in the aftermath of the accident, and they were able to function as parents in a way that he couldn't. He'd needed them to do that for him. It was all he could do to get out of bed in the morning.

But after six weeks, Travis told his friends that he no longer needed his dinners prepared. With visions of Kenneth Baker playing in his mind, he knew he had to take control over what was left of his life. He had to become the father he once had been, and, little by little, he did. Now, at the three-month mark, their lives were as normal as could be expected.

On the downside, since the accident, he'd left little time for Joe, Matt and Laird. While they still dropped by occasionally for a beer after the girls had gone to bed, their conversations were stilted. Half the time, everything they said seemed to be wrong somehow. When they asked about Gabby, he wasn't in the mood to talk about her. When they tried to talk about something else, Travis wondered why they seemed to be avoiding talking about Gabby. For the life of him, he couldn't escape his rage at the unfairness of it all. He wanted what they had and knew they would never understand his loss, no matter how hard they tried. He hated himself for thinking these things and tried to hide his fury, but his friends realised he'd changed. Gradually, their visits became more infrequent. He hated himself for that, too, for the wedge he was creating between them, but he didn't know how to repair it.

Sitting with Gabby, Travis glanced at his watch. It was coming up to two thirty, and normally he would be getting ready to say goodbye so he could be home when the girls came back from school. Today, however, Christine was visiting a friend's house, and Lisa was going to a birthday party, which was fortunate, since he needed to stay longer anyway. Later on he was meeting the neurologist and the hospital administrator.

He knew what the meeting was about, and he had no doubt they'd be in full sympathy mode, complete with reassuring tones. The neurologist would tell him that because there was nothing more the hospital could do for Gabby, she would have to be transferred to a nursing home. The administrator would note that unless Gabby was in the ICU, Travis's insurance covered only a three-month stay in the hospital. Essentially, by teaming up, they wanted to make sure they got their way.

Beneath the surface lurked the reality that while Gabby was in the hospital it was assumed that she would wake up soon, for this was where temporary coma patients always stayed. In a nursing home, it would be assumed that Gabby would never wake up. Travis wasn't ready to accept that, but it seemed as if he wasn't going to be given a choice.

But Gabby had a choice, and, in the end, his decision wasn't going to be based on what the neurologist or the administrator said to him. He would base his decision on what he thought Gabby would want.

Outside the window, he noticed that the pigeon was gone, and he wondered whether it went off to visit other patients, like a doctor making his rounds.

He leant his face close to Gabby's ear. 'I love you, Gabby, more than you'll ever know. You're every hope and dream I've ever had. I don't ever want to give that up. I can't. Can you understand that?'

He waited for a response, but there was nothing. There was always nothing, as if God were telling him that his love was somehow not enough. 'Please,' he whispered. 'You've got to wake up, sweetheart. Please? We're running out of time.'

'Hey,' Stephanie said. Dressed in jeans and a T-shirt, she looked nothing like the successful professional she'd become. She was the senior project manager at a biotech firm in Chapel Hill, but for the past three months she'd spent three days a week in Beaufort. Since the accident, she'd been the only one Travis could really talk to.

She crossed the room and leant over the side of the bed. 'Hey, Gabby,' she said, kissing her on the cheek. 'You doing OK?'

She pulled up another chair and slid it closer to Travis. 'And how are you doing, big brother? You look like hell.'

'Thanks.'

'You're not eating enough.' She reached in her handbag and pulled out a bag of peanuts. 'Eat these.'

'I'm not hungry.'

'Humour me, OK?' She forced the bag towards him.

Travis took it. 'Did anyone ever tell you that you can be a little bit too pushy at times?'

'Every day. And believe me, you need it. You're just lucky you have me in your life. I'm quite the blessing for you.'

For the first time all day, he gave a genuine laugh. 'That's one word for it.' He poured out a small handful of nuts and began to chew.

'So, when are you going back to work?'

'Soon,' he mumbled.

She reached into his bag of peanuts and popped a couple in her mouth. 'You're aware that Dad's not exactly a spring chicken any more?'

'I know.'

'So . . . next week?'

When Travis didn't respond, Stephanie folded her hands in front of her. 'OK, here's what's going to happen. You're going to start showing up at the clinic, and you're going to stay every day until one o'clock. You can close the office on Friday at noon. That way, Dad's only there for four afternoons.'

He squinted at her. 'You've been giving this a lot of thought.'

'Someone has to. And just so you know, this isn't just for Dad. You need to go back to work. If not for you, for Christine and Lisa.'

'What are you talking about?'

'Your daughters. Remember them? You have to show them that, no matter what horrible things happen in life, you still have to go on. After all, you haven't let them quit, have you? They're still in school, right?'

Travis said nothing.

'So, if you expect them to handle their responsibilities, then you've got to handle yours. They need to see you getting back to normal, and work is part of that. Sorry. That's life.'

Travis shook his head. 'You don't understand.'

'I understand completely.'

He brought his fingers to the bridge of his nose and squeezed. 'Gabby is . . .'

When he didn't continue, Stephanie put her hand on his knee. 'Passionate? Intelligent? Kind? Moral? Funny? Forgiving? Patient?

Everything you ever hoped for and imagined in a wife and mother?'

He looked up in surprise.

'I know,' she said quietly. 'I love her, too. I've always loved her. She's not only been the sister I never had, but my best friend, too.'

Unsure how to respond, he said nothing.

In the silence, Stephanie sighed. 'Have you decided what you're going to do?'

Travis swallowed. 'No,' he admitted. 'Not yet.'

'When's the meeting?'

'I'm supposed to meet with them in half an hour.'

She accepted that. 'OK. I'll let you think about it some more. I'll just head over to your place and see the girls.'

'They're not there, but they should be back later.'

'You mind if I wait around?'

'Go ahead. There's a key—'

She didn't let him finish. 'Beneath the plaster frog on the porch? I know. I'm pretty sure most burglars could figure that out, too.'

He smiled. 'I love you, Steph.'

'I love you, too, Travis. And you know I'm here for you, right?'

'I know.'

Standing, she reached for her bag and flung it over her shoulder. She was halfway out of the room when she heard Travis's voice again.

'How far should you go in the name of love?'

Stephanie half turned. 'You've asked me that question before.'

'I know.' Travis hesitated. 'But I'm asking what you think I should do.'

'Then I'll tell you what I always say to you. That it's your choice how you handle this.'

'What does that mean for me?'

Her expression seemed almost helpless. 'I don't know, Trav. What do you think it means?'

It was a little more than two years ago that Gabby had bumped into Kenneth Baker on one of those summer evenings for which Beaufort was famous. With live music playing, it had seemed like the perfect night to bring the kids downtown for ice cream. While they stood in line, Gabby mentioned that she'd seen a beautiful print in one of the stores they'd passed.

'Why don't you check it out,' Travis had said. 'I've got the girls.'

She was gone longer than he'd expected and, when she returned, her expression was troubled. Later, after they'd gone home and put the girls to bed, Gabby sat on the couch, clearly preoccupied.

'Are you OK?' he asked.

Gabby shifted. 'I ran into Kenneth Baker earlier today,' she admitted. 'When you were getting ice cream.'

'Oh, yeah? How's he doing?'

She sighed. 'Do you realise his wife's been in a coma for six years now? Six *years*. Can you imagine what that must be like for him?'

'No,' Travis said. 'I can't.'

'He looks like an old man. He's angry, too. It's like he resents her. He said he only visits her now and then. I got the sense that he wishes she were dead.'

Travis stared at Gabby. 'What's this about?'

'Would you visit me? If something like that happened to me?'

'Of course I would.'

Her expression was sad. 'But after a while, you'd visit less and, in time, you'd resent me.'

'I'd never resent you.' He shook his head. 'Why are we even talking about this?'

'Because I love you.'

She looked at him. 'I want you to promise that if anything ever does happen to me, you'll let me die.'

'We already have living wills,' he countered. 'We did those when we did our regular wills and power of attorney.'

'I know,' she said. 'But our lawyer retired to Florida, and as far as I'm aware, no one but the three of us knows that I don't want my life prolonged in the event I can't make my own decisions.' Her tone became more determined. 'And the thing is . . . I don't want to feel like I have to tell my parents or my sisters about the decision I made. The decision we made. I want to be able to trust that you'll do what I want. And that's why I want you to promise me that you'll honour my wishes.'

The conversation struck him as surreal. 'Yeah . . . sure,' he said.

'No, not like that. I want you to promise me. I want you to make a vow.'

Travis swallowed. 'I promise to do exactly what you want. I swear it.'

'No matter how hard it is?'

'No matter how hard.'

'Because you love me.'

'Because I love you.'

'Yes,' she said. 'And because I love you, too.'

The living will Gabby had signed in the attorney's office was the document Travis had brought with him to the hospital. Among other things, it specified that her feeding tubes were to be removed after twelve weeks. Today was the day.

Sitting beside Gabby in the hospital, Travis recalled the conversation they'd had that night. He'd replayed those words a hundred times, and as the three-month mark approached, he'd found himself growing ever more desperate for Gabby to wake up. As had Stephanie, which was why she was waiting for him at home. Six weeks ago, he'd told her about the promise he'd made—the need to share it had become unbearable.

Sometimes, during his imaginary conversations with Gabby, he'd tried to get her to change her mind. He'd argue that the promise hadn't been a fair one, that the only reason he'd said yes was that the prospect seemed so unlikely.

He would never be like Kenneth Baker. He felt no bitterness towards Gabby, nor would he ever. He needed her. He drew strength from visiting her. Earlier today, he'd been exhausted and lethargic; as the day wore on, his sense of commitment had only grown stronger, leaving him certain that he would have the ability to laugh with his daughters, to be the father Gabby wanted him to be. What he didn't know was how on earth he could go on, knowing that Gabby was gone.

Outside the window, the pigeon was back, pacing back and forth, making him think it was pondering the decision with him. There were times when he felt a strange kinship with the bird, as if it were trying to teach him something, though what, he had no idea. It showed no fear of him. Travis could tap the glass and the pigeon would stand in place. It was a curious situation that gave him something else to think about when sitting in the quiet room. What he wanted to ask the pigeon was this: am I to become a killer?

This was where his thoughts inevitably led, and it was what differentiated him from others who were expected to carry out the desires outlined in living wills. They were doing the right thing. Their choice was rooted in compassion. For him, however, the choice was different.

But for him, there would have been no car accident. He was the proximate cause of her injury, but she hadn't died. And now, with the flourish of some legal documents from his pocket, he could finish the job. Sometimes it seemed not only that God wanted Gabby to die, but that He wanted Travis to know that it had been entirely his fault.

The greyish afternoon light gave the walls a melancholy cast. Buying time, he removed the flowers from the windowsill and brought them to the bed. As he laid them across Gabby's chest and took his seat, Gretchen appeared at the door. She checked Gabby's vitals, then jotted something in the chart and smiled briefly.

'Is she going to be leaving us?' he heard her ask.

Travis knew she was referring to a transfer to a nursing home. But there was more to her question than Gretchen could possibly understand, and he couldn't summon the will to answer.

'I'm going to miss her,' she said. 'And I'm going to miss you, too.' Her expression was brimming with compassion. 'I mean it. It breaks my heart to see her like this. And you, too. The way you are with her. I know you're sad and angry, but I've seen you do the exercises with her. I've heard what you say, and it's like you and she have this connection that can't be broken.'

Travis felt his throat close.

'I guess what I'm trying to say is that you two make me believe that true love really exists. And that even the darkest hours can't take that away.' She stopped and turned away. A moment later, he felt her place a hand on his shoulder. Then she was gone, and Travis was alone with his choice once more.

It was time. Looking at the clock, he knew he couldn't wait any longer. The others were waiting for him.

Above her, the fluorescent light hummed and he wondered what he was going to do. He still didn't know. What he knew was this: she was still alive, and where there was life, there was always hope. He focused on her, wondering how someone so close and so present could remain so remote.

Today, he had to make his choice. To tell the truth meant Gabby would die; to tell a lie meant that Gabby's wish would be denied. He wanted her to tell him what to do, and, from somewhere far away, he could imagine her answer.

I already have, sweetheart. You know what you have to do.

It was more than he could bear, and he felt his mind begin to scream: please wake up! Do it for me. For our daughters. They need you. I need you. Open your eyes while there's still time.

And for a moment, he thought he saw a twitch, he would swear he saw her stir. He was too choked up to speak, but reality reasserted itself and he knew it had been an illusion. Watching her through his tears, he felt his soul begin to die.

He had to go, but there was one more thing he had to do. Like everyone, he knew the story of Snow White, of the kiss from the Prince that broke the evil spell. That's what he thought of every time he left Gabby for the day, but now the notion struck him as imperative. This was it, his very last chance. Despite himself, he felt a tiny swell of hope. He steadied himself and moved towards the bed, trying to convince himself that it would work. This kiss, unlike all the others, would fill her lungs with life.

He leant closer, feeling the heat of her breath mingling with his. He closed his eyes against the memory of a thousand other kisses and touched his lips to hers. He felt a kind of spark, and all at once he felt her slowly coming back to him. She was the arm that held him close in times of trouble, she was the whisper on the pillow beside him at night. It was working, he thought, it was really working . . . and as his heart began to race in his chest, it dawned on him that nothing had changed at all.

Pulling back, all he could do was lightly trace her cheek with his finger. His voice was hoarse, barely above a whisper.

'Goodbye, sweetheart.'

How far should a person go in the name of love?

Travis was still turning this question over in his mind when he pulled into the drive, even though he'd made his decision. Stephanie's car was parked out front. But, except for the living room, the rest of the house was dark.

The chill was biting as he stepped out of his car. He reminded himself to put out the girls' mittens and scarves so he wouldn't have to rush around in the morning. Tucking his hands in his pockets, he made his way up the front steps and went inside.

Stephanie turned when she heard him enter. She started towards him. 'Travis,' she said.

'Hey, Steph.' He removed his jacket.

'Are you OK?'

It took him a moment to respond. 'I don't know.'

She put her hand on his arm. Her voice was gentle. 'Do you want to talk about it?'

He sat on the couch and leant his head back. She sat next to him in silence. Finally she sighed. 'I want you to know that no matter what you decided, I'm with you, OK? I know how much you love Gabby.'

Travis turned towards the window. Through the glass, he could see the lights from his neighbours' houses. 'I couldn't do it,' he finally said. 'I thought I could, and I even rehearsed the words I would say when telling the doctors to remove her feeding tube. I know that's what Gabby wanted, but, in the end, I just couldn't do it. I love her too much to let her go.'

Stephanie gave him a wan smile.

'I know,' she said. 'I could see it on your face when you walked in the door.'

'Do you think I did the right thing?'

'Yes,' she answered without hesitation.

He swallowed. 'Do you think she'll wake up?'

Stephanie met his eyes. 'Yes, I do. I've always believed that. The two of you . . . there's something uncanny about the way you are with each other. I mean everything—the way she relaxes when you put your hand on her back, the way you both seem to know what the other is thinking—it's always struck me as extraordinary. With love like that, they say anything's possible, right?'

Travis let her words sink in.

'So what's next?' she asked. 'You need help burning the living will?'

Despite the tension, he laughed. 'Maybe later.'

'What about nursing homes?'

'She'll be transferred next week. I have to make arrangements.'

'Need help?'

He massaged his temples, feeling unbearably tired. 'Yeah,' he said. 'I'd like that.'

'Hey . . .' She gave him a little shake. 'You made the right decision. Don't feel guilty about a single thing. You did the only thing you could do. She wants to live. She wants the chance to get back to you and the girls.'

'I know. But . . .'

He couldn't finish his sentence. The past was gone, and the future had yet to unfold.

'I'm scared,' he finally admitted.

'I know,' she said, pulling him close. 'I'm scared, too.'

EPILOGUE

June 2007

THE MUTED LANDSCAPE of winter had given way to the lush colours of late spring, and, as Travis sat on the back porch, he could hear birds. Every so often a flock of starlings would break from the trees, flying in formations that seemed choreographed.

It was a Saturday afternoon, and Christine and Lisa were still playing on the tyre swing that Travis had hung the week before. He'd spent an hour that morning pushing the swing and listening to his daughters squeal in delight; by the time he'd finished, his shirt was slick with perspiration.

'Let Daddy rest for a few minutes,' he'd wheezed. 'Why don't you push each other for a while.'

Their disappointment lasted only moments. Soon they were squealing again. It warmed Travis's heart to see them playing so well together. He liked to believe that they would grow even closer in later years. At least that was the hope. Hope, he'd learned, was sometimes all a person had, and, in the past four months, he'd learned to embrace it.

Since he'd made his choice, his life had gradually returned to a kind of normality. Along with Stephanie, he'd toured half a dozen nursing homes, and, in the end, Gabby was transferred to one run by a man named Elliot Harris, only a couple of blocks from the hospital. She was given a gracious private room that overlooked a courtyard, and when Travis visited her, he rolled the bed towards the window and puffed up her pillows.

A week after placing her in the home, he took Stephanie's suggestion and began working until early afternoon five days a week; his father filled in after that. He hadn't realised how much he'd missed interaction with other people. Of course, working regularly meant he had to juggle his schedule with Gabby. After seeing the girls off to school, he went to the nursing home and spent an hour there. After work, he spent another hour with Gabby before the girls got home. On Fridays, he was there most of the day and at weekends he usually made it in for a few hours. Sometimes at the weekends, the girls joined him, but most times they didn't want to. Somehow, without the choice of whether Gabby would live or die hovering over him, their growing distance didn't bother Travis as much as it once had. His daughters were doing what they needed to do to heal and move on, just as he was.

And then, one afternoon, nine weeks after Gabby had been admitted to the nursing home, the pigeon appeared at Gabby's window. At first, Travis didn't believe it. Truth be told, he wasn't even positive it was the same bird. Who could tell? And yet, staring at it . . . he *knew* it was the same bird. It *had* to be.

He watched it in wonder, and the following day he brought some bread and scattered a few pieces on the sill. After that, he glanced at the window regularly, waiting for the pigeon to reappear, but it never did. He liked to think that it had come to tell him not to give up hope, that in the end his choice had been correct.

On the back porch, remembering that moment, he marvelled that he could stare out at his happy daughters and experience so much of their joy himself. He barely recognised this sense of well-being. Had the appearance of the pigeon heralded the changes that took hold of their lives? He supposed it was only human to wonder about such things, and Travis figured that he'd be telling the rest of the story as long as he lived.

What happened was this: It was midmorning, six days after the pigeon had reappeared, and Travis was working at the clinic. He was suturing a mutt that had received a gash while crawling through barbed wire. He had just finished the final stitch, when an assistant entered the room.

'It's Elliot Harris,' she said. 'He says it's urgent.'

Travis told the assistant to finish up. He walked to his office and closed the door. Thinking back, he wasn't sure what he'd expected to hear. It was the first—and the only—time Elliot Harris had ever called him at the office.

'Travis Parker speaking,' he said into the phone.

'Dr Parker, it's Elliot Harris,' the director said. His voice was calm and unreadable. 'I think you should come down to the nursing home as quickly as you can.'

In the short silence that followed, a million thoughts raced through Travis's mind.

'Is Gabby OK?' he finally asked, the words sounding choked.

There was another pause, only a second or two. But the brief words that followed made him drop the phone.

He was eerily calm as he left his office. At least, that's what his assistants would tell him later. Everyone, from the staff to the pet owners who'd brought their animals to the clinic, knew that Travis's wife was in the nursing home. Madeline, who was eighteen and worked at the front desk, stared at him with wide eyes as he approached her. By that point, nearly everyone in the office knew that the nursing home had called.

'Would you call my dad and tell him to come in?' Travis asked. 'I have to go to the nursing home.'

'Yes, of course,' Madeline answered.

As she punched the number, Travis stood as if paralysed. The waiting room was silent; even the animals, it seemed, knew something had happened. He heard Madeline speaking to his dad as if from a great distance. It was only when she hung up the phone that Travis saw the fear on her face. Maybe because she was young and didn't know better, she asked the question everyone was thinking. 'What happened?'

Travis saw concern etched on the faces in the waiting room. Most of the people had known him for years; some had known him since he was a child. Yet he didn't know what to say. He put his hand on the counter to steady himself. All he could do was mimic exactly what he'd heard on the phone only moments before.

'She's awake,' he finally said.

Twelve minutes later, Travis broought the car to a halt at the entrance to the nursing home, his head spinning with alternating scenarios of hope and despair.

Elliot Harris was waiting for him inside. 'The physician and the neurologist are going to be here in a few minutes,' he said. 'Why don't you go up to her room?'

'She's OK, right?'

Harris put a hand on his shoulder, ushering him forward. 'Go see her,' he said. 'She's been asking for you.'

Someone held the door open for him. He bounded up the stairs. On the first floor, he pulled open the door and saw a nurse and an orderly waiting with excited expressions. He leant against the wall to steady himself, then took another step towards Gabby's room. It was the second room on the left, and her door stood open. As he got closer, he heard the murmur of people talking. He stepped inside and Gretchen's face lit up.

'I was at the hospital next to the doctor when he got the page, and I just had to come see—'

Travis barely heard her. All he could register was the sight of Gabby propped up weakly on her hospital bed. She seemed disorientated, but her smile when she saw him told him everything he needed to know.

'Travis,' she croaked. Her voice sounded scratchy and hoarse from disuse. Travis moved slowly to the bed, his eyes never leaving hers, unaware that Gretchen was already backing out, shutting the door behind her.

'Gabby?' he whispered in near disbelief. He sat on the bed.

'Where were you?' she asked, the words full of love, unmistakably full of life. Awake. 'I didn't know where you were.'

'I'm here now,' Travis said, and at that he broke down, his sobs coming out in heaving bursts. He leant towards Gabby, aching for her to hold him, and when he felt her hand on his back, he began to cry even harder. He wasn't dreaming. Gabby was holding him. It's real, was all he could think. This time, it's real.

With Travis unwilling to leave Gabby's side, his dad covered for him at the clinic for the next few days. Travis had only recently returned to something resembling a full-time schedule, and at weekends like this, with his daughters running and laughing in the yard and Gabby in the kitchen, he sometimes caught himself grasping for details of the past year. His memories of the days he spent in the hospital had a blurry, hazy quality to them, as if he'd been only slightly more conscious than Gabby.

Gabby hadn't emerged from her coma unscathed, of course. She had lost a great deal of weight; her muscles had atrophied and a numbness persisted on most of her left side. It took days before she could stand upright without support. The therapy was maddeningly slow, and, in the beginning, she often grew frustrated that she could no longer do simple things she'd once taken for granted. She hated her gaunt appearance, though Travis always told her she was beautifu. He'd never been more sure of anything.

Christine and Lisa took a bit of time to adjust. On the afternoon that Gabby woke up, Travis's mother picked up the girls from school. The family was reunited an hour later, but, when they stepped into the room, neither Christine nor Lisa seemed to want to get close to their mother. Instead, they clung to Travis and offered monosyllabic answers to whatever Gabby asked. That night, after Travis brought the girls home, Christine asked whether Mommy was really back, or if she'd go back to sleep again. Though the physicians made it clear they were fairly certain she wouldn't, they hadn't ruled it out. Christine's fears reflected his own, and whenever he found Gabby sleeping, Travis's stomach would clench. He'd nudge her gently, growing increasingly panicked until she finally stirred. While Gabby accepted his anxiety in the beginning, it had begun to drive her crazy. Last week, with the moon high in the sky and crickets chirping, Travis began to stroke her arm as she lay beside him. Her eyes opened and she focused on the clock, noting it was a little after three in the morning. She glared at him.

'You've got to stop doing this. I need my sleep. Unbroken, regular sleep, like everyone else in the world! I refuse to live the rest of my life knowing that you're going to nudge me awake every hour.'

That had been the extent of her comments, but it struck Travis as so . . . *Gabby-like* that he breathed a sigh of relief. If she no longer worried about slipping into a coma again—and she swore she didn't— then he knew he shouldn't, either.

They were all adjusting and he knew that would take time. Lots of it. They had yet to talk about the fact that he'd disregarded the living will, and he wondered whether they ever would. He had yet to tell Gabby the extent of the imaginary conversations she'd had with him while she was in the hospital, and she had little to say about the coma itself. She didn't remember anything, she said. 'It's like time just . . . *vanished.*'

But that was fine. It was all as it should be. Behind him, he heard the screen door creak open, and he turned. In the distance, he could see Molly, the collie, lying in the tall grass off to the side of the house; Moby, old guy that he was, was sleeping in a corner of the porch. Travis smiled as Gabby spied her daughters, noting her content expression.

As Christine pushed Lisa on the tyre swing, both of them giggling madly, Gabby took a seat in the rocker beside Travis.

'Lunch is ready,' she said. 'Do you think maybe later, when Stephanie gets here, we can all head over to the aquarium? And maybe have some pizza afterwards? I've been dying for pizza.'

He smiled, thinking he could stay in this moment for ever. 'That sounds good. Oh, yeah, that reminds me. I forgot to tell you that your mom called when you were in the shower.'

'I'll call her back in a little while. And I've got to call about the heat pump, too. The girls' room just wouldn't cool down last night.'

'I can probably fix it.'

'I don't think so. The last time you tried to fix it, we had to buy a whole new unit. Remember?'

'I remember you didn't give me enough time.'

'Yeah, yeah,' she teased. She winked at him. 'Do you want to eat out here or inside?'

He pretended to debate the question, knowing it wasn't really important. Here or there, they would all be together. He was with the woman and daughters he loved, and who could ever need or want anything more than that? The sun shone bright, flowers were blooming, and the day would pass with a careless ease that had been impossible to imagine the winter before. It was just a normal day, a day like any other. But, most of all, it was a day in which everything was exactly the way it should be.

Nicholas Sparks

Profile

Born: Omaha, Nebraska, New Year's Eve, 1965
Current home: New Bern, North Carolina
Previous job: pharmaceutical salesman
Pets: three dogs
Favourite authors: Stephen King, Ernest Hemingway
Website: www.nicholassparks.com

Nicholas Sparks—once dubbed 'sexiest author' by *People* magazine—is the kind of man most women would love to marry because he is a romantic to the core. It is a facet of his personality that shines through in his writing, for he's not afraid to draw on his own personal experiences and emotions in his novels. In keeping with many of his best-selling love stories, *The Choice* resonates with a heartfelt appreciation of marriage and children that comes straight from the author's personal life. He and his wife Cathy—who he calls 'Cat'—met while at college and have been married for nineteen years. Five children later—Miles, Ryan, Landon, and twins Lexie and Savannah—they are still very much in love. 'Cat and I have loved each other since March 1988,' declares Sparks, 'and my feelings for her have grown only stronger over the years. I think that enduring, committed love between a married couple, along with raising children, is the most noble act anyone can aspire to. It is not written about very much.'

Nicholas Sparks usually sets his novels in his current home state of North

Carolina, and when he writes of loss and sadness, the depth of feeling he draws on is also very real for he knows all about losing loved ones. In 1989, his mother died suddenly following a horse-riding accident; seven years later his father was killed in a car crash; in 2000, his sister, Dana, succumbed to cancer at the age of thirty-three. Despite these personal trials, Sparks's outlook has remained relentlessly life-affirming—another hallmark of his fiction. 'As hard as it's been,' he says of his losses, 'I know that in many ways I'm fortunate. My wife and children are proof of that.'

According to Nicholas Sparks, Travis Parker, the sporty vet who stars in *The Choice*, is based on his own brother Micah, but sport plays a large part in Sparks's own life, too. Never one to do things by halves, he was so devoted to running at high school that he won an athletic scholarship to the University of Notre Dame, where he still holds a track-and-field record. He runs thirty miles a week, coaches track and field at the local high school, and regularly lifts weights. He also boasts a black belt in tae kwon do and competes at both regional and national levels.

'I think that enduring, committed love between a married couple, along with raising children, is the most noble act anyone can aspire to. It is not written about very much.'

The Choice is Nicholas Sparks's thirteenth novel and the product of a pretty intensive writing schedule. He says that he usually works five or six days a week and, on average, aims to write about 2,000 words a day, which can take as little as three hours or as many as eight. On occasion he has been known to write day and night.

One question that women are keen to ask a male author is how he feels about writing love stories. 'The love story is one of the oldest and most explored genres in literature,' is Sparks's reply. 'Because of the requirements in this particular genre—originality, universality of character and setting, and a plot interesting enough to keep the pages turning, and the fact that the conflict of the story is generally internal—it's among the most difficult genres in which to work. I love the challenge.'

So what does Nicholas Sparks do to relax? Well, he has recently discovered an interest in parasailing, which he features in *The Choice*, but mainly he just enjoys spending time with his family or reading. And this indefatigable romantic claims to get through more than 125 books a year!

Jane Eastgate

Little White Lies

BERNADETTE STRACHAN

Billie Baskerville is the last person you'd ask to manage a bridal shop, because she just doesn't believe in the white wedding thing. The frothy dresses, bridesmaids and confetti of wedding dreams seem more like nightmares to her. But when Great-Aunty Babs begs Billie to run her seaside boutique, the chance to change her life completely is just too tempting to resist.

ONE

BILLIE BASKERVILLE was running away. Again.

Last summer she ran to her parents' bungalow, but that hadn't been far enough, so now she'd pulled on her trusty trainers and run all the way to the sea. Drizzly, dozy Sole Bay, a fly speck on the East Anglian hump of England, was to be her Fresh Start.

On the threshold of Barbara's Brides, Billie finally stopped running. Not the sort of girl to be easily dismayed, Billie was optimistic, resourceful, with a sincere belief in the restorative powers of the oven chip, but even she had to admit that the imaginary roll of drums she'd awarded this moment didn't seem merited. The shop was dimmer, dirtier and more neglected than she'd expected. Great-Aunty Babs's letter had been frank: *It needs a little TLC, dear. But don't we all?*

The building looked like Billie had felt for the past few months. A little TLC wouldn't do it: the place needed bulldozing. The original shopfront was handsome enough, with its twin bow windows curving out into the narrow street like a cantilevered Edwardian bosom. They flanked a recessed door, approached by a tiled porch. The windows presented two lopsided mannequins. One, headless, was naked except for a lace glove, and the other—jaunty red wig obscuring a felt-tipped face—modelled a nylon crinoline whose Daz whiteness had long ago faded to the colour of freshly exhumed bone.

Taking all this in, as her bruised but hopeful heart descended in some slow internal lift to her feet, Billie didn't notice the door opening.

'You must be Billie!' sang the girl in the doorway. Dotted with freckles, the stranger had the bright eyes of a Disney character and swingy, shiny, red-gold hair. Her smile reached her eyes and beyond, as if there wasn't room on her face for it. 'Come in, come in!' she squealed, doing a good impersonation of somebody who'd been waiting for Billie and her tattered luggage all her life.

Stepping into the shop, its interior every bit as grubby and forlorn as its exterior promised, Billie suddenly felt what her Great-Aunty Babs might have described as 'queer'. As if she had been blessed with X-ray vision, standing in the middle of the sticky floorboards, Billie could see right through the brown paint, the woodchip, the stock flown in from the 1970s Soviet Union. She could discern the room's elegant bones, the beauty of its panelling and the perfection of its proportions.

It was unexpected, this fluttering in her chest, as if a pigeon was trapped in her Wonderbra. This was Billie's first real excitement since she'd fled home to her family's mock Tudor corner plot last August.

Maybe, Billie marvelled, the fluttering was more than mere excitement. She shook herself. It couldn't be love at first sight with a decrepit, mouldering ruin of a shop. It was absurd and Benny Hill-like, like a busty teenager lusting after a toothless pensioner.

Besides, Billie had fallen in love at first sight once before and that had caused more uproar than a kangaroo at a funeral. It was the reason she'd laced up those trainers again. 'You must be Dot,' she smiled at the girl, remembering her manners. 'According to Great-Aunty Babs's letter you keep this show on the road.'

'Oh, well,' blushed Dot, 'I wouldn't say that.'

Looking around her, neither would Billie. The premises were obviously rarely troubled by Hoovers, dusters or, she suspected, customers. Dot's own outfit was also slightly dusty, being the kind of tie-dye dress that invariably smells faintly of incense. Garnished with cheesecloth scarves and an armful of jangling metal bangles, Great-Aunty Babs's assistant was pure hippy: cut her slender frame in half and it would say 'Peace and Love' all the way through, like a stick of Glastonbury rock. Hippies made Billie come out in hives, but something about this sunny girl made Billie answer Dot smile for smile.

Deep down, Billie envied girls like Dot, who wore exactly what they liked and looked comfortable in it. A slave to trends, Billie hitched a lift on every bandwagon going. She'd persevered with baseball caps even though the effect was less Posh Spice and more ASBO, and she owned so much fake fur she suspected her Top Shop bomber jacket had pupped. With an unruly bosom and unrulier hair, Billie had never cracked dressing to flatter her good points, whatever they might be.

They weren't her legs—a touch too short, a touch too healthy—nor her hair. Kind friends might say 'Sarah Jessica Parker' but they were thinking 'sci-fi candyfloss'. Her bottom didn't qualify as a good point either: handy for keeping her warm on bus-stop benches, it brought to mind a bag of spanners when introduced to Lycra.

If pressed, Billie *might* admit that her eyes were the sort of sea-green that could make men look twice, or that her curves erred on the right side of Rubenesque. But you had to press very hard indeed.

Dot was burbling on. 'Babs has arrived safe and sound in Sydney. Her pen friend picked her up at the airport. Terribly handsome, apparently, and ever so good for eighty-four. He's driving her into the outback.'

'Do you mind me coming to look after the shop while she's away?' Billie asked. 'After all, I'm sure you could manage on your own.'

'I so couldn't!' hooted Dot. 'I'm hopeless! I'm worse than Babs and that's saying something! Tea?'

The electric kettle was as battered as the shop. As it coughed itself to a climax, Billie followed Dot on a tour of her new fiefdom. Her elderly relative had a weakness for dark brown gloss, and it covered everything that the woodchip didn't. A narrow, treacherous staircase at the back of the shop led up to the chaotic stockroom, stuffed with aged white dresses, folded like weary ghosts. Beyond these stairs, on ground level, was an unfeasibly dinky loo and an equally teeny kitchenette, home to a collection of tannin-streaked mugs.

'Babs is very particular about our stock,' Dot was saying. 'She likes to feel we have something for everyone.'

Everyone, thought Billie, with a man-made-fibre fetish and a secret desire to be mistaken for a Russian prostitute. The shop floor was crowded with rails, which in turn were crowded with the ugliest selection of wedding dresses Billie had ever seen. She was no fan of weddings, but even the most dewy-eyed romantic would find little inspiration in Babs's dingy cream puffballs and Day-Glo sheaths.

'We write all the signs ourselves, to save money,' boasted Dot, gesturing to a piece of inside-out cornflakes packet that invited the browsing punter, in thick red strokes, to FINNISH OFF YOUR OUTFIT WITH A TIARAR.

Satin slippers, now a tide-marked grey, slumped in corners waiting for the right foot. Creased veils sat in a glass cabinet, watched over by a white glove on a dummy hand which seemed to be making a rude gesture at the shop floor. 'Don't tell me that's the till?' Billie backed away from the mahogany and brass monster that dominated the counter.

'Isn't it marvellous? No horrid computery bits, so it's easy to operate. Although,' Dot added, 'you do have to convert everything into pounds, shillings and pence and back again. Oh, and don't open it!' she warned suddenly. 'Jenkins is asleep in there.' She responded to Billie's dumb look. 'My mouse. He's not been well.'

The warm tinkle of the old bell over the door announced a newcomer. Out of the dusk of Sole Bay materialised a tiny woman in a formal coat that had seen better days. White-haired head resolutely down, she negotiated the forest of disgusting dresses.

'Annie,' whispered Dot. 'Our most loyal customer.'

The elderly lady halted, flustered. 'Am I intruding?' she asked, in a high, fluting voice steeped in genteel timidity.

'Of course not, Annie,' said Dot. 'This is Billie. She's Babs's great-niece, and my new manageress. Tea?'

'No. Just the usual, please, my dear.' Annie held out a small notebook.

Dot removed a fiver from between its pages, scribbled in it, signed it, and handed the notebook back. 'See you next week.'

'Goodbye,' said Annie. The shop bell jangled again as she left.

'What was all that about?' asked Billie.

'Annie's saving up for a wedding dress. She's been bringing in a few pounds every now and then for quite some time.'

'Is the dress for her? She's a bit *old* to be buying a wedding dress.'

'I suppose she is,' admitted Dot, incuriously, as she tweaked a faded frock. 'Have you noticed our Gallery of Happiness.'

A pinboard over the register was studded with yellowing wedding photographs. Fat, thin and in-between ladies in white grinned down at them, gripping bouquets and sprays, accompanied by posses of brides-maids and flower girls and pages and best men and matrons of honour and, of course, the occasional groom, whose faces generally seemed to be sending out mute cries for help, like a hostage in a strangely ornate and well-dressed kidnapping. 'Mugs,' Billie whispered, sadly.

'Sorry?' Dot evidently thought she'd misheard.

'Nothing.' Billie felt ashamed. Now was not the time to lay her personal history on this friendly girl. The Story could wait. 'Dot, enough about the shop. Tell me about *you*.'

'Oh. Ah.' Dot seemed wrong-footed, as if she was unaccustomed to talking about herself. 'I love animals. I believe in reincarnation, you see, so that worm you tread on could be your great-grandfather.'

There being no answer to that, Billie said, 'Boyfriends?'

'Oh, boy*friend*. I live with Jake.' Inner lighting clicked on behind Dot's eyes and she assumed a look of bliss. 'He's wonderful. An artist. So talented. A genius. I'm so lucky, so very lucky.' She paused, before sighing, 'We're very much in love.'

It was an avalanche of romance. 'That's nice. Getting married?' It seemed an appropriate question to ask in their surroundings.

The inner light flickered. 'No. But I'm sure he'll marry me one day.'

That phrasing struck Billie as peculiar. A modern female might be expected to say '*We'll* marry' rather than use Dot's passive language. 'Wouldn't worry about it.' Billie gave her a conspiratorial wink. 'It's overrated, you know.'

'Are you married?' asked Dot.

'Jesus, no.' That came out very fast, very scornful. Billie hated the acid that had crept into her tone since last summer. 'I mean, no,' she repeated, more gently. 'Not really my cup of vodka. I'm single. Very, very single. About as single as you can be without being a dead nun. You might as well know from the beginning, Dot. I'm anti-weddings.'

'Oh.' Dot eyed her disbelievingly. '*All* women like weddings.'

'Not this one. I'm allergic.' With a wicked look, Billie teased, 'We're a fine pair to run a wedding shop. One immune to the lure of a white dress, the other living in sin.'

'We'll do all right.'

Hoping that Dot's calm confidence was contagious, Billie followed Dot into the kitchenette and accepted a cup of tea from her. Wandering back into the shop, she asked, 'Do you have bank stuff and keys for me?'

'Oh, yes, of course. Babs set up an account for you.' Dot came into the shop and, rummaging along the curtained shelves beneath the cash register, produced a pile of bank bumph. 'She thought you might like to make a few improvements, as well. Though I can't see how.' Dot shrugged. 'We like Barbara's Brides the way it is, but Babs said you're to have a free hand with it. Is there anything you'd like to change?'

Instead of baying, '*Everything!*' into that shining face, Billie marvelled at how unbusinesslike the two women were. And how much they loved this shop. 'What's the turnover?' she asked, having learned the word in a book called *Shopkeeping for Dummies* on the train journey.

'The . . .?' Dot looked like a Neanderthal faced with a microwave.

'Customers,' Billie simplified it. 'How often do you sell a dress?'

'Ah. Hmm.' Dot pouted. 'Let me see.' She wrinkled her nose. 'We sold a dress in January. No. I tell a lie. It was November.'

'*A* dress?' queried Billie. 'Last November?'

'Yes. And somebody bought a marked-down veil the other week.'

'I see.' So how on earth did Great-Aunty Babs sustain this place?

As if she'd read her mind, Dot said comfortably, 'Babs often jokes that it's lucky she doesn't rely on the shop to keep her. The husbands left her well off, she says.'

Ah. The husbands. The reason Billie's mother regarded Great-Aunty Babs as a geriatric Antichrist. Babs's history (or 'career' as Nancy Baskerville termed it) of marrying wealthy gents in the twilight of their days ('last legs' if you were Nancy) had raised eyebrows at family gatherings. There had been three husbands, each older, more doddery and with more capital than the last. They died happy and with airtight wills.

Billie bent to gather up her belongings. It was five thirty, closing time, and outside the shop Sole Bay was already dark. 'I'm ready to drop now, Dot. It's been a lot to take in.' She gathered up her bag and laptop. That innocuous computer inside its carrying case contained a ticking bomb that had plummeted, unannounced and unwelcome, into her email inbox two weeks ago. A fortnight of mustering courage to read it had got her nowhere. Glowing as if it contained kryptonite, the laptop taunted her: it knew she'd run out of excuses and that tonight, on the threshold of her Fresh Start, Billie would finally read *that* email. 'Do I reach the flat through the stockroom?'

'Flat?' Dot looked perturbed. 'What flat?'

'*The* flat. Great-Aunty Babs's flat. The one she said I could stay in.'

'Oh, no.' Dot's distress gained momentum. 'Oh, no no no no,' she wailed. 'Babs lives on the front, but she's let out her house. There's no flat upstairs, just the stockroom. Unless Babs meant you could sleep on the camp bed. But it's all bent. And it's freezing at night. And a pigeon kind of lives up there. And he's not been himself lately.'

'I get the picture.' Billie exhaled slowly. She'd misunderstood her great-aunt's ramblings. 'Where's the nearest hotel? The nearest *cheap* hotel,' she added, aware of her purse's shortcomings. This setback was a blow, but Billie could do this. She could drown out the family chorus of doubt, she'd find a way to make this Fresh Start work. Anything, was better than another evening watching her parents rehearse their latest amateur dramatic roles in *Chicago*: she would rather sleep in a wheelie bin than witness her mother's shimmy shake once more.

'You can stay with us! In Jake's cottage.'

'Oh, I couldn't . . .' Billie's fight was feeble. An artist's cottage sounded cute and comfy. And cheap. She imagined downy beds.

Practically jumping up and down in her Doc Martens, Dot insisted she could. 'Look! Here's Jake now!' she sang delightedly, as the door opened to admit a tall, lean man. She took his hand. 'He'll persuade you. Jake, meet Billie. She's going to stay with us for a while.'

Gangling, stooped and pale, Jake had babyish curls of translucent, greenish blond. His face was taut and guarded behind a beard.

Hooded eyes the colour of pondwater met Billie's and a bolt of vehement antipathy crackled between them. Her decision was made. 'Honestly, it's fine. I'll go to a hotel. I don't want to be any trouble.'

'Tell her, Jakey. We'd love to have her, wouldn't we?'

Still silent, Jake regarded Billie with rude frankness. Dressed in an eclectic assortment of second-hand garments that would guarantee a fancy-dress first prize as the Artful Dodger (or the Pretentious Tosser), he pulled his military greatcoat round him and finally said, 'OK.'

'Please.' Billie tried not to beg. 'Just point me at a hotel.' Something told Billie that this man's cottage would have no downy beds.

'No, no, you can have the spare room,' Dot insisted, leaning on her scarecrow-ish swain. 'As long as you don't mind sharing with Mrs Fluff. Our cat. Well, our baby, really.'

Next to cats, Billie's deepest dread was of cats that were babies 'really'. She sensed Jake's spare room creeping nearer and she flailed, looking for escape. Help came from a surprising quarter.

'I know of a place you can stay.' Jake had an impressive assortment of speech impediments, and he spoke low, so that Billie had to lean in to hear. 'It's beautiful. It's free.' He paused. 'But you might be too narrow-minded and bourgeois to appreciate it.'

'Try me,' said Billie.

Billie loved beach huts. She was mad about their cheerful décor, their dinky dimensions and their unabashed kiss-me-quick vulgarity.

Mind you, she'd never considered living in one before.

'I won't allow it.' Dot was horrified. 'You'll never fit all your things in there.'

In the sleet-lashed dark of the March evening outside the chalet, Billie jiggled the bag and laptop in her arms. '*This* constitutes my things. And it's so pretty,' she murmured, taking in the jaunty blue and white stripes of the tiny hut and the geraniums on its abbreviated deck. *Herbert's Dream II* announced the hand-painted nameplate. 'Who was Herbert?'

'Oh, some ex-husband,' explained Dot. 'The last one, or the second to last. He had a racehorse called Herbert's Dream, apparently.'

'Hence the two.' Billie nodded, satisfied.

'Never mind Herbert, there's no electricity!' Dot yelped. 'And no running water! You'd have to use the public loos!' She upped the cajoling when there was no change in Billie's smitten expression. 'What about telly?' She attempted sternness, but it wasn't her forte: Dot's voice was calibrated for cooing at kittens. 'I never watch it, but you might.'

'Going without television will be refreshing. I can read, and . . .' Actually, panicked Billie, what *would* she do without her *Corrie* chums, her *Sex and the City* gal pals and those irrepressible EastEnders? 'And, erm, embroider,' she claimed, nimbly inventing a Victorian alter ego.

Scrabbling for inspiration, Dot found it close to hand. 'The hut is practically in the sea!'

That was the wrong argument to choose. 'Yes, it is, isn't it?' Billie smiled. The line of huts sat where Sole Bay dwindled into the surf, at the foot of broad concrete steps leading down from the promenade. Only a few hundred yards of pebbly beach separated Herbert's Dream II from the North Sea. Scared of weddings but unafraid of sleeping with her feet in salt water, Billie told Dot, 'I've always loved the ocean.'

'It's illegal to live here,' Dot declared. 'Babs' lease only allows daytime use. You could be arrested. And you'd be in the papers. And you'd be—'

'Burned at the stake?' smiled Billie. 'I've made up my mind. Dot, please don't worry. It'll be all right. Somehow.' She felt exhilarated, like the time she'd tried paragliding on holiday. Hopefully this venture wouldn't end with Billie crying and covered in jellyfish, trying to find the Greek for, 'Please remove this sea urchin from my bra.'

Two gulls the size of spaniels woke Billie next morning. Raucous as the dregs of a hen night, they swapped seabird gossip on the window sill.

Disorientated, Billie gripped the duvet as her ragged, drowsy thoughts rearranged themselves. She came to and realised that the gulls weren't monsters and the duvet wasn't a duvet: it was a crochet blanket in toning shades of sludge donated the night before by Dot.

The sun bounced off the sea, in through the tiny window to illuminate every corner of the whitewashed hut as brightly as a searchlight. Wincing, Billie made a mental note to organise curtains.

Swinging her legs out of the camp bed rescued from the stockroom, Billie found herself on her knees with the bed closing on her back, like a turtle. She made a mental note to organise a decent bed.

Ten more minutes prompted ten more mental notes. Billie's new home needed, in no particular order, somewhere to wash, somewhere to cook, and somewhere to sit.

Scavenging a Bounty from her bag, which could usually be relied upon to supply an overlooked chocolate bar, Billie surveyed her home. The economical white wooden space was, at most, one Nigel by two Nigels. Nigel had been her first boyfriend. He'd been exactly six foot tall and, ever since, Billie had found imagining a row of prostrate Nigels to be a handy way of calculating distance.

The beach hut was calm, it was cute, and the gentle shushing of the waves was a welcome substitute for the lupine howls of her mother 'getting into character' as Roxie Hart. Bare and white, the room suited Billie's state of mind. She was a clean page, waiting for life to scribble on her again. She had, Billie promised herself urgently, packed away the pain of the last few months. She would be sensible, careful, wise. She would *not* be—she recalled her family nickname—Batty Billie.

'It's basic,' Billie told the seagulls, as she locked the padlock of the door behind her. 'But it's mine. All mine!'

A door two huts down banged, and Billie jumped. Standing on the step of a pristine hut was a tall, fair man.

Billie tried to look nonchalant. She couldn't do Nonchalant very well, so she tried Cocky. When that, too, fell flat she opted for Furtive and scuttled up the steps.

Clear, watery sunshine drenched the small town of Sole Bay as Billie walked to work. The blues and whites and pinks and creams of the houses and shops suited this mild weather perfectly. Her four-minute meander through the awakening streets contrasted pleasingly with the sweaty commute she'd endured until two days previously. Billie had started every day in her snot-coloured suburb in a foul mood.

Today, though, Billie found herself nodding a cheery, 'Good morning!' to the people she passed. The town affected her that way, as if she'd been rinsed in the waves overnight, and woken up not as a grubby Londoner, with bad manners and a permafrown, but as an extra in a gentle black and white comedy of English country life.

Sole Bay was a pocket of charm and Englishness. Its narrow streets veered off the cobbled main square at crazy, pre-town-planning angles, and Billie took a wrong turning or two before she discovered Little Row, where the shop waited for her.

Barbara's Brides squatted dead centre in a sedate strip of genteel businesses. To the right was a butcher's, with sawdust on the floor. A red-faced man in a striped apron winked at Billie as she glanced in. She allowed herself a private preen, even though the butcher made her Gramps look hot. When a girl has been shrouded under dustsheets for the best part of a year, she appreciates any and all winks.

On the other side of her great-aunt's establishment was a sweet shop. Home-made fudge peeped out through the Georgian-style mullioned window. Its sugary charms weren't lost on Billie, who leered in.

'Sweet tooth?' asked a voice from the doorway. A chubby lady, between sixty and a thousand, stood sweeping her porch.

'Not really. Kind of.' Billie's sweet tooth wasn't something she readily admitted to.

'Taste that.' A cube of fudge was produced from the woman's pinny pocket and held out. 'Just made it. New recipe.' Her hair was Elvis black, though the style owed more to the *Bride of Frankenstein*.

Billie made an entirely new sound: vowel-less and fruity, it was impossible to translate but denoted dangerous levels of bliss.

'You the great-niece?' Billie's new neighbour looked her up and down.

'No secrets in this town, are there?' laughed Billie.

'You'd be surprised.' The woman didn't laugh. Her round face was doughy, and her eyes were like two raisins sunk in it. Raisins don't usually glitter, but these two certainly did. 'Nowt like Babs, are you?'

'Not really. Sorry.' Billie held out her hand. 'I'm Billie.'

The woman shook her hand heartily. 'Zelda.' Her sweeping resumed. Evidently, the interview was terminated, for Zelda had started to sing to herself, a falsetto version of 'Don't Cha Wish Your Girlfriend Was Hot Like Me?'

The handwritten CLOSSED sign was still showing on Barbara's Brides' door. Billie had a quick game of push-me-pull-you with the big rusty key in the old lock, before falling in and wading through the pizza delivery leaflets and a pamphlet for a donkey sanctuary addressed to Dot. Righting herself, Billie switched on the lights, noting how little impact they made on the soupy gloom at the back of the shop.

Swinging her laptop on to the counter, Billie unzipped it slowly. She'd run out of excuses. The lack of electricity in Herbert's Dream II had given her a reprieve, but it really was time to confront her email.

'Morning!' Dot clattered in on rainbow-coloured clogs.

'Morning,' echoed Billie. Tucking away the laptop, she told herself piously that she needed privacy to read the email.

'Your crash course in wedding-dress shoppery starts here,' beamed Dot, as she held up one forefinger. She pressed down on the switch of an ancient radio on a high shelf. 'East Coast FM. Always on in the background,' she explained, as a Beatles track tinnily filled the room.

'Right.' Billie nodded. She nodded again when Dot picked up the kettle and filled it sl-o-wly from the tap, as if Billie might have been new to the complex world of the cuppa.

Remembering to nod and say 'Got it' at intervals, Billie's mind wandered as Dot pottered about, putting the change (and the mouse) in the till, primping the tired stock and waking the shop up for the day ahead. Rescuing Great-Aunty Babs's letter from under the make-up, mobile, magazines and sweet wrappers in her bag, Billie looked it over again.

The letter had arrived out of the blue. Kept apart by her mother's disapproval, Billie and her great-aunt hadn't met for ten years. Postcards had been exchanged but this chatty, intimate letter had been a surprise.

I'm being very cheeky, Great-Aunty Babs had written, *but if you cud take some time out of your bizy life to help me, I'd be so greatfull.*

'Bizy.' Huh. How Billie had snorted the first time she'd read that at her desk in the telesales office. Since last summer Billie's 'bizy' life had been one long round of banging her head against the wall trying to forget last summer, to a backdrop of her mother's suggestions that she go on a diet, try Botox, buy a smart raincoat.

To earn some running-away money, Billie had taken a job so dull that a letter from an OAP counted as kicks: she flogged double-glazed conservatories over the phone, extolling their virtues from a laminated list as if they were the Taj Mahal rather than glorified lean-tos.

By contrast, her great-aunt's life had sounded packed. *I long to meet an Australian gent I have been corisponding with,'* Great-Aunty Babs had explained. *'I have high hopes of Colin, so I may stey for six months. Or longer. Or less. Or forever. Cud you help me out and look after the shop? I can pey you, and you'll have a free hand with any improovments. Your the boss! If you say yes, it would be a lifeline.* Suddenly the A5 Basildon Bond had morphed into Billie's passport to her Fresh Start.

Trapped in suburbia, wearing a phone headset in an air-conditioned, fluorescent-lit box, Billie had yearned for beauty, adventure . . . and a reason to get out of bed in the morning.

She folded the letter into its well-worn creases, then looked out at Little Row. 'It's time we dressed that poor bint in the window,' she said, taking her first step as a fledgling manageress.

'Okey-dokey.' Dot handed her a cup of tea before stepping up into the window display. 'What shall we put her in? A shepherdess gown?'

Billie plucked a simple white nylon shift off the rails. Just carrying it across the shop floor made her hair stand on end; it could easily combust during the first dance. 'Let's try this.' She clambered up beside Dot and they began to dress the naked mannequin.

The ting of the bell above the door stopped the action in the window. A heavy-hipped, middle-aged woman with a perm was grinning coyly up at them. Knowing that paying customers were rarer than guitar-playing chickens, Billie smiled back, then looked towards Dot.

'Your customer, Miss Billie,' Dot said, a faint challenge in her eyes.

'Of course, Miss Dot.' Taking up the gauntlet, Billie clambered out of the window. 'How can I help?'

'I'm getting married!' the woman told her. 'Me! Imagine.'

'Congratulations,' said Billie. From her lips it sounded ever so slightly like 'Condolences'. She shot a look at Dot for support. 'When's the big day?'

'As soon as I can get over there. He's from the States, you see.'

'Any idea which style you're after?' Billie asked, hoping the customer preferred the dated, the hideous or the downright Barbara Cartland, as that was all the shop had to offer. When her question provoked a blank, almost scared, response, Billie asked helpfully, 'What kind of dress does your fiancé like to see you in?'

'Oh, he's never seen me. We met on the internet. I knew immediately that he was the one. I've written to other men on Death Row but none were as sensitive as him. Maybe you've heard of him? The Mississippi Mutilator?'

After a surreal half-hour, Cheryl, the bride-to-be, bounced off carrying a magnolia Terylene drop waist that fitted her like a glove and needed no alteration, and a surprisingly pretty diamanté headdress.

As the door clanged shut, Billie punched the air. She'd made her first sale. And to a serial killer's fiancée. She swivelled round to Dot. 'Have you ever heard anything like it?' she gasped. 'I could hardly believe it.'

'Me neither,' sniffled Dot. She held up a picture of a hedgehog with a plaster on its snout. 'All the suffering in this crazy old world of ours.'

TWO

A WHOLE WEEK had passed since Billie had jumped feet first into the world of weddings. A celebratory pasty had been bought from Mr Dyke the butcher to mark the occasion in the best possible way.

'Mr Dyke makes a mean pasty,' mumbled Billie through greasy lips.

Watching her sorrowfully, her vegetarian assistant—who apologised to quark before eating it—said, 'There's been a Dyke in Sole Bay for generations. This town is built on Dykes.' If she was aware of her pile-up of double entendres, she didn't show it. 'You can trust a Dyke.'

'Indeed,' giggled Billie.

'Although,' began Dot, in an undertone, lips pursed, 'he is a bit of a one. Kept a few beds warm over the years, according to my gran.'

'The butcher?' Billie was incredulous. 'But he's got ruddy cheeks and a round tummy and a handlebar moustache. And he's married.'

'Poor Zelda had'—Dot lowered her voice when she realised that Zelda was outside, washing her windows—'had her heart broken by him years ago. Nobody knows what happened, but people say that's why she's the way she is. She's been driven wild with sexual jealousy.'

Billie had to protest. 'Zelda? She wears surgical stockings!'

'Evidently, they are no barrier to passion,' said Dot, sagely.

'I don't know if I can look his meat in the face again,' sighed Billie.

And there the double entendres ended for the time being, as Billie's mobile chirped at her from across the room.

'Oh. *You*.' Ashamed at her own disloyalty, Billie was reluctant to pick up when she read her caller ID. Blood is thicker than pasty, however, so she pressed a button and said a cheery, 'Hi, big bro.' It was advisable to sound cheery around Sly: he homed in on misery like a cruising vulture.

'Sis,' cooed her brother in the silky tone he'd cultivated since setting himself up as a motivational guru. 'I'm worried about you.'

This was a standard opener. Sly claimed to worry about everybody, from his nearest and dearest to bus conductors. Billie had long rumbled his global concern as a way of opening people up. Opening people up was a vital part of Sly's trade. 'Why?' she asked. 'I'm fine.'

'Mum and Dad are worried, too.'

That meant that Mum was worried—very vocally—and that Dad had nodded over the top of his newspaper. 'I called her last night and told her everything was great.'

'She tells me you're living in a shed? Are things really that bad?'

'It's not a shed, it's a beach hut, er, house.' She could have told her brother that she felt liberated, that she was sleeping well for the first time in a long time, that feeling was returning to various numb parts of her. Billie contented herself with, 'I'm enjoying myself, honest.'

'So you're going ahead with this whole shop stunt?'

Stiffening, Billie launched into what she could remember of her yoga breathing. 'Yup.' Years of deference to her older brother, the Goldenballs of the Baskervilles, meant she could never defend herself properly.

'Are you sure it's healthy?' Healthy was one of Sly's professional buzz-words, along with 'nourishing', and 'major credit cards accepted'. 'Mum tells me the shop is a mouldy old dump off the beaten track.'

Unable to argue with that, Billie simply said, 'Well, I like it.' Then she surprised herself by saying, 'It feels like home.'

'I'm coming up to the back of beyond to see for myself,' announced Sly. 'Hey! Does your shop have a workforce?'

'It's got a Dot, if that's what you mean.'

'Tip top. We'll hold an Inner Winner seminar!'

'Noooo!' Billie reacted as if her brother had offered her a cup of sick.

'It's on the house, don't worry,' said Sly, magnanimously. 'My seminars are proven to improve productivity one thousand per cent. Bye.'

Two more pounds were dropped into the tin allocated for Annie's fund. Once again she politely refused tea. After she left, in her dignified shabby coat, Billie said approvingly, 'What a nice old girl.'

'Huh!' Zelda's sour honk from the corner startled Billie. She hadn't seen her neighbour come in, nor heard the shop bell. 'Why do old people have to be *nice*? Nobody expects youngsters to be nice,' she cawed, one false fingernail toying with a lock of unlikely black hair. 'I was never nice and I don't intend to take it up now.'

Smiling, Dot insisted, 'Oh, you *are* nice, Zelda. You're lovely.'

Who, Billie wondered, would be considered less than lovely in Dot's universe? Jack the Ripper? 'We like you just the way you are, Zelda,' she laughed. Zelda was omnipresent, like God and Lulu, as much part of the fixtures and fittings of Barbara's Brides as the flammable dresses.

'How's that Jake treating you, darlin'?' Zelda asked Dot.

'You know Jake,' answered Dot dreamily.

'That's why I'm asking,' growled Zelda. 'If he doesn't do right by you then . . .' She left her sentence unfinished, but managed to induce visions of medieval martyrs being boiled alive in oil in Billie's mind. Zelda's attention was diverted, suddenly. 'Hey! You!' she shouted, darting into the street. '*Maneater!*' she howled at the slowly disappearing back of an anorak on a shaky mobility vehicle.

'A love rival,' Dot explained. 'Mrs Davis has been linked with Mr Dyke in the past.'

Billie shadowed Dot, hoovering up every detail of running Barbara's Brides. She had fallen in love with this neglected old treasure and had stopped trying to talk herself out of it. Her feeling for the shop was the rocket fuel for her new plans . . . plans she hadn't yet shared with Dot.

Billie's fears that nobody ever crossed the threshold were unfounded. Locals popped in all the time. They chatted, drank tea and doled out home-made biscuits. Almost the only activity they didn't indulge in was buying.

The two plump ladies who did the alterations dropped in with some flapjacks and told Billie how much they disapproved of Great-Aunty Babs's practice of holding a sizable stock of ready-to-wear dresses for the last-minute bride, an idea which struck Billie as unusually sensible.

She was less impressed with the 'fibbing tape', a special tape measure for the larger customer, which took two inches off all vital statistics.

'That's treating women just like silly girlies,' protested Billie.

'We're protecting them,' corrected Dot, placidly.

'Who says they need protecting? If they ate the cakes they can face up to the inches. Why does everybody assume that women's brains dribble out of their ears when a wedding is mentioned?' Billie harrumphed, pushing the tape to the back of a drawer. 'Perfect weddings are just another stress, another impossible ideal that we can't live up to.'

'Well, I love weddings,' said Dot, happily.

'I loathe them,' Billie said, emphatically. 'I mean, why do we agree to lose a third of our body weight and truss ourselves up in white lace? Why do we put ourselves into debt so that uncles we've never met can cruise the buffet in a stripey marquee? What's so special about a white dress anyway?'

'I reckon you'll give in and get married,' persevered Dot. She was, Billie had come to realise, a persevering perseverer. 'One day. Bet you.'

'I promise that if I ever get married I will hand you a million pounds.'

'Ooooh!' beamed Dot. 'I'll open a badger sanctuary!'

Marvelling at the differing ways to blow a million—Billie's own dream scenario involved a sports car, a mews house and a forthright offer for a few hours of George Clooney's down time—Billie began to rearrange a rail of squeaky man-made fabric dresses. One stood out as a real Babs special. It was a nightmare of ruffles and bows and flounces and frills. Billie laughed, holding it against her for Dot to see.

Usually reliable for a giggle, Dot was straight-faced. 'Can you honestly say,' asked Dot, gazing penetratingly at her boss, 'that you've never even fantasised about what you'd wear at your own wedding?'

'Well . . .' Billie shoved the hanger back on the rail. Perhaps it was time for Billie to tell Dot her story. *The* Story. The one that defined her these days, much as she kicked against that fact. 'I didn't just fantasise.'

'You had a wedding!' Dot squawked. 'But you said—'

'I said I'm single.'

'So . . .' Dot trod carefully. 'So, you're divorced?'

'Nope. The Story's better than that.' Billie conjured up a pallid smile. 'My wedding day went like clockwork, Dot.'

Dot gasped. She really was an excellent audience.

'The 23rd of August last year. James's parents' anniversary. Our local church was garlanded with lilac and white flowers. It looked stunning. My mother's new facelift hadn't quite settled down—she still looked mildly startled—but she looked stunning, too. And, somehow, so did I,' said Billie wonderingly, remembering her reflection in the mirror of her five-star hotel suite. 'I'd lost pounds to get into a vicious brocade monster of a dress that laced up the back and cut off my breathing, but took years of sitting on my bum off my bum. The bridesmaids were excited. My brother was ushering for all he was worth. Only one detail fell short of the required perfection.' She turned a grubby veil over and over. 'No groom.'

'He jilted you?' Dot put a hand to her mouth. 'At the altar?'

'Not quite. It doesn't even qualify as your archetypal jilt.' Billie attempted a laugh. 'There was a note, just before we were due to leave for the church. Cold feet, all the way up to the neck. No real reasons, just excuses. But there was a desire to run, to be free, between every line.' Billie's brightened expression wouldn't fool a cat, let alone a sensitive soul like Dot. 'All for the best really. I mean, if a person can do that to you, they're not really marriage material, are they?'

'Now I get it,' Dot said softly.

'Weddings are just a con, a charade, an excuse to part gullible lovebirds from their money.' Billie tossed the veil into the air for punctuation and it spiralled slowly to the brown floorboards.

'If you believed that,' Dot said carefully, 'you wouldn't love this place as much as you do.'

Shutting up shop, Billie gingerly shooed Zelda's cat from her porch. A malignant black bathmat, Raven glared up at Billie with glowing orange eyes and stayed where he was.

'Off!' shouted Billie, refusing to be bested by what looked like an abandoned hat. Eventually, she stepped over him, glowering down. 'Who do you think you are?' she hissed at him.

The look that Raven gave her suggested that he knew exactly who he was, thank you, and what's more, he knew all about her and what a coward she was. The flat-faced cat had seen her put away her laptop, once again, without reading James's email.

Herbert's Dream II had been made over. A fortnight had transformed him from a drab bachelor to a jaunty hut-about-town.

The entire innards had been painted with a job lot of brilliant white. A blitz on Sole Bay's charity shops had furnished it with change from a twenty-pound note. Arranging a mishmash of striped and flowery cushions on her new, narrow but comfortable, wrought-iron bed, Billie thanked God for the out-of-touch matrons who ran charity shops: they had never heard of shabby chic and priced accordingly.

The challenge was to shoehorn in mod cons without obliterating Herbert's seaside-y charms. A 'rescued' deckchair was recovered in chintz. A second-hand camp table supported a camp stove. Beneath the table sat a washing-up bowl and a washing-Billie bowl, their bright colours contrasting cheerily with the gingham curtains Dot had run up. Billie's scant collection of clothes hung around the walls on hooks, Shaker style.

A water container squatted alongside the table. Filling it from the communal tap was a chore that Billie had come to dread. Hobbling back over the pebbles, the container banging against her shins, she imagined bystanders doing double takes and hissing, Sherlock Holmes-like, 'Hold hard! Isn't that a mighty large receptacle for an individual permitted to use the premises for recreational purposes only?'

Battery-powered lanterns slung from the beams cast a forgiving light over Billie as she read herself to sleep each night, from her new library of second-hand books. Fear of encountering a bogey on each page couldn't spoil the contrasting delights of Jane Austen and Jackie Collins.

Now that she had a modicum of comfort, Billie relished returning to her kooky little haven after a day of toil at Barbara's Brides. Two weeks into her Fresh Start, she was still comparing her journey home through Sole Bay with the commute back at her parents'. She had swapped a dark walk home along deserted streets, looking over her shoulder and imagining burly ne'er-do-wells in the bushes, for a trot past candy-coloured house fronts, guided by the swishing petticoats of the sea.

Reaching the broad steps that led down to the darkness of the beach, Billie looked left and right, studiously casual and screamingly obvious. With scant acting skills inherited from her mother, Billie minced down the first two steps as if she didn't have a care in the world, then broke into a gallop on the second two.

After a brief tussle with the padlock, Billie was in, and soon the kettle was whistling. She switched on the lanterns, turned on East Coast FM and clambered into her pyjamas. The evening phone-in swirled about the hut unheard as Billie lay back on her charity cushions with a soothing mint tea to contemplate her bedtime reading.

No Regency coyness or bonkbuster knicker-ripping tonight. Billie had sought out Sole Bay's library earlier in the day and had used the facilities to print out James's email.

Even the most dedicated coward has to give in and face the music sometime. Billie was a noted coward, her craft honed through long years forging notes for the PE teacher (her periods were eligible for the *Guinness Book of World Records*), telling boyfriends it wasn't them it was her (even though it was *definitely* them), reassuring her mother she didn't look too old at fifty-eight to play Sandy in *Grease*, and avoiding her rear view in those cruelly comprehensive movable mirrors shops install in their changing rooms these days. But that was the old Billie.

The new, businesslike model faced up to things. Folded in her hand, the printed-out email looked innocuous.

Opening it, she winced. The title in the subject box was 'Sorry'. Just a short word, but it towered over Billie like Ayers Rock. A 'sorry' email usually arrived when somebody had to cancel lunch, or they'd lost the tattered Marian Keyes she'd lent them: it couldn't begin to cover what had gone on between Billie and James.

Billie was nonplussed, and she much preferred being plussed. With a tiny mew she dipped her toe in the freezing water.

Hi there. How's tricks? Long time no see!

Billie reread that first line. James was addressing her as if they'd once attended an Esperanto evening class together. She swallowed. The 'sorry' of the title turned out to be punily anticlimactic:

Sorry I haven't been in touch!

Of course he hadn't been 'in touch'. The break-up had been bloodier than *The Texas Chainsaw Massacre*. Those exclamation marks made her pout. James loathed them, yet here he was scattering them willy-nilly. Billie read on, the suspicion dawning that her ex-fiancé had swapped his sober, accountant's personality with a surfer dude.

I've joined a gym! Yes, me! I pump iron and feel the pain and generally make a tit of myself on all the scary expensive equipment. Afterwards I go for a curry and down a few beers—that's what you're meant to do, isn't it?!

I've got a new job. Won't bother telling you about it because it's every bit as boring as my last job, and your eyes used to glaze over whenever I used the word 'work'. I get more money and a comfier chair and the post boy thinks I'm important, so that's good enough for me. Still haven't got round to fixing the boiler—the shower continues to belch out five seconds of boiling water, before going stone cold. Still haven't gone to New York. But I did get to the Isle of Wight for a mini-break. Does that count?

And you? Still flogging conservatories? Can't see that somehow . . . How are your folks? Still crazy as ever, bless them?

Bless them? James had never, ever blessed her family. Neither had he used the word 'crazy' about them in a jocular, aren't-they-funny way: he'd used it in a perfectly serious, can't-we-get-them-looked-at way.

Are you still reading this? Hope so. I've got this mental image of you brandishing a crucifix at the screen and bellowing 'begone satan'. It's taken me weeks to pluck up the courage to write, and you've probably deleted it without reading. Oh well. You thought I was quite nice once. And I rather liked you. The odd email can't hurt. Can it?

James

That email took a while to digest. Newsy and breezy, it didn't do justice to what they'd been through together. It was as if Hitler had texted Churchill to suggest nipping out for a pint.

Restless, Billie wrapped herself in one of her knitted blankets and wandered outside. Her bottom padded by an ancient cushion, she sank onto the pebbles. The sea would make things better.

Their almost-wedding day had bent her out of shape, transforming James into a not-actual-size presence in her life. She never wanted to see him again, never wanted to reprise that particular and peculiar pain. In a strange way this distaste showed James the appropriate respect: it was the only possible response to the magnitude of their shared drama.

James was evidently made of sterner, or weirder, stuff. He was over her. He could talk to her as if she was a nice girl he'd once known, not somebody he'd last glimpsed on the deck of their very own *Titanic*. No doubt he saw her as a blip in an otherwise successful life.

He was laughing at her. That yellow-haired bloke was laughing at her from the deck of his beach hut as he leaned his lanky frame against it.

He knew. Hair dishevelled, heart pumping, Billie tore up the steps and plunged into the warren of streets that made up Sole Bay. One phone call to the council and her Fresh Start could be thrown off course. Her lonely vigil on the beach last night had made her more, not less, determined to keep on track.

She risked a look back. Shit. He was still looking. And laughing. He was certainly handsome. She'd never gone for that peroxidey, punky look, though. Just as well. It wouldn't do to fancy your nemesis.

Billie was early, but Dot was even earlier. They kept the CLOSSED sign up as they supped their instant choco-crappo-low-cal drinks.

'Fancy joining us for Sunday lunch?' Dot's even little teeth flashed.

The correct answer, given Jake's inevitable involvement, was 'No' but Billie was well brought up and managed, 'I'd love to.' She was interrupted by a loud banging on the locked door. 'Oh Gawd,' she muttered, quickly turning away from the rough-looking teenager rapping angrily on the glass. 'I don't like the look of that one. Ignore her.'

Already halfway across the shop, Dot was saying delightedly, 'It's our Debs!' and then the furious girl was in.

'Where's Babs?' The newcomer was a formidable sight, her cannily bright eyes slanted into half-moons by the pull of her vicious ponytail, and her meaty legs grazed by her stonewash denim mini. 'And 'oo the fuck is she?' She pointed a growing-out nail extension at Billie.

Dot told her, 'That's our lovely Billie,' regarding the girl with misty fondness and not as if she was one of the scariest examples of British girlhood that Billie had seen since she'd last witnessed a fight in a pub car park. 'Babs has gone away for a while. This is her great-niece.'

Something in those coldly analytical eyes told Billie that Debs didn't think Billie was all that great. 'Are you a . . . past customer?' Billie sounded doubtful. Not only were Babs's customers an endangered species but this nose-studded Amazon didn't seem the marrying kind.

'You what? I'm your fucking Saturday girl, you gibbon.'

The gibbon was taken aback. 'But I don't have a . . .' She noticed Dot's freckles darkening in a blush. 'Ah. I do. And it's *you*,' she finished, dragging up the end of the sentence and the corners of her mouth. She felt like a new prisoner being introduced to the lifer who ran her cell block. Extra-politeness seemed the best way to handle somebody so large and so malevolent. 'Brilliant! Great! Glad to have you on board!'

Unimpressed, Debs tore off her squeaky nylon parka. 'I go for two weeks in Faliraki and everything's changed.' She cracked her knuckles and both Billie and Jenkins jumped.

According to Dot, Debs was their good-luck token. 'We've never had so many customers!' she whispered, thrilled, as they watched a fidgeting woman and her daughter paw the dresses.

Billie suspected the recent trickle was due to the dusting and the hoovering and the removal of dead flies from the window display. 'Is Debs OK?' she said, in an undertone. Snippets of her Saturday girl's sales patter had reached her ears—'No way. Rubbish. You're never a size fourteen, love'—and she was feeling uneasy.

'She's a diamond,' Dot assured her. 'Come on, let's help these ladies.'

Swallowing her doubts about the wisdom of sleepwalking up the aisle to manacle yourself to an under-qualified Prince Charming, Billie matched Dot coo for coo as the two women tried to choose a dress.

Crumpled with anxiety, the mother's mantra was, 'I just dunno, love,' as her daughter paced the floorboards in frock after frock. 'I think I preferred the one with the lacing at the back.'

When the long-suffering girl clambered once more into the one with the lacing at the back, her mother put her hands to her head and wailed, 'I just dunno! What about the strappy one?'

'The first one you saw? An hour ago?' Billie double-checked.

'I dunno!'

Some psychological sleight of hand was called for. 'I shouldn't really be doing this,' Billie began, her low-key delivery grabbing the two women's attention. 'But something tells me I can trust you two.' She was silent for a moment, semaphoring 'deep thought' by means of putting her finger to her chin. 'We have a dress in the stockroom that isn't on the rails yet.' She ignored Dot's bafflement. 'It's unique. It's . . .' She looked to the ceiling, a fervent look on her face. '*Stunning.*' She looked from one customer to the other, gravely. 'You must tell nobody that you have seen this dress. Nobody! I could get thrown out of the Grand Association of Wedding Dress . . . er . . .Procurers just for showing it to you.' Clicking her fingers, Billie commanded imperiously, 'Miss Dot! The dress!'

Luckily Dot had cottoned on and snatched up the first dress she saw in the stockroom, a simple design in white with organza sleeves.

'Oh God!' moaned the older woman. 'That's the one!'

'Yes! Yes!' Her daughter tore at her zip in the middle of the shop floor. 'I have to have it, Mum. Stu will die.'

Shortly the two women left, grinning like television evangelists, and the magical dress was folded up and ready to go to the alteration ladies.

Channelling Dick Emery, Dot chided, 'You are awful, Billie.'

'It was the nicest dress in the shop!' Billie defended herself stoutly. 'They believe they have the best dress in the world and, apparently, Stu will die. It's just one more little untruth on the way to the altar. It's less of a lie than promising to love someone for ever.'

'I'm not listening.' Dot popped the cups of a threadbare satin bra over her ears. 'I believe in love. I believe in marriage. I—'

Interrupting this pink torrent, Billie raised one 44G cup to ask, 'Do you believe in nipping next door for a sausage roll? I'm starving.'

'No spirit of romance,' tutted Dot, setting off for Mr Dyke's.

'Strange, that, for somebody whose *wedding day ended in their old single bed at their mum's!*' Billie hollered the last bit. Sometimes she had to remind Dot of The Story. And herself. Because the customer really had looked beautiful in the dress. Funny how a length of white fabric could make you rethink all your hard-won knowledge.

'I don't do washing up,' stated Debs baldly.

During that long Saturday she had told Billie she didn't do errands, she didn't do tidying and she didn't do smiling.

'I presume you do getting paid?' Billie held up a couple of tenners.

'Yup.'

The tenners were snatched and stuffed into a bum bag. It seemed an opportune moment to warn the girls that they would have to attend her brother's team-building seminar.

'Semin-what?' snapped Debs suspiciously. 'Will it hurt?'

'Sly's never lost a seminarian yet,' Billie reassured her.

'What does Sly stand for?' asked Dot as Debs swayed out of the shop on her Ugg boots. 'Is he a Sylvester, like Sly Stallone?'

'Not exactly.' Billie hesitated. She might as well tell her. 'Actually, Sly was named after the character my dad was playing in the am-dram production when my mum fell pregnant. Just like me. Mum was playing Mina in *Dracula* when she found out she was expecting, hence . . .'

'*Wilhelmina.*' Dot nodded knowingly, sympathetically, with a slight wince. 'So what was your dad playing?'

'It was *Peter Pan*. Dad was one of the pirates.'

'Oh.' Dot looked chastened. 'Slightly.' She gulped. 'Oh dear.'

'Oh dear indeed,' agreed Billie. 'Sly changed his name by deed poll as soon as he got to secondary school. There's only so many beatings with a damp towel a boy can take.' She yawned. 'Time to go home, Miss Dot.' Switching off lights, Billie asked wryly, 'Any more members of staff to come out of the woodwork? Or is Debs as bad as it gets?'

'Babs is very fond of Debs,' said Dot reprovingly. 'One of the last things she said was to keep an eye on her. Debs has a heart of gold.'

'And a face of granite. She scares me.'

'She wouldn't hurt a fly. Well,' Dot rethought that statement. 'Apart from the vicious wounding and the aggravated assault. But that's all behind her since she gave up the alcopops.'

April was too early in the year to expect the lavender dusk to be warm. Billie speeded up as she neared the sea, pulling her cord jacket tightly around her. That padlock was a moody bugger and Billie unleashed a few choice words as she battled with it. 'Bums,' she muttered. 'Willies.'

'Ssssh!'

The hiss had come from the beach behind her. She spun round. At this hour the row of huts were deserted. The darkening shore was empty. Did murderers shush before they pounced? Did ghosts? The key slipped from Billie's fingers and she scrabbled on the ground.

'Need a hand?' The voice was a London drawl full of lazy life.

Jerking upright, Billie looked around wildly again. There was a figure standing in one of the weather-beaten boats that lay around the beach.

'I'm fine, thanks,' mumbled Billie, recognising him. It was that distinctive punky guy again. Her nemesis.

'You should be careful,' he said, climbing out of the boat and ambling towards her. 'Somebody might see you.'

'Doesn't bother me.' Billie turned her back on him, cursing the key for getting smaller and her fingers for getting thicker.

'But you're breaking the law, love, aren't you?'

Billie gave up with the padlock, cleared her throat in readiness for a damn good scream, and faced the man. He was nearer and more distinct, although he stayed down on the pebbles. He was very tall and very slender and his eyes were locked on hers. 'Am I?' she asked.

'You know you are, you dirty little squatter, you.' Light, mocking, his tone seemed to lack spite but he didn't let her off the hook.

'It's a fair cop.' Billie smiled, and her lips stuck to her teeth.

'I've always wanted to say this, so bear with me.' The stranger cleared his throat and ruffled his already spiky hair. 'Blackmail's an ugly word.' He grinned happily, showing very white teeth.

Billie noticed that his molars were pointed. Vampiric, even.

'You leave me no choice,' he went on. 'Unless you come out for a drink with me I'll be forced to, how does one put it? I'll be forced to *squeal*.' He folded his arms. 'How about it?'

'Erm . . .' Billie wondered if he meant it.

'If you're wondering if I mean it—I always mean it.'

Years of conditioning had prepared Billie for this moment. *Don't talk to strange men*, her nursery school teachers had warned. Her mother had related grim fables of girls who accepted a Werther's Original in the street and ended up in a harem. Nobody, she reasoned, had ever mentioned blackmailing vampires. She risked a half smile.

'I was right about you.' With this open-ended compliment, her nemesis approached her. 'I'm Sam, by the way. I know your name. We blackmailers pride ourselves on that kind of detail. Next Saturday. Eight o'clock. Here.' He stopped, and held out an elegant hand. 'Deal?'

I must be mad, thought Billie. 'Deal,' she said, and took his hand.

THREE

'Mmmm.' Billie sniffed the air as Jake dragged the door of the cottage open. Like everything else in his house it didn't quite do the job it was designed for. 'Something smells . . .' There was no polite word to cover the scents wafting towards her, so she hung up her jacket on a coat stand fashioned from rusty drainpipes. 'What's the roast?'

'*Rrroast?*' Jake roared. 'You came here expecting a celebration of death?'

'Well, perhaps a chicken,' mumbled Billie. 'It *is* Sunday.'

Loftily, Jake told her, 'We don't eat and kill our friends in this house.'

Billie bridled at his pomposity. 'I'll go and see if Dot needs any help.' She headed for the back of the house and squinted into the gloom of the no-mod-cons kitchen. The romantic-sounding artist's cottage was created in Jake's image. The tiny two-up two-down near the front was chaotic, dirty and belonged to another era, just like Jake's beard. Half-finished canvases of sludgy khakis and browns loitered in every room. Billie was glad to see Dot's radiant little face in the murk.

'It's dark in here,' commented Billie, handing over a bottle of the off licence's second-cheapest Australian white.

'Jake painted the windows black a while ago,' explained Dot. She seemed to find nothing strange in this. 'Said the sunlight was evil.'

'Right.' Billie stared into the pot of gloop that Dot was stirring on the blackened Aga. 'What's for lunch?'

'Nettle soup to start,' Dot told her. 'Wine?'

'So yes.' Billie sat down at the table.

'Try this.' Dot handed her guest a foaming glass poured from an unlabelled urn. Billie raised it to her lips, barely listening to Dot's description of the wine until she heard, 'Jakey makes it in the bath. With his—'

'DON'T SAY FEET!' yelped Billie, slamming the glass on to the table. The table, a recycled toilet door, took her mind off the wine. The plates, stamped *Brockington Insane Asylum* took her mind off the table. The cottage was a multilayered nightmare, a spider's web of Jake's obsessions. Dot, with her peachy skin and swingy hair, was utterly out of place there, like Snow White sharing a squat with Pete Doherty.

When the swampy soup was set out, Jake joined them.

Perched opposite Jake on a fourteenth-century birthing stool, Billie learned a lot about him. Over a main course of salad and a slab of rubbery tofu, Billie discovered that he didn't believe in the establishment, money, status, blinkered suburban values or God. Reading between the lines it was also clear that Jake had never believed in paying his way, lifting a finger, listening or combing his hair.

But Dot believed in Jake. Billie watched her gaze, rapt, at her shambling boyfriend as he pontificated. He didn't repay the compliment. Oblivious to Dot's hard work in that wreck of a kitchen where the sink was made from a horse trough and the saucepans may have belonged to Jesus, he sat on his bony behind throughout, even when Billie attempted to shame him by offering to wash up.

Rinsing the madhouse crockery, Billie broached a subject she'd been dreading. 'Dot, I've had an idea. A big idea. I phoned Great-Aunty Babs last night and she's agreed. Now all I need is your blessing.'

'Sounds serious.' Dot turned her honest little face to her friend.

'Barbara's Brides is going to be reborn.' In her excitement, Billie tripped over her words. 'I'm going to rip it all apart and start again. The whole place will be brightened up, refreshed. All the old stock will go. There'll be elegant, funky new dresses and shoes and bags and veils and underwear and *everything*. It will be modern, clean and inviting, but with all the charm of the past.' She answered Dot's frown with one of her own. 'Well? Are you in, Dot?'

'Course,' said Dot, easily. 'Sounds like fun'.

'Fun?' queried Billie, anxious that her assistant had heard properly. 'A complete refurbishment? On very little money? The whole place stripped and painted? New stock? New everything? Just the two of us doing all the work?'

'Yeah,' nodded Dot. 'Fun.'

Hmm. Billie would have to educate Dot about fun. It was traditionally found around wine bars and sweet shops, not up ladders. A thought struck her. 'Where are the portraits of *you* around here?' She'd seen plenty of half-finished, muddy faces looming out of canvases, but none that reminded her of Dot's piquant little mush.

'Oh, there aren't any.' Dot shrugged, not quite disguising the discomfort she obviously felt. 'Jake doesn't see anything special in me. I'm just ordinary. Not like you.' She twiddled a strand of the strawberry-blonde hair that gleamed like a hostage sunbeam in the grotty room.

'He's a better manipulator than my brother, and Sly's a professional,' sighed Billie. She lifted Dot's chin with one forefinger. '*I* see something special in you, Miss Dot.' And she did. She saw a friend.

Eyes glistening with tears, Dot said sadly, 'Oh, it's heartbreaking.'

'It's not heartbreaking. It's about bloody time,' huffed Billie, as another unspeakable dress joined its miserable compatriots on the shop floor. This brutal clearout was the official start of the refurbishment. They'd rushed round to the shop as soon as the last plate was put away and now a meringue mountain, a kind of wedding-dress slag heap, obscured the light from Barbara's Brides' windows.

'Such a shame,' murmured Dot, placing an off-the-shoulder, off-white, off-the-scale-disgusting creation tenderly on the pyre.

'Good riddance, you mean,' snorted Billie robustly. She marvelled at the price tags as she consigned white frock after white frock to its fate.

'Why do little girls dream of growing up to wear one of these? You can get a fortnight in Magaluf for the same money.'

'It's a dream,' said Dot. 'You can't put a price tag on a dream.'

'No, but you can pay a man with a trailer to take it to the dump.' Billie's gaze fell on a small trunk she hadn't spotted before. 'What's in that box? More of these monstrosities, I suppose.'

'Those are *really* old stock,' Dot told her. 'Babs didn't consider them trendy enough for her clientele.'

Intrigued at the thought of designs too dowdy for Babs, Billie surfed over the doomed wedding dresses to open the trunk. 'But these are beautiful . . .' she gasped, unearthing gown after gown. 'Feel the fabrics!' The velvets and silks and crisp cottons were balm after handling Barbara's nylon. Tiny covered buttons inched up the backs of expertly pleated and tucked dresses. Understated and chic, the curiously time-less designs contrasted strongly with the dog's dinners that had crowded the rails. 'Ooops.' Billie's heart sank as her finger poked through a moth hole. The dresses were showing their age.

Of the twenty-two creations in the trunk, only three were still intact. Tiny labels, surely sewn in by fairies, read RUBY WOLFF. 'Old Ruby knew her stuff,' pondered Billie, elbow-deep in sensual fabric.

Dot found a yellowed and crumpled receipt. 'Look at the curly, old-fashioned handwriting. According to this, Ruby lived just round the corner at 12 Richmond Villas.'

'These must be forty years old at least. See how this moves.' Billie held a simple white velvet dress, luxuriously lined in silk, in front of her. 'I'll stick this in the window when we reopen.' Holding it to her body, she did an experimental swish. The fabric moved like water.

'Shame you hate weddings so much. White suits you.'

'Makes me look drawn.' Billie folded the dress brusquely.

'No. It suited you. You lit up when you looked in the mirror,' per-sisted Dot. 'Even you can be seduced by a white dress.'

Billie plonked a veil on her head and simpered, 'You've seen through me. I admit it. I'm just waiting for Mr Right to come along.'

A loud knock on the door made them jump.

'Afternoon, ladies, I'm Mr Wright!' bawled the toothless old man, his creased and filthy face pressed against the glass.

Eyes wide and mouths wider, Dot and Billie stared at each other for a long second before collapsing among the wedding dresses, gripped by the kind of hysterical laughter rare outside toddler puppet shows.

'Coming, Mr Wright,' gasped Billie, her chest sore, as she crawled across the shop on all fours. 'I've been waiting for you!'

As Ernie Wright, Sole Bay's premier odd-job man, hauled away the rejected dresses in a trailer that stank of mackerel, Dot and Billie recovered enough to self-prescribe Magnum ice lollies.

Blanked-out windows hid frantic scenes from Little Row: of a screaming Dot executing perfect figures of eight on the hired sander, and Billie falling off a ladder and acquiring a bruise shaped uncannily like the Tube map of Greater London.

The ambitious scheme was great on paper. Barbara's Brides would be a cool white space, with distressed floorboards and recessed lighting. The panelling, the counter and the cornicing would be born again under a few coats of slick white paint. 'A virgin cube,' Billie murmured to herself, breaking open a packet of sandpaper.

It was the first packet of many. She'd envisaged herself wielding a dainty brush, her hair caught up in a scarf and a cute smudge of paint on her nose, but the *Reader's Digest Book of Home Improvement* had spoilt that fantasy. It preached that preparation was everything and Billie's fingernails were the first casualties as she attacked the acres of brown paintwork with the coarse paper.

A vision in Billie's head kept her going, even when she was crying with exhaustion and Dot was face down in a pile of dustsheets. It was a vision of 'her' shop, of the regenerated Barbara's Brides. White, clean, brand new and full of hope.

Billie had come to the conclusion that Barbara's Brides could actually turn a profit. It was the only wedding shop for miles. That meant that there was a scrum of potential customers out there who didn't even know that Barbara's Brides existed.

Pulling off her interior-designer hat for a moment, Billie had tried on her PR hat for size: it was a little too big, and the sequins didn't suit her, but she came up with some ideas. Leaflets were hastily printed at the Kall Kwik on the high street, and sat in a conscience-pricking pile by the shop door. Dot's aunty, who ran the biggest paper shop in Sole Bay, slipped one into every bridal magazine, and Dot cruised the surrounding villages in her Robin Reliant, placing ads in newsagents' windows.

The Barbara's Brides PR machine was cranking into gear. Slowly.

Limping to the butcher's on Friday morning, Billie was in search of a savoury snack to blot out the pain.

'My favourite young lady!' beamed Mr Dyke, red cheeks bulging.

Now that Billie knew of the passions lurking beneath his apron, she responded with a prim, 'Good morning.' As she browsed the pasties, another customer came in.

'Good morning to *you*, Mrs Davis.'

Billie looked up surreptitiously. Something more than gallantry had entered the butcher's voice.

Tittering, Mrs Davis, regally seated on her mobility vehicle with a three-legged Yorkshire terrier tucked in at her feet, responded with a girlish, 'What have you got that's tasty?' and a toss of her rain hood.

'I seem to recall my pudding always goes down well with you.'

Dentures whistling only slightly, Mrs Davis whispered, 'Oh, a length of your pudding sets me up for the day, Mr D.'

Billie froze. Mr Dyke was holding up a foot-long black pudding in an indisputably saucy manner. Good God! The man was waggling it!

And now the lady on the scooter was laughing coquettishly, before it turned into a smoker's cough. 'Just eight inches now,' she choked.

This was quality banter. Billie had parachuted in on *Carry on Butchering* and couldn't wait to report to Dot. Another customer joined them, blocking the light from the door. Billie saw the shadow cross the butcher's face and, in a very different voice, he said guardedly, 'And what can I do for you?'

'Oh, I think you've done enough.' Zelda stalked across the black and white floor tiles. 'And you, Mrs Davis,' she snarled, looking down on the little woman, 'I would have thought your pudding days were over.'

'Ooh. Perhaps I'd better . . . just a cutlet, Mr D,' muttered Mrs Davis, trying to restrain her little dog who was growling at Zelda. 'Shush, Peter!' she begged, avoiding the fudge-maker's eye.

Parcelling up a cutlet, Mr Dyke asked, resigned, 'Did you actually want to purchase something, Zelda?'

'Yes, *Mr D*,' taunted Zelda. 'A nice bit of sirloin for Raven.'

'You spoil that cat, Zelda,' murmured Mr Dyke mildly.

'He's no ordinary cat,' said Zelda, defiantly. She noticed Billie. 'All right, my lovely?' she asked, with genuine warmth, before turning back to the butcher to issue a haughty command. 'Put it on my slate.' Zelda sauntered out, humming.

Billie relayed the little scene to Dot.

'Don't ever get on Zelda's wrong side,' advised Dot. 'Has the evil eye, according to the old folk.'

'What? Like a witch, you mean?' Billie demanded clarification. 'Never. There's no room for a witch in the modern world.'

'But this isn't the modern world,' Dot reminded her. 'It's Sole Bay.'

'True.' Billie sat down on the bottom stair, sending up a mushroom cloud of dust. 'But surely somebody with supernatural powers would do a better job of colouring their hair than Zelda does.'

'She was always very sweet to my mum,' said Dot, looking at the denuded wall but seeing past it.

'Oh, Dot, I didn't know. Is your mum . . .?'

'Yes. A while ago,' nodded Dot.

Billie could sense she didn't want a kind word: those kind words can break a carefully constructed dam. She stayed quiet until Dot spoke again.

'Sometimes I think Zelda could sense it.'

'Could sense what?'

'About my mum.' Dot turned to her. 'My mum was abandoned on the steps of Sole Bay vicarage. She was wrapped in a little blanket, with a biscuit in her hand. The vicar gave her to his cleaning lady. Adoption laws must have been more relaxed in those days.'

'Did she ever find her real parents? Your grandparents?'

'No, never. There's a whole chunk of my family missing,'

'I wish my family would go missing,' muttered Billie.

'This is a surprise,' said Nancy Baskerville, archly. 'A phone call from my runaway daughter. What brought this on?'

'I just wondered how the first night of *Chicago* went?'

'A triumph,' said Nancy, blithely. 'Your father's groin trouble came back during his solo but nobody noticed. The *Surbiton Enquirer's* drama critic called me, oh, what was it?' Nancy wasn't a good enough actress to pretend she hadn't learned the accolade by heart. '*A rare gem in a suburban setting.* Pity you couldn't be there, darling.'

'I'll come to the next first night,' promised Billie recklessly. She waited for a question about the shop, about the hut, about her.

'When are you coming home, sweetheart? We worry so.'

'I know, Mum,' sighed Billie. 'I know.'

Saturday arrived. Another day of sanding and scraping and undercoating and dealing with electricians, it was also, possibly, Billie's last day on earth if her date turned out to be a psychopath.

Keeping such thoughts to herself, she toiled alongside Dot all morning. The street was hidden to them, thanks to the newspaper stuck over the windows, but hectic screams and shrieks had both Billie and Dot racing to the door.

Avoiding their toes by centimetres, Mrs Davis sped past, hollering, on her mobility trike. Flames followed her, lurching out of the shopping basket strapped to the back of her vehicle. Zigzagging across Little Row, belching fire like a dying Spitfire, Mrs Davis was hysterical.

In marked contrast, Zelda, leaning on the door jamb of her fudge shop, was calm. To Billie's eyes she looked smug. And guilty as hell.

Dot bent to scoop up Peter, Mrs Davis's three-legged terrier, who had presumably been flung from the speeding trike for his own safety.

A distant jangling, like panic set to music, sounded, and Billie stood up straighter. A fire engine. That meant firemen.

As a fire engine turned down the narrow street, a striped blur raced out of the butcher's. Mr Dyke, apron askew, bolted after his customer, who was now wailing, her hands off the wheel and covering her face.

The engine drew up, wheezing hard, and figures in yellow and blue leaped down. It's hard to concentrate on anything else when tall men in helmets have arrived, but Billie's attention was diverted by Mr Dyke.

As Mrs Davis's crazed trike turned back on itself, heading for the small crowd of onlookers, the butcher made a heroic leap and got a toe-hold on its footplate. He balanced, one hand on the wheel, the other on the canopy, like those sexily nonchalant boys who operate fairground dodgems, and managed to turn off the ignition.

The little vehicle screeched to a halt, as firemen galloped towards it with foam extinguishers. Mr Dyke folded Mrs Davis into his arms and tenderly lifted her out. With her white perm standing on end, Mrs Davis clung to her hero until he deposited her carefully on a chair provided by the tea room opposite.

A low growl sounded close to Billie, and it wasn't Peter. Zelda was pawing the ground like a bull, a dangerous sparkle in her black eyes.

'Zelda,' said Billie, warningly, and reached an arm round the old lady's shoulders. 'Leave it.'

Little Row breathed again. The shopping basket was a damp, sudsy mess, but Mrs Davis had been reunited with Peter, whose three-legged dance of joy was moving.

Pulsing with fury, Zelda was glaring at Mr Dyke. In a deep register, she muttered, 'Curse that man.' Her eyes were shimmering and Billie tightened her grip round her shoulders, remembering Dot's tale of Zelda's powers. Billie looked closer: Zelda's eyes were full of tears, not hate, but before she could say anything a male voice was asking her, 'Is she yours?'

The tall, broad and unfeasibly handsome fireman gestured at Zelda with a laconic movement of his thumb.

'No,' said Billie, self-conscious under the scrutiny of two eyes as dark and desirable as cheap chocolate. 'Zelda's my neighbour.'

'Right.' The fireman, who had started off so assertively, coughed. His face was flooding with red, as if somebody had whispered a rude joke in his ear: his (Billie couldn't help noticing) perfectly shaped ear, round which a stray brown curl had snaked. He turned to Zelda. 'I don't know what went on here, and we're not going to ask too many questions. But do I have your word you won't waste our time again, love?'

It could have been a nod, but it could equally have been a shrug. Zelda took the fire-fighter in, then turned to Billie. 'A looker, ain't he?'

The looker, whose blush had faded slightly, turned back to Billie. 'And your name?' he asked, brusquely.

'My name?' repeated Billie, surprised.

'Yes. Just for, erm, the paperwork.' The fireman bit his lip.

'I'm Billie Baskerville,' she told him, wishing she didn't have white gloss in her eyebrows.

He raised an eyebrow. 'Good name.'

Never had such a lukewarm compliment caused such tumult in the recipient. The fireman was flirting with her. 'Thanks,' Billie muttered.

Steering the arsonist into the chaos of Barbara's Brides, Billie reminded herself that the shop demanded her fidelity. Fancying a fire-fighter would be two-timing. Which made her a two-timer.

Her date was on time. Sunglasses on despite the dark, he lounged, long legs crossed at the ankle, against a powerful-looking motorbike near the top of the steps that led down to the beach huts.

Billie patted her hair and tugged at her waisted cord jacket as she approached. She could tell he was staring at her from behind those shades, taking in the jeans and shirt and flattie pumps: could he tell she'd chosen clothes she could run away in? 'Hi,' she said, insouciantly, as if meeting dangerous men in indecently tight trousers was a habit.

'Hi yourself.' That wide mouth smiled, and creased Sam's broad, strongly drawn face into a welcome, rendered wolfish by those razor-like canines. 'Hop on.'

'On?' queried Billie, uncertainly. 'Hop?'

Tossing her a helmet, Sam nodded. 'The pubs here are hopeless. I can't take another horse brass.' He took off his glasses and unleashed those blue eyes of his. They were beautiful. 'Come on, don't make me ring my contact in the council offices,' he threatened.

I shouldn't be doing this, thought Billie, swinging a leg over the bike.

It was like flying. Noisy and bullish, the bike roared through the lanes where Sole Bay petered out into countryside proper.

The outskirts of Neeveston, the nearest big town, materialised under their wheels and soon the suburbs yielded to the urban clutter of car parks and high-rises and deserted malls.

All, Billie couldn't help noting, prime murder sites.

The street they stopped in looked deserted, its paving stones stained Lucozade yellow by the streetlights, one of which flickered.

'This is us, Billie-pops,' said Sam. 'That door, there.'

That black, blank, anonymous door beyond which was . . . what? Billie hesitated, but Sam guided her firmly towards the door with a hand on her elbow. He pressed a bell, the door opened, and they were ushered into the low lights and velvet seating of a members-only club.

Billie hypothesised that this busy, buzzing, über-trendy venue was an unlikely murder scene. Cocktails were brought to their Perspex table by Dolce & Gabbana-clad staff. In a smoked-glass mirror wall opposite, Billie could see that although the helmet had flattened her hair into a style that brought to mind a knitted snood, she looked stylish enough to complement her surroundings. Beside her, Sam's broad shoulders filled out his misleadingly casual tee—Billie knew that the simply cut top had cost more than Dot took home at the end of a week.

'Cheers.' Sam lifted his glass to her, a mocking look in his eye that seemed to be his default setting.

'Cheers.'

'You're going to be my girl, Billie-kins.'

Aaaargh. Billie began to stutter. 'Hmm. Well. Now. Ah ha. The thing is. Oh God, Sam, are you mental? I mean, are you going to kill me, at all?' Clocking the lifted eyebrow which was as close as that laconically handsome face could get to astonishment, she raced on. 'No, you're not, are you? But you might tell on me. Well, do it then. I'll move out of the hut. Because I'm not ready for a relationship. I'm not looking for one.' Here, the tall fireman popped briefly into her head and was smartly ushered out again. 'You're gorgeous and everything, but I don't want . . .' she slowed—Sam was biting his lip in a way that usually denotes a suppressed guffaw—'a boyfriend.'

'Darling,' Sam said, taking her hand. 'I. Am. Gay. You really didn't notice? Any gayer and I'd be straight. I'm so gay I make other gays homophobic.' He paused, perhaps enjoying the shades of mortification, embarrassment, regret and acute desire for alcohol chasing each other across his companion's features. 'And please don't say *relationship* out loud like that without warning me. I'm going cold turkey and I'm looking for a mate.' He pointed at her. 'That's where you come in.'

'But you said you want me to be your girl,' insisted Billie.

'Down your drink. I do want you to be my girl. You're different.' He magicked another round. 'You don't fit in at Sole Bay.'

Bridling, Billie disputed this. 'I bloody do.'

'Not really. Your jeans are at least two seasons ahead of the trendiest bird in the place. You appreciate a dry Martini. And you *enjoy* living in a beach hut, for crying out loud. No local would be caught dead doing that.' He waggled a forefinger at her. 'My dear, you and I are foreigners and we should stick together.'

Stung by his assessment of her status in her bolthole, Billie turned snippy. 'Friendships develop. Perhaps I don't like you.'

'Perhaps you don't,' agreed Sam. 'I'm not very nice. I'm loud. I'm rude. Apparently, I don't "recognise boundaries". Consequently, Billiver, I don't have that many friends. But,' he leaned forward, and that whiplash smile was inches from her face, 'the ones I do have, love me. And I look after them. And appreciate them.'

The kiss on her nose made Billie jump, but it also made her grin despite herself. 'So you'll be my "gay best friend" kind of thing? I'll tell you all about my emotional problems and we'll get drunk together and then you'll help me pick out new curtains?'

'Fuck off. I said I was gay, not Dale Winton. No curtains. Emotional problems only where appropriate. But lots of fun. Is it a deal?'

She looked at Sam for a long while.

'You want to say yes,' he told her, like a stage hypnotist. 'But something's holding you back.'

A gay psychic with a powerful motorbike and rock-god dress sense. The old Billie resurfaced for a moment. The one who believed in yesses. 'It's a deal,' she laughed, aware she might regret it, and not caring a bit.

Sam was an artist, he told her, as his outline grew oddly blurred. Billie wondered if it was a party trick of his, not thinking to blame the Martinis she was massacring.

'That hut is my studio.'

'You don't look like an artisht.' What Billie meant was that he didn't look like Jake. He didn't smell like him either: this artist smelt of discreetly expensive cologne. 'Are you successful?'

'Very,' said Sam, without pride. In fact, there was a noticeable curl to his full lip. 'I'm renting that big thatched cottage on the edge of the coast road for a few months. You know it?'

Billie knew it. 'Classy,' she slurred.

'Enough about me. I want to know about you, Billie-poos.'

'Oh. There's nothing to tell,' insisted Billie, not drawing breath until the staff diplomatically whispered that it was closing time.

The next week was arduous—and never-ending. With the paint still tacky, Dot and Billie were setting out the new stock at midnight on Friday. Dull months down the telesales saltmines had honed Billie's negotiating skills and she'd managed to fill the shop on credit. Thanks to this, the refurbishment had squeaked in on budget.

Pausing in the hanging of a simple satin strapless dress, Billie allowed herself a moment of pride. For the first time her head and heart were hand in hand. Not only did she love the bricks and mortar of Barbara's Brides, but she could see the potential in it. Batty Billie had pulled on a business suit and lo and behold, it fitted. Her heart had a bad credit rating, but this time it wasn't in charge. This time things would work out . . . wouldn't they?

Even the most anticipated days finally roll round. Saturday came and Billie woke early, due to a combination of bowel-loosening nerves and the booming of a furious sea. By the time she furtively left Herbert's

Dream II, the waves had calmed and the town behind her was serene, yawning in the struggling sun of late spring.

Turning into Little Row, Billie saw a stork-like frame up a ladder outside the shop. Jake was finishing the sign. Billie approached him sideways, reluctant to look up at his handiwork. She needn't have worried. The new sign was sharp, clear and professional: Jake evidently had unpublicised traditional skills. There was only one thing wrong with the elegant black lettering on a clean white background.

'That's not the bloody name of the bloody shop!' Billie shrieked.

Emerging from the shop, Dot answered for him. 'Oh, yes, it is! I OK'ed it with Babs over the phone.'

Billie stared up at the words. 'Oh, Dot,' she said, trying to control the smile that was threatening to engulf her whole head.

'Billie's Brides,' read Dot. 'Has a ring to it, don't you think?'

'Billie's Brides' resembled a still life. The clean white walls sang. Dresses bristled with all the thrilling potential of unworn clothes. The floorboards, repaying the girls' blood, sweat and swearwords, glowed.

The upmarket savoury bites offered themselves selflessly, like lingerie models at a footballer's penthouse, and the plastic champagne flutes marched in orderly rows. The new pink tissue paper was piled in optimistic towers. A brand-new, and as yet blank, Gallery of Happiness stared down from above the new, computerised cash register. GOOD LUK MY DEARS! shouted a postcard of a wallaby from Great-Aunty Babs.

In the centre of the still life, an unusual family portrait was arranged. Tense and upright, Billie wore her cleanest jeans and had chivvied her hair into an approximation of a bun. Dot, bullied into a plain navy dress that had neither a tassel nor an appliquéd butterfly to its name, was solemn. Debs had interpreted her new employer's request to 'dress classily' as an invitation to pull on a fluorescent-pink ruched tube dress. They were ready.

'Unlock the door, Miss Dot.' Billie nodded at her assistant, who was holding the key ready.

'Hello, Sole Bay!' sang Dot, and flung open the door with a flourish.

Peter, the three-legged terrier looked in, sniffed, and stumbled on.

'Can we start on the booze?' asked Debs.

'We're serving it, not drinking it, remember?' said Billie, but gently. 'Once the rush starts we won't have time to think about drinking.'

'**I**s she the rush?' asked Debs loudly, as Annie helped herself to a sausage on a stick.

'Sssh,' ordered Billie. 'Ask our customer if she'd like champagne.'

'Fancy it?' Debs waggled a chilled bottle in Annie's startled face.

'Oh.' Annie looked dismayed. 'I don't drink alcohol, dear.'

'I'll have one for you.' Debs could be very thoughtful.

'It's already midday.' Billie was fretting.

'Five and a half hours to go. Plenty of time for the crowd to build.' The glass was always half full to Dot.

To Billie it was humiliating, standing about with her staff in an empty shop. At least she could drink herself into amnesia on the beach with the leftover champers.

The shop bell had them all standing to attention.

Then they all slumped. 'Jake,' snarled Billie by way of welcome.

'It's dead in here,' he noted, with open satisfaction.

'Have a breadstick,' suggested Billie, popping one in his mouth.

The shop bell jangled again and, shyly, a young woman came in. Dot poured her some champagne. A couple followed, full of questions about bridesmaid dresses. As a gentle wave of custom began to ebb and flow through the shop, the horror of throwing a party that nobody came to receded. From her mingling, the new proprietor learned that there was a lot of intrigued local interest in the revitalised business.

'It was a bit . . . eccentric before,' ventured one woman.

'This is *tons* better,' gushed a chic twenty-something girl, slim and splendid in black. 'Even makes me consider getting married!'

'Oooh, don't get carried away!' laughed Billie, aware that this was the wrong tack for somebody whose livelihood depended on weddings. She would have to crank round her attitude to happy-ever-afters by a full 180 degrees. Professionally, at least.

So, for the next few hours, she heard a voice—just like her own but perhaps slightly higher-pitched—saying things like, 'After all, it's the happiest day of your life,' or, 'We all dream of our big day, don't we?'

Men were outnumbered by women, but some hapless blokes had been dragged in. The new stock was being whisked in and out of the revamped changing cubicles, as girls emerged from behind the white velvet curtains, confident of raising squeals from their companions.

A glass in each hand, Zelda was impressed. 'The place looks like a palace,' she said. 'Much as I love Babs, you could never accuse her of having taste. Mind you, I don't either!' Her tangerine trouser suit backed this up. 'That's why I never married. I always chose wrong 'uns.' She sipped at each glass in turn. 'Besides, I was too busy to get married. Too busy making love,' she confided to a woman in glasses who was trying on a white sheath. 'Love 'em and leave 'em. Who wants to face the same old willy every morning? Variety. That's the answer.' With this parting advice, Zelda shimmied off through the crowd.

On the fringes, Sam watched the scrum of brides over the rim of his champagne flute. He winked slyly at Billie and she giggled to herself. It felt reassuring to have his male bulkiness around, his creaking leather jacket contrasting starkly with the laces and silks of her new life. The embodiment of the wholesome cynicism that she wasn't allowed to express, Sam prowled the shop, raising his eyebrows at the gushing and gasping and emoting that a few white frocks could incite.

'Enjoying yourself, Annie?' Billie asked.

'It's a lovely party, thank you,' said Annie. She had homed in on the Ruby Wolff dresses. 'These are exquisite. Quite exquisite,' she said, softly. 'I used to be a seamstress, you see, so I appreciate quality.'

Billie was stopped by a firm hand on her wrist, a hand weighed down by a rock on the third finger that could be seen from space, and attached to a lanky blonde, obviously addicted to hair straighteners.

'I *love* your shop!' the blonde girl gasped. 'Don't we?' she went on, turning to a man at her side, built like a small block of flats.

'Yeah.' The big man seemed bored. 'How much for the wedding?'

This earned him a playful slap from his companion and a puzzled look from Billie. 'Don't ask straight out. Build up to it, Dean!' admonished the girl, who turned back to Billie. 'How much *is* it for the whole wedding?'

It took a moment or two of conversation to discover that there had been a misunderstanding. 'Miss Dot. Cooee, *Miss Dot!*' called Billie.

Reluctantly, Dot left the side of a couple who had fiercely opposing views on jewelled hairbands.

'Miss Dot,' began Billie, 'Dean and Heather here are telling me that we offer a comprehensive wedding package. Apparently we organise *everything*. Dresses, suits, venues, caterers, the lot. Apparently they discussed this with your good self.'

'Did they . . . ?' began Dot, vaguely.

'Yes, we did,' Heather said. 'You said this is a one-stop shop, and you arrange everything for the bride-to-be.' She pointed out to the street. 'The sign says Billie's Brides, not Billie's *wedding dresses*.' She stressed the distinction with an arch look, as if she was playing a lawyer in a Hollywood courtroom drama and had just nailed the defendant.

The defendant wasn't going down without a fight. 'Sorry, but you're wasting your time. We really don't organise weddings.'

'But you must!' Heather's face folded in on itself. 'It's the biggest day of my life and I don't know where to start. I've left it all too late. This shop tells me that you have perfect taste, like myself,' she claimed, wildly. 'I need you. *Please help me!*'

That glimpse of hysteria whisked Billie right back to her own wedding day. She wasn't revisiting that swamp of hormones and expectation. 'No. Sorry. Not at any price.'

'Dean. Get out your chequebook,' commanded Heather, regally. 'Write her a cheque right now for . . .Three thousand pounds.'

'Perhaps,' said Billie, 'if you really need me . . .'

FOUR

MONDAY BROUGHT BILLIE mixed feelings. There was relief that her scraping days were done, but fear that she and Dot might sit in their modern, pristine, white and down-lit Fresh Start all on their ownio.

Billie was glad to see the red light on the new answerphone glowing when she got in. 'That's a good start!' she thought, pressing the button. She jumped back when she heard Heather's voice, loud and unamused.

'Oh. I see. You're not there. You shut on a Sunday, do you? I'm having a crisis about the pageboy. I think he might be ugly. And you're still on for the meeting Monday afternoon, I hope?'

Dot breezed in, all lovebeads and sandals, and while she put the kettle on and chatted about the party, Jenkins's health and other Dottish topics, Billie noticed the laptop sticking out from behind the counter.

An image flashed through her mind. Of her drunken self, tapping out an email to James with one hand while the other one kept a rigor mortis grip on a plastic glass of flat champagne.

Billie went hot and then cold. What had she written? She was loquacious when drunk, always ready to ring up some bloke she'd snogged a decade ago and deliver a detailed autopsy of his personality. Sometimes she would tell men she barely knew that she loved them, other times it would be all vitriol.

Yes, that computer did have a smug air. It knew something she didn't. It knew whether or not she had made an absolute arse of herself in front of a man whose opinion still meant a lot.

That thought stopped her short. Even with thumbscrews, Billie would never have admitted that she cared what James thought any more. She flew at the computer and manhandled it out of its case. She poked at keys, tutted through its interminable blinking and whirring and the computer awoke, and then fearfully read what she'd written.

Baffled, she read it twice. It didn't sound like the insane ramblings that usually followed a cuddle from the alcohol fairy. It was more like the musings of a fond aunt to a schoolboy nephew.

Lovely to hear from you!

it began, as if The Story had never happened. Jauntily, it went on:

I've moved! To the loveliest little town!

Billie's vile drunken alter ego could be relied upon to spread chaos, but this twittering, gushing new persona was somehow creepier. It was as if her tipsy self had decided to play along with James and beat him at his own game. The language used was every bit as airy as his. Seen any good movies lately?—it asked the man she'd last seen drunk in his boxers, dividing up their paperbacks as if he personally hated each one.

Even without the lure of free comestibles, the shop was busy that first day. The crystal tinkle of the bell was music to Billie's ears, each note crooning, 'You haven't cocked up! Well, not yet!' to her bandaged self-esteem. She and Miss Dot listened to the needs and wants of the women who came in, with barely time to share a companionable biscuit.

Billie eyed a girl flicking through a rail. The thin, knock-kneed little scrap was surely a bridesmaid, not a bride. 'Need any help?' she asked.

'I need a wedding dress,' the girl mumbled, face turned away.

'Are you old enough to get married?'

'Yeah. I'm sixteen. And my dad's given his consent.'

Wonder if she's pregnant, thought Billie.

As if the accusation had come out of the side of Billie's head on ticker tape, the girl said firmly, 'I'm not pregnant.'

Billie showed her the updated ready-to-wear range. Simple, unfussy dresses that needed no alterations, they were also cheaper, and better suited to a teenager's pocket.

It was hard to shake off the feeling that she was colluding in what might be the biggest mistake of the sixteen-year-old's life. At that age Billie had painted her room black and daydreamed about going ice skating with Phillip Schofield. She shook herself, and accepted the tenners the girl extracted from her Bratz purse. This was a business transaction, pure and simple.

Tidy and respectable, the new housing estate sat primly on the edge of town. Heather Du Bois's house was square and neat, like its neighbours, except for the concrete Grecian columns that rose majestically either side of the double-glazed front door. *A very important person lives here*, they seemed to say, although Billie could also hear a whispered, *Somebody with no bleeding idea lives here*.

Welcomed by Heather, fluffy slippers complementing her sweatpant civvies, Billie was politely ordered to take her shoes off. 'New carpets,' explained Heather. 'Oatmeal wool/nylon mix. You understand?'

Billie padded after her hostess into a pale sitting room, all blond wood and white walls. With its plasma screen and careful arrangement of Buddhas, it was a room to pose in, rather than relax.

'Any chance of a guided tour?' Billie asked Heather. Congratulating herself on how professional it sounded, she enlarged, 'Your house tells me a lot about your personal style and preferences.'

'Like your thinking.' Heather pointed an acrylic nail at her.

Sounding professional was vital, because Billie felt distinctly amateur. She was in way over her head: the only other wedding she'd ever organised had ended with blood on the walls. Quite apart from the £3,000 fee, Billie would be responsible for spending lots and lots and lots of Heather's money: it was a sobering prospect.

After the zen reception room, the country kitchen was a surprise. Herbs swayed from polystyrene beams above the Aga. In the bedroom a four-poster swathed in machine-washable silk changed the mood again. The modern, noodle-eating woman of the sitting room, who'd morphed into a Domestic Goddess in the kitchen was now Mata Hari.

It wasn't very useful. Heather liked props, and playing a part. Which of these characters was the flesh-and-blood woman?

'Impressive,' Billie summed up as they seated themselves on the cream leather sofa, an instant coffee apiece. 'First things first,' she continued, as crisp and efficient as a girl who organises ten weddings before breakfast. 'What's the date of the wedding?'

'August the 23rd.' Heather frowned. 'What's that look for?'

'Nothing,' coughed Billie. 'That's a lovely date.' So lovely she'd chosen it for her own wedding. 'Tell me a bit about yourself, Heather. Your likes and dislikes. It all helps,' said Billie. 'Shame Dean isn't here.'

'Why?' Heather seemed baffled.

'So I can find out what he wants from his wedding day.'

'Oh, he wants what I want.'

It transpired that Heather was in IT. Billie understood alchemy better than she understood IT. Dean was a prison warder: 'Has all the top rapists and murderers,' Heather told her proudly. The bride-to-be was the adored elder daughter of parents who had given her a pony, an overbite and too much positive reaffirmation. Her mother had died some years ago, but, 'You'll love Granny,' prophesied Heather. 'Told me to tell you she'll watch you like a hawk and string you up in the church if everything isn't absolutely perfect!' In Heather's family this kind of threat apparently passed as humour. 'Shall I fetch the mood board?'

'Oooh, yes please.' Billie had no idea what a mood board might be.

'Taaa-daah!' Heather leaned behind the sofa and yanked out a large cork noticeboard, studded with pictures and swatches and cuttings. 'This is like the inside of my head!'

A pang of sympathy for Dean shot through Billie. It couldn't be easy living with a woman whose head was full of white horses with feathered plumes, roast beef and calligraphy. The mood board had an immediate effect on Billie's mood. It scared the offal out of her. 'Okaaaay,' Billie busked, floundering. 'You want all these things for your wedding?'

'Of course not! But the plumed horses are non-negotiable. This is just a starting point, to give you an idea of *the feel* of what I'm after.'

'The feel,' repeated Billie blankly, staring at a magazine photograph of a butterfly on a postbox.

'I'm thinking romantic but raunchy. Kylie Minogue meets Scarlett O'Hara. Roses. Orchids. Table diamonds. Candles. Doves.'

Wondering what the hell a table diamond was when it was at home, Billie threw Heather a practical question. 'How many bridesmaids?'

'Just a dozen.'

'Venues?' Billie asked, brightly.

Heather looked down at her lap, a self-absorbed look on her face. 'My dream venue is the old bandstand, near the pier. Do you know it?'

'I do.' One of Billie's favourite spots in Sole Bay, the bandstand was loaded with charm, weather-beaten and peeling: not terribly Heather.

'When I was little, when Mum was still here, she used to take us there with sandwiches and Cokes every Saturday. It's my absolute favourite place in the world. I dragged Dean there as soon as he proposed. Kind of, you know, to let Mum know.'

'Well, I doubt that the bandstand has a licence for you to get married there, but we can include your mum's favourite hymn in the service, or the flowers she liked in your bouquet,' Billie said softly.

The suggestions seemed to warm Heather. 'I never thought of that.'

Thanks to a frantic Google, Billie had some venues to consider. She promised to make enquiries. 'We can go along and check out the rooms, taste the catering before we make a final decision.'

'What about the cake?' asked Heather. 'Dean wants fruit cake. He's such an old woman. "Over my dead body, Dean Kelly," I said.'

'The *in* cake, the cake all the celebs are choosing,' began Billie, reciting parrot-fashion a paragraph from a catalogue, 'is a white chocolate mousse-based confection. It's topped with crème anglaise and darling miniature truffles. Catherine Zeta Jones had one.'

'Order it.'

All talked out about headdresses and invitation fonts and the oldest bridesmaid's allergies, Billie stood up to go. 'Let's meet up again next week,' she suggested, quelling a yawn.

'And you still think macrobiotic sushi is wrong for the reception?'

'You are not Madonna. Your guests are not from LA. British people will feel short-changed if they roll up to a reception and somebody hands them a raw prawn.'

'You're right,' Heather caved in. 'I just want to stun everybody, you know? I want the wow factor.'

'The main thing is marrying the right bloke,' Billie laughed. 'The rest is just detail.' Billie had managed to creep as far as the front door, and she leapt when it suddenly opened.

Heather's welcome for her husband-to-be was accusatory. 'You're early,' she said, suspiciously.

'I wanted to catch Billie.' Dean nodded an affable hello. 'All right? Has she nobbled you about the fruit cake yet?'

''Fraid so,' smiled Billie.

'Did you get to the jazz band?' he asked, hopefully.

'Dean, for the last time, we are not having jazz bastards at my wedding.' She turned to Billie. 'Can you get me a band that looks and sounds exactly like the Rolling Stones?'

'Hmm. Wouldn't that be the Rolling Stones?' Billie inched nearer the door and freedom. 'Let's discuss the music next week.'

Dean took off his jacket. 'Pity you can't hang around for dinner. You could meet my best man.' He pointed to a framed holiday snapshot by the coat stand. A crowd of lads, sunburnt and peeling, were holding up pints to the camera. 'That's Ed. On the far right.'

Politely, Billie glanced at the photo. Then she stared, struck by something. 'Is he a fireman?' she asked.

'Yeah. One in a million. Salt of the earth.'

'If I'd met Ed first . . .' Heather looked dreamy out at the distorted street through the dimpled glass of the front door. 'Poor old Ed,' she sighed, with a sympathy that seemed misplaced when discussing a physically perfect fireman.

'Poor? Old?' queried Billie, remembering the man who'd asked her name after the inferno of Little Row.

'He's so shy,' explained Heather. 'Goes red as a tomato when he speaks to girls he fancies.' Perhaps noting Billie's novel expression, which encompassed both a raised eyebrow and a dropped jaw, she asked, 'Did I say something?'

'No,' lied Billie. Refraining from chanting *Nah nah na nah nah the hunky fireman likes me*, she checked, 'He's single, then?' Ed's status shouldn't, and didn't, matter but she was window-shopping.

'Not for long,' said Heather, mysteriously.

'How come?' For a window-shopper, Billie was displaying a marked interest in the goods.

Pointing to another, larger, framed photograph, Heather said,

'Angela. My sister. Chief bridesmaid. She and Ed were meant for each other. I'm going to get them together at the wedding.'

With the look of a man who'd heard all this before, Dean snorted.

Billie studied the formal studio portrait of Angela.

'She's an angel. Clever. Witty. Has her own pest-control business.' Heather gazed admiringly at her sibling. 'A real catch for any man.'

The summer had hit its stride early. Sweetie-coloured houses along the front dazzled in the sun's glare. Pale, shy shoulders met the outside world for the first time in months, and blue-white legs marched proudly about in last year's shorts.

Being the boss of a growing business didn't just mean lounging about in luxury and drinking tea from bridal slippers. A distinct lack of minions meant that Billie did a little of everything, from cleaning to selling to putting on a funny voice to disrupt the East Coast FM phone-ins. Today she was delivering a boned bodice to an address near the front. Dot had offered the loan of her Reliant Robin, but Billie made it a rule only to drive cars with an even number of wheels.

'About time,' said the customer, closing the door in Billie's face.

'Not at all,' simpered Billie to the closed door. 'Any time.' She stomped off and took a wrong turning. 'Oh flip,' she muttered. Being new in town, she'd spent a lot of time exploring the byways and alleyways of Sole Bay, but this short, narrow street was new to her.

Too pragmatic to believe in fate—like fairies, fat-free biscuits and reliable boyfriends the basic premise was preposterous—Billie couldn't help humming *The Twilight Zone* music when she realised that this was Richmond Villas, the address on the Ruby Wolff invoice.

The other flat-fronted cottages could be forgiven for leaning away from mucky number twelve. A rotting tooth in a set of pristine gnashers, its net curtains were grubby and its front door peeling.

'Why not?' Billie dusted off one of her favourite sayings from the old days, before life had stepped in and shown her exactly why bloody not. Pressing the doorbell, she jumped back from the step, startled by the clamour the innocuous ding dong had set off in the house. A great huffing and puffing began, and she could hear things being pulled and dragged and kicked out of the way. All this noise and fury delivered a tiny, scowling, gnome of a man onto the step. He pulled the door carefully behind him, as if to hide some secret that the dark, uninviting interior might hide. 'What?' he asked, with ill humour.

'Oh,' began Billie, with her customary élan. 'Is your wife in?'

'Don't have no wife,' growled the man. He wore an impeccably cut and sensationally filthy three-piece suit.

'I'm sorry.' So Ruby must have passed on. Billie suddenly felt sorry for this dishevelled little man, who was finding it hard to cope alone, if the stink of whisky was anything to go by. 'I didn't know.'

'No need to be sorry,' snapped the gent, obviously insulted by her sympathy. 'Wives are nothing but trouble. One hand in your purse and the other on your manhood.' He shook his head vehemently.

'Well, Ruby was certainly a talented lady. I run the wedding shop in town and I was going to ask her if she wanted to start making dresses again.' Until that moment, Billie had no idea that she'd been going to ask Ruby any such thing. 'But, sadly—'

Mr Wolff grunted, 'I'm Ruby, you halfwit.'

Billie blinked. 'But you're not . . .' She didn't finish the sentence.

'Reuben.' He stabbed a nicotine-stained finger at her. 'Reuben Wolff. You silly chit.'

'Sorry to disturb you.'

The door had slammed before she got to the full stop.

'I couldn't leave her at home,' reasoned Dot, looking down at the chicken scratching about on the newly painted boards. Lowering her voice to a whisper, she confided, 'She's been getting worse. Mood swings. Suicide attempts on the garden rake. Depression is one thing but this . . .' she waved a hand in the direction of the chicken, who was now pecking at a grosgrain shoe, 'is quite another.'

'I can see she's going through a tough time,' cooed Billie.

'Aw, can you really?'

'No, I can't. It's a bloody chicken, Dot.'

Dot bent to say, 'Julia, ignore her. She doesn't know you like I do.'

The chicken scuttled across the shop floor in a crazy zigzag.

Considering a short homily, centring on the incompatibility of neurotic chickens and wedding-dress shops, Billie decided against it. 'Try and keep her out of the way,' was all she said.

'I think you'll find that discretion is Julia's middle name.'

'And mine is Mug.'

Julia's middle name turned out to be Idiot. When Sam dropped in at lunchtime, she was refusing to leave Billie's handbag.

'Lunch, Billie-knickers?' he asked, when Julia had retired, huffily, to the bin. Glasses shaded his strobe eyes.

'Why not?' Leaving Dot in charge, Billie steered him towards the square. 'Let's have something in the Swan.'

'Oh God, more chintz.' Sam looked about him, crossly. 'It's so damn clean here. Christ, I miss London.'

Billie was only half listening. 'Look!' She pointed across the road at the bookstore, which was housed in a drunkenly tilted half-timbered building. 'In the window. That poster looks like . . .'

'It is,' growled Sam, lowering his head.

Whooping, Billie dashed across the road. 'It's you!' She gestured wildly at the window display of books and posters. 'You're *that* Sam Nolan!' She stopped, awestruck. 'You are the creator of Tiddlywinks the velvet rabbit.' She took a step back from him. 'Sam, you're famous.'

'If you happen to be four, I'm famous.'

'I know people who are four. So you're famous to me.' Billie's drawn-out, 'Awww,' was profoundly Dot-esque. 'You're Tiddlywinks' daddy.'

Sam was glaring in at the piles of books as if he wanted to break the window and ransack the shop.

'But, Sam, Tiddlywinks must have made you rich.' Billie pointed at the adorable soft toy in the window, holding its little grey velvet paws wide. 'He's the world's favourite rabbit. The books have been turned into a TV series. You're probably like a millionaire, or something.'

'Yes,' sighed Sam. 'As well as destroying my credibility as an artist for ever, the little git's made me a millionaire a few times over.'

'In that case,' Billie took his arm. 'The ploughman's is on you.'

Back at Billie's Brides, Billie roamed the Internet winkling out purveyors of horses with feathers on their heads. She dipped into her email for some distraction. James had replied. She twitched, but only slightly.

> Hi Billie, Thanks for replying. Glad to hear you're living by the sea. You always wanted to. Well done!

Billie winced. James had a tendency to be patronising, and that 'well done' was a bit condescending. Or maybe, she reconsidered, I am being paranoid and oversensitive and he is merely being nice.

The sea had a profound effect on us whenever we managed to escape London. Remember that weekend in Cornwall? The sky seemed huge over our heads and there wasn't a single cloud. As we drove home we realised we hadn't argued once and decided the sea must have calmed us. Remember?

Relaxing slightly, Billie puzzled at the unmistakable note of yearning that ran through the email. She remembered that weekend as if it were yesterday. It had been great. Just great. Perhaps he missed her a little, teeny, tiny bit after all.

By the way, did I mention my girlfriend?

And then again . . .

She's great. You'd like her.

Billie clenched and unclenched her fists. Suddenly she had the demeanour of a woman who had been sucking a lemon since puberty.

She's a doctor, a real brainbox. (So *Hollyoaks* omnibuses are out!)

Those omnibuses had been the highlight of their week, recalled Billie, feeling unaccountably bruised by how easily her ex-fiancé had relinquished two and a half hours of quality television.

She keeps me in line, I can tell you. It's early days yet, but we'll see how it goes. She kind of reminds me of you in a way.

How? boggled Billie. Presumably they had the same number of heads, but there, surely, the comparison must end between herself and a telly-hating intellectual who saved lives during the day and kept James in line at night.

But not as mad, obviously!

Obviously. Nobody, thought Billie bitterly, is as mad as me, are they, James? Harrumphing, she read on.

And you? How's the love life?

There it was. The booby trap she'd been dreading. So casual, so conversational. It was like a hot brand on her skin. Ed popped, unbidden, into her mind. He was very welcome but he was just a daydream and no match for a sexy lady doctor.

Tell me about Billie's Brides. I can't imagine you running a shop, but I bet you're good at it. What kind of customers come in?

Already composing her reply in her head, Billie thought of all the characters who would figure in it. She could imagine how he'd laugh at the serial killer's fiancée. She knew how to tickle James's funny bone. Smugly, Billie decided, on no evidence, that the lady doctor didn't make him laugh. She stopped short, warning herself to 'hold on'. Why on earth was she competing with a woman she would never meet for a man she used to love?

Isn't it kind of strange, though—a wedding shop? I mean, after what happened. Look, it'd be nice to hear from you again but I'll understand if it's too, well, tricky, OK?

Billie stood up and sat back down again. She coughed. She drummed her fingers on the table. Then she shouted very loudly, and quite unnecessarily, at Julia, who was optimistically squatting on a small handbag to see if it would hatch.

The days passed in an unfolding panorama of measuring women's bumpy bits, eating ice lollies and drinking with Sam.

It was a sluggish Friday afternoon. Out on the pavement, a male shape caught Billie's eye. She gave a little miaow of surprise. Although she'd been thinking about him, it was a surprise to see his face. She stepped out into Little Row.

'Mr Wolff. You look different.'

Reuben Wolff was clean. His face, free of stubble, was arresting in an old-fashioned, biblical, large-featured way. Tamed and combed, his white hair sat in dated waves upon his head, and his elegantly cut suit was no longer dirty. Chest puffed out, he carried his five foot four frame as if he was an archduke. Stiffly, he told her, 'I've come to talk to you about your business proposition.'

'Proposition?' Billie was puzzled, and wary.

'Unless I'm mistaken, you commissioned me to design and make wedding dresses for your establishment.'

'Not exactly,' fudged Billie, uneasily. 'I only said—'

'My word is my bond. Is yours?' snapped the dapper little man.

'Yes.' Billie was insulted by the old man's insinuation. 'A Baskerville's word is her bond. Come inside, and we'll talk about it.'

By the time Reuben Wolff left, Little Row was dark and he had an order for five wedding dresses based on the designs in the trunk. He had insisted that Billie find him an assistant. But he had also talked eloquently about his passion for making dresses that made women feel beautiful, and Billie decided she really rather liked him.

Watching his progress down the street, Dot said dreamily, 'Isn't Ruby lovely? What a gent.'

'You wouldn't have thought that if you'd seen him before,' muttered Billie. 'He looked like a tramp and he reeked of booze.'

'Loneliness is very corrosive. Isolated people are never happy.' Dot turned to her boss. 'Are they?'

FIVE

TALL, BROAD AND CORN-FED handsome, Sly Baskerville posed with feet planted far apart and hands on hips, displaying the gold silk lining of his jacket. He exuded a confidence so palpable that it could have been his twin. The eyes, nose and jaw were vaguely reminiscent of his sister's, as if Billie's features had been fed into a Super Hero machine.

The shop was transformed into what Sly called his arena. A row of three chairs faced him, behind him stood a massive flip chart, and an easel supporting a studio portrait of his lovely self. With an airbrushed cheesy smile, this laminated Sly pointed at them, both hands cocked like pistols. YES! YOU! it said underneath.

Already cringing at the tinny strains of 'Things Can Only Get Better' from her brother's mini speakers, Billie squirmed. Other people were blessed with run-of-the-mill families, she thought. How come fate had drop-kicked her into the Baskervilles?

Slowly, Sly was studying the faces of his expectant audience. 'Ladies, ladies, ladies,' he drawled, in a mid-Atlantic accent. 'Here, in front of me, are three fine examples of twenty-first-century womanhood.'

Really? thought Billie. She peered sideways at Dot, whose organic hemp skirt was exuding a gentle hint of the cattle barn, and at Debs, who was scratching 'Baz' on her forearm with a compass. Such raw material was unusual for Sly.

'I can see, just by looking at you,' began Sly, looking at them, 'I can see that you all have an Inner Winner (trademark applied for).'

'We do?' Breathless, Dot was leaning forward.

'You do.' She was rewarded with a killer smile from Sly: his teeth were not standard-issue idiosyncratic Baskerville originals, and he liked to get value for money by blinding clients with them. 'I can smell originality and creativity and MAGIC in this room!'

'I think that's Dot's skirt,' mumbled Debs.

'A quick exercise.' Suddenly Sly ripped off his jacket. 'Up!' He clapped his hands and only Debs ignored him, Dot jumping up as if her seat was electrified. 'Debs, isn't it?' Sly asked, bending towards her.

'Yeah.'

'I know you want to succeed, you want to fulfil your potential.'

'After I've finished me tattoo.'

'I'm going to tattoo your soul.'

Debs looked up at him dubiously, pulling her shirt together.

'With one word,' Sly enunciated carefully. 'Success.'

'Naw.' Debs enunciated slowly, as if talking to a foreigner. '*Baz*.'

'The sooner you get up, the sooner you'll get home,' sighed Billie.

Up jumped Debs.

'We're going to work on trust. All organisations need trust,' Sly stated, emphatically.

'Lust?' queried Debs.

'Sorry, ladies, I'm taken.' Sly winked at Debs and Dot, and ignored Billie's cringe. 'Seriously, though. You need absolute faith in each other to work together productively. Build the team, build the dream.'

'So true,' sighed Dot.

Sly split the seminar into pairs ('Debs and Billie, myself and Dot') and instructed them to catch each other as they fell backwards. 'You must fall back with your arms folded across your chest, fully confident that your partner will catch you.' Sly demonstrated with the aid of Dot, who looked like a very pretty eleventh-century martyr as she dropped, calm and trusting, into his arms.

'Now you two,' he said encouragingly to Debs and Billie.

'I'll catch you, yeah?' Billie got this in quickly.

'No, no, no.' Sly waggled a finger. 'That's not how it works. This is about trust, not leadership. *You* fall, and your assistant catches you.'

'You sure about this?' Debs frowned. 'She must be all of eleven stone.'

'I'm nine eight!' yelped Billie, who was ten two.

'Ladies.' Sly had brought his voice right down. 'Begin.'

A long moment followed, where Billie did not fall backwards.

'Begin,' said Sly again.

Another little while. Billie just couldn't bring herself to drop into Debs's grasp. She didn't, she realised, trust or even know this girl.

'Begin.' A hint of irritation was tickling the edges of Sly's delivery.

Billie gulped, shut her eyes and fell back. Debs caught her.

Billie opened her eyes, looked up into Debs's upside-down features, and breathed a heartfelt, 'Thank you.'

And then Debs dropped her. 'You never said nothing about hanging on to her.' Debs, over the wails, was unrepentant. 'She's fucking heavy.'

They were all punching the air. '*I wanna win!*' they were shouting.

Not shouting terribly loudly because of her headache (those floorboards were hard). Billie didn't really sound as if she wanted to win.

'*What do you want?*' yelled Sly, pacing like a panther.

'*I wanna win!*' Dot was surprisingly loud, and even Debs was getting into it, now that her iPod earpiece had been rumbled.

'What do we hate?' Sly whispered, fervently.

'*Negativity!*' shrieked Billie's fellow drones.

Punching the air, Sly bawled, '*Where are we going?*'

The answer wasn't '*Straight home to bed!*' as Billie would have preferred, but, '*To the top!*'

'Time for the Ball of Blame (trademark applied for)!' Sly bounded among them. 'You throw this little ball to each other, and you have to say something you dislike about the person you're throwing it to.'

'Me first.' Debs grabbed the squashy little leather ball.

Putting up her hand, Billie queried, 'Isn't this a little . . . negative?'

'It's all within the protective framework of the seminar.' Sly traced a tent with his hands, but Billie couldn't see a framework. 'We accept and absorb, because we are *building*, not destroying.'

'Fat arse,' shouted Debs, tossing the ball, rather hard, at Billie.

Struggling to accept and absorb, Billie flung the ball back at her. 'Clock-watcher.'

A flicker of hurt, unmistakable and totally unexpected, showed in Debs's eyes. 'Too nice to animals,' she said, throwing the ball at Dot.

'Oh God, no no, I can't. I love Debs. I love Billie.' Dot accepted the ball as if it was a flying baked potato. 'Can I throw it to myself?'

'Throw,' commanded Sly, mercilessly.

'Ohhhhh.' Dot closed her eyes and slung the ball in Billie's direction. 'Occasionally a bit rude, just a bit, not much, to my boyfriend.'

Over the next few minutes, Billie learned that Dot thought she was slightly, slightly, slightly not much but slightly impatient about the problems with the new till, and that Debs thought she was 'narky', 'snotty' and 'should wear jeans a size up'.

Absorbing this, even within a protective framework, was taking some doing, so Billie was relieved when Sly moved on.

'Remember, people, that you are the fuel that drives this company. Without fuel in the tank, there ain't no money in the bank. Winners never quit, quitters never win. Am I right?'

'*Yes!*' shouted Dot, quite alone.

How Billie longed to quit. And if that meant she'd never be one of Sly's Inner Winners—heck, she could live with that.

Sly shook his head. 'Mum was right. It's a shed, Bill.' His weighty presence shrank Herbert's Dream II to the dimensions of a Wendy house.

'I like it,' said Billie, mulishly. She didn't, she *loved* it. Fear of ridicule prevented her sharing that with Sly: small, shabby, mod-con-free, it would never appeal to a status snob like her brother.

'Please, love, come home. Everyone's worried about you.'

'There's no need. I'm . . . happy. Things are going well. I'm actually taking my job seriously for the first time and I like that.'

'And yet you think your customers are mugs?'

Ouch. 'It's not that I look down on them. I just mean that . . . I can't fathom why they want to buy what I'm selling.'

'You should be careful,' warned Sly, stretching and almost smashing the window. 'They'll catch on. And they'll stop buying.'

'Not a chance. I'm a lone voice in the wilderness. Everybody loves weddings. And the thought of a happy ever after. I'm out of step. Most people get married. Look at you and Sana.'

'Yes, we're very happy. Very very happy. A team. A partnership. Along with the kids we form a Trust Triangle.'

Disappearing into the sooty dark that began at the end of the verandah, Sly called, 'Good night, Billie. Don't forget next Sunday at Mum
and Dad's. No excuses, now.'

By the time he'd got to his Merc, Billie was locating her Inner Slob
(no trademark necessary) with the aid of a kindly Wagon Wheel.

'My subconscious has had a creative eruption,' Dot announced.

'You mean you've had an idea.' Exposure to Sly made people sound
as if they'd been fed into shoddy translation software. 'Spit it out.' Billie
paused in her grooming of a mannequin's ash-blonde wig.

Dot said, 'Henceforth you are the Billie's Brides wedding fairy.'

Billie frowned. 'Fairy.'

'You'll wear wings. And you'll carry a wand. And you'll scatter glitter
everywhere.'

'Me?' Billie double-checked. 'Glitter? Wings?' She paused. 'Wand?'

'Don't be negative,' scolded Dot. 'Here.' She rifled the cloth bag covered in beads and tassels and shards of mirror that went everywhere
with her. 'I made these for you.' Dot produced wings and a wand that
betrayed their humble genealogy of chicken wire, chopsticks and last
year's Christmas decorations. 'Try them on.'

Glowering, Billie tied the ribbons of the wings under her bosom. She
steeled herself to look in a changing-room mirror. 'Good grief,' she
muttered. 'I draw the line at the wand,' she said, belligerently.

'Of course you don't,' protested Dot. 'How else can you work your
magic?' She pressed the wand into Billie's limp grasp and stood back to
admire her handiwork. 'Every inch a fairy.'

'I don't work magic. I sell wedding dresses. If I wanted to be a fairy
I'd call myself Rupert and hang around Old Compton Street.'

'Shush, now.' Dot put a finger to her lips. 'Only positivity, please,
from those fairy lips.'

'I warn you, Dot—'

The threat would never be uttered. A girl of about twenty and her
mother came in at that moment and both women put their hands to
their mouths and squealed when they spotted Billie.

'A fairy!' shrieked the mother, who was old enough to know better.

'A wedding fairy!' screamed the younger one, who was on Dot's
wavelength. 'Oh Mum, I love it. Don't you love it? Mum?'

'I do, darling. I love it.'

Standing up straight and holding her customised chopstick less like a weapon and more like a wand, Billie said, with the animation of one being forced at gunpoint. 'Hello. I'm the wedding fairy.'

A cascade of glitter, thrown by Dot's expert hand, fluttered down on them all. Only some of it went in Billie's eyes.

SIX

SATURDAYS USED TO MEAN lie-ins and hangovers and mooching around, but now they were the busiest day of Billie's week.

Hopping from foot to foot on the tiled porch as Billie approached, Heather was the first customer. 'Is my dress altered? Is it ready?' she gabbled, as Billie tried to get the door open without dribbling a melting Mivvi into her bag.

'Fetch!' As the door opened, Billie pointed to the gown that hung, swathed in plastic like a kinky backbencher, on the banisters.

Heather tore into a changing room, and Billie prayed her client would be satisfied with the dress, a beautiful ivory velvet, with sheer sleeves.

Billie opened the post, made a cup of tea. She was on her third Jammie Dodger before she remembered she wasn't alone. Perhaps Heather had gone through the back of the changing room into Narnia. 'Heather?' she asked, at the brocade curtain. 'Everything all right?'

'Mm hmm.' Heather sounded like a lamb, with a blocked nose.

Gently, Billie pulled the curtain aside. Heather was gazing at her reflection. The dress fitted and flattered her, translating her bony hips into curves. Even her face was transformed by the radiance of the fabric, and softened by the tears on the edge of her lashes.

'Damn. I promised myself I wouldn't be one of those stupid girls who cry,' she bleated. 'But my mum should be here . . .' She tapered off, pursing her lips to control her voice. 'It *is* all right, isn't it?'

'Your mum would love it,' said Billie softly to Heather's reflection.

A tear splashed on the forgiving velvet, sank in and disappeared.

The Gallery of Happiness was filling up. Resisting Billie's suggestion that they rename it the Gallery of Hapless Delusion, Dot pinned up snap after snap of Billie brides.

Late again, Debs had the decency to explain. 'Man trouble,' she said, treating Billie to a view of her chewing gum looping the loop round her fillings.

'Right. Well, don't, you know, do it again. Or whatever.' Billie turned away, biting her knuckles. 'And tidy the changing rooms!' she ordered, when Debs was safely on the other side of the shop. She had to show Debs who was boss.

Shocked, Debs said, 'Gimme time to finish me nails,' effortlessly showing Billie exactly who was boss. 'Why are you all made up?'

'Am I?' asked Billie, through lips the colour of crushed roses. 'No reason.' She surreptitiously checked her hair in the mirror.

Before Heather had left, she had turned out her handbag in a fruitless search for a vital photograph of a bridesmaid dress. Her casual, 'I'm seeing Ed later. I'll tell him to pop it into you,' had been received noncommittally by Billie, who had leapt like a maddened gazelle to her make-up bag as soon as Heather left.

The mirror told Billie that her hair was behaving, but, like a grenade, it could go off at any minute. To drown her suspicious subconscious questions about why a random fireman's opinion of her was suddenly so important, she applied herself to a discussion about sashes with a permed woman. Billie had to raise her voice above the strains of 'Do Ya Think I'm Sexy?' from Zelda, who had come in to give them the latest on Raven's health.

Billie's attempts to help her customer were disrupted by Jake.

Vinyl shorts squeaking, he sloped in and collapsed onto the chair meant for customers. 'I'm in hell,' he groaned.

'Not quite yet,' whispered Zelda, who'd stopped singing.

Dot laid a hand on his forehead. 'Poor baby. He's got a block. Can't paint. Just lies there. Can't do anything.'

Hands on hips, Zelda approached Jake. 'Paint this little beauty,' she suggested, putting an arm round Dot. 'God knows, she does everything for you. Why don't you do something for her for once?'

'Hmm.' Jake looked Dot up and down, as if he'd never seen her before. She was sucking her lips, staring at the floor, her discomfort obvious. 'Nah,' he said, finally. 'She's just not inspiring.'

Flinching just once, as if she'd been hit, Dot bounced over to Billie and brightly joined in with the sash symposium.

'You want to watch it,' said Zelda, quietly to Jake. Some thing about her posture reminded Billie of Raven watching the sparrows. 'One day you might have to answer for the way you treat that lass.'

About five o'clock the day bottomed out. Billie flicked her wand carelessly about. 'What's in that bin bag, Debs?' she asked dubiously.

'A job lot of these.' Debs pulled out a handful of L-plates. 'Thought you could flog them for hen nights.'

It sounded like a good idea to Billie, but there was one detail she didn't like. 'A job lot?' As far as she was aware, Debs was not a DVLA executive. She ventured a word she'd heard on *The Bill*. 'Are they hot?'

Debs said solemnly, 'I swear on little Monty's life that they're legit.'

Wondering who Monty was—a younger brother?—Billie doled out a couple of fivers, as a loud rumble drew them all to the window.

'Ooooh yessss!' Debs sounded husky. 'Firemen!'

Blocking the daylight through the bay windows was a red engine, every bit as big and shiny as any five-year-old boy could hope. Out jumped a smorgasbord of firemen, some tall, some taller, and all every bit as rugged as any twenty-eight-year-old girl could hope.

Striding towards the door, Ed was tugging at the shiny buttons on his double-breasted navy jacket. Billie gulped, and tore her wings off.

The door opened, and an avalanche of testosterone swamped the tranquillity of the bridal shop. Men in bright-yellow waterproof dungarees filled all the available space.

Billie was pulling in her tummy, sticking out her chest and trying to rearrange her thoughts in a way that didn't involve Ed minus his waterproofs. 'Hello, boys,' she said. 'Are we on fire?'

'I sodding am,' hissed Debs, who was twirling her ponytail

'Debs, haven't you got something else to do?' Billie said meaningfully.

'Absolutely not.' Debs seemed sure of this. 'Nope.'

'When the lads heard where I was stopping off, they insisted on coming in.' Ed looked rueful. 'They're a bit like that. Sods, I mean.'

'The more the merrier.' Crikey. Where was this dialogue coming from? Billie seemed to be wired up to How To Embarrass Yourself In Front Of Hunks dot com. 'Do you have a picture for me?'

The clipping of a high-waisted peach horror was handed over, to a rowdy chorus of, 'Ooh, is that what you'll be wearing, Ed?' and, 'He's got the legs for it.' Was that why Ed was glowing like a nuclear tomato? Perhaps not, thought Billie, as their eyes met and his creased warmly.

'There's another reason why we came in.' Ed burrowed in a pocket, pulling out a small wad of paper. 'We're short of women for our disco next week, in aid of the local kids' charity.'

'We'll be there.' Debs moved purposefully and snatched the tickets.

'Short of women? Really?' queried Billie. This seemed unlikely.

'Short of the right women.' Ed said this quietly. Only Billie could hear. And consequently only Billie's insidey bits pirouetted.

An unexpected email arrived that blistering Monday, while the Sole Bay sun melted daytrippers' 99s in record time. It was from Billie's long-lost, much-mourned, old friend Jackie.

'Jacks!' gasped Billie, opening up the message with an anticipatory smile. 'She never changes,' thought Billie, settling herself more comfortably on the hard chair up in the stockroom and shaking her head as she read an account of Jackie's last few months.

While Billie had been selling double glazing and withstanding her mother, Jackie had fitted in a serious boyfriend, a not particularly serious boyfriend, and much random how's your father with barmen, not to mention a new job, being sacked from her new job, and a much-regretted haircut that made her look like 'Carol Vorderman's evil twin'.

It's time we met up, wrote Jackie, baldly and plainly, just as she spoke. I miss you. We can't let a man spoil a friendship, can we? Just because James introduced us, it doesn't mean he gets to keep me after the break-up, I'm not a fucking futon!

There was always plenty to talk about with Jackie. Catnip to men, she was a brunette Amazon, with non-stop legs and curvy hips, who left a trail of destruction like a modern Helen of Troy: Helen of Battersea, perhaps. A trust-fund girl who didn't need to work, she did it anyway for the thrill of stealing office stationery.

A lone voice of dissent during the chorus of sentiment in the run-up to the wedding, Jackie had asked, coolly, 'Are you two quite sure about this?' When Billie had paraded in *the* dress, Jackie had murmured, 'Not really *you*, is it, darling?' But then, after the wedding had imploded, their friendship had suffocated. James loomed metaphorically over them and Billie had been relieved when they'd both given up the pretence of being able to carry on.

And now here was Jackie, reaching out of the ether like James had done. Billie missed the chaos, and knowing that her old mate wanted to see her was a welcome prop for her self-esteem. And yet . . . the snug rhythms of her new days were important to her, and Jackie had a habit of dynamiting her way into people's lives.

Billie peered past the empire-line dress in the window to spy on Annie, who was browsing the 50p paperbacks outside the Nearly New shop opposite.

'I still haven't found out Annie's story,' Billie mused. 'She's going into The Tasty Treat! This is my chance!' She dashed out

Skidding to a halt outside the café, Billie composed herself to look surprised when she saw Annie. She wasn't much of an actress: like her deluded mother she tended to overemphasise and exaggerate.

Stepping inside, she breathed 'Annie!' like Maria Callas, and half the tea room swivelled to look. 'Fancy seeing you here!' she enunciated too carefully. 'Let's sit down and I'll order us a nice cream tea.'

Annie, flustered, nodded and sat down abruptly. Congratulating herself, Billie positioned herself on the squeaky plastic banquette opposite.

It was hard going at first. The old lady couldn't meet Billie's eye and replied very economically to attempts at conversation.

And then the scones arrived. Escorted by a jug of thick cream and a silver bowl of rudely red strawberry jam, they sent a visible shudder through Annie's skinny frame.

'Help yourself.' Billie pushed the plate towards her guest.

'I shouldn't.' Anne shook her head.

'I insist.' Billie played her trump. 'I'll be offended if you don't.'

So Annie reached out a white hand. For such a modestly built woman she could put away a surprising amount of scone. The first one seemed to hit like heroin, and she slumped a little in her seat, turning a gooey smile on Billie.

'So, Annie, where do you live?' began Billie, starting with the innocuous, and oblivious of the hot-chocolate moustache she'd acquired.

Spilling nicely, Annie revealed she'd lived in Sole Bay all her life. 'I'm widowed,' she said, simply. 'Twenty years I've been on my own now.'

A sadness the chocolate couldn't diffuse reached across the doilies to

Billie. That was a long time to get up, and go about, and climb back into bed on your own.

'We love seeing you in the shop, you know,' said Billie, truthfully. 'Do you mind telling me why you're saving for a wedding dress?'

'I didn't have a wedding dress of my own. Too plain, you see.'

Not quite comprehending, Billie asked, 'Your dress was too plain?'

'No. I was. Mother said we shouldn't waste money on finery for me, so I just wore my Sunday coat.' Annie looked up, with a watery smile. 'I was never much to look at, dear.'

Billie quivered with indignation. The warm brown eyes, the delicate skin—how could a mother call that little face plain? She said, 'I bet your husband thought you looked beautiful. You must miss him.'

'I wish I did,' sighed Annie. 'Oh, I mean, he was a good man. Hard, mind you. He had to be. He didn't have an easy life. But, no, dear, he didn't think I was beautiful. Nobody ever thought I was beautiful.'

Billie was overcome by sympathy. 'So,' she asked. 'You're searching for the wedding dress you never had?'

'I suppose I am. I try to put more pennies by, but something always gets in the way. The roof needed doing last year. And now the cooker's gone all peculiar.' The scones were just crumbs, and a curtain of inhibition dropped over Annie. 'Thank you for a splendid tea. I must be going.'

'Hold on a mo, Annie.' Billie had had an idea. It was perfect.

Annie wasn't so sure. 'I haven't sewn in years, dear,' she said.

'You admired his dresses yourself,' Billie reminded her. 'Ruby Wolff needs somebody to help. You'd be eligible for a staff discount.'

Sharply, for such a meek woman, Annie said, 'I don't want charity.'

'And I wouldn't dream of offering it,' claimed Billie, who would gladly have given Annie a free dress. 'How about for—fifty per cent?' That discount wiped out any profit. 'Say yes, Annie.'

And Annie did.

Heather elbowed her way in front of the woman holding up a basque, and reeled off a list of questions at Billie, ending with, 'Homestead Hall?'

'All booked for Wednesday. We're going to meet the owner, see the function room and have dinner.'

'Right.' Heather had another question. 'Hen night?'

'Getting there. The limo's booked.' She handed Heather the hen guest list to check as Sam popped his shock of hair round the door.

'Liquid lunch?' he suggested.

'Busy,' mouthed Billie, pointing to Heather behind her back.

Heather turned and studied Sam intently. 'You're . . .' she said.

'Am I?' asked Sam, beaming archly. 'Hang on. No, I've checked and I'm not.'

'He's Sam Nolan, if that's what you mean.' Billie spoilt Sam's fun.

'Oh my God!' Heather turned to Billie. '*He's famous!*' she yelped. She pulled a disbelieving face at Billie as if to say, *You know him?*

'Yeah.' Billie shrugged. 'It's easy.'

'Come to the wedding!' she blurted at Sam. Turning to Billie, she ordered, 'Invite him to the wedding.' She wrestled her mobile phone from her bag and rudely pushed past Sam to get out into the street. 'Wait till my goddaughter Tiffany Beulahbelle hears about this.'

Sam pointed at Billie. 'Are you? You are, aren't you?'

'Gasping for a drink? Yes.' She put on her jacket and shoved him out of the shop.

Billie was replying to James's latest email, borrowing James's breezy style.

> Hi, James. Just a few lines, it's pretty hectic here in Sole Bay!
> Glad to hear you've got yourself a girlfriend. It's about time, after all.

She gritted her teeth. Slowly, painstakingly, she typed:

> She sounds lovely.

and took a deep breath. That hurdle negotiated, Billie thundered on.

> I've got my eye on a fire-fighter. He seems to be interested, but it's early days. For the moment I'm enjoying being young, free and single. I'm too busy with Billie's Brides to think about lurve, to be honest. I've taken to shopkeeping. I love it. I especially love helping women find that perfect dress, the one that makes them feel special, and beautiful, even if in their everyday life they feel dowdy and ordinary. You can sense their empowerment, they seem to grow a couple of inches in front of you. It goes without saying that I can't empathise with the 'happy ever after' aspect of it, but it's what they want and I can't criticise them for being starry-eyed about love. I wish I still was . . .

No, thought Billie fiercely, that had to go. She backspaced the last five words. A change of tone was called for.

Maybe the best way to give you a taste of what life's like in a wedding shop in the middle of nowhere is to describe a few of our customers.

A sketch of Annie was followed by a vaudeville version of Mrs Serial Killer. Grinning as she typed, Billie got into a riff, the way she'd used to at the end of the day when she lived with James. Telling him about her exploits as he sat, exhausted, on the sofa, his tie yanked undone and a glass of something in his hand, she'd known how to build a scene so that he'd eventually splutter Rioja all over the rug. Back then, Billie had often had the curious feeling that things hadn't really happened to her until she'd recounted them to James.

She stopped typing. That memory made her unbearably sad.

Things were happening to her now. She had no need, she reminded herself, to filter them through *anybody*. Her new life in Sole Bay was colourful and absorbing, without James. She typed:

Got to dash. Bye for now. Don't do anything I wouldn't do.
Like getting over us, for instance.

It was time for elevenses on Friday morning, but the Munchmallows preparing to meet their maker were enjoying a reprieve. Billie and Dot were waiting for a man.

'Mr Wolff is late,' pointed out Annie, whose concession to the heat-wave was to wear a slightly less heavy coat.

'Only fifteen minutes.' Billie was lenient, aware that she didn't apply the same rules to Debs's timekeeping.

'Here he is!' Dot jumped up to let Ruby in.

Introductions were made, and then Dot and Billie moved discreetly away. Not so far away that they couldn't earwig. That would be silly.

'Are you any good?' asked Ruby, bluntly.

'Well. Dear me. What a question.' Annie did her twittering thing.

'Why can't a woman answer a straight question?' blustered the old man. His appearance may have been tidied, but his manners could do with a blow-dry. 'Are you any good, madam?'

'Mr Wolff,' quavered Annie. 'I am very good.'

'You'd better be.' Ruby handed over a carrier bag. 'Here's your first pattern pieces. I've put instructions in.' He turned to go, without a goodbye, but turned back when Billie called to him. 'What?'

By various gesticulations and wide-eyed, silent-movie gestures, Billie managed to convey that the carrier bag was far too heavy for Annie.

'Oh.' Ruby ran a stubby hand over his heavy features. 'Women!' he growled, snatching back the bag. 'Come on, what's-your-name, Annie. I'll walk you back with this.'

'There's no need,' protested Annie, who obviously didn't want this little oddball's company on her way home.

'I insist,' said Ruby sourly, ushering her out.

The owner of Homestead Hall was posh. The historic Tudor manor house was his, courtesy of aggressive ancestors who had ruthlessly fought off all comers over the centuries. These days Homestead Hall welcomed all comers, and Visa.

As the host showed Billie, the bride and groom, Ed and Angela to some vacant sofas in the vast drawing room, Billie noticed that Heather's accent had scrambled up a few rungs of the social ladder. Suddenly, her client was a lot less Argos and a touch more Fortnum & Mason.

As the owner ambled off to check on their table, Heather said approvingly in her new voice, 'Now, *this* is refained.'

At the other end of the pleasingly tatty Chesterfield, Dean offered a morose, 'Bit poncey, if you ask me.'

'But I didn't, did I?' bit Heather, her old tones surfacing.

As a venerable grandfather clock struck disaster, Billie realised that she had inadvertently chosen exactly the wrong evening for the test-run wedding meal. She wasn't to know that the happy couple had had a row minutes before leaving the house, but she would soon find out.

Before the alluring Martini on the low table got even halfway to Billie's eager lips, Heather dragged her off to the fussy splendour of the powder room and delivered an unexpurgated and slightly overlong account of the row. Murmuring words of empathy, Billie hustled Heather back to the drawing room as quickly as possible.

As they approached, Dean and Ed were laughing extravagantly, whacking the arms of their seats. The other member of their party was looking a little left out. Angela was nothing like her sister. Where Heather was angles, Angela was curves. A marshmallowy blonde in a buttoned dress that was straining to do its job, her wide, pearly face was not improved by its burden of make-up.

'Angela,' snapped Heather. 'Sit beside Ed. He doesn't want to listen to Dean's so-called jokes all night.' She wasn't wasting any time embarking on her matchmaking duties.

The look of alarm that transformed Ed's face lasted a split second, but it wasn't lost on Billie. Nothing about Ed was lost on her: she'd been watching him like a private detective since they'd all met up.

Every word he'd uttered (and there hadn't been many) had been weighed and rated and valued. He was polite. He was eager to please— that smile was flashed often. He was perfect, easy company. But Ed was maddeningly difficult to work out. So far he'd said nothing surprising, nothing idiosyncratic, nothing that would make Dean turn to Heather and laugh, 'Oh, that's *so* Ed!' He'd make a good poker player. But Billie didn't want to play poker with him. What did she want from him? she wondered, eyeing him up as he discussed the weather with Angela. Billie studied his face.

It was rare to come across features so symmetrical, so ideal. His nose was narrow, his bottom lip was full and slightly petulant, and his delicious colouring was the icing on his rather sexy cake. Billie was a fool for black-haired men with brown eyes. Strange, then, that she should have found herself engaged to a blond guy with green eyes.

Leaning towards her prey, Angela was employing techniques she may have learned at the Sledgehammer School of Flirting. She was directing her impressive—some might say terrifying—embonpoint at his nose, and baring her teeth, only some of which had lipstick on them, in a seductive smile. She seemed to find everything he said funny, even though he said so little.

Cowering on inherited cushions, Ed was a man valiantly trying to look calm. Billie could sense the disquiet seeping from him.

She took a gulp of Martini. Fancying Ed was fine. Going any further was not. She had a plan for the next year, and it could be précised as work, more work, with a little work thrown in for fun. She had finally found something she could get serious about and she was determined to apply herself.

And yet, it might be fun to apply herself to that hard chest . . . Billie put the Martini down. It wasn't helping. She was pro-romance only in her professional capacity as a wedding fairy. Personally, romance had shipwrecked her and left her clinging to the life raft of her parents' bungalow: she never wanted to be that sodden victim again. 'Look at him and see James,' she ordered. The James who had sworn to love her for ever and who was now sending her gossipy emails about his new bird.

It was difficult to impose James on Ed's contours. Her ex was a strong character, whose aura, according to Sly, shouted 'success'. James was opinionated, forceful and funny. This man opposite, despite the gym-honed packaging, was a pushover, she could tell.

Despite the fact that Ed could carry grown adults out of burning buildings, he looked mildly alarmed by the world. Like a crab, he had a shell he retreated into.

Contriving to puff out her chest like an inflatable dinghy, Angela was teasing her prey. 'You should wear a suit more often. *Suits* you.'

'Don't really like them,' muttered Ed, his gaze flickering everywhere except Angela's beleaguered bra. He was, Billie noted with a stab of pleasure that shamed her, perfectly pale, with not a hint of a blush.

'Know what you mean,' simpered Angela. 'I prefer to be naked, too.'

Now Ed *was* red. But, rationalised Billie, so am I. Even Dean turned pink. 'If God had meant us to eat naked, he wouldn't have invented soup,' chirruped Billie, hoping to rescue Ed from the swamp of sexual innuendo Angela was leading him into.

That got a laugh from Ed and a giggle from Dean, but Angela's mouth turned down at the ends. She didn't seem to welcome another woman straying into her territory.

The dining room was stylish. 'It's too dark,' complained Angela, as they took their seats. A button of her dress was undone.

Acting on strict instructions from Dot, Billie raised her glass. 'Here's to your happy ever after!' she toasted, toothily. There was a moribund echo from her fellow diners, and Billie was grateful for the distraction of the menu. 'Ooh, yum. It all looks so good,' she chanted, before she'd even focused on the curly calligraphy.

'Steak.' Dean crossed his arms and didn't open the menu. 'Chips.'

'Oh shit, it's in French,' moaned Ed, shedding brownie points with Billie: she liked her men to have a sense of adventure.

'Oysters to start,' mouthed Angela, predictably. 'Although I won't be held responsible for what happens later.'

You'll smell of fish, predicted Billie comfortably.

Heather waved a waiter over. Offering up a silent prayer that the others would be ravenous and provide cover for her greed, Billie went first. Weeks of existing on canned things carefully burned over a camping stove meant that she was giddy with anticipation of proper food, at the appropriate temperature, lacking strange black bits. After her impressive list of wants, the waiter turned to Heather.

'Nothing for me,' said the bride-to-be decisively, handing the menu back. Gentle protests from the others were met with a raised hand and a shrill, 'I have to lose half my arse by August!'

'But Heather . . .' began Billie, genuinely troubled. This woman was already spare: a further ten pounds would render her dipstick-like. 'The whole point of this evening is to sample the food.'

'Food is full of evil. I have to drop a dress size for the wedding.'

'I'll eat for two, then.' Dean opened up the menu and chose some accompaniments for his steak. His order made Billie's look restrained, and she was grateful to him.

Conversation was stilted during the starters and the main course. Billie was glad when Angela perked up, and began to join in with the general conversation instead of murmuring sweet somethings at Ed.

Even if her opener was a baffling, 'I see holes.'

'Eh?' queried Billie, her mouth full of hot calories.

Sagely, Angela went on, 'Rattus Rattus. Our little Norwegian friend.'

Billie didn't have Nordic friends of any stature. 'I'm sorry, I don't . . .'

'There are holes in that skirting board ple-e-nty big enough for rats,' Angela informed them all, calmly. 'And the patterned carpet would easily disguise droppings.'

'Of course. You're a pest-control lady.' Billie caught her drift.

'I am an operative in the pest-control arena,' Angela informed her. 'What I don't know about maggots isn't worth knowing.'

Throwing down his knife and fork with a clatter, Dean glared at Angela. 'Every dinner time. Like bloody clockwork. Out come the maggots.' He turned to Billie. 'It'll be regurgitative digestive juices next.'

At this, even Billie put down her cutlery, and previously she had assumed that nothing short of a hail of bullets could achieve that. 'I'm sure we don't have to worry about hygiene in a place like this,' she said.

'Oh, believe me, you wouldn't want to see inside the average restaurant kitchen.' Angela popped another button in her enthusiasm for her subject. 'Don't get me started on cockroaches.'

'Nobody, but nobody, has any intention of getting you started on cockroaches.' Heather had the look of a geyser ready to erupt.

'The German ones are great climbers,' Angela told Ed with an air of confidentiality, as if imparting priceless gossip.

Standing up, Heather said commandingly, 'Take me home, Dean.'

Presumably, in Heather's vision of the next few moments, Dean would leap up and guide her tenderly out of the hotel. The reality was that he scowled, told her not to order him around and said, 'You're old enough to get home on your own. I want my pudding.'

Billie tailed the furious Heather out of the room, flinging back a pleading glance at Ed as she went. It was time for his best-man duties to start with some groom pep-talking.

Despite Billie's pleas, mouse-like even to her own ears, Heather marched off, down the gravel drive, leaving Billie on the steps.

Tugging off his tie, Dean appeared and followed her, after the merest of pushes from Ed. The best man was evidently taking his position seriously. Watching Dean hurtle after his disappearing fiancée, Ed said to Billie, 'Don't worry. This is nothing.' They were the first direct words he had spoken to her. 'They can argue over a frozen pea.'

'That I'd like to see.' She considered. 'Actually,' she grinned up at him (he really was thrillingly tall), 'I wouldn't.'

'No, you wouldn't,' confirmed Ed. He grinned back and wasn't there . . . yes, Billie could see a definite wash of red invade his face.

This close she could feel his breath on her face in the balmy night air. She shivered slightly, unsure if it was caused by the bareness of her shoulders or his proximity. There was no hiding out here in the glare of the moon: Billie wanted this man.

And to judge by his ketchup colouring, he wanted her. Ed was silent, but he didn't look shy. He looked like a man about to kiss a woman.

Billie leaned up. Ed leaned down. And Angela clattered out on her six-inch mules to join them, with an impatient, 'Can we please get back indoors and finish our dinner?'

'Yes! Yes!' Billie jumped back, coughing.

'Er, yeah.' Ed cleared his throat and wriggled his shoulders.

They both looked supremely shifty but Angela didn't notice their demeanour, or else chose to ignore it. 'Come on.' She grabbed Ed's arm and spun him efficiently back towards the entrance. 'That silly pair have made up already. Let's get back indoors and hit the liqueurs.'

Slightly deflated at seeing her very own fireman taken so abruptly off her hands, Billie turned to see her clients making their slow way up the crunchy gravel. Now Heather was leaning into Dean, a rueful smile softening her equine features. His head was bent, kissing her forehead, and Billie guessed he was whispering one of those secret incantations that couples concoct for making up.

SEVEN

HAVING SENT DEBS OFF with her wages Billie suggested adjourning to the Swan. 'Come on, Dot. You've been run off your recyclable espadrilles all afternoon.'

'Better not,' said Dot. 'I'd love a cider, but you know Jake.'

Billie did know Jake, and he seemed an excellent reason not to go home. 'I'm sure he can manage not to play with matches or stick his finger in the light sockets long enough for you to have one drink.'

A patina of hurt washed over Dot's face. 'By the way, I don't know whether I can come to that silly disco. Jakey would worry.'

Counting to ten didn't dampen Billie's urge to shout, *'He's a manipulative, hairy-faced swine!'* So she counted to thirty-four before she reminded Dot how much they'd both been looking forward to the 'silly disco'. 'And why on earth would Jake worry?'

'He says I can't be trusted. After all, I don't know where I come from, do I? My real grandmother could have bad blood.' Dot pouted. 'Wish I knew who I really was.'

Crossing the floor to cash up, Billie detoured to give Dot a squeeze. 'I know exactly who you are, and you are a woman who can be trusted to control her wild lusts at a church-hall disco, Dot.' The sums wouldn't add up properly, she kept arriving at a twenty-pound shortfall that couldn't be right. As she re-counted the twenties and the tens, Billie felt eyes boring into her back. She realised that Dot was gazing upon her with the same exaggerated sympathy she lavished on small mammals with eczema. 'What?' asked Billie.

'I was just thinking that Saturday is the night for lovers to be together. And you'll be sitting alone in that hut.'

'Me and Herbert's Dream II like our Saturday nights in,' said Billie, as a high-pitched chorus of 'Bat Out Of Hell' preceded Zelda's entrance.

'Get a load of my new rig-out, girls!' Zelda twirled in a ruffled, tiered, beribboned gypsy number that should have been viewed through smoked glass for safety's sake. 'Babs lent it to me before she left.' The twirl ended badly, with one of Zelda's support socks slipping down. 'I'm swinging by the British Legion. They won't know what's hit them.'

That, thought Billie, was true enough.

'You never go out, do you, love?' Zelda asked suddenly. 'You're a sad little singleton, aren't you?'

'I wouldn't quite put it—'

'Could you babysit Raven? Only he's got another one of his colds.'

'I'd love to. But I'm going round to see Sam tonight.'

Saving the day, Dot took Raven home in a basket.

Too relieved to be guilty, Billie dignified the fib by going to Sam's. 'Hi, honey, I'm home!' she yelled through the letterbox of the pink thatched house in half an acre of sumptuous garden on the rim of Sole Bay.

Through the rectangle of letterbox, Billie saw bare legs stumble up the hall, tripping over themselves. Opening the door a crack, somebody who looked just like Sam but had spent the last twenty years in a skip peeped out. 'Christ, it's you, Billage.' He opened the door, and trotted, naked, down the hall ahead of her. 'Better slip some knickers on.'

When pants, jeans and a Clash T-shirt had all been slipped on, Billie and Sam settled down to the serious culinary business of ordering a fast-food delivery.

'What kind of beauty régime do you follow to look this good?' teased Billie, snuggling down on the luxurious sofa. Like the house, it was top quality and very attractive, but definitely not Sam's style. It was as if a surly teenage layabout had snaffled the keys to his rich grandma's.

Rubbing his eyes, which had shrunk to the size of Tiddlywinks' button ones, Sam said, 'I was up all night working.' He stole a look to see how that was going down, then admitted, 'All right, I was up all night working at drinking. I'm good at it.'

Over the detritus of two extra-large pizzas, Billie asked, 'Got any drawings to show me?' She knew his deadline for book number twelve was weeks away, and had cast herself as his conscience.

'I don't show works in progress of Tiddlywinks to anybody,' sulked Sam. 'Let's not talk about him.'

'OK. Let's talk about why you're exiled in this chi-chi bolthole, then.' Billie was keen to know more about this man who had become such an important part of her days. Walks on the beach were more vivid with Sam, and his plush rental cottage had become a haven for her, fully stocked with Jack Daniel's, cynicism and fond teasing.

And yet she didn't know enough about him. She gabbled on about herself, only noticing at the end of the evening that he'd been listening, lobbing grenades of dour insight and keeping her glass topped up, without giving anything away about himself.

'The usual reasons,' winked Sam, bounding on to the sofa and laying his head on her lap. Even after a night on the booze and a day under the duvet, he smelt good. 'I'm not good at relation-whatsits.'

'Same as me.'

'I prefer lots of sex with the widest possible cross section of the male populace, some of it outdoors.' Sam sighed.

'Eeeyurgh. Not the same as me.'

'No, you dull little straight.' Sam grinned up at her. 'Thank God for poofs. We're the last people in Great Britain having fun.' He composed his face again. 'Although there is such a thing as too much fun.'

'Did you burn out?'

'Yes, I suppose I did.' He settled his cranium more comfortably in Billie's denim lap. 'All the things that are bad for me, i.e. all the things I enjoy best i.e. strong liquor and small blokes called Raoul, are too available in London. I had to escape before I ended up as a stain on the carpet.' He knitted his brows, looking almost serious. 'It got too much one morning and I jumped on a train. Can't really explain it.'

Billie could. Even sybarites like Sam have their limits, she reasoned. 'Is it evil to want another giant pizza?' she ventured.

'I'm so glad you said that.' Sam leaped up to grab the phone. 'That's why I knew you were the girl for me: matching weaknesses.'

Over the cheesecake that Sam accidentally ordered with the second pizza, Billie told Sam The Story. It was time.

As expected, he didn't offer a shoulder for weeping purposes. 'Good riddance,' he said, through a mouthful of New York Vanilla. 'James? An accountant? I know the type. All cold sheets and pinstriped knickers. He did you a favour by jilting you. It would have blown apart sooner or later. All that happy-ever-after shit is a myth.'

'Do you ever get lonely in this big house, Sam?'

'Haven't you been listening, Billo? I'm not the tortured artist. I'm the slacker who came into money. I'm not lonely. I've got you.' He lifted his eyebrows at her. 'And perhaps, when I finish the book, I'll have that cute little guy in the post office who doesn't know he's gay yet.'

Bowing out when the tequila bowed in, Billie made for the sea. Tequila unleashed her inner traffic-cone-on-head wearer, and she didn't want to face her parents the next day with a hangover.

Or would it help? She slowed, but instead of retracing her steps, she nipped down Little Row, for a moonlit tryst with the virtual world. With her jacket still on, she typed:

> James, it's late and you're probably canoodling with the lady doctor. Tried to explain to somebody tonight about why I'd rather eat my own spleen than have Sunday lunch at my parents', but he didn't get it.

Expecting Sam to be cynically sympathetic, Billie had treated him to a few of her meatier family anecdotes, but he'd surprised her by drawling, 'Sounds to me as if you're trying to replace your family with a new one down here without giving the originals a chance. Zelda, Dot, Sam—just add water. Instant Family!' He'd rolled his eyes when she hadn't laughed. 'Billie-willy, we've all got mad families. Mine think I can be cured of homosexuality by sitting me next to girls with large breasts. But I still visit them. How bad can your lot be?'

James knew how bad they could be.

> *Chicago* is finished, and they're rehearsing a Noël Coward play. You understand what that means, don't you?

It was a risk to compose an email like this. There were no exclamation marks, no inanity, no Redcoat enthusiasm. She was just communicating with somebody who used to know her very well, and who could be trusted to understand. Perhaps James would shy away from this new honesty, but right now it was comforting to vent her frustrations.

James was a veteran of Baskerville get-togethers. He'd been there during the run of *Hamlet*, when her father had strolled about the house in black forty-denier tights with a low-slung gusset; he'd endured being served Nancy Baskerville's 'famous hotpot' on every single visit because he'd manfully finished his first portion (Nancy's hotpot was a culinary Jade Goody—famous for all the wrong reasons); he'd watched as Nancy's face stiffened with Botox over the years yet still managed a sneer for her daughter's progress through life.

> Sorry again. Get back to your snogging!!

Exclamation marks are a tricky habit to break completely.

It's a long way from Suffolk to Surbiton. A Sunday paper lay in Billie's lap. She neglected it in favour of the scenery dashing past the train window. Settling herself more comfortably, Billie recalled the unexpectedly speedy email reply from James. Just one line, but it had made her laugh: Shall I fetch Blankie?

Nobody else knew about Blankie. A tattered old tartan thing, James used to tuck it over Billie when she was assailed by period cramps and had self-prescribed lying on the sofa watching black and white films. Blankie's scope grew, and soon James flourished him whenever Billie had a hangover, an argument with her mother, or got the £200 question wrong on *Who Wants to Be a Millionaire?*.

'**H**ello, Aunty Billie. I thought you were dead.'

'So did I, Moto, so did I.' Bending down to kiss her four-year-old nephew at the front door of the Baskerville bungalow, she marvelled again at his good looks. With sleek black hair and tilted dark eyes, Moto and his sister were proof that God approved of the British and the Japanese getting it on. Relinquishing the squirming Moto, Billie wished that her sister-in-law had been allowed to name both kids: an almond-eyed beauty called Deirdre was all wrong.

The kitchen door burst open at the other end of the long hall and a haughty beauty, straight from the roaring twenties, sprinted down the gaudy carpet, a cigarette holder between her perfect teeth. 'Dahhhling!' she squealed, the black feather on her sequinned headdress fluttering, 'It was too too splendid of you to come.' As she bent to kiss her guest she added, 'You're late,' in an undertone.

'I've come all the way from Suffolk, Mum. You look lovely.'

'Tish!' The volume was better suited to the stage than the narrow hall. 'Bless you, angelic one, for your kindness.' Tarantula false eyelashes fluttered in a face expressing constant lazy surprise, thanks to the Botox. Nancy led the way to the kitchen. She was tall, and had the kind of looks that used to be called 'handsome'. Old black and white pictures revealed the strong-featured, long-limbed beauty that she was desperately trying to prolong. With the wind in the right direction she was still striking, with her full head of curling hair and her artfully arched brows. 'Be a poppet, darling girl, and stir the gravy, do.'

The chatter might be Twenties, but the décor was pure Seventies. Billie peered through the amber glass of the sliding doors to the sitting room as she stirred. She could make out the bulk of her father and Sly, side by side on the sofa, newspapers up like shields.

The doors juddered apart, and Sana joined the ladies. Hugging her sister-in-law warmly, Sana whispered, 'What play are we in today?'

'We're with Noël Coward and his chums.'

Making a small noise, possibly Japanese for, 'Oh cack,' Sana tweaked a fold in her taupe cashmere wrap and asked how the shop was going.

Billie said, 'Fine. Good, in fact.' It was always hard to find the puff to blow her own trumpet between these walls.

Sly joined them. 'Sis! You made it at last!' His hug was all-enveloping. 'So, the seminar helped, then?'

A gong sounded. Her mother's talent for amassing props was formidable. 'Luncheon is served!' she trilled.

Like the Mad Hatter's tea party, they all fussed over where to sit. When Roger Baskerville spotted his daughter, he patted the seat next to him. 'Daughter! Sit next to your old pater.' He had the tones of Noël Coward to a T, though his monocle kept falling off. 'What kept you?'

Crikey, thought Billie, kissing the top of her father's brilliantined head, did all the Baskervilles have clocks where their hearts should be? 'You look very dapper, sir.' The smoking jacket had been resurrected from the costume trunk, so the room smelt of mothballs.

'Splendid to see you. Top hole.'

'How are things, Dad?'

'Super-duper.' And that, Billie knew, was as much detail as she would wring out of her father.

The gravy was thin, but the beef was thick. It was a traditional, badly cooked roast dinner and Billie could feel it warming her right through. She smiled inwardly at her mother's attempts to twinkle *and* stop Deirdre anointing Moto with creamed horseradish.

'Now, now, my cherubs, my darling tots,' she tinkled, her feather bending backwards, lured by the extractor roaring away in the kitchen.

'Kids!' boomed Sly, making the whole table jump. 'Cut it out!'

Deirdre's head bent over her plate, and Moto slumped onto his mother for comfort. Trying and failing to catch Sana's eye, Billie was puzzled. Sly prided himself on his patience with the younger axis of his Trust Triangle. Her mother's voice interrupted her thoughts.

'Billie, dahhhhling, even though you got Granny's legs, it would be nice to see you in a skirt once in a while.'

A safe conversational gambit was required, to draw friendly fire away from Billie's legs, hair, nose, teeth, work, lack of a man and lack of a proper home. 'How are rehearsals going?'

'Sublime!' Surgery had put paid to grins, but Nancy did her best. 'You will attend our first night, won't you, babycakes? You know how your mama needs your support.'

Before Billie could answer, Deirde put down her knife and fork to ask, 'Will you sell your own wedding dress in your shop, Aunty Billie?'

'Deirdre!' Sana had always trod very carefully around the subject of Billie's non-wedding. 'That's none of our business.'

'I think your grandma cut it up for dusters,' Billie told her niece.

'There was precious little point keeping it.' Nancy sawed away at her beef. 'She's hardly likely to risk another wedding after *that* debacle.'

Deirdre wasn't finished. 'Why haven't you got a boyfriend, Aunty?'

'You don't *have* to have a boyfriend, Deirdre,' Billie said.

'So brave.' Nancy wiped a tear from a carefully kohled eye. 'You're among family, my angel. No need to pretend with us.' She sighed before adding in a very modern tone, 'You do know I'd pay to have your nose done, don't you?'

'Mum!' It was Billie's turn to raise her voice.

'Heavens, such temperament!' Nancy flounced back to the Twenties.

Billie wasn't listening.

The knowledge that she was quick to anger around the other Baskervilles, that she was partly to blame for the descent of family meals into bloodbaths, didn't help with the knowledge that she was mired at the bottom of the bungalow's rigid pecking order.

Her folks' worry manifested as criticism. What if I were to stand up now, she thought, thump the table and announce that things are going right for a change? That I'm enjoying my work, that I'm making a success of it, that I'm spreading some happiness while I'm at it? I could tell them I'm sleeping well, that I'm making friends, that I'm carving a little Billie-shaped space in a strange town. I could even amaze my mother with the stop-press news that somebody, a *male* somebody, is interested in me. Despite my hair, my nose and Granny's legs.

Tuning back in briefly to hear Sly refuse, uncharacteristically, to talk about his latest seminars, Billie took her daydream further. She stole a look at her mother.

Nancy's beauty was undeniable, despite Harley Street's intervention, but Billie felt unable to offer her mum a compliment because the older woman expected fulsome praise at all times and just gobbled it up without listening. Billie would have liked to tell her mother how she'd loved the shape of her pre-surgery eyes, and the way they used to crinkle with sympathy when Billie told her about her latest disaster at school.

What if she was to be completely honest with her mother? To say, 'Mum, things aren't going wrong, but I do need your help? I need you to help me straighten out my frazzled feelings. I need you to advise me, like a woman, not a character from a play, about whether I'm ready to fall again. Whether I deserve another chance. Or whether I should stay in the shadows until I'm stronger.' Wishing she could say it out loud, she said gently, 'I need you, Mum,' with the tender voice in her head that was never heard at this reproduction dining table.

'A little smidgin for dessert?' Nancy turned to Billie, and didn't seem to notice the plea in her daughter's eyes. 'Billie?' She paused. 'Better not, my cherub. We don't want to be at home to Mr Double Chin.'

'I'd better catch my train,' Billie said, standing up abruptly among the post-lunch debris. Her mother walked her to the door.

'Goodbye dah-ling,' she said, in a swooping voice, air-kissing her daughter. 'Darling,' she suddenly said, in her usual voice, as Billie stepped on to the crazy paving. 'Darling . . .'

'Yes, Mum?' Billie looked hungrily at her.

'Nothing. Just, you know.' She ground to a halt. Nancy was no good at speeches unless somebody else had written them. 'I do worry, you know,' she finished in a small voice. 'Do you have to go so soon?'

'Mum, it's a long way from Surbiton to Suffolk.'

Thank God.

A brief 'thank you' was necessary. After all, James had cheered her up on her way to her date with doom (and roast beef): Thanks. I miss Blankie.

Oops. That was a little intimate for their fledgling correspondence. A little revealing. Billie shrugged—missing Blankie didn't mean she missed James—and pressed SEND. She was far too busy flogging white frocks to spend much time on emails to an ex.

The week crawled, dragging its feet through the mud of paperwork that had been piling up in the stockroom. Staring dumbly at pro forma invoices and carriage notes in the stockroom, Billie shouted down to

Dot to check that she was definitely coming to the fire-service disco.

'We-ell . . . It's not really fair to Jakey. It's not his kind of thing. I should stay home with him.' Dot shouted for corroboration. 'Shouldn't I?'

'You might as well be married,' yelled Billie. 'Love isn't about binding yourself together with ropes and padlocks. Does he love you?'

'Of course he does.'

'Well, then.' Billie stalked to the top of the stairs and squatted there. 'Where's the harm in dancing around your handbag for an hour or two, while he sits at home and makes portraits out of unlikely ingredients?'

'Jake's not like other men,' said Dot. 'If you'd heard about his child-hood, you might understand him. Like I do. I'm precious to him and he doesn't trust the universe to let him keep me. He just holds on a bit too tight sometimes, that's all.'

Billie was wrong-footed. 'You really love him, don't you, Dot? But you're still entitled to do things you want to do, if they don't hurt him. Do you want to go to the firemen's disco?'

'Yes,' admitted Dot, with a guilty grimace.

'Well, then.'

'What are you wearing?' Evidently, Dot was as shallow as her boss in some departments. 'I have some gorgeous dungarees in the wardrobe.'

'And that's where they'll stay,' decreed Billie. She was relieved. Dot was her posse. She needed Dot to provide cover for her stalking of Ed.

Sam arrived to escort them to the disco in a sharp black suit. 'Debs,' he breathed, taking in her strapless, backless Lycra. 'You're a goddess.' He had a soft spot for his friend's unruly Saturday girl, considering her to be a work of art every bit as relevant as any old tent Tracey Emin ran up on her Singer. 'You just don't care, do you, sweetheart?'

Unaware of her status as post-modern icon, Debs told Sam, 'Your roots need doing.'

'Ooh, I love her,' smiled Sam.

Discarding her wings, Billie clattered up the bare wooden stairs. 'I'm just popping up to the stockroom to get changed,' she shouted. 'Then how about a little glass of something to get us in the mood?'

'Maybe,' sighed Dot. Billie didn't know if Dot was angsting over deserting Jake for the evening, or angsting over the eighteen-pound shortfall in the till, or angsting over some challenged mammal, but angsting she was. It wasn't the first time the takings had been out by that kind of amount, but Billie had decided to defer her own angsting until after tonight: tonight was all about Ed.

'I don't need nothing to get me in the mood,' Debs announced. 'I've been in the mood since I clapped eyes on that ginger fireman.' She jiggled the acres of chest only loosely reined in by her dress. 'He hasn't got a chance.'

'By the way,' said Billie, halfway up the stairs and therefore a safe-ish distance from her Saturday girl. 'You were half an hour late again this morning, Debs. What was all that about?'

'Oh.' Debs' voice lost its previous animation. 'Yeah. Couldn't help it.'

Leaving a pause for the 'sorry' that would never come, Billie gave up and carried on upstairs to where her new black trousers and a silky wrap top were waiting. One day she'd tackle Debs about her timekeeping, but it would have to wait until she had the time. And the muscles.

Hopping on one foot as she cajoled her toes into a strappy silver sandal, Billie leaned over her laptop and opened an email from James.

So, how was lunch? As bad as you feared? Or only as bad as being torn apart by stampeding elephants?

Billie giggled. He understood.

Thanks for being nice about the new girlfriend. I kicked myself for telling you about her. Even she reckoned it was 'a tad sadistic'. I didn't mean it that way. So I was relieved when I got your reply.

Reading on, the giggles were switched off abruptly.

When I told my Significant Other about Blankie, she demanded one too. Have I found the secret way to the modern woman's heart?

Significant other. Billie harrumphed. Significant bloody other, I ask you. James had been reluctant to award her the anaemic title 'girlfriend' until they'd been going out for a year and Billie had pointed out that either she was his girlfriend or a very unusual poltergeist was leaving tampons in his bathroom cabinet.

Outlining her lips in the sliver of cracked mirror that was available to her, Billie harrumphed again. Why did James have to go and tell his significant other about Blankie? The little tartan rag was part of their shared past, too special to be bandied about with highbrow medical women. She squinted down at the rest of the message.

Work's busy, but I'm enjoying it. I keep meaning to book a week away somewhere. Can't decide if I want to lie on hot sand or dash around looking at ruins. I'd better get on with it—the summer will be over before we know it.

There was a page of this vanilla fluff. Billie could read the invisible ink between the lines. James was laying boundaries, glaring enough for even her short sight. He didn't want intimacy, or nostalgia, or her cutesy whines about missing Blankie, just an olive branch, after months of discord, from one friend to another.

Fine. Billie put the matt peachy lipstick back in her bag. *That's fine.* She filled in her pout in scarlet. *Absolutely bloody fine by bloody me.*

Somebody was banging energetically on the door down in the shop. 'Tell them we're closed,' Billie hollered down the stairs. Tutting at Dot's soft-heartedness, she heard the shop bell clang. This set off an explosion of chatter downstairs, followed by loud hoots of laughter. Billie stopped dead. She knew that voice. 'Jackie?' she yelled.

'Billie!' the voice shouted back.

'Oh my God, Jackie.' Half falling down the stairs, Billie threw her arms round her old friend. 'Where did you spring from?'

Tall and curvaceous, the statuesque brunette had lips like a bouncy castle. 'All the way from London, darling.' Jackie's accent was pure Belgravia, but her vocabulary could stray to the fishmarket. 'What an arse of a place this is. No fucking taxis at the station.' Regally, she handed Debs her linen coat, and Debs was so surprised she took it. 'I jumped on a bus and here I am!'

Billie had forgotten how exhausting just listening to Jackie could be. 'But . . .' she stammered. 'You didn't warn me, you didn't—'

'Thought I'd surprise you. I'm unemployed now, and bored.' Jackie's background allowed her to work when she felt like it. 'You always loved surprises,' beamed Jackie, her eyes lighting on the bottle of wine that Debs had been wrestling the cork from. 'Ooh, I've arrived in the nick of time. No doubt you'll be needing some help with that, folks.'

Out came the plastic glasses and the home team, even Sam, were silent as Jackie held court. They heard the stirring tale of her latest amour. 'Said he'd leave his wife when the time was right yada yada yada. I fell for it, hook line and hotel room. It's my fault, I just can't resist a man who's spoken for. You know?' Jackie raised a waxed eyebrow at Dot, who shrugged nervously and took another gulp of wine.

'Not everybody likes to break the rules,' Billie reminded her old mate, whose bosom and personality seemed to have swelled in the months they'd been apart. 'Which hotel are you at?'

'I thought . . .' Jackie threw a questioning glance Billie's way. 'I thought wrong, obviously,' she laughed, looking a little flustered.

'Oh, you want to stay with me?' Floundering, Billie said, 'Of course, yes, it's just that . . . I know people say their places are small, Jack, but mine is minuscule. There isn't room.' She threw a desperate glance Sam's way: his cottage had bedrooms to spare. He was looking away. And down. And up. Billie got the message. Perhaps he didn't want a lodger whose charisma rivalled his own. 'But we'll make do somehow.'

'Perhaps we won't need to,' said Jackie, musingly. 'You slappers are off out somewhere, aren't you?' She listened to the details of the disco. 'Firemen! Oh, for fuck's sake,' she roared. 'As if I'll need a bed tonight. I'll be rolling around some fire-station bunk.' She knocked back the dregs of her cheap wine. 'Lead me to the fire-fighters!'

Typhoon Jackie had hit Sole Bay.

Fairy lights had magically transformed the village hall into a village hall with a few fairy lights slung round it. The music throbbing through the small wooden building had to compete with the gobby seagulls and the dull whump of the night sea.

'I hope Jake will be all right on his own,' fretted Dot, as their little group approached the bar. She pulled at the form-fitting dress Billie had foisted on her.

'Oh, he'll be fine.' Billie was short on sympathy.

A round of drinks was plonked down on the chipped Formica bar.

'Be honest,' asked Jackie, who had roughed up her hair and hitched up her skirt. 'Do I look like an easy lay?'

'Oh, I wouldn't say that,' said Dot, shocked.

Billie nodded.

'Excellent!' Jackie scanned the crowd. Only a few brave pioneers were dancing, and everybody had the furtive look common to the sober, early part of a British night out.

Tugging at Sam's elbow, Billie whispered, 'You don't like her.'

'Of course I don't.' Sam looked at Billie as if she was mad. 'Jackie's a bosom-shaped battering ram.' He looked over to where Jackie was preening herself, preparing for the chase and the kill. 'The way you tell it, she dropped poison in James's ears all through your engagement and then walked away backwards when everything went pear-shaped.'

'Nah. You've got her wrong. She's wild, not bad.'

'Whatever. So long as you remember,' he bent to whisper, his breath hot in her ear, 'I'm your gay best friend and I trump your slaggy blast from the past, OK?'

'OK.' Billie dead-legged him.

Then it was Jackie's turn to tug at Billie's elbow. 'Gay, right?' she nodded in Sam's direction. 'Shame.'

As a Bucks Fizz song that even Bucks Fizz's mothers had forgotten blared out, Debs' teetering mules took her off across the sticky lino. 'There he is!' she hissed, heading for her marmalade-headed prey in a smoky corner. '*Oi, gingernut!*' she bawled. 'Get your hose, you've pulled!'

Bemused at the lack of champagne—'Are you quite sure? Could you look again, darling?'—Jackie was buying the second round. As she turned to dole out the Lambrusco, her eyes narrowed and she reminded Billie suddenly of Raven. 'Oh my,' she drawled huskily, looking across the room. '*He* is so mine.'

'No, you don't, sister.' Alarmed by her own vehemence, Billie watched Ed push his way through the crowd. 'That one's spoken for.'

EIGHT

'Hi,' said Ed.

'Hi,' said Billie.

'Are you all right?' asked Dot, sweetly. 'You look a bit red.'

Billie put her mind at rest. 'It's the lighting. He's fine.' She threw a questioning glance at Ed. 'Aren't you?'

'I am now.'

Jackie had already introduced herself. 'Can't hang around, I'm afraid. Other fish to fry.' She leaned in to say smokily near Ed's ear, 'And you're off limits. Unfortunately.' With a wink at Billie, she sauntered away, as confident as a huntsman off to shoot fish in a barrel.

Winching Ed's attention back from the departing jelly on springs that was Jackie's backside, 'Dance?' Billie asked.

'If I must,' he gulped, and followed her quietly.

Somehow, Ed's dancing was both sexy and funny. Mincing to the Scissor Sisters, he did his best to get down with his bad self.

Ed's treatment of Dot was another plus. Sam had gracefully retreated, aware that something was brewing, but Dot had no such instincts. Chatting above the music about llamas and recycling, she was a gooseberry so large and green she was visible from France. Patiently, Ed listened, and bought her drinks, and danced alongside her as she swayed like a Thai temple dancer with eccentric little moves of her own.

Making her way round the dance floor, Billie watched Ed. He looked great. He smelt better. He glanced up from Dot and his eyes found hers across the acres of chewing-gum-pitted floor: the thread between them was taut. But was Ed a good bet for a love affair? After years of buccaneering, Billie wanted a decent man. She'd found one in James, and, give or take a devastating heartbreak, she'd rather liked it.

'The Birdie Song' finally broke Ed. 'I can't. The lads would never let me live it down.' He gestured to a mob of blokes, all fairly wobbly of leg, who had been shouting a running commentary on his dancing.

'Let's have a drink.' Billie looked around for Dot, but she was being chatted up by a man at least eighteen times as attractive as Jake.

Billie's own horizons had shrunk to the space between her and Ed. She reasoned that only he could answer the big question. 'Ed,' she began, 'are you nice?'

'This is girl speak,' he said immediately, leaning back as if she'd pulled a knife on him.

'Aw, Ed, come on. Level with me. Are you nice?' persisted Billie, laughing.

He wasn't laughing. He seemed uncomfortable, his chocolate-drop eyes flitting here and there. 'Well, I wouldn't murder anyone,' he admitted, finally. His mouth relaxed into a smile. 'Yes, Billie, I'm nice.'

'Knew it!' Billie was triumphant. And intrigued. And riddled with lust. She smiled up at him, dancing on the spot, wriggling her hips.

'Don't do that. It does funny things to me.'

Looking away to hide her excitement, Billie finally faced facts. This man was hers if she wanted him.

'Do what?' she asked, wide-eyed. 'This?' And she shimmied again.

Ed pulled her to his side with one arm. 'Don't. I won't be responsible for my actions.'

His arm was like a red-hot wire across her skin. She tensed. An hour in, and already the end of the evening seemed a foregone conclusion. 'I should find Sam. And Jackie,' she muttered. 'Don't you want to spend some time with your mates?' she asked, almost aggressively.

'Trying to get rid of me?' Ed was trying to smile.

Evasively, Billie replied, 'No, no. I don't want to monopolise you.' She looked down into her drink. 'They'll think something's going on.'

'Something *is* going on.' Was there a hint of temper in the downward curve of Ed's lip as he put his pint down with a thud on the bar? He turned and shouldered his way through the tipsy mob.

Cutting off her companion mid-lousy-chat-up-line, Dot burrowed through the crowd. 'What did you say to Ed?' she accused, slamming down her dandelion and burdock, and bundling Billie into a quieter corner. She was a formidable bundler, despite her size. 'He looks upset.'

'I just said I should look after Sam and Jackie and maybe he should find his mates.'

'That's the same as telling him you're bored with him! Sam went home ages ago, and Jackie's sitting on the bar.' She looked horrified. 'Ed's been so brilliant, buying us drinks, putting up with me, dancing . . .' She petered to a stop. 'He'll think you don't like him.'

'Well, I don't. Particularly.' Billie shrugged.

'You're scared.' Dot was scornful and Billie was startled, as if a Teletubby had sworn.

'I am not,' she laughed.

'I don't get it.' Dot shook her head. 'You have the guts to turn a dying business round, to live in a shed, but you can't face your own feelings.'

'I told you, Dot, I'm not scared. I'm just not that into him.'

'You are into him.' Dot sounded sad. 'And he's into you. You are allowed to have fun, you know. You can have a romance. You can even fall in love if you want.' Dot's mouth fell open, a perfect circle. 'That's it! You think you might fall in love with Ed. *That's* what's scaring you!'

Dot was right. Billie didn't deny it. A quick roll in the hay was scary enough, but loving a man—that was too much of a risk.

It would replace James once and for all.

'All right,' whispered Billie. 'I'm scared.'

Dot hugged Billie. 'We're all scared,' she breathed against Billie's hair.

'But we do it anyway.' She broke away and held Billie at arm's length. 'He's over by the fire exit, looking all Heathcliff. Go and tell him.'

'Tell him what?' How the hell did Dot start calling the shots?

'I don't know.' Dot gave Billie a shove. 'Tell him you like him.'

The impetus of the shove sent Billie stumbling through the herd. She kept going until she reached the fire exit. Ed gazed moodily out through the half-open door, with its bar across it, ignoring her.

'Ed . . .' she began. He didn't turn, but gazed resolutely out. 'I like you.' She put her hand to her mouth.

That got his attention. Ed turned quickly to her, and reached up to pull her hand away from her lips. Grabbing her by the waist, he lifted her out on to the gravel, the fire door swinging heavily shut behind them. 'And I like you, Billie's Brides,' he murmured.

The scratch of his stubble and the velvety feel of his lips were sensory overload after Billie's long drought. She responded with a whole-body shudder of pleasure. It was the first kiss since James. And one of her best kisses ever. She was in the hands of a natural.

'I've been dying to—' Ed tilted his head to whisper, but Billie pulled it firmly back with a patrician, 'No talking!'

'Ohh,' she gasped, eventually, when they really had to stop or die.

'Christ.' Ed was looking urgently into her eyes. 'You're—'

'And you're—'

Whatever they both were would have to wait, because Ed pounced again, a broad hand on either side of her face. Superglued together, they lingered, delighting in all the spooky sexiness of their first embrace, until a rogue band of wandering, beer-sodden firemen happened upon them and launched into a medley of rugby songs.

Polishing up his credentials as an A1, tip-top, twenty-four-carat prospective boyfriend, Ed insisted on walking Dot home.

Watching her let herself into the cottage, Billie said, 'You're very gallant. I heard tell of a lock-in.'

'Hmm.' Ed wrinkled his nose. 'Thirty hairy fire-fighters and an endless supply of booze. Didn't fancy it.'

Billie knew who would fancy it. 'Jackie will be crowned queen of Sole Bay before the night is out.' She'd noticed her friend getting very cosy with Debs's red-haired victim, and could imagine the girls fighting over him, like King Kong and Godzilla in heels. She knew who she would bet on: Jackie had an unbroken record. 'I hope that ginger bloke can stand the pace.'

'Chugger can look after himself,' Ed assured her.

'Chugger? Is that his surname?'

'Nickname,' Ed explained. 'All our watch have them.' Ed screwed up his eyes. 'There's Humpty. Moggsy. Fried Egg. Oh, and Ronnie the Pig.'

'And you?' Billie leaned into him, slightly surprised at how natural this felt. Distracted by his sharp, gorgeous, hormone-rousing smell, she recovered to ask, 'What's your nickname?'

'Unfortunately, I'm Treacle,' said Ed, in a voice thick with meaning as he snaked his arms round Billie in the lamplight.

Slipping away from him, Billie raced down the quiet street.

'*Oi!*' echoed round the sleeping houses as Ed took off after her.

A good runner, even in heels, Billie stayed in front until they reached the steps leading to the beach. 'Thought you'd never catch me,' she panted, as Ed's hands delved into her hair and pulled her face towards his. Kissing dreamily, they edged towards Herbert.

Perhaps Ed was impressed, but he could also have been dismayed. 'This is really where you live?'

'It's snug,' conceded Billie, still grasping Ed's bulk.

'Do you think I'll fit?' Ed pressed himself lasciviously against her.

Without warning, Billie disentangled herself and took one rapid step back. Ed had moved things on and suddenly she saw herself as if viewed from above. The girl down there by Herbert's verandah, with her hair all messed up and her cheeks flushed, looked defenceless.

'I'm sorry,' she started.

'No, I am.' Ed backed off, hands in the air as if Billie was flammable and could go up at any moment. 'I'm rushing things.'

'No, you're not . . .' spluttered Billie, floundering. Seeing Ed recede panicked her and now she felt herself missing his warmth. 'But it's been a while and—'

'I understand.' Well, that made one of them. 'I'll drop by the shop in the week. See how you're doing.'

'I'd like that.' Billie smiled at Ed, suddenly shy. He was trying so hard. He was being so *nice*. 'Do I get a good-night kiss?'

'Oh, you get that all right.'

All kissed out, Billie fell into her narrow bed alone, sighing with pleasure and happy exhaustion. The sea answered her, sigh for sigh.

The knocking seemed to have been going on for hours. Billie surfaced through sticky layers of sleep, wondering if the seagulls had turned nasty and were beating down her door to demand protection money. Shaking herself, she got up, tugged on her dressing gown and dragged Jackie inside.

'Bloody hell,' she hissed. 'You'll wake the whole town. I'm not supposed to be living here, remember?'

'Oh. Yeah. Sorry.' Jackie didn't look sorry. Jackie looked as if she'd been dragged through a hedge backwards, forwards, then backwards again, before being diligently sandpapered. 'Forgot.' Billie knew that the dishevelment meant that Jackie had been bouncing up and down for most of the night with a gentleman caller.

'Good night?'

'Oh, not good,' leered Jackie, who had all the attributes of a male philanderer bar the willy. 'Great.' She threw her arms in the air and arched into a long stretch. 'These firemen are *fit*, girl!'

'I wouldn't know,' simpered Billie, hoping to elicit questions.

She was disappointed. Jackie had moved to the mirror. 'Christ. Did I really walk through the town with mascara down to my chin? What do I look like?'

'Shagged, Jackie, is how you look,' laughed Billie. 'At least, that's the technical term. Is Chugger still alive?'

'Ah, Chugger!' Jackie threw her head back in nostalgia. 'A man every bit as intoxicating as his name suggests.' She picked up a comb from the shelf and made a start on detangling her sex-dreadlocks. 'What a conversationalist. I now know everything I'll ever need to about smoke alarms.'

'He saved you the price of a hotel room,' Billie reminded her.

Jackie put down the comb. 'Have some human decency and give me cotton wool and make-up remover, would you?' she pleaded. 'And stick the kettle on. Can I smoke in here?'

'No, you slattern, you can't. Only minutes in the door and I'm slaving for you. Would you like a croissant with your tea, Your Majesty?'

'And jam. All right if I lie on that bed? I haven't had a wink of sleep.'

For the rest of that Sunday morning, Billie catered to her hung-over guest. They caught up efficiently: Billie's year had been pretty samey whereas Jackie had a complex tale to tell.

Listening to the litany of lovers, Billie felt the familiar mixture of amusement, admiration and repulsion. She didn't aspire to Jackie's score card, but hearing the details, told with such relish and such complete lack of remorse, always made her laugh. Mention of wives and girlfriends dampened the fun: Billie hated the emotional carnage Jackie wreaked so carelessly.

'I saw James and his new bird the other night,' Jackie said casually. 'Should I be careful about this stuff, or are you OK with it?'

Assuring Jackie that she was 'OK with it', Billie did her best to be. Suddenly unwanted details were flying at her like bats in a Hammer horror movie. She now knew that James's new girlfriend was called Antonia, had long blonde hair, long brown legs, great dress sense, and pots of money. Perhaps realising that none of this was what an ex would want to hear, Jackie added, 'No balls, though. Nothing like you. She's a big step down.'

Archly, Billie said, 'James reckons she reminds him of me.'

Looking flabbergasted, Jackie queried, 'You're in touch? You and James? Christ.'

'It's not that amazing.' Billie reconsidered. 'Is it?'

'After what happened . . .' Jackie began to retouch her face in the mirror. 'I'm amazed you're talking. Glad, but amazed. Maybe you can be better friends than lovers.'

'That's the idea,' said Billie. 'Do you think it's possible to forgive that kind of thing?'

'For James's sake, darling, we must hope so,' Jackie said absently. 'Anyway, you're moving on. There are plenty more fish in the sea.'

'Well, I already have somebody. Remember?' Billie felt sure that Jackie couldn't have forgotten Ed: Ed was not forgettable.

'Oh. You mean what's-his-name, Ed. Yeah, him, but I mean somebody special. Not just some pretty boy.'

'He's special.' Billie was wounded.

'But you haven't . . . have you?'

'No, but that's not the be-all and end-all.' Properly riled, Billie went waspish. 'They're not all in it for the sex, you know.'

'Hmmm.' Pouting at her reflection, Jackie left that opinion hanging in the air. 'You sure about that?'

'You're annoying me. May we change the subject?'

'Sure, darling. Why don't you perform a short mime for me about how on earth one pisses in this hovel. I'm *bursting*.'

'**D**ot, why are you hovering?' grouched Billie. 'You know I'm dangerous when I'm working out VAT.' She lifted her head from the pile of invoices she had brought up to the stockroom to stare at in mute horror. 'Was Jake all right when you got home? Didn't have a go at you?'

'He never has a go at me.' Dot corrected her boss mildly. 'He was already in bed. Had a terrible stomach ache. Thought it was peritonitis.'

Tosser-itis, diagnosed Billie, meanly. 'Poor him,' she said, acidly.

Dot fingered her embroidered hem. 'Seeing Ed soon?'

Billie sighed, 'You'll have to work on your casual questions, you know. Yes, Dot, I *am* seeing him again. And, before you ask, I don't know when. OK? Some time this week is all he said.'

'Today, I reckon.' Dot clambered downstairs, in answer to a hopeful shout of, 'Yoo hoo! I'm desperate for a crinoline!' from the shop floor.

After successfully evading thoughts of Ed all morning, Billie was ambushed. She could conjure up the gentle sandpaper of his chin, the curve of his lips in the moonlight. VAT paled into insignificance as her skin's memory reproduced the pressure of his hands on her back.

'What does "this week" mean?' Billie was plunged back into the dating girl's universe of second-guessing and motive evaluation. Did Ed mean literally a week? Therefore, should she worry if he didn't drop in by the time the shop closed on the coming Saturday? Or was it a looser version of a week? A man-time week, perhaps?

Billie knew from what felt like centuries of experience that man-time runs to a very loose calendar. 'I'll call you soon' could be translated as 'I'll call you after your teeth have dropped out'. 'See you around' could mean 'See you around' but in man-time it also meant 'Now that I have achieved sexual congress with you I will avoid you as if you are leprous'.

The perils of trying to mix and match man-time with her own more straightforward diary had been one of the reasons Billie had always avoided commitment, scorching blokes before they'd had the opportunity to do the same to her. Until James, that is, and his refreshing approach to time. 'I'll call you later,' meant that she'd hear from him later that day, and, 'Let's go for a drink this week,' had always resulted in clinking glasses before seven days were up.

'He's not James,' she reminded herself. It was self-evident, but it needed saying. Mind you, Billie realised that she'd been saying it a lot. Everything Ed had said and done so far had been compared to James: his score was good, but it worried her that she was keeping score.

Standing up to pace the tiny stockroom, she told herself it was unhelpful to compare the two men.

Billie reapplied herself to the VAT. Down in the shop, the bell over the door sang. Freezing, Billie only relaxed when she heard a female voice ask for a refund on a bolero. This anticipation was *horrible*. Billie hated the way she watched the door, scanned the street, mistook every red Ford Fiesta for a fire engine. Why couldn't she be cool?

Because she cared about Ed. Already, after a few salty seafront kisses, she was bovvered. There was somebody she wanted to tell. Before she had the opportunity to examine this impulse, she had bashed out James's email address. *Guess what?* she asked her ethereal ex, floating out there on the worldwide web like a stray astronaut. *I've found somebody, too.*

This had to be carefully judged. James had set very clear guidelines for their new correspondence. She must keep her touch light.

The fireman finally came across. But, he doesn't remind me of you at all. Who knows what will come of it? Nothing, perhaps. But for now, it feels good. Right, enough hearts and flowers. Can you help me with a VAT problem?

James had been so important to her once that it seemed right to be telling him how she felt. And the VAT query would make him laugh. If she still held that power.

The bell jangled again. Billie shot up. Ed's voice was asking, 'You on your own, Dottie?'

'No, no, she's not.' At the bottom of the stairs before Ed had finished his question, Billie smiled, broad and soppy. 'How are you?' she asked.

'Recovering.' Ed was smiling too, almost as broad, almost as soppy. 'I wasn't a pretty sight yesterday. Hangovers get worse as you get older, don't they?'

Nodding, Billie hid her puzzlement. She hadn't realised that Ed had drunk enough to merit a punishing hangover. Perhaps he'd been sozzled when he kissed her? Perhaps he regretted it?

Casting a furtive look at Dot, who wasn't making a very good job of pretending to be interested in a bridal underwear catalogue, Ed held up a small bunch of white flowers.

The gremlin disappeared in a puff of green smoke. Regretful men tend not to buy flowers, reasoned Billie. 'Are they for me?'

'Well,' Ed looked around the room. 'Unless Dot wants them.'

The bell jangled again and Heather materialised between them, like a panto witch. 'God, it's hot,' she moaned, demonstrating her mood to be somewhat panto witch-like, too. 'Oh.' She took in Ed's presence. 'What are you doing here? Did I ask you to pop in?' She looked from Ed to Billie and then back to Ed again. 'Flowers, Ed?' she queried.

A number of thoughts flashed across Billie's consciousness like text messages from her psyche. HTHR MST NOT KNOW OR MY LIFE OVR, one read, recalling her client's plans for Ed and Angela. Then, in even bigger letters: PLSE DNT TELL HR!!!

'Yeah,' conceded Ed, looking down at the freesias. 'Flowers.' He looked at Heather for a long while. 'For my mum,' he said finally, in a voice that suggested he didn't even believe himself. 'She's not well.'

'Oh, isn't he nice?' Heather grabbed the tall man and chucked his chin. With a sly look, she said, 'Angela is a sucker for flowers.'

'I'll keep that in mind,' promised Ed, not looking at Billie.

'Anyway, run along,' ordered Heather. 'I have a million and one things to talk to Billie about.'

'See you around,' said Ed. Behind Heather's back, Ed shrugged exaggeratedly at Billie, and pulled a sad face over the flowers.

'See you!' said Billie, casually, attempting to imply by subtext that when she did see him she would snog him until he begged for mercy.

'Horses,' proclaimed Heather.

'Booked. Two. White. Gorgeous.'

'Plumes?'

'Fuchsia.'

'Carriage?'

'Silver.' On a gasp from Heather that turned into a violent cough, Billie added, 'But will be sprayed lilac for the big day.'

'Oh, I love you!' gabbled Heather, as her throat seized up.

So you should, thought Billie wryly. She had made more phone calls about those horses and their sodding feathers than President Bush had made about foreign policy. 'Don't worry, everything is under control.'

'Of course I'm worried!' snapped Heather. 'According to my schedule, it's almost time to panic.'

This was familiar territory. Billie remembered her own sweaty palms and thudding heart every time her mother opened the wedding folder that had lain on the coffee table for months. Fear of her dress going out of fashion had kept her awake at night, and she had almost punched a second cousin who turned vegetarian after the menu was finalised.

There was no time for a cup of something reviving after Heather had left. A new customer took her place. The accent was eastern European. The voice was a throaty growl. The lipstick was bright. And the breasts were not as God made them. 'Is best quality, yes?' asked the prospective bride, snatching up a tulle skirt between silicon talons.

'Is best quality,' mimicked Billie, unwittingly. She was keeping a safe distance from this woman, who had the unpredictable feel of a lioness.

'And this?' The customer snatched up a posy, delicately fashioned from silk flowers. 'Will rot?' She rolled her Rs like a circus master.

'Will not.' It was a novel feeling, but Billie wished that Debs was there. 'When's the big day?'

The insignificant man trailing the statuesque foreigner answered merrily, 'As soon as possible!' His myopic eyes twinkled and his sandy moustache quivered as, daringly, he reached out a hand the size of a child's to take his fiancée's claw. 'We can't wait, can we, my passion-flower?' His milky face gazed up adoringly.

'God, always you paw me, Clifford,' snapped his passionflower, shrugging him off. 'I need quick dress, so we can get married before his mother stops us. What is most dearest dress?' she asked, peremptorily.

'The Angelica.' Motioning to a raw-silk extravaganza in the window, Billie added, 'But it's over three thousand pounds.'

'I try on.' The bride-to-be headed for the changing room. She was already undoing her top.

The gown looked wonderful, despite the sour look on the customer's haughty face. 'Is not worth the money,' she stated, baldly.

'The silk is French and the lace is handmade,' said Billie, doing up the last tiny button. 'Look at this stitching.' But the woman was busy checking her teeth in the mirror.

'You think these front teeth too big?' she demanded. 'Clifford buy me crowns. I think they are too big, like mouth of camel.'

From outside the curtain, her generous groom insisted, 'No, no, Ivanka, my love. Your teeth look wonderful.'

Lowering her voice, the woman confided, 'He think I look wonderful if I have sanitary towel on head. He know nothing about woman. Is like making sex with an oven glove.' She dragged the dress off and thrust it at Billie. 'I take this one,' she declared, loudly.

'Really, my love?' Clifford's voice sounded weak from the shopfloor. 'Won't you try on some . . . not so, um, I mean, less extravagant ones?'

'You mean cheap?' roared the woman, tearing the curtain aside and striding out into the shop in her scarlet underwear. 'OK, bring me the cheap rubbish. I will wear nastiest dress in shop on most special day in life!' she howled. 'I am not worth three thousand pounds! Clifford would rather keep it in the bank!'

'No, no, not at all.' The little man's translucent pallor was compromised by two throbbing dots of red on his alarmed face.

'Perhaps you do not wish to marry your Ivanka?' Hands on hips, his Ivanka glared at him, her rock-hard breasts of unlikely proportions roughly at the height of his watery eyes. 'You can go to your mother and say, "Old woman, you were right. I should stay home with you and spend life savings on static caravan."' She paused for a moment, then sneered, 'And I suppose you want your tits back.'

'Don't talk like that, Ivanka.' Clifford seemed close to tears. 'Have the dress. And shoes to match. And a tiara. And a veil to cover your beautiful face. Only, please, my love, don't shout at your Clifford any more.'

'OK.' As insouciant as a teenager who's just had their Big Mac supersized, Ivanka turned to Billie. 'Show me best shoes in shop.'

Lounging against the counter with Zelda, idly snaffling fudge from her bag, Billie watched Dot fling glitter over the window display. Her aim was a little shaky, thanks to the muttered running commentary from Jake, sprawled like a daddy long-legs on the floorboards.

'I shouldn't be surprised when you behave like a Jezebel,' he was saying, in a disappointed voice. 'Who knows what blood is in your veins?'

A quiet growl sounded from Zelda at Billie's side.

'Your grandmother could have been a lunatic. Or a sex maniac,' Jake carried on, sadly. 'After all, what kind of woman abandons a baby? She can't have loved your mum much to do that to her.'

Chewing, Zelda pointed out, 'You shouldn't talk about a lady you know nothing about.' She skewered Jake with a narrow-eyed gaze.

'It's none of your business,' Jake told her, lazily.

Defiantly, Zelda said, 'If Dot's grandmother were here she'd love her, just like we all do. Everybody loves that girl.'

Jake carried on dreamily, almost under his breath, 'If Dot wants to kick our relationship to death there's nothing I can do about it.'

Now Dot was galvanised into action. Not the sort of action Billie would have taken, involving Jake's beard and a box of matches, but a gentle, reproving, 'Oh, Jakey, don't.'

'Perhaps we're not meant to be.' Jake assumed a look of mock misery, unbent his limbs and made for the door. He left the shop, but not before Billie had seen Zelda throw Jake a look so venomous, so vengeful, so *murderous* that Billie gasped.

'**I**'ve chosen,' said Annie, looking amazed at her own effrontery. '*That,*' she pointed to a dress hanging near the stairs, 'is the one for me.'

'Ooh, Annie,' cooed Billie. 'That's my favourite, too.'

The Ruby Wolff design was regal. Cream velvet, with an austere, high-buttoned collar and a puddling train, the dress had a purity and simplicity that drew Billie to it. She was constantly tweaking it, rehanging it, nuzzling against its luxurious fabric. 'I'll put it away for you.'

Annie, pink and delighted, trotted out to meet Ruby in the street, but he darted back to the shop, leaving her on the pavement.

'Mum's the word,' he croaked, surreptitiously passing Billie a fiver.

'Oh.' Billie looked down at the crumpled note. 'That's so sweet of you, Ruby. So how is your new seamstress coming along?'

'I've never seen such exquisite work,' enthused Ruby. 'The woman has a wonderful touch.' He shuffled out to join Annie on the pavement.

'Aww, look,' simpered Dot. 'He's taken her arm.'

There was no time to dwell on Ruby's rehabilitation: the VAT beckoned. 'I want calories. Now,' insisted Billie, shuddering at the thought of the pile of papers upstairs. 'Fudge, Dot. Fetch fudge.'

'Noooo,' whined Dot. 'Please don't make me. I can't bear to see Raven at the moment. He looks ill. I'm so worried about him.'

Not so concerned about the devilish moggy, Billie joined the queue in Zelda's shop. Somebody stepped in behind her and she budged up slightly. Then she realised who it was. 'Ed!' she quacked.

'Billie.'

'What are you doing here?'

He bit his lip. His lovely, fleshy, slightly moist lip. 'Buying fudge?'

'Of course you are, it's a fudge shop.' For some reason Billie was shouting. Then she laughed. Much too loudly, as if fudge shops were intrinsically funny. Ed's charms short-circuited her conversation wiring.

'Sorry about the flowers.' As usual, it was left to Ed to steer them to saner conversational waters. 'I guessed you wouldn't want Heather to know.' He swallowed. 'About us.' He swallowed again. 'If there is an us.'

Billie said, 'I hope there is.' And that was it. She'd chosen. There was going to be an us. A smile broke out and ran riot all over her face.

An answering grin rendered Ed even more handsome. 'When can I see you again?' he whispered.

'Dinner at my place?' It came out before Billie had time to think. Her place was a bad place for dinner, but it was too late. Ed had nodded happily and she was committed to cooking and serving a romantic meal in a space smaller than the average lift. 'Saturday?'

Crinkling up his eyes, Ed said slowly, 'Ye-es, I'm off Saturday night.'

NINE

IT FIRST STRUCK BILLIE halfway through cashing up one evening: the till had been short only on Saturdays. The amounts had all been similar.

It *had* to be Debs. Only the three of them had access to the till, so unless Billie had had some kind of amnesia, she could rule herself out; the world would topple from its axis if Dot ever stole, which left Debs.

Two things stopped Billie from confronting her Saturday girl: lack of hard evidence and her surly, aggressive demeanour.

'I'll just have to tell her she can't use the till,' Billie resolved, as she opened up the shop. 'Simple as that. No need for bad feeling.'

'Nice day,' sang Zelda, as she put out her FRESH FUDGE HERE sign.

'Lovely!' The weather was mentioned every day on Little Row, even though scorching days were commonplace, the summer's success anointed with a hosepipe ban. As if Billie had summoned up Debs by thinking about her, her Saturday girl sauntered to the door.

Trying not to stare at the web of white strap marks across the irradiating sunburn on Debs's chest, Billie preceded her in. 'You're early.'

'Yeah.' Debs never explained anything. 'There's bird cack all down the window. I ain't cleaning it up,' she added, lest there be any doubt.

'Of course not.' Billie strode out back for a bucket. 'The very idea.'

Billie scrubbed at the poop as Debs dealt with the first customer.

'Boss!' yelled Debs raucously. 'Get in here! The till's stuck!'

Not stuck, but locked. It was time to tell Debs that she couldn't use the cash register. Bracing herself, Billie strode back in.

'This one 'ere needs a refund.' Debs jerked a thumb in the direction of a pale, pained woman in her thirties, who was clutching a Billie's Brides bag between reddened fingers. 'She's been dumped.'

The woman's self-possession cracked and she started to sob. Slipping an arm around the distressed jiltee, Billie suggested Debs should put the kettle on.

'Bloody hell, I've only just got in!' yelled Debs, dragging herself out to the back of the shop. She stopped in front of the woman to ask, in a kinder voice, 'It was for someone younger, prettier, yeah?' Her only answer was harder sobbing. 'Thought so.'

The day was a blur of white fabric and veils. Billie barely had time to take Debs to one side and ask her to please wipe the hair-removal cream on her upper lip.

'But I'm going out tonight!' moaned Debs.

'I don't care!' answered Billie, emboldened by her suspicions.

A brief face-off ensued, but Debs lost the cream. The showdown over the till had been an anticlimax too: 'Not bothered,' she'd shrugged, when told she would no longer take payments.

Billie was a powerhouse that Saturday. Those promised few hours with Ed at the end of the day shimmered like light at the end of the tunnel. Getting to know him better, getting to kiss him again, would be her reward after this demanding day.

One of the demands it made on Billie was twenty minutes alone with Jake. 'Dot's not here,' she told him, as he sloped into the shop, his floral kilt a touch too short for her liking. 'She's delivering some shoes.'

Jake uttered the terrible words, 'I'll wait,' and settled himself on the chair reserved for customers.

Billie found herself trying to make conversation. 'Been painting?'

'You don't like me, do you?' whispered Jake. 'Do you want to know what I think of you? You're a bad influence. You unsettle Dot.'

'I'm Dot's *friend*.' Billie stressed that last word.

'You lead her astray.'

'You sound like a puritan papa. Why are you so hard on her, Jake?'

'Haven't you noticed by now? She's the moon and stars to me. She's my night and day. I can't breathe when she's not near me. It's like being trapped in an abyss.' Jake slumped, spent.

'Do you tell her that?' asked Billie, quietly.

'She knows.'

And now Billie knew, too. Perhaps Jake's childhood had left him tongue-tied, a foreigner to the language of affection. That outburst had been the only positive thing he'd ever said about his girlfriend. Heartfelt, eloquent, loving, the speech had been profoundly non-Jake.

The old Jake returned soon enough. 'From the back,' he told Billie, 'you could be a man.'

The CLOSSED sign was finally slapped over.

A peek at her watch told Billie she had an hour to wash, change, civilise her hair and make-up her face. She paid her little team and shooed them out just as her mobile phone buzzed.

'Sam,' she said, speed-walking in the direction of Herbert's Dream II.

'Drink?' he asked.

'No.' Billie tried not to sound as if she'd won the lottery. 'Date!'

'Oh, I forgot. The fireman.' Sam tutted. 'Have fun, I suppose, you little turncoat. Where are you cooking for him?'

Billie cut Sam off and walked into a lamp post. How could she have forgotten she'd promised Ed dinner? She'd been fantasising solidly for twenty-four hours about this date and the most important detail had slipped her mind. She broke into a run.

By twenty-five to six, Sole Bay High Street was shuttered and shut. But Billie wasn't downhearted. She was headed for Tesco Metro, which kept urban hours and could be relied upon to dispense dinner-party-style titbits until at least 9 p.m.

Skidding to a halt outside the small supermarket, she pushed her way through the crowd gathered outside. With a twitch of foreboding she recognised them as staff. 'What's going on?' she asked.

A chain-smoking lady garlanded with gold chains said, 'Them fool Saturday boys larking about. They've only flooded the place.'

'But you're not . . . shut?' Billie grasped the lady's flabby arm.

'Of course we're shut, love. It's like *The Poseidon Adventure* in there.'

Billie stopped whimpering and beetled off in the direction of the only other establishment that would be open at this hour.

Garage forecourt shops are cornucopias of plenty if you want a *Daily Mirror* and a squeegee, but Billie suspected celebrated socialites don't rely on them when entertaining. 'Oh Lord,' she sighed, grabbing at the limited selection of foodstuffs on the shelves. 'I can't offer him biscuits for a main course,' she muttered, suddenly loathing the Jaffa Cakes and Digestives and Jammie Dodgers that she usually greeted like long-lost chums. 'Ah ha!' A break at last. 'Pringles. That's the starter sorted.'

Looking around at the dusty pastels of her tiny home, softened and polished by countless tealights, 'Dreamy,' Billie murmured, approvingly. The beach hut now constituted a serious fire hazard, but at least her guest would know what to do if the gingham curtains went up.

The faithful black trousers understood about Billie's bum, and the strappy top showed off her fashionably pale shoulders nicely. Even her hair was cooperating, acquiescing meekly when introduced to a clip.

The fly in the evening's ointment was the food. James had always cooked when they'd invited mates round. Billie had been in charge of taking coats, passing around nibbles and getting tipsy.

Tonight, flying solo, she arranged Pringles on a melamine picnic plate with the confidence of one who has handled nibbles before. The surly teenager behind the garage counter had answered, 'Tarama-wot?' when quizzed about dips. The Pringles would have to fly solo as well.

The scrape of male feet on Herbert's verandah startled her. *He's early!* she squealed to herself, running in all directions yet getting nowhere. The rap at the door was loud. Billie slapped herself suddenly round the face and breathed in so hard the candle flames wavered. 'Coming!'

'I'm early.' Ed's even, stolid voice was apologetic.

'Are you?' Billie managed to look amazed. 'No problem.' She accepted the bottle of wine and the supermarket flowers with exaggerated delight. 'So beautiful!' she breathed over the drooping heads of carnations that would all be dead by dessert.

Looking around him, Ed said, 'It's bigger than I thought.'

Hoping he wasn't referring to her arse, Billie invited him to sit down.

By the time Ed's Grade A bottom hit the deckchair, Billie had uncorked the wine. 'Cheers!' she said, dismayed at just how twitchy his proximity made her. There was an intimacy to having this long-legged, broad-shouldered man in her home that she hadn't anticipated.

Almost horizontal in the deckchair, Ed seemed relaxed and content, even when a plastic platter of Pringles was thrust under his nose. 'No, ta,' he said mildly. 'I've never liked them.'

Shit. They're the best bit, panicked Billie, as she picked up her wine-glass. 'So,' she began, a little too loudly, 'how's work?'

'You look very sexy tonight, Ms Baskerville. I like your hair up like that.'

'Nah, it's too fluffy.' Ed's comment had pleased her more than he could possibly know. Billie's hair was a natural phenomenon that only James had admired. His fascination with it—'You've got the best hair'—contrasted nicely with her mother's 'Dear God, you could keep owls in that. Get it cut!,' Billie gulped at her wine. 'My hair's always a mess,' she insisted confidently, as the red wine hit her empty tum. 'Rescued anybody from certain death this week?'

'Not really.' Ed drew his legs in.

Oblivious to the eloquent body language, and somehow missing the neon signs saying STOP! DON'T GO THERE! Billie rambled on. 'Your job fascinates me. I mean, everybody runs from a fire. But you run *towards* it.'

'Hmmm.' Ed's face was set like granite in the candlelight.

'I mean,' Billie repeated, 'you're a hero!'

'Not what I'd call myself.' Ed stood up and crossed the room to tower over her. 'Look,' he said. 'Can we talk about something else?'

'Of course. Anything you like.' His nearness and his sudden seriousness threw Billie again. 'Politics? Religion?' She scrabbled. 'Fruit?'

Taking her hands in his, Ed kept his voice low.

'I don't give a toss what we talk about. I'm with the best-looking girl I've met in a long time, and I want to get to know her. OK?'

'OK.' Her hands felt small in his. The little homily calmed her.

'Let's eat. I'm starving.'

It was Billie's turn to go grave as she 'served' dinner. She produced a selection of processed cheese triangles, a Pop-Tart, and a stick of Peperami, cut into varying lengths. 'Bon appétit,' she sighed.

Hot, sated, they lay back on her little iron bed, in a kind of swoon, swapping stupefied looks of delight.

'That was . . . so good,' groaned Billie.

'No, Bill, that was the best.' Ed had melted into the mattress.

Not post-coital bliss, but the eerily similar post-chip bliss.

Licking his fingers, Ed suddenly turned to her, and kissed Billie full on the mouth. 'You taste of salt and vinegar,' he whispered.

She couldn't whisper anything. 'I never thought I'd say this, but that kiss was better than chips,' she eventually told him.

He leaned in to do it again. The charity-shop cushions got in the way, but were soon dispensed with. Greedily kissing, Billie and Ed held each other close, their bodies joined from lip to toe.

'You're lovely,' he muttered, with a huskiness that prompted her to press herself even harder against him. He put his fingers to her trouser zip, while his tongue explored her mouth with explicit desire.

Lurching upright, Billie gasped, 'We can't! It's too quick.' She was scrambling off the bed. 'It's not right. It doesn't feel right.'

'It does.' Ed reached out to her. 'You know it does.' He was seductive again, although his face was clouded. 'Come on,' he added, anxiously, as if he could see something wonderful slipping away.

'No, I'm sorry.' Billie suddenly wished he'd go. 'It's me, not you.'

It was Ed's turn to hear The Story.

Over the last of the wine, Ed listened, with far more patience than a man with an erection might be expected to. He nodded in the right places, said, 'Aww,' when he should, and even threw in a, 'If I could get my hands on him . . .'

'It's too soon, Ed. I mean, I was just about to be *married*. I'm still raw. Do you understand?'

Smiling regretfully, Ed nodded. 'Of course I do.' He sighed. 'Shame, though.' He shrugged. 'Looks like it's cold showers for me for a while.' He looked intently at her. 'Not for ever, though, eh?'

'Not for ever, Ed,' she promised, to herself as much as him.

'Is cuddling forbidden?'

'It's mandatory.' Billie held out her arms, and he filled them beautifully. Some of the candles had guttered out and the hut was darker, its corners secret again. Lying on the bed, with Ed snuggled into her embrace, Billie ruffled his hair. She'd been aching to ruffle his short, puppyish hair, and it was every bit as enjoyable as she'd imagined.

'How come you're so nice?' she said softly.

His voice was loud, too loud for the moment. 'Don't say that.'

'But you are,' she insisted, in the same gentle tone.

'Don't start.' The traditional male plea was muffled by the headlock.

'All right. I won't,' Billie humoured him, and relinquished her hold.

All the signs were there. Billie was humming to herself, bestowing extravagant welcomes on the trickle of Monday customers, pausing to gaze into the middle distance, drifting off in the middle of sentences.

'If you ask me you're in love,' Dot opined.

'As if.' Billie knew exactly where she was on the Everest of her new relationship. She was in the foothills. She'd left base camp, but she was still on the relatively easy slopes. No snow yet. No crevasses. 'It's brand new. I couldn't possibly have deep feelings for Ed yet.' She couldn't admit, even to Dot, the effect he'd had on her. Ed was on her mind: the feel of his mouth was on her lips.

'I knew Jakey was the one straight away. Did Ed stay late?'

'If dawn is late.'

'Oh.' Dot studied her fingernails. 'Did you talk a lot?'

'Loads. When we weren't kissing.'

'Kissing?' Dot reacted as if this was a novel first-date activity. 'Right. Just . . . kissing?'

Feigning ignorance of the question that Dot was too decorous to ask, Billie tortured her with, 'Oh, kissing and stuff.'

'Big stuff?' Dot asked idly.

'Medium stuff.' Billie frowned in thought. 'You know, biggish.'

Just then the shop door opened enough for Sam to insert his artfully dishevelled head. 'Shag 'im?'

'No.'

Sam withdrew his head.

It was like one of those dreams where you know you're dreaming and you long to wake up. You struggle and strain but you remain in an absurd other world. That was how Billie felt when she realised that Zelda had been sitting on the chair meant for customers talking about her troubles with her feet for three-quarters of an hour.

The phone rang and Zelda's feet receded when Billie heard Ed's voice. This man didn't run on man-time: he ran on demigod-time. He made a date for Wednesday.

'Dating', with no promise of sex at the end of the evening, was quite liberating: for a start, Billie didn't bother to shave above her knees. She felt like Doris Day as she buttoned up her striped sundress in Herbert's Dream II on Wednesday evening. Although Doris Day never had to beat her hair with the hairbrush to calm it down.

For a reason locked in the vaults of Billie's psyche, she was sticking to her newfound celibacy. It wasn't because she didn't fancy Ed: she would have gnawed through a dungeon door to get a glimpse of his gluteus maximus. It was hard to pin down and name her motives, but they had something to do with self-preservation. Perfect though he was, Ed was still a man and as a man he held the power to disrupt her carefully ordered new life.

If Ed could wait, perhaps he would be worth risking it all for.

Sole Bay had a selection of pubs and, as Sam had pointed out, they were all big on horse brasses. And fishing nets. And witches' balls. And pewter tankards. Billie had never been in the Sailor's Lament before and she looked round nervously.

There he was by the bar. Still beautiful. 'Hello, sir,' she said, eyes twinkling overtime: Ed made her feel giddy.

'Matron,' he responded, in an attempt at a Kenneth Williams.

Perhaps it was nerves, but that was the first of a handful of impressions that peppered their evening. Billie smiled dutifully, and even laughed (albeit for the wrong reasons) at his Frank Spencer, his Billy Connolly, his John Wayne and his Sean Connery: 'I'm going to the little boysh room. Shtay there.'

It didn't make any difference to her feelings. Something told her that when they eventually got down to rude and dirty business, it would be all Ed and no Frankie Howerd. Missus.

'I can't wait for you to get to know Sam. And my friend Jackie.' She loved this part of the process, the light and airy bit with the stabilisers still on. 'You'll love them,' she said confidently. 'What are you doing tomorrow night?' she asked, three vodka and tonics emboldening her. 'You could meet my folks if you want. They're in a play, this amateur crap, and I'm going, so you could come, but I didn't mean, you know, inverted commas, *meet the folks*.'

'Don't panic,' smiled Ed. 'I know what you meant. You're the one putting the brakes on, not me.'

'We'd have to set off in the afternoon. They live on the outskirts of London.'

'I'm working tomorrow night. You're going to learn to hate my bloody shifts,' prophesied Ed. 'A fireman's girlfriend always does.'

'Fireman's girlfriend.' Billie giggled. 'Ooer.'

'You'll hate it. You'll just laugh at everything. Why did you come?'

'Because you invited me.' Sam, lounging on the first-class train seat like a broken toy, lifted his sunglasses to add, 'Because I'm the only layabout who could leave town this early to go to a play.'

Billie was a veteran of West End opening nights: west end of Surbiton. Looking around her in the over-lit foyer of the community centre Billie saw all the usual first-nighters, a veritable who's who of Surbiton. The only face missing was Sly's. He had to work, he'd told Billie on the phone. It was the first opening night he'd ever missed. Hitching Sam to a Jack Daniel's and Coke, Billie ventured backstage.

Following the trail of the loud 'LALALALALALALALALA!' of her mother's vocal exercises, Billie opened a scuffed door, adorned with a sign ordering: CHECK WITH JANITOR IF DAMP.

Nancy Baskerville sat at an improvised dressing table. A desk lamp shone on a mirror leaning against the centre's cleaning rota. She had stopped caterwauling and was staring at her face as if she'd never seen it before, with an expression so unusual that her daughter almost didn't recognise her. Nancy jumped and looked around. 'My lucky charm! You made it, you utter angel!'

The first act was long and, as played by the am-dram troupe, confusing. During the interval, in the cupboard-sized bar, Billie asked what Sam thought of her parents' endlessly rehearsed posh accents.

'Oh, it's in English?' Sam seemed surprised.

After a challenging second act, in which the nervous man playing Nancy's lover forgot every single one of his lines and improvised with all the easy confidence of a coma victim, the curtain fell to rapturous applause. There were cheers, whistles and bravos. Sam, catching the mood, jumped up and hollered, '*Nancy, I love you!*'

Back in the bar, the cast trickled out to join their friends, looking diminished in everyday clothes. Last to emerge, of course, were the Baskervilles, who milked the applause until Billie's palms were sore.

'How was I?' Scurrying over to Billie, this was Nancy's first question. She was clutching a glamorous silk wrap around her and was still wearing her stage make-up. 'Was I too much? Or too little? Was it awful?'

Sam, sunglasses firmly off, leaned over and took Nancy's hand to kiss it. 'You were magnificent,' he said, throatily.

Laughing artificially like a trunkful of china dropped from the top of a skyscraper, Nancy, whose appetite for praise was similar to Billie's for pasties, pretended to be overwhelmed. 'How kind,' she simpered. 'You are . . . ?'

Lying, thought Billie disloyally. She introduced them, and Nancy leapt like a mountain goat to the wrong conclusion, saying, 'I always hoped she'd meet a creative type one day.'

'No, Mum, no, Sam's not my boyfriend.' She wondered whether or not to tell all: she risked it. 'Although I *am* seeing someone. A fireman. He couldn't come tonight.'

'A fireman?' Nancy examined the idea and evidently found it wanting. 'Each to their own. I've always preferred artistic men.'

In Herbert, balanced between sleep and wakefulness that night, Billie was thinking about her mother. As the waves chased each other outside, she recalled her mother's expression in the mirror.

It came to her—that look was fear. Outspoken, ball-breaking Nancy had been terrified of her own face. In that little snapshot Nancy was a woman, not a mum. What's more, she was a woman who had always been judged on her looks and who could now see them changing, morphing, disappearing, leaving her an old lady with no currency left.

This was strange territory for a daughter. Although obvious, it had never registered with Billie that Nancy had been a woman long before she was a mother. A woman whose life hadn't turned out the way she'd planned: the young Nancy had dreamed of the professional stage, not the local community centre.

They had something in common. Disappointment squatted like a stone in both their hearts. Billie, feeling sorry for her mother for the first time ever.

Passing the market cross on her way back from delivering a strapless gown, Billie stopped. Sole Bay had short-circuited; a detail was wrong.

'Jackie?'

Jackie also stopped short. 'Billie,' she said. 'There you are.'

'What are you doing here?' asked Billie rudely.

'Aren't you glad to see me?' teased her friend, who was, as usual, a Technicolored, slightly-larger-than-life, sight for sore eyes in a clingy red sundress and platform sandals. 'I thought you could take the day off and sit on the beach with me.'

'I can't,' protested Billie, still computing Jackie's presence. 'But I can do an early lunch.'

Thanks to Dot's understanding nature, Billie was down on the pebbles at noon, decanting loot from the organic delicatessen onto a blanket filched from Herbert. 'How's things? You look tired,' she said.

'I am.' Jackie's vivacity was stilled.

'Anything wrong?' Billie opened some juice. 'Can't be man trouble.'

'You'd be surprised.' Jackie was looking out to sea. 'It would be nice, wouldn't it, Billie, if just occasionally one of them proved us wrong?'

'How do you mean?' Billie held out a tumbler of juice.

'Once in a while one comes along and you think, Please, please, don't be a sod. But they can't help it.'

'That's fine talk for a heartbreaker.'

'I knew you'd say that.' Jackie sounded bitter.

'Jackie, are you annoyed at me? Have I done something?'

'You? No.' It should have been reassuring, but the way Jackie spoke was verging on aggressive.

'You're doing my head in. What is it, Jackie?'

'Nothing. I'm sorry.' Jackie made a visible effort and took the juice. 'Cheers!' she said, her old self once again.

The D-Day landings were a doddle compared with coordinating twelve girls for a hen night. Counting heads outside the shop, Billie raised her voice, 'We're one short, ladies! Who's not here yet?'

Dot, despite Jake's misgivings, was present, tie-dye smock tucked into tie-dye skirt (Billie couldn't rule out the possibility of tie-dye knickers). Debs was there, sullen and sexually available in a brief denim skirt and a T-shirt with a misspelt diamanté slogan: BICTH. Heather was there, bedecked with L-plates, cheap veil and scowl.

'Angela's not here. Anybody know where Angela is?' Even to her own ears, Billie sounded like an exasperated geography teacher on a field trip, and she wasn't surprised the hens were more interested in each other's PVC shorts and body glitter than they were in listening to her.

As she turned the corner of Little Row, the reason for Angela's lateness was explained: the tightness of her plastic nurse's outfit, low cut and two sizes too small, made any walk faster than a purposeful mince impossible.

'Ange, you look *gorgeous*,' Heather shrieked.

'Bloody hell,' murmured Debs. 'There's less meat in Mr Dyke's window.'

A white stretch limo was negotiating the corner. Its arrival on Little Row set off the kind of whooping and dancing that Billie would have expected only from women who had been kept in a darkened room all their lives and had never heard tell of the combustion engine.

Heather led the gang into the vehicle. It was like a little white night-club, with leather seats, fluffy carpet, music blaring and a minibar. Champagne was opened, champagne was spilt, legs were kicked in the air and every comment was greeted with guffaws.

To find a venue that pandered to the whims of hens, Billie had cast her net outside Sole Bay, the Sailor's Lament being short on oiled male bar staff. The flashing neon scribble of the Shady Ladies sign in Neeveston encouraged the girls' communal blood pressure even higher as they all piled out of the limo.

'Ooooh!' and 'Yesssss!' they hooted, clattering to the entrance. Waved through by the bouncer, they were led through the bar, giggling. It was an ordinary sort of bar, enlivened by winking lights and swags of silver fabric. At the back was a row of booths, with leatherette horseshoe banquettes round circular tables. The VIP booth, which differed by virtue of the thin chain across its opening, was theirs.

'Cocktails!' chanted one of the girls, whose top half was dressed as a nun, and whose bottom half had forgotten to get dressed at all. 'I want a long slow screw against the wall!'

A waiter who had dispensed with his top, but hung on to his bow tie, took their order. Rolling his eyes good-naturedly at the hilarity involved in asking him for a Screaming Orgasm or a Slippery Nipple he was taken aback only by Dot's request for a dandelion and burdock.

The music cranked up a few decibels and conversation from then on had to be shouted. After the first round of cocktails, the shots began. Billie passed hers to Debs, who knocked them back like an expert.

The bar filled up and the place throbbed with sweaty energy. It was a long, long time since Billie had set foot in such a pulling palace.

'I love these girls,' Dot confided to Billie, over the din. 'Such lovely, sweet people. Especially Angela,' she said, gazing up fondly at the lumpen nurse high-kicking on their table.

'How many shots have you had?' asked Billie, taking in Dot's eyes, which were nearly crossed.

'Hmm? Dunno.' Dot peered into her glass. 'Are they alcoholic?'

'Oh dear.' Billie did another head count. 'Where's Debs?'

'I saw her leave half an hour ago,' said Dot. 'She didn't look like a bunny happy. A bappy hunny.' Dot hiccupped. 'She looked shad.'

'Charming.' There was no time to focus on Debs's customary rudeness: Billie had to help Angela down from the table when her stethoscope caught in the glitter ball and she almost garrotted herself. As designated grown-up, quite a few tasks fell to Billie over the evening. It was she who had to convince the half-nun not to punch the slag staring her out across the bar: 'That's your reflection,' Billie yelled. And it was Billie who frogmarched Heather to the Ladies when the inevitable happened and her hysterical laughter segued into hysterical tears.

'Come on, come on, you're all right,' soothed Billie, taking the crumpled girl into her arms by the cruelly lit mirrors. 'It's overwhelming, I know.' And she did know. She mopped Heather's streaked and smeared face, remembering how her own hen night had ended in a bare-knuckle fight between her and Jackie over an Opal Fruit.

'I don't want to do it,' wailed Heather. Other punters were washing their hands a tad too slowly, one eye on this unexpected sideshow.

'Do what? We can go home if that's what you mean.'

'The wedding!' shouted Heather, impatiently. 'I'm not ready. I'm too young! I've got too much life to live!'

'No, no,' cooed Billie. 'You love Dean. It's a match made in heaven.' Running the shop meant that such gooey phrases were second nature to her now.

'But I don't know if I do really love him!' Heather's words were delivered with tears cascading down her face. 'I can't go through with it. Don't make me!' she begged Billie.

'Let me through, I'm a porno nurse.' Angela barged through the rubberneckers and wrested Heather from Billie. 'There, there,' she said, breathing 100 per cent proof fumes over her sister.

'An affair!' Heather yelped. 'I could have an affair! A last fling.'

The drink was talking, and as usual it was talking crap. 'Think about that tomorrow,' advised Billie, a geography teacher once more. 'Let's get back to the table. You've still got a surprise to come tonight.'

'It's perfect! A fling!' Heather fell back onto Billie. 'And I know just the man. Don't tell *her*,' she hissed, pointing at Angela who was now recalibrating her breasts in a mirror. 'She'd kill me, but he fancies me and he's gorgeous and he's decent and he's good and he's got to be better in bed than Dean.' She hiccupped.

'Too much information,' said Billie decisively, and propelled Heather back towards their VIP booth.

Checking her watch, Billie scanned the crowd. It was past midnight. Spartakiss was late: perhaps it was misguided to expect punctuality from a man who called himself Spartakiss but she felt she deserved some professionalism for her seventy pounds. 'You can't miss him,' the agent had promised. 'Six foot two and dressed as a Roman slave.'

Darting back to the loos, Billie pecked out the agency's number on her mobile, only to reach an answerphone. Tutting, she made her way back to the booth, suddenly cheered by the leering bellows coming from it. She guessed that her strippergram had arrived.

Oiled and gyrating, Spartakiss towered over the delirious hens, who were clapping and stamping as he removed a tiny suede loincloth to reveal an even tinier thong.

'Excellent bum,' thought Billie admiringly, as she inched through the crowd towards his back view. The excellent bum was wiggling plenty hard enough for seventy pounds of any woman's money, and the front view had evidently rehabilitated Heather's mood completely: the bride-to-be was being restrained from clambering up beside Spartakiss.

The bored agent had asked Billie if this was an 'all the way' booking. Billie had given this some thought: personally she had no need to see the regenerative organs of a complete stranger, but she'd guessed that a dozen drink-fuddled hens would feel cheated without a genital grand finale. 'Yes,' she'd said.

Inching onto the banquette beside Dot, Billie almost choked on the fog of drunken female desire. Dot, who was clapping out of time to Spartakiss's routine, shouted above the howls: 'He sheems a lovely man.'

The lovely man was inviting Heather to pull off his thong and she was being pushed towards Spartakiss by her friends. Yelling, 'No, no, I can't, I can't!' she was getting closer to the stripper all the same.

'*Off! Off! Off! Off!*' the pagan hens chanted. Even Dot was chanting, albeit quietly and with her head on the table.

Billie, now a geography teacher desperate to be liked by the fifth form, chanted too. '*Off! Off!*' she shouted, then, more wildly, '*On! On!*' She'd dragged her eyes up from Spartakiss's hard-working loins and had taken a proper look at his face in the glare of the glitter ball. '*Sly?*'

she yelped, and batted Heather's hand away from him: she hadn't seen her brother's machinery since they'd been bathed together twenty-seven years ago and now was not the time to discover how much he'd grown.

'*Oi!*' Heather shoved Billie away and grabbed for Sly's equipment.

Paralysed at hearing his name, Sly stopped in mid-grind as if somebody had pulled out his plug and stood, eyes locked on Billie's.

'What the hell is going on?' shouted Billie.

'*Yesssss!*' A communal hiss of triumph went up as Heather whipped off the thong. Sly cupped his manhood in his hands and leaped from the table. Hunched over, he darted through the throng.

'Get back here!' cried Billie, taking off after him.

Sly careered through the door of the Gents toilets, hotly pursued by Billie. An arm barred her way when she tried to follow him.

'I don't fink so,' said a bouncer.

'Please. I've got to talk to Spartakiss,' gabbled Billie.

'Yeah. Talk.' He turned Billie round by her shoulders.

'But . . .' Billie could think of no 'Buts' that would get her into the Gents, so she waited. She waited until it occurred to her to ask the bouncer if there was a way out through the loos.

'Yeah. You can get out to the car park.'

Surmising that Sly had stashed his clothes in the toilets, Billie realised she'd lost him. Dazed, she dragged her feet back to the table. They were still discussing her brother, in terms no sister wants to hear.

'The size of it!' Angela was marvelling. With the air of an expert, she slurred, 'You only normally see that kind of thing abroad.'

Heather looked as if she might cry, throw up, burst into song, or a mixture of all three. Leaning over, Billie whispered, 'Do you want me to get you home?'

Nodding, Heather let herself be extracted from the cackling hens, who now seemed to be moving with many limbs but just one brain, an amoeba on the pull. Gathering up Dot, Billie herded her two charges into a minicab.

'I'm gonna do it,' promised Heather, settling her head on Billie's tense shoulder. 'I'm gonna have 'im.'

'Who?' asked Billie.

'You know who,' leered Heather, her sentence clipped by a snore.

And suddenly Billie did. The only good-looking, decent man that appeared in the Venn diagram of Heather, Billie and Angela was Ed. My boyfriend, thought Billie, peering at her client. Heather had seemed very confident that Ed would take her up on her offer of a last fling.

'Are we in Kansas?' asked Dot.

TEN

ED'S PROPHECY was coming true. Billie hated his shift schedule. She hadn't reckoned on the fact that when he came off a night shift he would sleep the whole day. Monday rolled round and she still hadn't had a chance to kiss him insensible.

Leaving a penitent Dot in the shop—'I wasn't a total embarrassment at Shady Ladies, was I?'—Billie walked to Ruby's house to drop in some stiffened organza. As she waited for Ruby to answer the door, she couldn't help noting that his net curtains were dazzlingly clean.

'This is a surprise,' said Ruby, without a growl or a snuffle. He was as spotless as his curtains and he surprised Billie by inviting her in.

The house looked bright and inviting, not at all the dank pit she'd glimpsed the first time she'd knocked on the door. 'In here. We're just having afternoon tea.' Ruby preceded her into the dated kitchen, where Annie was setting out thin sandwiches on patterned china plates.

'Hello,' said Annie, looking coyly up from the magnificent spread that boasted a teapot and a tiered cake plate displaying fondant fancies.

This didn't look like two tailors hard at work. Billie looked from one to the other: Ruby and Annie both seemed to be trying not to giggle. Suddenly she was the oldest in the room and she had two naughty children on her hands. 'Ruby,' Billie began, 'do you want to explain that smudge of lipstick on your cheek?'

Ruby's hand flew to his face and he stared at Annie. They shared a wide-eyed moment before he said, 'You can be the first to know. After all, you brought us together. Annie has agreed to be my wife.'

Annie flinched at the scream that Billie unleashed, but she allowed herself to be kissed and hugged and then kissed again as Billie scattered congratulations. 'This is the best news ever!' she gasped.

'It's all down to you, young lady.' Ruby took her hand. 'Will you do us the honour of being a witness?'

'I'd be proud to.' Billie was trying to get away with wiping her eyes surreptitiously. 'When's the big day?'

Annie laughed, 'As soon as possible. We've booked the registry office for the 14th of August. There'll be no frills, no fuss. We can't afford them. But there's no sense in waiting.'

'I want her here. With me.' Ruby gazed across the fondant fancies at his fiancée, and she looked demurely down. He reached into his pocket and withdrew his wallet. 'Here's another twenty towards the dress.'

Taking it, Billie wanted to throw the notes in the air and yell, 'Have the dress for nothing!' but she knew that that wouldn't be acceptable to these pensionable lovebirds. She toasted their health with tea and left them as soon as she could. Any fool could tell they wanted to be alone.

As she made her way back to the shop, Billie thought about the messages she had left for her brother. She'd progressed from: *Please call me when you get this message* to: *Sly, you were waving your cock in public! I'd like an explanation!*

Being angry with her big bro didn't come easy. Sly was a pompous ass and a hard family act to follow, but he had always been a fixed point in her universe and she wanted him to stay that way.

When her mother had called on Sunday, Billie had tried some discreet probing, but nothing revealing had been gleaned.

By Friday there was still no response from Sly. Telling Ed how she encountered her brother naked on a table top made a good story as they strolled, entwined, along the front in the kind dusk. Listening to Ed hoot, Billie felt hollow.

'Anyway,' she said, lightly and without emphasis as they approached the Sailor's Lament, 'what have you been up to?'

Maybe it wasn't as light as she thought, because Ed's dark face clouded and he asked, uneasily, 'What do you mean? Up to?'

'Calm down!' laughed Billie. 'I'm not the FBI. How has work been?'

'Fine. Quiet. The usual.' He shook off her grasp and held her at arm's length. 'The boys were right.'

The boys, Billie knew, were seldom right when it came to their mates' girlfriends. 'What have they been saying?' she asked dubiously.

'That I've got to watch myself,' smirked Ed. 'Going out with a bird who runs a wedding shop.' He puffed out his cheeks. 'Gotta be careful. You sound like a wife, checking up on me.'

Perhaps he hadn't been listening properly when she'd told him The Story. She frowned. Ed had misunderstood a fundamental detail about her. 'Now, listen,' she began, all lightness of touch forgotten.

'Oh shush, I'm only teasing.' Ed smothered her with a hug, cutting off her defence. He kissed her ear, and whispered, 'Although, remember, you did try to introduce me to your folks the other night.'

That wasn't fair. 'No,' Billie protested, feeling this was important stuff to get right while still in those relationship foothills. When Ed kissed her neck, he accidentally located her amnesia zone and she gave up defending herself and got on with some serious canoodling.

Later, walking home along the dark, breezy front, sharing freshly made chips, Billie squeezed Ed's broad back. 'We're having the archetypal seaside romance. Just like couples did back in the Fifties.'

'Right down to the last detail.' Ed lifted an eyebrow down at her in the yellowy umbrella of a flickering street lamp.

Billie knew what he meant. 'Soon,' she heard herself say. Not, 'Now!' But, 'Soon.' Lunging for and securing a particularly big chip, she asked fearfully, 'Are you sick of waiting for me?'

'We're only getting to know each other,' said Ed, reassuringly. 'Don't be daft.' And then they got to know each other some more on a bench.

The first phone call of Saturday was, predictably, Heather. 'You're sure the bridesmaids' satin pumps are light lilac and not medium mauve?'

'As sure as when you called me last night,' said Billie. 'Chill out.'

'Chill!' yelped Heather. 'Out! I still have eight pounds to lose!'

'The dress will look awful if you're too thin,' warned Billie.

'Thanks.' A stifled sob could be heard as the phone slammed down.

'Gee, ain't weddings just magical,' grimaced Billie to the empty shop. She stiffened as Debs arrived. Partly because the till had still been twenty-two pounds down last Saturday despite keeping Debs away from it. And partly because Debs had a head full of hair extensions.

'Your hair's nice,' Billie managed to say.

'Ta.' Debs did not seem to need Billie's approval.

'What happened at Shady Ladies?' coughed Billie. 'You disappeared.'

'Yeah, I did.' Debs chewed a hair extension and leaned against a shelf that needed dusting. A middle-aged woman wandered in and Debs asked loudly, 'Do you want me to do 'er?' then dragged her feet across the shop floor to enquire, 'You the bride? Or the mother?'

Watching her, Billie's dilemma sharpened. Money was disappearing. A showdown was inevitable. Even if Billie discounted the thieving, there was the timekeeping, the belligerence, the rudeness.

A hair extension had detached itself from Debs's head, and lay across the counter. Billie prodded it gingerly. How, she wondered, could Debs afford such luxuries? Great-Aunty Babs's exhortation to 'keep an eye on Debs' was taking on a very different hue.

As Billie was trying Sly's number yet again, Dot turned up.

'Dot,' began Billie uncertainly, guiding her out to the kitchenette by the elbow. 'I think Debs might be stealing from the till,' she whispered. 'Did Great-Aunty Babs ever mention anything about having suspicions?'

'Babs loves Debs,' said Dot. 'Debs is part of this place.'

'And I suspect she takes part of this place home with her at night.'

'She has a lot on her plate,' said Dot, quietly.

A familiar face disrupted this lopsided character analysis. 'Hello there!' Billie recognised one of 'her' brides. 'How's married life?'

The sixteen-year-old's face looked different without her scowl. She was a rosy, sunny girl today. 'It's great. I wanted to, you know, thank you. You made me feel special, and then the wedding was brilliant. It was the best day of my life.'

'You've made my day,' beamed Billie. 'No, my week.'

'I can't bear to put away my dress and my headdress. It feels funny to put them in the loft when they've only been worn once.'

'S'pose so,' said Billie sympathetically, remembering that she had drop-kicked her tiara into the hotel swimming pool. She sat up, animated by sudden inspiration. 'I've just thought of a way they could be a part of somebody else's big day as well.'

After the teen bride had left, Billie dug out the customers' address book. Maybe Annie was going to get a few frills after all.

A queue, excitable, lively, and on the whole no taller than three feet, snaked down the street from the door of the bookshop. Inside, the book-cluttered room was dominated by large posters of Sam.

Beneath the posters sat the hero of the massed abbreviated humans.

His hair a jagged white pineapple above their curls and ponytails and Alice bands, Sam was signing book after book. The dim interior of the cosy shop hadn't moved him to ditch the dark glasses, and the leather collar of his jacket was turned defiantly, moodily, Fonzily up.

Plucking a hardback of *Tiddlywinks and the Naughty Ragdoll* from a teetering pile, Billie joined the queue, looking round for Heather and her godchild. Billie had made a loose arrangement to meet them. Perhaps, she thought, they'd already been.

Another reason for the kids to pogo and yelp was the presence of Tiddlywinks himself. Six foot of grey velvet, with buttons for eyes and a nose of hard black plastic, Tiddlywinks waddled round his weeny fans.

Nearing the top of the queue, Billie witnessed Sam's technique with his diminutive worshippers.

'Name?' he'd bark, like an eastern European border guard. Having scribbled rapidly in his incomprehensible hand, Sam held out the book between two fingers as if it was diseased. 'Enjoy. Next.'

Finally at the head of the queue, Billie laid her book down.

'Name?' Defeated, Sam didn't even lift his head.

'Wilhelmina Baskerville. Aged four.'

The glasses were snatched off. Sam lifted tired eyes to hers, suddenly full of gratitude and hope. 'A person!' he gasped. 'At last.'

'Come on, sign,' chided Billie.

Having scratched a few words on the title page, Sam swivelled *Tiddlywinks and the Naughty Ragdoll* round for her to read: *Create diversion (poss set fire Tiddlywinks) & regroup in pub.* 'There's a tenner in it for you,' he hissed.

'Try and be brave,' laughed Billie. 'I'd do anything to have this kind of adoration in my life.'

'Short-arsed groupies,' he sneered. 'I sold my soul for this.'

'Take a leaf out of Tiddlywinks's book.' Billie gestured at the man-sized soft toy bounding about, a crocodile of children tailing him.

'Oi! Tiddlywinks!' Sam beckoned him over. In a low voice that only Billie and the 'resting' actor imprisoned in eight metres of furnishing fabric could hear, he menaced, 'You are a toy rabbit, not a clubber. You're making me look bad. Tone it down, OK?'

Off sloped Tiddlywinks, self-esteem trampled.

'You weren't kidding when you warned me you were hard to like,' murmured Billie, picking up her book and turning away.

'You love me, though,' said Sam, taking the next eagerly proffered book. Ignoring the shiny-faced tot grinning up at him he asked Billie's back, 'Don't you?'

Without turning round, Billie admitted with a regretful smile, 'For some reason I can't fathom, yes, Sam, I do.'

The fire station was an angular shed of a building on the road that led to Heather's housing estate. A couple of hours after having her book signed and now AWOL once more from the Saturday crush of Billie's Brides, Billie felt guilt as she approached it. She'd hastily pinched her cheeks and pulled the straps of her camisole down to achieve a wanton look: her plan was to ask to see Ed and then kidnap him for a snog down an alleyway before scuttling back to her dream-peddling duties.

The territory was against her: Billie could see no alleyway. She would have to content herself with smouldering at him in the reception area.

Except there was no reception area. Discouraged, Billie was on the verge of leaving, when two fire-fighters stepped outside. 'All right?' shouted one of them across the primly clipped front lawn.

'Chugger!' Billie was glad to see Debs's paramour. 'Can you tell Ed I'm here? I want a quick word.'

'Ed? He finished as I came on,' said Chugger. 'A good hour ago.'

'You sure?' Nothing about this saucy visit was going right. 'I thought . . .' Then she realised: book signings were probably low on Ed's agenda. 'Thanks, anyway.'

So Ed fibbed to get out of meeting her friends. That wasn't so nice. Disappointed, and feeling mug-like, Billie headed back to the shop.

There were no customers, but the ranks had been swelled by Zelda, who had thoughtfully brought Raven for a visit. Billie didn't want to know. 'I'll be upstairs, tackling the VAT,' she lied.

Shopfloor chatter drifted up as Billie tried Sly's number again without success. Sighing, she flicked open her laptop. Expecting to find an email reply from a company that had let her down over a delivery of stockings, she 'Oh'ed in surprise as she opened up a message from James. 'Blimey.' It was *long*. She scanned the first few lines:

Re: your VAT problem. I think I know the answer. Let me begin by explaining the basic premise of Value Added Tax.

And that's what he did. At length.

'Thank God,' breathed Billie when she reached the end, 'for firemen.'
She pressed REPLY:

> Thanks for the VAT advice. I shall fill in my forms exactly as you suggest so
> hopefully I won't get thrown in prison anytime soon. How come I understand
> VAT when you describe it, but go all cross-eyed when I read the leaflets? If
> only you could deal with other aspects of my life so succinctly. Like whether or
> not my Saturday girl is nibbling at the profits. And whether or not I'm ready to
> get serious with the fireman. It feels right, but I'm out of practice and a bit
> scared. Well, very scared. Oh, just ignore me, James.

Billie pressed SEND then ventured downstairs, where all was calm.
She crossed to the till and checked the takings. They were twenty-one
pounds short. In response to the eloquent plea in Dot's eyes, Billie paid
Debs at home time and said nothing, but once the girl had gone she
warned her assistant, 'Dot, I *have* to tackle Debs soon.'

A man who can look sexy playing crazy golf is a man worth hanging
on to. Ed was just such a man. He even bought the ice creams afterwards. His post tutti-frutti lips planted strange but thrilling cold kisses
on Billie's neck and she wriggled ecstatically. It was a good Sunday.

They'd met at nine on Saturday night and the evening had been
clouded by dark imaginings, gradually chased away by Ed's behaviour.
He was so attentive and fond that she felt ashamed of her suspicions
and had relaxed. But she'd gone to sleep untinkered-with again.

Now, as the sun drowned in the bay at the end of the weekend, Ed,
snuggled up to Billie on Herbert's verandah, confessed, 'I used to think
Sam was your boyfriend, you know.'

Billie laughed. 'I've got entirely the wrong equipment for him.'

'I was well chuffed when I found out he was a bender.' Ed paused,
then said, as if risking it, 'And a twat.'

Billie elbowed him in the ribs. 'Oi, he's one of my very best friends
and he's not a twat.'

She wanted to add that she didn't think 'bender' was the right word
to apply to a beautiful and manly man like Sam, but she took the
coward's way out and absolved Ed on the grounds of working with men
all day: his vocabulary was bound to be a bit crude. Besides, she was
perversely glad that he'd admitted his dislike of Sam: now she had a
credible motive for his fib about his shift.

Hi Billie,

I'm really flattered that you think I have potential as an Agony Uncle, but I can't agree with you. I'm not the right person to advise you about getting 'serious' with your fireman. Sorry! If it feels right, just do it—that's the best I can come up with.

Hope you're well. Me and the significant other have just booked a short trip to Marrakesh.

Love, James

He'd upgraded his sign-off to 'love', Billie noticed. Perhaps it was to soften the blow that the rest of his email could be paraphrased as: *Are you mad, woman? Don't involve me in your love life. It's like asking your murderer to say a few words at your funeral!*

'Marra-bloody-kesh,' she muttered to herself as she bounded down the stairs in response to Dot's: 'Your mobile's ringing!'

At long last. Grabbing the phone greedily, Billie couldn't keep the irritation out of her voice. 'About time, bro. What's going on?'

'I can't believe you were there,' he began. 'The booking was in the bride's name, you see.'

'*You* can't believe *I* was there!' echoed Billie unhelpfully.

'I thought you never ventured out of Sole Bay these days.'

'I get let out occasionally, Spartakiss.' Billie was surprised at her own annoyance. 'Why are you dancing on tables?'

'If you must know,' Sly sounded peevish, as if he'd hoped she could be fobbed off. 'I'm broke. Bust. Kaput.'

'Pardon?' For the first time in many years Billie used one of her mother's preferred words.

'Inner Winner Incorporated collapsed weeks ago. Nobody knows. Except you. And my bank manager.'

'And Sana, obviously.'

'Well, no,' Sly admitted. 'I've been protecting her.'

'Lying to her, you mean. Please don't tell me you pretend to go to work every day?'

'As far as she's concerned I've still got the office and I still travel to organise seminars.'

Billie asked, 'Where were you on Mum's first night?'

'I was at a twenty-first birthday party in Brighton.'

'As Spartakiss?'

'No. That night I was the Horny Highwayman.'

'Sly, you can't keep this up. Stripping can't be nearly as well paid as, er, guru-ing.'

'Billie, I'm going to lose everything. The house. The private schools. The holidays.' Sly sounded defeated. He had located his Inner Loser. 'I've failed. I'm going to lose the whole fabulous lifestyle I've built up.'

'Success isn't just about money.' Billie had never noticed anything 'fabulous' about the lifestyle Sly promoted: a better car, a bigger house, a longer job title. 'There's more than one way to be fabulous.'

'Sana will leave me the moment she finds out.'

'That's not true. Tell her, Sly. Tell her today. She deserves to know. I bet you any amount of money you like that she surprises you. Sana is made of stern stuff.'

'You think so?' Sly was asking her opinion. On an important issue.

'I honestly think so. Besides, you can't go on like this for ever, leading the silliest double life in the history of double lives.'

'You're right.'

Another first. 'You'll tell her?'

'I'll tell her,' said Sly with his beautifully modulated motivating voice.

'Attaboy, Spartakiss.'

'**B**y the way, Ivanka rang,' Dot said. 'Reckons you can have her veil for Annie. We have to collect it. Said she's on honeymoon in the Swan and she's not leaving room service for anything.'

Billie picked up her trusty fake Gucci bag and headed out.

The receptionist at the Swan, Sole Bay's celebrated old coaching inn which sat, sure of itself, on one side of the main square, rolled her eyes when Billie asked for Ivanka.

Announcing herself with a surly, 'You! Lady at desk! Please to change the bed in my suite. It is hard, like bloody coffin,' the new Mrs Clifford Larkin appeared. Wearing a cantilevered feather-trimmed negligée, she approached Billie, holding out an exquisite veil. 'This is for penniless bat you speak of,' she said, bored already.

'I'm so grateful, Ivanka.' Billie folded the veil. 'How's married life?'

Ivanka lowered her voice, 'Tell me. Is possible to die from sex? If you are oldish man?' She sighed, then whined, 'Oh, don't bother. I know answer. *Nothing* will kill him. Is just my luck.' She peered out through the undulating ancient glass in the front window of the Swan. 'Vot is happening out there? Everyone running about like blue-arse fly.'

A giddily excited boy stuck his head round the main door. 'The Galleon's on fire! It's brilliant!' he yelled, before dodging out again.

'A ship on fire?' Ivanka was puzzled.

'A tea shop,' Billie clarified. 'The old timbered one across the square.'

Reception emptied as everybody dashed out into the sunshine. Tea-shop customers, some clutching Pyrex cups of tea, stood about, gazing back into the little tea room that was now the centre of attention.

The fire was pulling in the crowds. Billie saw Dot near the front of the semicircle keeping a respectful distance from the Galleon, and pushed through the onlookers to reach her. Ivanka, bouncing along behind in her negligée was nearly as fascinating as the fire to gentlemen in the crowd of a certain age.

Billie had never been so close to a real conflagration. From halfway across the cobbles, she felt as if her nose was melting. Flames quivered and jumped in the heart of the building.

Her hand to her mouth, Dot was white despite the heat. 'Jakey sometimes has a reviving doughnut in the Galleon. What if he . . .'

On the far side of Dot, Zelda's expression could be translated by any casual observer as, 'Would that be so bad?' Frowning at her, Billie put an arm round Dot. 'He'll be safe somewhere,' she said, confident of Jake's self-preservation skills. 'In fact . . . there he is!' Billie pointed him out on the other side of the square, sketching the fire, a doughnut clenched between his teeth. Beside him stood Debs.

Behind Jake and Debs, Sam, shades firmly on, was watching the free show, too. He waved at Billie. This close, the fire was awe-inspiring. She could sense its power as it doubled and redoubled.

Billie trotted through Ed's schedule in her mind. She was almost certain he was on duty. The fire, more visible now, showing off by pushing out a window here and spitting out a jet of sparks there, seemed too formidable for mere men to tackle. She hoped she was wrong about Ed's shift. Wryly she recalled that she'd been wrong before.

A banshee wail announced the arrival of the fire engine. It braked on the cobbles and spat out a handful of fireman. Their sudden activity added to the tumult and townspeople backed away to make space.

A figure strode round the engine, his face obscured by breathing apparatus. Billie would know that bottom anywhere, even in yellow waterproofs. '*Ed!*' she shouted. All at once, the drama was very real.

'Is your boyfriend?' queried Ivanka, squinting over at Ed.

'Yeah,' whimpered Billie.

'Can I interest you in swap for Clifford?' Ivanka showed all her expensive crowns in an operatic laugh. 'Only joking!' she yelled.'

Ed's trained. He'll be fine, Billie assured herself. There was a fresh purpose to the way he and two of his colleagues were double-checking their breathing apparatus: she could sense that this was it.

Suddenly, the three fire-fighters made for the Galleon's narrow doorway. All chatter stilled, as if by decree. Every eye stayed on that dark slit as the crowd waited for the men to reappear.

Standing alongside time, Billie's next few minutes seemed to take a year, ticking off on some slow, cold clock of their own. The fire belched and gulped and carried on, gleefully devouring the dry old bones of the poor tea shop. Every now and then a loud thump sounded, as the red and gold flames, insolently leaping out of the windows, ate away at a framework that had survived Henry VIII, two World Wars and the advent of reality television. Sole Bay held its breath but the doorway remained empty, and the fire staggered drunkenly on.

And suddenly there they were. The three firemen trotted out into the square, tearing off their masks. 'Clear!' shouted Ed.

A burst of applause competed thunderously with the flames. A bubble of relief and pride broke in Billie's throat and she could breathe again. Beside her, Dot was, of course, sobbing. Even Zelda dabbed her eyes and popped some fudge.

Milling around the fire engine, fire-fighters unfurled a giant hose, and yelled incomprehensible instructions to each other. Busy, focused, they seemed unfazed by the danger.

A shrill cry made the crowd turn. '*Peter!*' Bobbing up and down on her mobility vehicle, old Mrs Davis was pointing up at the stricken building. '*My Peter!*'

All eyes followed her arthritic finger up to where Mrs Davis's terrier was framed in a jagged window opening. He looked as though he might jump.

Shielding Dot's eyes—it would take years of hot chocolate and whale music to rehabilitate her if she witnessed a canine suicide—Billie looked up at Peter, horrified at his predicament.

Her gaze clicked to Ed. Like everybody else in Sole Bay, he knew how Mrs Davis felt about Peter. The dog was her constant companion.

Ed was staring over at Mrs Davis, hyperventilating on her vehicle.

Billie was already whispering, '*Don't,*' as Ed pushed the breathing gear back over his face, ignored the shouts from his mates and raced back through the coffin-shaped door of the tea shop.

A cheer, louder than the fire, louder than the blood beating in Billie's ears, went up. It was a cheer worthy of England winning the 1966 World Cup, but it was all for a tall, staggering figure clutching a sooty three-legged dog in his arms.

'He's a hero!' burbled Dot, jumping up and down, while Zelda took the opportunity to smother Mr Dyke in a fleshy embrace. The whole of Sole Bay seemed to be dancing, but Billie stood very still as Ed delivered Peter safely to a weeping Mrs Davis.

Tearing the safety mask from his face, Ed crossed the square in a handful of strides. The sea of people parted as if he was a modern-day Moses, and Ed made straight for Billie. Without speaking, he took her face in both his blackened hands and kissed her full and hard on the lips. Then, he turned and marched back to his crew.

Staring dumbly after him, her face smudged with black, Billie supposed that she might as well die right now, as she would never top this.

A couple of candles lit the darkness of Herbert's Dream II. Hugging her knees on the iron bed, Billie lost herself in their flickering prettiness. Her thoughts were formless and flirty, like the shadows dancing on the boarded walls. Neither happy nor sad, she felt *right*. She was the right temperature, in the right place, waiting for the right man.

A tap sounded at the window. Her face lit up. He'd come, just as she'd known he would.

Ed was framed in the door. 'For once, you've got to let me say it. My hero,' she whispered. She reached out her arms and he bent into her hug. She could smell his shampoo. It excited her more than any cologne.

The expected tearing-off of her (deliberately) flimsy clothes didn't happen. Ed freed himself and sat at the little picnic table. 'Got any beer?' he asked.

This was deviating from the script. 'Well, no,' said Billie. She wrapped her arms round him. 'I thought we'd . . .'

Coldly, Ed shrugged her off. 'What is all this?' he snapped, bursting her candlelit bubble.

'Don't you want to . . .' Billie blushed. 'After today, I thought we could . . .' She looked over at the bed, meaningfully.

'You want to shag a hero, is that it?' Ed stepped back.

'It wouldn't be a shag,' Billie suddenly hated that word. 'I want us to make love, yes. Don't you?'

'I want to have sex with you. *You.*' Ed stabbed his finger at her viciously. 'Not some fucking fairy tale. I was doing my job. I'm not a hero. It was a dog. A dog with three sodding legs. And I got bollocked for going in on my own and putting the guys in danger.' He looked at Billie, almost pleading. 'If you say I'm nice or a hero once more, Billie, I swear I'll . . .'

'I won't, I won't!' promised Billie placatingly.

Ed exhaled exhaustedly. 'I'm being a bastard, Billie, I know. Days like today . . .' He closed his eyes. 'I don't have the right words. All I can tell you is that they make me feel funny. Not proud. Not happy. Kind of hollow.' He looked at her. 'Sad, if I'm honest.'

'I think I understand,' Billie said, carefully. 'We can just sit and chat. We don't have to do anything saucy.'

Ed smiled. He looked devilish. 'Come here,' he said.

'Are you sure?'

'Are you going to come here or do I have to come and get you?'

'I rather suspect you're going to have to come and get me.'

Billie flung herself back on to the bed. She was swiftly followed by Ed, and for the next few hours the little iron bed proved itself to be the bargain of a lifetime.

It was just a four-minute walk to work but in Billie's head it was a fully choreographed Technicolor Hollywood musical with lights, music and extras. She could have danced through the bandstand, swung from the lamp posts, pirouetted past the shops, with a special tap solo for the gutted tea shop, before running, leaping and jumping down Little Row to the front door of Billie's Brides. The song in her head had limited lyrics, and they scanned and rhymed abominably, but to Billie's ears they were sweeter than anything *The Sound of Music* had to offer: 'My boyfriend is Ed—at last we went to bed—he's even sexier than I thought—and I thought he was very sexy indeeeeeeeeeeeed!'

As she unlocked the door, snapshots of the previous evening flashed in her head. The kissing, the nuzzling, the delicious lingering had been

worth the wait. Ed put out fires for a living, but even he'd been surprised by the one he'd started in the beach hut last night.

'Don't do that with anybody else but me for the rest of your life,' he'd
told her, as he kissed her goodbye.

'Careful,' Billie had chided him. 'Don't go all silly on me.'

Now, picking up the post, Billie felt a bit silly herself. She would
allow herself one morning's mooning about, one morning's member-
ship of the girlie club that insisted on drawing hearts with arrows
through them and looking up his star sign, but that was all. Her soul
was still ring-fenced.

She was glad she'd waited, and even gladder she'd stopped waiting.
Making love with Ed had brought them closer, she could feel it.

James would want to know the latest, she told herself. He'd be glad
that she'd decided to 'get serious': there was no need to be more spe-
cific. James wanted her to be happy, and no, of course she wasn't typing
out a long, detailed description of Ed's daring rescue just to rub in how
gorgeous, brave, sexy and—she could use the word when Ed wasn't
around—*heroic* her boyfriend was. She just wanted to put him in con-
text. He wasn't a doctor; he was tons better than a dull old doctor.

One pair of white elbow-length gloves had already been sold before
Billie remembered to check the answerphone. Bracing herself for a slew
of Heatheresque demands, she pressed PLAY. The voice she heard was
quite unlike Heather's. 'Ah. You're not there.' The deep, hoarse, evidently elderly man sounded dismayed. 'Can you hear me? If I speak,
will you get this?' She recognised Ruby's signature mix of rudeness and
politeness. 'Billie, dear, I can't deliver the finished dress today. I'm afraid
we've had bad news. I'll be spending the day at the hospital with Annie.
Now what do I do? Does one say goodbye? Or over and out—'

The merciless machine cut Ruby off, leaving Billie staring at it.

Shoulders sagging in his bespoke suit fashionable forty years ago,
Ruby asked, 'How did she look to you?'

They were on a bench outside the hospital. A few feet away traffic
thundered along the main road, belching fumes over the demoralised
flower beds. Neeveston felt a million miles away from Sole Bay.

'Small,' said Billie, truthfully. Annie's head had been a little apostro-
phe on the pillow, barely denting it. She'd lain with her eyes closed,
as if unwilling to take in what was happening to her. 'Where is the

tumour?' That word felt clunky and angular in her mouth.

'Her stomach.' Ruby sounded angry. 'Those fools can't even tell me if it's benign or the other thing.'

'They're doing their best.' Billie decided never to use the word 'malignant' in Ruby's hearing: if he couldn't face it, she wouldn't force him to.

'Apparently, they open her up,' he grimaced at the phrase. 'Once she's strong enough. My poor girl's anaemic, you see. And they remove the . . . the thing, and do a biop-whatchamacallit. The damn results won't be in until the next day.'

'We've got to think positive, Ruby.' Billie was adamant.

'Positive?' scoffed the old man. 'I wait seventy-eight years for something good and when it comes along—psssssssfft!'

'We'll get through it.'

'I tell you this right here and now.' Ruby's gnarled old face was shaking with emotion. 'If that lady has to suffer, I'll never set foot in a synagogue again. And if she goes,' he looked Billie defiantly in the eye. 'I go.'

'It won't come to that.' This was that mushy, flabby talk that Billie railed against, but she didn't know what else to offer in the face of Ruby's fears. 'You're getting married. You have plans. We won't let a silly old tumour mess that up.'

'Didn't you hear the date of the operation?' Ruby sounded almost triumphant, as if long-held suspicions about God's sarcasm were being proved. 'That's right. The day of the wedding.'

Groaning inwardly, Billie just clutched his arm tighter. 'You and Annie are getting married. It'll just be a little later than planned. Hang on to that.'

It was hard telling Dot the news about Annie because they had to keep breaking off for her to sniffle, gasp or squeak, 'No, not Annie!'

'She's not going to die,' declared Billie. 'I won't let her. She's going to be all right and she's going to get married and that's that.'

'Yes.' Billie's certainty seemed to be catching. 'Annie is not *allowed* to die!'

'Exactly.' Billie paused. 'She still owes us for that wedding dress.' She flicked Dot with a veil. 'Don't look at me as if I just ate Julia. I have to be cynical, it's how I am.' Billie knew it would help her get through. She looked at her watch. 'Nip off and see Annie, if you like. Give Ruby a break. We're going to have to be Annie's family, Dot.'

Dot nodded. As she was leaving, she reminded Billie to ring Heather. 'She sounded agitated.'

Billie dialled Heather's mobile.

Confusingly, Dean picked up. More confusingly, he said, 'Heather?'

'No, no, Dean, it's Billie. What's going on?'

'She's gone.' Dean sounded stunned. 'She's left me.' He gulped. 'The wedding's off.'

ELEVEN

PERHAPS BILLIE'S MOTHER was right to worry constantly. The last few hours had certainly borne out the perils of being too happy. The post-coital glow had been chased from Billie's cheeks, and she looked back to that morning as a golden era of carefree joy when the only concern she'd had was whether to straddle Ed on the floor or the bed. That reminded her: she needed a new picnic table. There had been casualties in among the yelps of pleasure.

Speed-walking on wedge sandals is tricky, but Billie was heading for the sea as fast as she could. She knew exactly where to find the Missing Presumed Bonkers bride, and as she neared the neglected bandstand she could make out a lanky shape in the shadows.

Leaning back against the central pillar, a cut-price French Lieutenant's Woman, was Heather. She'd wrapped her long arms round herself like the sleeves of a straitjacket. 'Go away,' she murmured, as Billie climbed the rotting wooden steps.

'Good afternoon to you, too.' Billie put her hands on her hips and looked at Heather. She'd known a girl just like her once: herself. Except Billie had kept all the angst and fear and disillusion inside, whereas Heather was externalising it nicely. 'Got to you, then, all this nonsense?'

With a flash of her customary arrogance, Heather said, 'I know what you're here for. I'm not going back. The wedding's off.'

'Dean deserves to know why.'

'He knows. Deep down.'

'Is it to do with the fling you were threatening?' Billie couldn't help remembering that Ed's mysterious absence from his shift had coincided with Heather's no-show at the book signing. 'Have you fallen for somebody else?'

Heather snorted. 'I got turned down, didn't I? In front of quite an audience. Surprised you haven't heard all about it from that stinky boyfriend of Dot's. It's nothing to do with another man. It's about me. I want to see the world. I want to sow my wild whatsits.'

'Go on, then.' Billie folded her arms. 'Cancel it. I'll do it all for you. You don't have to lift a finger.'

'Good.' Heather was looking at Billie out of the corner of her eye.

'The world won't end. Tall buildings won't crumble. Sole Bay won't fall into the sea. Life does not stop at the end of your nose, Heather.'

'Hang on,' began Heather, straightening up a little.

Ignoring her, Billie trundled on. 'This wedding has been your life for the past few months, but for most people it's just an invite perched on their mantelpiece and a last-minute panic about whether or not to have their matching dress and jacket dry-cleaned. You need to get things in perspective.' Billie's tone heated up a little. 'I just left a sick woman in Neeveston Hospital. She's planning to get married . . . if she lives. That'll be a wedding of love and devotion, and it won't matter a bit whether the bride's bouquet matches the bridesmaid's eczema.'

Heather's unconcerned expression was unconvincing.

'So go on, break Dean's heart. Destroy something, if you feel the need. He'll survive. I know that from experience. But he'll be changed for ever.' She swallowed. 'And so will you.'

Achieving quite a stomp on the bandstand steps, Billie left her client alone. Billie hoped that Heather had recognised the pompous, ill-thought-out speech as coming directly from her heart.

'**P**oo,' said Billie. Ed's mobile was on voicemail. A plump plop of rain hit her in the middle of her forehead. She was dashing towards Billie's Brides to appropriate some of the stock: it had been a long time since she'd felt the need for fishnets. White ones would have to do.

More raindrops followed the advance party, which had already fluffed up Billie's hair to Ronald McDonald proportions. She scurried to the shop, and let herself in.

Having successfully rifled the stockings drawer, and put the right money in the till, Billie's shoulders slumped as she gathered up her bag. It looked as if a disaster movie was being filmed in Little Row. The rain lashed viciously down, bouncing high off the pavement. With no umbrella, Billie was forced to sit in the dimly lit shop and gaze out at the deluge, trying Ed every couple of minutes to no avail.

Bored, she remembered her laptop. As she'd expected, there was an email from James. It made her smile. He was impressed with Ed.

That kind of bravery is a mystery to me. I'm not sure if I could rescue my own mother. Hang on to this guy. He sounds like one in a million. We've moved on, haven't we, Billie? That's a good thing, isn't it?

The beep of her mobile phone made her jump, and the sight of the word 'ED' in caller ID made her slam shut her laptop and forget all about James. 'Hello,' she said seductively.

'You've been calling?' Utterly unseductive, Ed was surrounded by the telltale noises of the fire station.

'You're at work,' pouted Billie, plans scuppered. She changed tack, lowering her voice to a sultry purr. 'Here I am, all alone, thinking about you and what I'd like to do to you, and you're at work.'

'Ye-es.' Ed seemed to have caught her drift. 'So behave yourself.'

'But I want to be naughty,' she growled, trying not to laugh. Countless magazine articles were adamant that men loved this play-acting stuff. 'I want to be verrrrrry naughty.' Were those trilled Rs too much?

'Do you now?' Apparently not, if the hoarse interest in Ed's voice was anything to go by.

'Will you punish me if I'm a bad, bad girl?' To her own ears she sounded educationally subnormal, but it had the desired effect.

'Just you wait,' he warned.

The storm outside was flexing its muscles. The heavy clouds bullying each other above Sole Bay darkened the streets, even though it was only seven o'clock. Not ready to go home, she turned up, bedraggled and wet, at Dot's door. 'I could do with some company,' she explained when Dot dragged the door open.

'I know what you mean,' said Dot with a wide, sympathetic smile. 'Come in and get dry. Jake's just made some delicious soup.'

Soup à la Jake had the consistency of wet cement, but rather less flavour. Luckily, Billie couldn't really see it, as the electricity had flickered and died just as she walked through the door. Jake was of the opinion that it was connected to Billie's arrival, and the electromagnetism of female eroticism, but she preferred the more prosaic probability that the bad weather had caused problems with the supply.

The kitchen defied Billie's theory about candles: it was *not* improved by their influence. The dark corners grew and shrank boisterously, offering glimpses of the jagged junk that Jake accumulated.

Even Dot seemed affected. She was quiet, and her face had a sewn-up look to it. She was making no attempt to big up the dismal soup.

'So how's the big love affair?' Jake asked, leaning back on his chair to survey Billie through half-closed eyes. 'Wonderful? Marvellous?'

'I wouldn't use any of those words,' said Billie, as pleasantly as she could. 'It's fine, thanks. I'm enjoying getting to know him.'

'Good. I'm happy for you.' This sounded as likely as if Jake had said, 'I am a part-time model for Calvin Klein.'

'Thank you.' It was best not to provoke Jake. As Billie took another slurp of her muddy main course, she learned she didn't have to.

'He might surprise you, you know.' Jake's tone implied that this surprise wouldn't be a nice one. 'I've seen him with somebody that might surprise you.' He grinned, a proper happy grin. Breaking people's hearts cheered him up, apparently. 'Getting very cosy.'

'I know all about it.' Billie stayed calm. She felt furious at this man's need to drag her down, but his tepid revelations about Ed and Heather couldn't hurt her. 'Sorry to disappoint you,' she couldn't help adding.

'Oh.' Jake was no actor: his dismay showed. Even his beard drooped. He pushed his plate away and retreated to an only partly eviscerated soft chair on the fringes of the candles' reach.

A tile slipped off the roof and landed in the garden with a splashy crash. Dot jerked her head upright and Billie was alarmed to see real fright in her eyes.

'It's only a tile,' said Billie, soothingly.

'I hate rain like this,' said Dot through gritted teeth.

'It's just water.' Jake's sulky voice drifted over from his shadowy chair.

'I do know what rain is,' said Dot, veering closer to irritation than Billie had ever witnessed. 'My mum always told us it was a night like this, a really filthy night, when she was abandoned.' She bit a nail. 'Bad things happen on nights like this.'

Shivering slightly, Billie frowned. 'Stop it, Dot. I'm getting spooked.'

'Sorry.' Dot's face mellowed. 'I think the whole Annie and Ruby thing is getting to me. I don't know whether to hope for the best or . . .'

From the armchair, came a flat voice, 'We all die. We must all face death alone.'

'I had a chat with the nurse,' said Dot. 'She told me that the operation itself is quite an ordeal for somebody like Annie.'

'You mean there's a chance she might never wake up?' Billie wanted to run from that much-too-real thought. 'That would kill Ruby.'

'They wouldn't even be married.' Dot sighed.

Like a spider, Jake unbent his body to lean into the circle of light. 'You can gas on about this as much as you like, but if she dies, she dies.'

'We love Annie,' protested Billie, hearing the tiny cry that Dot made. 'We need to talk about her.'

'Love,' Jake sneered. 'You don't love her. You hardly know her.'

Galvanised, Dot said in a shaky voice, 'We're all she's got. Our shop gave her something to hope and plan for. And we introduced her to Ruby. Maybe we do hardly know her but I know how I feel, and I love her, in my own way.'

Jake was silent, his face unreadable in the gloom.

So was Billie. She'd never witnessed Dot standing up to him like that.

Turning to Billie with glassy eyes, Dot changed the subject. 'I saw Dean on my way home. He was very pale. Looked all confused. Jilting is a terrible thing to do to anybody. I hope they get back together.'

'Hmm.' Billie tried not to sound as if she agreed or disagreed. Perhaps the pain Heather was spreading around was preferable to years of a bad marriage. Look at her and James: they both knew they'd had a close escape. She was at last believing there was life after jilt. But then she thought of Dean and what he'd be going through.

'Why should you care?' asked Jake. 'Or do you love them, too?'

At that moment, a loud clap of thunder boomed over the cottage. Dot leapt to her feet, her hands over her ears, and the back door crashed open. In ran Julia, clucking as if her tail feathers were on fire.

'Julia!' shrieked Dot, trying to catch her feathery friend.

Another clap of thunder seemed to rock the whole house, driving Julia behind a basket of dolls' heads and Jake to his feet.

'It's you!' he screeched, his face gaunt and terrible in the candlelight. A bony finger pointed at Dot, who had bent to gather Julia to her chest.

'You've caused this storm with your negative feminine menstrual energies! Stop it! Stop the storm, you witch!'

Looking fearfully at Dot, Billie was ready to scoop her up in her arms and steady her. But Dot didn't need any such help. She shouted back, 'Get out! Get out of my life, you mean little man!'

Jake couldn't have looked more astonished if Julia had answered him. 'This is my house,' he said feebly. 'You can't throw me out.'

'Watch me!' yelled Dot. 'Out!' She rushed Jake. 'Out you go! Out!'

All Jake's cocky self-assurance dissolved in the face of this new, all-shouting, all-ranting Dot. He scuttled for the front door.

'And take your fucking hat!' Dot bowled a top hat towards him.

Finding his voice, Jake spat, 'This is *her* fault,' gesturing at Billie. 'I said no good would come of your having friends.'

'Get. *Out*.'

And out Jake got.

The effort of finally standing up to her persecutor drained Dot. After a contemplative hour, Billie left her to get to bed and await Jake's return.

Fighting the wind, Billie trudged through the storm. The thunder was becoming more insistent, its complaints closer together. The lightning was flexing its muscles, lighting up Sole Bay for a second or two at a time. Head down, Billie made for Herbert.

Her route took her down Little Row. Squinting at the spitting insults of the weather, Billie saw lights gleaming foggily from the back of Zelda's shop.

Zelda, despite her bizarre ways, had a nose for unhappiness. Tonight Billie could do with some of her special treatment. She knocked boldly on the door of the fudge shop.

Inside, the light flickered and moved. Billie could hear sounds of upheaval, but Zelda didn't appear. Billie knocked again, louder.

Bangs, crashes, a sudden bright light through the crackled glazing of the door to the parlour. Billie peered into the shop. She could see a shape moving about, hunched, as if dragging something heavy. '*Zelda!*' she shouted, over the fury of the storm.

Heavy-footed in her wide-fit sandals, Zelda plodded towards the door. She opened it an inch and poked her nose through. 'Who's that?'

'Me. Billie,' said Billie. 'Is everything all right?' Those loud noises had disturbed her, and Zelda didn't seem her usual self. She was twitchy.

'Everything's fantastic!' Zelda grinned. 'Tonight's the night, child. I'm inspired. I can feel the fudge in my veins. I feel like Doctor Frankenstein.' The lightning obligingly flashed at this point, illuminating Zelda's lined, gleeful face. 'Out of tragedy comes forth sweetness.'

'Like I always say,' laughed Billie. Mad as she was, Zelda would be company so she tried a casual, 'Fancy a cup of tea?'

'Tea?' Zelda was shocked. 'I can't stop now. I'm possessed.' And she looked it as she shook her unnaturally black hair out of her eyes.

'Maybe tomorrow,' said Billie, bravely.

'Good night, petal.' Zelda put up one hand to push an unruly cowlick back from her forehead: her arm was stained dark red to her elbow. 'You can be the first to taste my new recipe in the morning.'

'Good night,' said Billie to the slammed door. Thunder crashed above her head. In the confused lighting of the storm, that red on Zelda's arms had looked like gore. 'Must be the famous secret ingredient,' mused Billie, heading for the shelter of Billie's Brides' porch.

Drenched and defeated by the angry rain, Billie decided she could go no further and let herself into the shop. Looking murderously out at the monsoon she decided she'd sit it out in the dry, safe interior.

The light switches were impotent. Billie lit a fat candle she found in the kitchenette, and wondered if she could read her emails despite the blackout. Happily charged up, her laptop glowed and purred, and displayed three messages she hadn't had the time to open when they'd arrived.

The third was James. He was in advice-giving mode.

Try not to panic about Annie. Don't assume the worst until you have to. Think positive. If I know you, you'll be chewing your fingernails down to the knuckle. You always get so involved. Annie sounds like such a sweetie, I hope the prognosis is good.

Billie braced herself for mention of the doctor bird. It came.

My girlfriend might be able to answer some of your queries. I could let you have her email address if you like.

And this man has the cheek to call me mad, thought Billie.

Marrakesh is cancelled. Well, the holiday is. I feel confident that the place is still there. I can't get the time off work. Sound familiar?
It's very late, and it's raining hard.

Spooky, thought Billie.

As you often said, rain doesn't suit a minimalist loft apartment. It feels reassuring when it falls on a thatched roof, but it's intimidating when drumming on my metal balcony. I've had a whisky, and I've had a shower, and I'm feeling very mellow. And a bit sad. Perhaps it's your little Annie getting to me.

With all the dark thoughts of the past few months, Billie had forgotten how caramel-soft James could be underneath the accountant's carapace. There was a PS.

I've been taping the Hollyoaks omnibus to watch when my girlfriend is working nights. Does this make me a bad person?

BANG! Billie tensed. The noise was the infuriatingly indefinable sort that only happens in the dark.

She picked up the candle and climbed the stairs to the stockroom.

BANG! Billie stopped halfway up, analysing the sound as the hair on the back of her neck stood on end. It could just as easily be one of Dot's animal chums bumping into something. Slowly she carried on, bemoaning the lack of a blunt instrument.

When the noise sounded a third time, all became clear and Billie sagged with relief. The tiny window that looked out onto the yard had been blown open by the wind and was now banging listlessly.

Billie balanced the candle on the nearest shelf. She pulled at the rotting window, which now refused to shut.

A movement outside in the long rectangles of yard caught her eye. Somebody was in Zelda's garden, a much nicer and better kept plot than Billie's Brides' bin colony. Pushing her hair out of her eyes, Billie strained to see through the teeming rain. Zelda wouldn't be gardening at this hour in this weather: whoever it was had to be up to no good.

As her heart banging loudly, Billie peered anxiously down at the grainy figure, moving among the rhubarb plants. A loud clap of thunder growled over Sole Bay, shadowed by a long bolt of lightning so powerful that the whole of Little Row was lit with a mercurial glow.

Down in next door's garden, Zelda stood by a narrow, deep hole. A lumpy bundle, covered with blankets and indistinct in the dark, lolled at her feet. As Billie watched, mesmerised, the old woman, hair streaming, threw back her head, brandished the shovel and unleashed a banshee howl up into the tempest, her eyes tightly shut.

The window chose that moment to have an encore bang. Like a cat sensing a mouse, Zelda's eyes flew open and locked on to the window. Flattening herself back against the wall, Billie blew out the candle. She stayed stuck to the wall until she heard Zelda's back door lock.

She hoped that Zelda hadn't seen her. Wedging the window shut, she examined that thought. Why was she suddenly scared of a woman she knew well? Was it the shallow ditch? The shallow, *grave-like* ditch? The suspicious bundle? Maybe the werewolf howl?

All of these things, decided Billie, setting off for Herbert.

When Dot appeared just before lunch, she was idly chewing, and wearing a hessian sundress that Billie had never seen before. No tear ruts down her face. No dishevelled misery hair.

'What time did he crawl back?' asked Billie, wryly. 'I hope you didn't let him off the hook too easily.'

'Oh, he didn't come back,' said Dot, easily. 'Fudge?' She held out a bag of pinkish fudge. 'Zelda's new recipe. It's . . . indescribably good.'

'No, ta.' Billie was perturbed. 'So, where is he?'

'I have no idea.' Dot, who worried about everything up to and including the welfare of passing flies, didn't sound worried.

'Dot, have you been taking drugs? How can you calmly tell me that you don't know where Jake, the love of your life, is?'

'He can look after himself.' Dot sounded ever so slightly bitter. 'Sure you won't have some fudge?'

Billie backed away from the outstretched bag. 'It's a funny colour.'

'Pink,' smiled Dot.

'More . . . flesh colour.' Billie shuddered.

'Don't say that!' Dot pulled a face. 'It's delicious. Very very moreish.' She was licking her fingers, and for some reason Billie was repulsed. 'I cleaned the cottage from top to bottom this morning. You wouldn't recognise it. I slung all the junk out into the garden, put flowers everywhere. I even used the Hoover. I never get the chance normally, because Jake says the noise reminds him of the tormented souls in Hell.' She paused. 'Dickhead.'

'Dot!' Billie was disorientated.

'Oh, that was awful of me.' Dot was blushing. 'I'm sorry. But it helps. With the anger. But he's not a dickhead.'

'No,' said Billie with dignity, adding, 'he's a twat.'

Going out with Ed had morphed into staying in with Ed. Their nights in were all spent in Herbert, as Ed's all-male house share was not relationship-friendly. 'If these walls could talk, they'd be X-rated,' giggled Billie on Wednesday night as she rearranged her clothing. 'You are damn good, Edward.'

'All part of the service.' Ed jumped up and stalked over to the water container to splash his face.

Billie watched him. The width of his shoulders and the way his torso narrowed down to his buttocks thrilled and delighted her. It was like owning a never-ending bag of sweets. Or fudge.

Ed asked, 'Have you tasted your neighbour's new fudge?'

Billie was startled. 'No. You haven't, have you?'

'Course I have. The lads are nuts about it. It's unusual. I love it.'

'It's bad for you,' she said.

'Since when do you turn something down because it's bad for you?' He grinned, towelling his face. 'Like me, for instance.'

'You're good for me,' said Billie. 'You are the fat-free biscuit I've been searching for.'

'You reckon?' Ed's face was obscured by her polka-dot towel.

'Yes, I do.' Billie didn't like this talk. Ed always shied away from being told how she felt about him. Her programming was different from the women who came into her shop: Billie didn't fast forward to a happy ever after. She'd had that beaten out of her and she appreciated a happy right now. But part of that happiness was the belief that Ed belonged to her in some small, non-freedom-threatening way, that they were experiencing something real and worthwhile. 'Why, don't you?'

'Hang on. This is girl speak. I don't do girl speak. I'll get sucked into a situation where I can't say anything right.' Ed chucked the towel at her with a masculine bark of laughter. 'This is dangerous stuff. You talk about weddings in your shop all day and that's scary for a bloke. I could fall asleep a bachelor and wake up married.'

Billie didn't answer, too busy computing the fact that Ed had misjudged something as integral to her personality as her attitude to marriage. 'You're quite safe,' she said, not entirely able to keep the acid out of her voice. 'This particular bird doesn't want to marry anybody.'

'See. I've cocked up already.' Ed knelt in front of her. 'Men and women shouldn't talk about anything important. It always ends in plates being thrown.' His chest was within touching distance.

So she touched it. 'No, you haven't cocked up, silly. Just let me tell you how I feel about you once in a while. You don't have to respond.'

Ed took Billie's face in his hands and stared into it for a delicious while. 'You're no ordinary woman, Billie Baskerville. What are you doing with me? I'm not as nice as you think, girl.'

'That started well,' smiled Billie, 'but frankly you've got to work on your endings.'

Later, as they lay entwined in the mess of blankets, Billie remembered a phone call she'd had that afternoon. 'Jackie's coming up on Saturday,' she told him in the darkness.

'Right.'

'Well, sound pleased. She's one of my best friends.'

'Hurray,' said Ed, limply.

'Do you want me to see her on my own?'

'Definitely.'

Disappointed, Billie changed the subject. 'Jake's still not back. Dot's taking it all very well.' She chose to interpret his silence as fascination, 'And we've started a rota for visiting Annie.'

If the continuing silence was anything to go by, Ed was *really* fascinated.

'Well?' Nudging him enthusiastically, Billie got her reaction.

'Ooof. Yes. Your sick old lady, lovely,' muttered Ed, sleepily.

'They're important to me,' grumbled Billie.

'Yes, darling.' Ed was cruising away, over the horizon.

Setting off on Saturday for the hospital, Dot asked blandly, 'Shall I take Annie some fudge?'

'No,' said Billie sharply, adding, 'she doesn't like rich things.'

Lurking by the door, ignoring a customer peering needily at her over a rack of dresses, Debs commented, 'That fudge is fucking wicked.' She was wearing a pair of denim shorts that didn't even begin to control the wild frontier of her bottom. 'All right, love, keep your hair on,' she advised the customer, who had coughed politely.

The queue for Zelda's new recipe stretched past the door of Billie's Brides. Looking out at it, Billie felt her wings begin to itch. 'Dot,' she asked carefully, 'have you been in touch with Jake's family?'

'They haven't seen him.' Dot was using the non-committal expression she'd cultivated since Jake loped off into the storm. 'Nobody's seen him. He'll come back when he's ready. He's doing this to worry me.'

'Is he succeeding?' Billie didn't buy this new, disengaged Dot.

'No,' Dot insisted. 'I'm not alone. I've got Julia. And Jenkins has been a tower of strength.'

'So you don't think anything bad's happened to him?'

'Like what?' asked Dot innocently.

Like being murdered, dismembered and buried by the overprotective sorceress who lives next door. Like being the secret ingredient in Zelda's best-selling fudge. Billie couldn't dismiss the gore on Zelda's hands that night, or that lumpy bundle on the ground. 'Oh, I don't know. He's probably licking his wounds somewhere.' Her murder/fudge scenario seemed ludicrous but still it nibbled at her peace of mind.

'I don't have time to worry.' Dot was determined to make the best of things. This steel spine was a revelation to Billie, who had supposed her friend to be composed of much floppier materials. 'I'll get myself some fudge. That'll cheer me up.'

Not knowing how to phrase *No! it's wrong to eat your boyfriend!* in an acceptable way, Billie opened the door to let her out.

The face was familiar. 'Cheryl!' Billie clicked her fingers as she nailed the customer's identity. 'How was the wedding?'

The new Mrs Mississippi Mutilator glowed. 'The wedding was perfect. The whole of Death Row cheered. And now . . .' Cheryl patted her tummy. 'I think I'm expecting.'

'Aw,' said Dot. 'A little Mutilator Junior!'

'I didn't realise they allowed you to . . .' Billie regretted starting that sentence. 'Erm, have conjugal, erm . . .' she faltered.

Cheryl cottoned on. 'Oh, they don't. Physical contact is strictly forbidden. But,' she continued, her face ablaze with the memory, 'the way he *looked* at me through the high-security plexiglas, the way his eyes *burned* into my body, I could feel our union deep within me.'

Billie trod carefully. 'Have I got this right? You're pregnant?'

Cheryl intoned movingly, 'I feel his babe quicken within me.'

Taken aback, Billie asked, 'When are you seeing Len again?'

'Oh, he's dead,' said Cheryl airily. 'He went to the chair right after the wedding.' She plonked a pair of white shoes on the counter. 'Sorry that it's taken me so long to get back to you, I've just got home from the States. Do you still need to borrow my shoes for your friend's wedding?'

'Not any more, I'm afraid,' said Billie. 'Although, then again . . .

Thanks, Cheryl, we'll accept them. I'll give you a ring when you can have them back.'

As soon as the perky bride/widow/expectant mother left, Billie rang the hospital. 'Is it possible,' she asked an administrator, 'to carry out wedding ceremonies in your hospital?'

Billie had to nip next door to Zelda's to ask for change. A bullish woman had insisted on paying cash for her satin two-piece and Billie had to break a twenty-pound note to give her the correct change.

'I'll serve this one!' Zelda elbowed her assistant out of the way to grin over the glass counter at Billie. 'What'll it be, my lovely?'

Billie couldn't answer. She was mesmerised by the battered top hat sitting at an angle on Zelda's exuberant, coal-black bouffant.

Sprawled on Billie's renovated deck chair out on Herbert's verandah, vodka in mitt, Jackie said, 'Seriously, though, when are you coming back to the action, babe?'

'I couldn't take any more action, thanks very much,' laughed Billie. She'd spent the last two hours of her working day ringing round the various companies she'd wheedled deals out of for Heather's wedding cancelling everything. Phone silence from Heather had confirmed that the jilt was going ahead. 'It might look peaceful, but Sole Bay is more eventful than your sex life.' Sitting on the boards, her knees to her chin, she looked up at Jackie mischievously. 'For one thing, Ed's been unfaithful, so I hear.' She would enjoy sharing the tale of Heather's doomed attempt to board the good ship *Fireman*.

'Oh.' Jackie sounded only vaguely interested.

'Jake told me Ed has been doing something I'd be surprised at.'

'Yeah?' Still Jackie wasn't intrigued.

Billie ploughed on. 'With *somebody* I'd be surprised at,' she said archly. Surely Jackie, who had heard many tales of Heather's arrogant high-handedness would guess. 'But I already knew all about it! Can you take a wild guess at who the someone is?'

'Christ, you bore me.'

Billie reacted as if she'd been slapped. 'You what?' she frowned.

'Listen to you.' Jackie mimicked her vindictively. 'Ed's been unfaithful, who with, oooooh!' She stood up, hands on hips, and looked down at Billie, still on the floor. 'Why not just have it out with me? The bearded weirdo snitched on us, so why not say so?'

From a long way away, a skinny idea suddenly piled on the pounds. 'Jackie . . .' was all Billie said, too unhappy to continue.

'Yes, I shagged him,' declared Jackie. 'OK? Got it? I shagged him the night I met him and I've been shagging him, train schedules permitting, ever since. As if you don't bloody know.'

'I didn't,' said Billie quietly, standing to face her. 'Bloody know.'

Jackie blushed. 'What was all that about, then? You were torturing me.'

'I thought Jake was referring to Heather. She told me she chased him.' Billie folded her arms, a mutinous look on her face. 'But she obviously can't run as fast as you.' It was as if Jackie had mutated before her eyes into another creature altogether. The bouncy hair looked overdone and the full lips looked ravenous. 'I thought you were my friend.'

'Shit.' Jackie sank back into the deck chair. She looked up at Billie and, incredibly, she was biting her tongue, trying not to laugh. 'You mean, I just confessed all for no reason?' She shook her head. 'You weren't supposed to find out, ever. We didn't want to hurt you.'

'Spare me the clichés,' growled Billie. 'You're boring *me* now.'

'It's true. It's not like Ed and I have been having some wonderful love affair behind your back. It's just sex. We don't discuss you. Honest. And we don't talk about our feelings or any of that crap.'

'Gosh, I feel so much better now.'

'Listen, Billie. This doesn't have to mean the end of you and me. Or you and Ed. Can't we put it behind us? You know I'm a greedy cow.' She hesitated. 'And you went and found yourself a greedy guy, too.'

'I can't get my head round this.' Billie needed some details. 'You've been coming here without me knowing?'

'A handful of times.' Jackie was able to hold Billie's gaze. 'That time we bumped into each other and had a picnic, I was heading for the cab office after spending the night with Ed.'

'Where?' Billie's mind raced. Then she knew. 'At his place?'

'Yeah. What a dump. Lad Central.'

'I've never even been to his flat.'

'You're the girlfriend, I'm just the bit on the side. His flat's not good enough for you.'

'Are you, *you*, trying to make me feel better?' scoffed Billie.

'Wouldn't dare. You've got the moral high ground and you're galloping about on it on your high horse. You needn't believe this, but I really wanted to tell you after the first time. Looking back I wish I had. You wouldn't have gone out with him at all.'

'When was the first time?' said Billie, sounding as if she was falling asleep. She was weary of this evening and its tacky revelations.

'The first time I met him. The night you kissed him.' Jackie seemed to be willing herself to be as plain as possible. 'The night of the disco.'

'But he came back here . . .' Billie woke up.

'And you sent him packing.'

'You stayed with Chugger that night.'

'Nope. Your chavvy assistant did. You never really asked me, so I never really told you.'

So, Debs's 100 per cent success rate was safe. This news also explained Ed's mysterious hangover the day after the disco. The implications for Billie's feelings for Ed, for her peace of mind, for her faith in her own judgment were looming and taking shape in the lilac evening. He was another Mr Wrong, after all. That million pounds she'd have to hand over to Dot if she ever tied the knot was safer than ever.

'Go, will you, Jackie?'

Standing up, hauling her oversized back up from the boards, Jackie said, 'It's only a man. It's only sex. It's not important. I wouldn't have done it if I thought it would split you and me up.'

Shrugging, Billie could only offer, 'You did do it. And you'd do it again. I'm just a casualty of your quest to have fun now.'

Jackie stamped angrily down onto the concrete. 'I hate that tone you use. You want everything to be just so, like that dreadful perfect wedding you tried to organise for yourself. Billie, life is a mess. I make messes because I live. I cry over it then I carry on. I don't bury myself in a backstreet shop that doesn't even belong to me, reaching out a virtual hand every so often to a man who shouldn't matter any more. I don't eulogise some common-or-garden bloke with a hard-on as The One. I'm a real person. And I choose life, every time. I don't say "no", I don't say "maybe", I grab it with both hands. And if you don't like real life and its messes, that's your problem.'

Fuming, Billie watched Jackie clatter off in shoes she'd thought fabulous a few hours ago but now considered ridiculously inappropriate. 'Apology accepted!' she yelled, before going back inside Herbert for a really good, really long sob.

TWELVE

THERE'S ONLY SO MUCH CRYING a girl can do before she wants to buy a hatchet. Luckily for Ed, there were no hatchet shops in Sole Bay, so Billie resorted to phoning him. And phoning him. And phoning him.

Ed was not picking up. His partner in crime had warned him that the unwitting filling in their sex sandwich had rumbled them.

Replaying recent history in her head had made for a troubled night. First she'd re-examined the times she'd spent with Ed to discern if his feelings for her were real. Then she'd looked for clues that he had no feelings for her at all. Ashamed, but unable to stop herself, she then tried to prove that he preferred her to Jackie. 'As if that matters,' she thought miserably.

The shadow cast by Jackie's betrayal polluted their history: her vocal scepticism before Billie's non-wedding was starting to look malevolent rather than playful. Perhaps Billie would discover that Jackie had been instrumental in the horrific, historic jilt. Best not examine the past in that case, decided Billie, who had enough to deal with just now.

Ed had deceived her, used her and turned his high-pressure hose on her self-confidence. But Billie needed to hear in his own words what had gone on between him and Jackie. Perhaps there was some consolation to be found, some reasoning that she couldn't fathom.

However, apparently, Ed did not need to meet up with her. At first she assumed he was at work, out on a call, asleep, pinned down by pygmies. Slowly it became obvious that he simply wasn't answering.

Standing patiently in line, waiting for Mr Dyke to finish flirting with a woman bent over on two sticks and sporting a prewar, microwave-sized hearing aid, Billie had high hopes for the Scotch egg in her sights. Lolling on its chaise longue of cress, that egg didn't know it yet, but it was going to make her Feel Better: a task beyond the brisk sales in the shop, the sun splitting the trees outside, and Dot's call to East Coast

FM's *Chit-chat With Charlie* posing as a Zambian cross-dresser.

A talon dug into her shoulder. Billie spun round to meet Zelda, eyeball to evil eyeball.

'Haven't seen you for a while, love.' Zelda raised her drawn-on brows. 'You avoiding old Zelda?' She tittered hoarsely.

'No, no,' Billie tittered back. 'Just been busy with the shop.'

'You haven't had a nibble of my special fudge.' Zelda slowly tweaked open a small paper bag and insinuated it under Billie's nose.

Zelda seemed to be watching her more closely than one human offering another human a sweet might be expected to.

'I'm on a diet.' Billie had her fib ready.

'Really?' Zelda looked down at Billie's jeans. 'Might be for the best.' She folded the bag over and put it back in her apron pocket.

'Still no sign of Jake,' said Billie, boldly.

'Wouldn't be the end of the world if he never came back.' Zelda didn't take her eyes from Billie's. 'Would it?'

A shout of 'Next!' from the counter saved Billie from answering. Her saviour wasn't Mr Dyke, but a peachy-looking boy of about nineteen with a cap of indie curls.

'My grandson, Darius,' explained Mr Dyke. 'He was born into meat.'

Darius dissuaded Billie from the Scotch egg she had her eye on, pointing to the one behind it. 'Fuller shape. Crispier breadcrumbs.'

'That Dot,' he said abruptly, wrapping her Scotch egg. 'She got a boyfriend?'

Unsure how to answer—possibly with a 'Yes, but he's in this lady's pocket'—Billie narrowed her eyes. 'Why?'

'Cos she's the prettiest thing in Sole Bay, that's why.'

Pushing rudely past Billie, and almost knocking the other customer off her walking sticks, Zelda rapped on the high glass counter and hissed, 'You keep that pup of yours away from our Dot, Dyke.'

'Ah, Zelda,' said Mr Dyke indulgently. 'Boys will be boys.'

Déjà vu of an unpleasant kind assailed Billie as she crossed the lawn in front of the fire station. The last time she'd visited Ed here, he'd been across town, busy between her friend's legs. Loitering outside, she looked up at the windows of the recreation room. Ed had pointed them out to her, describing how the watch spent their time there.

The door in the side of the building clanged open, spitting out two men in navy-blue fire-fighting basics. One of them was patting his pockets in search of cigarettes. He found them as Billie approached.

Shyly, she asked, 'Excuse me. Do you know Ed? Is he on duty?'

'Treacle?' laughed the bloke putting a cigarette to his lips. 'Everyone knows Treacle. Yeah. He's on.' He stopped suddenly. 'At least, I think he's on.' He turned to the man beside him, who had found something of great interest down on the grass. 'Is Treacle in there?'

'No idea,' snapped his colleague without looking up.

'Could you do me a big favour?' asked Billie nervously, aware that her face and demeanour simply screamed 'chucked bird'. 'Could you tell him Billie's here to see him?'

'Course.' Putting his unlit cigarette regretfully back in the packet, the man hurried back into the fire station, leaving Billie with his colleague.

In no time, the door swung open again, and Billie, hopeful despite her fears, suppressed a groan when her messenger reappeared alone.

'I was wrong,' he said, too loudly. 'No sign of him. Sorry, love.'

'Never mind, I'll catch him later,' she said, as brightly as she could manage, even adding a cheery, if trembling, 'Thanks!' before she sauntered off, delivering an unconvincing portrait of a girl who didn't care.

Billie lugged her laptop along the lane to Sam's cottage. His computer had 'gone apeshit' and Billie had offered him the use of her machine.

Opening the gate to the manicured front garden, Billie spotted Sam sunbathing on the emerald-green grass.

He sat up, his brown torso glistening. 'Any word from Ed?'

'Ed who?' Billie passed him and let herself into the cottage. She made for the kitchen, and hoisted the computer on to a granite island. 'I went to the fire station,' she told Sam sheepishly, as he padded in after her.

'Oh dear. Something tells me he didn't run out and smother you in a thousand tiny kisses.'

'His mates pretended he wasn't there.' Billie's body executed a kind of Mexican wave of shame. 'It was one of the worst moments of my life.'

'It's time to give up with the calls and the turning up at his work, Billie-dillie.' Sam's eyes fixed hers as he pulled on a dressing gown. 'We've got to roll with the punches. You'll drive yourself mad if you keep looking for answers and reasons and explanations.'

Pretending to concentrate on the computer screen, Billie said, 'I can't just walk away. It's unfinished business.'

'Life is full of unfinished business,' argued Sam. 'My God, Ed comes out of this looking like the perfect gent compared to the way I've chucked blokes in the past.' He leaned against the worktop, remembering. 'One guy fell asleep in a cab and I got out at the lights. Little Manolito turned up at my flat to discover I'd sublet to Mormons. The Greek guy I shagged for a fortnight couldn't track me down because he thought my name was Cedric Tattybye. Do you hate me yet?'

'No, Cedric, I don't,' laughed Billie. 'But I should. Those are people's hearts you're playing with.'

'Nah.' Sam shook his white-blond head. 'I only play with other parts of their anatomy. And I've heard some of your stories, young lady. I know you've trampled on feelings before and never looked back.'

'And karma got me, fair and square.' Billie's face crumpled. 'I was enjoying being normal again. Being part of the human race. And now it's all been whisked away.'

'All?' Sam sounded testy. 'I'm here. Dot, God bless her irritating little hen-loving ways is still here. The shop is here. You're down one fireman who couldn't keep his cock in his underpants: good riddance.'

'But having a boyfriend again was reassuring, as if I was a fully paid-up Earthling again, after months of living as a freak,' whined Billie.

'Listen to you,' snapped Sam, evidently unmoved. 'You sound just like one of those needy, self-deluding women you rant on about.'

'Don't expect me to make sense right now,' whinged Billie, 'I'm going through emotional trauma.'

'Your pride is hurt. Your libido is disappointed. But your heart isn't broken, so don't come the emotional trauma bit with me.'

'Where are the hugs? The "you're too good for him"?' Billie was almost shouting. 'What kind of a gay best friend are you?'

'The real kind, Billious,' laughed Sam. 'What are you typing?'

'Just a quick email before I hand this over to you.' Billie had composed a few angry lines to James.

The fireman has shat on me from a great height with your lovely friend Jackie. Thank you sooooo much for introducing us. Not.

'There. All yours.'

'Ta. I've got to scan my latest drawings and send them to my editor.'

'May I see them?' asked Billie, hopefully.

'No,' said Sam flatly. 'It's bad enough drawing the little sod without watching people go all gaga over him.' He draped an arm round her shoulders. 'Listen, Billie, you've helped me so much by being your delightful, contradictory, soft-as-butter self. You've made this whole rural idyll bearable. If it's hugs you want'—Sam folded her into his dressing gown and squeezed—'How's that?'

'Nice,' smiled Billie. She leaned against him, liking the solid warmth.

'For you,' Billie heard a deep voice saying down in the shop, and got to the bottom step in time to see Darius Dyke handing a bouquet to Dot.

It was a lovely tableau, the strapping young lad offering a love token to the dainty young woman. But then Dot recoiled with, 'Oh, yuk!'

The bouquet was a selection of meat. A scarlet lamb chop nestled among sausages and a turkey drumstick, all tied up in a red bow.

Intervening, Billie told the puzzled Darius, 'Dot's a vegetarian.'

Still looking away, Dot managed to say, 'It was a kind thought.'

As Darius left, his chop drooping, Billie advised quietly, 'Why not go the conventional route next time and try a bunch of roses?'

'What kind of woman prefers a rose to a sausage?' marvelled Darius.

'Virtually every kind of woman,' Billie called after him. Coming back in, she dissolved into giggles with Dot. 'Lucky you, though. Another gentleman caller already.'

Her giggles braked when she saw the distress on Dot's face. 'I don't want any other man, I want my man. Oh, Billie, I'm starting to worry now. It's been so long.'

'He'll be back,' said Billie, hoping she sounded convincing. Dot's face, so woebegone when she let her guard down, haunted her. When should Billie speak up? When should she tell the police about the cigar-shaped hump in Zelda's yard, now sprouting a fine crop of weeds?

Dot was biting her nails as Billie put down the phone. 'Did he say yes?'

'Finally,' said Billie. Her shoulders sagged. The consultant had taken some convincing that Annie's situation merited a hospital wedding, and without his say-so it couldn't happen.

Dot sagged with relief. 'You're a genius,' she told Billie.

Debs was out in the kitchenette making tea. Billie could hear her nattering to Dot, and risked a hearty, 'Where's my cuppa?'

Emerging from the back of the shop with a mug in her hands, Debs said, loudly and quite slowly, 'What on earth is that up the tree?'

Crossing to the window, Billie peered up into the tree, an overgrown specimen outside Dyke's. 'I can't see anything.'

'Oh my God!' gasped Dot, coming up behind Debs. 'It's Raven. Poor Raven. He's stuck up the tree!'

Next door's arthritic old cat hadn't been around for a while, and Billie doubted that he could make it up a tree. 'I still can't see him.'

'Look!' persisted Dot, waggling a finger. 'There!'

'Yes!' Debs nudged her and Billie went flying into the window display. 'There.'

'You're not pointing at the same spot,' puzzled Billie.

'I'll get the ladder,' said Debs, very decisively for a girl who usually shirked lifting anything heavier than her eyebrows.

The three of them stepped out into Little Row, which was in shade at this time of the day. 'Still can't see him,' complained Billie.

Plonking the ladder against the trunk, Dot motioned to her to step on it.

'Why me?' asked Billie. Raven would probably sink a claw in her jugular if she tried to manhandle him down from a tree.

'I'm scared of heights,' Dot said.

'So am I.' Debs wasn't scared of pit bull terriers or stealing from under her boss's nose, but she couldn't face climbing a ladder.

'Oh, all right.' Billie couldn't be bothered to fight. She clambered awkwardly up the ladder, her wings waggling. 'Where is the little sod?' she asked, squinting into the mass of greenery.

'Go to the top of the ladder,' shouted Dot. 'And then he's on the end of that thick branch. Yes! That one. Just ease yourself onto it.'

The ladder wobbled as Billie reached out for the bumpy branch. 'Ohhhhh God,' she muttered, swinging a leg inelegantly over the rough extended arm. Straddling it, she looked down and mewled. The tops of Debs and Dot's heads were a long way away. 'I still can't see him,' she said, but shakily this time. With a shriek, she squealed, 'What are you doing?'

'Nothing,' said Dot innocently, as she and Debs grappled the ladder away.

'I need that to get down!' Billie pointed out the obvious, holding on to her branch as if it was a runaway stallion. 'Debs!' she yelled, as she saw her Saturday girl stab the same digit three times on her phone.

and a penny dropped loud enough to be heard at sea. 'Don't!'

'Fire brigade,' Debs was saying into her phone. 'Could you come quickly? There's a cat stuck up a tree on Little Row.' She looked up at Billie. 'And hurry. Poor dumb pussy's in a right state.'

'Your shout, Treacle!' yelled Chugger, who leapt off the fire engine before the others and had the first look up the tree.

Up among the leaves, Billie straddled her branch, her bum now familiar with every knot and bump. Back straight, lips thin, she was attempting to hold on for dear life while appearing carefree, relaxed.

There was the thud of a ladder against the trunk and the yobbish laughter of Ed's mates. Then her branch swayed in rhythm to Ed's feet as he climbed the rungs. Billie shook her hair (which was unwashed) and licked her lips (which were unglossed) and steeled herself.

Refusing to look at him, preferring to be mesmerised by a distant leaf, Billie only faced Ed when he said flatly, 'You're not a cat.'

Turning to meet his gaze, she was reminded just how brown his eyes were. 'You're a hound, though.' She sighed. 'This wasn't my idea.'

'Really?' Ed seemed sceptical.

'Yes, really.' Billie shifted on the knotty bark. 'I'm not desperate, Ed. I know I turned up at the fire station and everything, but—'

Ed said, 'I'm sorry about that. That was low of me.'

'Yeah. It was.' She paused. 'Did you care about me at all, Ed?'

Ed gave a tiny sigh and leaned on her branch, resigned. 'Don't start,' he said, morosely.

'Eh?' Flabbergasted, Billie became shrill. 'What did you expect? That I'd just shrug? Say, "Oh well, never mind"? You're going to have to put up with some "girl speak", mate. I slept with you, I trusted you and you lied to me, over and over again.'

'You make it sound so dramatic.'

'I happen to think it is dramatic. What you did was unforgivable. Don't you realise how hurt I am?'

'Keep your voice down. My mates are lapping all this up.'

'Ed!' It was like talking to a small boy about a broken window. 'I need some answers. Why did you—' Billie stopped short of accusing him of breaking her heart: he wasn't guilty of that. 'Make a fool of me?'

Simmering, Ed spoke impatiently, as if the truth was so obvious that she was daft to ask. 'Because it was there. It was on a plate. I didn't have to lift a finger.' Eyes down, Ed let the story out in a rush. 'After the disco, when you weren't coming across, I looked in at the lock-in, and Jackie came over like a guided missile. She was all over me.'

'So it's all her fault. You couldn't say no?'

'I'm a man,' he said, simply.

'Not every man would have taken her up.'

'You sure about that?' asked Ed, cynically. 'She's a persuasive girl.'

'I'm sure. My hero,' she snorted.

'I told you I wasn't one of them,' said Ed. 'You wouldn't listen.'

'Oh. Now it's my fault. I'm so sorry. Remember that word?'

Ed said, 'I *am* sorry. I wish I'd done things differently. But I didn't. Look, does it have to be over?'

'Which script are you reading from?' spluttered Billie. He'd told more lies than Billie had at Weight Watchers, he'd trashed an important friendship, and he'd avoided her as if *she* was the villain of the piece.

'OK. Dumb question.' Ed held out his arms and the gesture brought tears to Billie's eyes: it no longer meant what it used to. 'Ready? We're wasting the guys' time.'

Into his arms she slid, tucking herself over his shoulder. A small cheer went up from Debs and Dot at the foot of the ladder. Billie blinked a hot tear from her lashes. Those strong hands were touching her for the last time.

As she approached Herbert, Billie saw somebody tall and man-shaped nip up on to the verandah, round the far side facing the sea.

'Sly!' The bulky stranger was her brother.

'I took your advice.' Sly dispensed with hello's. 'And here I am.'

'You don't mean Sana threw you out?'

'As soon as she took the call from the bank, I was history.'

'Hang on.' Billie cocked her head. 'So she found out from the bank?'

'Well. As soon as the bank told her it was withdrawing credit and calling in the overdraft, I sat her down and told her everything.'

'As soon as you had no choice, in other words.' Shaking her head, she opened the door. 'Get in, you big lummox.'

It became clear that Sly was properly broke. He had no money at all.

'So I can stay? Just until I get on my feet?'

Billie said. 'What about your sideline? Spartakiss?'

'I gave that up,' said Sly curtly. 'It's not a job for the faint-hearted.'

'It's far too hot for a leather jacket,' Billie chided Sam when he dropped in to return her computer.

'A leather jacket is a state of mind.' Sam turned his collar up. 'It's never too hot for one.'

'Not if you're a narcissistic poser,' smiled Billie. Sam proved that there was life beyond relationships. With him around, Billie didn't stick out like a sore thumb. 'Did your editor like the drawings?'

'Loved them.' Sam mimed vomiting. 'Particularly Tiddlywinks kissing all the other toys on the bed and saying "nighty night".'

'Oh, that sounds so sweet!' sang Dot, oblivious to Sam's feelings.

'Drink tonight?' suggested Billie. 'Many drinks? Too many drinks? Far, far too many drinks?'

'I'm going to use an unusual word here.' Sam enunciated, 'No.'

'I demand to see the real Sam Nolan immediately,' gasped Billie.

'Deadline, Billita.'

Sly burst in at that moment, with some of his old bravado. 'The fudge from the lady next door is quite exemplary,' he said, his face creased with admiration. 'Try some.'

Backing away, Billie shook her head. 'It's very bad for you.'

'Is it the secret recipe?' An evil glint lit up Sam's eye as he took a square. 'Mmmmm!' he enthused, savouring it. 'I'd kill for that taste.'

As Dot reached out her hand, the grotesque possibilities became too much for Billie. 'Don't!' she yelped, slapping away Dot's hand.

Dot yanked her hand away from Billie. 'Why did you do that?'

'Yes, Billie, *why*?' echoed Sam, enjoying himself enormously.

'It's fattening. And it's a sin to eat between meals,' gabbled Billie.

Sly said sorrowfully, 'Do you and Dot need to revise some of the trust exercises we explored during the Inner Winner seminar?'

'No,' said Billie. 'Sorry, Dot. I just didn't want you to . . . feel sick.'

'That's OK,' said the saintly Dot. 'I suppose I am overeating.' She looked uncomfortable as she added, 'I'm missing Jake, to be honest.'

As Billie knew he would, Sam leapt right in with a solicitous, 'In a funny way, do you feel closer to him when you eat fudge?'

'Out.' Billie held the door open. 'You've got a deadline.'

As Sam left, Sly said thoughtfully, 'You've got some work to do on your leadership style, sis.'

Humbly, Billie agreed. And gave him fifty pence pocket money for the afternoon.

A handful of emails waited to be read. The message from Jackie was erased without reading it. The last one was from James.

> Typical. Even hundreds of miles away, your latest disaster is all my fault. I'd forgotten how it feels to be responsible for everything and to be in the wrong twenty-four hours a day. Thank the Lord we never married.

There was no sign-off. No news. No sympathy. It sounded final.

It was Saturday. Seven days since Billie had had a moment to herself, an evening with Sam, or an email from James.

She was ratty. Perhaps that is unfair to rats. Billie was more wounded hippo-y as she charged through Sole Bay to the shop. One sight of Dot's pale face, soiled with worry, cranked her stress up another notch or eight. Strapping on her wings, she asked menacingly, 'Debs late again?'

'Now, don't be too hard on her,' said Dot by way of reply.

'When am I ever hard on her? She's late, she alienates custom, she steals the takings and won't make me a cup of tea, yet I barely tell her off. Dot, you look terrible. Have you thought any more about . . .'

'The police?' Dot shook her head. 'It's too early. He'll be somewhere.'

Guilt was closing its tentacles over Billie, as if *she'd* been the one in the yard with the shovel. Debs slouched in, mobile to her ear.

'You're late,' growled Billie, calling on her inner wounded hippo to face up to Debs. 'And today I want an explanation.'

Debs held up an imperious finger for Billie to wait.

With a sigh that parted Dot's hair, Billie tapped a flip-flop ostentatiously until Debs clicked her phone shut. 'Thank you,' said Billie acidly. 'Now, are you going to tell me why you're late? Again?'

'Gotta go,' replied Debs, retracing her steps. 'Man trouble.'

Billie's mouth dropped open. 'I don't believe it. Oi! Hey!' she yelled after Debs, who jogged off down Little Row without turning back. Billie turned to Dot. 'Right. Where does she live?'

'Hang on,' said Dot, gravely. 'Don't be hasty.'

'Hasty!' yelped Billie. 'Dot. *Where does Debs live?*'

There was only one grotty shop in Sole Bay, and Debs's flat was over it. 'Honest Bob the Bookie' operated from a dark hole, lit by one fluorescent tube. The bored men inside, smoking roll-ups and concentrating on the TV screens suspended from the damp ceiling, didn't even glance at Billie as she barged through the room and up the stairs at the rear.

'Debs!' she shouted, as she banged on the door. 'It's Billie.'

The door opened a centimetre or so and a narrow slab of outraged Debs showed itself. 'What're you doing here?' she demanded. 'I'm busy.'

'You should be busy at work,' spat Billie. 'Man bloody trouble? What kind of excuse is that to walk out?'

'I suppose you better come in.' Sullenly, Debs took the chain off the door and preceded Billie into the room that constituted her flat.

It was very untidy and very drab. The curtains were yellowing with age and the carpet was past retirement. Brightly coloured building bricks provided a splash of colour on a rug.

'This is Zac.' Debs bent down and scooped up the rolypoly one-year-old. 'He's my man.' She playfully nipped his nose. 'And you give me no end of trouble, don'cha?'

Silenced, Billie stared at Zac. Gurgling and giggling, he cheered up the miserable room. 'I didn't know,' said Billie, uneasily.

'Why should you?' replied Debs. 'He's my business.' She bit her lip. 'He doesn't like to leave me. Since he was born, you see, it's been me and him. His Dad . . .' Debs shrugged, as she sat on the arm of the sagging armchair. 'Not interested. My family are hopeless. Bunch of drunks. So we're a pair, aren't we, Zac?' Zac said 'ploop' or similar, and Debs carried on. 'At college he goes in the crèche four days a week, but on Saturdays he goes next door to my mate. But he doesn't always settle. And she's not exactly patient with him, so I have to rush back.'

'What are you studying at college?' Billie asked.

'Childcare.'

Another surprise. This burly girl, with her glitter pumps and her barely there denim mini, was full of them.

'Listen, Debs. I know about the money.'

'What money?' Debs challenged.

'The money you've been taking from the till.'

'I'm sorry, right?' shouted Debs. 'I didn't set out to be a thief. It's not what I want for him.' She pressed Zac's head to her bosom and he squeaked. 'I just can't make ends meet. He always needs something. And I won't let him have the childhood I had. No cuddles, no shoes, all the kids laughing because all I had was my school uniform.'

Billie'd come here to sack her surly, useless, maddening shop assistant. Now she sat here admiring Debs for her tenacity and her courage.

For being able to hold on to this grotty flat, for making sure there were some primary colours in it, for keeping Zac fit and healthy and secure. She felt almost envious of the chubby little boy, suffocating against his mother's boob tube: Zac knew he was loved.

'Listen, I've got an idea,' she began.

'**B**abs knew.' Billie had reassessed that 'keep an eye on Debs'. 'But she turned a blind eye. I think it was her way of helping.'

'I think your way is even better,' said Dot approvingly.

As expected, Dot had 'Oooh'ed and clapped her hands all the way through Billie's news. From now on, Debs would come in to the shop on Thursdays, her day off from college and, luckily, a busy-ish day at Billie's Brides. The extra money would ease her financial problems and Zac would accompany her to work, where Dot and Billie would muck in to help with him. 'But she's not allowed to use the till,' Billie warned Dot. 'She knows that and she's cool with it.'

'She's going to earn our trust,' beamed Dot, whose belief in happy endings was unshakable, whatever the proof to the contrary.

'**O**nly a few days to go,' said Billie to the figure in the bed.

Annie looked a little dazed, her white curls tossed. 'I can't quite believe it's really happening, to be honest.'

'Ooh, not getting cold feet, I hope,' Billie teased.

'It's an awful lot to do on one day,' worried Annie. The doctors had pronounced her fit enough to undergo the operation as planned. 'Will you drop in on Ruby, if anything happens?'

That shorthand. 'I'll be dropping in on both Mr and Mrs Wolff.' Billie was having no nonsense. Annie would be all right. She had to be.

'**W**heeeeeeee!' shrieked Billie, her hair trailing from under the motorbike helmet. 'Whoooooooo!'

'SHUT UUUUUUUUUUUP!' bellowed Sam from the front seat, guiding his monster of a machine down a lane so leafy and green it might have been underwater.

They stopped at the end of a track, where the woods petered out and gave way to tussocky, tangled grass. The sea shimmered coyly in the distance, and the green slopes as far as the eye could see were a long, warm bath for the senses.

Stretching out beside Sam, Billie looked up at the taut, perfect blue sky and whispered dreamily, 'This is so beautiful.'

Sam put his hands under his head. 'The countryside is dull. It's all a myth, that garbage about open spaces being good for you. I know what's good for me and it's illegal.'

'I wonder how Heather is,' said Billie, almost to herself.

'Thrashing about, spreading the pain,' said Sam, with notable lack of sympathy. 'God, she embarrassed me that day.'

'At the shop?' Billie smiled: the episode had been so Heather-ish. 'She was excited. She'd never met a real-life celebridee before.'

'No, when she offered me her body in the Sailor's Lament.'

Billie sat up, as if she was on a spring. 'Offered? Body? Lament?'

'I told you.' Sam could be infuriating. 'Oh, I didn't? You're going to love this. I was having a tête à tête with a JD and Coke, trying to ignore the stares from across the room of our beardy friend, now Missing Believed Fudged. In saunters Heather, dressed to impress. Although the only people who'd be impressed would be heterosexuals who long to see a horse dressed as Mariah Carey. Anyway, she's on her own and she sits beside me. Buys me a drink. Asks me about myself. And I realise I'm being chatted up. Me! I haven't been chatted up by anybody with working nipples since I was a teenager. So I let her down gently.'

Wincing, Billie had to ask what Sam's version of letting a girl down gently was.

'I told her I was very flattered, but the female front bottom is my sexual equivalent of Disneyland: I've never been there and I can't begin to understand the people who have. She wasn't pleased.'

'I can imagine. You were destined to be her last big fling.'

'She told me. In among the tears. God, she was like a burst pipe.'

'Were you nice to her? Did you comfort her?' asked Billie, warily.

'Of course. I'm not totally inhuman.' Sam seemed affronted. 'When she'd stopped crying and saying things in an incomprehensible, mucus-heavy way, she said she hoped we could be friends.'

'That's nice.' Billie could just imagine Heather's desperate face.

'I told her I didn't have a vacancy for a friend at the moment but if one came up I'd let her know.' Sam watched Billie's expression from the corner of his eye. 'I did warn you, back at the beginning. I'm not very nice, I said. I do what it says on the box.'

'It also says on the box that you're lovely to me. And besides, you're the only other fearless freedom fighter facing the world with a balanced view of love and its pitfalls.'

Scrambling to his feet, Sam nodded in the direction of the bike and handed Billie her helmet. 'Don't go romanticising us, Billificacious. We're misfits, that's all. Misfits who happened to find each other.'

THIRTEEN

It was Annie's big day. Bigger than the average wedding day, as she would be a bride in the morning, and the star of her own biopsy in the afternoon.

With the shop defiantly CLOSED, the bridesmaids took off in Dot's Reliant Robin. 'I wish I felt happier,' complained Dot, as the car belched along, taking corners at an unfeasible angle on the road to Neeveston.

'I know.' Billie was holding her door shut by hanging on to the handle, trying not to care that their three-wheeler was cutting up a Saab on the hospital roundabout. 'There's a cloud hanging over us.' A big, murky, cancerous cloud.

All hospitals smell much the same: bleach; soap; fear. Neeveston Hospital embraced them with sterile arms as they clattered down long linoleum corridors searching for the private room the conspiratorial nurses had somehow wangled for the day. The staff loved the tiny lady in the end bed and the story of her wedding had touched them all.

Armed with scrounged finery, pots of make-up and a set of heated rollers, Billie felt like a guerrilla as she roamed the hospital, looking for the room where she would detonate her romance bomb. She found it, and they rushed in to kiss and hug and embarrass Annie.

'I don't want any fuss,' was her first line, with trademark modesty.

'Boy, are you in the wrong place,' laughed Billie. 'This room is now the world capital of fuss.' She knelt in front of Annie, upright in a wipe-clean wing chair. 'I'll be on hair. Dot, you do nails.'

There was no champagne for this bride-to-be, no French manicure.

Operating-theatre etiquette insisted on nil by mouth and clean nails, so Dot would just file and shape and buff.

'Nervous?' asked Billie.

'I'm far too old to be nervous,' said Annie, whose hands were shaking so much that Dot could barely file the nails. 'I hope Ruby's all right.'

Tweaking a curtain, Billie was able to reassure her. 'I can see him down on the lawn with his best man. They're smoking cigars the size of small trees.' Sam with his shades and pointed boots and wraparound misanthropy might have been an unusual choice for best man, but he'd leapt at the chance. His grey velvet suit had impressed Ruby, who'd studied the lapels carefully and pronounced them 'quality *schmutter*'. For reasons of his own, Ruby hadn't invited his family to the ceremony: Annie simply had none. Apart from, that is, the raggle-taggle band that had closed ranks round her in this pastel-toned private room that looked like the best en suite in a mid-priced B&B.

Head heavy with rollers like a chrysanthemum, Annie stood up to be buttoned into her gown. It was stiff and magnificent, each pleat perfect.

Arms straight at her sides, Annie was silent and still, like a tiny statuette strayed from the top tier of a wedding cake. She looked beautiful. Her parchment skin was enhanced by the sheen of the material, and her regal posture made the most of the gown's design.

'I've never seen such a lovely bride,' said Billie, glad that she never cried at weddings.

Something seemed to be disturbing Annie as Billie backcombed her fluffy, rollered white hair into a respectable Princess Anne-ish bouffant.

'Have we fulfilled the rhyme?' she asked, fearfully. 'Something old, something new?'

'Well, the dress is forty years old,' mused Billie. 'Your wedding ring is new.'

Dot lifted the veil: 'Borrowed,' she said.

'Oh dear. Where's the something blue?' Annie was wringing a tissue between her hands.

Billie had to confess that there was nothing blue.

'I didn't take it seriously at my first wedding,' said Annie, agitated. 'Mother warned me I'd be sorry. And I was.'

Mother must have been a bundle of laughs. 'It's just a rhyme, Annie,' soothed Billie, pinning the veil carefully onto Annie's hair. Taking advantage of Annie's distraction to rub some pink stain on her thin lips,

Billie glanced at her watch. 'Go get Ruby,' she commanded. 'Just got to get the headdress on.'

Dot took off on oiled clogs.

The door opened and Billie spun round with a happy 'Ta daa!', which melted on her lips when she met the eyes of Annie's specialist. 'Oh. Sorry. Thought you were the groom.'

The consultant stood staring at Annie. 'What . . . oh, of course. The bloody wedding,' he muttered.

'Obviously,' said Billie. 'She doesn't always dress like this.'

'I'll have to move this.' The doctor whipped back the veil. 'Say aah.'

Frowning, Billie asked, 'Do you have to do this now? The registrar is already late. He'll be here any minute.'

Impatiently, the doctor replied, 'This lady is having an operation later. Would you rather I didn't check her over?' He had finished shining his tiny torch down Annie's throat and was now pointing it into her eyes, smudging the careful eye shadow Billie had just applied. 'My patient needs all her strength. Is this carry-on really necessary?'

'Not necessary, but rather wonderful, don't you think?'

Finishing up and patting Annie on the shoulder, the doctor asked, 'Remind me of the divorce statistics?' as he headed out of the door.

Dot had crept back in. 'Sounds like you,' she commented casually.

That exact thought had occurred to Billie. She rearranged Annie's veil.

At last, their work was done. Annie stood, holding on to the edge of her bed, her other hand cradling her posy of blush-coloured roses.

Chips of happiness from other big days completed Annie's wedding outfit. The borrowed shoes raised her, the borrowed veil protected her, the borrowed circlet on her head glistened like a halo. Women she had never met had reached out to wrap their arms round the little bride. Flanked by Sam, Ruby appeared. They were chortling and some instinct told Billie that a dubious joke had just been shared. They straightened up like altar boys when they felt her reproving gaze upon them.

Then Ruby saw his girl. 'Look at you,' he said, his rough voice full of emotion. 'Oh, my dear, you are a beauty.' He took her arm carefully.

Nurses crowded into the room, talking and giggling and lining the walls as they called out, 'Good luck, Annie!' and, 'What a stunner!' The registrar, a circular man in bottle-end glasses, was swept in with them, and he soon exerted his authority by requesting, 'A bit of 'ush.'

A respectful quiet fell over the guests and he welcomed them, then read from a card: 'Are you, Reuben Daniel, free legally to marry Anne Madeleine?'

Ruby was, and he said so. Annie was, too.

Billie smiled approvingly as Ruby slipped the ring onto Annie's finger, reciting the approved text: 'Anne Madeleine, I give you this ring as a token of my love and a symbol of our marriage.' He paused, before adding his own words: 'If we have one day of married life or a hundred years, I promise to love you and look after you always.'

When Ruby lifted the veil to plant a tentative, boyish kiss on Annie's lips, laughter and applause broke out, like glass shattering. Sam was crouching in front of the Wolffs with a Polaroid camera and Dot hissed at Billie, 'Confetti! We forgot confetti!' in a paralysed whisper.

The wedding planner struck her forehead, just as the room filled with a swirling snowstorm of paper dots, slung overarm by the gaggle of nurses. Billie plucked some out of the air. It wasn't confetti: it was a slew of tiny discs of paper from a hole punch. The nurses must have raided the office and filled their pockets. The tiny discs fluttered slowly down around the newly-weds in crazy meandering spirals, and Billie's disobedient tears fell with them.

In the midst of all this, Annie was wilting, like a lily on a stalk. Ruby guided her back to her chair with, 'Take a seat, Mrs Wolff.'

The improvised confetti had to be picked up and Billie bumped heads with one of the nurses as they stooped. 'Sorry,' she laughed, straightening up to find it wasn't a nurse. 'Oh! You got my text, then?'

'I crept in near the end.' Heather had lost even more weight and her face verged on sepulchral. 'This is the hospital my mum died in.'

'Oh, Heather.' Billie sucked her lip. 'I didn't know. What did you think of the ceremony? Not your average wedding, was it?'

'It was lovely.'

'And not a plumed horse in sight.'

The ward sister shooed the guests out. 'This lady has another appointment today and we need to prepare her.'

They loitered, enjoying Sam's impersonation of the registrar, until Annie was trundled out in a wheelchair in a papery NHS nightie. 'Wish me luck,' she said as, one by one, her wedding party bent to kiss her. 'I wish we'd fulfilled the rhyme,' she fretted. 'I can't help thinking . . .'

'Enough about something blue, Annie,' Ruby said. 'You're going to be fine. I'll be holding your hand again in a little while.'

'You've had something blue all along, Annie,' Sam drawled. Pointing to her sparrow-like legs, just visible beneath her gown, he said, 'Varicose veins, darling. They're blue. You're sorted.'

Nobody laughed until Annie did. Then they all felt free to giggle as she was pushed down the hall in her wheelchair, waving happily.

It was time to go. There was no band, no first dance. 'Ruby,' Billie intruded on his thoughts. 'Can we drop you home? We'll drive you back when Annie gets out of theatre.'

Looking affronted, Ruby said, 'No, I'll wait here. It's my place to be close by when she wakes up.'

'Call us the minute there's news,' said Billie, closing the door.

They plodded to the car park and Sam and Billie squeezed into the back seat of Dot's Reliant Robin.

'Shall I drop you off at your sister's?' Dot asked Heather, who was sitting beside her in the front.

'No.' Heather leaned back on the headrest and closed her eyes. 'Take me home, please.'"

One of Billie's deepest held beliefs was that people never fundamentally change. She knew that she would never, ever get married, and now that the Du Bois/Kelly extravaganza was back on, she knew that Heather would still hanker after the whole glossy shebang.

Lip service had been paid to the moving simplicity of Annie and Ruby's wedding, but now Heather was back off the carbs and back on the warpath. Not for her a stripped-back, bare and beautiful swapping of heartfelt oaths: Heather was yelping once more about ponies and doves and hors d'oeuvres that would 'show' her relatives.

The phone was busy. Billie knew she could do this now. These days she could confront a to-do list that reared at her like a spitting cobra, confident of her ability to wrestle it to the floor.

The only truly feared call had been taken by Dot, the day after the improvised hospital wedding. Picking up the phone, she'd muttered, 'Hello, Billie's erm, Brides things.' Phone technique wasn't her strong point. 'Ruby!' she'd gasped, fluttering her hands in Billie's direction.

Dropping a customer midway, Billie crossed the shop in two strides. It was hard not to wrest the phone away from her assistant, but she controlled herself and listened to Dot's uncertain, 'Ye-es,' and her anxious, 'Right,' and finally her jubilant shout of 'BENIGN!'

In the back of her mind, Billie had imagined that the Debs who turned up for her first Thursday in the shop would be a subtly changed girl, meeker and less prone to comment on others, gratitude for her second chance apparent in her demeanour. Debs's first full sentence had been, 'I had a bad biryani last night so don't come too close.'

Zac settled in right away, sitting happily on the desert island of his play mat, tickled every other minute by a besotted Dot.

Fresh from a visit to the weak but recovering Mrs Wolff, Billie's fingers twitched with the desire to email James about Annie's recovery. After the last exchange she wasn't welcome in his cyberspace any more. Spam filters were all very well, but Billie yearned for a twat filter, which would refuse to send her dafter missives. Blaming James for the squalid mess that Jackie and Ed had made was absurd. And childish. And petty. And cruel.

Childish pettiness was nothing new in her life but James had always absorbed her bad behaviour.

'That was back when he loved me,' she reminded herself. James had been patient with Billie's protracted growing-up: he'd been amused by her kicks against the constraints of a serious relationship, and generous when the inevitable tearful apologies kept him up half the night. The self-control that she'd lampooned had stopped him yelling at her when she'd rolled in hours later than she'd prophesied, and restricted his anger to a rolling of the eyes when she'd accused him of 'clipping her wings' if he asked her to phone when she was going to be late. From a distance, James's armour was taking on a white glint.

She had left James behind. It was a blessing that their wedding had been derailed at the last minute. He was pompous, bossy, detached . . . she scrabbled for her stock criticisms of him.

These were serious crimes indeed. If tried in front of an all-female, premenstrual jury James might get life. But he could plead that he would never, ever do what Ed had done: James was faithful to the core.

The memory of James explained Billie's confidence when she'd assured Ed that not all men would have taken up Jackie's Special Offer. James wouldn't have dispensed with his trousers and his principles so eagerly. And he would have been gallant with Annie on her big day. And he would have listened to her theory about Jake. Oh, she pinched herself, hoping to inject a little reality to her thought processes, this mythical James was faultless: at this rate he would have massaged her feet at the end of the day, fed her truffles and done the washing-up. Absence made her heart grow forgetful: the real James was no knight in shining armour, but an overworked accountant who took the mickey all through *Grand Designs*.

Billie accepted that she still had a lot to learn about the wedding-dress world, but even she knew that it was bad for business to have a boy in a blood-stained overall mooning about the shop.

Darius had it bad. He dropped in countless times a day, for change, for some sugar for his tea, to check the time.

One afternoon, despite several nudges, hints and an outright, 'Darius, *go home!*', he was still hanging about at closing time. 'Did I tell you I'm in the running for Junior Slaughterman of the Year?' he asked.

Dot didn't answer. She was especially quiet that afternoon.

Out of the corner of her eye, Billie saw Zelda leave her fudge emporium and head their way. She tensed.

'I reckon I'll win this year.' Darius nodded, reaching into his overall pocket. 'I've got a secret weapon, see.' Slowly he pulled out a long, crooked sausage. 'I call it the Dot. No toes, no snout, no genitals. Just pure meat.' Like a knight of old laying down his sword before his lady, Darius gracefully held out the sausage in both hands to Dot.

Swooping in like an avenging angel (albeit one with an Elvis bouffant) Zelda snatched the Dot. Not giving it the respect a prize-winning meat product deserves, she thrashed Darius with it. 'Take your chipolatas, sonny, and stick 'em! This girl's heartsick. She don't need you'— Zelda punctuated the 'you' with a particularly hard thwack to Darius's retreating bottom—'and your meat bothering her.'

Billie watched in disbelief as Zelda, at least a foot and a half smaller than Darius, manhandled him out of the door and onto the pavement, slinging the now detumescent Dot after him. 'Get back to your grandfather's dump of a shop and stay there!' she yelled. 'Like grandfather like grandson. Always poking your sausage where it's not wanted!'

There was never a good time to ask Sly what his plans were. He didn't seem to have any, beyond endlessly circuiting Sole Bay like a gull.

One word changed the way Billie felt about Sly, and she suspected it was one he'd never used to her before. Picking at burnt beans on toast on Herbert's balmy deck, Sly said, out of the blue, 'Thanks.'

Looking around for the hidden camera, Billie queried, 'Eh?'

'Thanks,' said Sly, as if he said it every day. 'You've been taking the flak for me. I heard Mum giving you a hard time on the phone the other day and you could have snitched but you didn't. Thanks.'

'It's OK.' Billie felt like bursting. Sly had noticed. He'd noticed that she'd plodded on in her traditional role as family problem, absorbing her mother's scattergun affection/abuse and protecting him. If Billie was honest, she was also protecting her mother, that other mother she'd glimpsed in the mirror. Such a fragile, vulnerable woman couldn't cope with her hero son's fall from grace. 'Thanks.' She realised that she was thanking Sly for thanking her, but she couldn't stop herself.

'You've done pretty well with that shop, you know.'

This was entering the realm of fantasy: Sly was praising her.

'Really?' she goggled.

'It's ticking over nicely,' Sly conceded. 'You're making a lot of customers happy.' He hunter-gathered a baked bean. 'Well done.'

This was a surprise. Scanning her in-box for a vital missive concerning the health of one of the plumed horses, Billie saw an email from James.

> I don't want to leave things like this between us. I over-reacted to your over-reaction. If I'd taken a minute to think about it, I could have imagined how hurt you were by Jackie. (I've heard the whole story since, from the horse's mouth, and even with Jackie's spin on it, it sounds dire.) You needed to lash out.
>
> And then I felt got at. So I wrote back, just as hot-headed, just as nasty. I should have been more grown up, and I regret it now.
>
> Talking of being grown up, I can't do this any more, Bill. Keep in touch, I mean. It's harder than I imagined. Some things should stay buried. I've been re-examining the past and it's confusing, depressing, unsettling—generally bad for us, I think.
>
> Let's wave goodbye as friends. At least we can console ourselves that we did better than last time, eh?
>
> J

Billie sniffed, whether dismissively or sadly it was hard to tell. 'Good,' she said to herself. 'Good good good.' She closed her eyes. Her features sagged with sadness, heavy as the linen bag of Sole Bay pebbles that held open the door of Billie's Brides. She opened her eyes, said one more weary 'good' and went back downstairs to the shop.

A plague of disease-ridden vermin were rampaging through the stock-room. This was how Billie saw it. Dot preferred to say that some nice mousey types had come to stay for a while. Before Billie got busy with traps, Dot had begged for a chance to persuade them to leave.

Downstairs in the shop, Billie was pottering as Dot murmured at her rodent friends. Billie was an expert potterer and she was just getting into it—easing the tissue-paper pile a centimetre to the right, putting the pens in the pen tub the right way up—when she turned, profes-sional smile in place, at the sound of the shop bell.

It was a ghost.

'Jake!' breathed Billie, taking a hasty step backwards.

'Dot in?' he asked, as if he'd come from across the road and not from beyond the grave. His beard was shaggier than Billie remembered and the bones of his face more pronounced.

'You're alive,' she gasped.

Jake frowned. 'Yes,' he nodded. 'Dot in?' he asked again.

'Where have you been?' Billie was struggling to take in this healthy, three-dimensional Jake, perfect in every detail right down to the speech impediments and the dirty toenails. He was carrying a large stretched canvas, wrapped in a sheet.

A burst of song from upstairs tugged Jake's gaze upwards. He moved slowly across the shop, as if he was sleepwalking. At the foot of the stairs he turned and said, 'Wish me luck.'

Perhaps, thought Billie, he *is* a ghost. The original Jake would never have admitted to needing anything so mundane as luck.

Now that Zelda was suddenly exonerated of murder most foul (albeit most understandable), Billie nipped next door to bring her up to date. Deserting her post, Zelda waddled back to Billie's Brides.

When two people share the same vice there's no need for polite pre-tence, so Zelda and Billie eavesdropped shamelessly, huddling together by the stairs and straining to hear what was going on above their heads.

Unfortunately they couldn't discern words, just a low murmur. And then tears. A deluge of tears.

'I'm going up,' grunted Zelda, setting one foot on the stairs.

'No, listen,' grinned Billie. 'They're happy tears!' The next moment she and Zelda had to fly across the floorboards and affect nonchalance by the till: Dot and her prodigal boyfriend were coming down.

'He's back!' Dot's innocent happiness was almost catching.

Almost. 'So I see,' sighed Zelda, looking Jake up and down as if he'd just applied for the post of Chief Handbag Stealer. 'You took my advice, then?' She nodded at the canvas that Dot was clutching.

'Yup.' Jake was taciturn. He was greedily focused on Dot.

She was something to see. The pallor had disappeared, her posture had straightened and her hair had somehow perked itself up. She was displaying all the attributes Cruft's looks for in a puppy: sparkling eyes, rude health and a loud yap.

'Look at this! Just look at this!' She spun the painting round.

The full-length portrait of Dot was more realistic and straightforward than Jake's usual tricksy style. She was wearing a gauzy gown through which the slender lines of her body could just be glimpsed, and her gaze out at the viewer was direct and frank and loving. He had caught the sweet expression in her eyes perfectly.

'It's beautiful,' said Billie. 'I didn't realise you could paint like this.'

'I don't normally have a subject like Dot. I've never felt so inspired.'

Billie checked Jake for telltale signs of facetiousness but couldn't discern any: he'd given Dot an honest compliment, the very one she'd been yearning to hear for years. 'Why don't you trot home and hang the picture?' she suggested. A reunion is an intimate thing, and besides, Jake smelt like a cabbage-processing plant.

'What did you mean,' Billie asked Zelda as soon as the intertwined pair left, 'when you said he took your advice?'

'The night Dot threw him out, he banged on my door,' Zelda elucidated. 'What a state. Soaked through. Sobbing. Wittering about killing himself. I was tempted to encourage him, or even drive him to Beachy Head myself. But then I thought of Dot, and I tried to help. Said he had to value her. Appreciate her. I gave him a good telling-off. He was whining about how he couldn't tell her how he felt and he didn't have the right words. So I told him to paint her. To show how he felt through his art. I would never have suggested it if I thought the bugger was going to take me seriously. She's better off without him. The little sod wouldn't tell me where he was going, wouldn't say when, if, he'd be back. He ran off so fast he left his stupid hat behind.'

'Did you see how happy Dot looked?' asked Billie, wonderingly. 'As if she'd glimpsed heaven. It won't last, of course. He'll start insulting her again. Bullying her. Walking all over her.'

'It won't matter,' said Zelda. 'She loves him. What I didn't know before today, is that he loves her.' She shrugged. 'Who would have thought he could paint like that? Beauty in every brushstroke.'

That was inarguable. 'It's easy to believe that Jake loves her: Dot's so completely and utterly nice. But what does she see in him?' Billie was tussling with an old topic again. 'He doesn't deserve someone like Dot.'

'People don't deserve love,' said Zelda. 'If that counted for anything, half the world would be on their own. You can't explain it. We just choose to love somebody and that's that. I loved the same man for fifty years but I'd happily run him over with a tank if I got the opportunity.' Zelda fixed Billie with a searching look. 'People choose love. They always do. You're a smart girl, Billie. You knew that, didn't you?' She slid one hand into the pocket of her apron. 'About time you tried my special recipe.'

Billie took the fudge with a clear conscience. 'Oh. My. God.' She leaned back on the counter, cheeks flushed. 'I'd rather eat that than invite Brad Pitt to buy me at auction. What's in it?'

Ignoring her, Zelda mused further on the subject of the day. 'On paper, you should have loved that Ed. Handsome. Polite. Went like a rocket in bed, no doubt. But you didn't love him. And you never would. I knew that. Did *you* know?'

'Yes.' As soon as she said it, Billie knew it was true.

'Your heart is already taken. Hearts aren't like heads, they're not fickle.' Zelda paused. 'Nip next door and fetch me emergency gin, darlin',' ordered Zelda, with the expectancy of obedience dictators enjoy.

Billie nipped, the gin was opened, and the two women settled down in Billie's Brides with a glass each. 'The night of the storm—' Billie began.

'Oh, that evil night!' wailed Zelda, grabbing centre stage immediately. 'The night that wrenched my Raven away from me.' She hung her dyed head, after a fortifying sip of Mother's Ruin. 'I didn't let on about Raven's death. I know how Dot felt about him and I didn't want to burden her. She had enough to worry about. To know that cat was to love him. I buried him in the garden, so he'll always be close. I had to do something to keep me mind off him, so I finally got round to making my extra-special, tip-top fudge.'

'You'll laugh, Zelda, but I used to think you were a witch.'

'Well of course I'm a witch. That's how I kept my looks.' Zelda smiled and her dentures slipped. 'Pour us another gin, there's a good girl.'

Approaching Herbert's Dream II, Billie could hear voices.

Crouching, Billie tiptoed towards the tiny window and peeped in. She could see Sly standing with his head in his hands, and she could make out the shoulder of a smaller female standing in front of him. That shoulder gave the game away. Only Sana could wear linen so uncrumpled in a heatwave.

'About time!' laughed Billie, flinging the door open and crossing to kiss her sister-in-law. 'Have you managed to forgive him?'

'Nearly.' Sana shook her head in a kind of horrified awe. 'Honestly, Billie, men . . .'

Head now out of his hands, Sly's face was a medley of differing emotions. He looked ashamed, relieved, happy and suicidal all at once. Billie realised how much he'd been holding in during their enforced hut share. She was suddenly glad not to be a slab of testosterone, afraid to show weakness. 'Maybe now you can show him that money isn't everything.'

'Oh, it was never the money. It was the lies. Leaving the house for the office every morning. Saying he was holding a seminar when he was dancing about in a loincloth. Spartakiss! If only he'd trusted me, I could have come up with a much better name.' This seemed to annoy her more than the bankruptcy. 'I've got a job now,' Sana said, calm again.

'No. I told you the day we got married you'd never have to work,' said Sly vehemently.

Billie said, 'People say all sorts of crap on their wedding day, Sly.'

Sana said, 'I meant every word. I said I'd stand by you in sickness and in health, and you're certainly sick in the head, Slightly Baskerville.' Sana stood a little taller, 'And yes, I know you don't like your whole name, but I don't like being treated like a child by my own husband.'

Beneath the hut, tectonic plates were shifting. The power in this marriage was transferring. Sana told Sly that she had taken up a position as PA in a fashion importer's. 'The money is nothing like what you earned. Life won't be fabulous, but it will be OK. And as long as you and Deirdre and Moto are there, that's enough for me.'

The Inner Winner hugged his landlady and sat in the passenger seat as his remodelled wife drove him away.

The hut felt very small that night. Around Billie, souls were pairing off again. She was the outrider once more, flying the flag for independence and freedom. And for leaving the radio on all night because the silence of her four walls was just too much.

FOURTEEN

THE BIG DAY had arrived. For most, it was another ordinary Saturday. The 23rd of August. A day off, perhaps.

In Herbert's Dream II it was D-Day, a Red-Letter Day, the day Billie's Brides earned its stripes. It was Doomsday.

Billie had been up since first light, dosing herself with strong coffee in preparation for the trials ahead. She'd last heard from Heather at midnight when the bride-to-be had woken from her beauty sleep to fret about the registrar's breath.

Accessorising an oyster silk slip dress with Reeboks, Billie slipped her high heels into a capacious shoulder bag. Half-wedding guest, half-slave, the final sartorial touches would have to wait until her final 'to-do' list had been ticked into submission.

Ringing the doorbell at Heather's house at 10 a.m., Billie had already looked in at Homestead Hall, double-checked the arrival time for the open carriage, and bought a new pair of nude thirty-denier tights for bridesmaid number four.

The tiny house, bursting with people, was unrecognisable as the home Billie had spent hours discussing place cards in. Dean had been banished to Ed's, and both storeys were awash with women. The twelve bridesmaids were conducting whispered conversations asking what they had ever done to Heather to make her put them in drop-waist cappuccino taffeta with matching marabou boleros.

'*I need the bog!*' Heather was screaming at the closed toilet door, face half made up and rollers in her hair.

Billie approached Heather with cautious professionalism.

'Have you checked the—' Heather began.

'Whatever it is, yes. I've checked flowers, I've checked place settings, I've checked Dean's choice of underpants. I would check your blood pressure, but something tells me I wouldn't like it.' Billie had become very bossy since the wedding had been raised from the dead. Now that she matched Heather strop for strop they got along just fine.

'What time is it?' asked Heather, before banging on the toilet door again. *'Get out of there! I am getting married in three hours!* Doesn't anybody care? Billie! Sort out Granny's hat!'

Billie sought out Granny, chain-smoking down in the sitting room. 'I understand there's something wrong with your hat?' As far as Billie could see the hat was fine.

'I've gone off it,' announced the well-preserved woman, skinny as dental floss and about as much fun. 'It needs a flower on the brim.' She tossed the plain white boater across the room.

'I'll pick one from the garden,' said Billie, optimistically, bending down to retrieve the hat.

'I'm a martyr to hay fever.' Granny took a long, somehow malevolent drag on her cigarette. 'You can make one.' She put her head on one side. 'For three grand, dear, you can make me a flower, surely?'

'It'll be my pleasure,' Billie assured her, backing out on her trainers and pulling some swift, evil faces behind the door.

She shut herself in the utility room. The hat stared unhelpfully back from the top of the washing machine. Plain, white, unremarkable, it certainly needed something to cheer it up. Billie racked her brains.

Many times over the years she'd seen her mother fashion props out of the most unprepossessing raw materials.

What would Mum do? Billie asked herself. She rifled her bag, discarding tat. A packet of tampons lay at the bottom. Billie took one out. White, it matched the hat.

By unwrapping them, tying them all together, adding a few leaves cut from the green plastic lid of a detergent tub, and tweaking them carefully, Billie achieved a bold, modernist chrysanthemum. She fixed it to the band of the hat with bendy tags filched from Heather's selection of sandwich bags. 'Thanks, Mum,' she whispered.

Surprised, Granny managed a grudging, 'Very pretty.'

The make-up artist was powdering Angela's upturned face in the spare bedroom. As Billie passed the open door an 'Oi!' from Angela called her back. 'Are you bringing a plus one?' Angela wanted to know.

'No.' Billie smiled. 'Thank God.'

'For a while there,' said Angela, closing her eyes as they were powdered over, 'I thought you had your eye on Ed.' She opened one eye. 'Did you?'

Billie ditched honesty for a circumspect, 'Don't worry, he's all yours.'

Succumbing to eyeliner, Angela said complacently, 'We'll have matching tattoos by Monday.' She lowered her voice. 'How's my sister doing? Do you think she'll be all right?'

'Of course.' Billie seemed to know Heather better than her sibling did: all this hysteria would morph into glacial calm the moment she hit the church. 'This is the day she's been waiting for.'

'For some reason. I mean . . .' Angela pulled a face. '*Dean*. Would you?'

'I wouldn't, to be honest. But Heather would. She loves him.' Billie trotted out. She was too busy to discuss the basics of life with Angela. Heather's love for Dean was Heather's business. Just like Dot's feelings for Jake, they didn't need to be explained or justified. People fell in love, and they expressed it in different ways. Billie knew she would never want to celebrate love by dressing up in white and hiring a Rolling Stones tribute band, but she no longer scoffed at Heather and women like her.

No. Billie had realised, during the recent long nights alone in Herbert, that she envied those women their self-knowledge and the way they knew what to do when love came along. They treated it with respect. When Billie had been handed love she'd jiggled it and tossed it and left greasy fingerprints all over it. She knew better now.

'I have to get back to the shop,' Billie told Heather.

'You can't!' whined Heather. She sat on the edge of her bed, half dressed. 'I need you.'

'You've got all the help you need. I'm only in the way here.' Billie was expected back so Dot could visit Annie, who was still in hospital: under the new régime Debs couldn't be left in charge of the shop. She reached out and hauled in a passing bridesmaid. 'Lyndsey here will look after you. Won't you, Lyndsey?' she asked, nodding encouragingly.

'Of course.' Lyndsey patted Heather's arm. 'All you have to do is sit back and enjoy your day. Things will go wrong, of course. It doesn't matter one bit. As long as you enjoy yourself, that's the main thing.'

'Are you trying to kill me?' Heather shouted so loudly that Lyndsey leapt back and trod on Hamish the weeny pageboy. 'Do you want me to drop down dead in front of you? Things will go wrong? Have you any idea how much I've spent? I could have bought a street in Wales for what this fucking wedding has cost me!'

Blubbering in pain from the stab of Lyndsey's cappuccino stiletto, Hamish blundered backwards onto the hem of Heather's underskirt.

'No!' gasped Heather, darting down to examine the fragile silk. *'Get out, you troll!'* she bawled, an inch from the terrified pageboy's face.

Hamish was a blur as he sped down the stairs. Before she left for the shop, Billie gingerly placed his knickerbockers in the fast cycle of the washing machine.

'**I**s that what you're wearing?' asked Debs, frowning at the oyster-coloured slip dress.

'It looks better with the shoes,' said Billie, hopefully, doing up the delicate straps of her gold sandals.

'Yeah,' agreed Debs. 'Looks a bit less like underwear now.'

'Zac looks smart.' As smart as a doorman at a dodgy nightclub. Zac's baby tufts had been gelled into a Mohican and he was wearing a bow tie over his Babygro. Billie had been surprised when Debs received an invitation, but Heather had scattered them like confetti. Zelda was a guest (apparently she was a crony of some aunt or other), as was Mr Dyke. 'It was nice of Heather to invite you and the baby, wasn't it?'

'S'pose. Oh, look, it's your poof.'

Sam's suit was getting another outing. His hair was shorter.

'You've been clipped,' said Billie, approvingly. She was proud of Sam's looks in a maternal way, as if his broad shoulders and even teeth reflected well on her.

'We need to talk.'

'Blimey.' Billie was taken aback. 'If we were going out I'd assume you were going to chuck me.'

'I'm serious, Billie. We need to talk.'

'You called me Billie,' said Billie, slowly, studying him. 'You've never called me that before. Why are you so serious?'

'Can we get out of here?'

'Sure.' Billie could tell that Sam meant business. She turned to Debs and took hold of her hand. 'Debs, will you look after the shop while I talk to Sam?'

'But you said . . .' Debs was silenced by a squeeze from Billie's fingers. She thought for a second, then said, 'Yeah.' She squeezed back and a tiny laugh slipped out. 'And don't worry.'

'I'm not worried.' Billie enjoyed the little smile they shared.

His arm through hers, Sam marched Billie through Sole Bay. He'd slipped his dark glasses on. 'You're not going to like this. I'm leaving. I'm off to London straight after the wedding.'

Mid-march, Billie halted. Her heart was sideways in her chest as she pulled her arm from his. In a very small voice she said, 'Sam, you can't go.' She was losing her partner, her buddy, the only other soul in Sole Bay inoculated against love.

Refusing to stop, Sam forced her to scuttle after him. 'I've got to go. The book's finished. I need to see London again. I tried, but I can't live without casual sex and people being rude to me on public transport.'

Crushed, Billie noted the ease with which her Siamese twin could leave her. 'Oh. OK. Right.'

'Obviously I can't leave you on your own.' Sam hurried her on until they were at the bandstand. There he plonked her down on the rotting bench, then swung one foot up beside her. Leaning down into her face, he told her, 'I've found you a replacement.'

'Don't you dare inflict a cat on me, Sam,' Billie warned heatedly. 'I've got a few years left before I give in and get a cat.'

'It's not a cat, you fool. You've got to trust me, Miss Baskerville. I'm doing this for your own good, even if you hate me for it.'

'Will you stop being so damned cryptic!' Billie was ready to fly apart. 'What is this about?'

'Secrets.' Sam cocked an eyebrow. 'Know anybody with a secret?'

'Well, no,' blustered Billie, not liking this swerve of direction much.

'Somebody with a little white lie on their conscience perhaps?'

'I hope you're not talking about me, Sam Nolan. I'm an open book.'

An eloquent look suggested that Sam didn't believe her. 'It's home truths time. I could have just buggered off back to London without any of this, but I couldn't because . . .' Sam faltered. Sam, who was never lost for words, faltered. 'Because I love you, I suppose.'

'Aw!' Billie relaxed. 'Do you? I love you, you know.'

'All right, all right, enough. I'm going to give you some advice now, even though I don't believe in the stuff. Don't ignore me, doll. Once, a long time ago, I ignored somebody who was trying to help me. And I regret it.' Sam swallowed. 'I've never said that out loud before.'

'What do you regret?' Tense again, Billie sat up straighter.

'Years ago, a friend of my dad's took me to one side. I was so young. Eighteen. With hindsight I can see that he was gay. And he told me to think very hard about what I was about to do. He knew I wasn't the clean-cut young hetero my parents boasted about at the golf club. He saw the signs.' Sam smiled. 'Smelt the cologne. But I pretended I didn't know what he was on about. So I went ahead and got married.'

'No!' barked Billie. 'You were married?'

'I *am* married.' Sam nodded. 'She won't divorce me.'

'Who was she?' Billie was avid for detail. 'Where is she?'

'She was the girl next door. Literally. She chain-smokes in Guildford now. She never got over it either.' Sam shivered.

'So what was the marriage like?'

'The worst sex and the loudest rows in the history of the Home Counties.' Sam shrugged. 'It was a farce, and it was all my fault. I broke her heart. My first trophy.' He swallowed. 'One I didn't want. One that still makes me hate myself. All because I didn't listen.' He held up a long finger. 'So you listen to me, and you listen good.'

'OK.' Billie shrank a little.

'Don't hate me.' Sam took a deep breath. 'I read all the emails you and James sent to one another.'

'You what?' Billie spluttered and tried to jump up, but Sam put a strong hand on her shoulder and held her down. 'How? When?'

'Spare me the moral outrage. You know I'm lacking in niceties. I saw them when I borrowed your computer. Can we get over the fact that I read them and move on?'

Billie nodded. She was uncomfortable, as if Sam had been elbow-deep in her knicker drawer, but she was also curious. 'Go on.'

'Every one of those emails was a love letter.'

'Oh, come on! They were just badly typed nothings.'

'His weren't badly typed. And just like yours, they were love letters.'

Billie was having none of this. 'If you remember, he only got in touch to tell me he'd found somebody else.'

'Yes,' drawled Sam. 'Funny that. I mean, why bother? If he was sooooo over you, why bother?'

'To hurt me, I suppose.'

'To get a rise out of you. To rattle your cage. To get your attention.'

'He called her his significant other.'

'And you waxed lyrical about your brave fireman.'

'Exactly,' said Billie, defiantly.

'The very same fireman you couldn't bring yourself to sleep with.'

'That was definitely nothing at all to do with James,' said Billie.

'Of course not. And he sorted out your VAT,' Sam went on.

'Exactly,' said Billie, adding, 'again,' slightly sheepishly.

'Love letters!' Sam spluttered. 'Two stubborn fools who couldn't type what they really felt, pussyfooting about like Edwardian spinsters.'

'You're wrong.' Billie shook her head, wondering where this meandering conversation was headed. Was Sam going to suggest some sort of reconciliation? He wouldn't say that if he'd seen James's last email. 'If you remember, he advised me to hang on to Ed.'

'Jealous. Covering it up.'

'If he was jealous he would have been upset when I told him I was falling for Ed. Instead he went all snooty on me.'

'Duh,' said Sam. 'Of course he went snooty. I'm betting he always used to when you got him where it hurts? Yes?'

That was true. Billie recalled how James would suddenly morph into Prince Charles if she laughed at his tie. 'So what?'

'So what?' shouted Sam. 'So the poor guy was trying to build a time machine in every single email. All those *do you remember?*s He was trying to rekindle the old feelings. He was testing you. And what do you go and do, you daft lump?'

'I blame James for Jackie and Ed sleeping together.'

'Exactimundo.' Sam folded his arms, satisfied.

'But it doesn't matter. I don't know where you think this is going, but James and I have nothing more to say to each other.'

'Stick that chin any higher and a gull will land on it,' scoffed Sam. 'Are you telling me you didn't get a glow all over you when he said he'd fetch Blankie? And as for that last little exchange. Yours was a doozie, managing to blame him for Jackie's dropped knickers.' Sam unfolded his arms, and poked her in the shoulder. 'The biggest, baldest love letter of them all. You might as well have typed "come and rescue me"!'

'Rubbish,' insisted Billie, her head beginning to spin with the ramifications of what Sam was forcing her to confront. 'And he replied by thanking God we never got married.'

'Anger. Fear. The usual male stuff,' decreed Sam.

'You didn't see the last one,' said Billie, quietly. 'James told me he couldn't stay in touch. He killed us stone dead. Again.'

'And what reasons did he give?'

'Erm, confusion, or something like that.'

'You people . . . Thank God neither of you are detectives .'

'What are you saying. That I'm in love with James?' She swallowed. 'Still?'

'You've misdiagnosed yourself all these years. You're not allergic to love, or commitment, or even marriage. You're allergic to big, turn-off, fancy weddings, that's all. You don't think you had a lucky escape at all. You wish you and James had got married.'

Mouth dry, Billie longed to vault over the bandstand rail and throw herself in the sea. She didn't want to answer. She'd been running from that thought since August 23rd last year: today was its anniversary and she was tired of running. 'There's something you don't know,' she began. 'There's one detail I always fudge in The Story.'

Shutting her eyes, Billie remembered the cell that her hotel room had become last August. She'd been primped and prepared and deemed ready. Her dress was an extraordinary construction, designed to elicit a 'Wow!' from the hundred or so guests gathering at the church.

Decisions about cake, about colour schemes, about flowers, about hundreds of things Billie couldn't care less about had been extracted from her over the previous weeks. She'd flailed, not waving but drowning: nobody had noticed. Her mother was up to her haunches in estimates and invoices, and her girlfriends couldn't wait for the reception.

James's days were unchanged, whereas Billie had veered off the track of everyday life some time ago. Her waking hours (and even her lurid dreams) were dominated by marquees and honeymoon packages. James was going to work, playing tennis, watching documentaries about the Nazis, and suggesting sex at the exact moment she was too tired to contemplate it. He was on the horizon, with the normal folk, while Billie was marooned in the valley with the crazy wedding tribe.

That girl in the mirror, around whom the bridesmaids were fussing, had looked as unfamiliar to Billie as James did.

Back in the present, with Sam invading her space, Billie bit her lip and said, 'James didn't jilt me. I jilted him.'

'Yeah, I know,' Sam said glibly. 'He told me.'

Eyes wide, Billie yelped, 'You've spoken to him? So you know. You know I lied.' She was hot with shame.

'And I still love you,' Sam reassured her unsentimentally. 'More to the point, so does James. Now *that's* forgiveness.'

'Please, Sam, tell me what this is all about,' groaned Billie.

'I told you. I've arranged a replacement me.' Sam grasped her hand and tugged her off the bench. 'Come on!'

Dragging Billie along the front, Sam steered her towards Herbert's Dream II. Her hair was in her eyes and the sun was glancing off the pebbles, but Billie could see a figure on Herbert's verandah.

'You're a year late.' Sam stopped. 'But you're finally here. Go get him.' He propelled Billie towards her beach hut, where James waited.

Like a sleepwalker, Billie put one unsteady foot in front of the other. She pushed her hair out of her eyes and took him in as she drew nearer. James was the same as she remembered. Exactly. Fair. Solid. Firm jaw. Crooked front tooth. Green eyes that didn't waver. Arms open wide.

They held on to each other for a long time.

'I'm sorry,' croaked Billie.

'No, I am,' said James. 'I should have noticed.'

'No, I am,' insisted Billie. 'I was cruel.'

'You were scared.'

'And cruel.'

'OK.' James laughed into her hair. 'I give in. You can be sorry. But only if you let me be a bit sorrier.'

Pulling away, but no further than their arms would reach, Billie said, 'We were very far apart, weren't we? I was drowning in the wedding, and you seemed so distant.' Hastily, she qualified that with a, 'I'm not blaming you. It was me, all me.'

'Let's never get that far apart again,' said James, soberly.

'Can you really forgive . . . what I did?' Billie had spent a year believing she was a monster.

'The minute I understood you, I forgave you. But it took a hell of a long time to understand you.'

With too many tears for glamour, Billie asked, fearfully, 'What about your significant other?'

Shaking his head, James dismissed the poor girl. 'Not that significant. She wasn't really like you. Nobody's like you, Billie.'

Feeling as if she might take off and whizz around Sole Bay like a punctured balloon, Billie laughed giddily. 'I hope that's a compliment.'

'It is,' said James, 'and then again it isn't.' He kissed her, despite the wayward hair that was determined to come between them.

That kiss took her home. 'James, James,' she whispered, panic-stricken. 'I love you, I love you, James, I've always loved you, James.'

'It's all right,' soothed James. 'I've always loved you, too. It's over.'

'Are we back together?'

'At bloody last,' nodded James.

A cough interrupted them. Sam had joined them on Herbert's deck. 'We've got to find a way of gluing you two together so you don't come apart again,' he said, mock grave.

'No wedding!' wailed Billie, putting up an arm. 'I admit I'm in love but I haven't changed my entire personality. I'd rather slash my—'

'Yeah, yeah, yeah.' Sam flapped his hands to calm Billie down. 'We know. We get it.' He leaned towards her and spoke slowly. '*You don't like weddings.* Got it.' He took a piece of paper out of his pocket and waggled it. 'James and I have had an idea,' he said, grinning.

Billie had had a recurring nightmare along these lines. She was standing in all her bridal finery, and the entire congregation was staring at her. Just as they were now.

Unlike her dreams, this congregation consisted of just two people, Sam and James. Her finery was different, too. The bridal bouquet was a sprig of plastic roses filched from the window box of Herbert's Dream II's neighbour. The veil was Blankie, tied under her chin and making her ears rather hot.

'Are we ready?' asked the minister.

'Well?' James inclined his head doubtfully down at his blushing bride. 'Are you? This time?'

'Ready,' whispered Billie, pushing Blankie up her forehead.

'Then I'll begin.' The minister was new to his job. Until the previous evening he'd just been a millionaire illustrator with peroxide hair and an attitude problem. Now, thanks to an internet payment of fifty-five dollars, he was a fully paid-up minister of the Church of Jesus Christ Megastar. As he'd explained to Billie, 'We're an LA-based church, not as popular as our Catholic rivals but a lot more easy-going. We're very big on forgiveness. Which is just as well,' he had said.

Now Sam was solemn. 'Brethren, please take each other's hand.'

After a bit of tussling, Billie's hand lay prettily in James's larger one. She looked down at them, dewy-eyed, and regretted writing the phone number for the dry-cleaner's along her thumb that morning.

'Billie and James,' boomed Sam, over the wind and sea and gulls. 'I now pronounce you bird and bloke. Don't split up again. Amen.'

'Ayyyyyyyymen!' whooped James, whose accountant friends would not have recognised him.

'Amen!' blubbed Billie, who was becoming reconciled to the fact that, after years of believing the contrary, she was *exactly* the sort of girl who cried at weddings.

The last to arrive, Billie and Sam tiptoed like naughty children into the private chapel in the grounds of Homestead Hall and slipped into the back pew, skating down it on their bottoms to find the middle. Billie had never been so joyous and so restless, nor less inclined to sit still and listen to a vicar.

Wiggling on the hard bench, she squeezed Sam's arm. She giggled. She sighed. She shrugged. In short, she was hugely irritating.

'Do you adore James? Isn't he fantabulous?' Billie asked Sam, in a penetrating whisper.

'He's a good bloke.' Coming from Sam, this meagre compliment was meaningful.

'Yes, he is. He's the goodest ever bloke in the history of blokedom. Dot!' Billie noticed the sleek waterfall of strawberry hair in the next pew. Jake had earlier announced that his principles wouldn't allow him to enter a house devoted to the empty promises of a dead deity, and Billie had passed him in the churchyard stretched out on a tomb like a martyr in fancy dress. She leaned forward to yank Dot's hair.

Spinning round, Dot gave Billie a thumbs up. 'Everything looks great, well done!' she mouthed.

Everything did indeed look great. The small, mellow-toned stone chapel was all gussied up, its columns garlanded with freesias, its altar draped with ivy. Tasteful, rustic and charming, it resembled a still from one of the wedding magazines Billie flicked through with gritted teeth and heaving stomach: and it was all her own work.

'Gosh,' thought Billie, her vocabulary distinctly Sole Bay. 'I'm a *good* wedding planner.' It was indisputable: after a decade of avoiding the sack by judicious use of revealing tops and diligent buck-passing, Billie Baskerville was good at her job.

'Have you redone your make-up?' whispered Dot, twisting in her seat to steal a good look at her boss. 'You look about twelve.'

'I've redone my soul,' claimed Billie ebulliently. She wiggled again.

'Calm down,' hissed Sam, crossly. 'People will think you're on drugs.'

'I am!' Billie sat on her hands, as if they were belligerent drunks, and tried to focus on the other guests. The wiggling stopped when her eyes found the back of Ed's head.

In best-man finery, he was talking to the vicar at the front of the chapel. Billie took in the sexy cap of curls on his modelled skull, and the expanse of shoulder in a well-cut morning coat. He was inescapably graceful, holding his top hat as if he wore one every day down at the fire station, and yet he'd behaved so badly. There was no tug of desire, no tidemark of regret. When Billie looked at Ed, she saw a handsome, weak man. Not a bad man, and not a man she mourned.

A formidable woman in a strange hat was near. Zelda took up an awful lot of pew beside Dot, a glittering black confection of feathers and bows clamped to her head. She was chewing, her powdered and painted face sucking and chomping in a bovine way. Billie watched her waggle her bag of fudge across Dot's lap in Mr Dyke's direction.

Half turning, he shook his head genially and a hazy notion glimmered in Billie's head. A penny didn't drop, but it teetered on the edge. Mr Dyke's and Zelda's profiles faced each other, like cameos, over Dot's innocent head; cogs began to whirr in Billie's mind.

A wet wipe hit her squarely in the ear. Zac's chubby hands applauded his own aim, from the far end of the pew in front. Debs scolded him absent-mindedly, and Billie leaned across Sam to ask her, 'Lock up OK?'

'Yeah.' Debs, her lobster décolletage contrasting vividly with her lime-green sundress, added, 'I cashed up an' all.'

'Good.' Billie's radiance must have lapped out as far as Debs, because the girl smiled, really smiled, in response.

Under his breath, Sam hummed the *Crimewatch* theme, but he was drowned by the Wedding March.

Everyone stood up at once, as creaking double doors at the back of the church opened to let sunshine stream through the dusty chapel.

Heads turned to get their first view of the queen bee at the centre of the day, but before Billie craned her neck to see Heather, she intercepted the look Zelda threw at the oblivious Mr Dyke over Dot's head.

That look was an eloquent one: it gave away decades of secrets and longings. It was the look of a woman who had chosen to love a man decades ago, and who had never wavered. Perhaps happiness rendered Billie super-perceptive, but suddenly she saw that if she was to make a jigsaw out of Zelda's eyes, Mr Dyke's nose, Zelda's complexion and the butcher's affable air, the picture on the box would be Dot.

Oh Zelda, groaned Billie inwardly. The little woman had made a painful choice a long time ago: she'd given up her baby and watched her grow up unloved, but respectable. And now Zelda was looking over her granddaughter, her ferocious pride intensified by secrecy. The little trio in front of Billie was a family unit, but only one of them knew it.

Billie realised that the bride had reached the end of the pew. Head down, her long neck bent gracefully over her lilies, she took Billie's breath away. Horsy Heather, patron saint of the pretentious and spokeswoman for castrators everywhere, was a goddess. Ruby's forty-year-old gown worked its white-dress magic on her, and Heather was transcendent, transformed. Even the Chinese burn she was grimly administering to her nervous dad's wrist in an effort to slow him down couldn't dent her perfection.

Today Billie was indulgent, enjoying the gasps and grins Heather provoked as she passed by, truly gorgeous for once in her life. This was Heather's perfect moment and Billie watched without any of the rancorous postscripts on matrimony she normally scribbled to herself.

Sitting down, and standing up, Billie never let go of Sam's hand. She was making the most of him while she had him, knowing she'd soon lose him to the lure of KFC and same-sex adventures of the flesh. The readings, nervously gabbled by the more photogenic younger relatives, stressed love and fidelity and not coveting thy neighbour's ox.

'Thy neighbours' cocks?' queried Sam innocently, but quite loudly. Mr Dyke, or Dot's Grandpa as Billie now thought of him, turned round with a quelling look, but Billie saw Zelda's shoulders quake.

Dean's vows were long and comprehensive, especially when compared to Heather's blithe promise to 'love, honour and occasionally cook for'. An interminable poem extolling understanding and harmony was read out by a third cousin once removed who wanted to be an actor, allowing Sam to fit in a short nap. Nobody slept through the Italian screechings of the opera singer Heather had insisted upon.

Next, doves, dyed pink, were released by the Dove Master, as Billie had labelled the myopic little bloke in a Motörhead T-shirt who'd delivered them. Fluttering wings filled the chapel, coos echoed in the rafters. Vicious claws darted overhead, and the congregation ducked as the birds swooped, confused by the lack of space. Hamish's screams drowned out the medieval tune a step-cousin was picking out on a lute.

Billie bit her lip as she whispered to the cowering Sam, 'Not *quite* the effect Heather was after.' Thankfully, the bride was unaware of the perfect circle of dove plop on the train of her gown.

A triumphal organ struck up again, and the ceremony, agonised over for months, described in pie charts and schedules, was over. Heather was married, and, less vitally, so was Dean.

The bells were ringing. Children were laughing. The sun was highlighting the glints in the ladies' hair. Heather was crying with happiness. Taking Billie's arm as they processed out of the church, Dot challenged her, 'Go on, take the mick. What do you want to make fun of?'

'Nothing.' Billie shook her head. 'It's perfect.'

Dot looked suspicious.

'Honestly. It's exactly what Heather wanted.' Billie smiled, wryly. 'I can't pretend it's what *I* would want, but that doesn't matter.' She had already had what she wanted. An elastic band wound tight around the third finger of her left hand reminded her that James was waiting for her, that from now on he would always be there to go home to. Their ramshackle wedding hadn't been legal, but it had been binding. 'Each to their own,' she ended sunnily.

Sam informed Dot, 'She's been through a cynicism-rinse. It's all gone, every last drop. She really is the wedding fairy now.'

Heather could be heard inviting people to get into their places for photographs with a gracious, 'Oi! Move it!'

Zelda had a tight grip on Mr Dyke's arm, and obviously had no intention of speeding up. The sight of them strolling along together, and the thought of all the might-have-beens as they followed their granddaughter across the churchyard, stopped Billie in her tracks.

Until Sam propelled her, with the use of both hands on her well-cushioned behind, towards the photographer. Heather's hands sliced the air as she marshalled everybody, evidently not trusting the professional to do it to her taste. Billie knew exactly what her client was up to—the less attractive family members were being massed on the ends of the rows, so that Heather's scissors could edit the big-nosed, the bald and the bad-hatted out of her perfect day. It was unlikely that any of Dean's family would make the final cut.

Sauntering over to join them in his wedding finery of a suit made from tea towels, Jake scoffed, 'Our wedding won't be like this.'

'Our what?' asked Dot, amazed.

'You heard me.'

'Yes, we did,' murmured Billie, wondering whether to be pleased or horrified. Jake had made certain promises, had accepted certain changes since his return: he washed up, he made the bed, he tolerated Billie, and he was now only misogynistic on Tuesdays. Despite all this, Billie was suspicious. Just as a leopard can't change its spots, Billie suspected a Jake can't change his possessive ways. Billie took in Dot's face, shining like the lighthouse and plumped for pleased. For now.

The photographs took longer than the service, an irony not lost on Jake. Tuning out his morbid musings about the plasticity of romance, Billie watched Ed, dutifully smiling with each new permutation of guests and family.

Sam said provocatively, 'You've got to admit, the boy's a beaut.'

'If you like that sort of thing.'

'Billifer, who doesn't like that sort of thing?' laughed Sam. 'I wouldn't kick him out of bed for eating crisps.'

'Been there.' Billie lifted her nose, smug. 'Done that. I'm sorted for snogs, thank you very much.'

The guests meandered along in the wake of the carriage that was being drawn along a stony path by fairytale white horses to where the tinkling notes of a harp lured them all into Homestead Hall. When she arrived, Billie scanned the terrace, saw what she was expecting to see on a stone bench, and relaxed. 'He's there,' she said to Sam.

Sam bent himself far enough out of character to say, 'Of course he is.'

A flute of champagne greeted every guest in its indomitable fizzy way as the guests filed through high French windows into a sunny white and gold reception room.

Heading for the buffet, Billie found herself picked off from the herd: she was that knock-kneed antelope familiar from BBC wildlife programmes. The lion was Ed, and he stood purposefully in her way.

'Don't throw your drink over me, will you?' said Ed, quietly.

Billie laughed. 'Don't worry. I promise not to go all *Fatal Attraction* on you. I know how much that gear cost to hire.'

'You all right?' he asked.

'Fine!' Billie was being bright and perky and distant, defying Ed's attempt to draw her back into that bubble of intimacy that ex-lovers can always recreate. 'Watch your back. Angela's on a mission.'

'She's wasting her time,' said Ed, twitching slightly. 'She smells of

Chanel Number Five and fatal chemicals. Anyway, I'm off women.' He looked at his feet. 'Most of them. There is one, but . . .'

Billie stood on tiptoe to kiss Ed's cheek. 'Thank you, Ed.'

'For what?' He looked puzzled. 'Why don't you want to stab me?'

'Oh, don't get me wrong,' said Billie, sweetly, 'I do. But you've been an important part of my journey.'

'Is that girl speak?'

'Yup. Good luck with the speech.' Billie left him and his patronising references to girl speak behind. For ever, she thought, melodramatically. She felt she was owed a little melodrama, after what Ed had put her through. Turning, she almost bumped into the newly minted Mrs Kelly. 'Heather!' she squealed, throwing her arms round her.

'Mind the dress,' snapped Heather, before relaxing into the hug that Billie was determined to give her. 'How do you think it's going?' Her face, powdered, blushered, shadowed, highlighted, plucked and glossed, suddenly puckered like a squashed tennis ball. 'Is everybody happy? Did the doves work? Was the lute too much? Does Dean look like a monkey in his tailcoat?'

'Heather.' Billie took her squarely by the shoulders. 'Your wedding is going fantastically. Listen.' She cocked an ear, exaggeratedly. 'Laughter. Chatter. The chink of glass. The ceremony was wonderful. The photos will be beautiful. You look like Gwyneth Paltrow with a push-up bra. Your guests are happy.' Billie paused. 'Are you?' She asked, urgently.

Surprised, Heather thought. 'I suppose I am,' she laughed.

'I know you didn't believe it this morning, but that really is all that matters.' Billie braved the billowing veil, the lacquered curls and the make-up that could deflect bullets to kiss her client on the cheek. She said quietly, 'Your mum would be so proud of you today.'

At last Billie made it to the buffet, where thousands of calories were patiently awaiting her attention. From behind her, she heard Heather bawl, 'Outside, everyone! I'm throwing the bouquet!'

Billie was caught up in a stampede of new heels. Tutting inwardly, she gave up all hope of getting the wrong side of a vol-au-vent as she positioned herself on the lawn among the other hopefuls, all jostling like rugby fullbacks in their chiffons and linens.

Hurling overarm, Heather took a good run up and East Anglia's most discussed bunch of flowers left her grasp and headed for Billie's face.

Flattened by the lilies, Billie heard Dot say, as she helped her up,

'Billie's next! The wedding planner's going to get married next!'

Dusting herself down, Billie handed the bouquet to Dot. 'Too late!'

'Eh?' asked Dot, with a daft look.

'I owe you a million pounds.'

'Eh?' repeated Dot, before remembering the bet they'd made a long time ago when they were refurbishing the shop. 'You're married?' She gaped, a picture of befuddlement. 'But how? That's not possible!'

'Get me another champagne and I'll—' Billie saw James striding across the lawn. 'We'll tell you all about it.'

'A million pounds,' marvelled Dot. 'You'll make a lot of badgers happy.'

'And that,' said Billie, 'is the main thing.'

POSTSCRIPT

Billie and James
do not request the pleasure of your company
at the non-wedding
that already took place.
Please join us for the non-reception
at Billie's Brides
on 22nd September at 8 p.m.

No presents
No hats
No speeches
No top table
And <u>definitely</u> no white dress

Dear Great-Aunty Babs,

A whole month since the most discreet wedding in the history of the world and we finally got round to throwing a party. I know you're having the time of your life with your sheep shearer, but I wish you could have been there—it's all down to you and your bonkers offer of this shop. There were no gifts, no vows, lots of kissing, some woeful dancing and a lot of love.

It was a double celebration—Billie's Brides is in profit! Real, proper profit at last. I did what I guessed you'd want me to do in this situation: I gave Dot and Debs a raise. Dot did the catering for our bash, so we had quite a few tofu 'n' marmalade kebabs left over, but James's punch took the guests' minds off the food.

The bride wore red. A Ruby Wolff creation made especially for me! Annie sewed a tiny blue bow just inside the bodice—as she said, I can't be expected to supply my own varicose veins just yet. She seems much better, though Ruby enjoys fussing over her so much that Annie admitted to me that sometimes she pretends to be tired so that he can bring her cups of tea.

Our picture went up in the Gallery of Happiness. A Sam Nolan, it's a Biro sketch of me and James, laughing on the beach and showing off our elastic-band rings. At least, I think we're laughing— my hair is obscuring my face, and most of the groom's face, too. Those rings are still firmly on, albeit a bit grubby by now.

Well, back to the party. The new husband was resplendent in jeans and a T-shirt. He's a bit tired these days (that commute is a killer) but no less handsome. Hopefully he will find a position somewhere nearby, before too long. Living in Zelda's top-floor flat is rather different to his apartment—the carpet can make you faint if you look into its swirls for too long—but I appreciate all the luxuries I'd been living without.

The shop was packed with friends, family and customers, all trying to chat over the music Debs insisted on turning up every time my back was turned. Sam came all the way from London, leaving (according to him) a small taxi driver locked in his flat.

Like the best parties, things got a little out of control. After drunkenly confiding her fudge's secret ingredient (tomato ketchup!), Zelda forced Mr Dyke to sip home brew out of her slipper, and Jake stripped off to reveal the epic poem about the nature of love he'd daubed on his body in woad.

Clicking her red shoes together, Mum was in character for her latest starring role. She treated us all (unasked) to a performance of 'Over The Rainbow' which made Julia cack herself by the trifle. She spent most of her time keeping Dad's Cowardly Lion mane out of his punch, but she took me aside to let me know how furious she is with me for getting 'married' without her. 'I've still got the bloody hat from your first crack at it!' she complained. But she loves James, and something has changed since the non-wedding. I can't explain, but she looks at me differently, as if she's really seeing me. As if I've finally, officially, grown up. I look at her differently, too—I've stopped blaming her for everything. She's just a woman, a funny, lively, disappointed woman trying to make the best of things. Like the rest of us. I kiss her more.

Debs's nylon track suit matched Zac's. Did I tell you she's cashed up twice now and we're still solvent. And she's paid back every penny she stole: if only she could stop pointing out the customers' cellulite she'd be perfect.

As Ruby and Annie waltzed defiantly together to the Eminem that Debs insisted on playing, another past customer, Ivanka, attempted an us-new-brides-together chat with me. 'I thought marriage would be like owning pet,' she said, in her accent thick as Jake's soup. 'But is like being stuck in lift with . . .' She couldn't find an analogy bad enough, and just gestured at her husband, who was explaining caravan insurance to James. 'Well, with Clifford.' Before she left, she said casually, 'Perhaps I poison him.'

My first big client was there, brown from her honeymoon in Goa. Dean wasn't so brown; having caught a tummy bug, he spent his two weeks in paradise Sellotaped to a toilet. Heather took me to one side to tell me I'd helped make her wedding the best day of her life, and I hugged her and said, funnily enough, it was the best day of mine, too. When somebody thanks you, with tears in their eyes, for making their childhood dreams come true, you'd have to have a heart of stone not to feel something. No wonder you love this silly old shop so much, Great-Aunty Babs.

If you hadn't chosen to explore Australia, I would never have found this magical town. Thank goodness I accepted your offer. If we say 'yes' to life, it usually works out, doesn't it? Perhaps that was what Jackie was trying to say—or shout—when she delivered a character assassination instead of an apology. I'm starting to think she was right, that people's choices shape their lives. It's what we say 'yes' to that matters in the long run.

Sorry if I'm starting to sound evangelical and scary—a bit like one of Sly's seminars—but love finds a way, doesn't it? It pushes round the bricks and through the doors.

I mean, I shook my head when Dot took Jake back, but it was the right choice for her and he's behaving himself. So far.

Sly is washing up in Colonel Cluck's Chicken Parlour—but he is the best washer up they've ever had and he's finished in time to collect Deirdre and Moto from school. Deirdre is very impressed with her mummy's new job—perhaps she'll ask Santa to bring her a Career Barbie for Christmas.

Sometimes, our choices hurt ourselves most of all. Great-Aunty, I know about Zelda. I guessed. I would never have imagined that such an epic story of love and sacrifice and fudge was playing out next door to your shop. Zelda's my new heroine—she gave her baby away even though it must have broken her heart, she looks out for her granddaughter (even seeing off a potential incestuous suitor), and protects the good name and marriage of her lover. And continues to love him. No wedding for Zelda, but a lifetime of commitment—I hope I can be as loyal to James.

Well, the party eventually wound down and I found myself staring up at the Gallery of Happiness.

All those women made a choice, too. One that was beyond me. They chose to stand up in public, in a church or a registry office or a hotel, point to their man and yell, 'I LOVE HIM! AND I ALWAYS WILL! AND DON'T I LOOK GOOD IN WHITE!'

My wedding wasn't cut from the template supplied by the glossy magazines, but I do love him, Great-Aunty Babs, and I always will. And I look pretty shit in white, to tell the truth.

I'd better sign off now. James is perfect, but not so perfect that he'll let me get away with the washing-up. You'll love him, I know you will, and he hears so much about you from Dot and me that he feels like he knows you already. Write soon, and let Sole Bay know how their ambassadress to the Antipodes is getting on. But much as I love you, my darling Great-Aunty Babs, please don't come home too soon . . .

Bernadette Strachan

What led you to write *Little White Lies*?

Well, nine years ago, when I was a showbiz agent, I was engaged to a handsome voice-over actor whom I represented. A month before our wedding he ditched me—entirely out of the blue and with no explanation—and shortly afterwards he took up with chat-show queen Vanessa Feltz. I spotted them in a magazine, dancing together, and went straight into the last act of a Wagnerian opera. I was up the curtains, hysterical. It turned out he had once been at school with Vanessa.

Did it take you ages to recover?

Yes. I was very miserable for a long time, but then I met Matthew, a composer, also through my work, and put it all behind me. After we were married, I gave up my job on a dare from Matthew and began to write full time.

Were you ever tempted to open a wedding-dress shop?

No, but I did once run a wool shop in Fulham. It had just the same storage space upstairs as Billie's Brides has in the book. Actually, what really galvanised me into writing *Little White Lies* was my long-time obsession with beach huts.

Really? Do you own a beach hut?

I wish. Because you know what it's like when you walk down a beach and see people sitting in their huts, or on the steps, legs planted apart, with a nice little flask of tea, some sandwiches and a newspaper, and you think, 'Oh, I've got to go and sit on the sand now and get covered in it while you're having a great time.'

If you could buy one, where would it be?

Southwold on the Sussex coast. Sole Bay in the novel is based on Southwold. It's really lovely and it's utterly unselfconsciously English, in that it's not kiss-me-quick, but full of nice old retired majors. It's sand, sea and back-to-childhood, buckets-and-spades simplicity. I once dreamed of running away to a beach hut, painting it white and living there without radio, television or phone.

You often put spirited elderly ladies into your books. Is this deliberate?

Yes. I think it's partly rebellion against the Chick Lit thing, when lots of the action revolves around wine bars and other places where the young go. In my books, the people who surround the central character are often like substitute family and so you need to have older people there too. I find it easier to write about older women than older men, which is why you'll find more old ladies in my books.

And where did the firemen come from? You seem to know a lot about them!

My best friend moved to Brighton and got set up on her first evening there with a blind date who was a fireman. He's riotously handsome and he got me into the whole fireman psyche. They really do give one another terrible nicknames and his is actually Treacle, like Ed in my novel. I think that a sense of humour is a very necessary safety valve for them. They have to do terrible things in the course of their work—they're always running towards danger while the rest of us are running away from it. There's great camaraderie between them.

Talking of camaraderie, you've written a stage musical with your husband.

It's called *Next Door's Baby* and it's set in 1950s Dublin. I wrote it originally as a radio play and then adapted it for the stage. Matthew wrote the music and lyrics. It's more a light-hearted piece with music than a musical. It was staged at the Orange Tree Theatre in Richmond and had a rave review in *The Times.* We've started work on a new one, about Ruth Ellis, the last woman to be hanged in Britain. It's really nice to have something to create together. Even though we both work from home, sometimes we hardly see one another!

How do you relax?

I love cooking. I used to cook Mexican one night, Italian the next, but now I keep it simple. Anything that goes in one pot, like Irish stew (of course, since I'm Irish!) although I keep the potatoes separate and serve big, floury ones on the side. And I love messing about with Niamh, my daughter, and making up stories for her. At four years old, Niamh has a vivid imagination and now when she makes up her own stories, she says, 'Mummy, I'm working'.

What's your favourite way to spend a Sunday?

To cook a roast—lamb for preference, or chicken—and to ask people round. I like having a real mixture of friends round the table and watching it all ramble on late into the afternoon. And then, ideally, to have people magically know that I've got fed up of having them there, and leave! I need my Sunday evenings.

If you could change one thing about your life, what would it be?

I'd like somehow to have the sea in Kingston, where we have our home.

Anne Jenkins